C. Hart

W9-BDM-514

COMICS

The Classics Collection

EDITIONS

New York

Special thanks to Teri Avanian, Barbara Fullerton, Shawn Saunders, Ken Shue, and Dave Smith.

"Heigh-Ho"
Words by Larry Morey Music by Frank Churchill
©Copyright 1938 by Bourne Co.
Copyright Renewed
This Arrangement ©Copyright 1993 by Bourne Co.
All Rights Reserved International Copyright Secured

"The Caucus Race"
Words by Sammy Fain / Music by Bob Hillard
© 1949 Walt Disney Music Company

"I'm Late"
Words by Sammy Fain / Music by Bob Hillard
© 1949 Walt Disney Music Company

"How D'Ye Do and Shake Hands"
Words by Cy Coben / Music by Oliver Wallace
© 1951 Walt Disney Music Company

"The Walrus and the Carpenter"
Words by Sammy Fain / Music by Bob Hillard
© 1949 Walt Disney Music Company

"The Unbirthday Song"
Words by Jerry Livingston / Music by Mack David and Al Hoffman
© 1948 Walt Disney Music Company

"In A World of My Own"
Words by Sammy Fain / Music by Bob Hillard
© 1949 Walt Disney Music Company

"The Elegant Captain Hook"
Words by Sammy Cahn / Music by Sammy Fain
© 1951 Walt Disney Music Company

"You can Fly! You can Fly! You can Fly!"
Words by Sammy Cahn / Music by Sammy Fain
© 1951 Walt Disney Music Company

To maintain the authenticity of these reproductions, the content has been reproduced exactly as it first appeared.

Copyright © 2006 Disney Enterprises, Inc.

Library of Congress Cataloging-in-Publication Data on file.

Originally presented in magazine form in *Four Color Comics* #49 © Disney 1944; *Four Color Comics*, Volume 2, #12 © Disney 1942; *Four Color Comics* #17, © Disney 1941; *Four Color Comics* #331, © Disney 1951; *Four Color Comics* #442, © Disney 1953

No part of this book may be reproduced or transmitted in any form, or by any means, electronic or mechanical, including photocopying, recording, or by any storage and retrieval system, without written permission from the publisher.

For information address Disney Editions, 114 Fifth Avenue, New York, NY 10011-5690.
Printed in Singapore
First Edition
1 3 5 7 9 10 8 6 4 2
ISBN: 0-7868-4902-9

CONTENTS

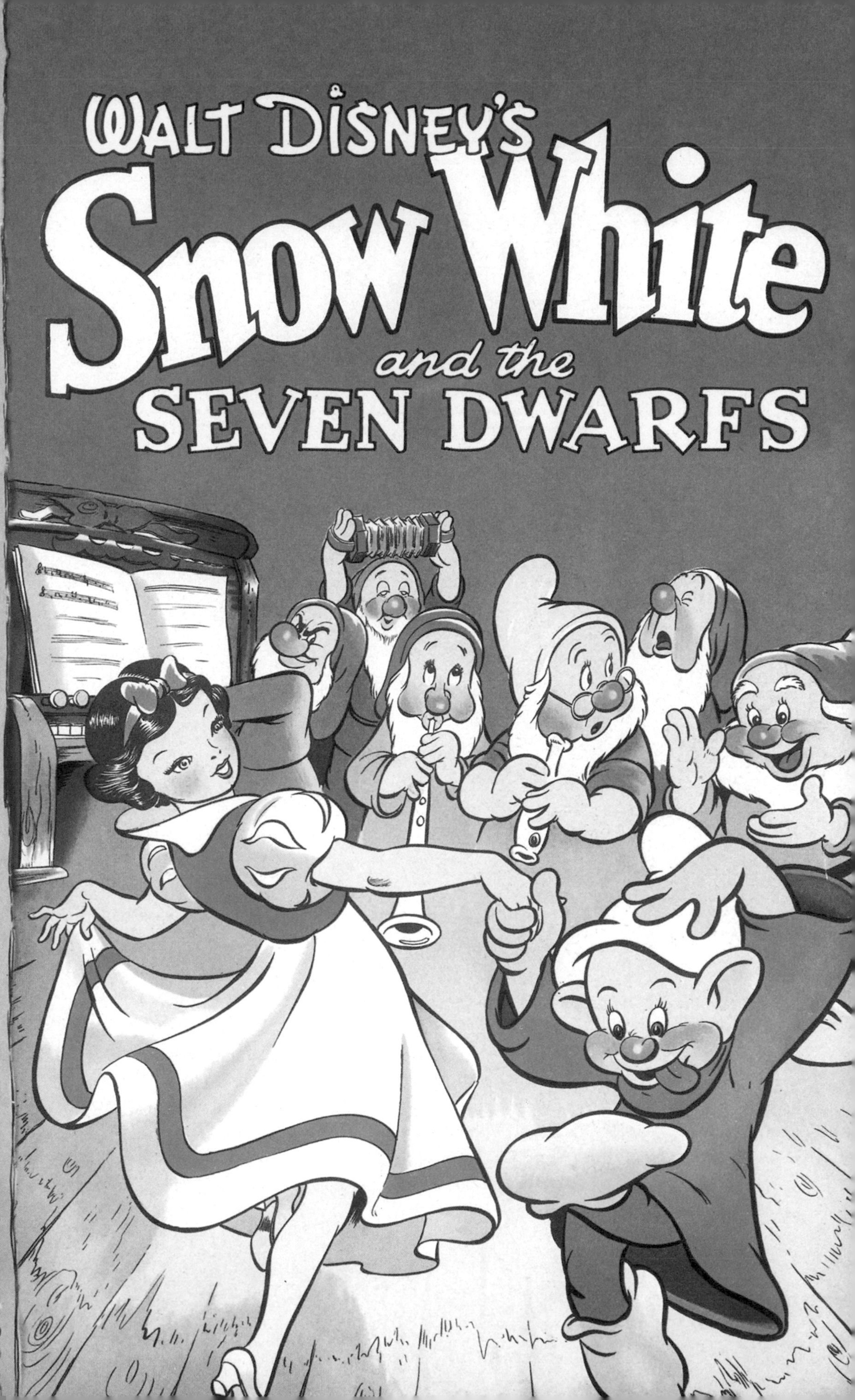
Walt Disney's
Snow White
and the
SEVEN DWARFS

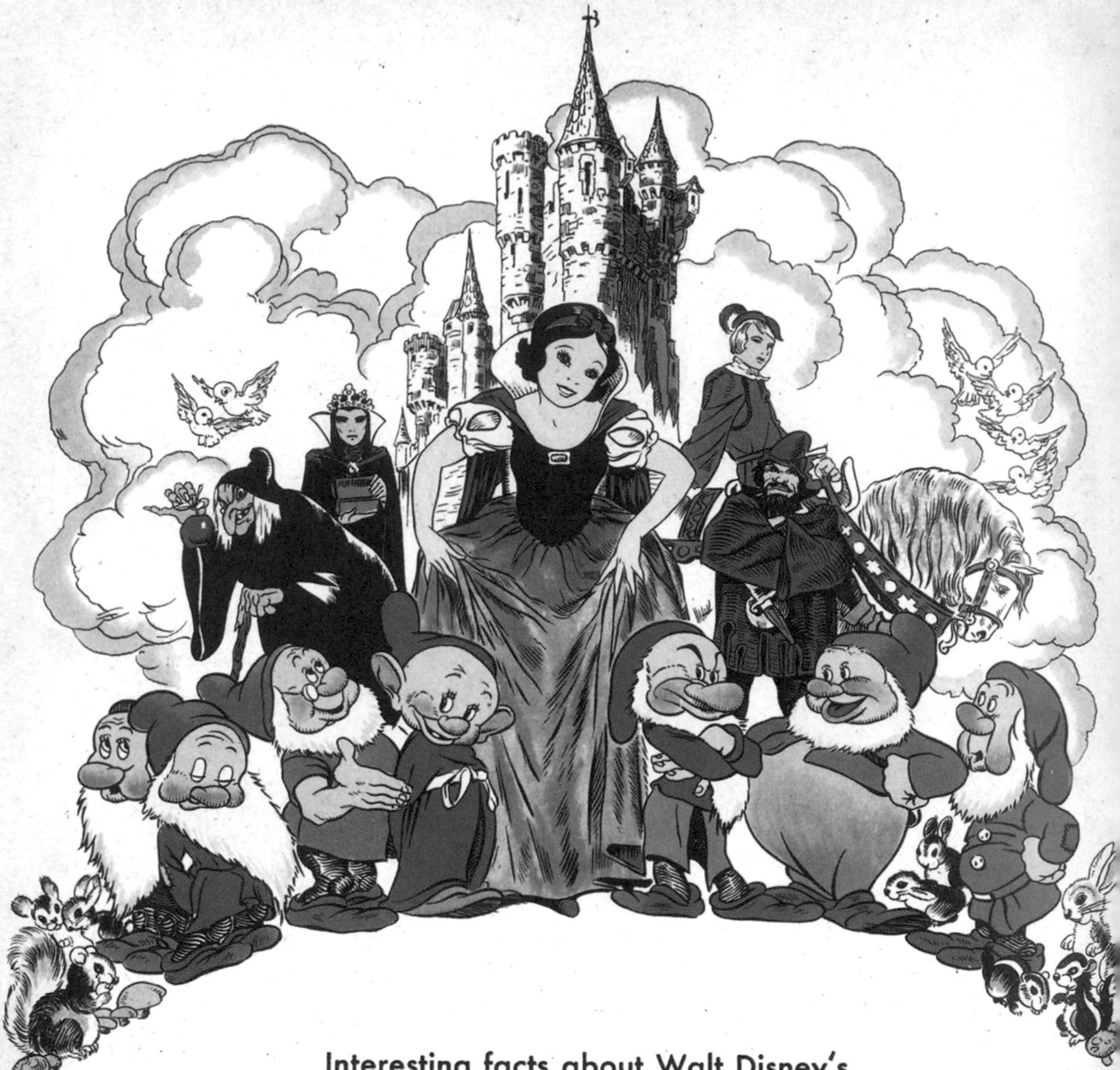

Interesting facts about Walt Disney's

"Snow White and the Seven Dwarfs"

This world-famous motion picture is based on the universally loved fairy tale of the same name. The picture took three years to make, employing the combined efforts of Walt Disney and over 600 artists, technicians, and musicians. More than 250,000 individual drawings were used. The entire picture is in Technicolor, with a complete symphonic musical score throughout. Every one of its songs became hit tunes and will live as long as good music is appreciated. Walt Disney's "SNOW WHITE AND THE SEVEN DWARFS" has been translated into practically every language and shown all over the world.

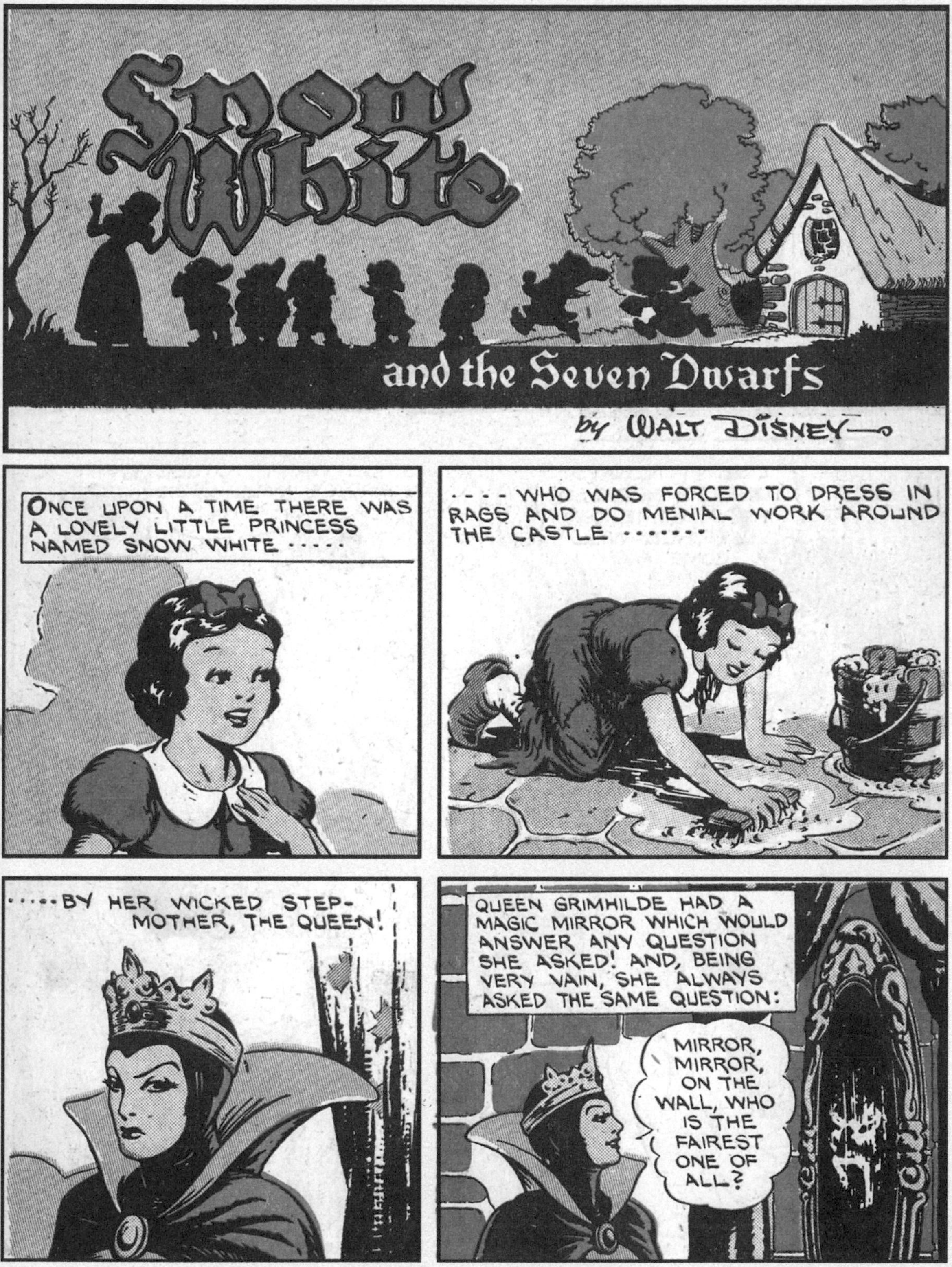
Snow White
and the Seven Dwarfs
by WALT DISNEY
ONCE UPON A TIME THERE WAS A LOVELY LITTLE PRINCESS NAMED SNOW WHITE -----
---- WHO WAS FORCED TO DRESS IN RAGS AND DO MENIAL WORK AROUND THE CASTLE -------
-----BY HER WICKED STEP-MOTHER, THE QUEEN!
QUEEN GRIMHILDE HAD A MAGIC MIRROR WHICH WOULD ANSWER ANY QUESTION SHE ASKED! AND, BEING VERY VAIN, SHE ALWAYS ASKED THE SAME QUESTION:
MIRROR, MIRROR, ON THE WALL, WHO IS THE FAIREST ONE OF ALL?

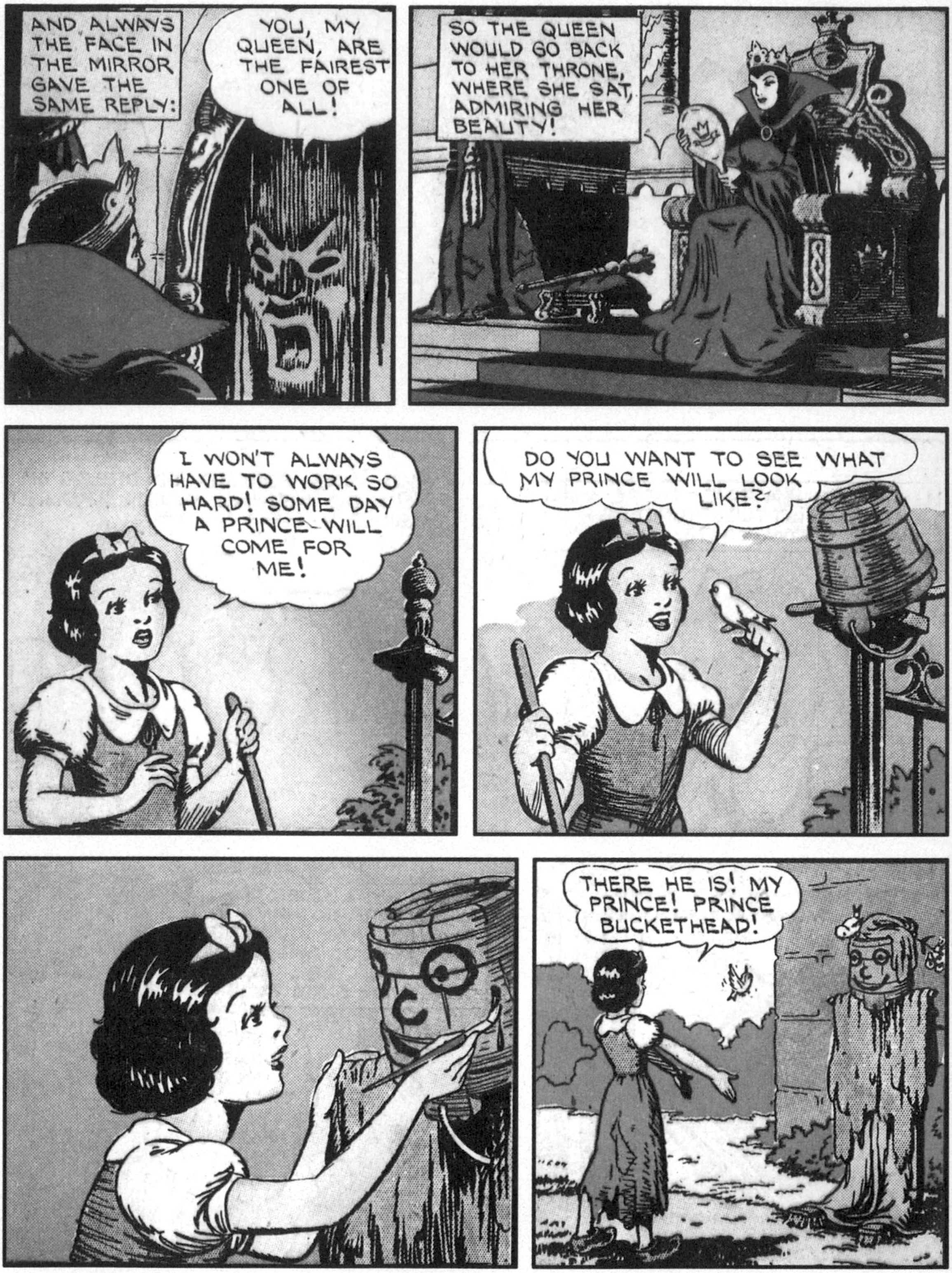
AND ALWAYS THE FACE IN THE MIRROR GAVE THE SAME REPLY:
YOU, MY QUEEN, ARE THE FAIREST ONE OF ALL!
SO THE QUEEN WOULD GO BACK TO HER THRONE, WHERE SHE SAT, ADMIRING HER BEAUTY!
I WON'T ALWAYS HAVE TO WORK SO HARD! SOME DAY A PRINCE WILL COME FOR ME!
DO YOU WANT TO SEE WHAT MY PRINCE WILL LOOK LIKE?
THERE HE IS! MY PRINCE! PRINCE BUCKETHEAD!

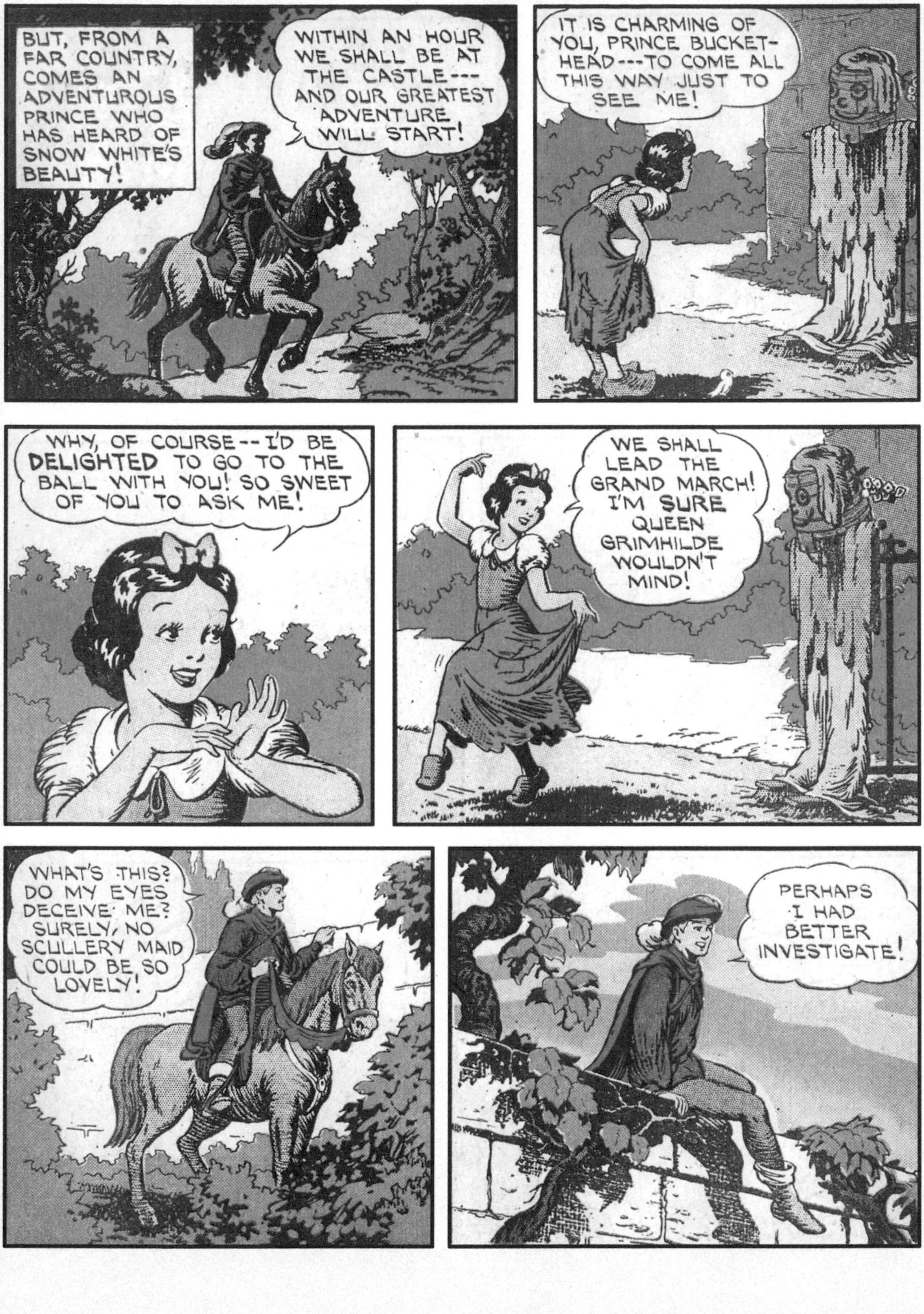
BUT, FROM A FAR COUNTRY, COMES AN ADVENTUROUS PRINCE WHO HAS HEARD OF SNOW WHITE'S BEAUTY!
WITHIN AN HOUR WE SHALL BE AT THE CASTLE--- AND OUR GREATEST ADVENTURE WILL START!
IT IS CHARMING OF YOU, PRINCE BUCKET-HEAD---TO COME ALL THIS WAY JUST TO SEE ME!
WHY, OF COURSE--I'D BE **DELIGHTED** TO GO TO THE BALL WITH YOU! SO SWEET OF YOU TO ASK ME!
WE SHALL LEAD THE GRAND MARCH! I'M **SURE** QUEEN GRIMHILDE WOULDN'T MIND!
WHAT'S THIS? DO MY EYES DECEIVE ME? SURELY, NO SCULLERY MAID COULD BE SO LOVELY!
PERHAPS I HAD BETTER INVESTIGATE!

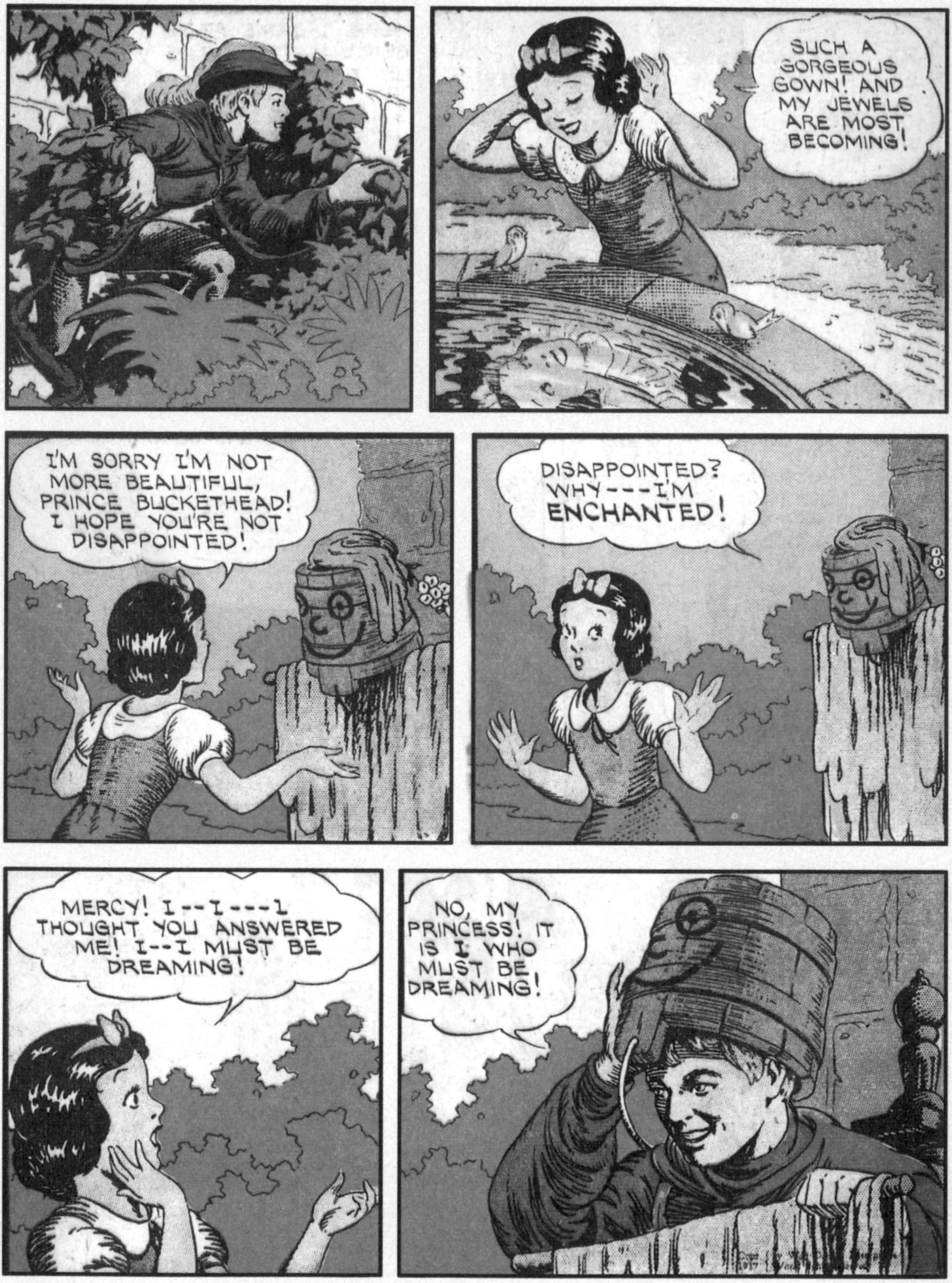
SUCH A GORGEOUS GOWN! AND MY JEWELS ARE MOST BECOMING!
I'M SORRY I'M NOT MORE BEAUTIFUL, PRINCE BUCKETHEAD! I HOPE YOU'RE NOT DISAPPOINTED!
DISAPPOINTED? WHY---I'M ENCHANTED!
MERCY! I--I---I THOUGHT YOU ANSWERED ME! I--I MUST BE DREAMING!
NO, MY PRINCESS! IT IS I WHO MUST BE DREAMING!

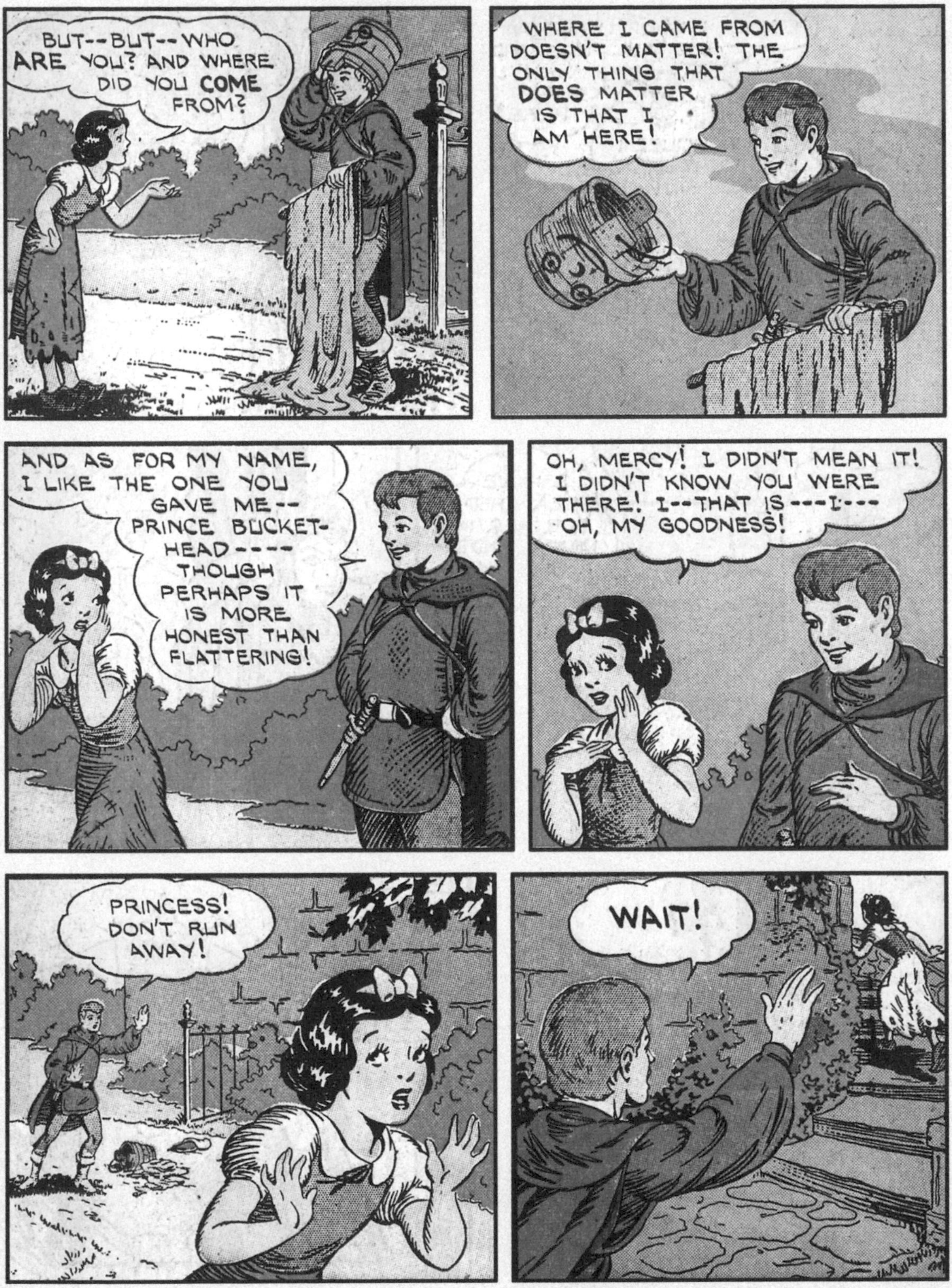
BUT--BUT--WHO ARE YOU? AND WHERE DID YOU COME FROM?
WHERE I CAME FROM DOESN'T MATTER! THE ONLY THING THAT DOES MATTER IS THAT I AM HERE!
AND AS FOR MY NAME, I LIKE THE ONE YOU GAVE ME--PRINCE BUCKET-HEAD----THOUGH PERHAPS IT IS MORE HONEST THAN FLATTERING!
OH, MERCY! I DIDN'T MEAN IT! I DIDN'T KNOW YOU WERE THERE! I--THAT IS---I---OH, MY GOODNESS!
PRINCESS! DON'T RUN AWAY!
WAIT!

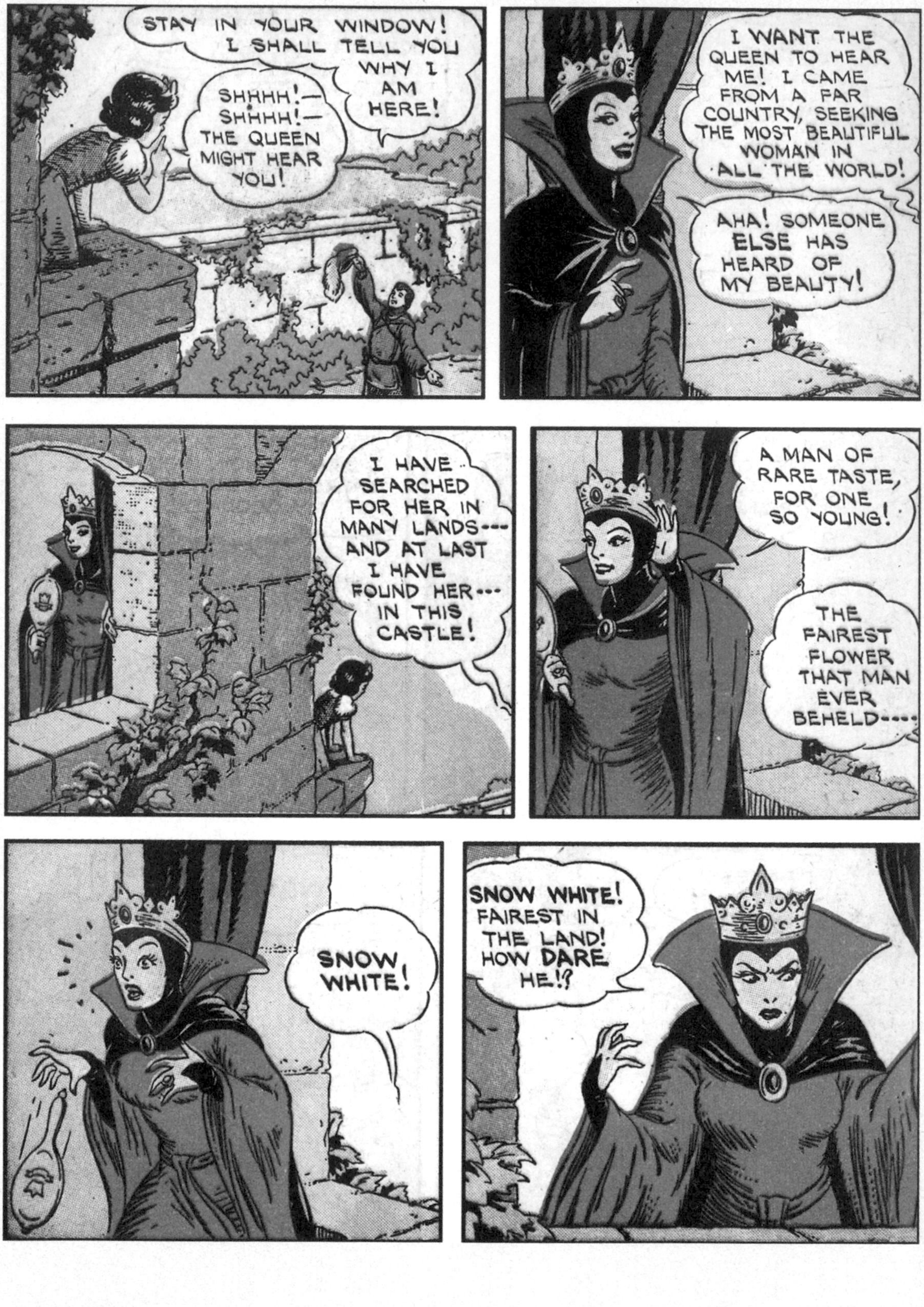

STAY IN YOUR WINDOW! I SHALL TELL YOU WHY I AM HERE!
SHHHH!— SHHHH!— THE QUEEN MIGHT HEAR YOU!
I WANT THE QUEEN TO HEAR ME! I CAME FROM A FAR COUNTRY, SEEKING THE MOST BEAUTIFUL WOMAN IN ALL THE WORLD!
AHA! SOMEONE ELSE HAS HEARD OF MY BEAUTY!
I HAVE SEARCHED FOR HER IN MANY LANDS--- AND AT LAST I HAVE FOUND HER--- IN THIS CASTLE!
A MAN OF RARE TASTE, FOR ONE SO YOUNG!
THE FAIREST FLOWER THAT MAN EVER BEHELD----
SNOW WHITE!
SNOW WHITE! FAIREST IN THE LAND! HOW DARE HE!?

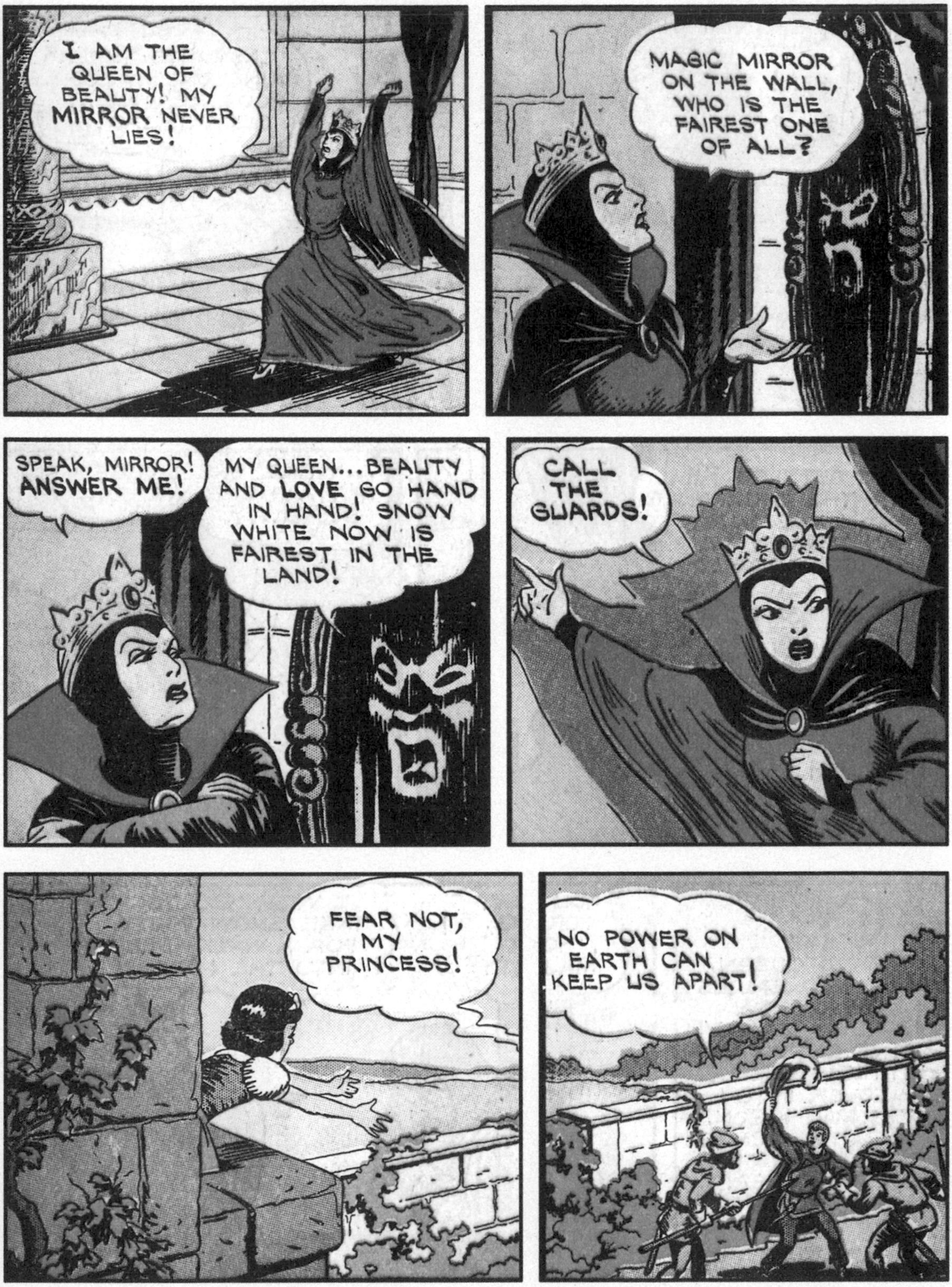
I AM THE QUEEN OF BEAUTY! MY MIRROR NEVER LIES!
MAGIC MIRROR ON THE WALL, WHO IS THE FAIREST ONE OF ALL?
SPEAK, MIRROR! ANSWER ME!
MY QUEEN...BEAUTY AND LOVE GO HAND IN HAND! SNOW WHITE NOW IS FAIREST IN THE LAND!
CALL THE GUARDS!
FEAR NOT, MY PRINCESS!
NO POWER ON EARTH CAN KEEP US APART!

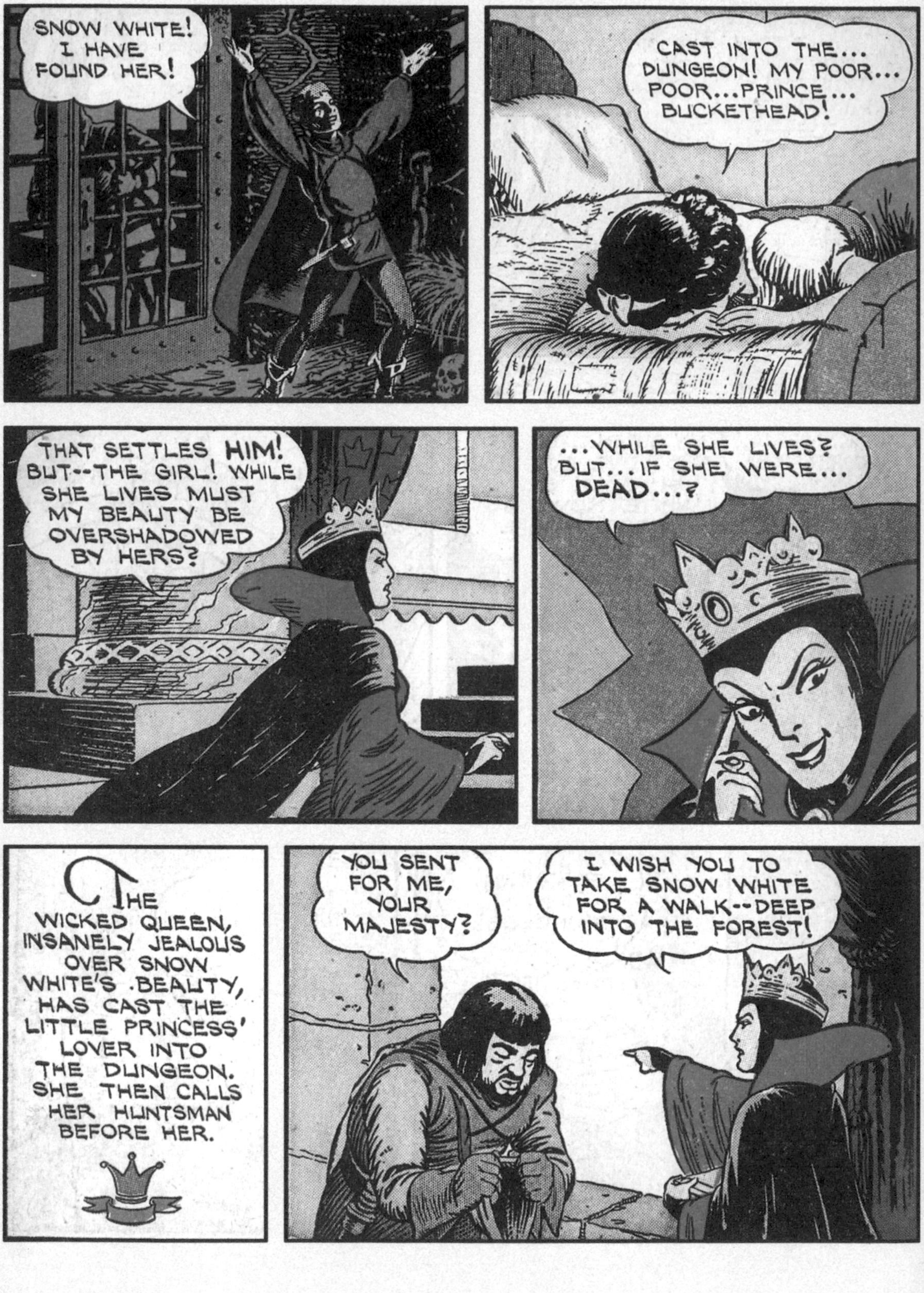
SNOW WHITE! I HAVE FOUND HER!
CAST INTO THE... DUNGEON! MY POOR... POOR...PRINCE... BUCKETHEAD!
THAT SETTLES HIM! BUT--THE GIRL! WHILE SHE LIVES MUST MY BEAUTY BE OVERSHADOWED BY HERS?
...WHILE SHE LIVES? BUT...IF SHE WERE... DEAD...?
THE WICKED QUEEN, INSANELY JEALOUS OVER SNOW WHITE'S BEAUTY, HAS CAST THE LITTLE PRINCESS' LOVER INTO THE DUNGEON. SHE THEN CALLS HER HUNTSMAN BEFORE HER.
YOU SENT FOR ME, YOUR MAJESTY?
I WISH YOU TO TAKE SNOW WHITE FOR A WALK--DEEP INTO THE FOREST!

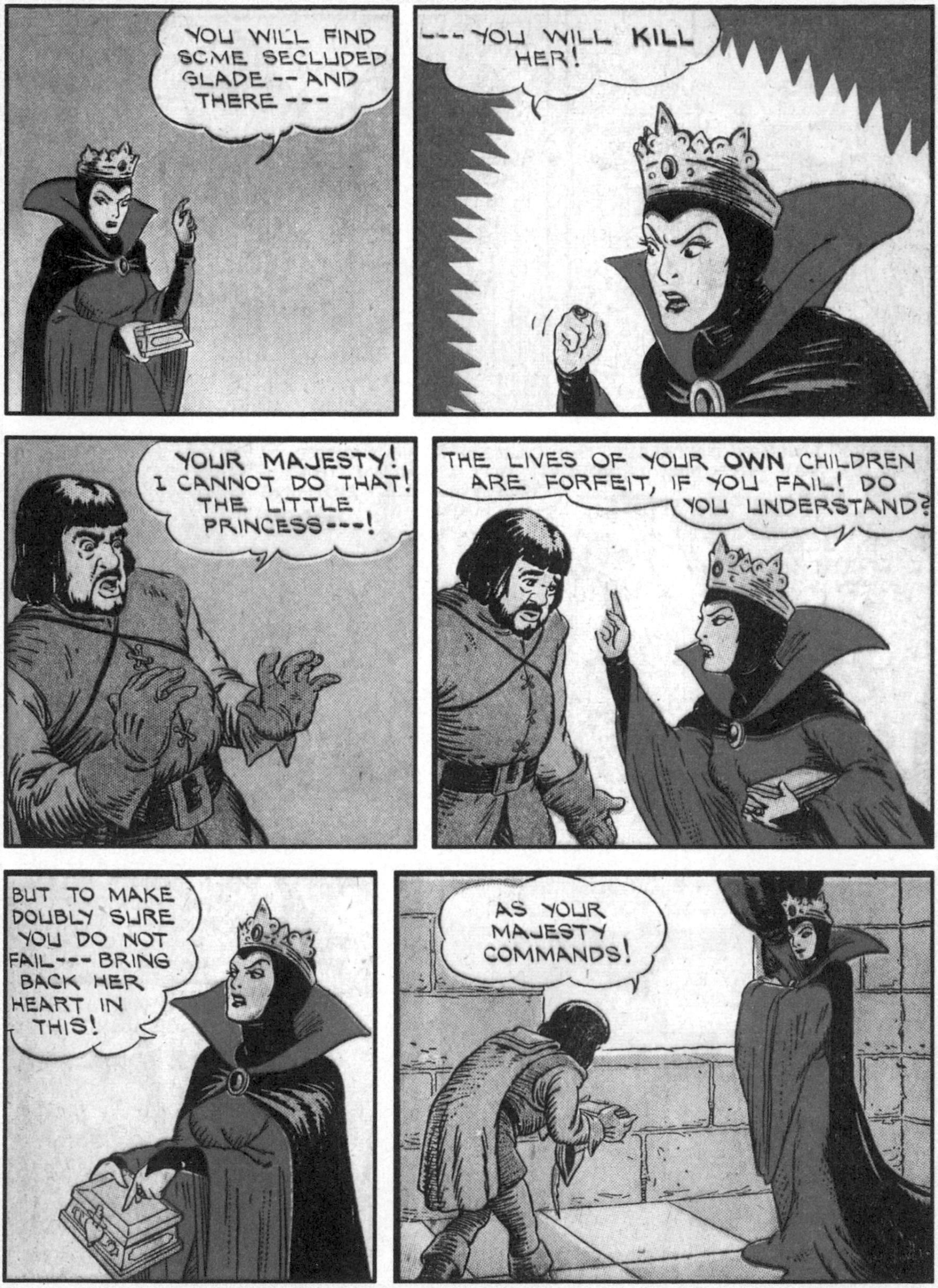
YOU WILL FIND SOME SECLUDED GLADE -- AND THERE ---
--- YOU WILL KILL HER!
YOUR MAJESTY! I CANNOT DO THAT! THE LITTLE PRINCESS---!
THE LIVES OF YOUR OWN CHILDREN ARE FORFEIT, IF YOU FAIL! DO YOU UNDERSTAND?
BUT TO MAKE DOUBLY SURE YOU DO NOT FAIL--- BRING BACK HER HEART IN THIS!
AS YOUR MAJESTY COMMANDS!

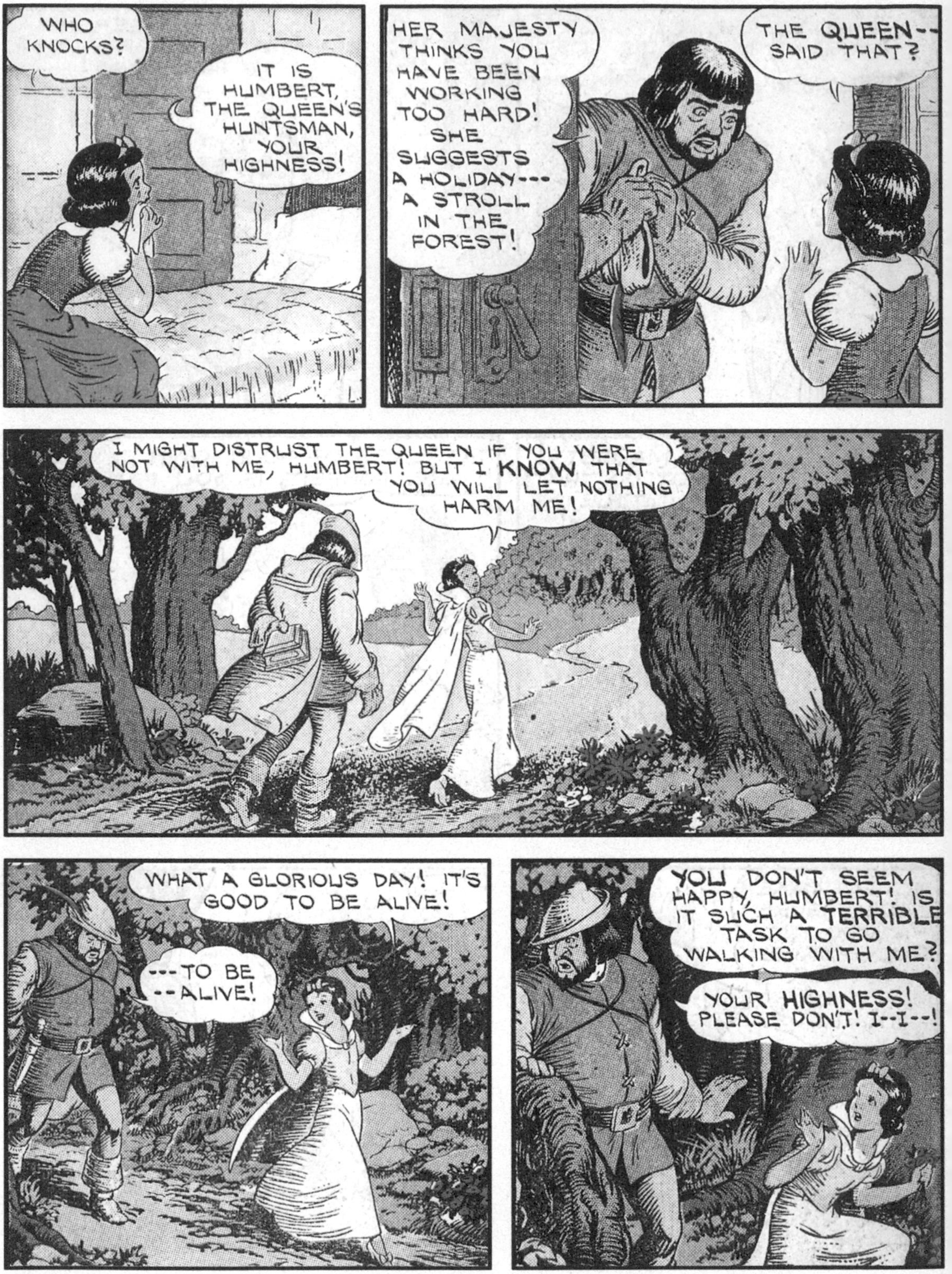
WHO KNOCKS?
IT IS HUMBERT, THE QUEEN'S HUNTSMAN, YOUR HIGHNESS!
HER MAJESTY THINKS YOU HAVE BEEN WORKING TOO HARD! SHE SUGGESTS A HOLIDAY--- A STROLL IN THE FOREST!
THE QUEEN-- SAID THAT?
I MIGHT DISTRUST THE QUEEN IF YOU WERE NOT WITH ME, HUMBERT! BUT I KNOW THAT YOU WILL LET NOTHING HARM ME!
WHAT A GLORIOUS DAY! IT'S GOOD TO BE ALIVE!
---TO BE --ALIVE!
YOU DON'T SEEM HAPPY, HUMBERT! IS IT SUCH A TERRIBLE TASK TO GO WALKING WITH ME?
YOUR HIGHNESS! PLEASE DON'T! I--I--!

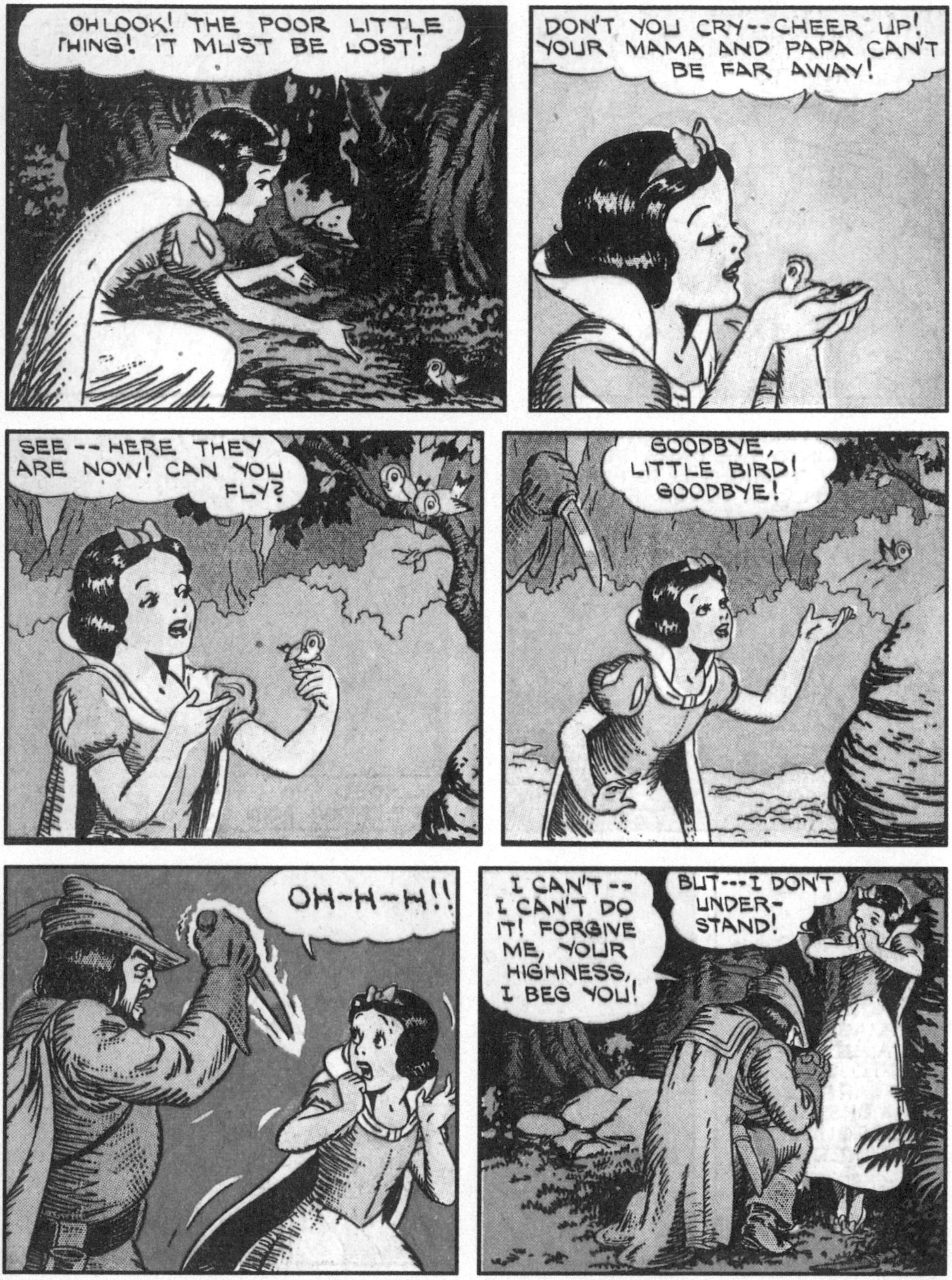
OH LOOK! THE POOR LITTLE THING! IT MUST BE LOST!
DON'T YOU CRY--CHEER UP! YOUR MAMA AND PAPA CAN'T BE FAR AWAY!
SEE--HERE THEY ARE NOW! CAN YOU FLY?
GOODBYE, LITTLE BIRD! GOODBYE!
OH-H-H!!
I CAN'T-- I CAN'T DO IT! FORGIVE ME, YOUR HIGHNESS, I BEG YOU!
BUT---I DON'T UNDER-STAND!

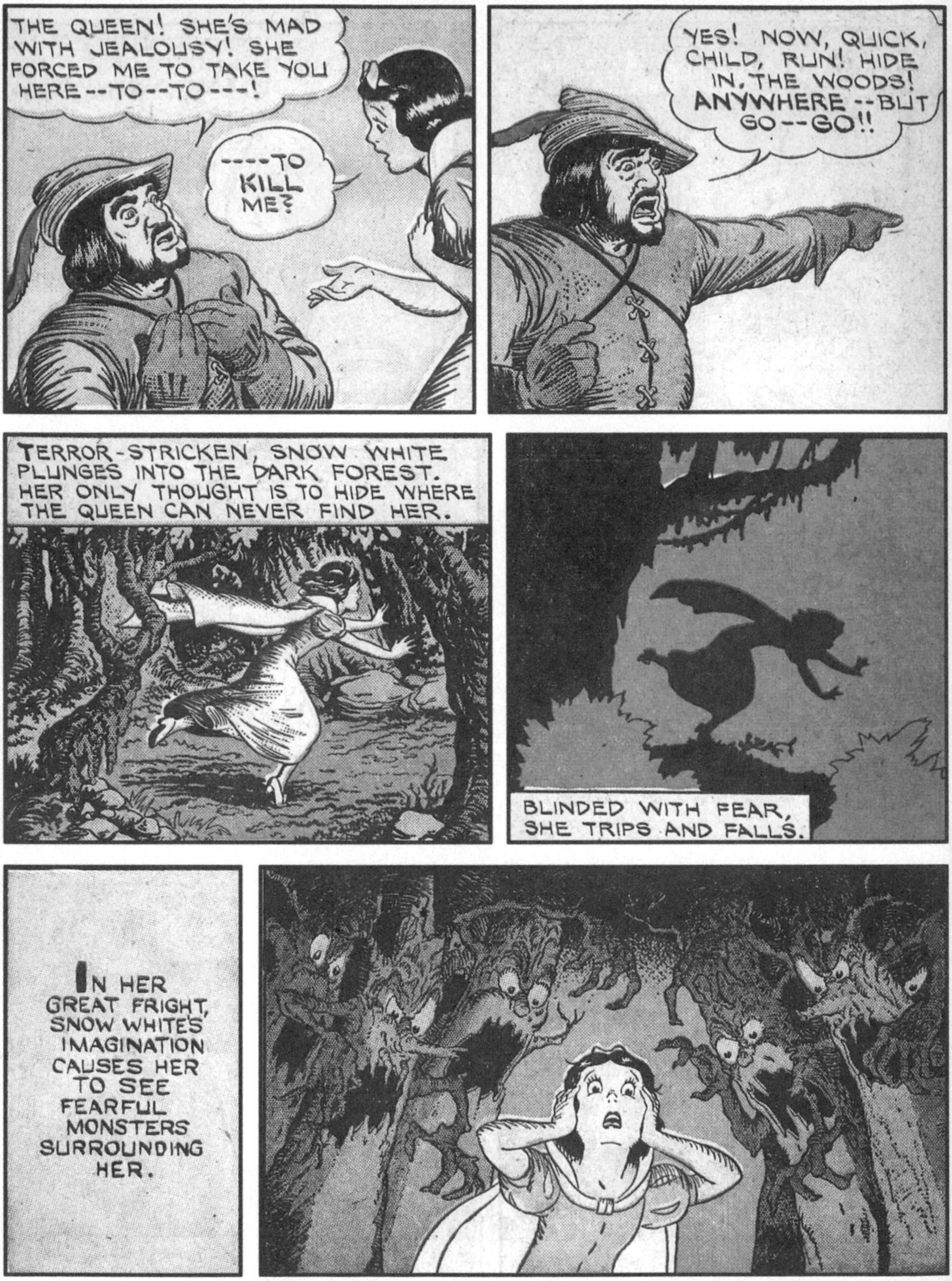
THE QUEEN! SHE'S MAD WITH JEALOUSY! SHE FORCED ME TO TAKE YOU HERE--TO--TO---!
----TO KILL ME?
YES! NOW, QUICK, CHILD, RUN! HIDE IN THE WOODS! ANYWHERE--BUT GO--GO!!
TERROR-STRICKEN, SNOW WHITE PLUNGES INTO THE DARK FOREST. HER ONLY THOUGHT IS TO HIDE WHERE THE QUEEN CAN NEVER FIND HER.
BLINDED WITH FEAR, SHE TRIPS AND FALLS.
IN HER GREAT FRIGHT, SNOW WHITE'S IMAGINATION CAUSES HER TO SEE FEARFUL MONSTERS SURROUNDING HER.

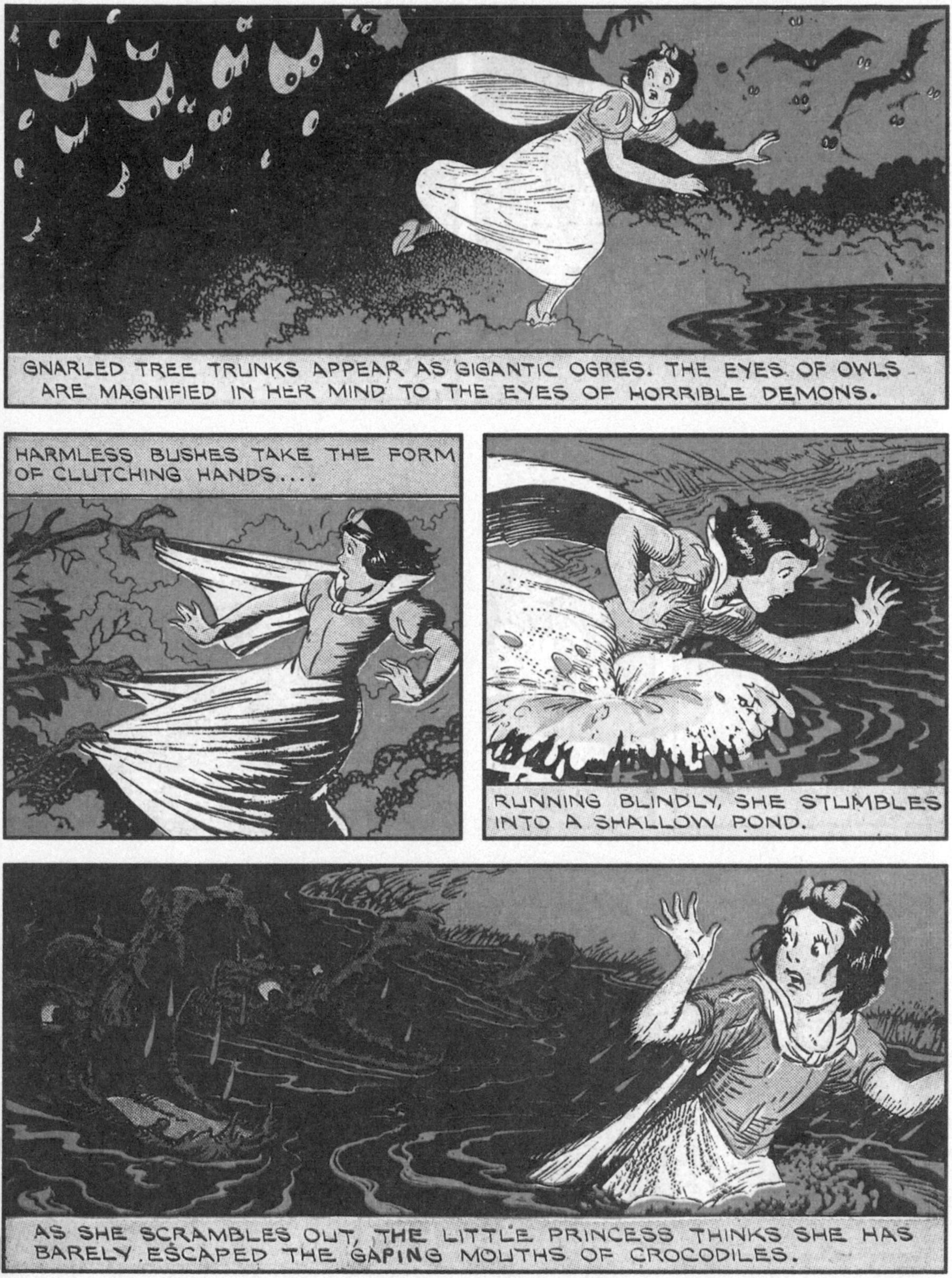
GNARLED TREE TRUNKS APPEAR AS GIGANTIC OGRES. THE EYES OF OWLS ARE MAGNIFIED IN HER MIND TO THE EYES OF HORRIBLE DEMONS.
HARMLESS BUSHES TAKE THE FORM OF CLUTCHING HANDS....
RUNNING BLINDLY, SHE STUMBLES INTO A SHALLOW POND.
AS SHE SCRAMBLES OUT, THE LITTLE PRINCESS THINKS SHE HAS BARELY ESCAPED THE GAPING MOUTHS OF CROCODILES.

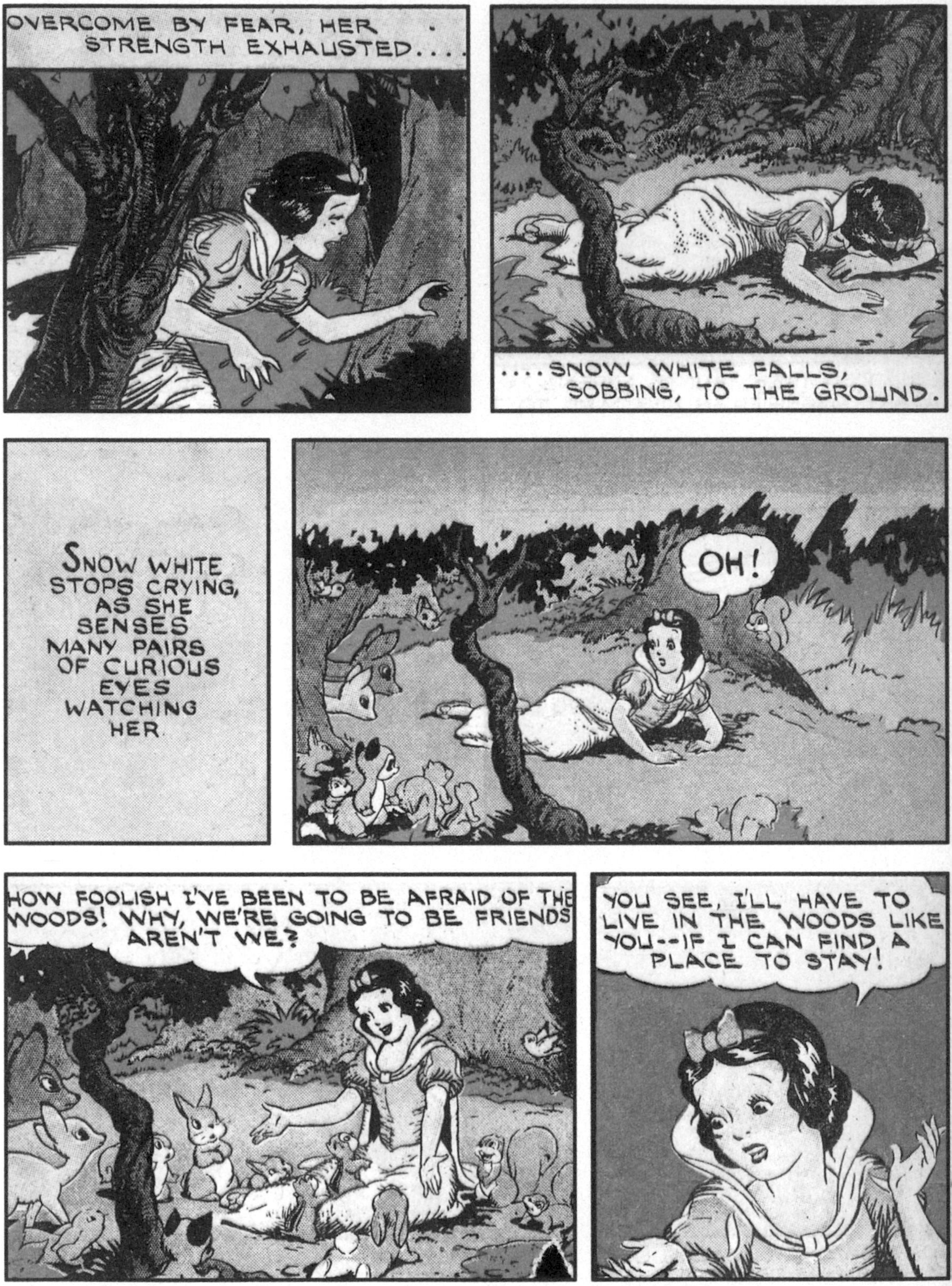
OVERCOME BY FEAR, HER STRENGTH EXHAUSTED....
....SNOW WHITE FALLS, SOBBING, TO THE GROUND.
SNOW WHITE STOPS CRYING, AS SHE SENSES MANY PAIRS OF CURIOUS EYES WATCHING HER.
OH!
HOW FOOLISH I'VE BEEN TO BE AFRAID OF THE WOODS! WHY, WE'RE GOING TO BE FRIENDS AREN'T WE?
YOU SEE, I'LL HAVE TO LIVE IN THE WOODS LIKE YOU--IF I CAN FIND A PLACE TO STAY!

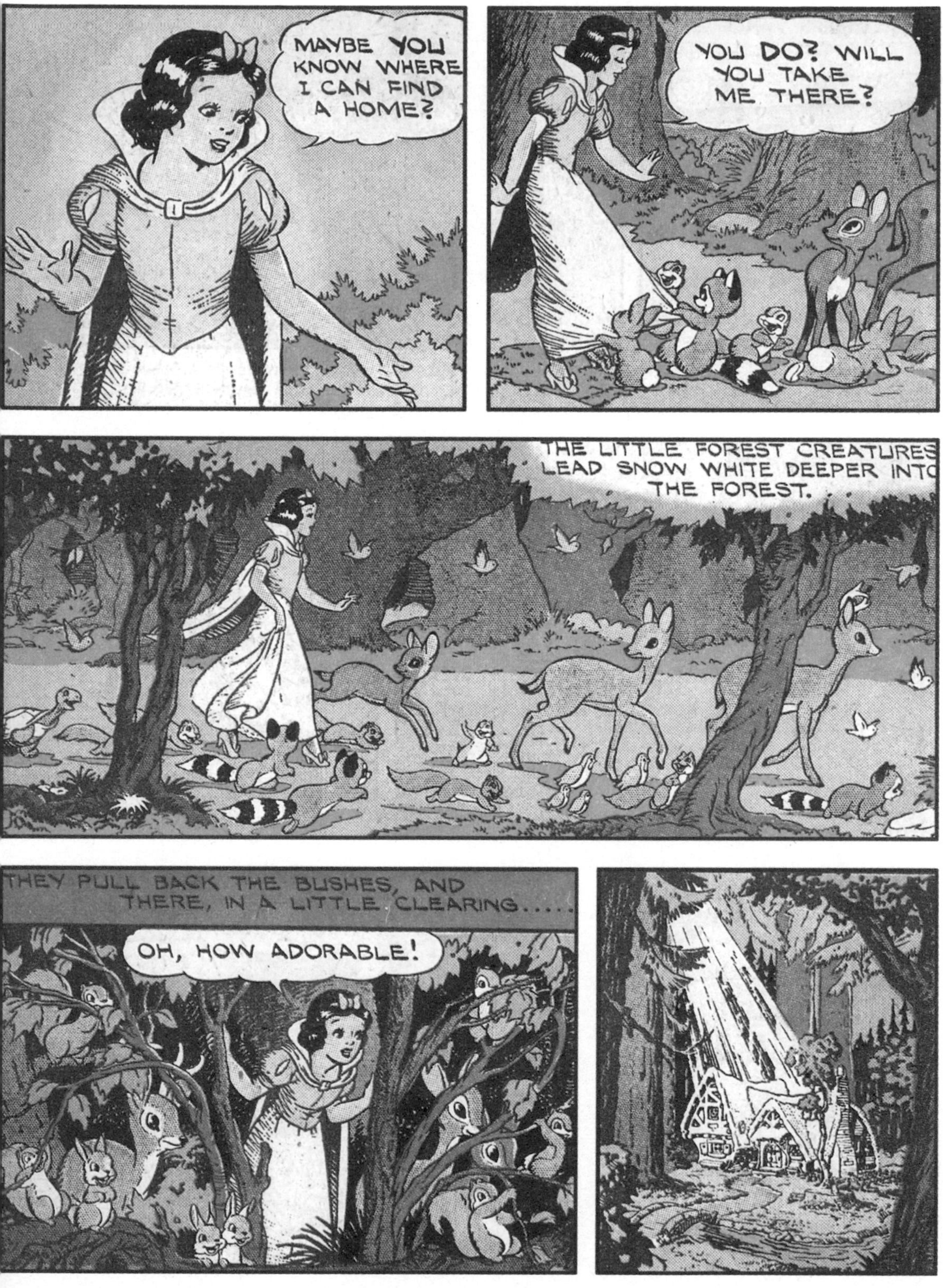
MAYBE YOU KNOW WHERE I CAN FIND A HOME?
YOU DO? WILL YOU TAKE ME THERE?
THE LITTLE FOREST CREATURES LEAD SNOW WHITE DEEPER INTO THE FOREST. . .
THEY PULL BACK THE BUSHES, AND THERE, IN A LITTLE CLEARING.....
OH, HOW ADORABLE!

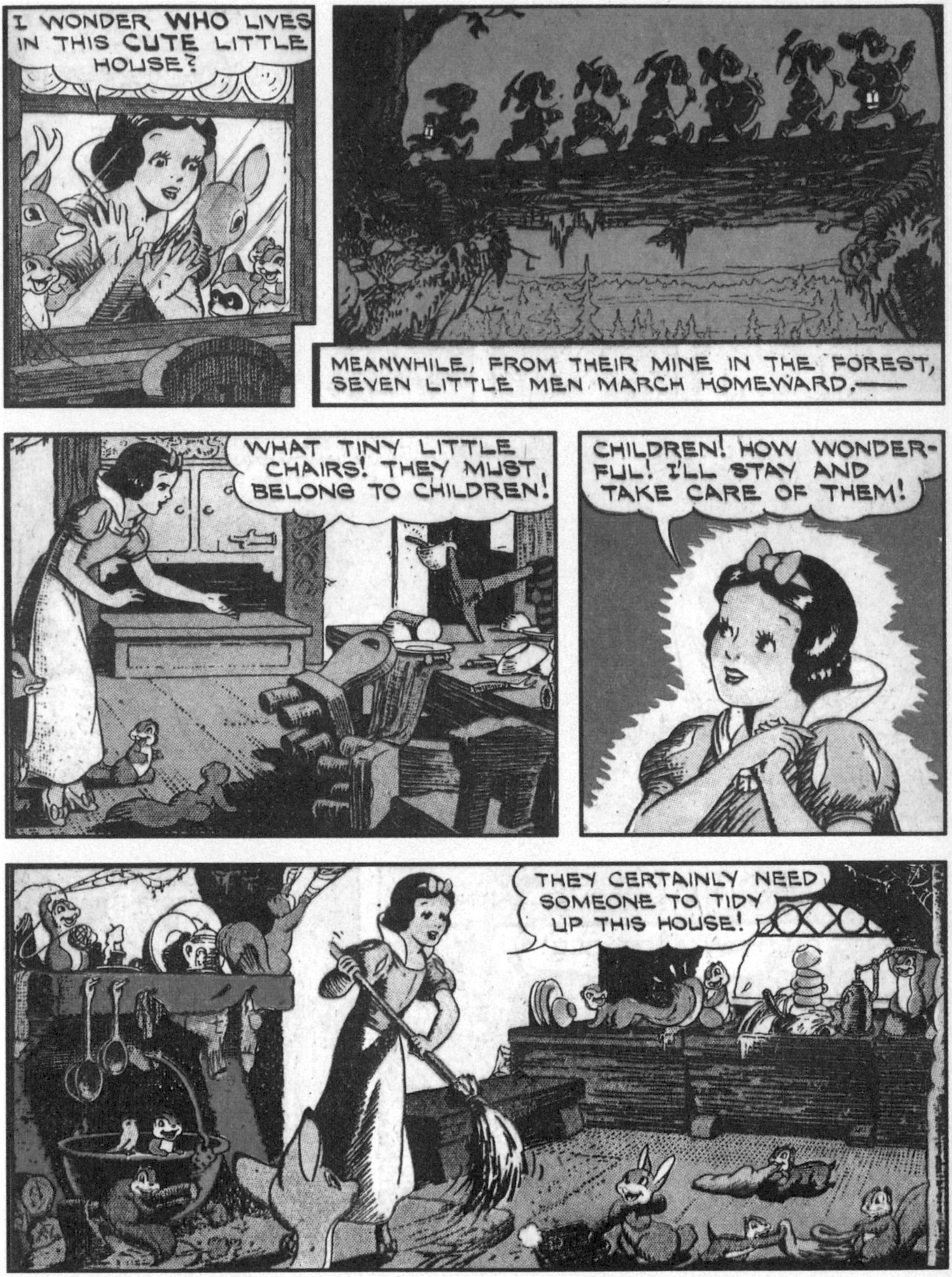
I WONDER WHO LIVES IN THIS CUTE LITTLE HOUSE?
MEANWHILE, FROM THEIR MINE IN THE FOREST, SEVEN LITTLE MEN MARCH HOMEWARD.——
WHAT TINY LITTLE CHAIRS! THEY MUST BELONG TO CHILDREN!
CHILDREN! HOW WONDER-FUL! I'LL STAY AND TAKE CARE OF THEM!
THEY CERTAINLY NEED SOMEONE TO TIDY UP THIS HOUSE!

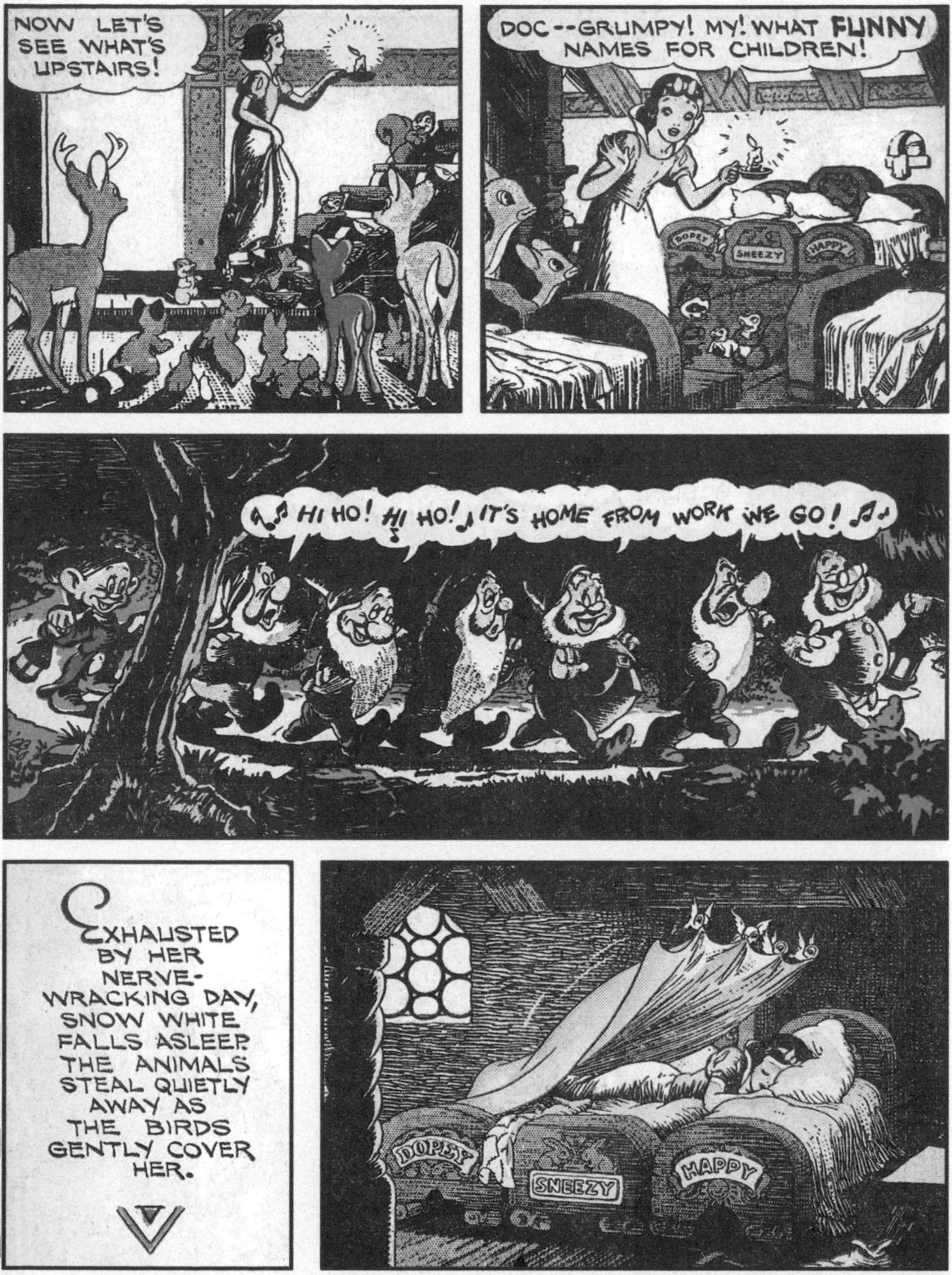
NOW LET'S SEE WHAT'S UPSTAIRS!
DOC--GRUMPY! MY! WHAT FUNNY NAMES FOR CHILDREN!
DOPEY
SNEEZY
HAPPY
HI HO! HI HO! IT'S HOME FROM WORK WE GO!
EXHAUSTED BY HER NERVE-WRACKING DAY, SNOW WHITE FALLS ASLEEP. THE ANIMALS STEAL QUIETLY AWAY AS THE BIRDS GENTLY COVER HER.
DOPEY
SNEEZY
HAPPY

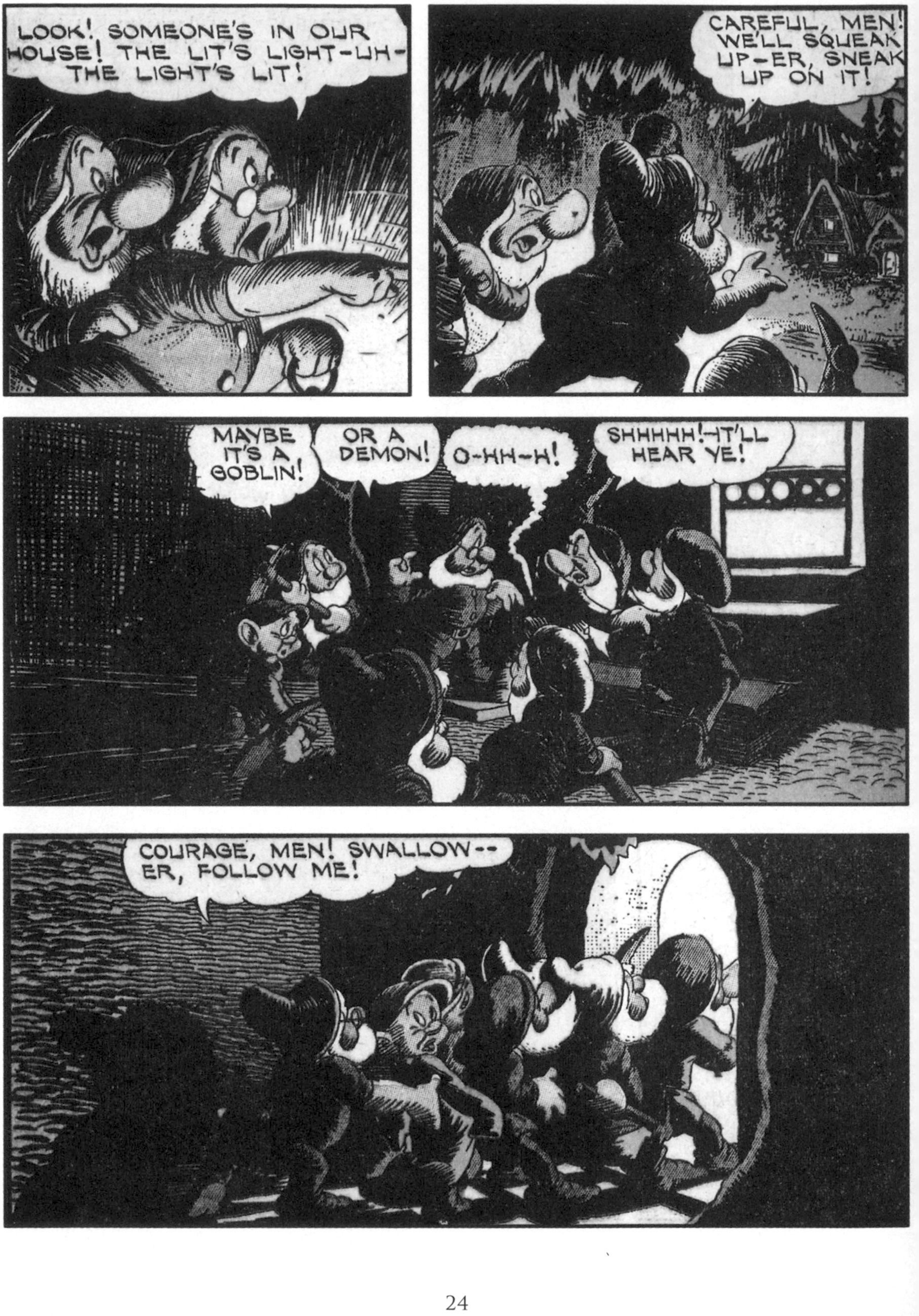
LOOK! SOMEONE'S IN OUR HOUSE! THE LIT'S LIGHT-UH-THE LIGHT'S LIT!
CAREFUL, MEN! WE'LL SQUEAK UP-ER, SNEAK UP ON IT!
MAYBE IT'S A GOBLIN!
OR A DEMON!
O-HH-H!
SHHHHH!-IT'LL HEAR YE!
COURAGE, MEN! SWALLOW--ER, FOLLOW ME!

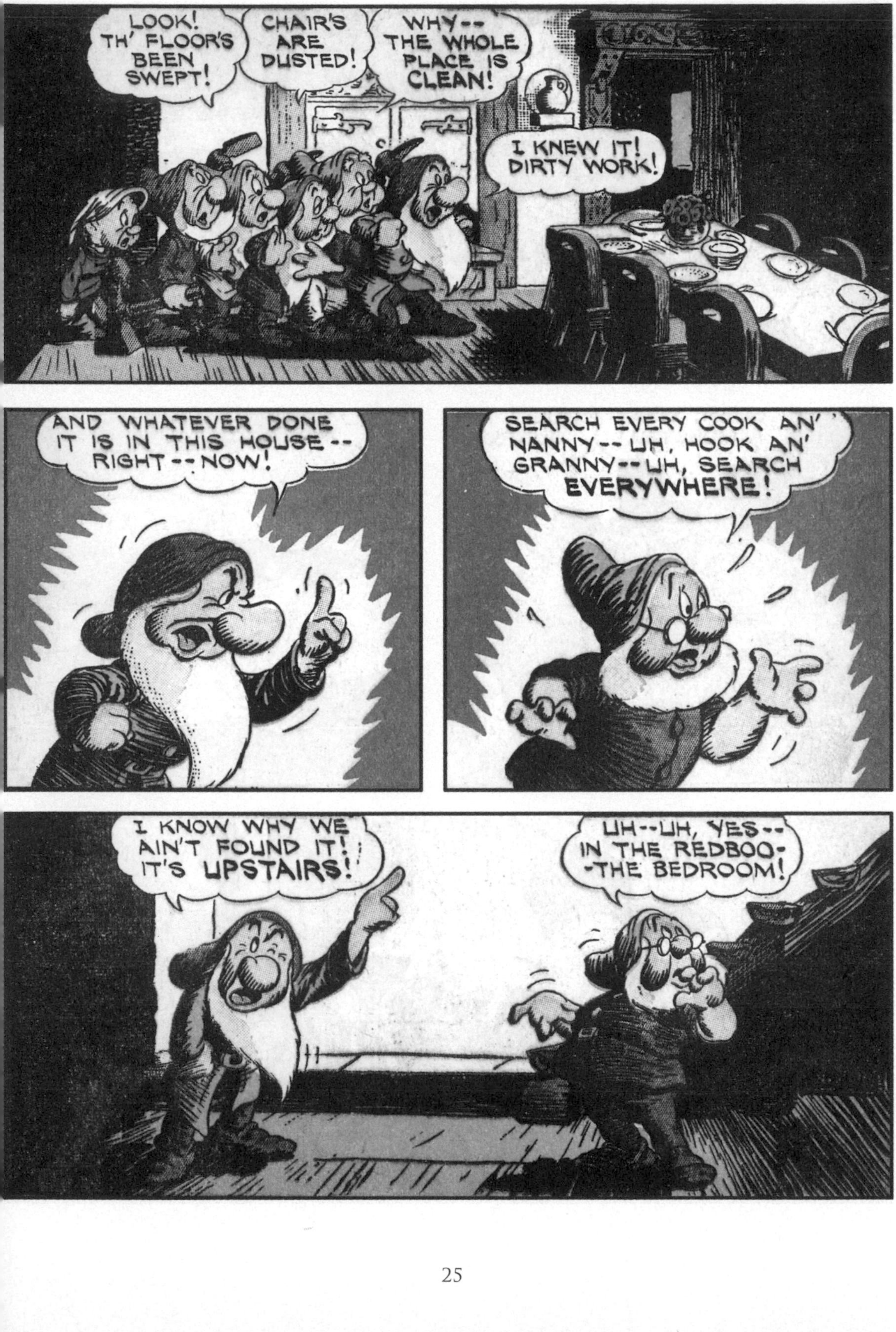
LOOK! TH' FLOOR'S BEEN SWEPT!
CHAIR'S ARE DUSTED!
WHY-- THE WHOLE PLACE IS CLEAN!
I KNEW IT! DIRTY WORK!
AND WHATEVER DONE IT IS IN THIS HOUSE-- RIGHT--NOW!
SEARCH EVERY COOK AN' NANNY--UH, HOOK AN' GRANNY--UH, SEARCH EVERYWHERE!
I KNOW WHY WE AIN'T FOUND IT! IT'S UPSTAIRS!
UH--UH, YES-- IN THE REDBOO- -THE BEDROOM!

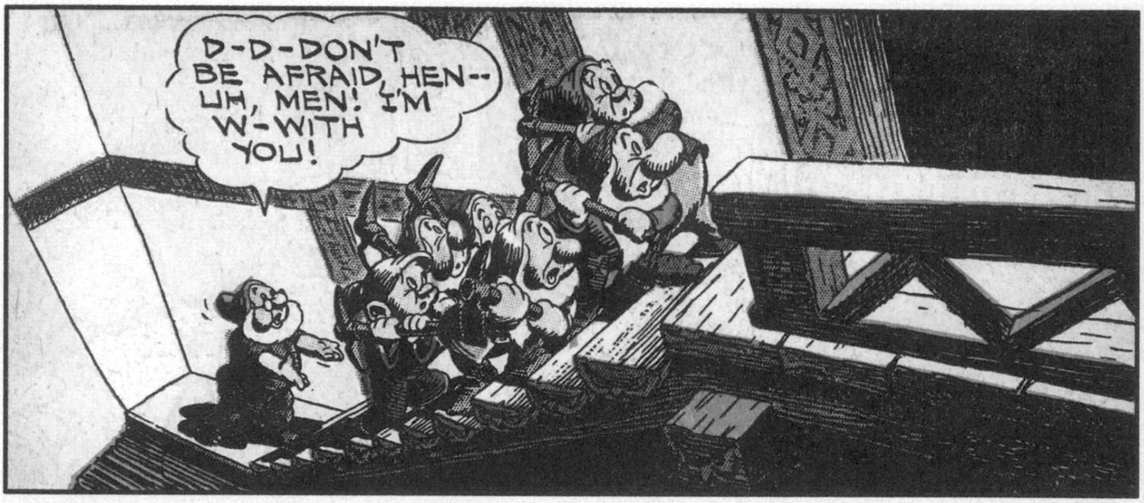
D-D-DON'T BE AFRAID, HEN-- UH, MEN! I'M W-WITH YOU!

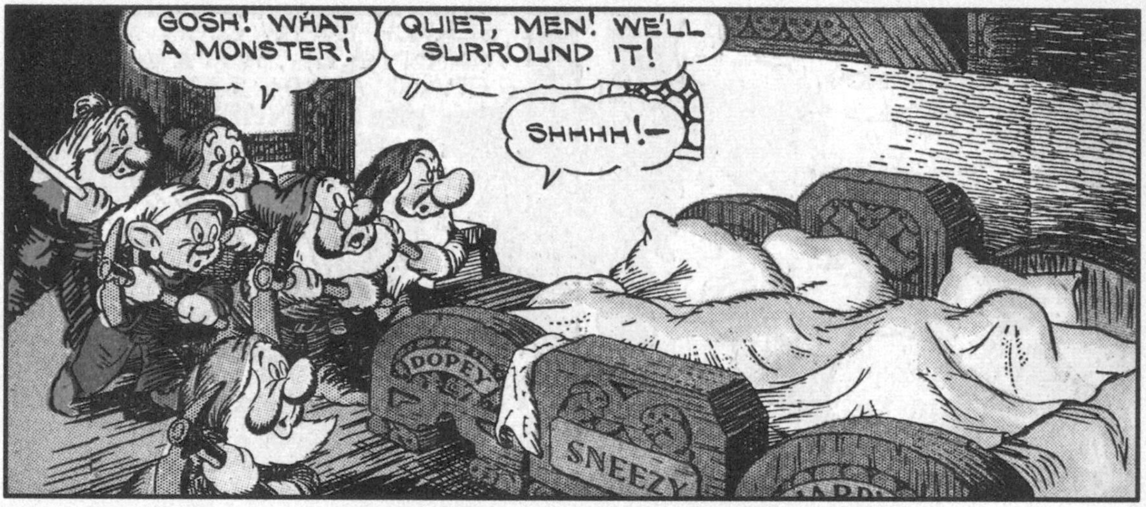
GOSH! WHAT A MONSTER!
QUIET, MEN! WE'LL SURROUND IT!
SHHHH!-
DOPEY
SNEEZY

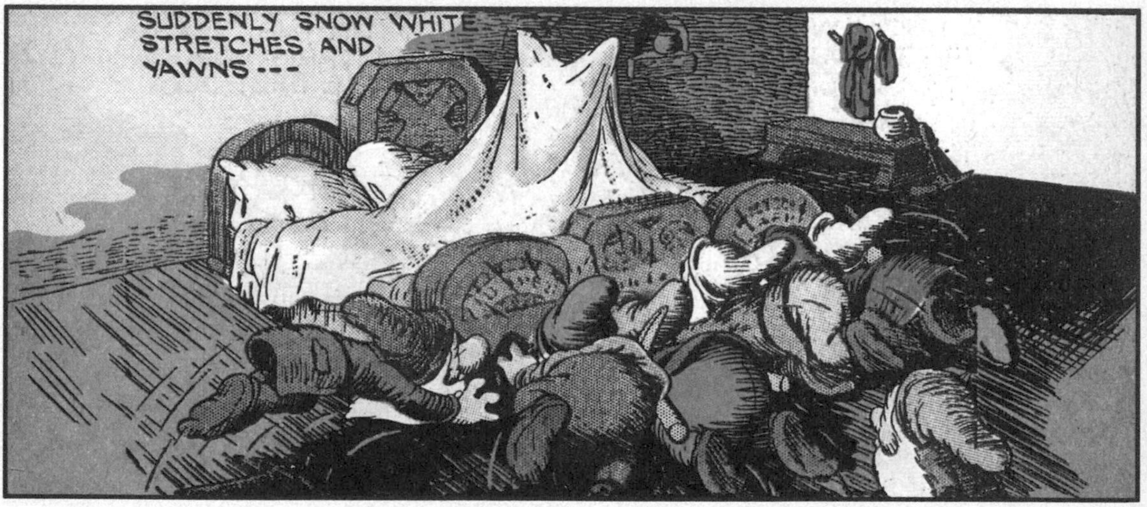
SUDDENLY SNOW WHITE STRETCHES AND YAWNS---

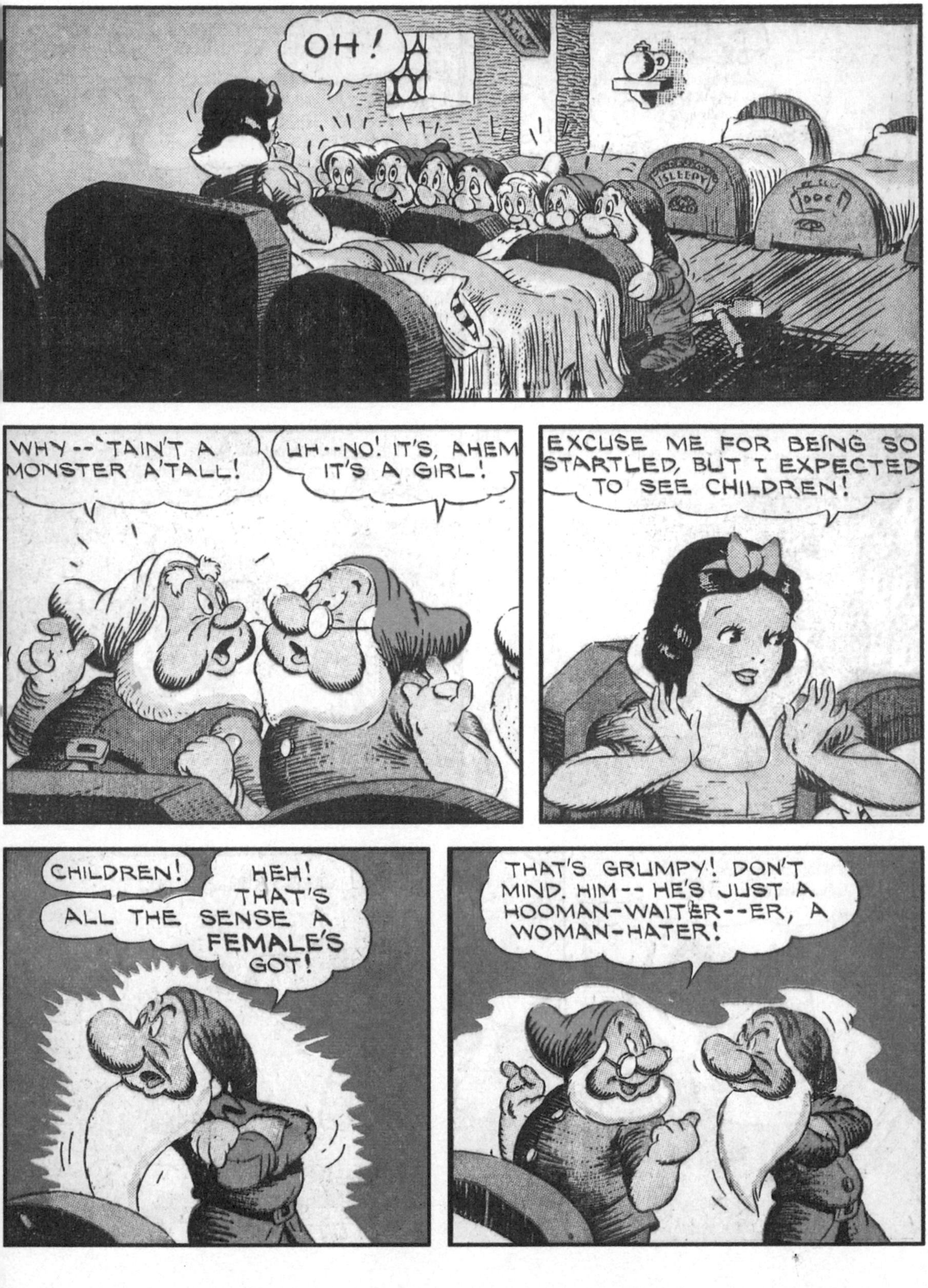
OH!
SLEEPY
DOC
WHY--'TAIN'T A MONSTER A'TALL!
UH--NO! IT'S, AHEM IT'S A GIRL!
EXCUSE ME FOR BEING SO STARTLED, BUT I EXPECTED TO SEE CHILDREN!
CHILDREN!
HEH! THAT'S ALL THE SENSE A FEMALE'S GOT!
THAT'S GRUMPY! DON'T MIND. HIM-- HE'S JUST A HOOMAN-WAITER--ER, A WOMAN-HATER!

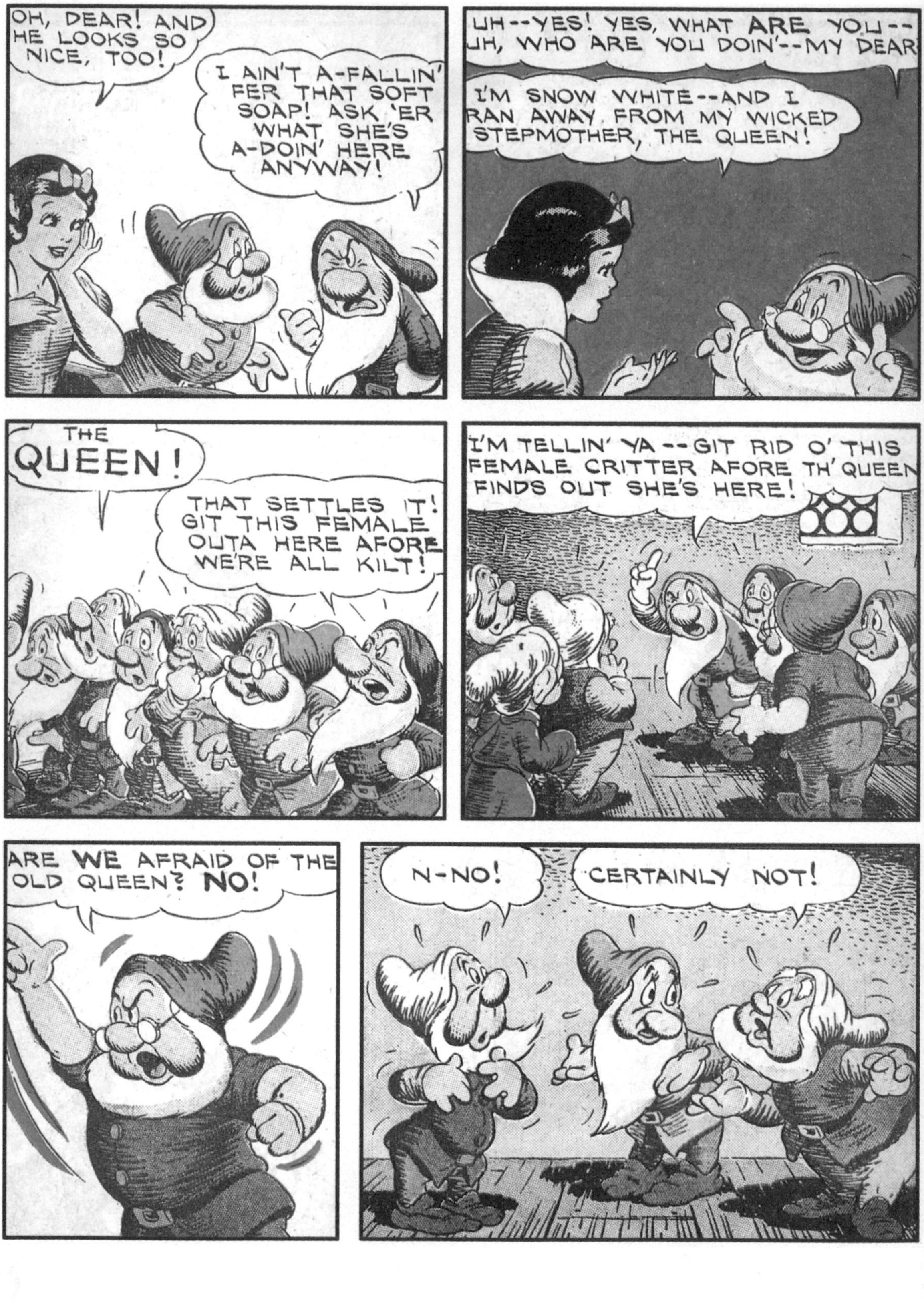
OH, DEAR! AND HE LOOKS SO NICE, TOO!
I AIN'T A-FALLIN' FER THAT SOFT SOAP! ASK 'ER WHAT SHE'S A-DOIN' HERE ANYWAY!
UH--YES! YES, WHAT ARE YOU--UH, WHO ARE YOU DOIN'--MY DEAR
I'M SNOW WHITE--AND I RAN AWAY FROM MY WICKED STEPMOTHER, THE QUEEN!
THE QUEEN!
THAT SETTLES IT! GIT THIS FEMALE OUTA HERE AFORE WE'RE ALL KILT!
I'M TELLIN' YA--GIT RID O' THIS FEMALE CRITTER AFORE TH' QUEEN FINDS OUT SHE'S HERE!
ARE WE AFRAID OF THE OLD QUEEN? NO!
N-NO!
CERTAINLY NOT!

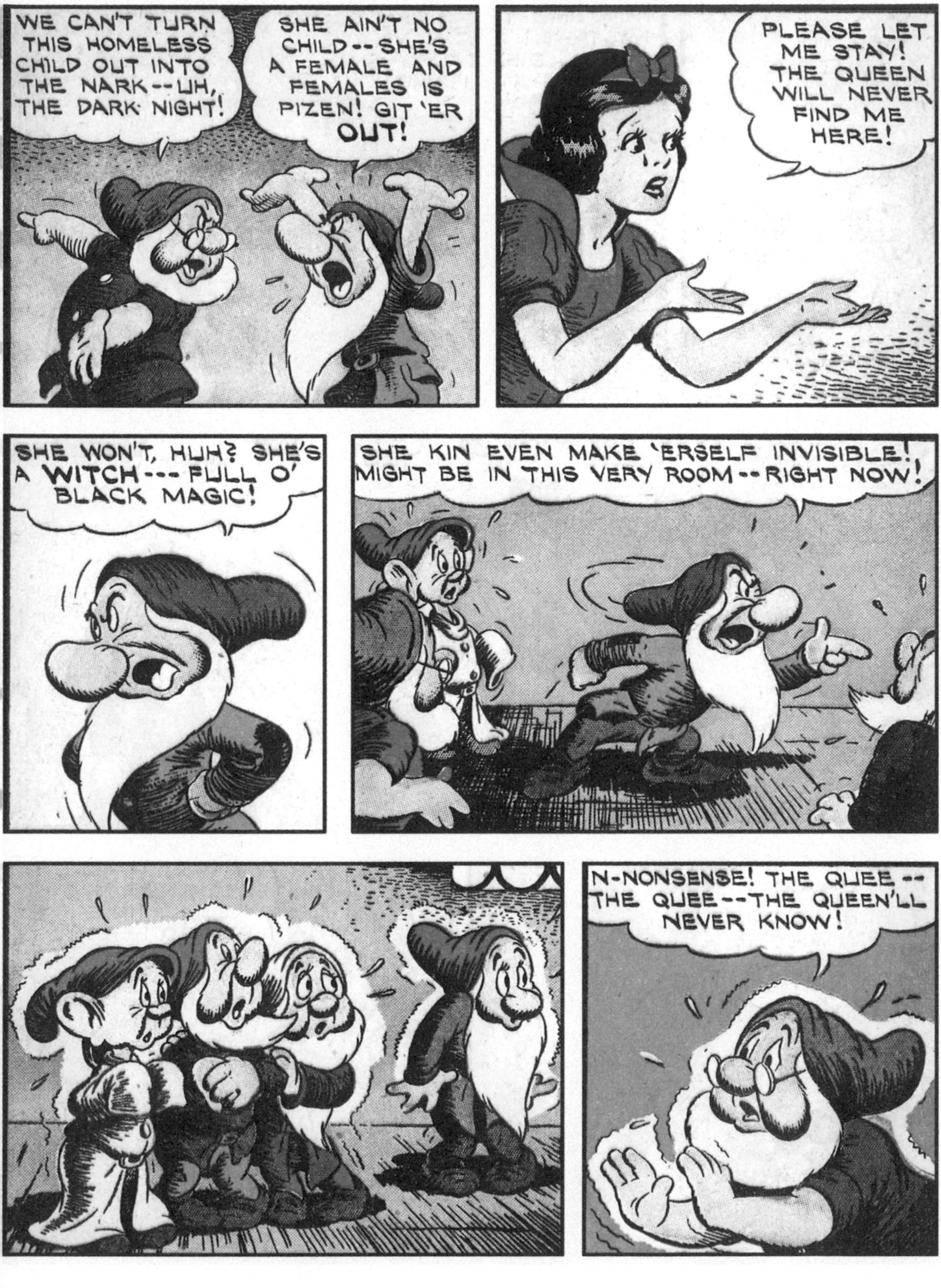
WE CAN'T TURN THIS HOMELESS CHILD OUT INTO THE NARK--UH, THE DARK NIGHT!
SHE AIN'T NO CHILD--SHE'S A FEMALE AND FEMALES IS PIZEN! GIT 'ER OUT!
PLEASE LET ME STAY! THE QUEEN WILL NEVER FIND ME HERE!
SHE WON'T, HUH? SHE'S A WITCH---FULL O' BLACK MAGIC!
SHE KIN EVEN MAKE 'ERSELF INVISIBLE! MIGHT BE IN THIS VERY ROOM--RIGHT NOW!
N-NONSENSE! THE QUEE--THE QUEE--THE QUEEN'LL NEVER KNOW!

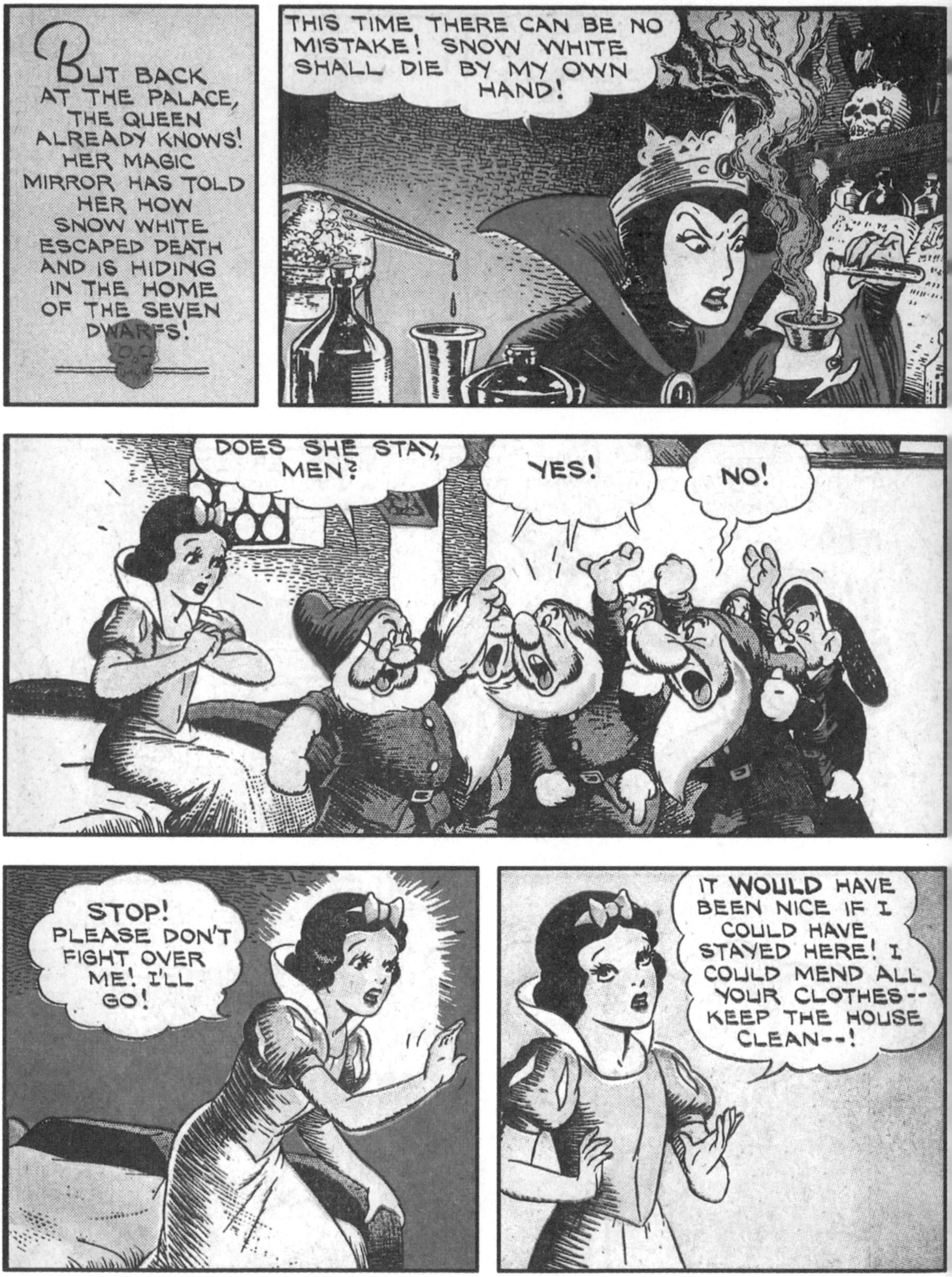
BUT BACK AT THE PALACE, THE QUEEN ALREADY KNOWS! HER MAGIC MIRROR HAS TOLD HER HOW SNOW WHITE ESCAPED DEATH AND IS HIDING IN THE HOME OF THE SEVEN DWARFS!
THIS TIME THERE CAN BE NO MISTAKE! SNOW WHITE SHALL DIE BY MY OWN HAND!
DOES SHE STAY, MEN?
YES!
NO!
STOP! PLEASE DON'T FIGHT OVER ME! I'LL GO!
IT WOULD HAVE BEEN NICE IF I COULD HAVE STAYED HERE! I COULD MEND ALL YOUR CLOTHES-- KEEP THE HOUSE CLEAN--!

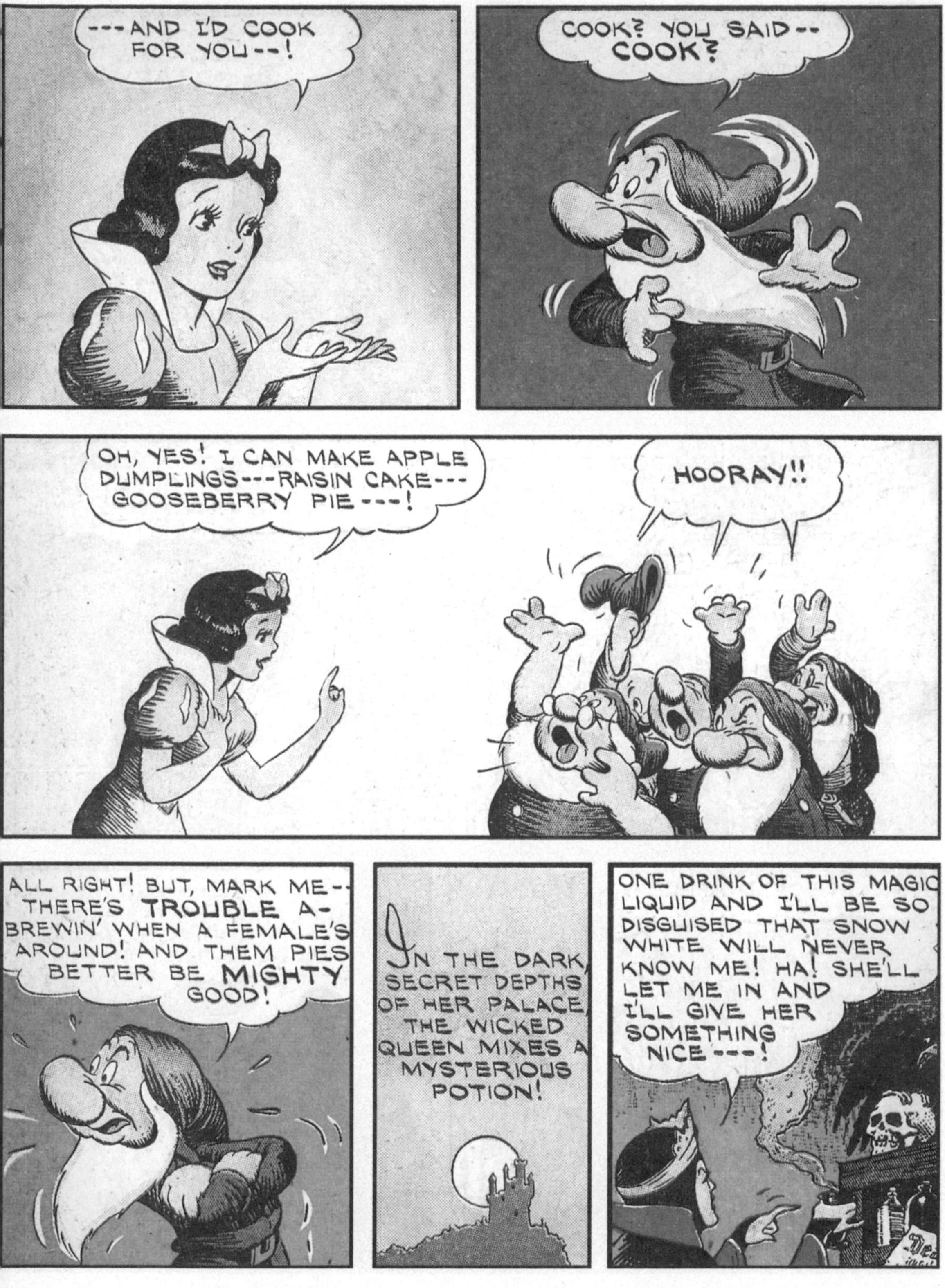
---AND I'D COOK FOR YOU--!
COOK? YOU SAID-- COOK?
OH, YES! I CAN MAKE APPLE DUMPLINGS---RAISIN CAKE--- GOOSEBERRY PIE---!
HOORAY!!
ALL RIGHT! BUT, MARK ME-- THERE'S TROUBLE A-BREWIN' WHEN A FEMALE'S AROUND! AND THEM PIES BETTER BE MIGHTY GOOD!
IN THE DARK, SECRET DEPTHS OF HER PALACE, THE WICKED QUEEN MIXES A MYSTERIOUS POTION!
ONE DRINK OF THIS MAGIC LIQUID AND I'LL BE SO DISGUISED THAT SNOW WHITE WILL NEVER KNOW ME! HA! SHE'LL LET ME IN AND I'LL GIVE HER SOMETHING NICE---!

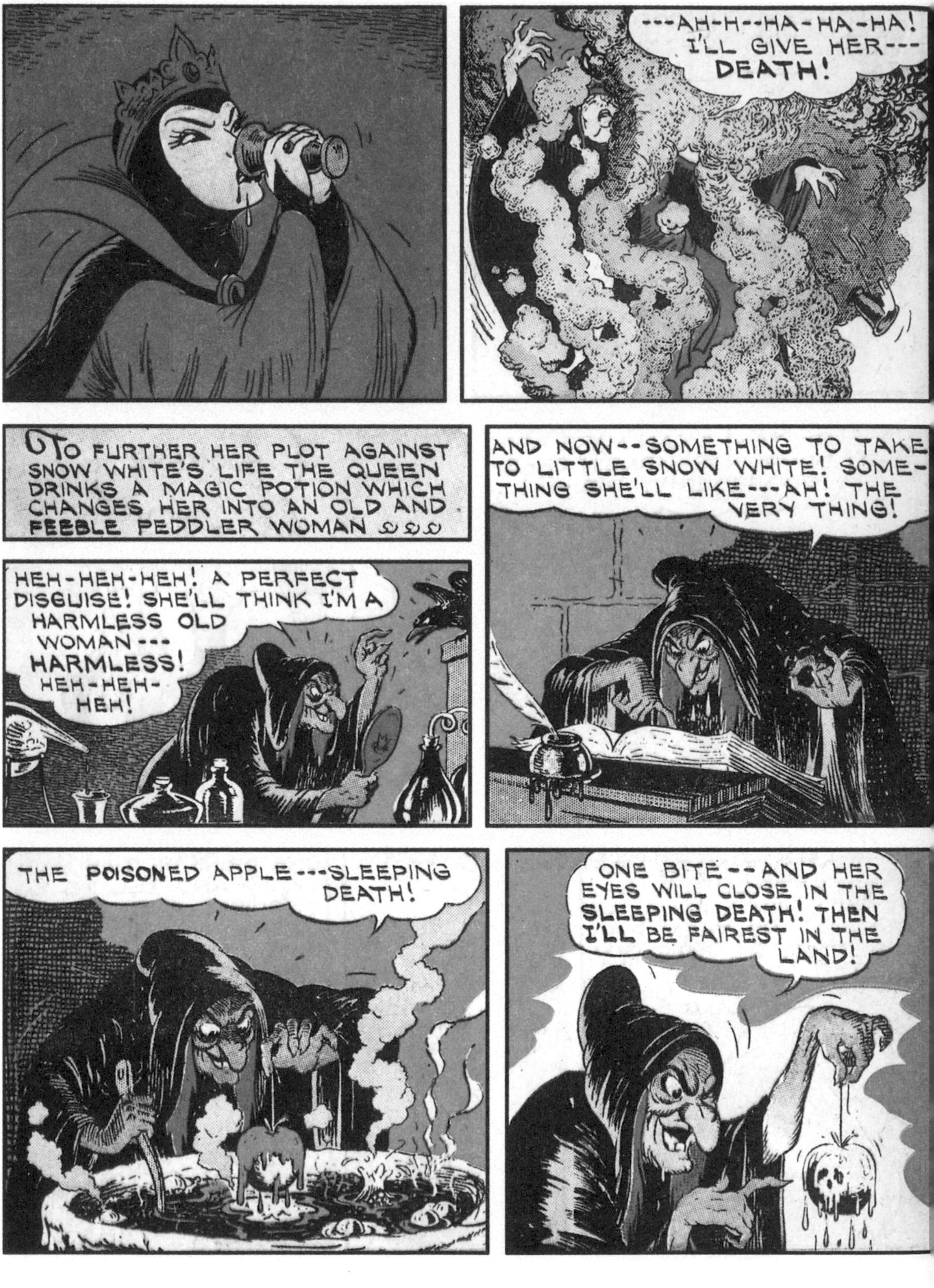
---AH-H--HA-HA-HA! I'LL GIVE HER--- DEATH!
TO FURTHER HER PLOT AGAINST SNOW WHITE'S LIFE THE QUEEN DRINKS A MAGIC POTION WHICH CHANGES HER INTO AN OLD AND FEEBLE PEDDLER WOMAN
HEH-HEH-HEH! A PERFECT DISGUISE! SHE'LL THINK I'M A HARMLESS OLD WOMAN --- HARMLESS! HEH-HEH-HEH!
AND NOW--SOMETHING TO TAKE TO LITTLE SNOW WHITE! SOMETHING SHE'LL LIKE---AH! THE VERY THING!
THE POISONED APPLE---SLEEPING DEATH!
ONE BITE--AND HER EYES WILL CLOSE IN THE SLEEPING DEATH! THEN I'LL BE FAIREST IN THE LAND!

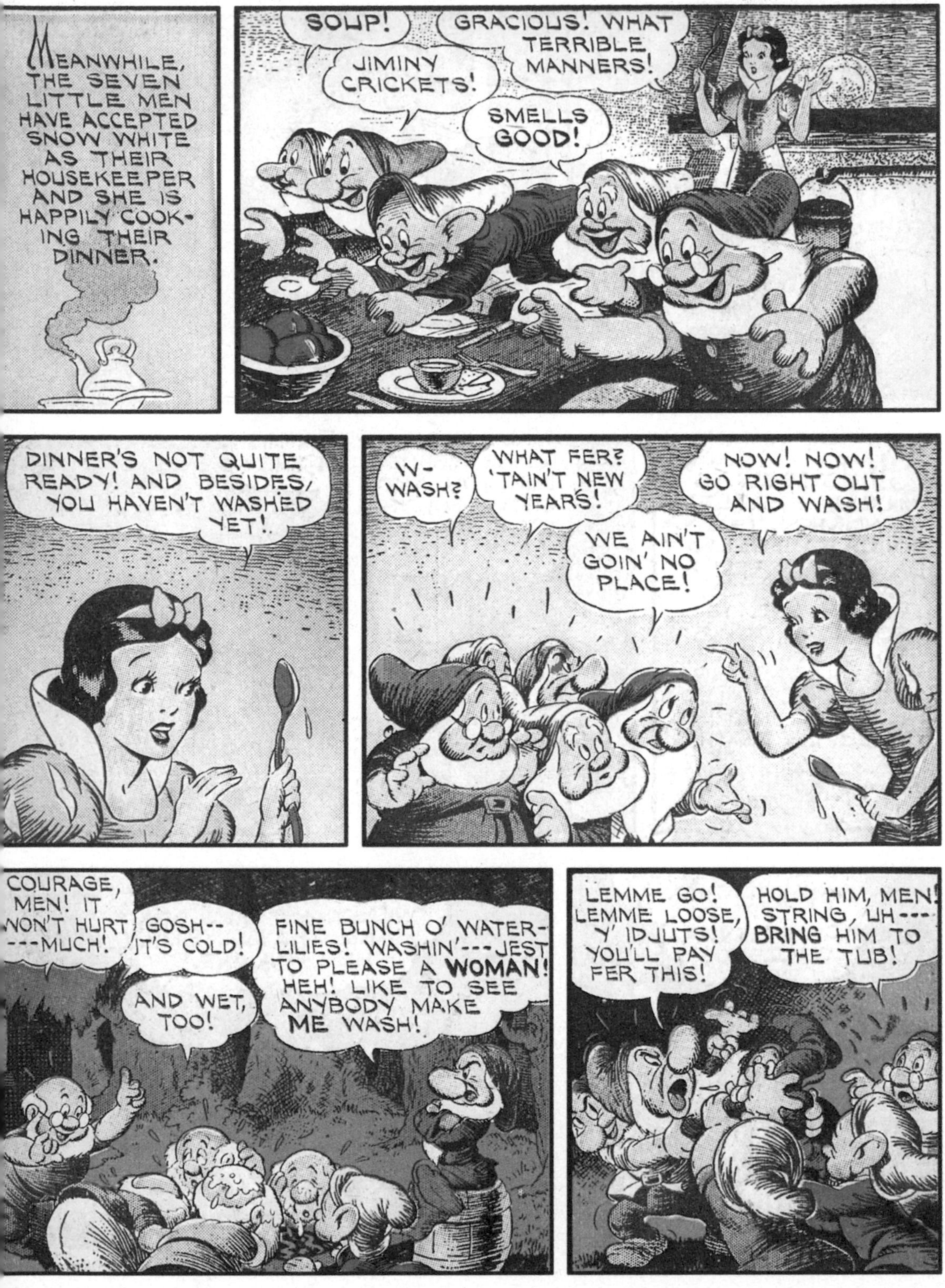
MEANWHILE, THE SEVEN LITTLE MEN HAVE ACCEPTED SNOW WHITE AS THEIR HOUSEKEEPER AND SHE IS HAPPILY COOKING THEIR DINNER.
SOUP!
GRACIOUS! WHAT TERRIBLE MANNERS!
JIMINY CRICKETS!
SMELLS GOOD!
DINNER'S NOT QUITE READY! AND BESIDES, YOU HAVEN'T WASHED YET!
W-WASH?
WHAT FER? 'TAIN'T NEW YEAR'S!
NOW! NOW! GO RIGHT OUT AND WASH!
WE AIN'T GOIN' NO PLACE!
COURAGE, MEN! IT WON'T HURT ---MUCH!
GOSH-- IT'S COLD!
AND WET, TOO!
FINE BUNCH O' WATER-LILIES! WASHIN'---JEST TO PLEASE A **WOMAN**! HEH! LIKE TO SEE ANYBODY MAKE **ME** WASH!
LEMME GO! LEMME LOOSE, Y' IDJUTS! YOU'LL PAY FER THIS!
HOLD HIM, MEN! STRING, UH--- **BRING** HIM TO THE TUB!

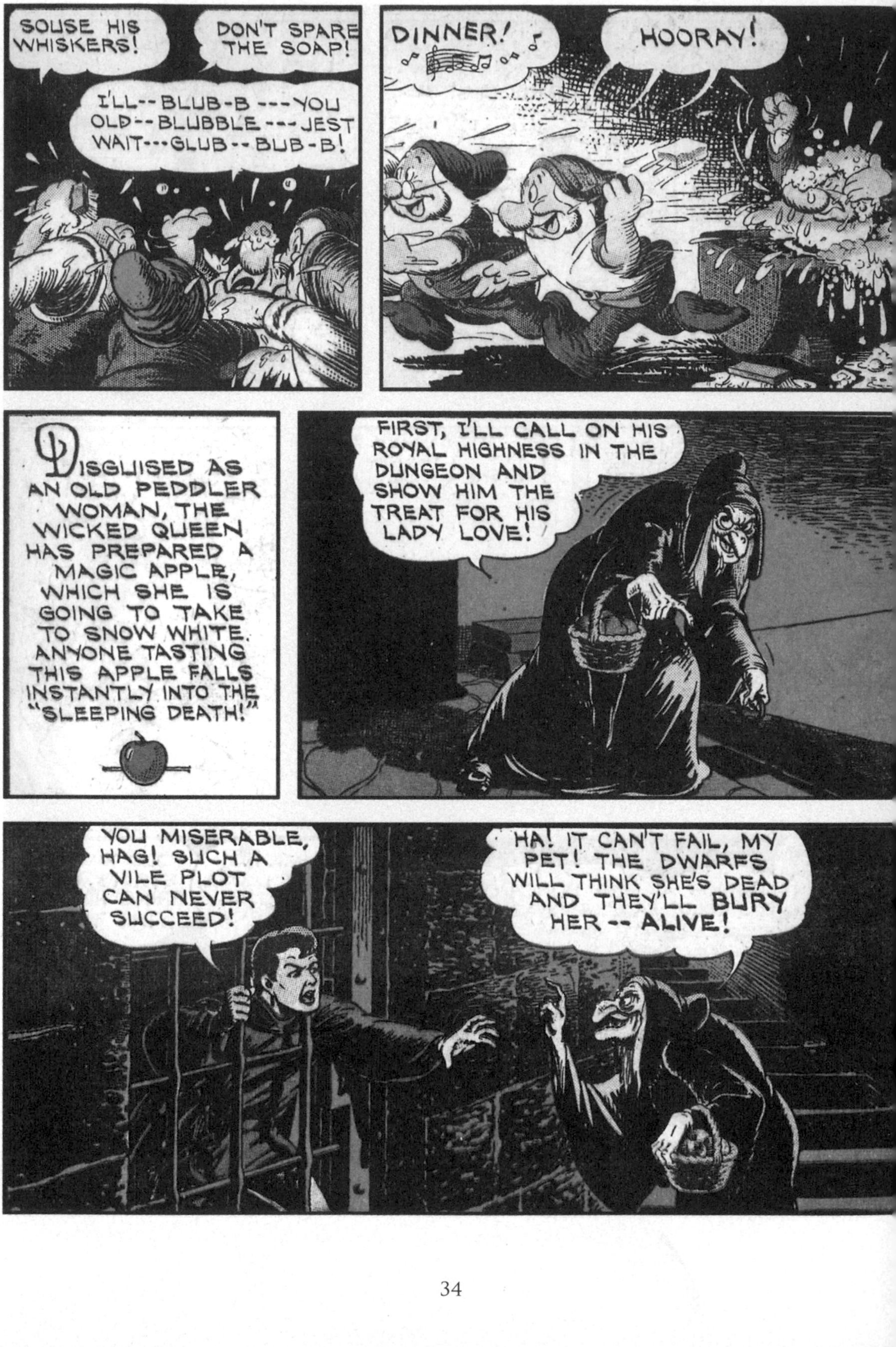
SOUSE HIS WHISKERS!
DON'T SPARE THE SOAP!
I'LL--BLUB-B---YOU OLD--BLUBBLE---JEST WAIT---GLUB--BUB-B!
DINNER!
HOORAY!
DISGUISED AS AN OLD PEDDLER WOMAN, THE WICKED QUEEN HAS PREPARED A MAGIC APPLE, WHICH SHE IS GOING TO TAKE TO SNOW WHITE. ANYONE TASTING THIS APPLE FALLS INSTANTLY INTO THE "SLEEPING DEATH!"
FIRST, I'LL CALL ON HIS ROYAL HIGHNESS IN THE DUNGEON AND SHOW HIM THE TREAT FOR HIS LADY LOVE!
YOU MISERABLE, HAG! SUCH A VILE PLOT CAN NEVER SUCCEED!
HA! IT CAN'T FAIL, MY PET! THE DWARFS WILL THINK SHE'S DEAD AND THEY'LL BURY HER -- ALIVE!

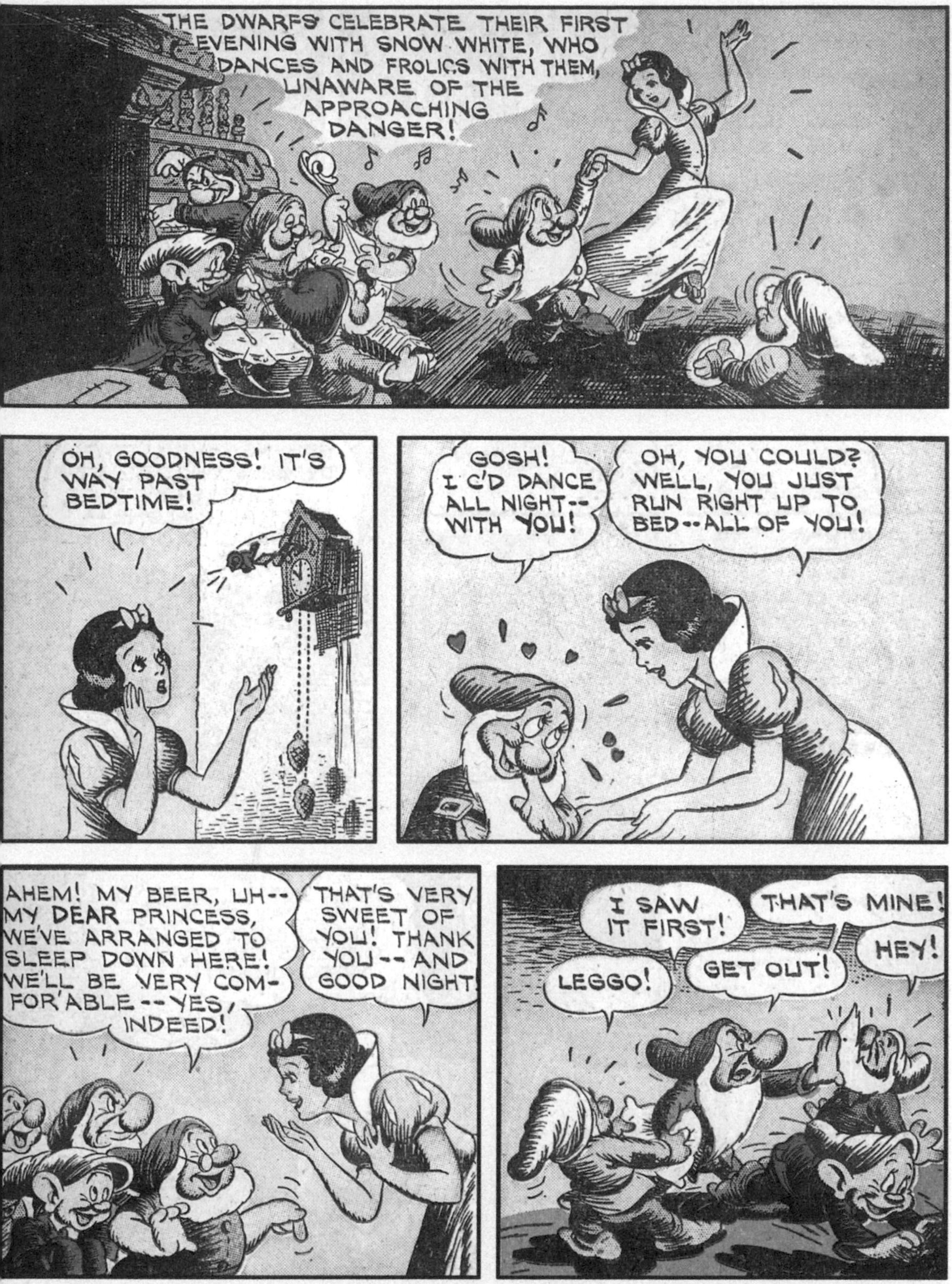
THE DWARFS CELEBRATE THEIR FIRST EVENING WITH SNOW WHITE, WHO DANCES AND FROLICS WITH THEM, UNAWARE OF THE APPROACHING DANGER!
OH, GOODNESS! IT'S WAY PAST BEDTIME!
GOSH! I C'D DANCE ALL NIGHT-- WITH YOU!
OH, YOU COULD? WELL, YOU JUST RUN RIGHT UP TO BED--ALL OF YOU!
AHEM! MY BEER, UH-- MY DEAR PRINCESS, WE'VE ARRANGED TO SLEEP DOWN HERE! WE'LL BE VERY COM-FOR'ABLE --YES, INDEED!
THAT'S VERY SWEET OF YOU! THANK YOU -- AND GOOD NIGHT!
I SAW IT FIRST!
THAT'S MINE!
HEY!
LEGGO!
GET OUT!

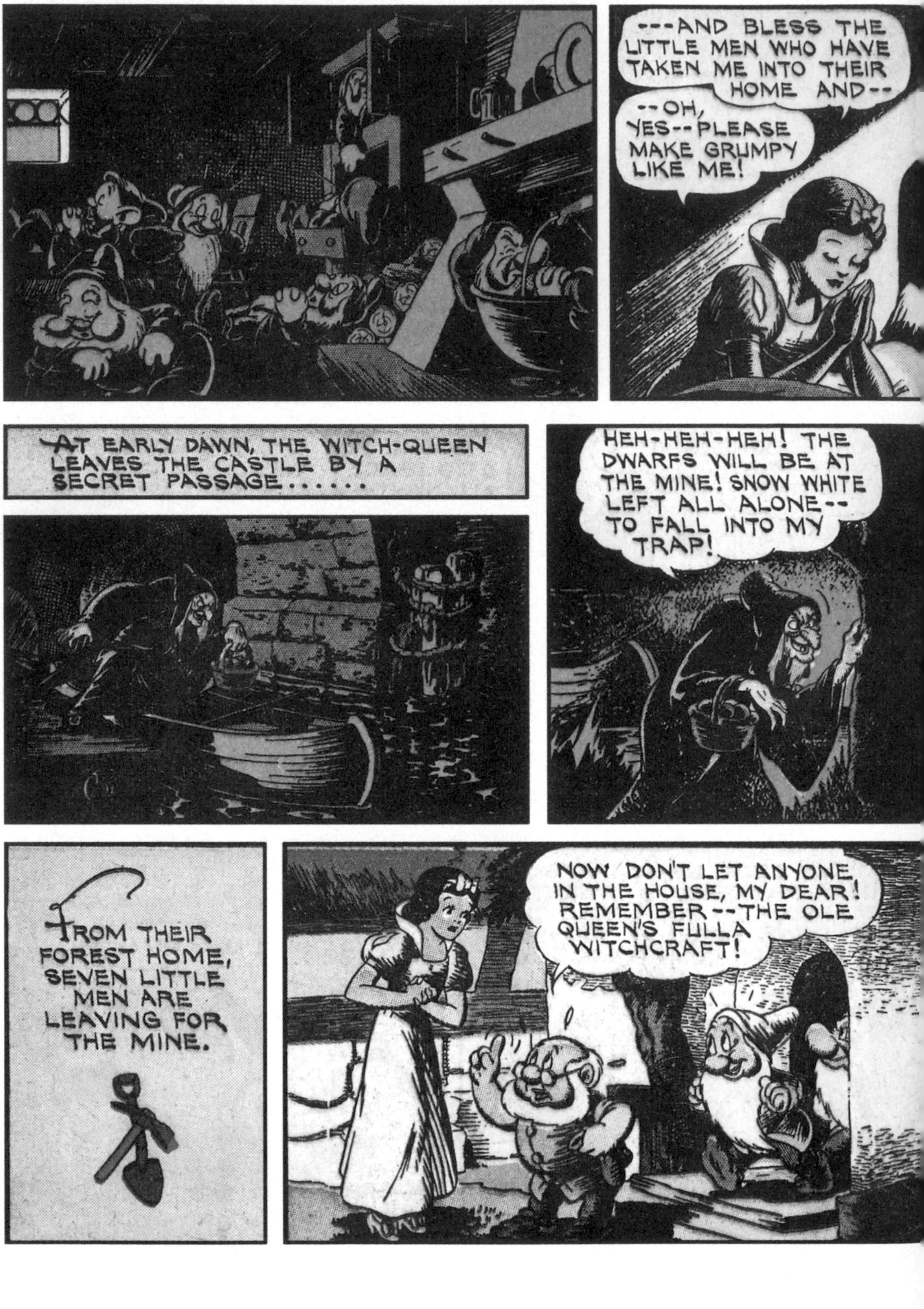
---AND BLESS THE LITTLE MEN WHO HAVE TAKEN ME INTO THEIR HOME AND--
--OH, YES--PLEASE MAKE GRUMPY LIKE ME!
AT EARLY DAWN, THE WITCH-QUEEN LEAVES THE CASTLE BY A SECRET PASSAGE......
HEH-HEH-HEH! THE DWARFS WILL BE AT THE MINE! SNOW WHITE LEFT ALL ALONE--TO FALL INTO MY TRAP!
FROM THEIR FOREST HOME, SEVEN LITTLE MEN ARE LEAVING FOR THE MINE.
NOW DON'T LET ANYONE IN THE HOUSE, MY DEAR! REMEMBER--THE OLE QUEEN'S FULLA WITCHCRAFT!

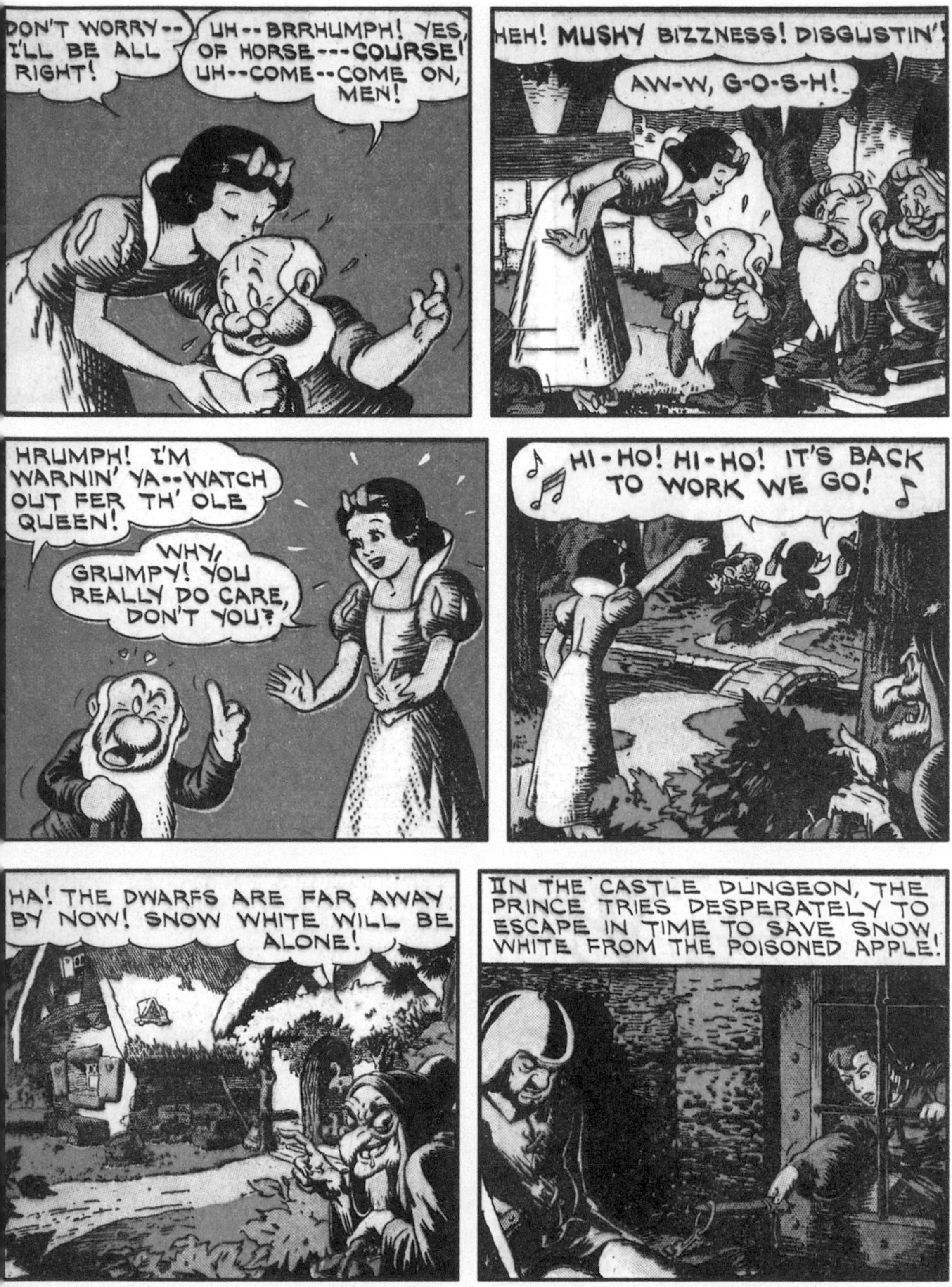
DON'T WORRY -- I'LL BE ALL RIGHT!
UH -- BRRHUMPH! YES, OF HORSE --- COURSE! UH -- COME -- COME ON, MEN!
HEH! MUSHY BIZZNESS! DISGUSTIN'!
AW-W, G-O-S-H!
HRUMPH! I'M WARNIN' YA -- WATCH OUT FER TH' OLE QUEEN!
WHY, GRUMPY! YOU REALLY DO CARE, DON'T YOU?
HI - HO! HI - HO! IT'S BACK TO WORK WE GO!
HA! THE DWARFS ARE FAR AWAY BY NOW! SNOW WHITE WILL BE ALONE!
IN THE CASTLE DUNGEON, THE PRINCE TRIES DESPERATELY TO ESCAPE IN TIME TO SAVE SNOW WHITE FROM THE POISONED APPLE!

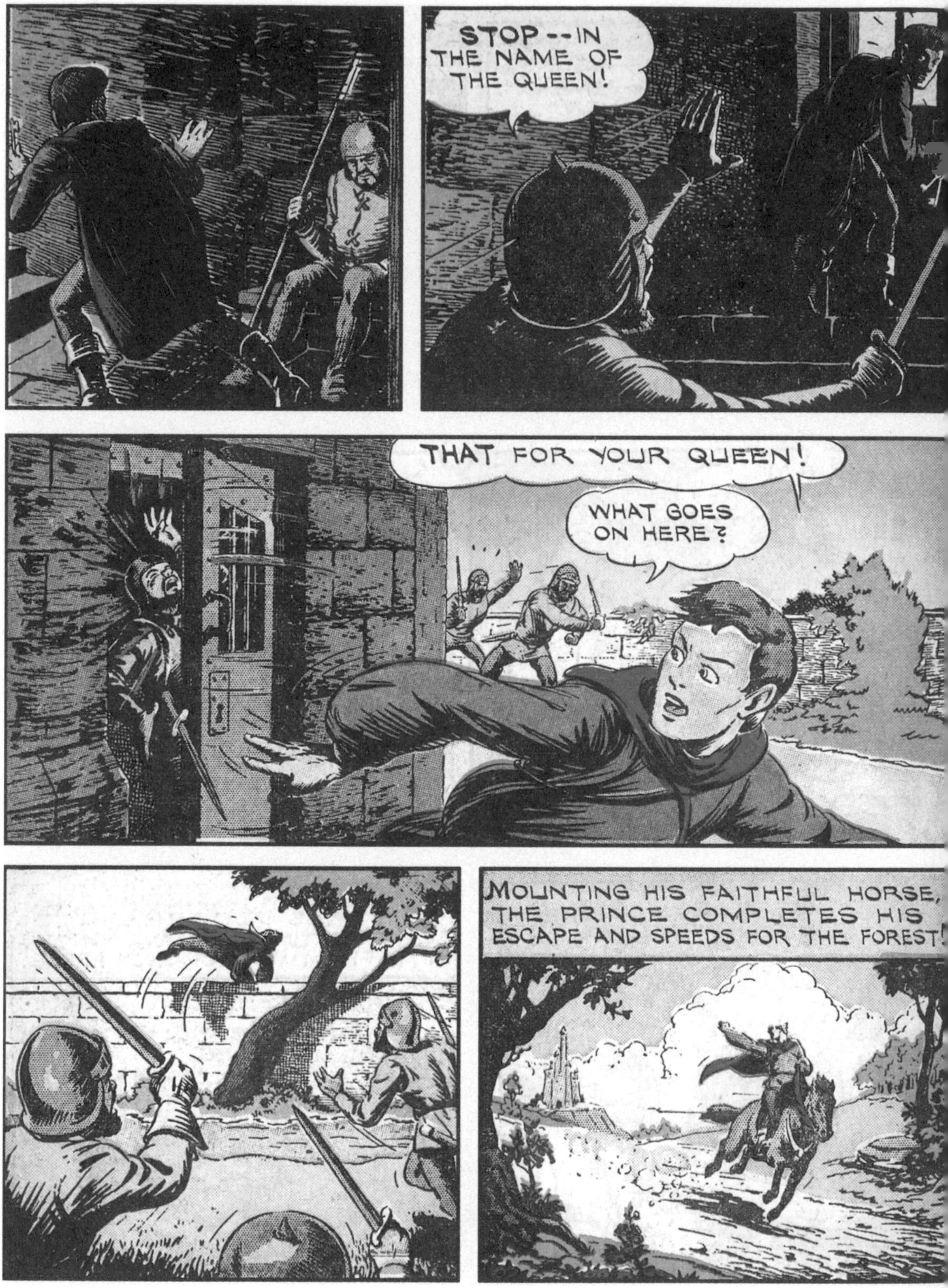
STOP--IN THE NAME OF THE QUEEN!
THAT FOR YOUR QUEEN!
WHAT GOES ON HERE?
MOUNTING HIS FAITHFUL HORSE, THE PRINCE COMPLETES HIS ESCAPE AND SPEEDS FOR THE FOREST!

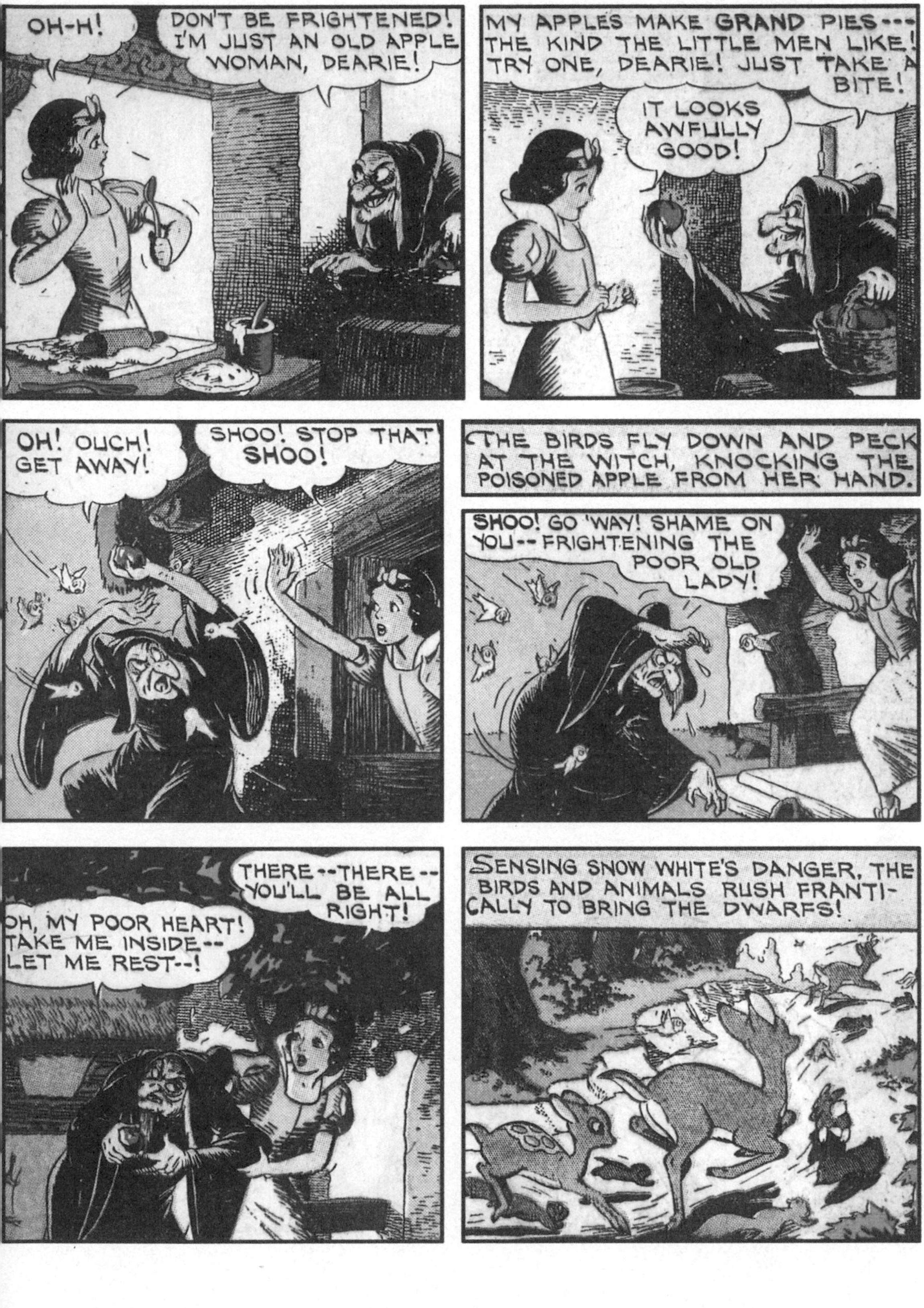
OH-H!
DON'T BE FRIGHTENED! I'M JUST AN OLD APPLE WOMAN, DEARIE!
MY APPLES MAKE GRAND PIES--- THE KIND THE LITTLE MEN LIKE! TRY ONE, DEARIE! JUST TAKE A BITE!
IT LOOKS AWFULLY GOOD!
OH! OUCH! GET AWAY!
SHOO! STOP THAT! SHOO!
THE BIRDS FLY DOWN AND PECK AT THE WITCH, KNOCKING THE POISONED APPLE FROM HER HAND.
SHOO! GO 'WAY! SHAME ON YOU--FRIGHTENING THE POOR OLD LADY!
OH, MY POOR HEART! TAKE ME INSIDE-- LET ME REST--!
THERE--THERE-- YOU'LL BE ALL RIGHT!
SENSING SNOW WHITE'S DANGER, THE BIRDS AND ANIMALS RUSH FRANTI-CALLY TO BRING THE DWARFS!

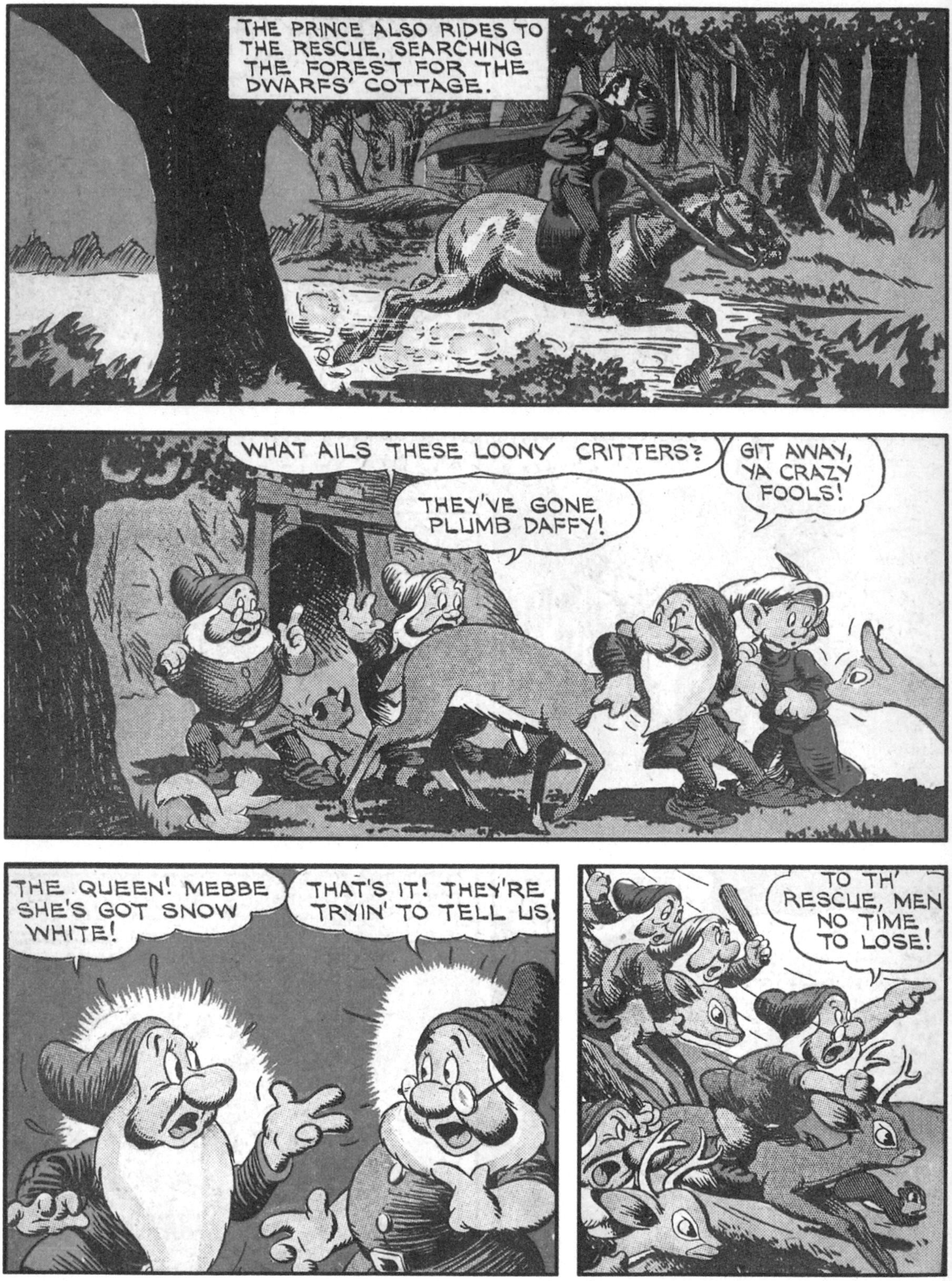
THE PRINCE ALSO RIDES TO THE RESCUE, SEARCHING THE FOREST FOR THE DWARFS' COTTAGE.
WHAT AILS THESE LOONY CRITTERS?
THEY'VE GONE PLUMB DAFFY!
GIT AWAY, YA CRAZY FOOLS!
THE QUEEN! MEBBE SHE'S GOT SNOW WHITE!
THAT'S IT! THEY'RE TRYIN' TO TELL US!
TO TH' RESCUE, MEN NO TIME TO LOSE!

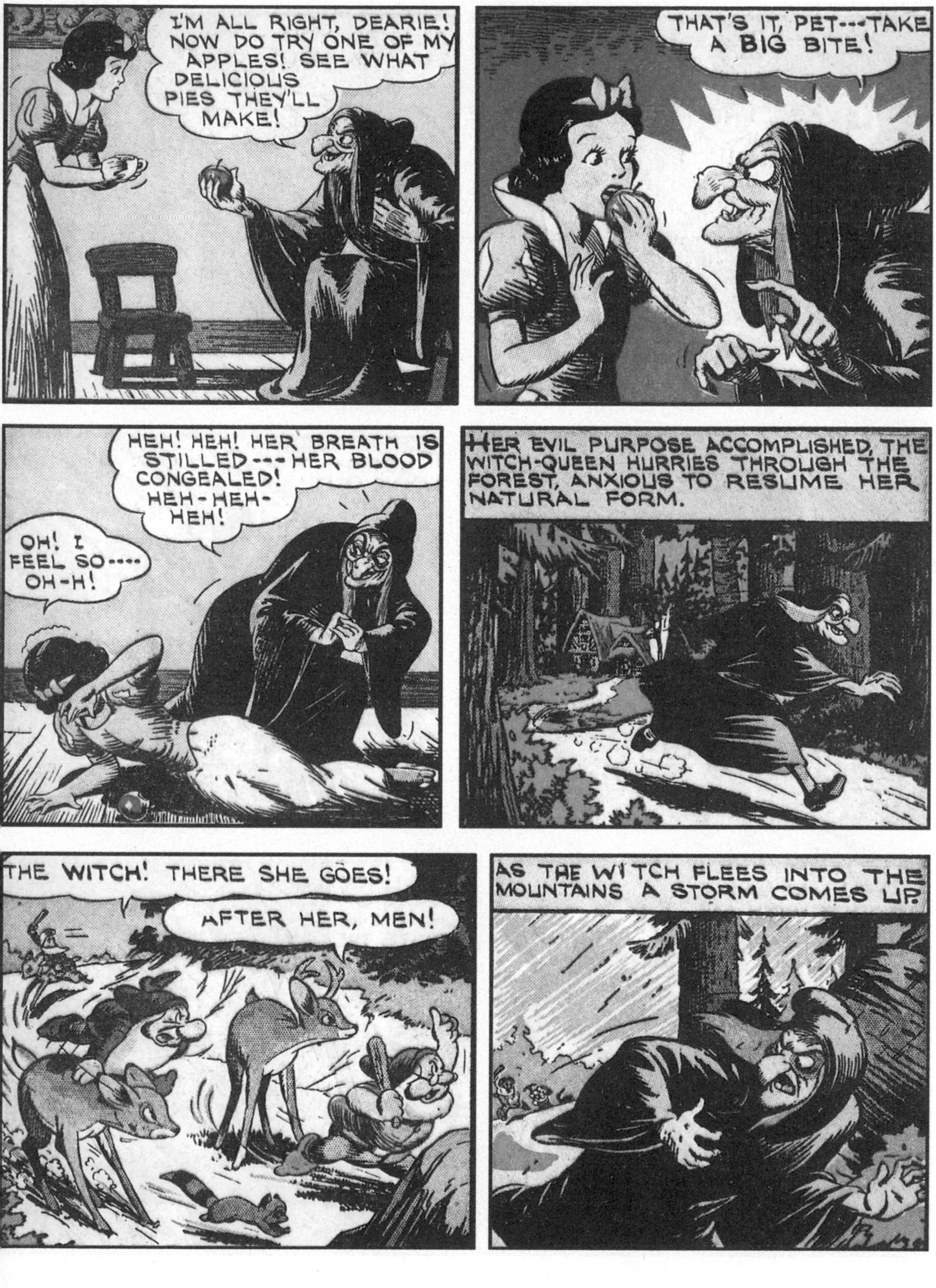
I'M ALL RIGHT, DEARIE! NOW DO TRY ONE OF MY APPLES! SEE WHAT DELICIOUS PIES THEY'LL MAKE!
THAT'S IT, PET---TAKE A BIG BITE!
HEH! HEH! HER BREATH IS STILLED---HER BLOOD CONGEALED! HEH-HEH-HEH!
OH! I FEEL SO---- OH-H!
HER EVIL PURPOSE ACCOMPLISHED, THE WITCH-QUEEN HURRIES THROUGH THE FOREST, ANXIOUS TO RESUME HER NATURAL FORM.
THE WITCH! THERE SHE GOES!
AFTER HER, MEN!
AS THE WITCH FLEES INTO THE MOUNTAINS A STORM COMES UP.

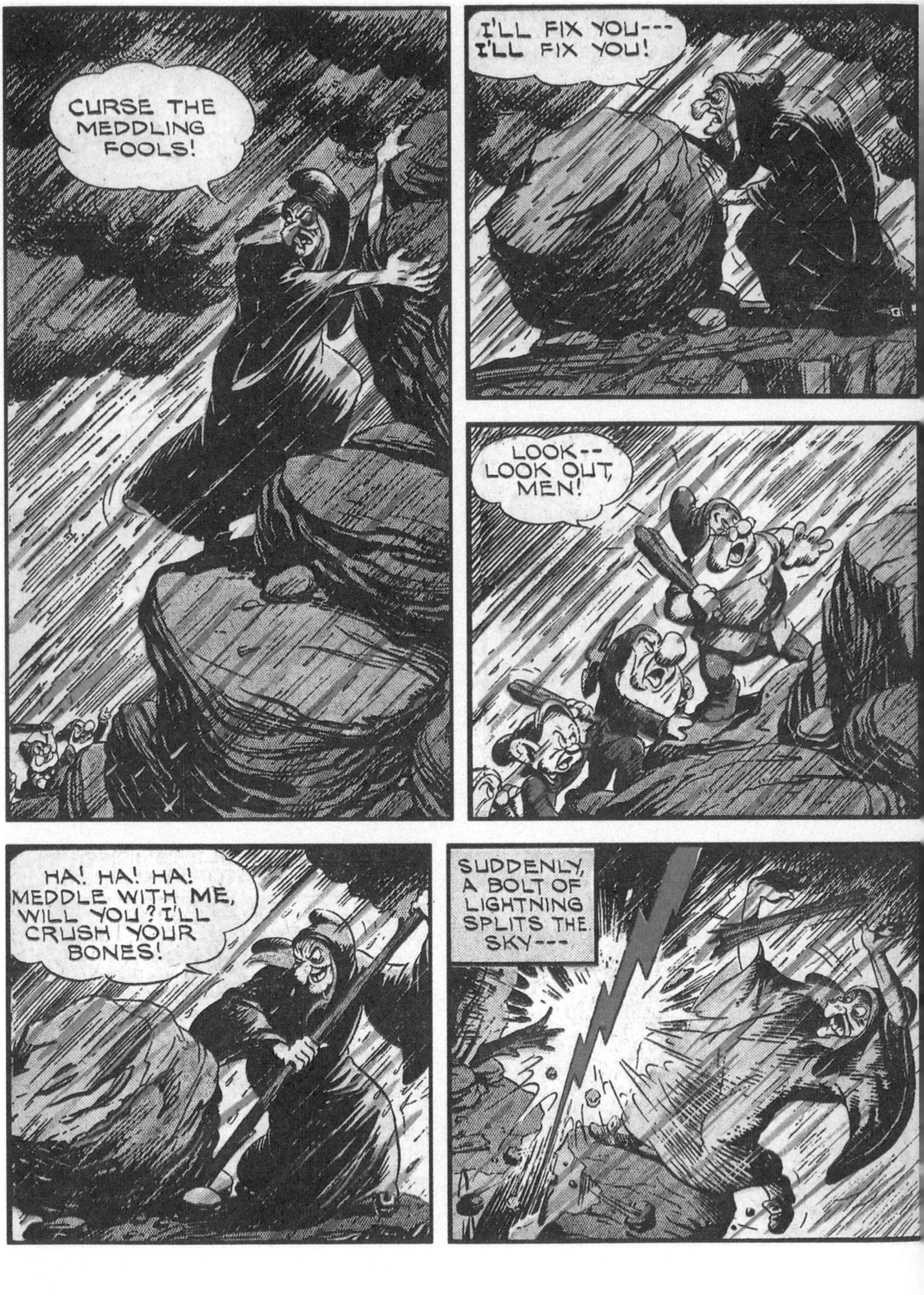
CURSE THE MEDDLING FOOLS!
I'LL FIX YOU--- I'LL FIX YOU!
LOOK-- LOOK OUT, MEN!
HA! HA! HA! MEDDLE WITH ME, WILL YOU? I'LL CRUSH YOUR BONES!
SUDDENLY, A BOLT OF LIGHTNING SPLITS THE SKY---

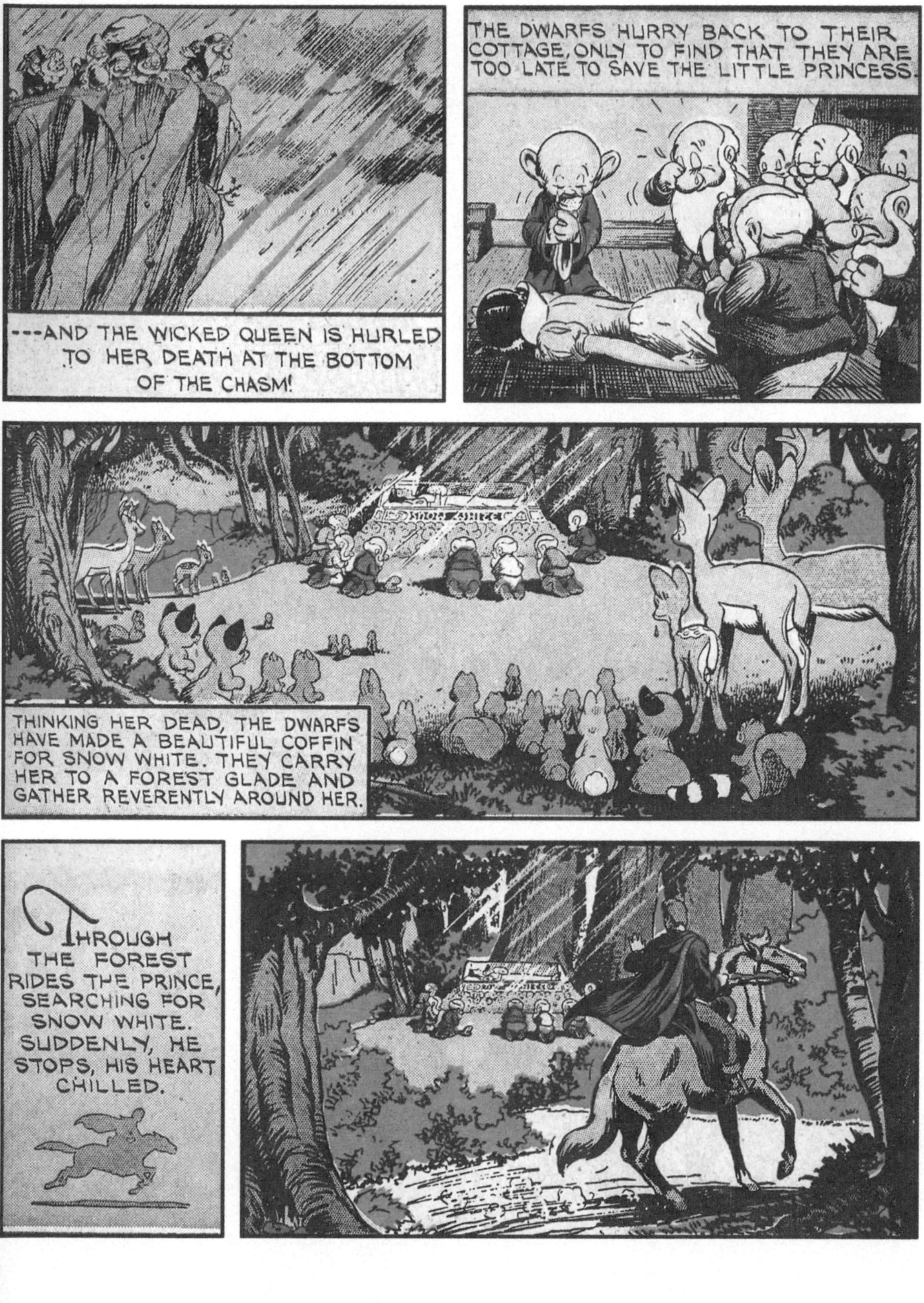
---AND THE WICKED QUEEN IS HURLED TO HER DEATH AT THE BOTTOM OF THE CHASM!
THE DWARFS HURRY BACK TO THEIR COTTAGE, ONLY TO FIND THAT THEY ARE TOO LATE TO SAVE THE LITTLE PRINCESS.
THINKING HER DEAD, THE DWARFS HAVE MADE A BEAUTIFUL COFFIN FOR SNOW WHITE. THEY CARRY HER TO A FOREST GLADE AND GATHER REVERENTLY AROUND HER.
THROUGH THE FOREST RIDES THE PRINCE, SEARCHING FOR SNOW WHITE. SUDDENLY, HE STOPS, HIS HEART CHILLED.

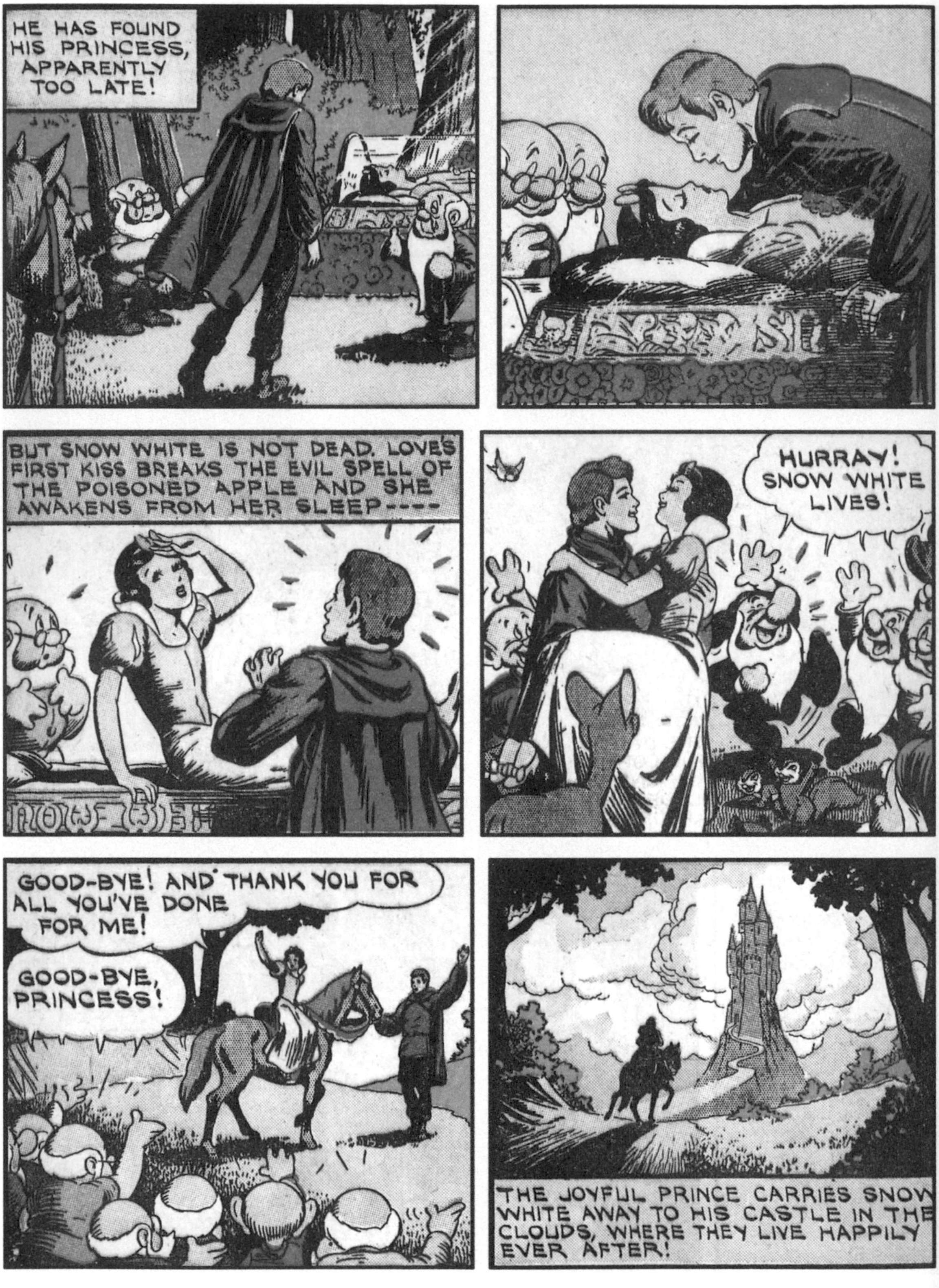
HE HAS FOUND HIS PRINCESS, APPARENTLY TOO LATE!
BUT SNOW WHITE IS NOT DEAD. LOVE'S FIRST KISS BREAKS THE EVIL SPELL OF THE POISONED APPLE AND SHE AWAKENS FROM HER SLEEP----
HURRAY! SNOW WHITE LIVES!
GOOD-BYE! AND THANK YOU FOR ALL YOU'VE DONE FOR ME!
GOOD-BYE, PRINCESS!
THE JOYFUL PRINCE CARRIES SNOW WHITE AWAY TO HIS CASTLE IN THE CLOUDS, WHERE THEY LIVE HAPPILY EVER AFTER!

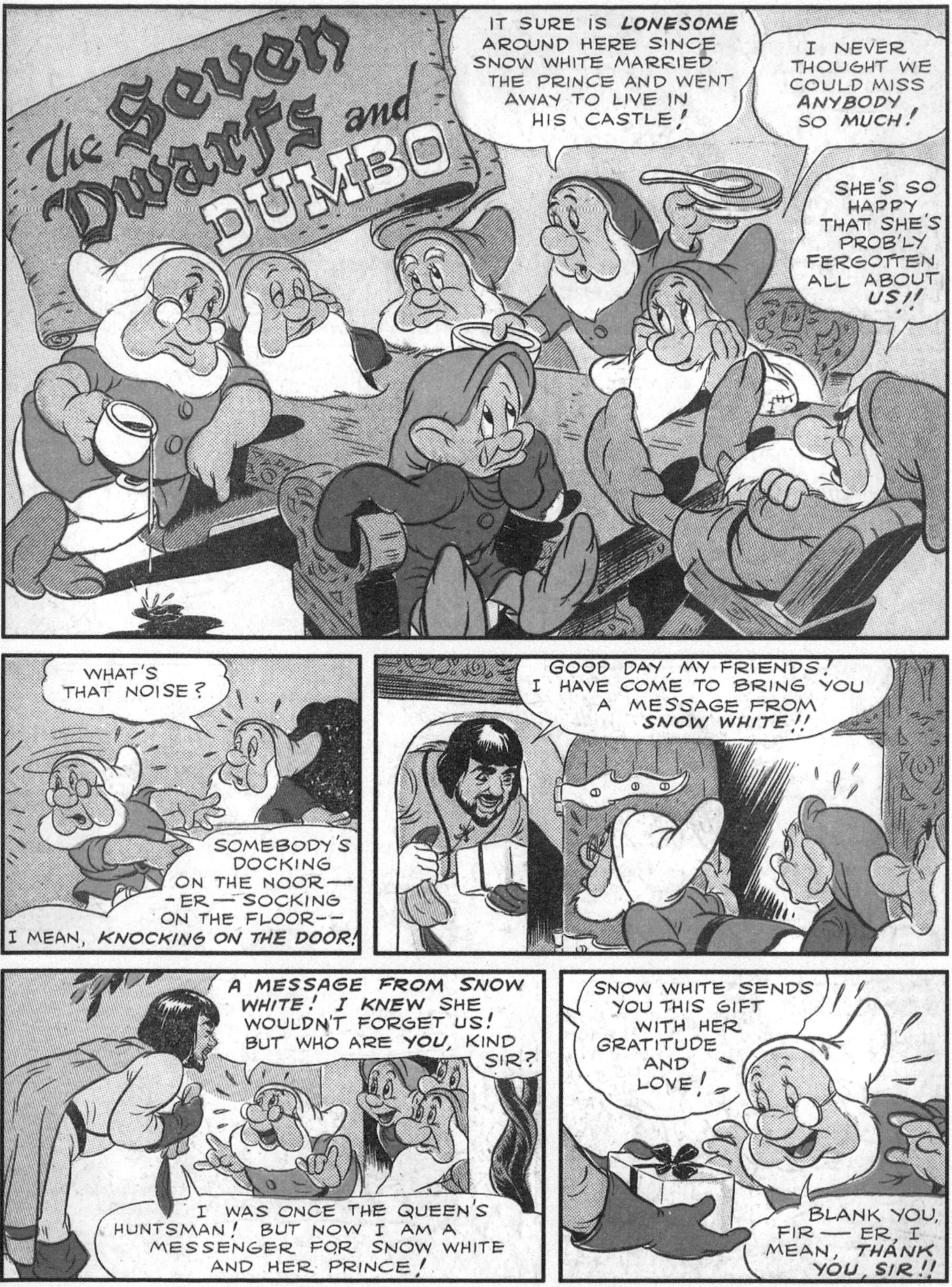
The Seven Dwarfs and DUMBO
IT SURE IS LONESOME AROUND HERE SINCE SNOW WHITE MARRIED THE PRINCE AND WENT AWAY TO LIVE IN HIS CASTLE!
I NEVER THOUGHT WE COULD MISS ANYBODY SO MUCH!
SHE'S SO HAPPY THAT SHE'S PROB'LY FERGOTTEN ALL ABOUT US!!
WHAT'S THAT NOISE?
SOMEBODY'S DOCKING ON THE NOOR— -ER—SOCKING ON THE FLOOR-- I MEAN, KNOCKING ON THE DOOR!
GOOD DAY, MY FRIENDS! I HAVE COME TO BRING YOU A MESSAGE FROM SNOW WHITE!!
A MESSAGE FROM SNOW WHITE! I KNEW SHE WOULDN'T FORGET US! BUT WHO ARE YOU, KIND SIR?
I WAS ONCE THE QUEEN'S HUNTSMAN! BUT NOW I AM A MESSENGER FOR SNOW WHITE AND HER PRINCE!
SNOW WHITE SENDS YOU THIS GIFT WITH HER GRATITUDE AND LOVE!
BLANK YOU, FIR — ER, I MEAN, THANK YOU, SIR!!

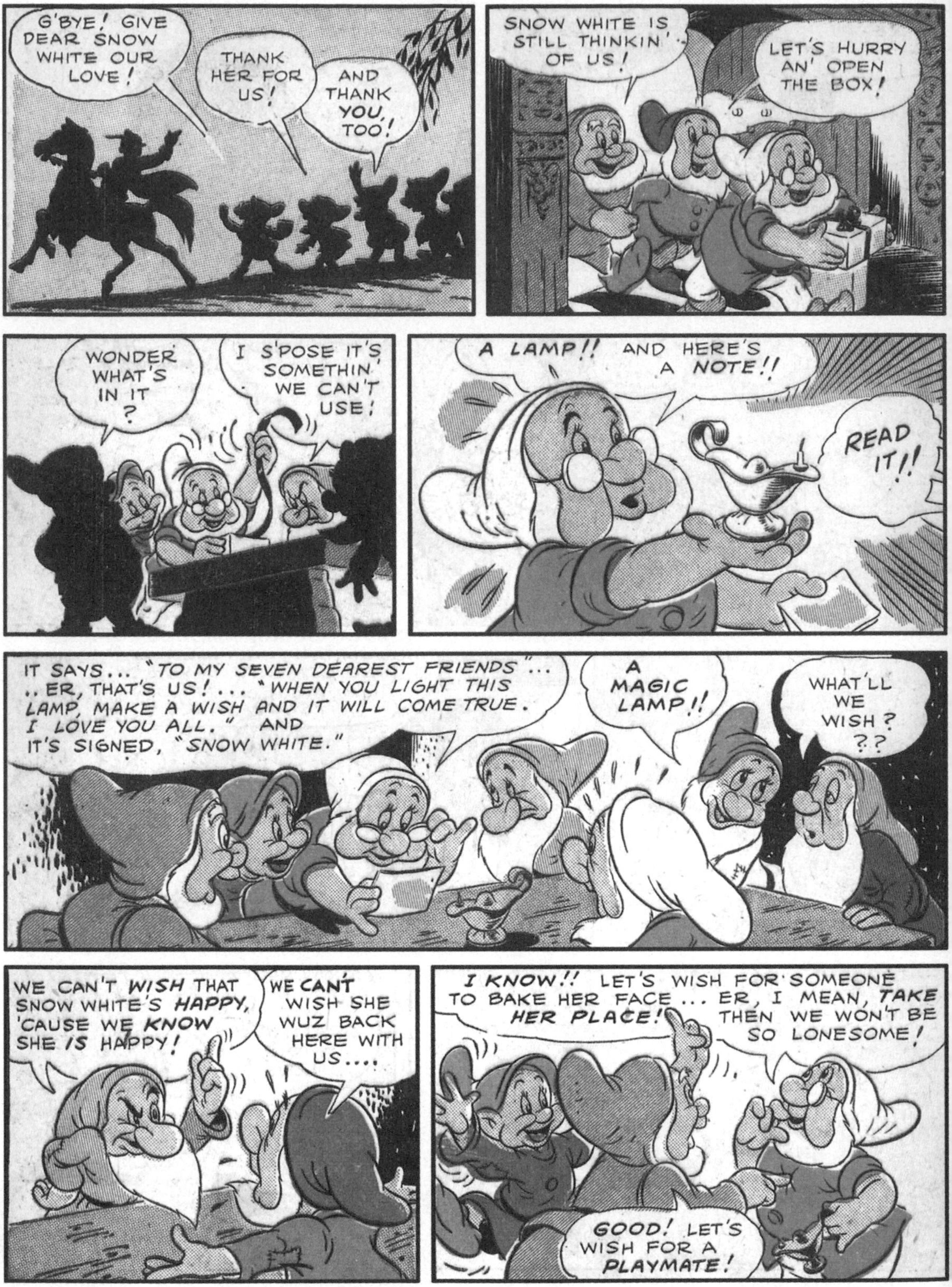
G'BYE! GIVE DEAR SNOW WHITE OUR LOVE!
THANK HER FOR US!
AND THANK YOU, TOO!
SNOW WHITE IS STILL THINKIN' OF US!
LET'S HURRY AN' OPEN THE BOX!
WONDER WHAT'S IN IT ?
I S'POSE IT'S SOMETHIN' WE CAN'T USE!
A LAMP!! AND HERE'S A NOTE!!
READ IT!!
IT SAYS... "TO MY SEVEN DEAREST FRIENDS"... ..ER, THAT'S US!... "WHEN YOU LIGHT THIS LAMP, MAKE A WISH AND IT WILL COME TRUE. I LOVE YOU ALL." AND IT'S SIGNED, "SNOW WHITE."
A MAGIC LAMP!!
WHAT'LL WE WISH? ??
WE CAN'T WISH THAT SNOW WHITE'S HAPPY, 'CAUSE WE KNOW SHE IS HAPPY!
WE CAN'T WISH SHE WUZ BACK HERE WITH US....
I KNOW!! LET'S WISH FOR SOMEONE TO BAKE HER FACE... ER, I MEAN, TAKE HER PLACE! THEN WE WON'T BE SO LONESOME!
GOOD! LET'S WISH FOR A PLAYMATE!

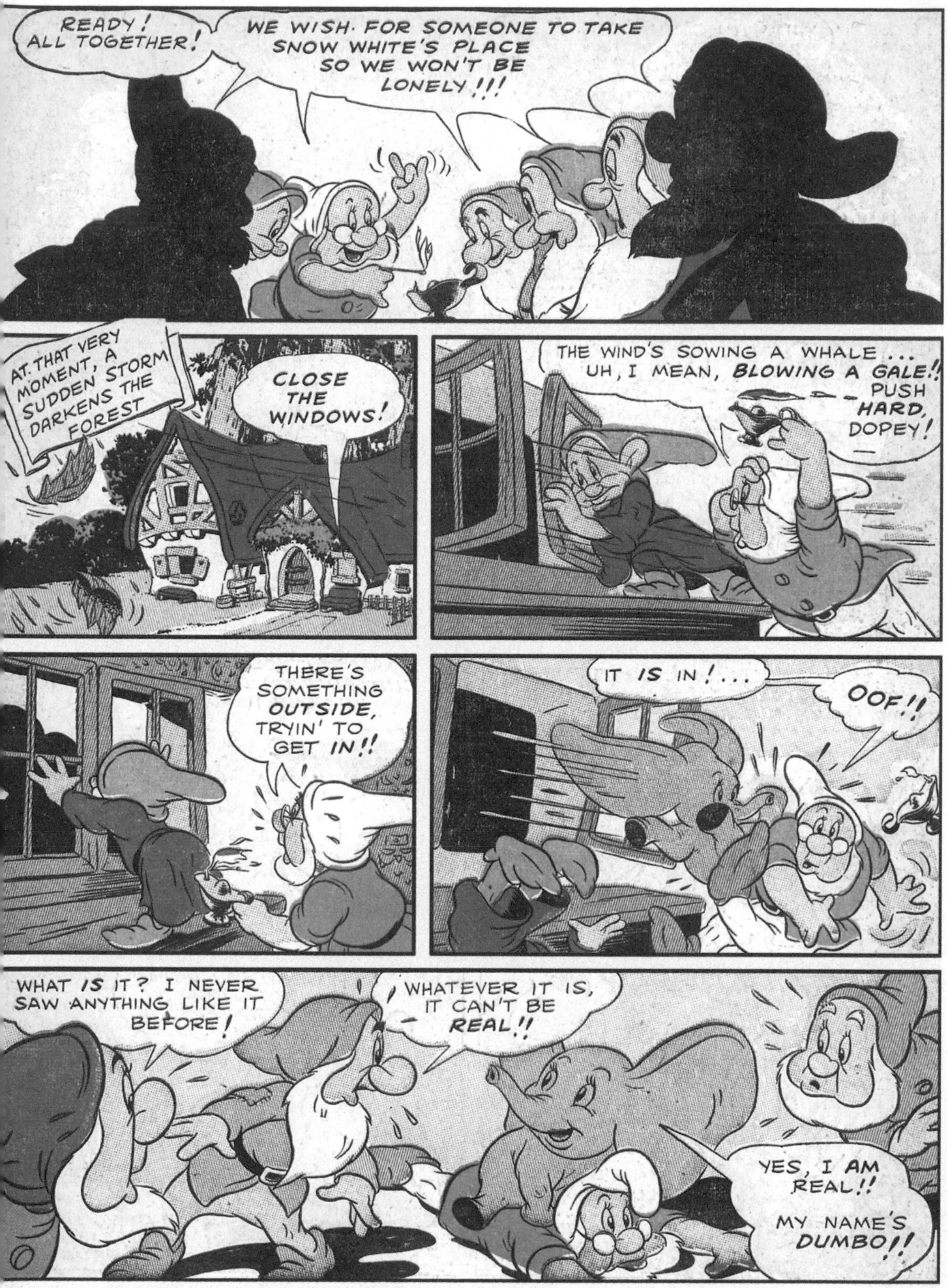
READY! ALL TOGETHER!
WE WISH FOR SOMEONE TO TAKE SNOW WHITE'S PLACE SO WE WON'T BE LONELY!!!
AT THAT VERY MOMENT, A SUDDEN STORM DARKENS THE FOREST
CLOSE THE WINDOWS!
THE WIND'S SOWING A WHALE ... UH, I MEAN, BLOWING A GALE!!
— — PUSH HARD, DOPEY! —
THERE'S SOMETHING OUTSIDE, TRYIN' TO GET IN!!
IT IS IN!...
OOF!!
WHAT IS IT? I NEVER SAW ANYTHING LIKE IT BEFORE!
WHATEVER IT IS, IT CAN'T BE REAL!!
YES, I AM REAL!!
MY NAME'S DUMBO!!

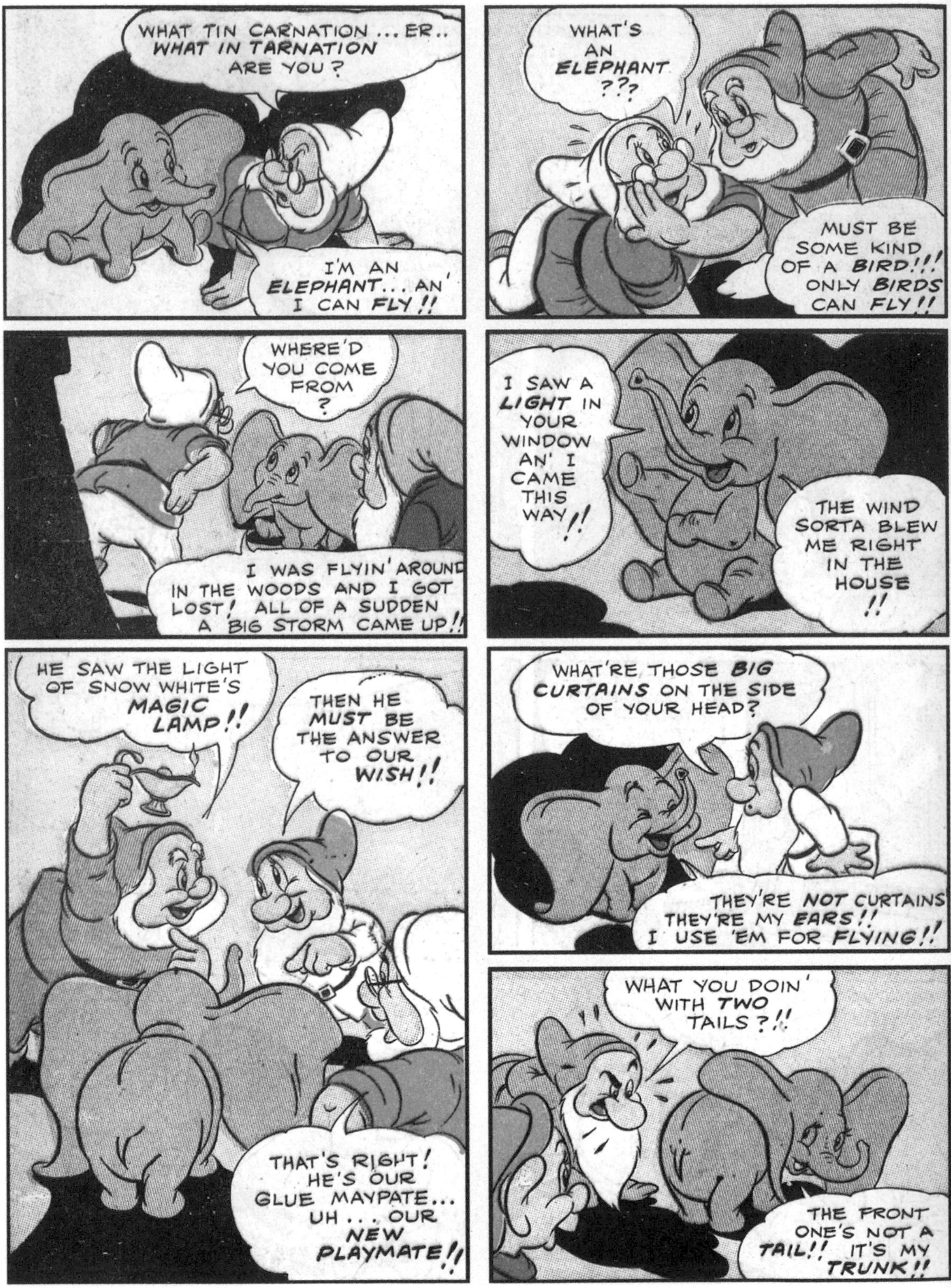
WHAT TIN CARNATION ... ER.. WHAT IN TARNATION ARE YOU?
I'M AN ELEPHANT... AN' I CAN FLY!!
WHAT'S AN ELEPHANT ???
MUST BE SOME KIND OF A BIRD!!! ONLY BIRDS CAN FLY!!
WHERE'D YOU COME FROM ?
I WAS FLYIN' AROUND IN THE WOODS AND I GOT LOST! ALL OF A SUDDEN A BIG STORM CAME UP!!
I SAW A LIGHT IN YOUR WINDOW AN' I CAME THIS WAY!!
THE WIND SORTA BLEW ME RIGHT IN THE HOUSE !!
HE SAW THE LIGHT OF SNOW WHITE'S MAGIC LAMP!!
THEN HE MUST BE THE ANSWER TO OUR WISH!!
THAT'S RIGHT! HE'S OUR GLUE MAYPATE... UH ... OUR NEW PLAYMATE!!
WHAT'RE THOSE BIG CURTAINS ON THE SIDE OF YOUR HEAD?
THEY'RE NOT CURTAINS THEY'RE MY EARS!! I USE 'EM FOR FLYING!!
WHAT YOU DOIN' WITH TWO TAILS?!!
THE FRONT ONE'S NOT A TAIL!! IT'S MY TRUNK!!

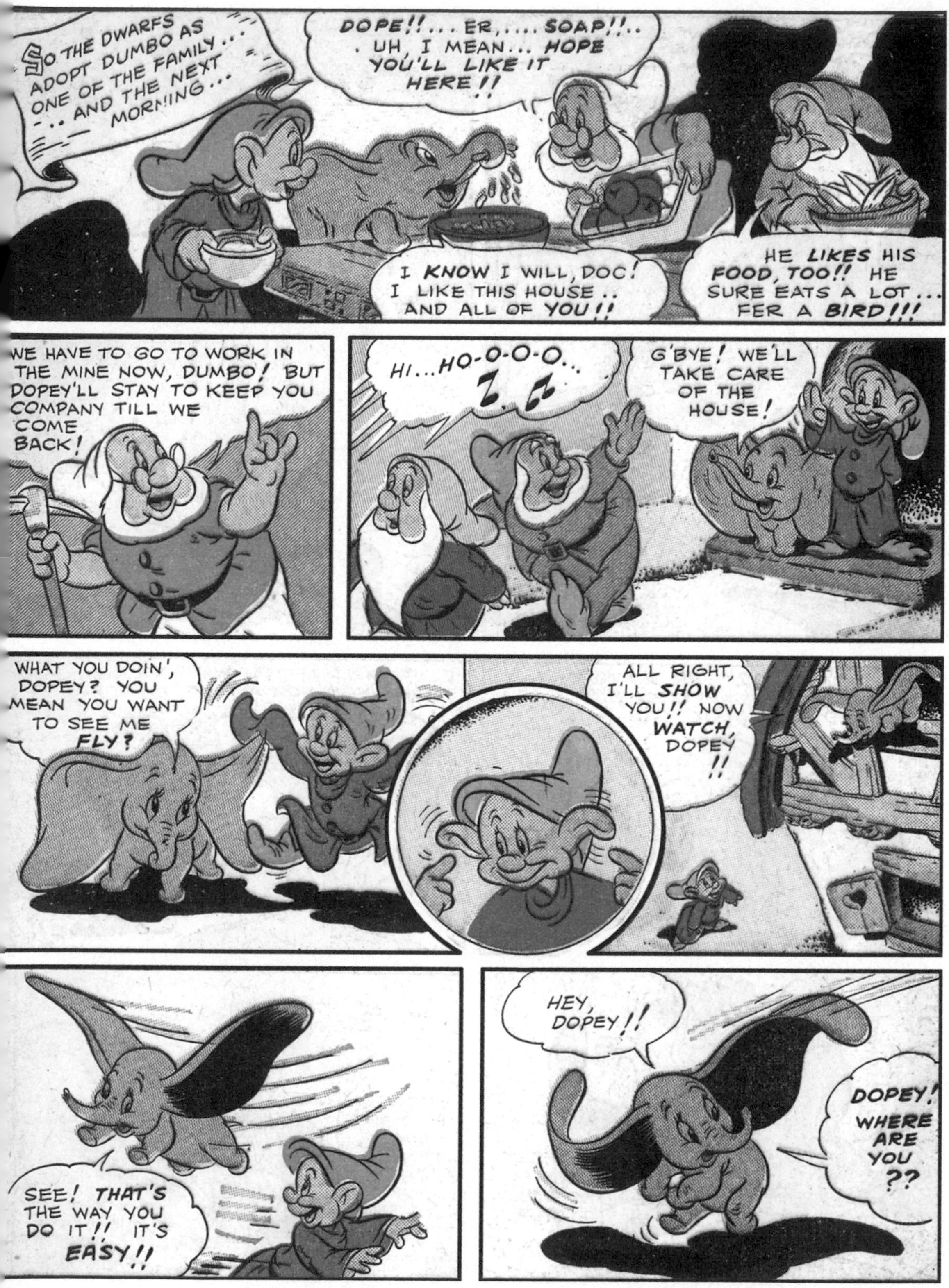
So the dwarfs adopt Dumbo as one of the family ... ... and the next morning ...
DOPE!! ... ER, ... SOAP!! .. . UH, I MEAN ... HOPE YOU'LL LIKE IT HERE!!
I KNOW I WILL, DOC! I LIKE THIS HOUSE .. AND ALL OF YOU!!
HE LIKES HIS FOOD, TOO!! HE SURE EATS A LOT ... FER A BIRD!!!
WE HAVE TO GO TO WORK IN THE MINE NOW, DUMBO! BUT DOPEY'LL STAY TO KEEP YOU COMPANY TILL WE COME BACK!
HI ... HO-O-O-O ... Z Z
G'BYE! WE'LL TAKE CARE OF THE HOUSE!
WHAT YOU DOIN', DOPEY? YOU MEAN YOU WANT TO SEE ME FLY?
ALL RIGHT, I'LL SHOW YOU!! NOW WATCH, DOPEY!!
SEE! THAT'S THE WAY YOU DO IT!! IT'S EASY!!
HEY, DOPEY!!
DOPEY! WHERE ARE YOU??

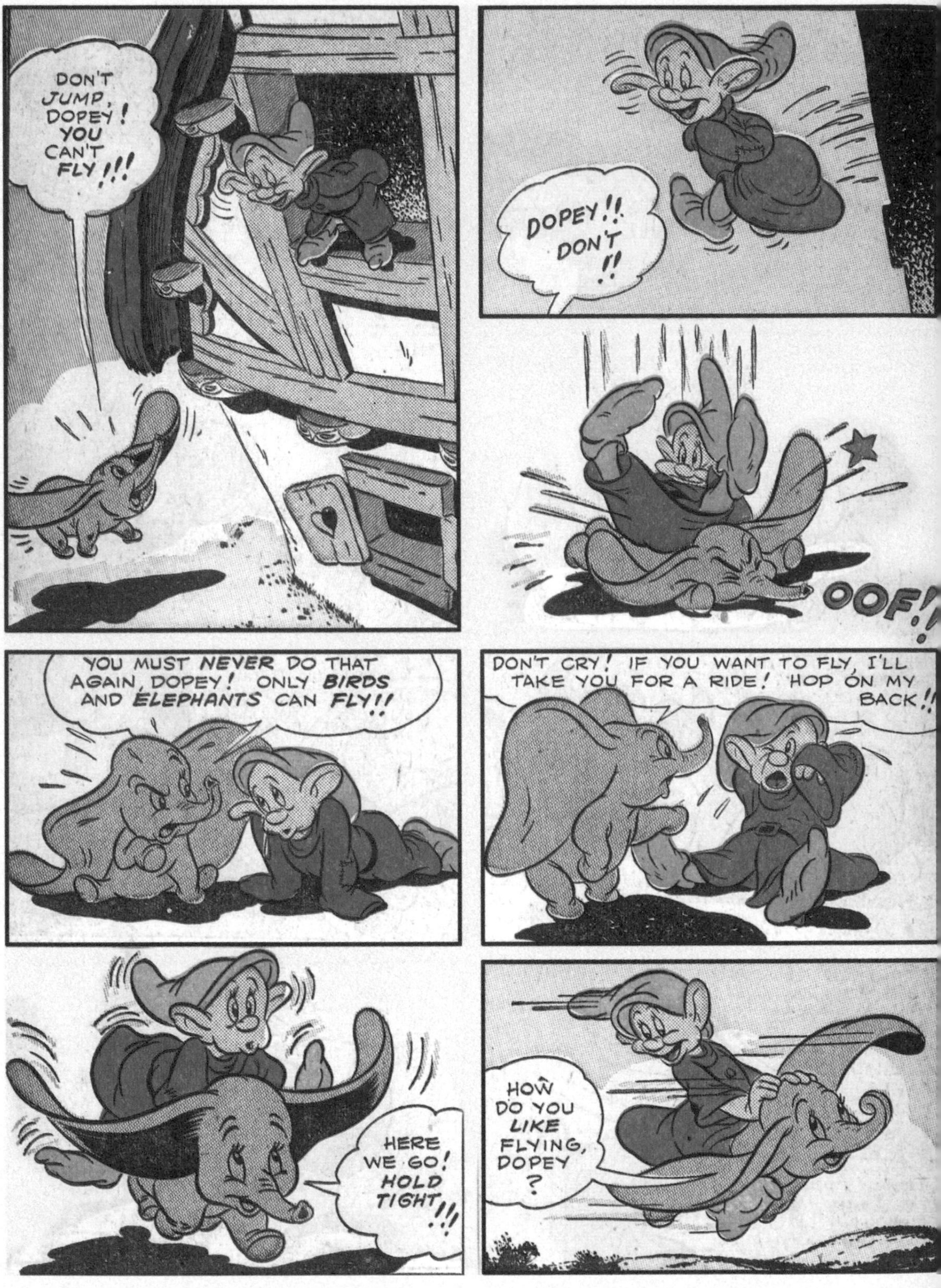
DON'T JUMP, DOPEY! YOU CAN'T FLY!!!
DOPEY!!! DON'T!!
OOF!!
YOU MUST NEVER DO THAT AGAIN, DOPEY! ONLY BIRDS AND ELEPHANTS CAN FLY!!
DON'T CRY! IF YOU WANT TO FLY, I'LL TAKE YOU FOR A RIDE! HOP ON MY BACK!!
HERE WE GO! HOLD TIGHT!!!
HOW DO YOU LIKE FLYING, DOPEY?

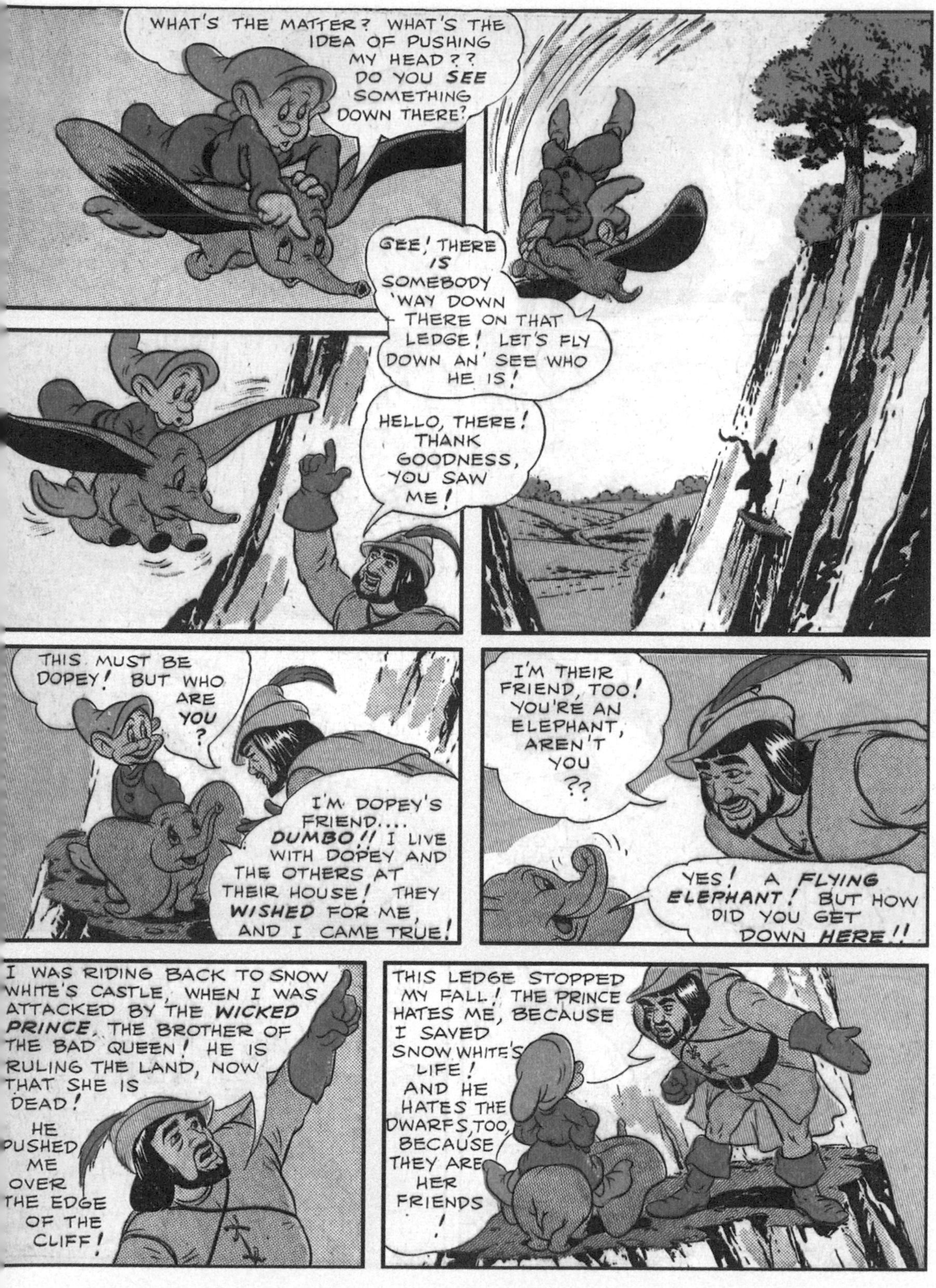
WHAT'S THE MATTER? WHAT'S THE IDEA OF PUSHING MY HEAD?? DO YOU SEE SOMETHING DOWN THERE?
SEE! THERE IS SOMEBODY 'WAY DOWN THERE ON THAT LEDGE! LET'S FLY DOWN AN' SEE WHO HE IS!
HELLO, THERE! THANK GOODNESS, YOU SAW ME!
THIS MUST BE DOPEY! BUT WHO ARE YOU?
I'M DOPEY'S FRIEND.... DUMBO!! I LIVE WITH DOPEY AND THE OTHERS AT THEIR HOUSE! THEY WISHED FOR ME, AND I CAME TRUE!
I'M THEIR FRIEND, TOO! YOU'RE AN ELEPHANT, AREN'T YOU??
YES! A FLYING ELEPHANT! BUT HOW DID YOU GET DOWN HERE!!
I WAS RIDING BACK TO SNOW WHITE'S CASTLE, WHEN I WAS ATTACKED BY THE WICKED PRINCE, THE BROTHER OF THE BAD QUEEN! HE IS RULING THE LAND, NOW THAT SHE IS DEAD!
HE PUSHED ME OVER THE EDGE OF THE CLIFF!
THIS LEDGE STOPPED MY FALL! THE PRINCE HATES ME, BECAUSE I SAVED SNOW WHITE'S LIFE! AND HE HATES THE DWARFS, TOO, BECAUSE THEY ARE HER FRIENDS!

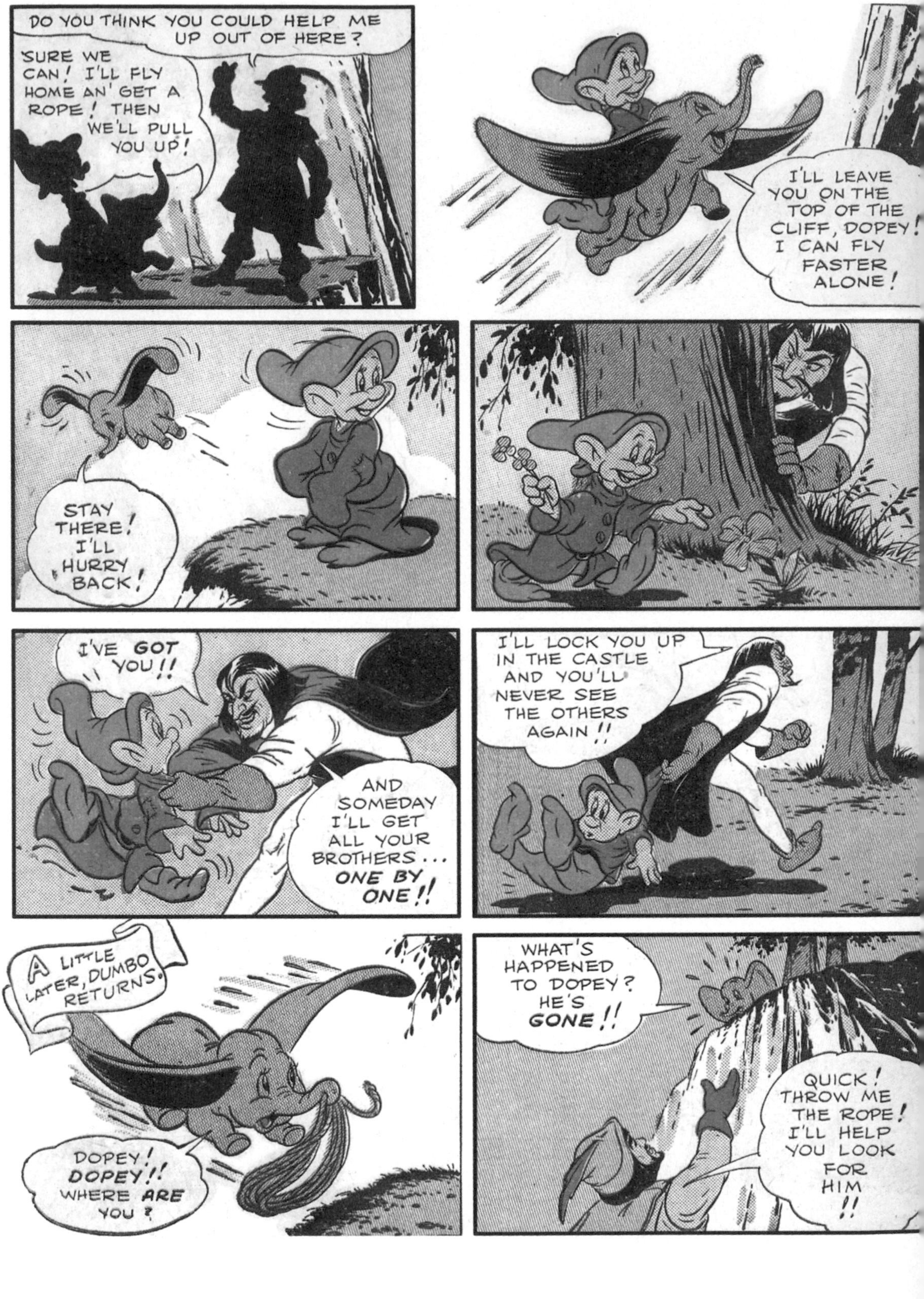
DO YOU THINK YOU COULD HELP ME UP OUT OF HERE?
SURE WE CAN! I'LL FLY HOME AN' GET A ROPE! THEN WE'LL PULL YOU UP!
I'LL LEAVE YOU ON THE TOP OF THE CLIFF, DOPEY! I CAN FLY FASTER ALONE!
STAY THERE! I'LL HURRY BACK!
I'VE GOT YOU!!
AND SOMEDAY I'LL GET ALL YOUR BROTHERS... ONE BY ONE!!
I'LL LOCK YOU UP IN THE CASTLE AND YOU'LL NEVER SEE THE OTHERS AGAIN!!
A LITTLE LATER, DUMBO RETURNS.
DOPEY! DOPEY!! WHERE ARE YOU?
WHAT'S HAPPENED TO DOPEY? HE'S GONE!!
QUICK! THROW ME THE ROPE! I'LL HELP YOU LOOK FOR HIM!!

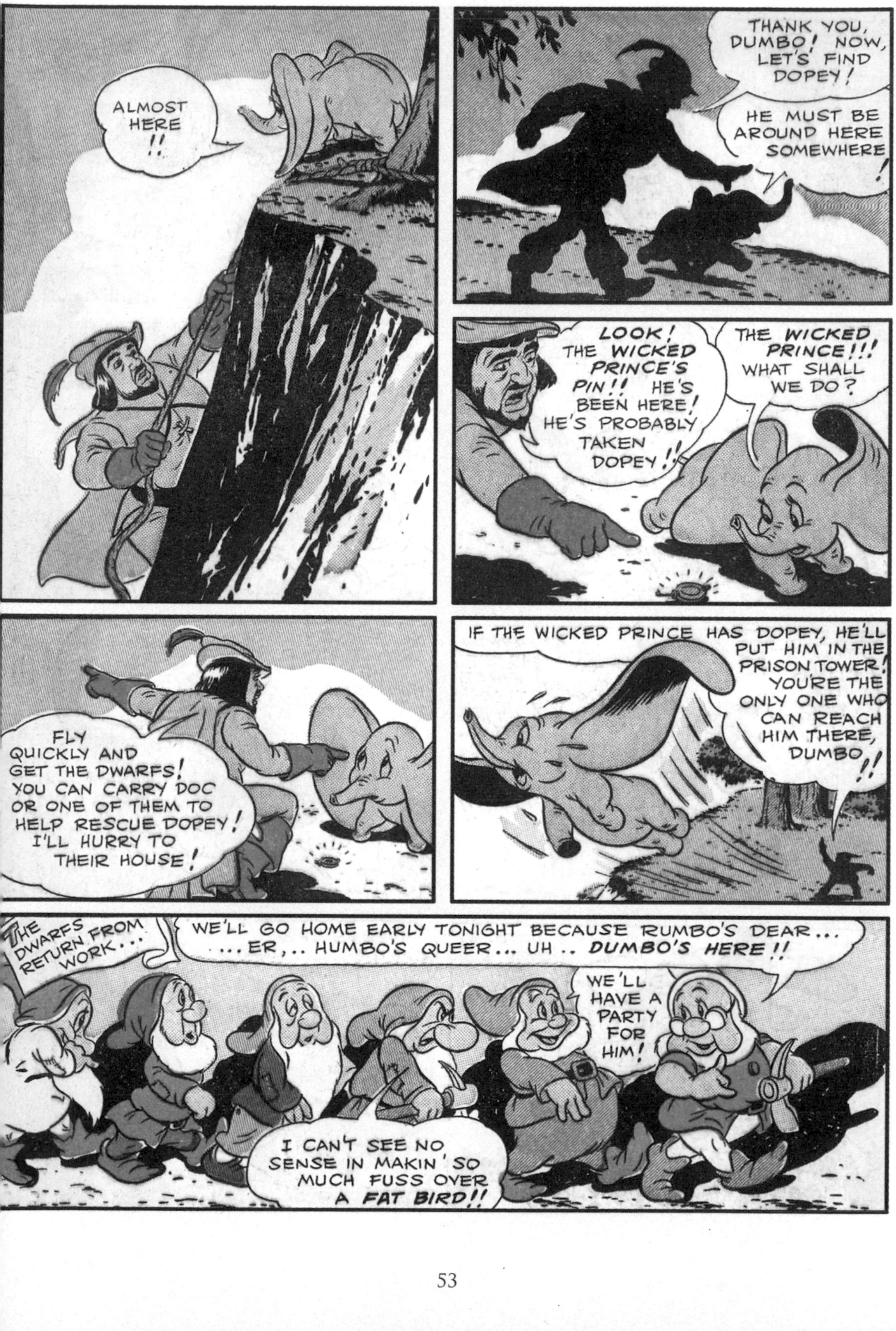
ALMOST HERE !!
THANK YOU, DUMBO! NOW, LET'S FIND DOPEY!
HE MUST BE AROUND HERE SOMEWHERE!
LOOK! THE WICKED PRINCE'S PIN!! HE'S BEEN HERE! HE'S PROBABLY TAKEN DOPEY!!
THE WICKED PRINCE!!! WHAT SHALL WE DO?
FLY QUICKLY AND GET THE DWARFS! YOU CAN CARRY DOC OR ONE OF THEM TO HELP RESCUE DOPEY! I'LL HURRY TO THEIR HOUSE!
IF THE WICKED PRINCE HAS DOPEY, HE'LL PUT HIM IN THE PRISON TOWER! YOU'RE THE ONLY ONE WHO CAN REACH HIM THERE, DUMBO!!
THE DWARFS RETURN FROM WORK...
WE'LL GO HOME EARLY TONIGHT BECAUSE RUMBO'S DEAR... ...ER,.. HUMBO'S QUEER... UH .. DUMBO'S HERE!!
WE'LL HAVE A PARTY FOR HIM!
I CAN'T SEE NO SENSE IN MAKIN' SO MUCH FUSS OVER A FAT BIRD!!

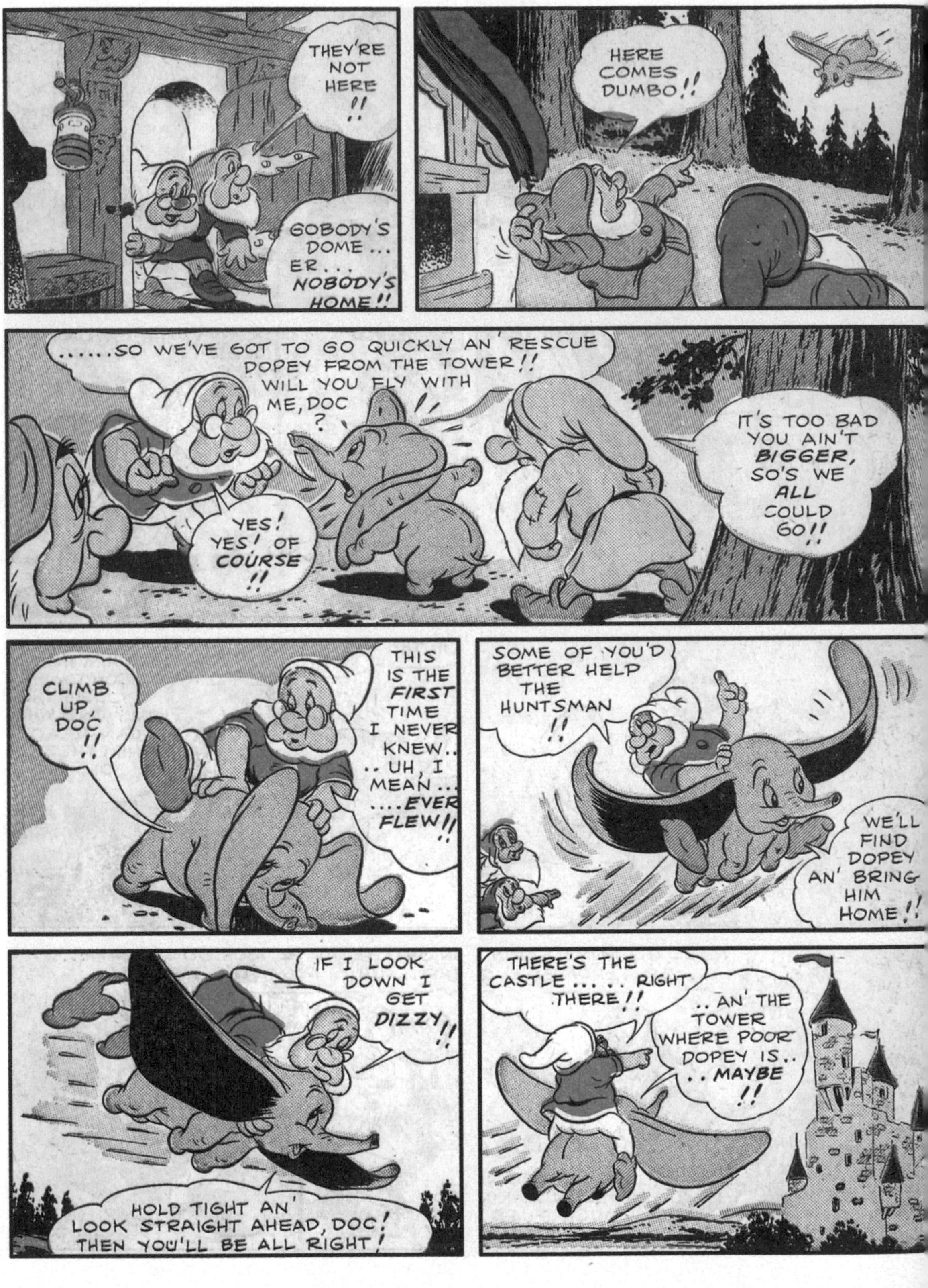
THEY'RE NOT HERE !!
GOBODY'S DOME ... ER ... NOBODY'S HOME !!
HERE COMES DUMBO !!
......SO WE'VE GOT TO GO QUICKLY AN' RESCUE DOPEY FROM THE TOWER !! WILL YOU FLY WITH ME, DOC ?
YES! YES! OF COURSE !!
IT'S TOO BAD YOU AIN'T BIGGER, SO'S WE ALL COULD GO !!
CLIMB UP, DOC !!
THIS IS THE FIRST TIME I NEVER KNEW.. .. UH, I MEAN ... .EVER FLEW !!
SOME OF YOU'D BETTER HELP THE HUNTSMAN !!
WE'LL FIND DOPEY AN' BRING HIM HOME !!
IF I LOOK DOWN I GET DIZZY !!
HOLD TIGHT AN' LOOK STRAIGHT AHEAD, DOC! THEN YOU'LL BE ALL RIGHT!
THERE'S THE CASTLE ..... RIGHT THERE !!
.. AN' THE TOWER WHERE POOR DOPEY IS.. ..MAYBE !!

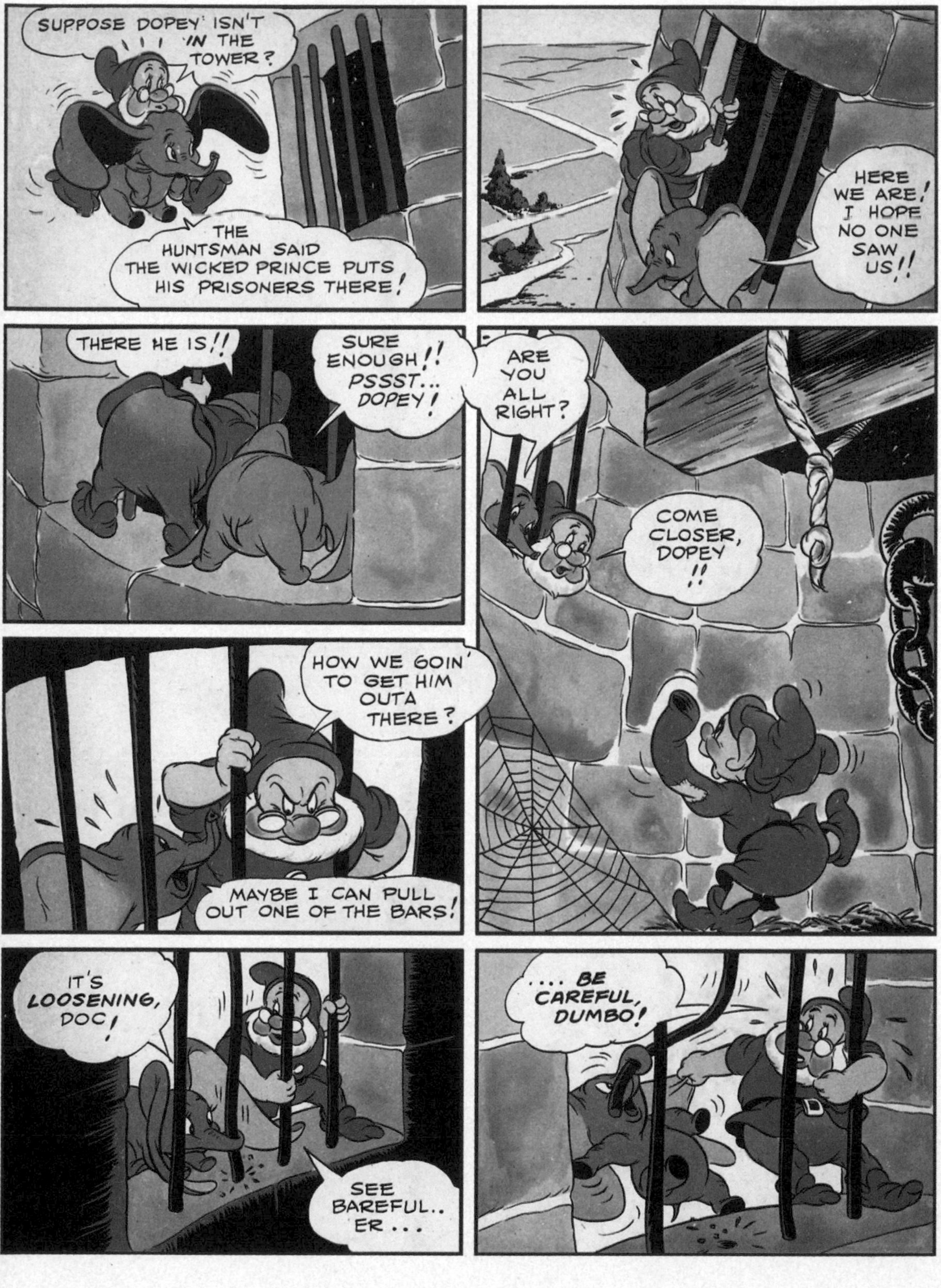
SUPPOSE DOPEY ISN'T IN THE TOWER?
THE HUNTSMAN SAID THE WICKED PRINCE PUTS HIS PRISONERS THERE!
HERE WE ARE! I HOPE NO ONE SAW US!!
THERE HE IS!!
SURE ENOUGH!! PSSST... DOPEY!
ARE YOU ALL RIGHT?
COME CLOSER, DOPEY!!
HOW WE GOIN' TO GET HIM OUTA THERE?
MAYBE I CAN PULL OUT ONE OF THE BARS!
IT'S LOOSENING, DOC!
SEE BAREFUL.. ER...
.... BE CAREFUL, DUMBO!

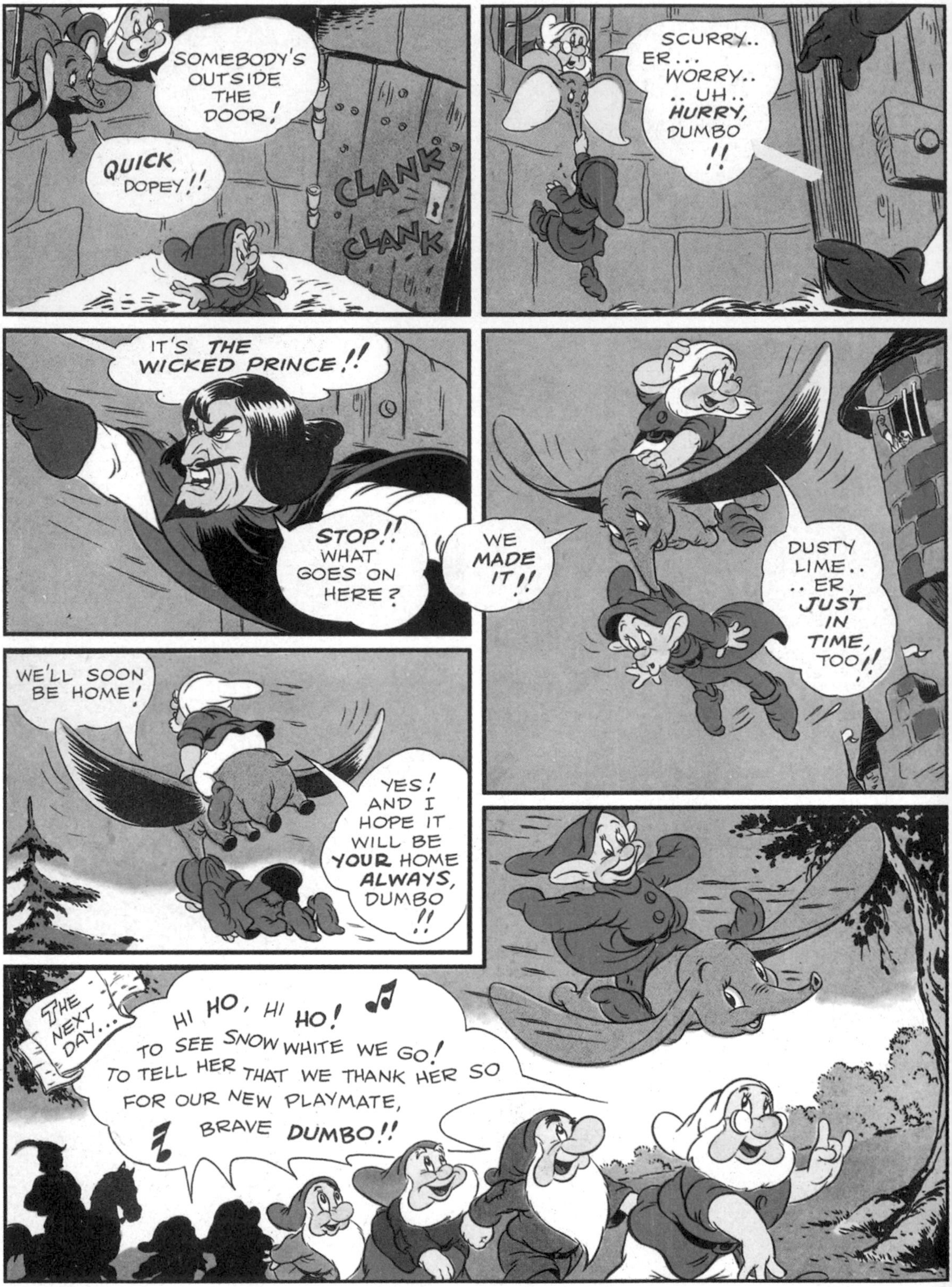
SOMEBODY'S OUTSIDE THE DOOR!
QUICK, DOPEY!!
CLANK
CLANK
SCURRY.. ER... WORRY.. .. UH.. HURRY, DUMBO !!
IT'S THE WICKED PRINCE!!
STOP!! WHAT GOES ON HERE?
WE MADE IT!!
DUSTY LIME.. .. ER, JUST IN TIME, TOO!!
WE'LL SOON BE HOME!
YES! AND I HOPE IT WILL BE YOUR HOME ALWAYS, DUMBO !!
THE NEXT DAY...
HI HO, HI HO! TO SEE SNOW WHITE WE GO! TO TELL HER THAT WE THANK HER SO FOR OUR NEW PLAYMATE, BRAVE DUMBO!!

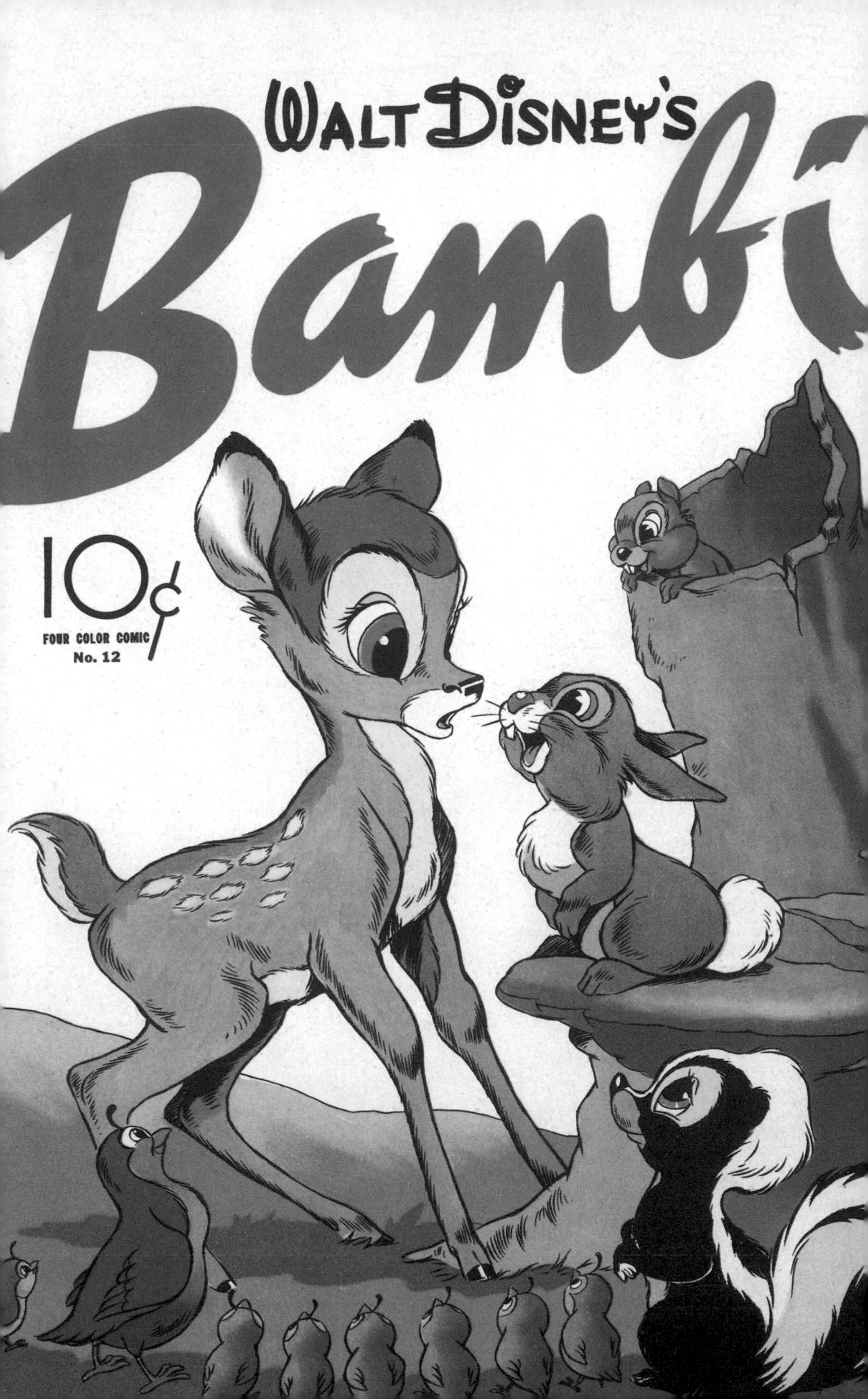

WALT DISNEY'S
Bambi
10¢
FOUR COLOR COMIC
No. 12

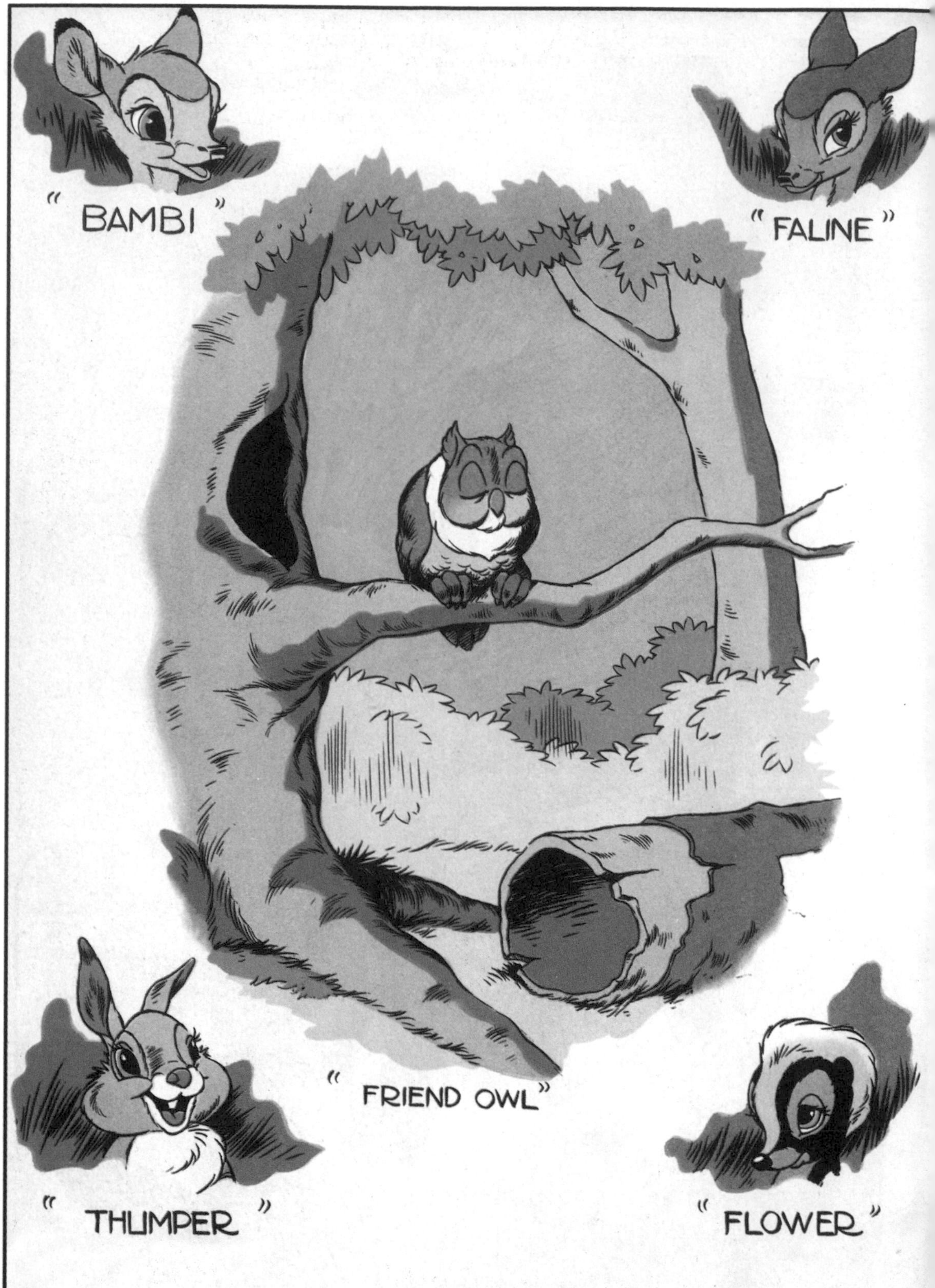
"BAMBI"
"FALINE"
"FRIEND OWL"
"THUMPER"
"FLOWER"

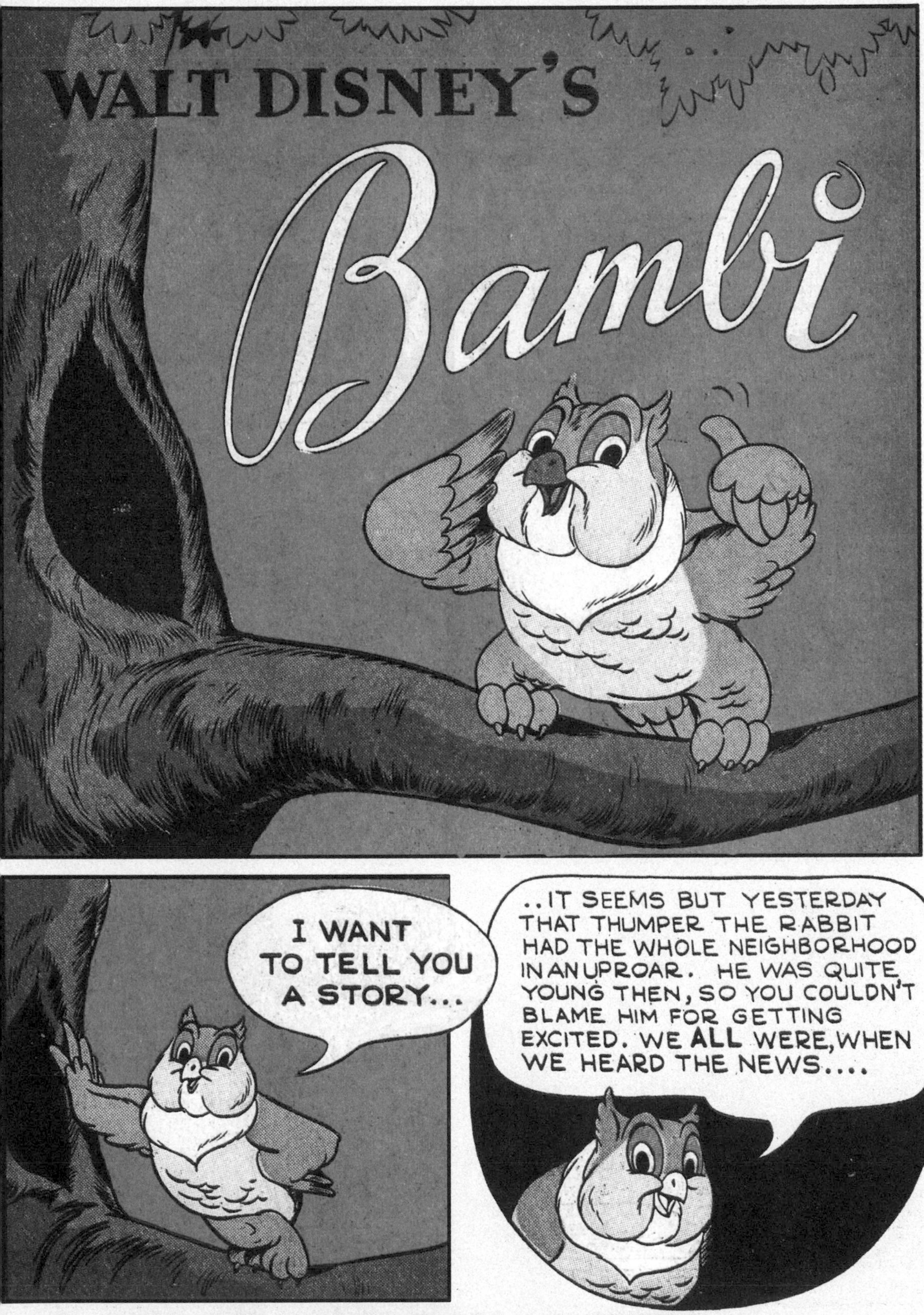
WALT DISNEY'S
Bambi
I WANT TO TELL YOU A STORY...
..IT SEEMS BUT YESTERDAY THAT THUMPER THE RABBIT HAD THE WHOLE NEIGHBORHOOD IN AN UPROAR. HE WAS QUITE YOUNG THEN, SO YOU COULDN'T BLAME HIM FOR GETTING EXCITED. WE ALL WERE, WHEN WE HEARD THE NEWS....

BUY WAR SAVINGS BONDS AND STAMPS

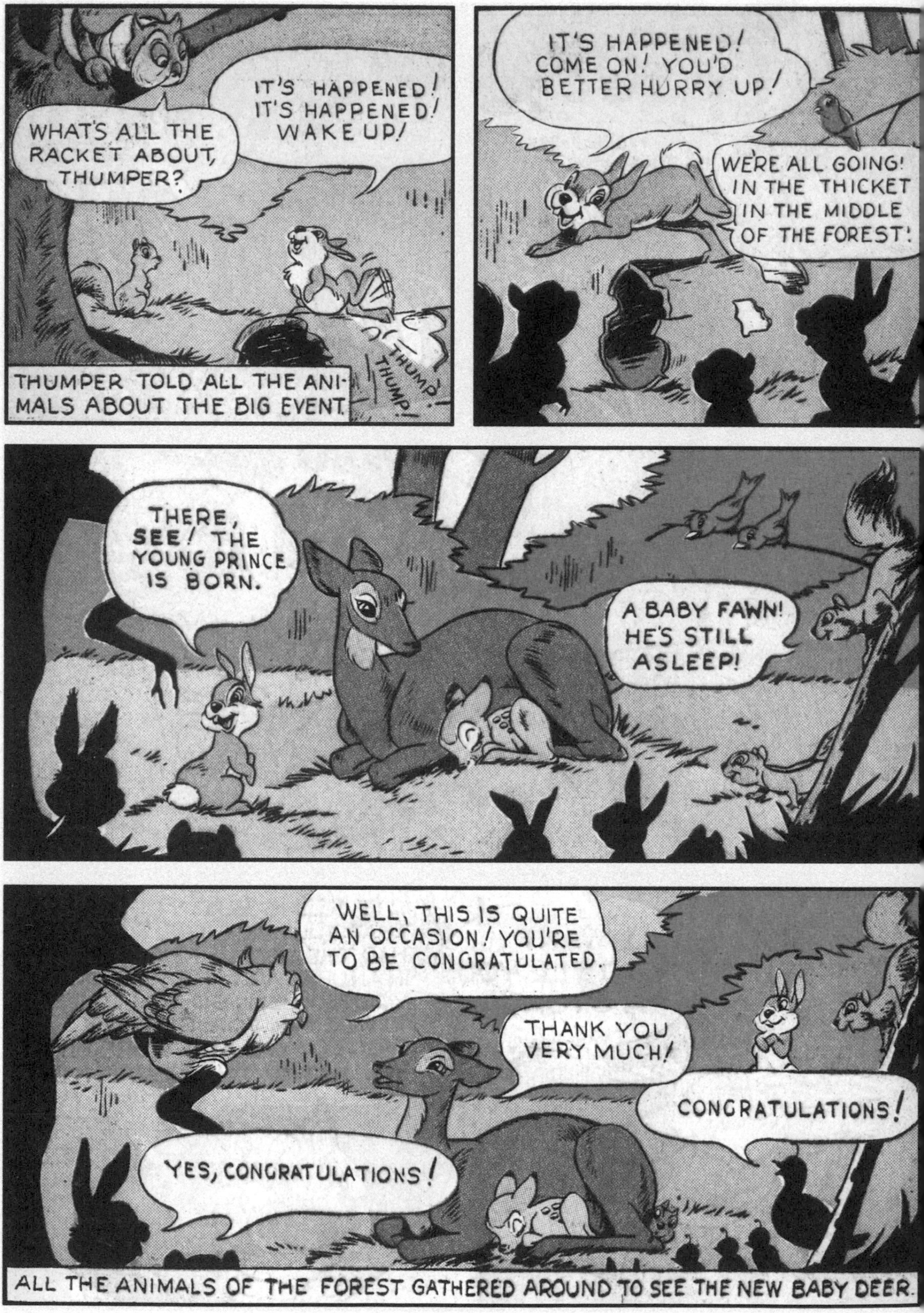
WHAT'S ALL THE RACKET ABOUT, THUMPER?
IT'S HAPPENED! IT'S HAPPENED! WAKE UP!
THUMP THUMP
THUMPER TOLD ALL THE ANIMALS ABOUT THE BIG EVENT.
IT'S HAPPENED! COME ON! YOU'D BETTER HURRY UP!
WE'RE ALL GOING! IN THE THICKET IN THE MIDDLE OF THE FOREST!
THERE, SEE! THE YOUNG PRINCE IS BORN.
A BABY FAWN! HE'S STILL ASLEEP!
WELL, THIS IS QUITE AN OCCASION! YOU'RE TO BE CONGRATULATED.
THANK YOU VERY MUCH!
CONGRATULATIONS!
YES, CONGRATULATIONS!
ALL THE ANIMALS OF THE FOREST GATHERED AROUND TO SEE THE NEW BABY DEER.

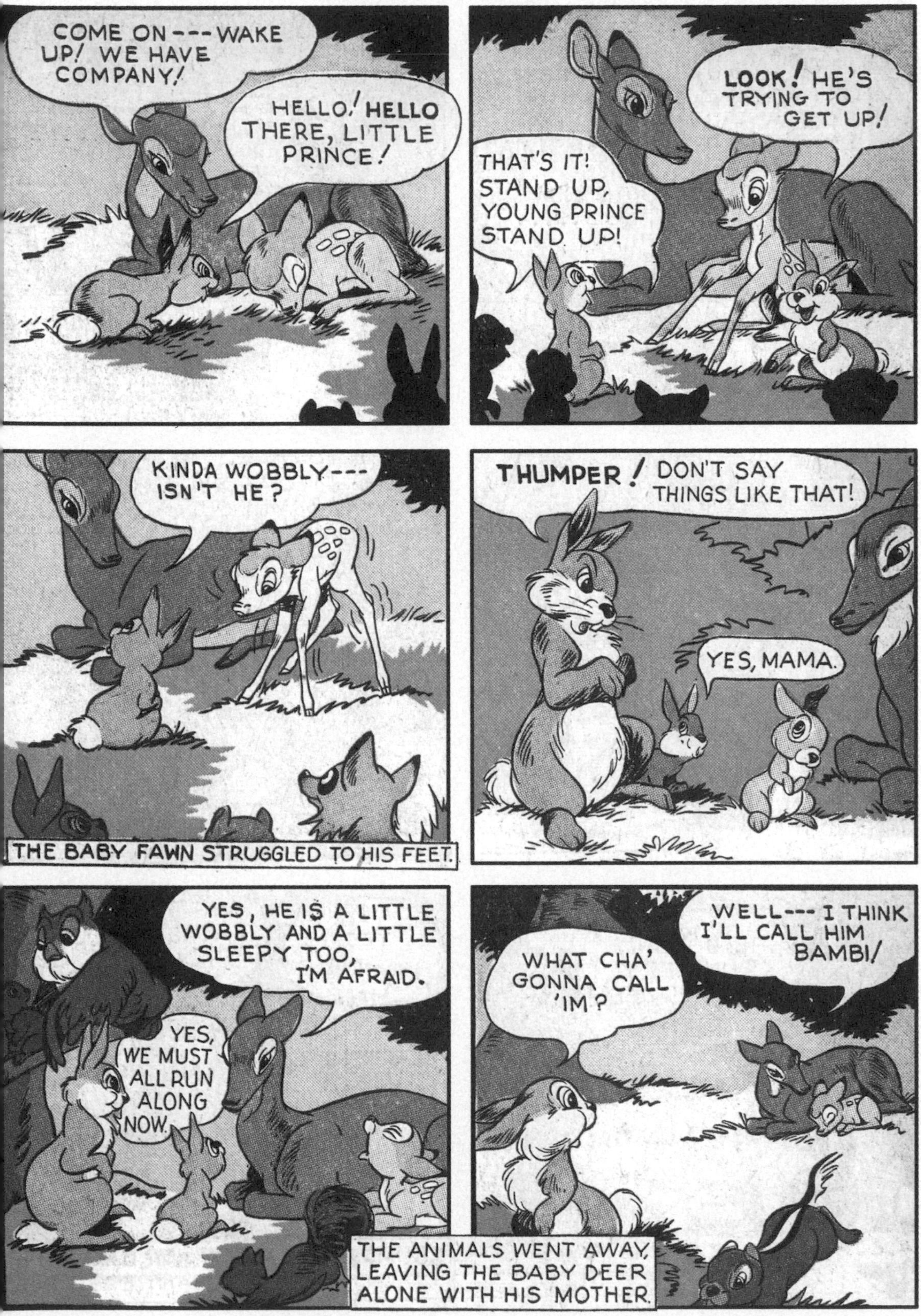
COME ON---WAKE UP! WE HAVE COMPANY!
HELLO! HELLO THERE, LITTLE PRINCE!
LOOK! HE'S TRYING TO GET UP!
THAT'S IT! STAND UP, YOUNG PRINCE STAND UP!
KINDA WOBBLY--- ISN'T HE?
THE BABY FAWN STRUGGLED TO HIS FEET.
THUMPER! DON'T SAY THINGS LIKE THAT!
YES, MAMA.
YES, HE IS A LITTLE WOBBLY AND A LITTLE SLEEPY TOO, I'M AFRAID.
YES, WE MUST ALL RUN ALONG NOW.
WHAT CHA' GONNA CALL 'IM?
WELL--- I THINK I'LL CALL HIM BAMBI!
THE ANIMALS WENT AWAY, LEAVING THE BABY DEER ALONE WITH HIS MOTHER.

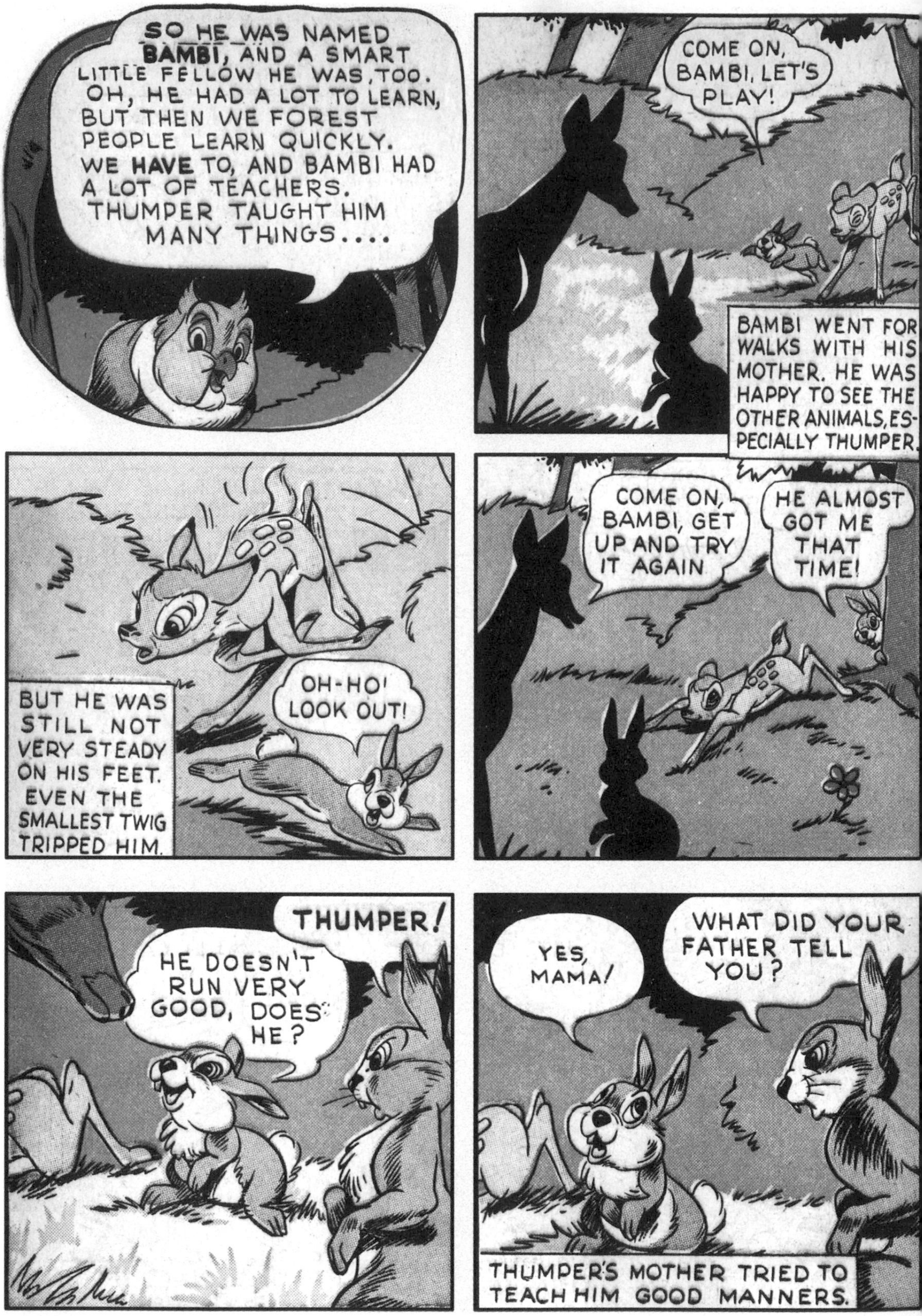

SO HE WAS NAMED BAMBI, AND A SMART LITTLE FELLOW HE WAS, TOO. OH, HE HAD A LOT TO LEARN, BUT THEN WE FOREST PEOPLE LEARN QUICKLY. WE HAVE TO, AND BAMBI HAD A LOT OF TEACHERS. THUMPER TAUGHT HIM MANY THINGS....
COME ON, BAMBI, LET'S PLAY!
BAMBI WENT FOR WALKS WITH HIS MOTHER. HE WAS HAPPY TO SEE THE OTHER ANIMALS, ESPECIALLY THUMPER.
BUT HE WAS STILL NOT VERY STEADY ON HIS FEET. EVEN THE SMALLEST TWIG TRIPPED HIM.
OH-HO! LOOK OUT!
COME ON, BAMBI, GET UP AND TRY IT AGAIN.
HE ALMOST GOT ME THAT TIME!
HE DOESN'T RUN VERY GOOD, DOES HE?
THUMPER!
WHAT DID YOUR FATHER TELL YOU?
YES, MAMA!
THUMPER'S MOTHER TRIED TO TEACH HIM GOOD MANNERS.

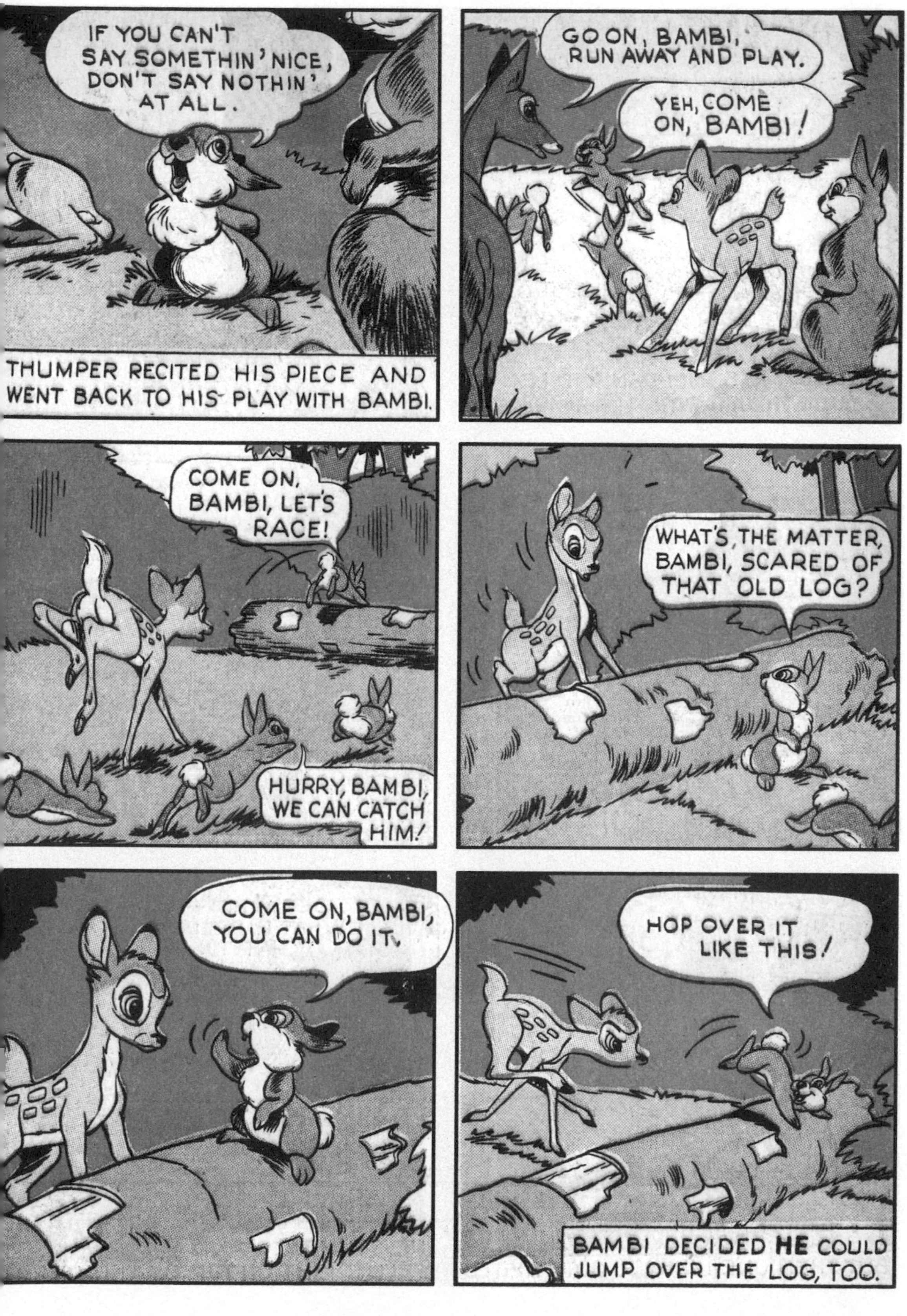

IF YOU CAN'T SAY SOMETHIN' NICE, DON'T SAY NOTHIN' AT ALL.
THUMPER RECITED HIS PIECE AND WENT BACK TO HIS PLAY WITH BAMBI.
GO ON, BAMBI, RUN AWAY AND PLAY.
YEH, COME ON, BAMBI!
COME ON, BAMBI, LET'S RACE!
HURRY, BAMBI, WE CAN CATCH HIM!
WHAT'S, THE MATTER, BAMBI, SCARED OF THAT OLD LOG?
COME ON, BAMBI, YOU CAN DO IT.
HOP OVER IT LIKE THIS!
BAMBI DECIDED **HE** COULD JUMP OVER THE LOG, TOO.

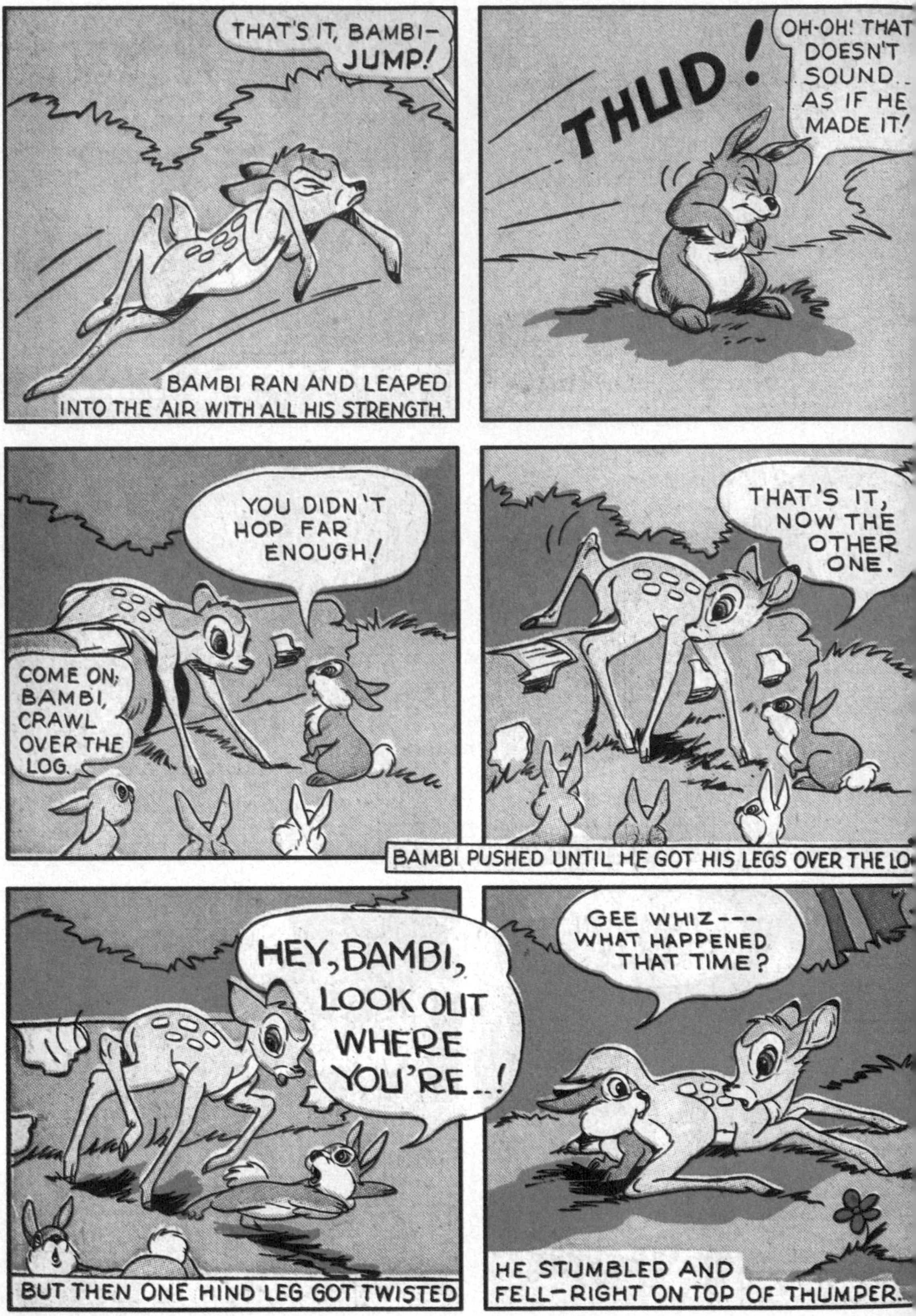
THAT'S IT, BAMBI— JUMP!
BAMBI RAN AND LEAPED INTO THE AIR WITH ALL HIS STRENGTH.
THUD!
OH-OH! THAT DOESN'T SOUND AS IF HE MADE IT!
YOU DIDN'T HOP FAR ENOUGH!
COME ON, BAMBI, CRAWL OVER THE LOG.
THAT'S IT, NOW THE OTHER ONE.
BAMBI PUSHED UNTIL HE GOT HIS LEGS OVER THE LO
HEY, BAMBI, LOOK OUT WHERE YOU'RE...!
BUT THEN ONE HIND LEG GOT TWISTED
GEE WHIZ--- WHAT HAPPENED THAT TIME?
HE STUMBLED AND FELL—RIGHT ON TOP OF THUMPER...

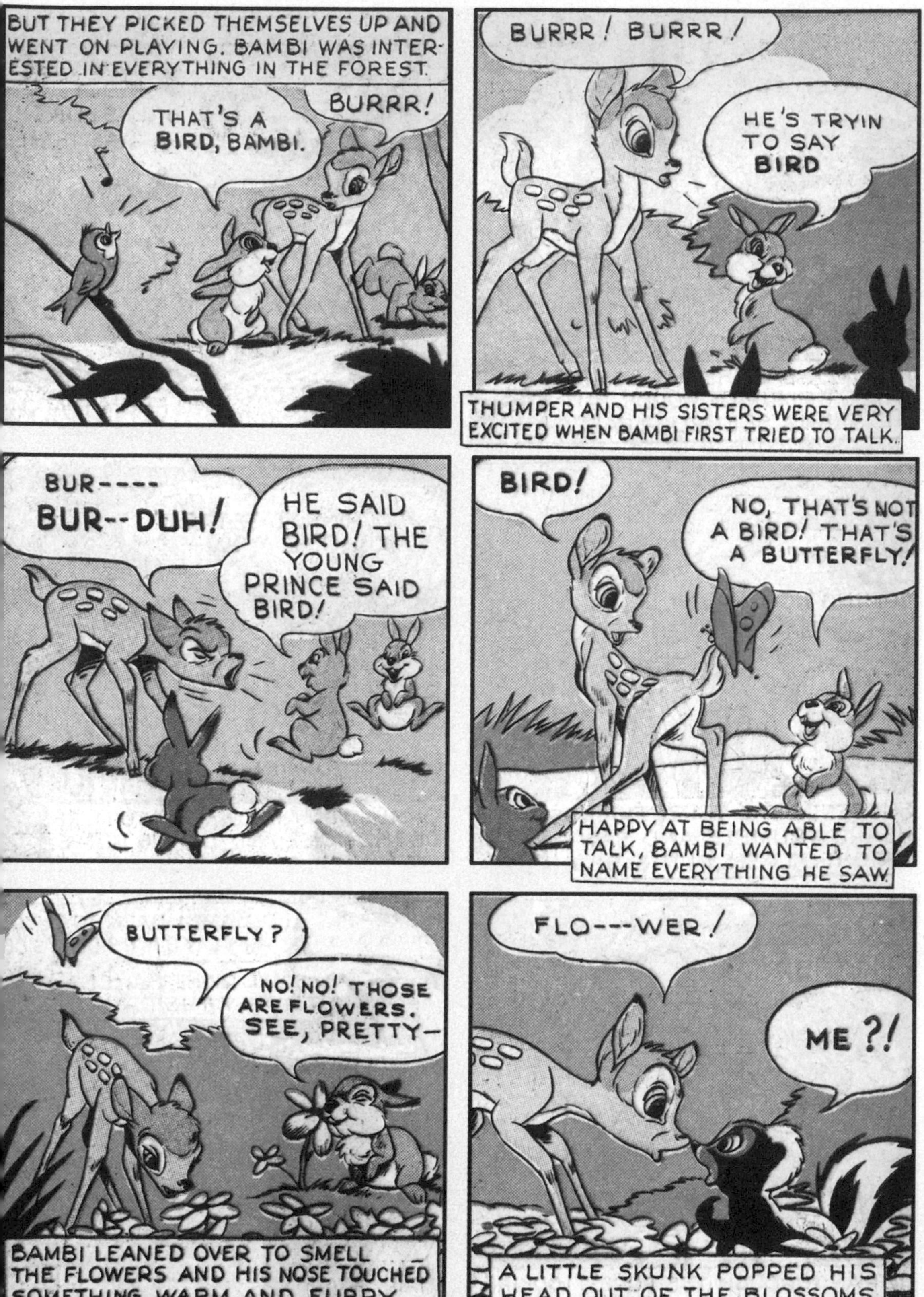
BUT THEY PICKED THEMSELVES UP AND WENT ON PLAYING. BAMBI WAS INTERESTED IN EVERYTHING IN THE FOREST.
THAT'S A BIRD, BAMBI.
BURRR!
BURRR! BURRR!
HE'S TRYIN TO SAY BIRD
THUMPER AND HIS SISTERS WERE VERY EXCITED WHEN BAMBI FIRST TRIED TO TALK.
BUR---- BUR--DUH!
HE SAID BIRD! THE YOUNG PRINCE SAID BIRD!
BIRD!
NO, THAT'S NOT A BIRD! THAT'S A BUTTERFLY!
HAPPY AT BEING ABLE TO TALK, BAMBI WANTED TO NAME EVERYTHING HE SAW.
BUTTERFLY?
NO! NO! THOSE ARE FLOWERS. SEE, PRETTY—
BAMBI LEANED OVER TO SMELL THE FLOWERS AND HIS NOSE TOUCHED SOMETHING WARM AND FURRY.
FLO---WER!
ME?!
A LITTLE SKUNK POPPED HIS HEAD OUT OF THE BLOSSOMS.

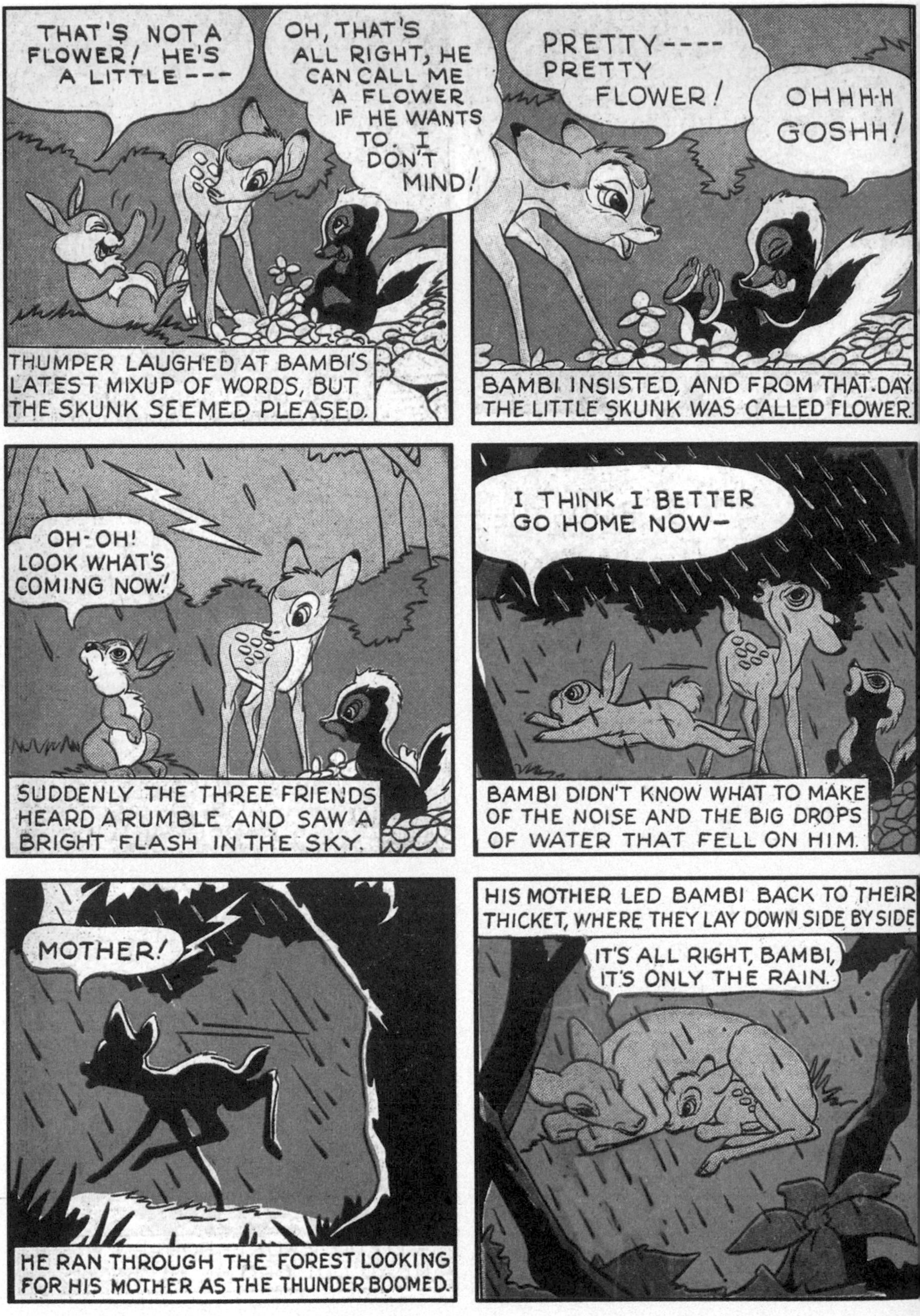
THAT'S NOT A FLOWER! HE'S A LITTLE---
OH, THAT'S ALL RIGHT, HE CAN CALL ME A FLOWER IF HE WANTS TO. I DON'T MIND!
THUMPER LAUGHED AT BAMBI'S LATEST MIXUP OF WORDS, BUT THE SKUNK SEEMED PLEASED.
PRETTY---- PRETTY FLOWER!
OHHHH GOSHH!
BAMBI INSISTED, AND FROM THAT DAY THE LITTLE SKUNK WAS CALLED FLOWER.
OH-OH! LOOK WHAT'S COMING NOW!
SUDDENLY THE THREE FRIENDS HEARD A RUMBLE AND SAW A BRIGHT FLASH IN THE SKY.
I THINK I BETTER GO HOME NOW—
BAMBI DIDN'T KNOW WHAT TO MAKE OF THE NOISE AND THE BIG DROPS OF WATER THAT FELL ON HIM.
MOTHER!
HE RAN THROUGH THE FOREST LOOKING FOR HIS MOTHER AS THE THUNDER BOOMED.
HIS MOTHER LED BAMBI BACK TO THEIR THICKET, WHERE THEY LAY DOWN SIDE BY SIDE
IT'S ALL RIGHT, BAMBI, IT'S ONLY THE RAIN.

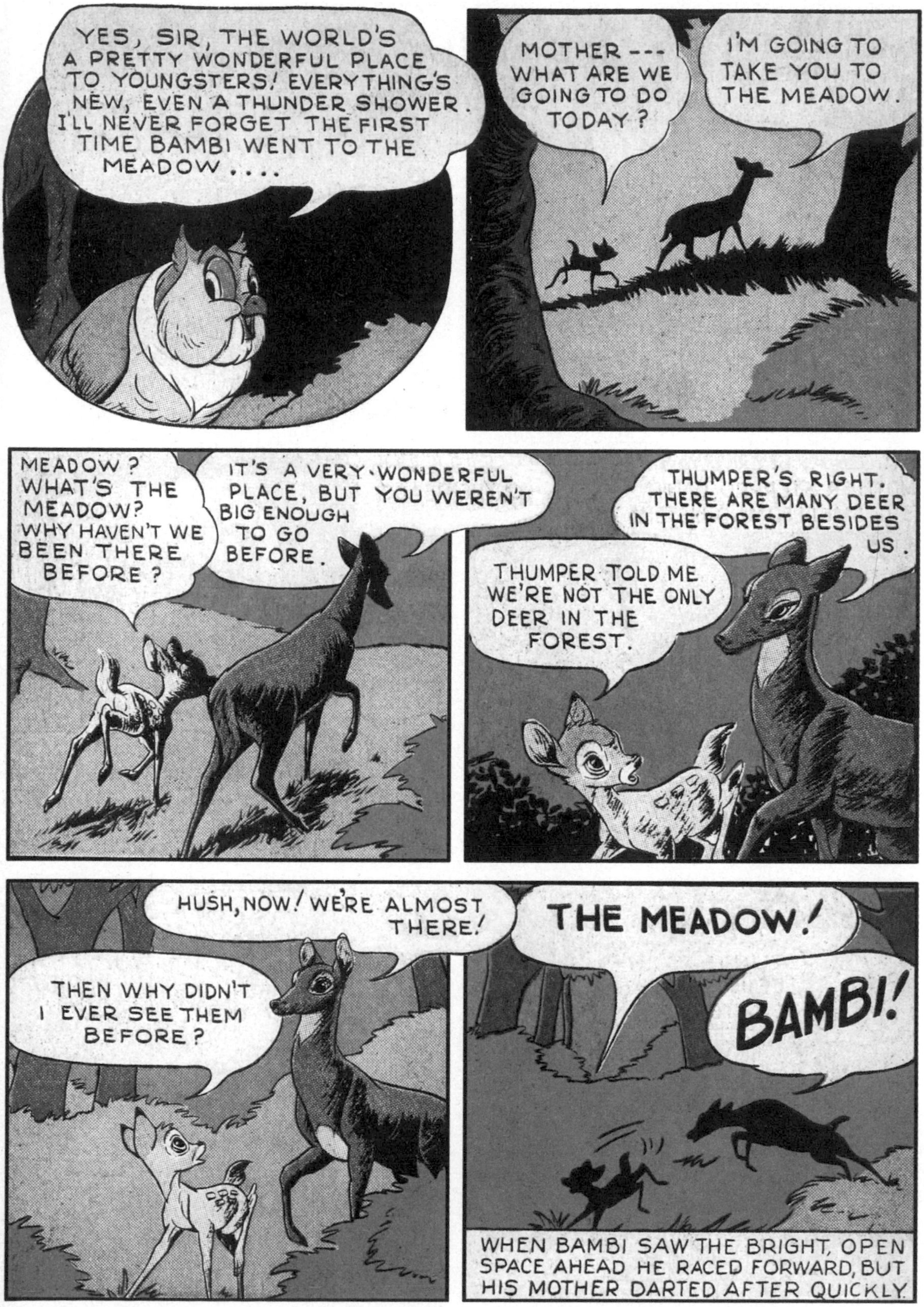
YES, SIR, THE WORLD'S A PRETTY WONDERFUL PLACE TO YOUNGSTERS! EVERYTHING'S NEW, EVEN A THUNDER SHOWER. I'LL NEVER FORGET THE FIRST TIME BAMBI WENT TO THE MEADOW....
MOTHER--- WHAT ARE WE GOING TO DO TODAY?
I'M GOING TO TAKE YOU TO THE MEADOW.
MEADOW? WHAT'S THE MEADOW? WHY HAVEN'T WE BEEN THERE BEFORE?
IT'S A VERY WONDERFUL PLACE, BUT YOU WEREN'T BIG ENOUGH TO GO BEFORE.
THUMPER TOLD ME WE'RE NOT THE ONLY DEER IN THE FOREST.
THUMPER'S RIGHT. THERE ARE MANY DEER IN THE FOREST BESIDES US.
THEN WHY DIDN'T I EVER SEE THEM BEFORE?
HUSH, NOW! WE'RE ALMOST THERE!
THE MEADOW!
BAMBI!
WHEN BAMBI SAW THE BRIGHT, OPEN SPACE AHEAD HE RACED FORWARD, BUT HIS MOTHER DARTED AFTER QUICKLY.

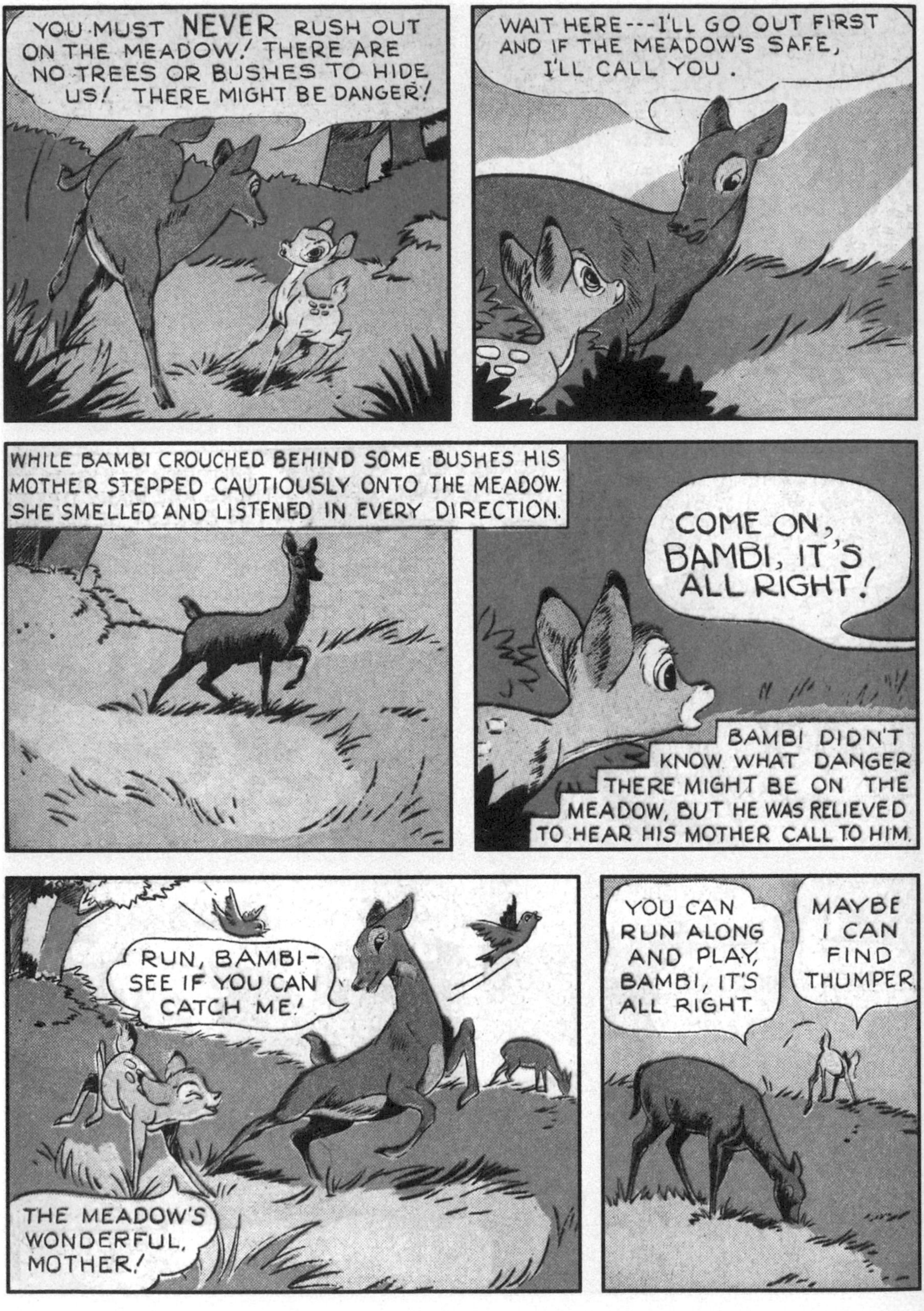
YOU MUST NEVER RUSH OUT ON THE MEADOW! THERE ARE NO TREES OR BUSHES TO HIDE US! THERE MIGHT BE DANGER!
WAIT HERE---I'LL GO OUT FIRST AND IF THE MEADOW'S SAFE, I'LL CALL YOU.
WHILE BAMBI CROUCHED BEHIND SOME BUSHES HIS MOTHER STEPPED CAUTIOUSLY ONTO THE MEADOW. SHE SMELLED AND LISTENED IN EVERY DIRECTION.
COME ON, BAMBI, IT'S ALL RIGHT!
BAMBI DIDN'T KNOW WHAT DANGER THERE MIGHT BE ON THE MEADOW, BUT HE WAS RELIEVED TO HEAR HIS MOTHER CALL TO HIM.
RUN, BAMBI- SEE IF YOU CAN CATCH ME!
THE MEADOW'S WONDERFUL, MOTHER!
YOU CAN RUN ALONG AND PLAY, BAMBI, IT'S ALL RIGHT.
MAYBE I CAN FIND THUMPER.

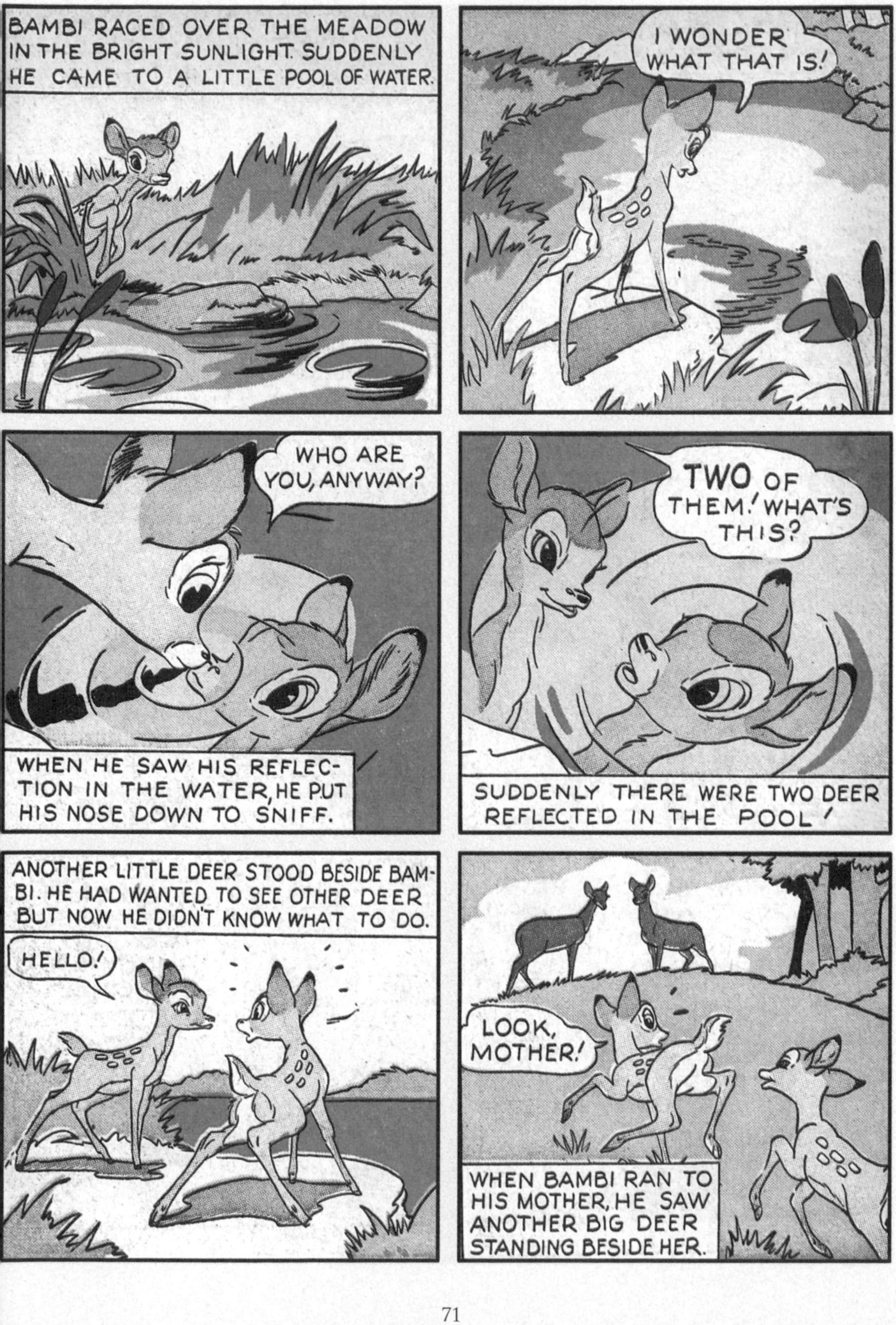
BAMBI RACED OVER THE MEADOW IN THE BRIGHT SUNLIGHT. SUDDENLY HE CAME TO A LITTLE POOL OF WATER.
I WONDER WHAT THAT IS!
WHO ARE YOU, ANYWAY?
WHEN HE SAW HIS REFLECTION IN THE WATER, HE PUT HIS NOSE DOWN TO SNIFF.
TWO OF THEM! WHAT'S THIS?
SUDDENLY THERE WERE TWO DEER REFLECTED IN THE POOL!
ANOTHER LITTLE DEER STOOD BESIDE BAMBI. HE HAD WANTED TO SEE OTHER DEER BUT NOW HE DIDN'T KNOW WHAT TO DO.
HELLO!
LOOK, MOTHER!
WHEN BAMBI RAN TO HIS MOTHER, HE SAW ANOTHER BIG DEER STANDING BESIDE HER.

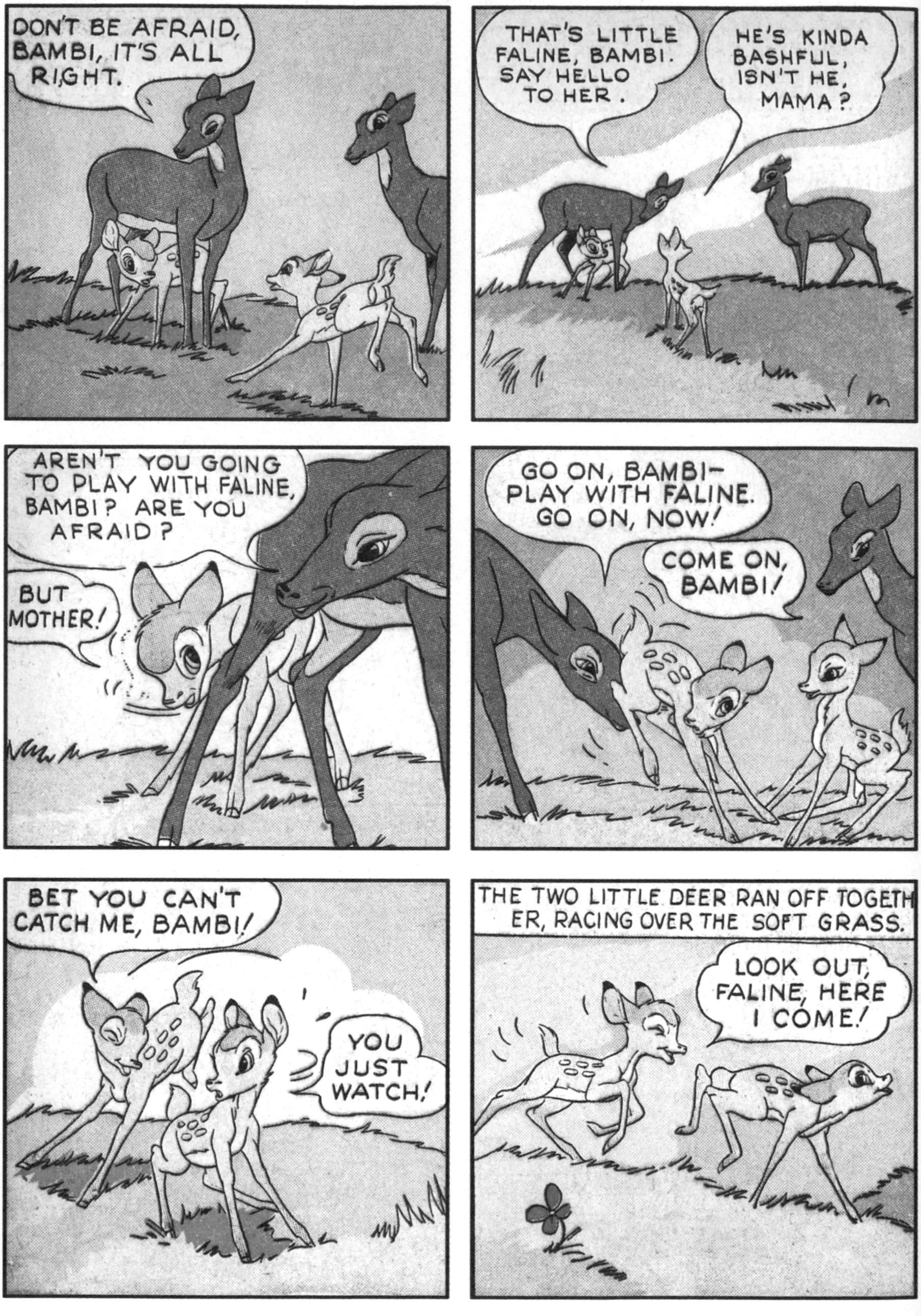
DON'T BE AFRAID, BAMBI, IT'S ALL RIGHT.
THAT'S LITTLE FALINE, BAMBI. SAY HELLO TO HER.
HE'S KINDA BASHFUL, ISN'T HE, MAMA?
AREN'T YOU GOING TO PLAY WITH FALINE, BAMBI? ARE YOU AFRAID?
BUT MOTHER!
GO ON, BAMBI– PLAY WITH FALINE. GO ON, NOW!
COME ON, BAMBI!
BET YOU CAN'T CATCH ME, BAMBI!
YOU JUST WATCH!
THE TWO LITTLE DEER RAN OFF TOGETHER, RACING OVER THE SOFT GRASS.
LOOK OUT, FALINE, HERE I COME!

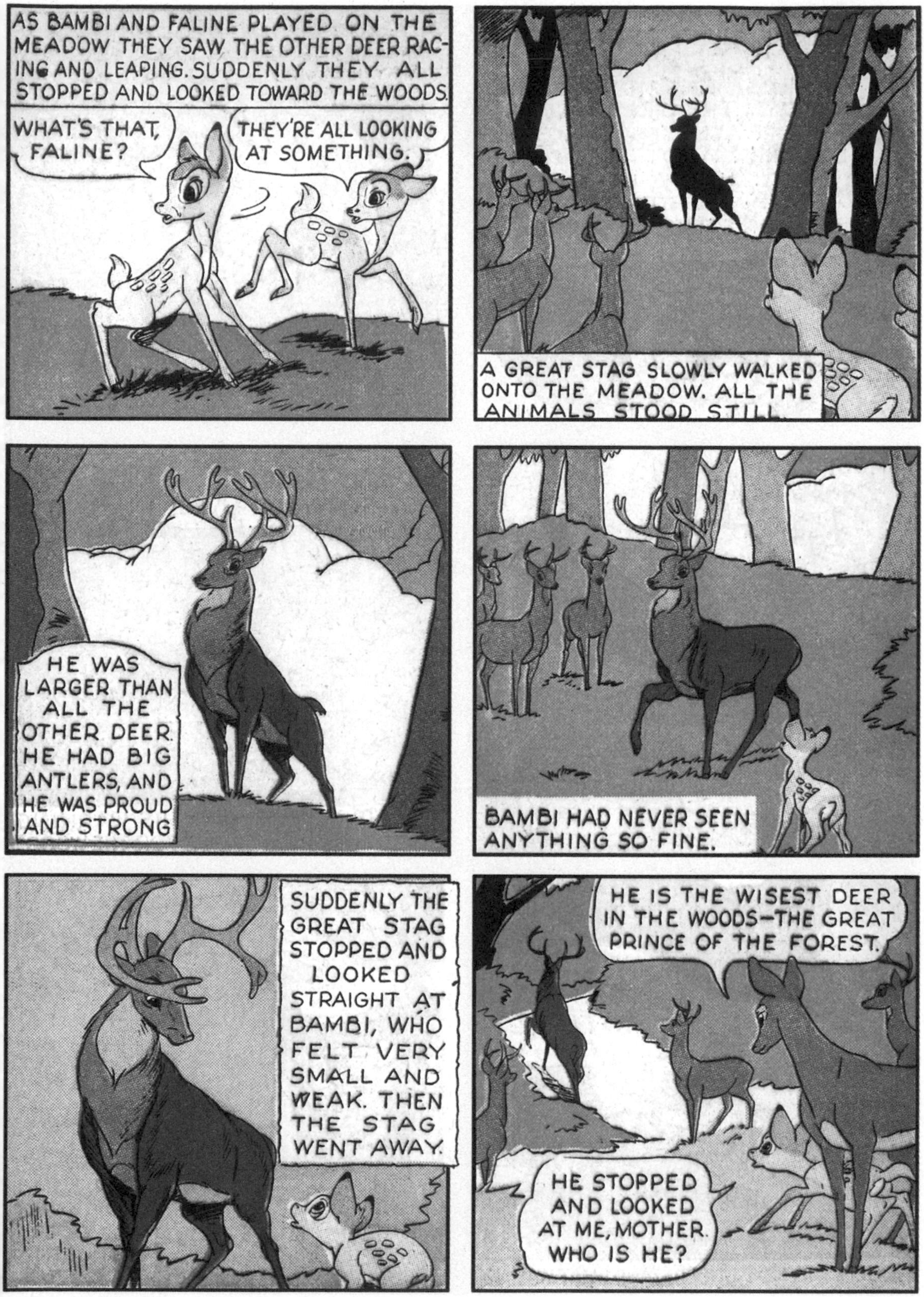

AS BAMBI AND FALINE PLAYED ON THE MEADOW THEY SAW THE OTHER DEER RACING AND LEAPING. SUDDENLY THEY ALL STOPPED AND LOOKED TOWARD THE WOODS.
WHAT'S THAT, FALINE?
THEY'RE ALL LOOKING AT SOMETHING.
A GREAT STAG SLOWLY WALKED ONTO THE MEADOW. ALL THE ANIMALS STOOD STILL.
HE WAS LARGER THAN ALL THE OTHER DEER. HE HAD BIG ANTLERS, AND HE WAS PROUD AND STRONG
BAMBI HAD NEVER SEEN ANYTHING SO FINE.
SUDDENLY THE GREAT STAG STOPPED AND LOOKED STRAIGHT AT BAMBI, WHO FELT VERY SMALL AND WEAK. THEN THE STAG WENT AWAY.
HE STOPPED AND LOOKED AT ME, MOTHER. WHO IS HE?
HE IS THE WISEST DEER IN THE WOODS—THE GREAT PRINCE OF THE FOREST.

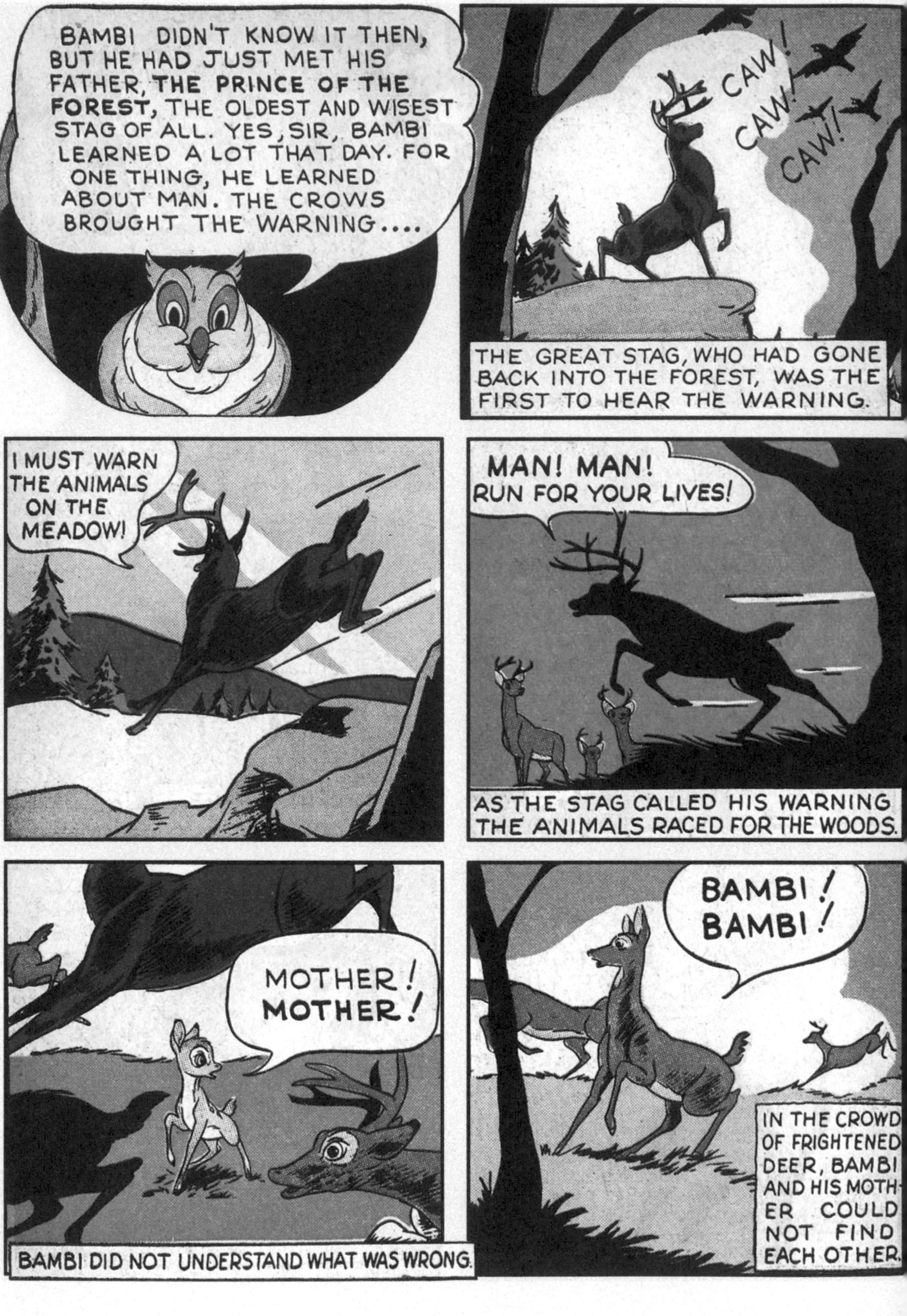
BAMBI DIDN'T KNOW IT THEN, BUT HE HAD JUST MET HIS FATHER, THE PRINCE OF THE FOREST, THE OLDEST AND WISEST STAG OF ALL. YES, SIR, BAMBI LEARNED A LOT THAT DAY. FOR ONE THING, HE LEARNED ABOUT MAN. THE CROWS BROUGHT THE WARNING....
CAW! CAW! CAW!
THE GREAT STAG, WHO HAD GONE BACK INTO THE FOREST, WAS THE FIRST TO HEAR THE WARNING.
I MUST WARN THE ANIMALS ON THE MEADOW!
MAN! MAN! RUN FOR YOUR LIVES!
AS THE STAG CALLED HIS WARNING THE ANIMALS RACED FOR THE WOODS.
MOTHER! MOTHER!
BAMBI DID NOT UNDERSTAND WHAT WAS WRONG.
BAMBI! BAMBI!
IN THE CROWD OF FRIGHTENED DEER, BAMBI AND HIS MOTHER COULD NOT FIND EACH OTHER.

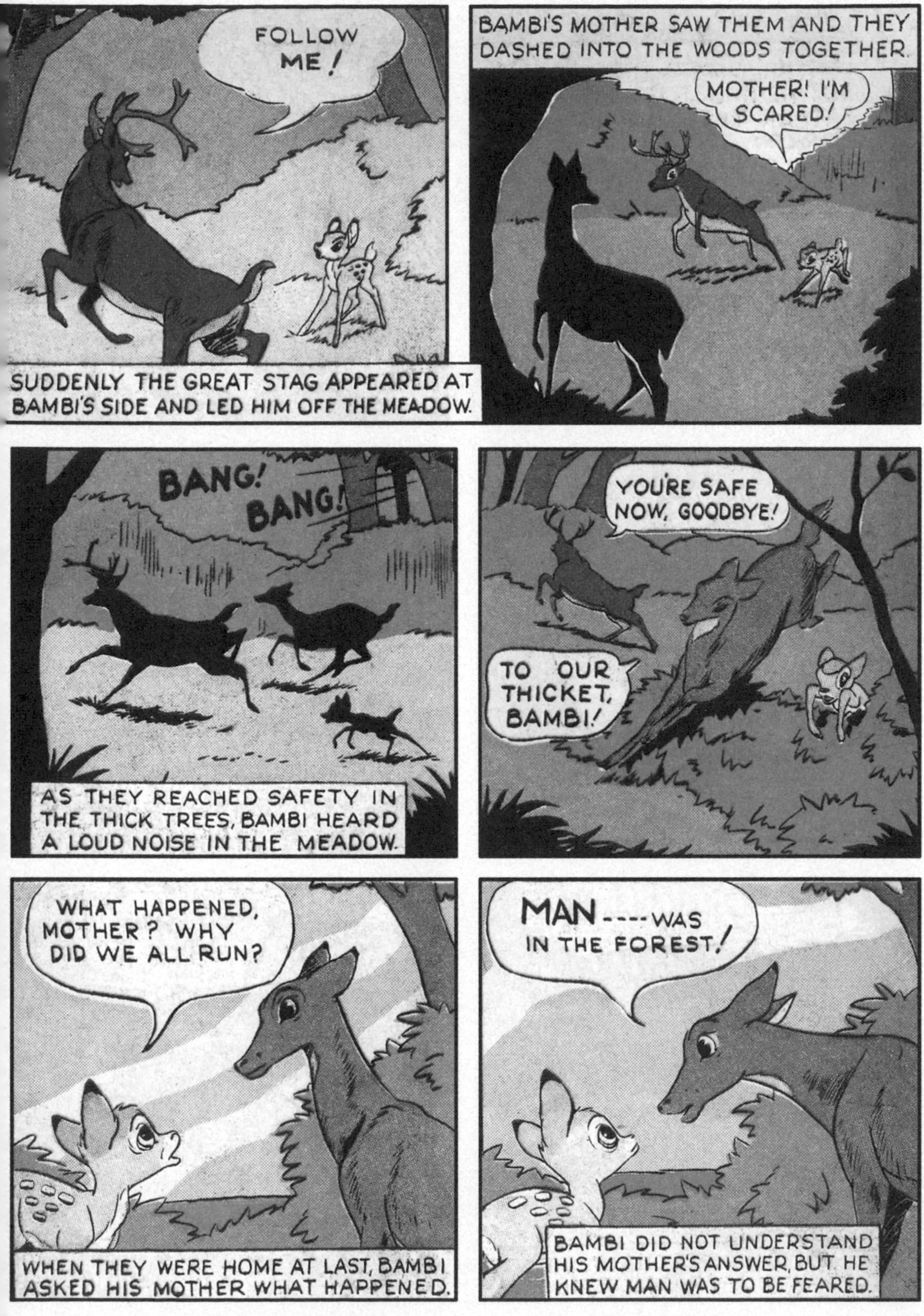
FOLLOW ME!
SUDDENLY THE GREAT STAG APPEARED AT BAMBI'S SIDE AND LED HIM OFF THE MEADOW.
BAMBI'S MOTHER SAW THEM AND THEY DASHED INTO THE WOODS TOGETHER.
MOTHER! I'M SCARED!
BANG! BANG!
AS THEY REACHED SAFETY IN THE THICK TREES, BAMBI HEARD A LOUD NOISE IN THE MEADOW.
YOU'RE SAFE NOW, GOODBYE!
TO OUR THICKET, BAMBI!
WHAT HAPPENED, MOTHER? WHY DID WE ALL RUN?
WHEN THEY WERE HOME AT LAST, BAMBI ASKED HIS MOTHER WHAT HAPPENED.
MAN----WAS IN THE FOREST!
BAMBI DID NOT UNDERSTAND HIS MOTHER'S ANSWER, BUT HE KNEW MAN WAS TO BE FEARED.

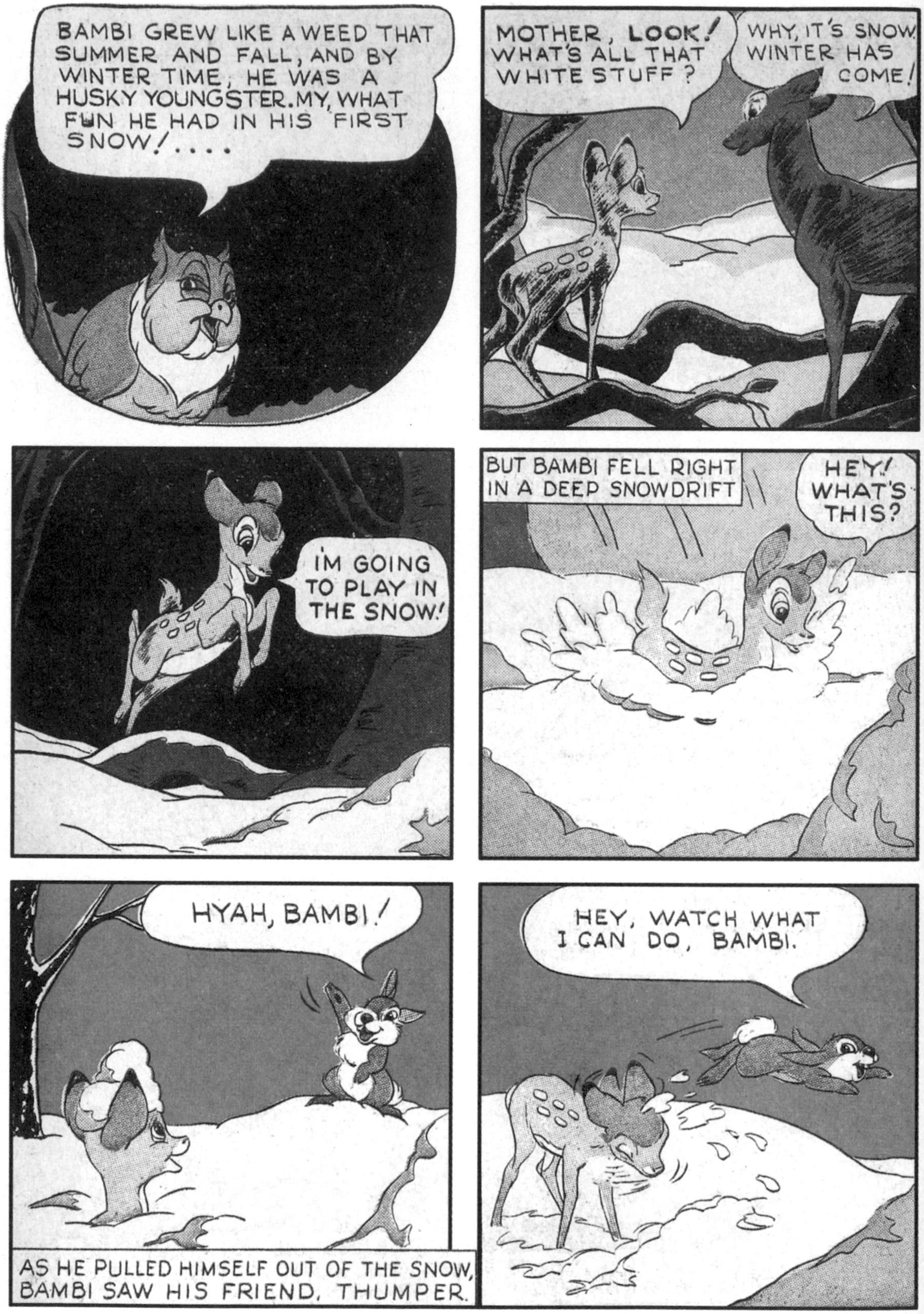

BAMBI GREW LIKE A WEED THAT SUMMER AND FALL, AND BY WINTER TIME, HE WAS A HUSKY YOUNGSTER. MY, WHAT FUN HE HAD IN HIS FIRST SNOW! ....
MOTHER, LOOK! WHAT'S ALL THAT WHITE STUFF?
WHY, IT'S SNOW. WINTER HAS COME!
I'M GOING TO PLAY IN THE SNOW!
BUT BAMBI FELL RIGHT IN A DEEP SNOWDRIFT
HEY! WHAT'S THIS?
HYAH, BAMBI!
AS HE PULLED HIMSELF OUT OF THE SNOW, BAMBI SAW HIS FRIEND, THUMPER.
HEY, WATCH WHAT I CAN DO, BAMBI.

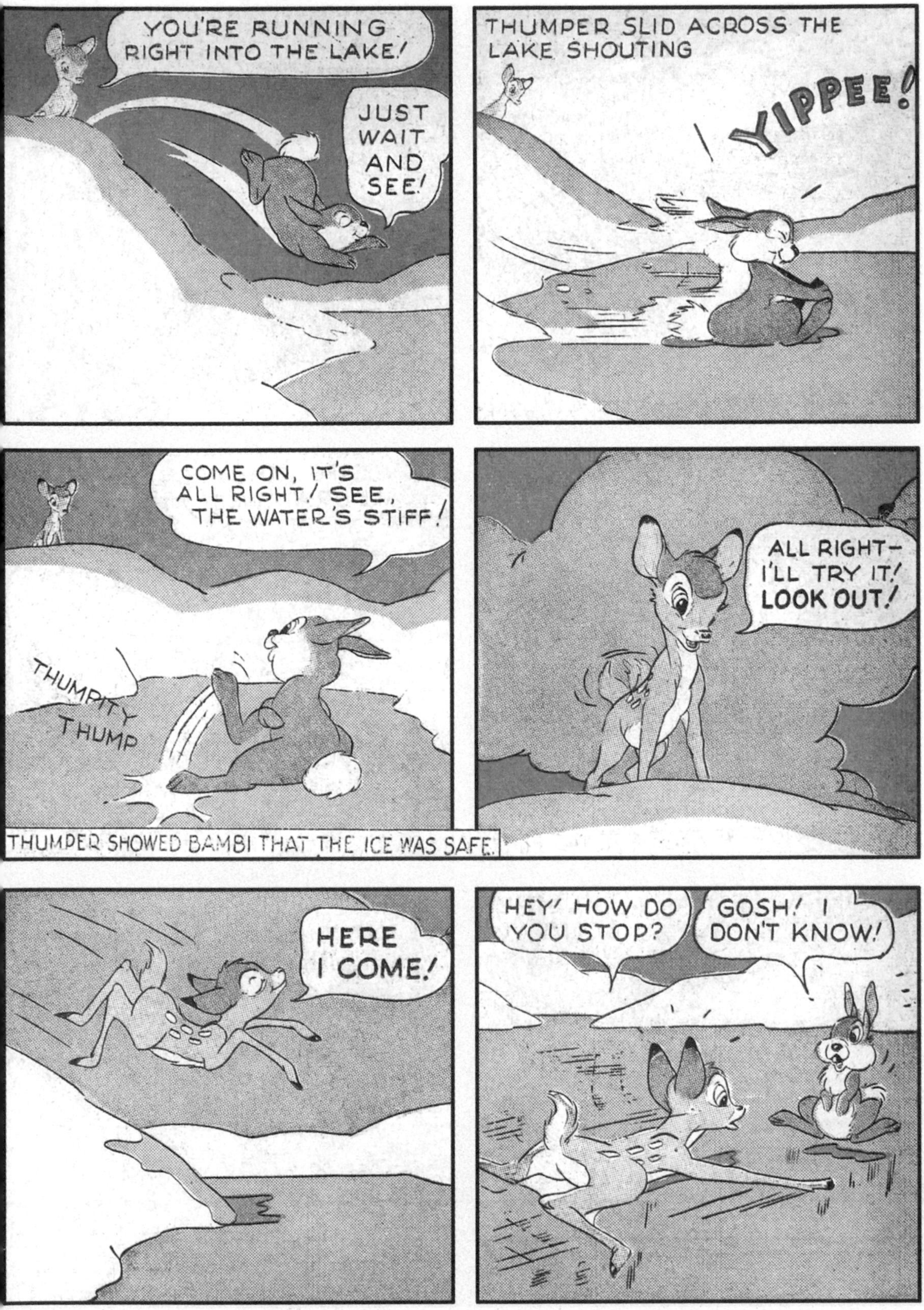
YOU'RE RUNNING RIGHT INTO THE LAKE!
JUST WAIT AND SEE!
THUMPER SLID ACROSS THE LAKE SHOUTING
YIPPEE!
COME ON, IT'S ALL RIGHT! SEE, THE WATER'S STIFF!
THUMPITY THUMP
THUMPER SHOWED BAMBI THAT THE ICE WAS SAFE.
ALL RIGHT— I'LL TRY IT! LOOK OUT!
HERE I COME!
HEY! HOW DO YOU STOP?
GOSH! I DON'T KNOW!

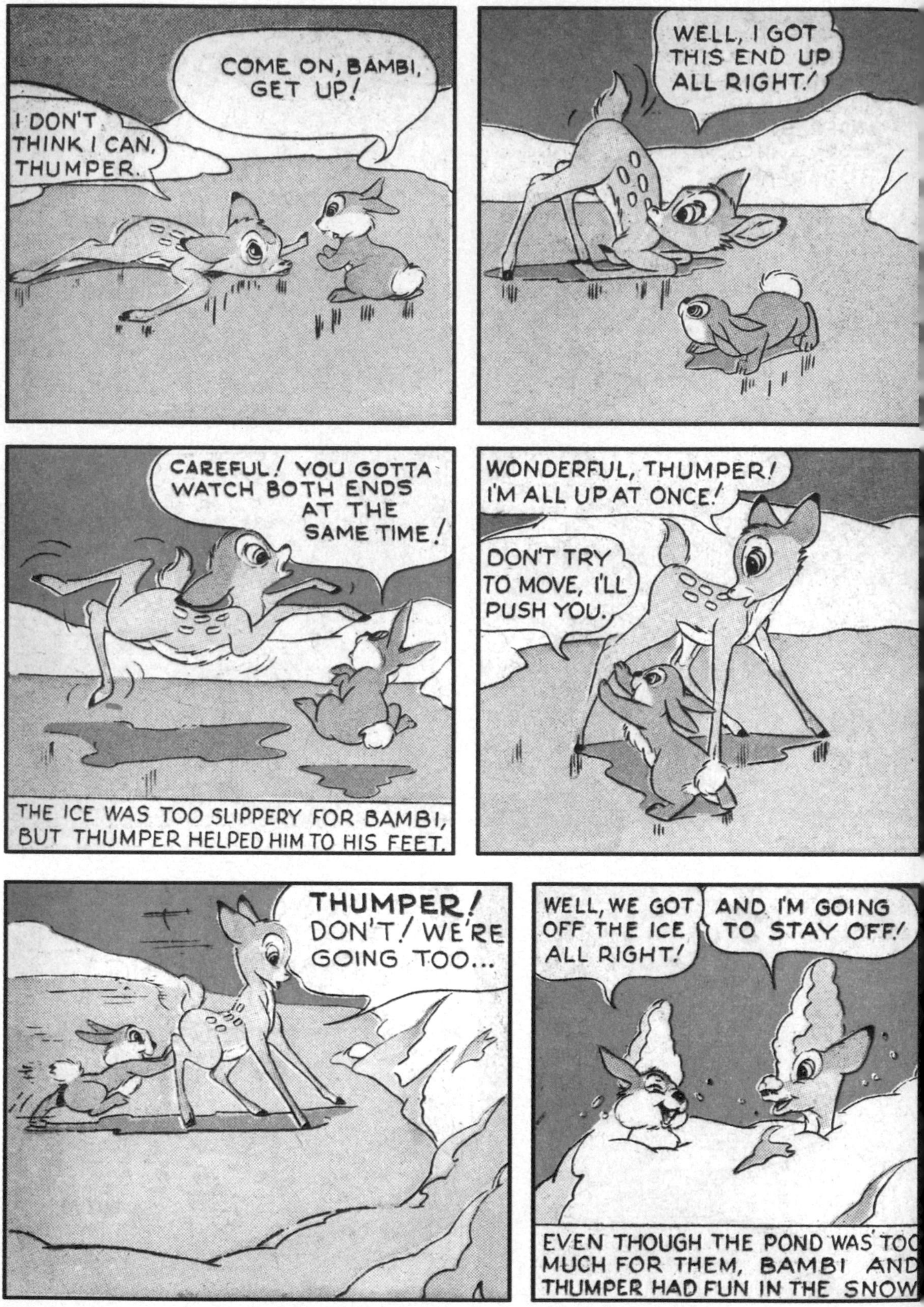
COME ON, BAMBI, GET UP!
I DON'T THINK I CAN, THUMPER.
WELL, I GOT THIS END UP ALL RIGHT!
CAREFUL! YOU GOTTA WATCH BOTH ENDS AT THE SAME TIME!
THE ICE WAS TOO SLIPPERY FOR BAMBI, BUT THUMPER HELPED HIM TO HIS FEET.
WONDERFUL, THUMPER! I'M ALL UP AT ONCE!
DON'T TRY TO MOVE, I'LL PUSH YOU.
THUMPER! DON'T! WE'RE GOING TOO...
WELL, WE GOT OFF THE ICE ALL RIGHT!
AND I'M GOING TO STAY OFF!
EVEN THOUGH THE POND WAS TOO MUCH FOR THEM, BAMBI AND THUMPER HAD FUN IN THE SNOW

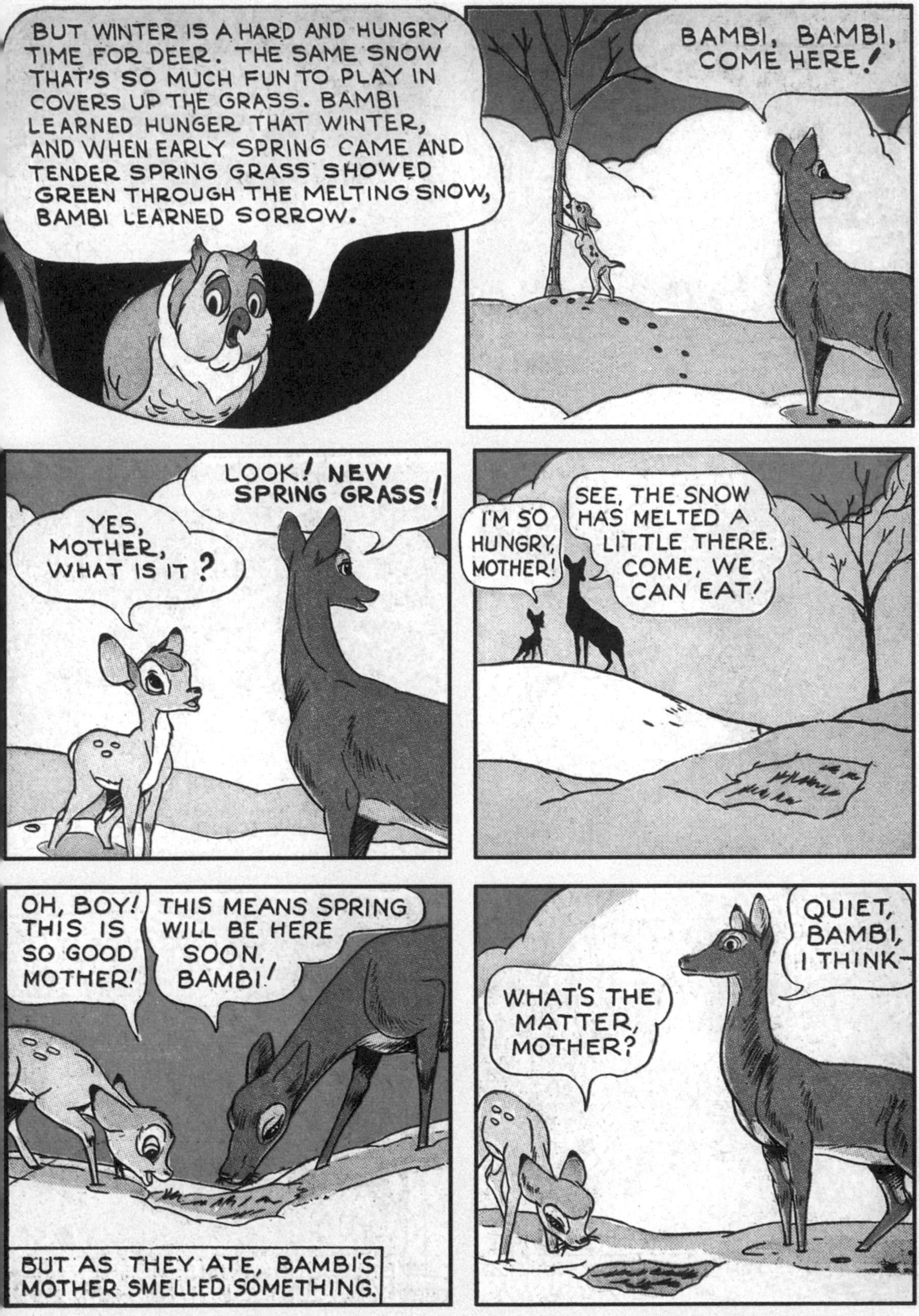
BUT WINTER IS A HARD AND HUNGRY TIME FOR DEER. THE SAME SNOW THAT'S SO MUCH FUN TO PLAY IN COVERS UP THE GRASS. BAMBI LEARNED HUNGER THAT WINTER, AND WHEN EARLY SPRING CAME AND TENDER SPRING GRASS SHOWED GREEN THROUGH THE MELTING SNOW, BAMBI LEARNED SORROW.
BAMBI, BAMBI, COME HERE!
YES, MOTHER, WHAT IS IT?
LOOK! NEW SPRING GRASS!
I'M SO HUNGRY, MOTHER!
SEE, THE SNOW HAS MELTED A LITTLE THERE. COME, WE CAN EAT!
OH, BOY! THIS IS SO GOOD MOTHER!
THIS MEANS SPRING WILL BE HERE SOON, BAMBI!
BUT AS THEY ATE, BAMBI'S MOTHER SMELLED SOMETHING.
QUIET, BAMBI, I THINK—
WHAT'S THE MATTER, MOTHER?

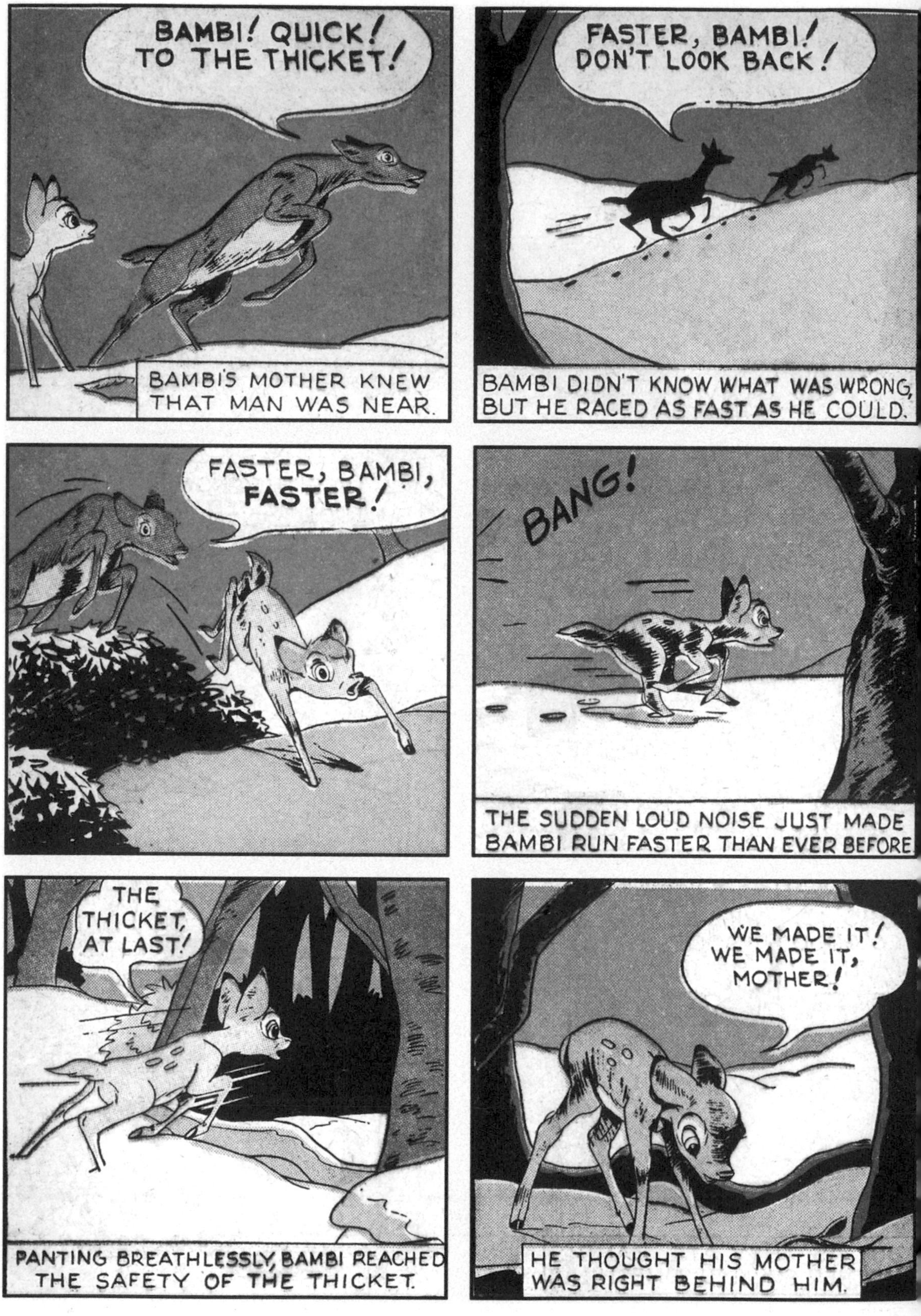
BAMBI! QUICK! TO THE THICKET!
BAMBI'S MOTHER KNEW THAT MAN WAS NEAR.
FASTER, BAMBI! DON'T LOOK BACK!
BAMBI DIDN'T KNOW WHAT WAS WRONG, BUT HE RACED AS FAST AS HE COULD.
FASTER, BAMBI, FASTER!
BANG!
THE SUDDEN LOUD NOISE JUST MADE BAMBI RUN FASTER THAN EVER BEFORE
THE THICKET, AT LAST!
PANTING BREATHLESSLY, BAMBI REACHED THE SAFETY OF THE THICKET.
WE MADE IT! WE MADE IT, MOTHER!
HE THOUGHT HIS MOTHER WAS RIGHT BEHIND HIM.

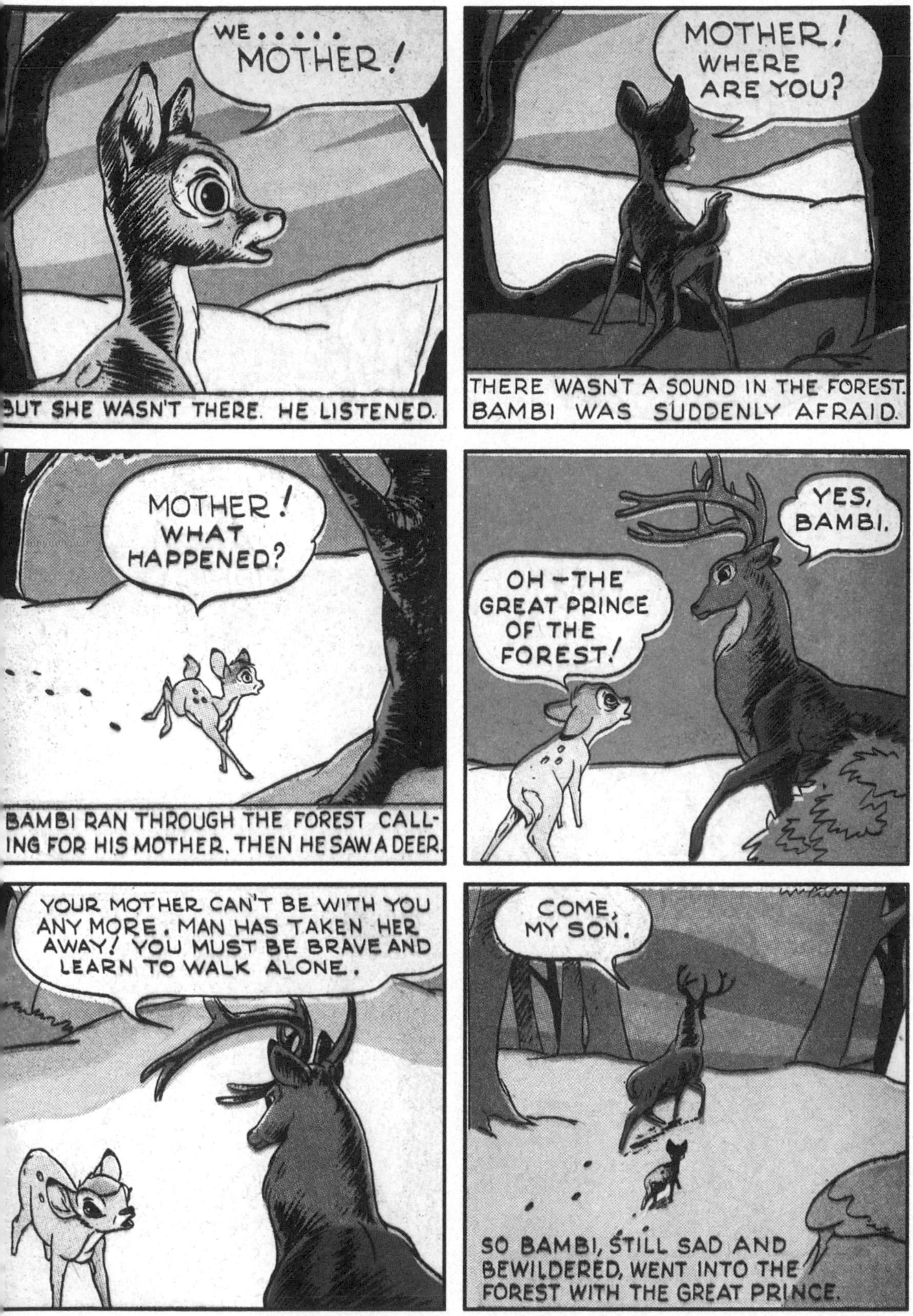
WE..... MOTHER!
BUT SHE WASN'T THERE. HE LISTENED.
MOTHER! WHERE ARE YOU?
THERE WASN'T A SOUND IN THE FOREST. BAMBI WAS SUDDENLY AFRAID.
MOTHER! WHAT HAPPENED?
BAMBI RAN THROUGH THE FOREST CALLING FOR HIS MOTHER. THEN HE SAW A DEER.
OH—THE GREAT PRINCE OF THE FOREST!
YES, BAMBI.
YOUR MOTHER CAN'T BE WITH YOU ANY MORE. MAN HAS TAKEN HER AWAY! YOU MUST BE BRAVE AND LEARN TO WALK ALONE.
COME, MY SON.
SO BAMBI, STILL SAD AND BEWILDERED, WENT INTO THE FOREST WITH THE GREAT PRINCE.

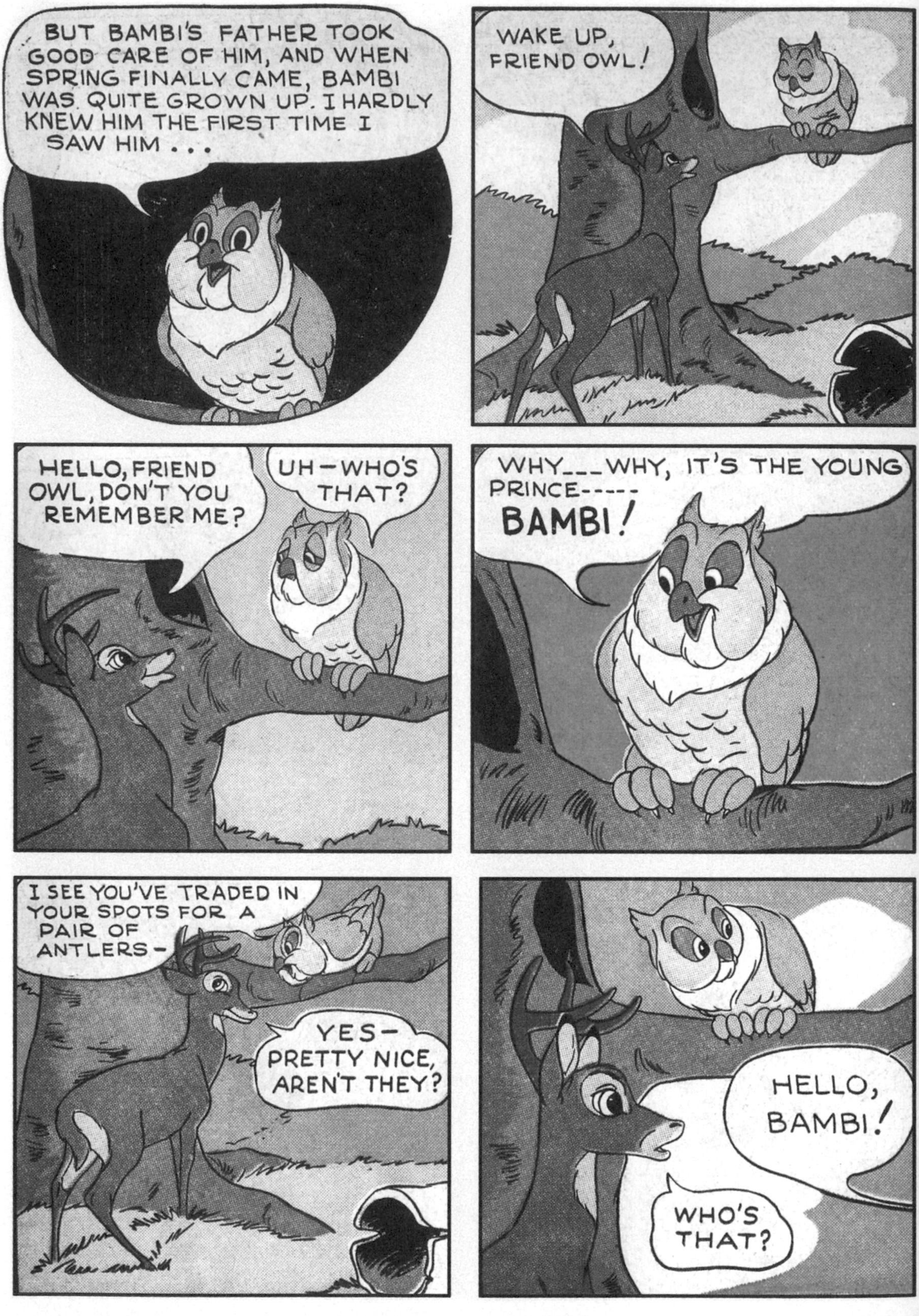
BUT BAMBI'S FATHER TOOK GOOD CARE OF HIM, AND WHEN SPRING FINALLY CAME, BAMBI WAS QUITE GROWN UP. I HARDLY KNEW HIM THE FIRST TIME I SAW HIM ...
WAKE UP, FRIEND OWL!
HELLO, FRIEND OWL, DON'T YOU REMEMBER ME?
UH—WHO'S THAT?
WHY___WHY, IT'S THE YOUNG PRINCE----- **BAMBI**!
I SEE YOU'VE TRADED IN YOUR SPOTS FOR A PAIR OF ANTLERS—
YES— PRETTY NICE, AREN'T THEY?
HELLO, BAMBI!
WHO'S THAT?

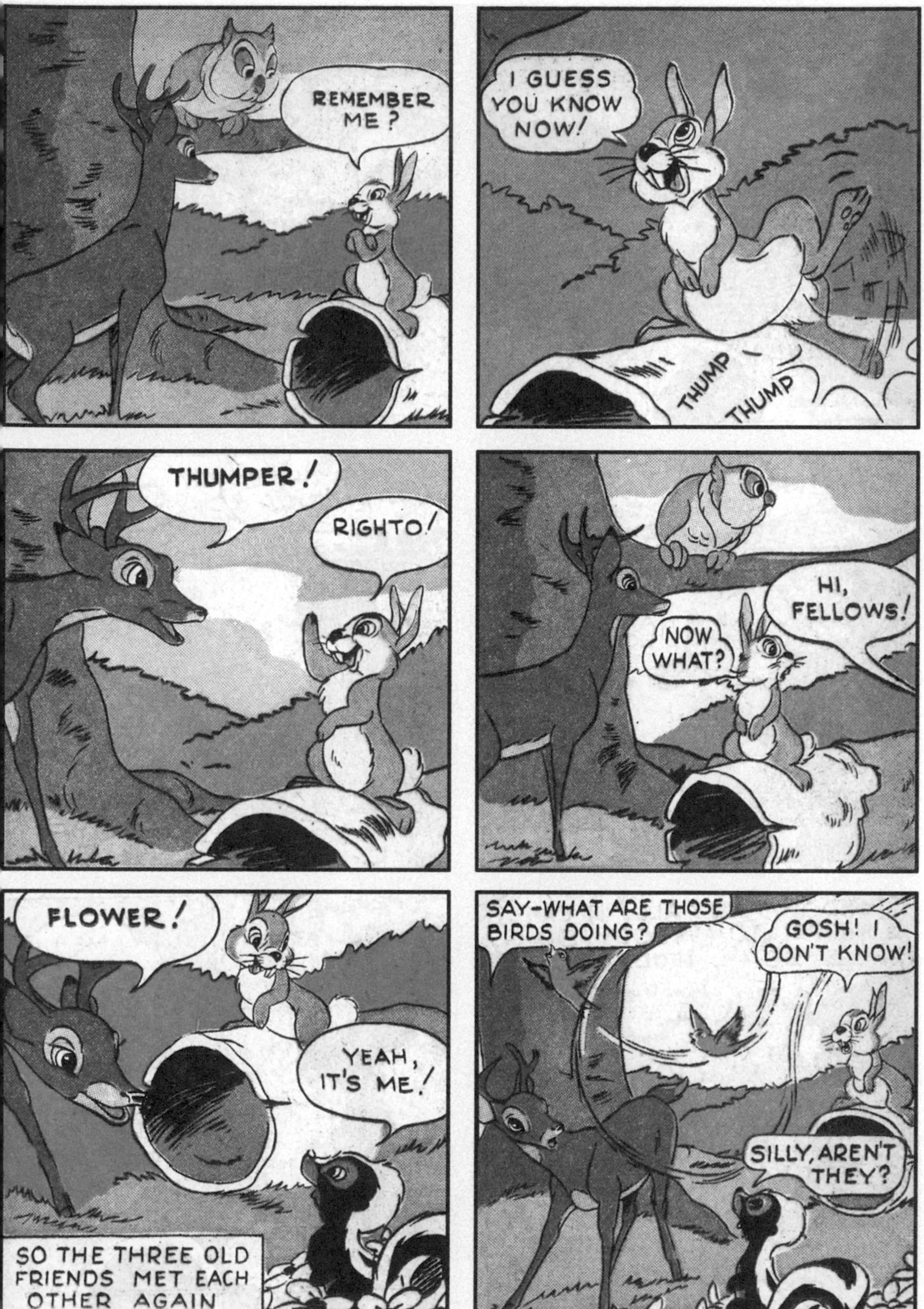
REMEMBER ME?
I GUESS YOU KNOW NOW!
THUMP
THUMP
THUMPER!
RIGHTO!
HI, FELLOWS!
NOW WHAT?
FLOWER!
YEAH, IT'S ME!
SO THE THREE OLD FRIENDS MET EACH OTHER AGAIN
SAY-WHAT ARE THOSE BIRDS DOING?
GOSH! I DON'T KNOW!
SILLY, AREN'T THEY?

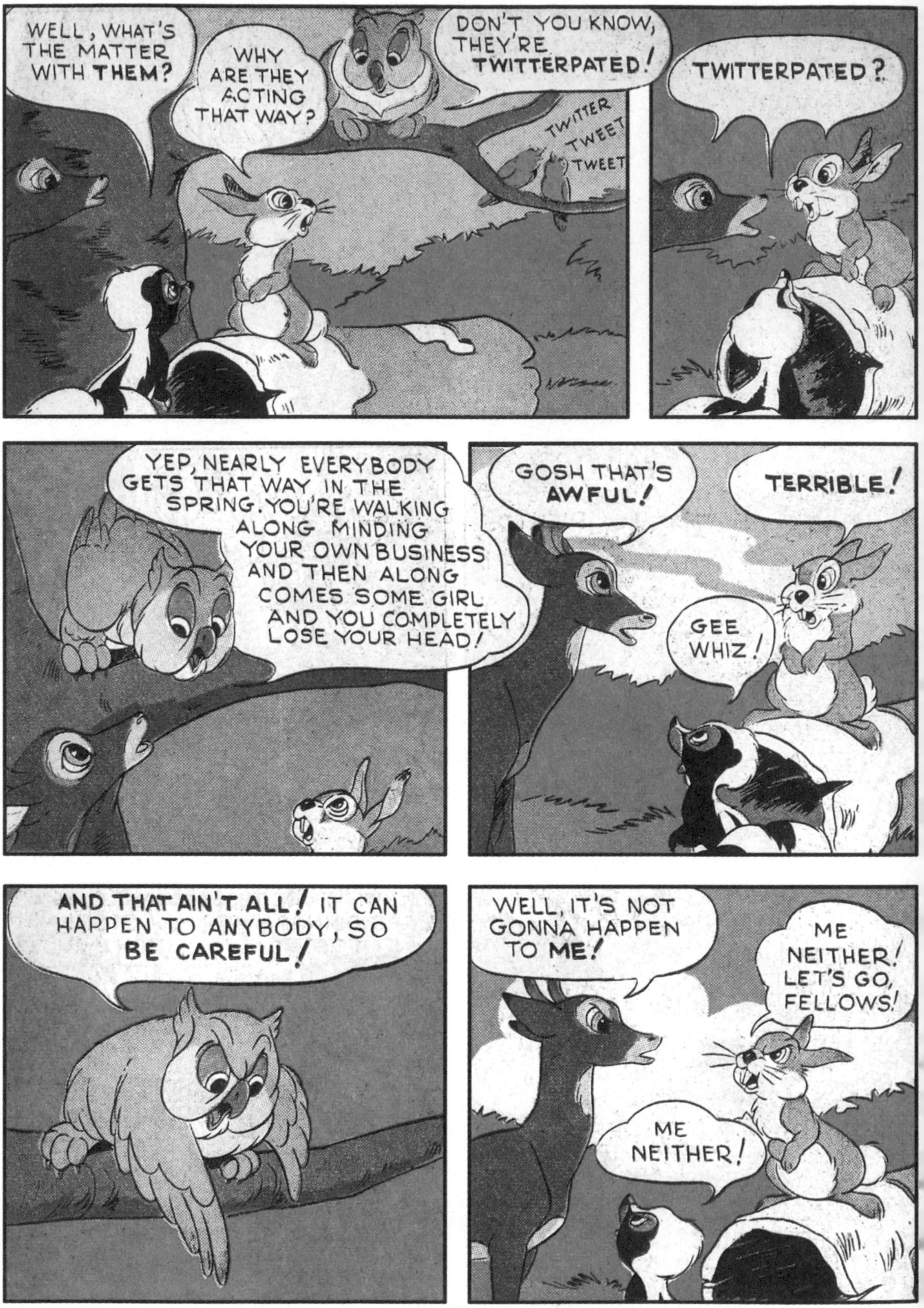
WELL, WHAT'S THE MATTER WITH THEM?
WHY ARE THEY ACTING THAT WAY?
DON'T YOU KNOW, THEY'RE TWITTERPATED!
TWITTER
TWEET
TWEET
TWITTERPATED?
YEP, NEARLY EVERYBODY GETS THAT WAY IN THE SPRING. YOU'RE WALKING ALONG MINDING YOUR OWN BUSINESS AND THEN ALONG COMES SOME GIRL AND YOU COMPLETELY LOSE YOUR HEAD!
GOSH THAT'S AWFUL!
TERRIBLE!
GEE WHIZ!
AND THAT AIN'T ALL! IT CAN HAPPEN TO ANYBODY, SO BE CAREFUL!
WELL, IT'S NOT GONNA HAPPEN TO ME!
ME NEITHER! LET'S GO, FELLOWS!
ME NEITHER!

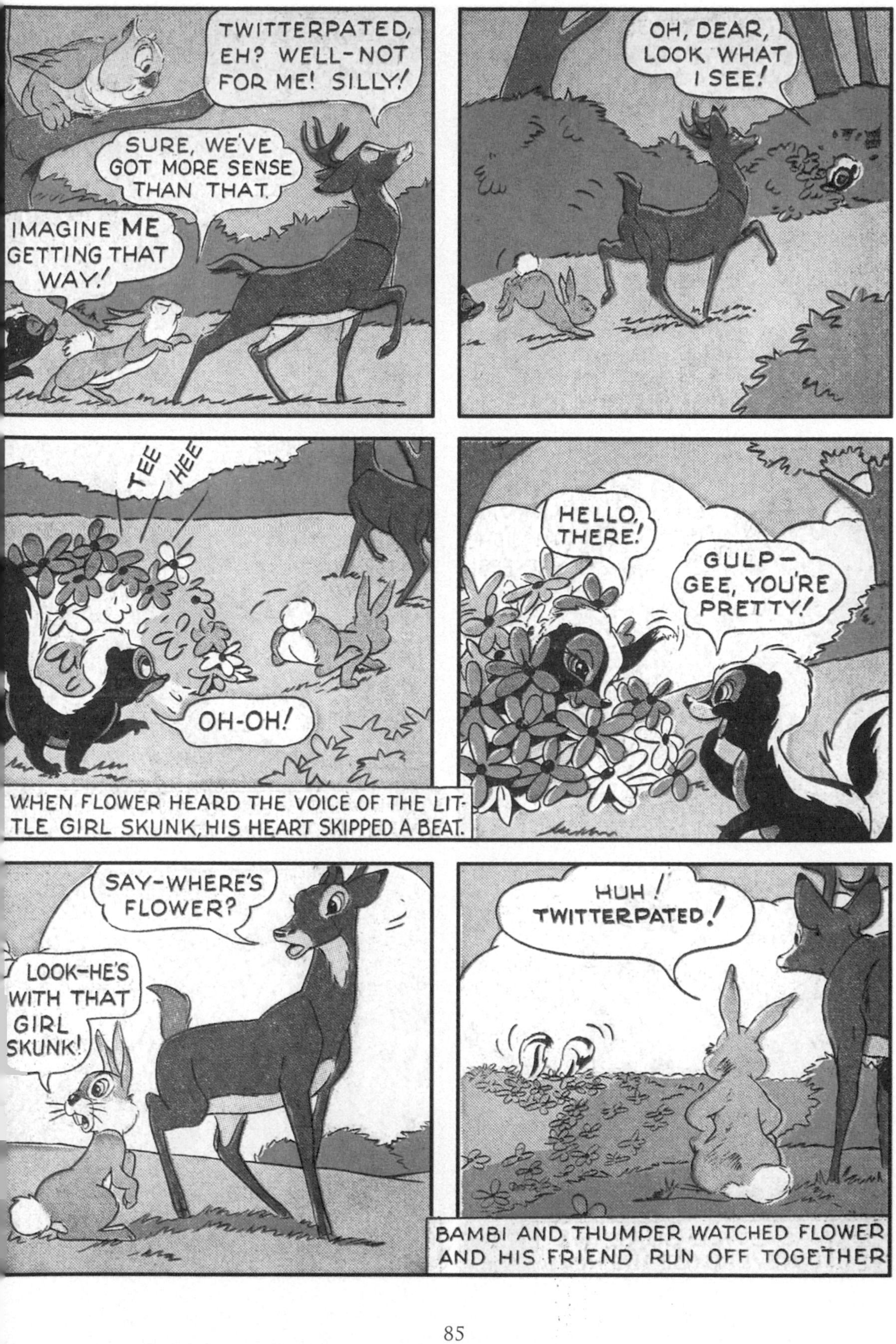
TWITTERPATED, EH? WELL-NOT FOR ME! SILLY!
SURE, WE'VE GOT MORE SENSE THAN THAT.
IMAGINE ME GETTING THAT WAY!
OH, DEAR, LOOK WHAT I SEE!
TEE
HEE
OH-OH!
WHEN FLOWER HEARD THE VOICE OF THE LITTLE GIRL SKUNK, HIS HEART SKIPPED A BEAT.
HELLO, THERE!
GULP-GEE, YOU'RE PRETTY!
SAY-WHERE'S FLOWER?
LOOK-HE'S WITH THAT GIRL SKUNK!
HUH! TWITTERPATED!
BAMBI AND THUMPER WATCHED FLOWER AND HIS FRIEND RUN OFF TOGETHER

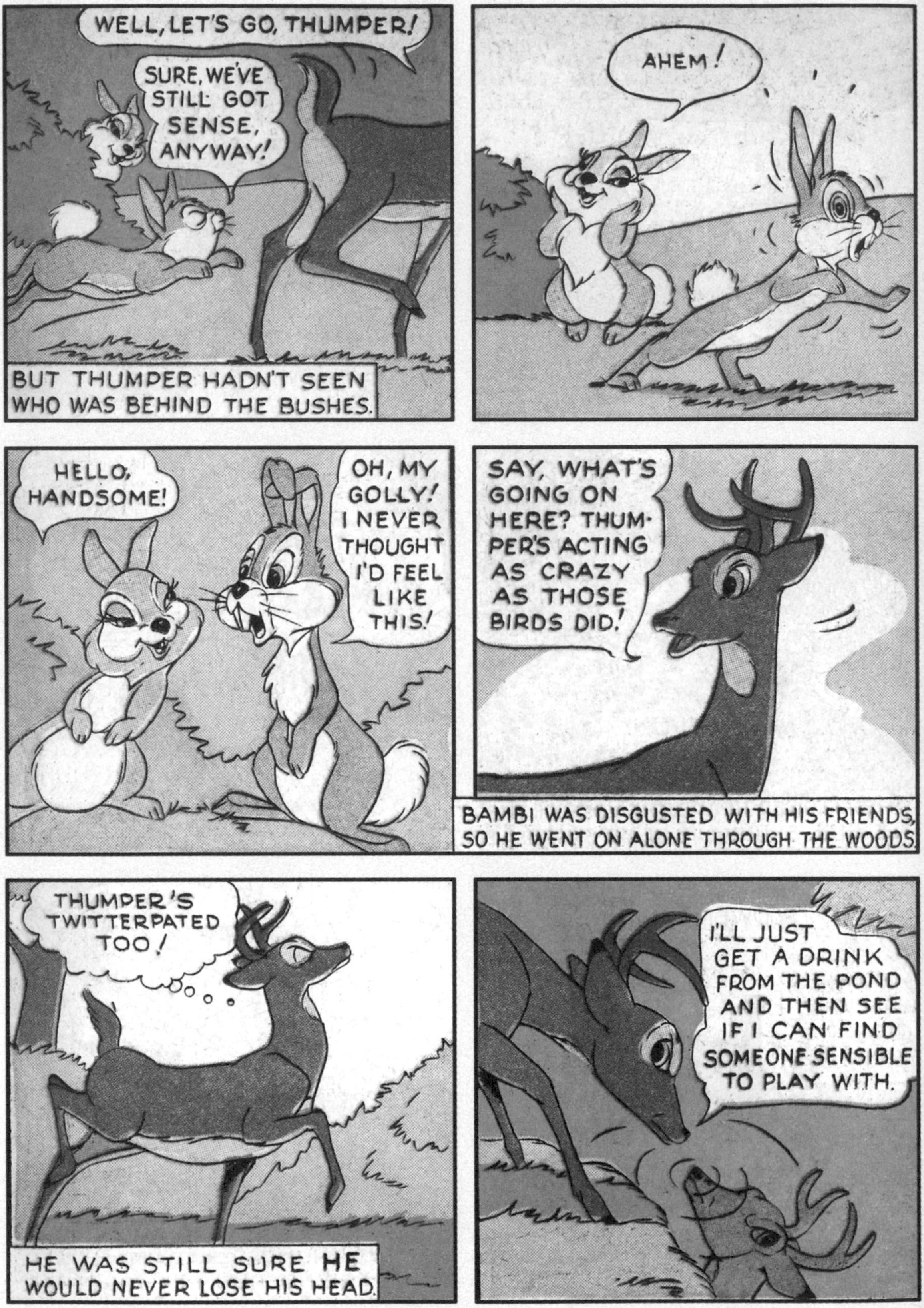
WELL, LET'S GO, THUMPER!
SURE, WE'VE STILL GOT SENSE, ANYWAY!
BUT THUMPER HADN'T SEEN WHO WAS BEHIND THE BUSHES.
AHEM!
HELLO, HANDSOME!
OH, MY GOLLY! I NEVER THOUGHT I'D FEEL LIKE THIS!
SAY, WHAT'S GOING ON HERE? THUMPER'S ACTING AS CRAZY AS THOSE BIRDS DID!
BAMBI WAS DISGUSTED WITH HIS FRIENDS, SO HE WENT ON ALONE THROUGH THE WOODS.
THUMPER'S TWITTERPATED TOO!
HE WAS STILL SURE HE WOULD NEVER LOSE HIS HEAD.
I'LL JUST GET A DRINK FROM THE POND AND THEN SEE IF I CAN FIND SOMEONE SENSIBLE TO PLAY WITH.

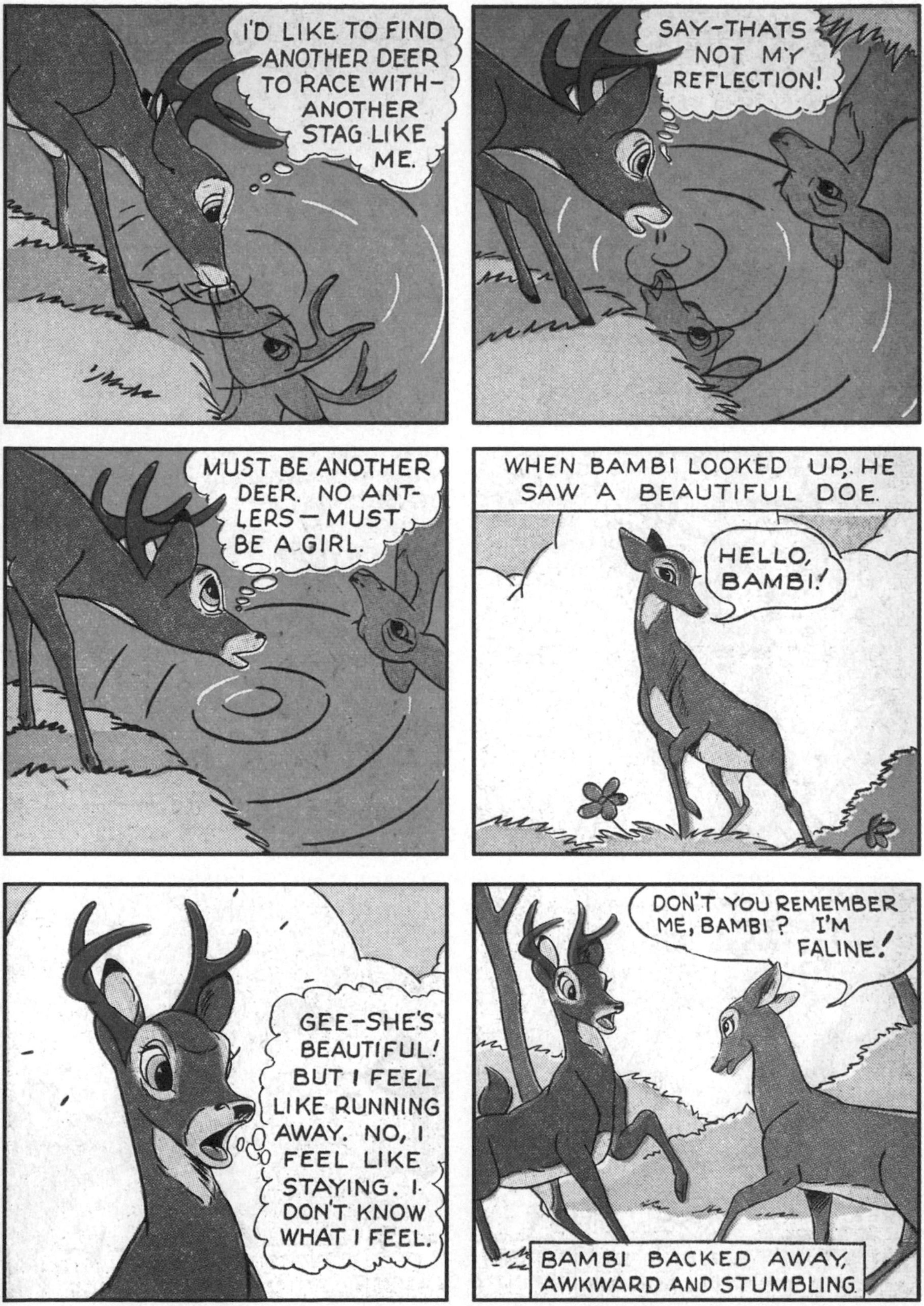
I'D LIKE TO FIND ANOTHER DEER TO RACE WITH—ANOTHER STAG LIKE ME.
SAY-THATS NOT MY REFLECTION!
MUST BE ANOTHER DEER. NO ANTLERS—MUST BE A GIRL.
WHEN BAMBI LOOKED UP, HE SAW A BEAUTIFUL DOE.
HELLO, BAMBI!
GEE-SHE'S BEAUTIFUL! BUT I FEEL LIKE RUNNING AWAY. NO, I FEEL LIKE STAYING. I DON'T KNOW WHAT I FEEL.
DON'T YOU REMEMBER ME, BAMBI? I'M FALINE!
BAMBI BACKED AWAY, AWKWARD AND STUMBLING.

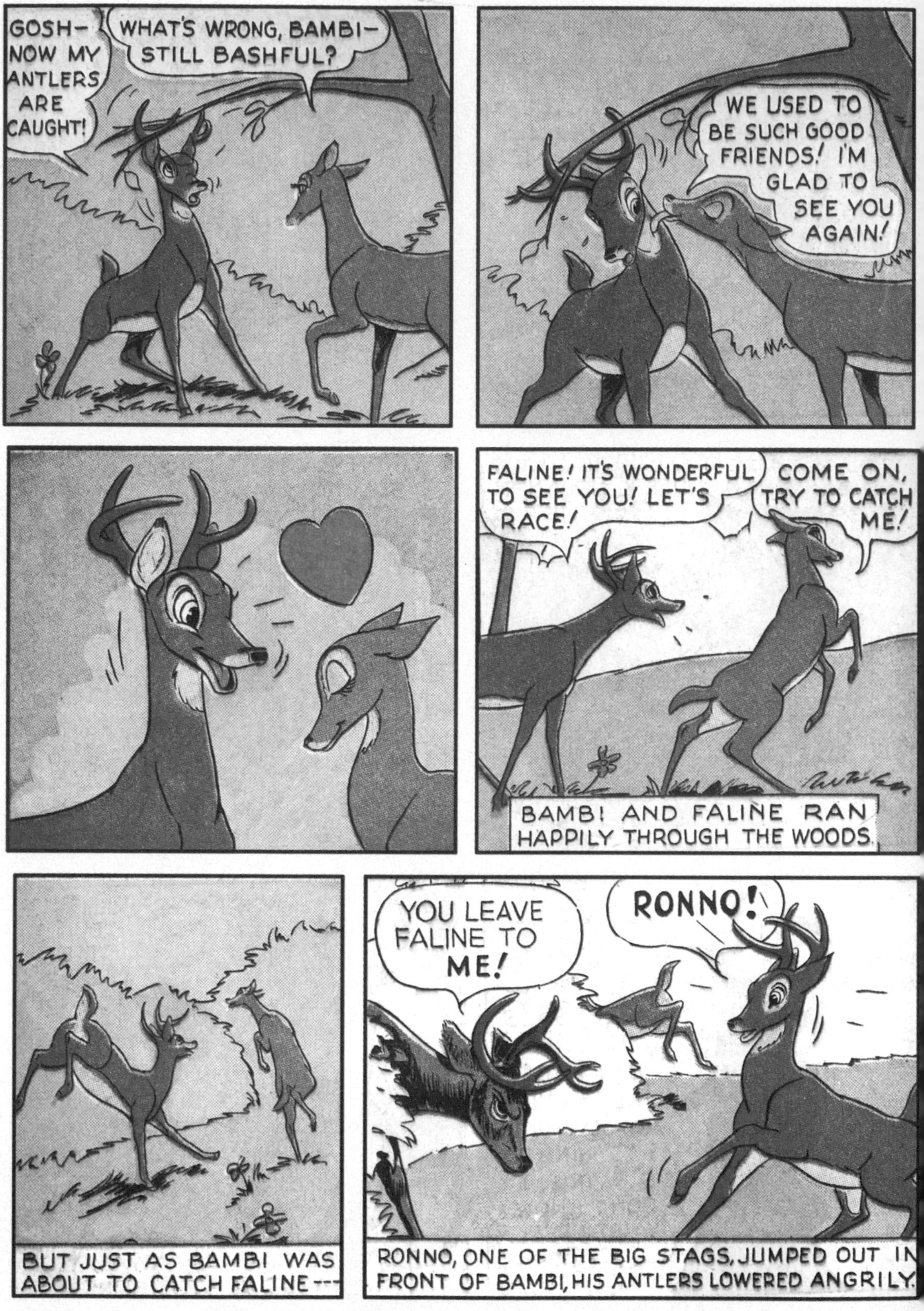
GOSH— NOW MY ANTLERS ARE CAUGHT!
WHAT'S WRONG, BAMBI— STILL BASHFUL?
WE USED TO BE SUCH GOOD FRIENDS! I'M GLAD TO SEE YOU AGAIN!
FALINE! IT'S WONDERFUL TO SEE YOU! LET'S RACE!
COME ON, TRY TO CATCH ME!
BAMBI AND FALINE RAN HAPPILY THROUGH THE WOODS.
BUT JUST AS BAMBI WAS ABOUT TO CATCH FALINE---
YOU LEAVE FALINE TO ME!
RONNO!
RONNO, ONE OF THE BIG STAGS, JUMPED OUT IN FRONT OF BAMBI, HIS ANTLERS LOWERED ANGRILY.

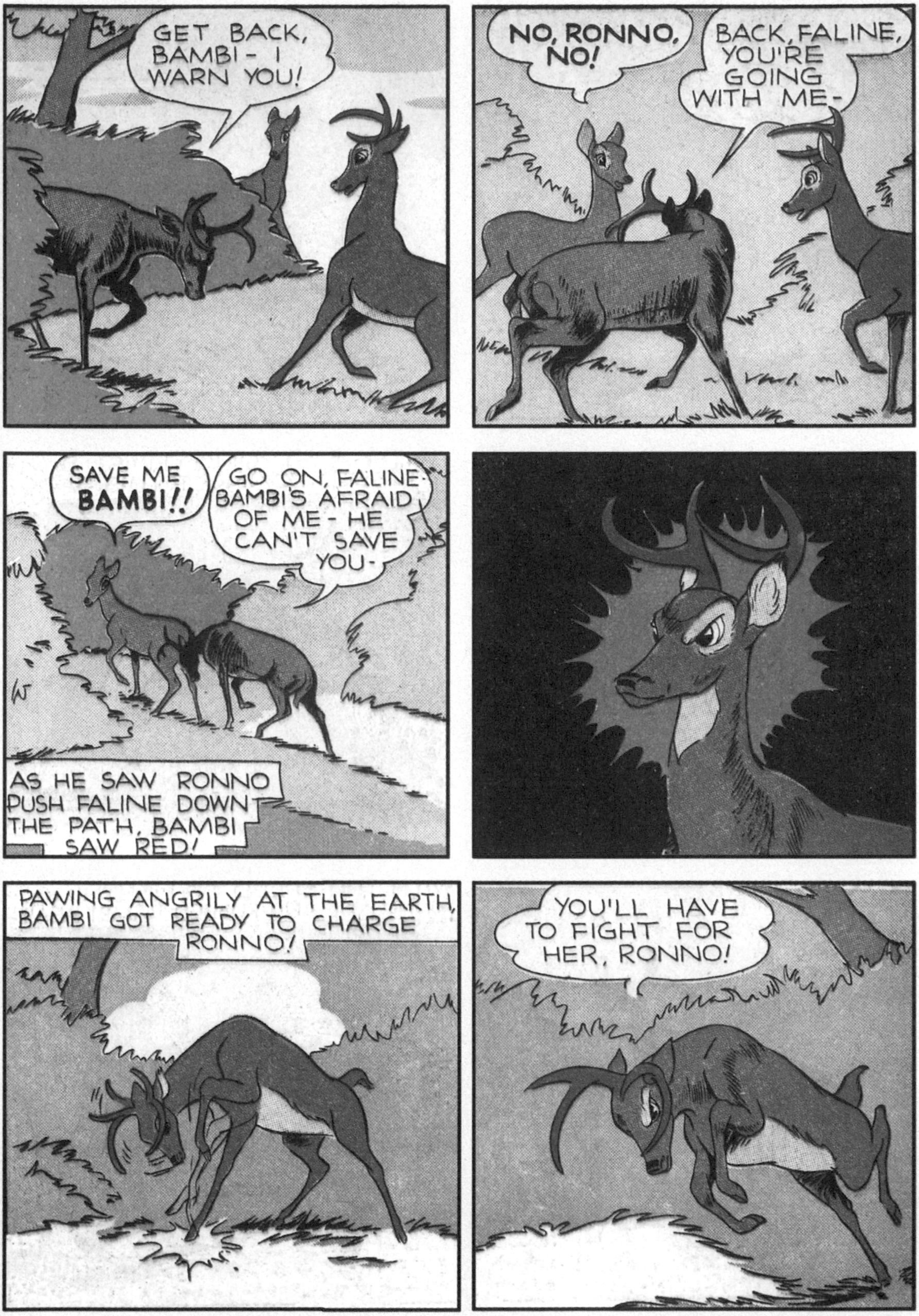
GET BACK, BAMBI - I WARN YOU!
NO, RONNO, NO!
BACK, FALINE, YOU'RE GOING WITH ME-
SAVE ME BAMBI!!
GO ON, FALINE- BAMBI'S AFRAID OF ME - HE CAN'T SAVE YOU-
AS HE SAW RONNO PUSH FALINE DOWN THE PATH, BAMBI SAW RED!
PAWING ANGRILY AT THE EARTH, BAMBI GOT READY TO CHARGE RONNO!
YOU'LL HAVE TO FIGHT FOR HER, RONNO!

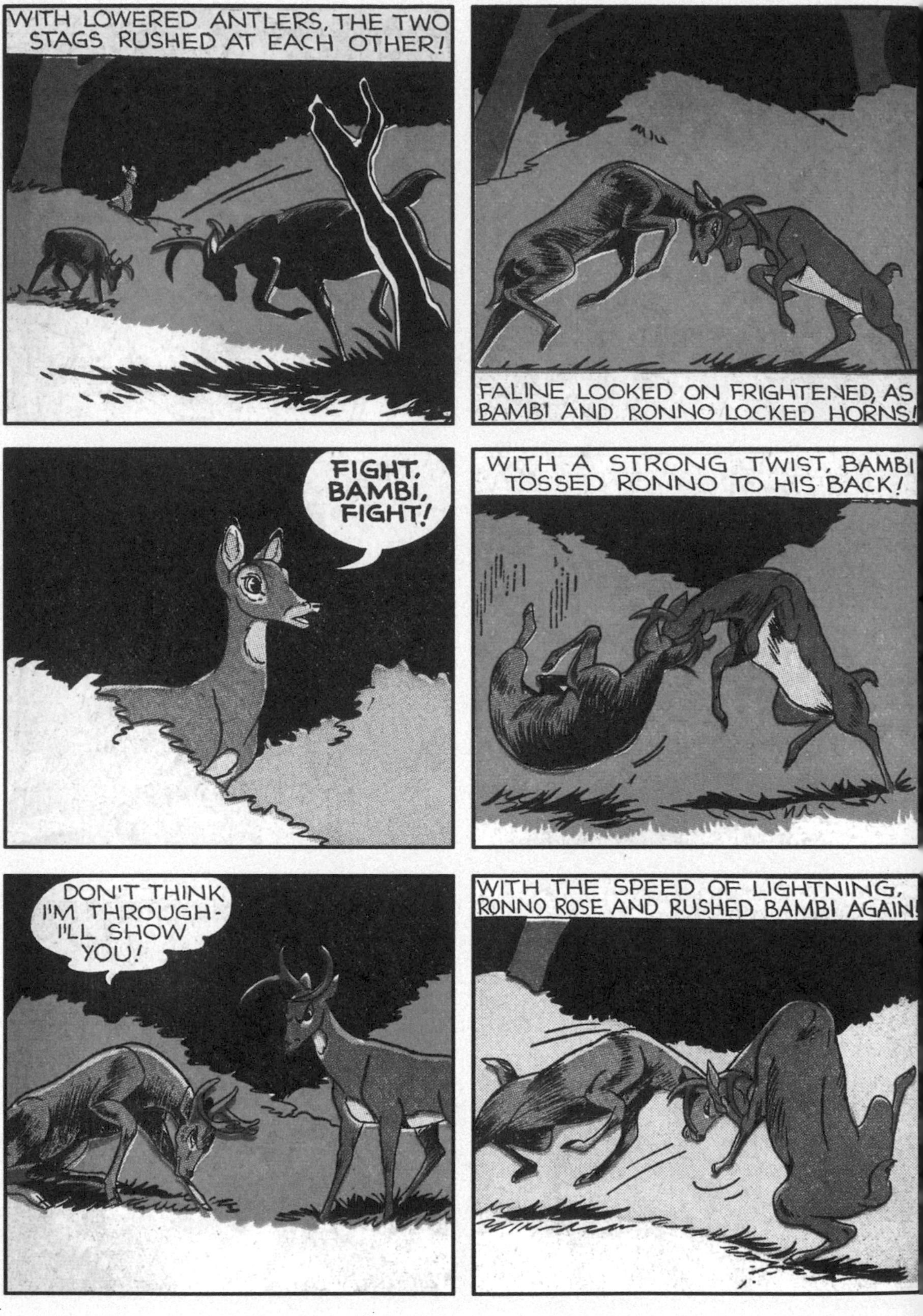
WITH LOWERED ANTLERS, THE TWO STAGS RUSHED AT EACH OTHER!
FALINE LOOKED ON FRIGHTENED, AS BAMBI AND RONNO LOCKED HORNS!
FIGHT, BAMBI, FIGHT!
WITH A STRONG TWIST, BAMBI TOSSED RONNO TO HIS BACK!
DON'T THINK I'M THROUGH- I'LL SHOW YOU!
WITH THE SPEED OF LIGHTNING, RONNO ROSE AND RUSHED BAMBI AGAIN!

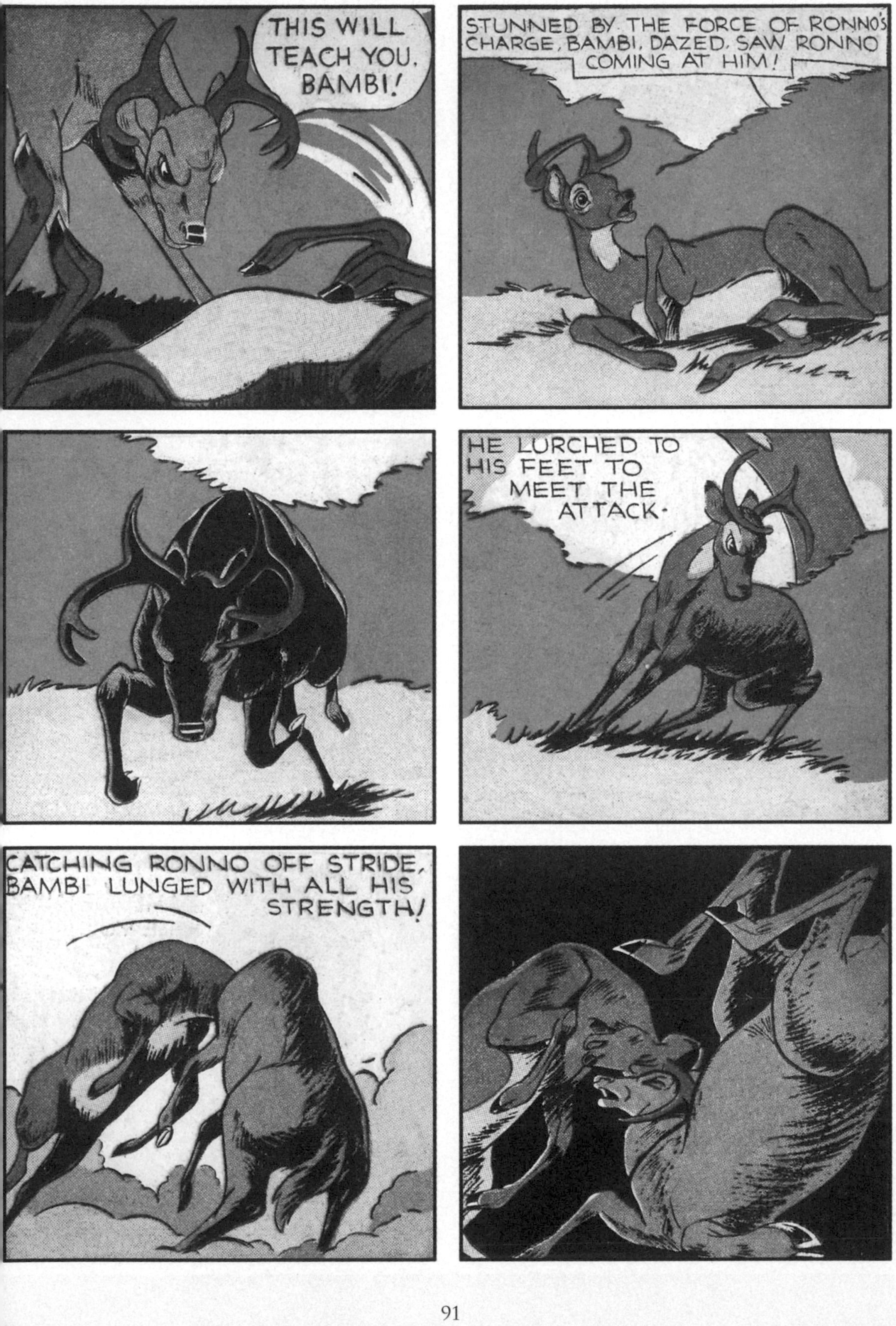
THIS WILL TEACH YOU, BAMBI!
STUNNED BY THE FORCE OF RONNO'S CHARGE, BAMBI, DAZED, SAW RONNO COMING AT HIM!
HE LURCHED TO HIS FEET TO MEET THE ATTACK.
CATCHING RONNO OFF STRIDE, BAMBI LUNGED WITH ALL HIS STRENGTH!

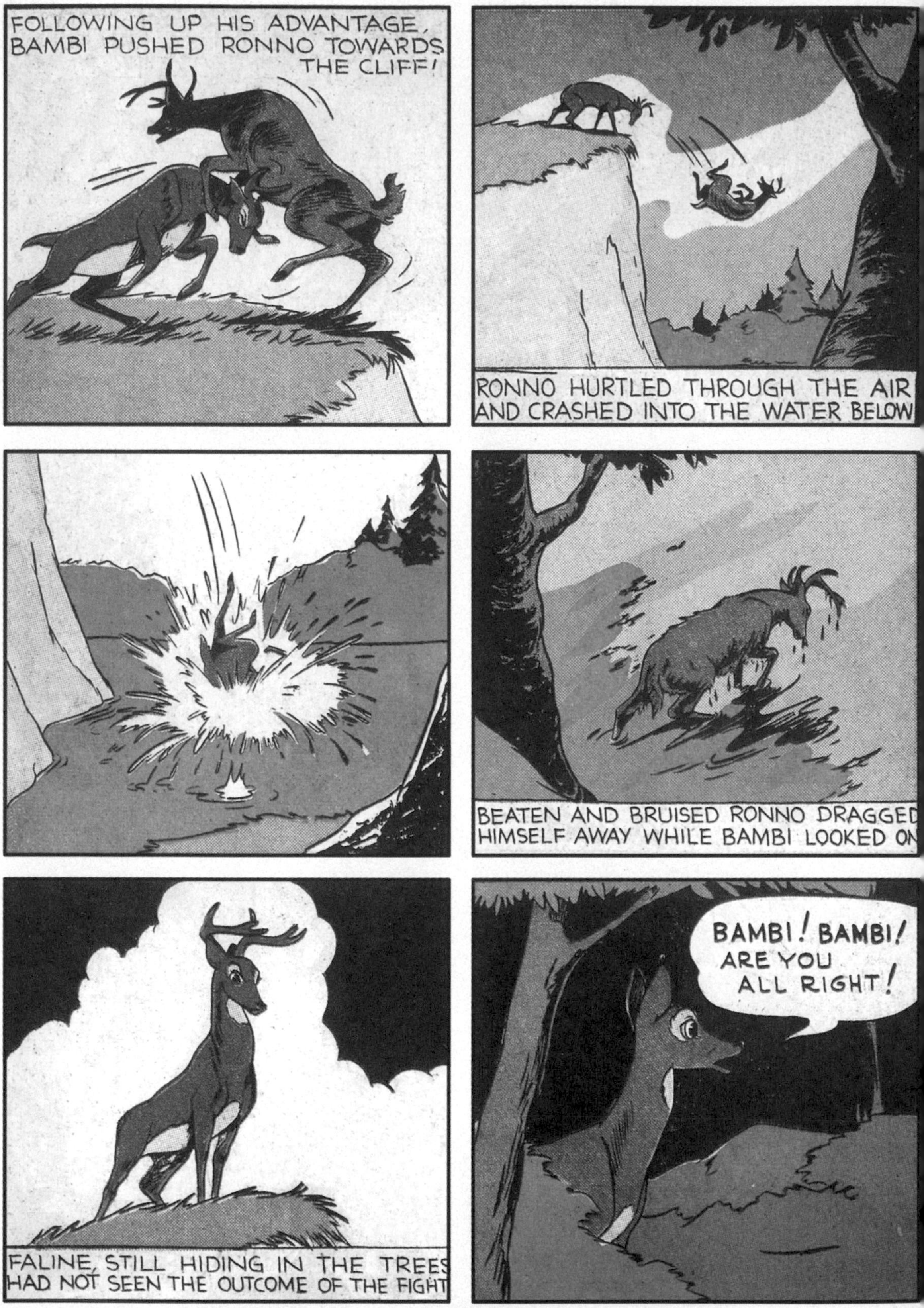
FOLLOWING UP HIS ADVANTAGE, BAMBI PUSHED RONNO TOWARDS THE CLIFF!
RONNO HURTLED THROUGH THE AIR AND CRASHED INTO THE WATER BELOW
BEATEN AND BRUISED RONNO DRAGGED HIMSELF AWAY WHILE BAMBI LOOKED ON
FALINE, STILL HIDING IN THE TREES HAD NOT SEEN THE OUTCOME OF THE FIGHT
BAMBI! BAMBI! ARE YOU ALL RIGHT!

BUY WAR SAVINGS BONDS AND STAMPS

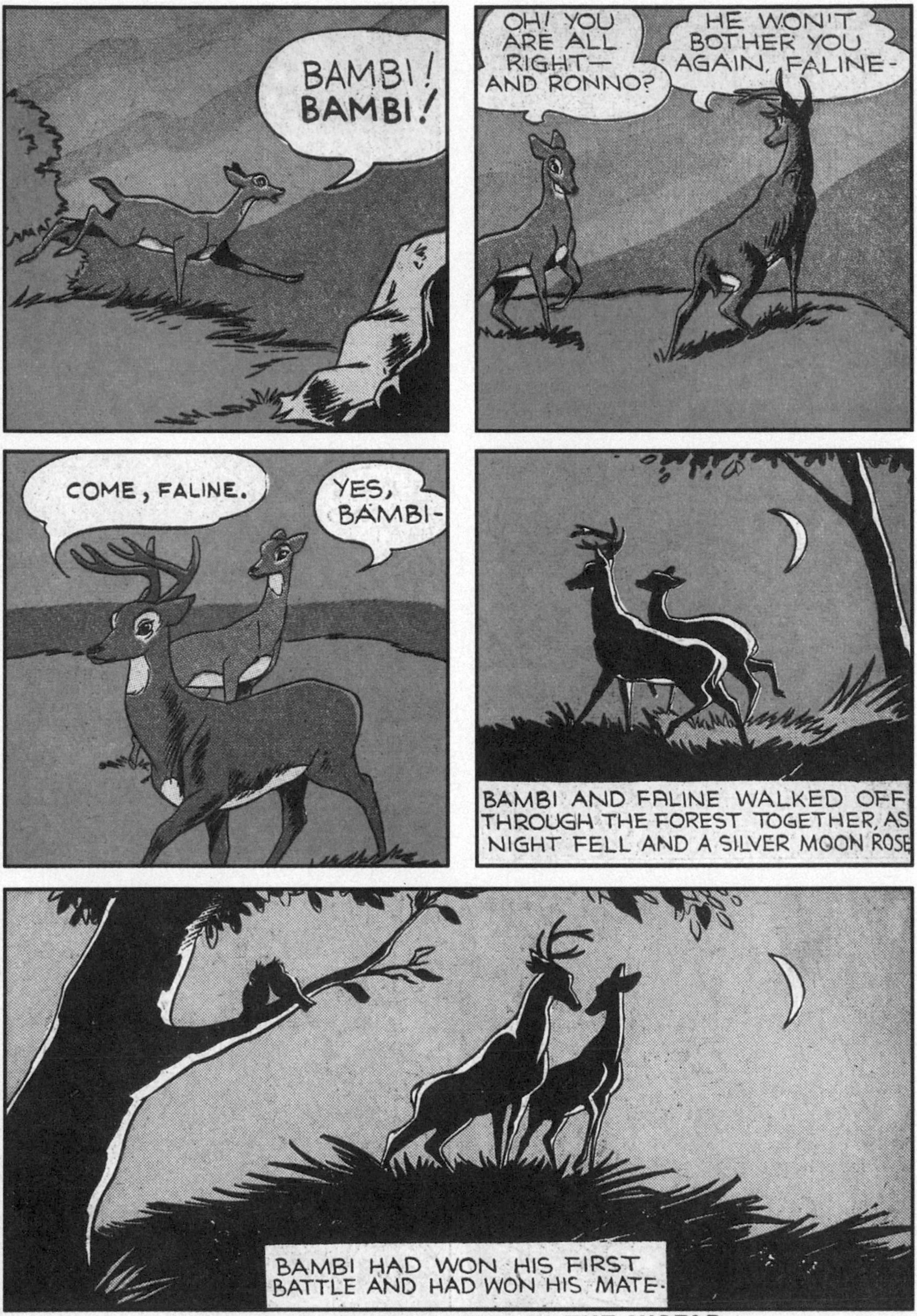
BAMBI! BAMBI!
OH! YOU ARE ALL RIGHT— AND RONNO?
HE WON'T BOTHER YOU AGAIN, FALINE-
COME, FALINE.
YES, BAMBI-
BAMBI AND FALINE WALKED OFF THROUGH THE FOREST TOGETHER, AS NIGHT FELL AND A SILVER MOON ROSE
BAMBI HAD WON HIS FIRST BATTLE AND HAD WON HIS MATE-

THE BEST INVESTMENT IN THE WORLD

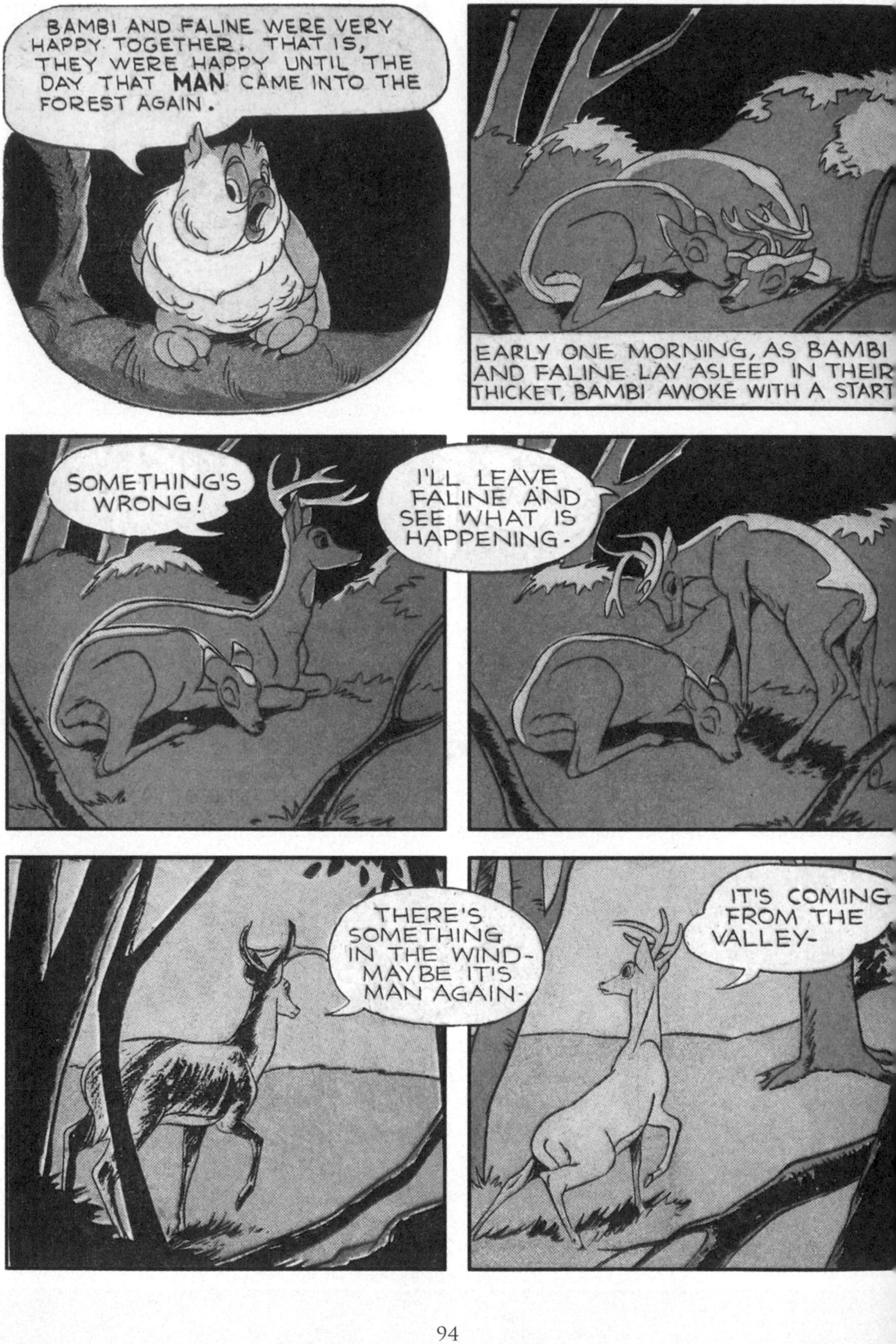
BAMBI AND FALINE WERE VERY HAPPY TOGETHER. THAT IS, THEY WERE HAPPY UNTIL THE DAY THAT MAN CAME INTO THE FOREST AGAIN.
EARLY ONE MORNING, AS BAMBI AND FALINE LAY ASLEEP IN THEIR THICKET, BAMBI AWOKE WITH A START
SOMETHING'S WRONG!
I'LL LEAVE FALINE AND SEE WHAT IS HAPPENING-
THERE'S SOMETHING IN THE WIND- MAYBE IT'S MAN AGAIN-
IT'S COMING FROM THE VALLEY-

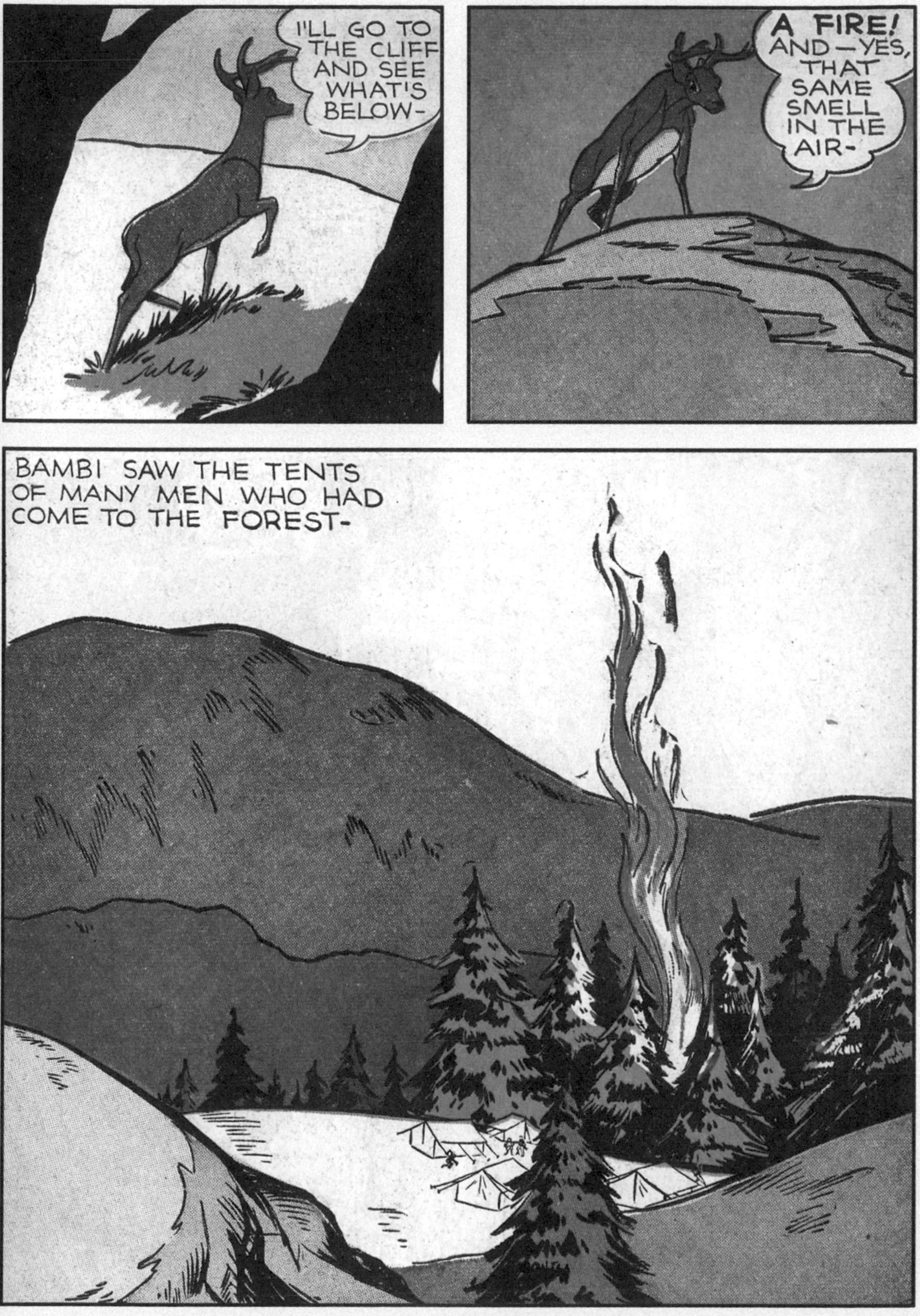
I'LL GO TO THE CLIFF AND SEE WHAT'S BELOW-
A FIRE! AND—YES, THAT SAME SMELL IN THE AIR-
BAMBI SAW THE TENTS OF MANY MEN WHO HAD COME TO THE FOREST-

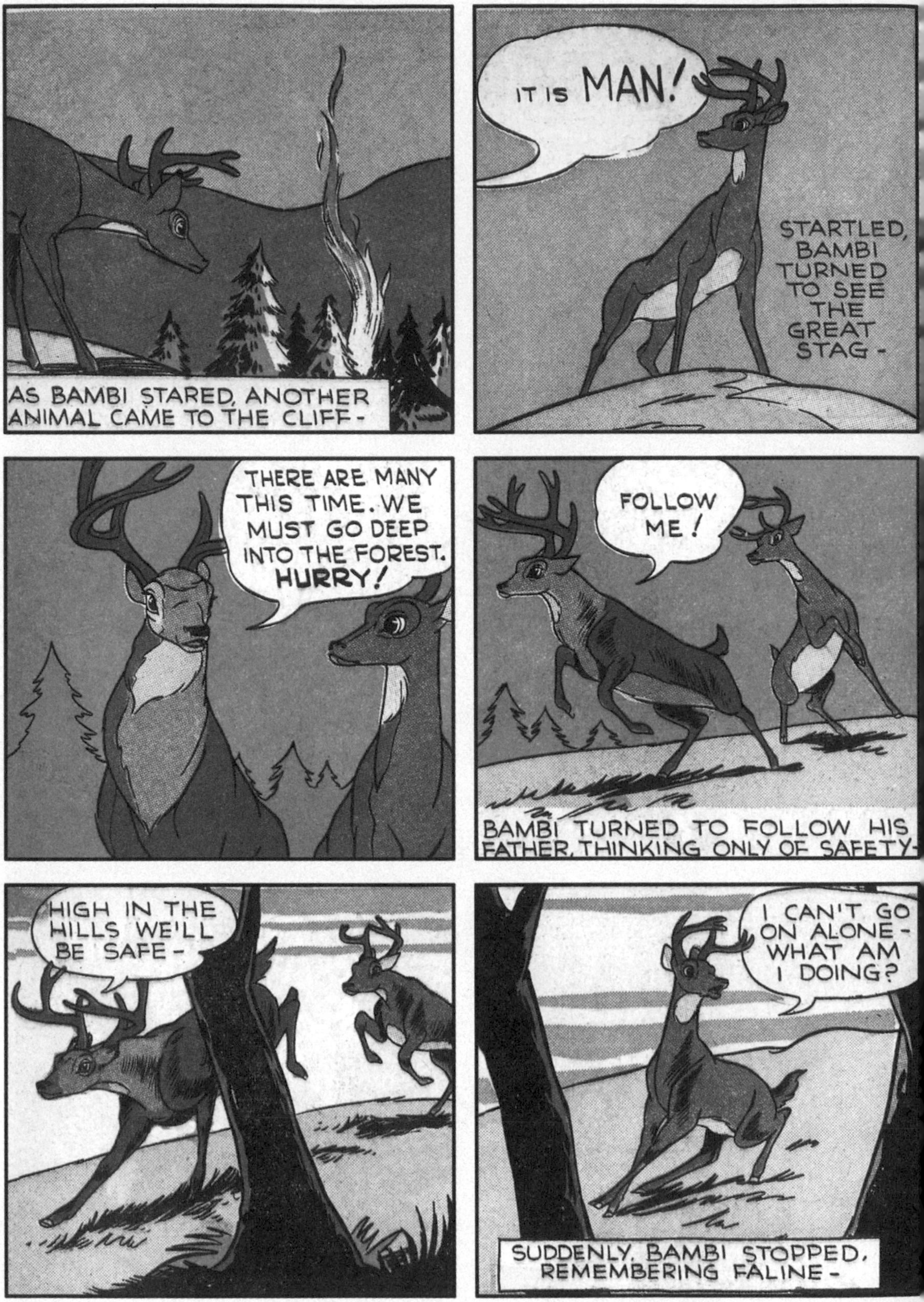
AS BAMBI STARED, ANOTHER ANIMAL CAME TO THE CLIFF -
IT IS MAN!
STARTLED, BAMBI TURNED TO SEE THE GREAT STAG -
THERE ARE MANY THIS TIME. WE MUST GO DEEP INTO THE FOREST. HURRY!
FOLLOW ME!
BAMBI TURNED TO FOLLOW HIS FATHER, THINKING ONLY OF SAFETY-
HIGH IN THE HILLS WE'LL BE SAFE -
I CAN'T GO ON ALONE - WHAT AM I DOING?
SUDDENLY, BAMBI STOPPED, REMEMBERING FALINE -

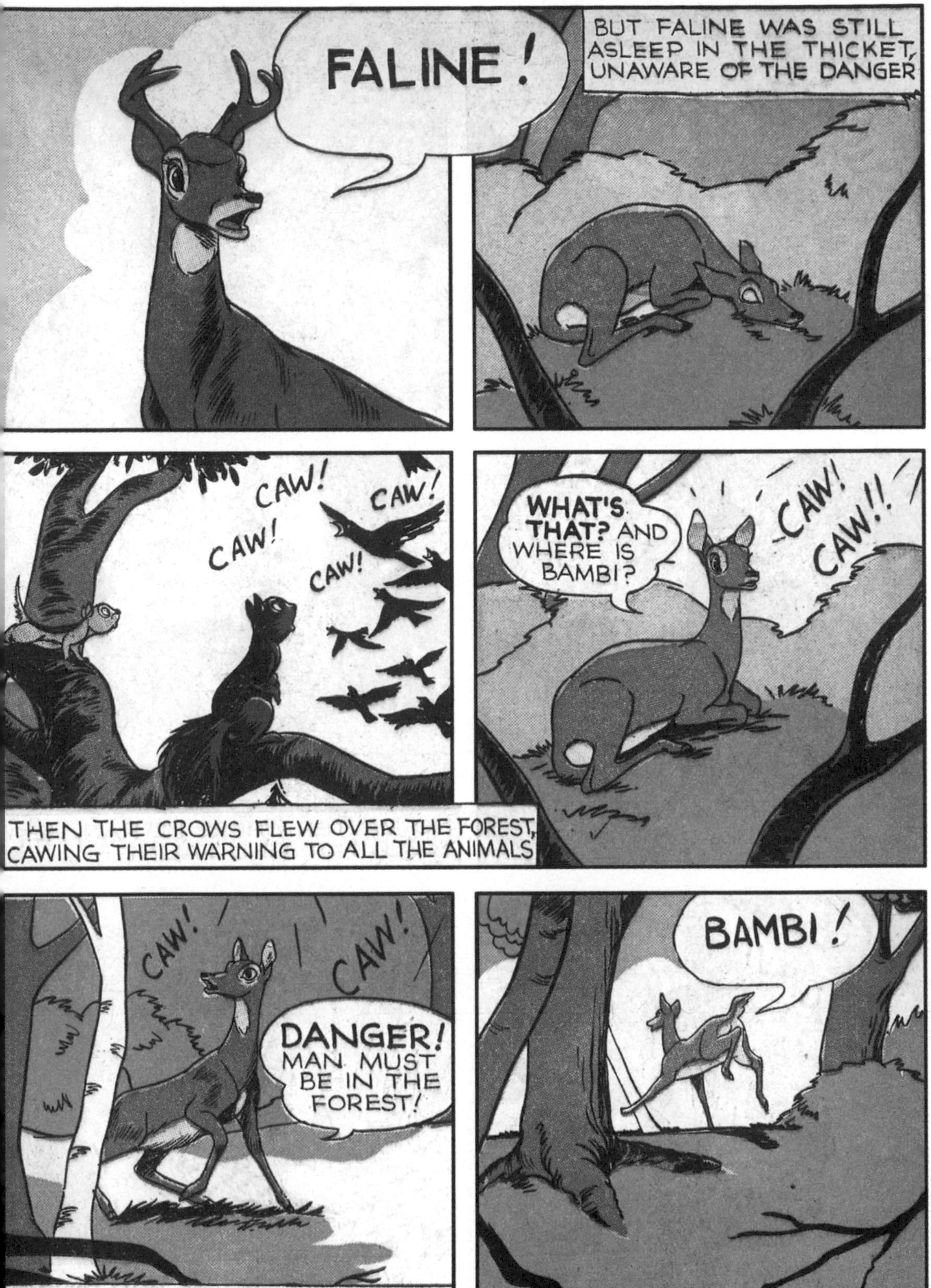
FALINE!
BUT FALINE WAS STILL ASLEEP IN THE THICKET, UNAWARE OF THE DANGER
CAW!
CAW!
CAW!
CAW!
THEN THE CROWS FLEW OVER THE FOREST, CAWING THEIR WARNING TO ALL THE ANIMALS
WHAT'S THAT? AND WHERE IS BAMBI?
CAW!
CAW!!
CAW!
CAW!
DANGER! MAN MUST BE IN THE FOREST!
FRANTICALLY, FALINE SEARCHED FOR BAMBI-
BAMBI!

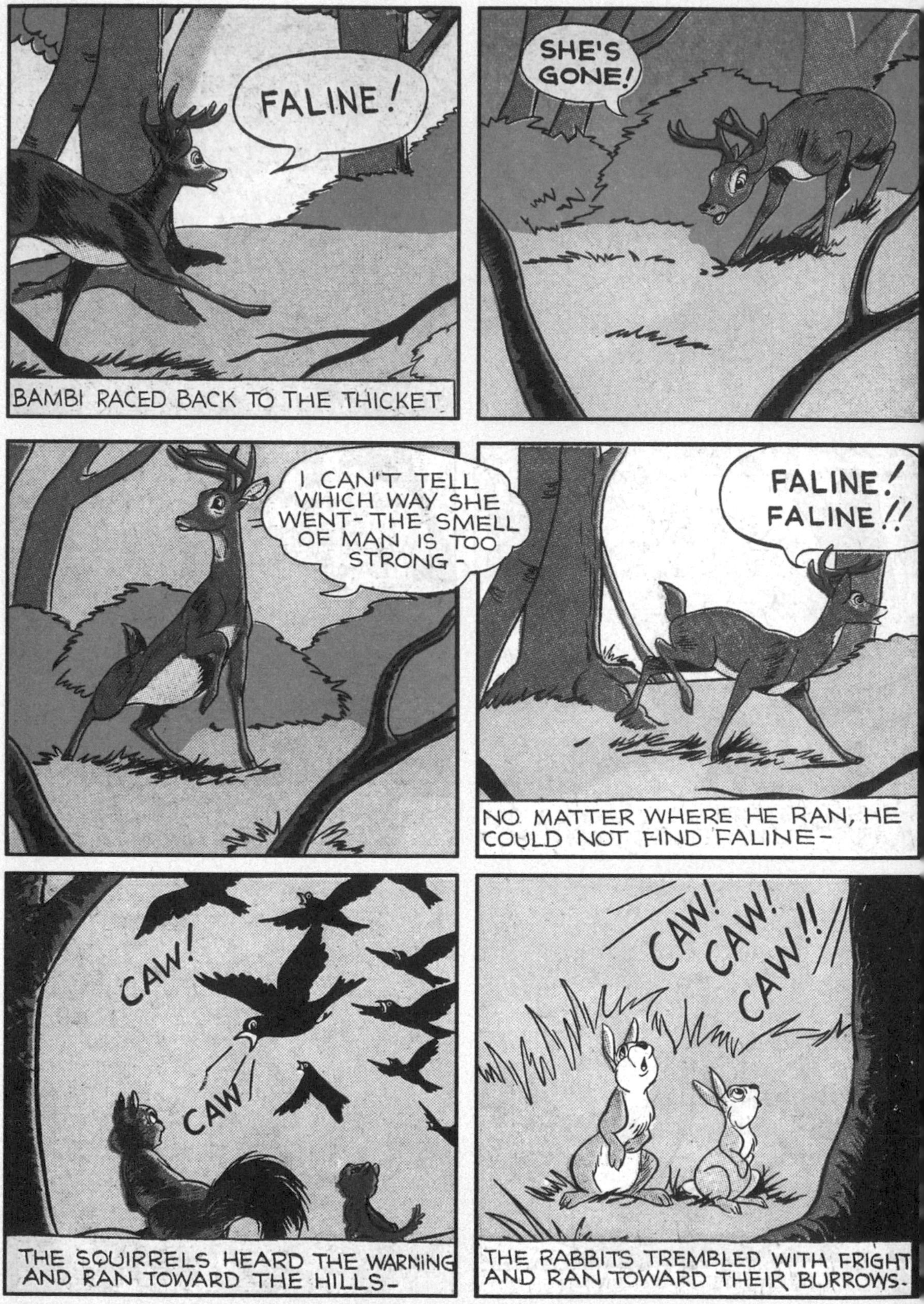
FALINE!
BAMBI RACED BACK TO THE THICKET
SHE'S GONE!
I CAN'T TELL WHICH WAY SHE WENT- THE SMELL OF MAN IS TOO STRONG-
FALINE! FALINE!!
NO MATTER WHERE HE RAN, HE COULD NOT FIND FALINE-
CAW!
CAW!
THE SQUIRRELS HEARD THE WARNING AND RAN TOWARD THE HILLS-
CAW! CAW! CAW!!
THE RABBITS TREMBLED WITH FRIGHT AND RAN TOWARD THEIR BURROWS-

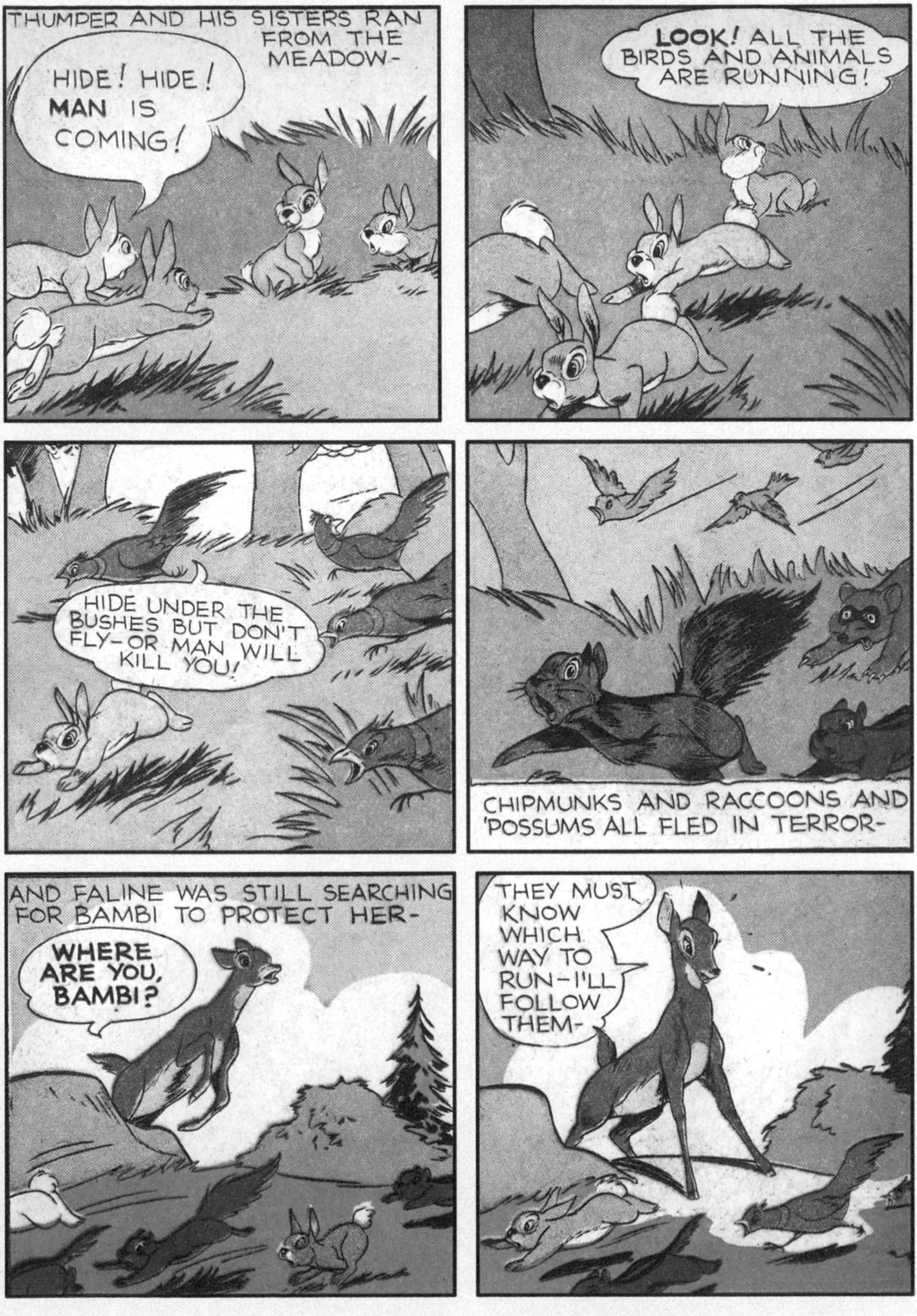
THUMPER AND HIS SISTERS RAN FROM THE MEADOW-
HIDE! HIDE! MAN IS COMING!
LOOK! ALL THE BIRDS AND ANIMALS ARE RUNNING!
HIDE UNDER THE BUSHES BUT DON'T FLY-OR MAN WILL KILL YOU!
CHIPMUNKS AND RACCOONS AND 'POSSUMS ALL FLED IN TERROR-
AND FALINE WAS STILL SEARCHING FOR BAMBI TO PROTECT HER-
WHERE ARE YOU, BAMBI?
THEY MUST KNOW WHICH WAY TO RUN-I'LL FOLLOW THEM-

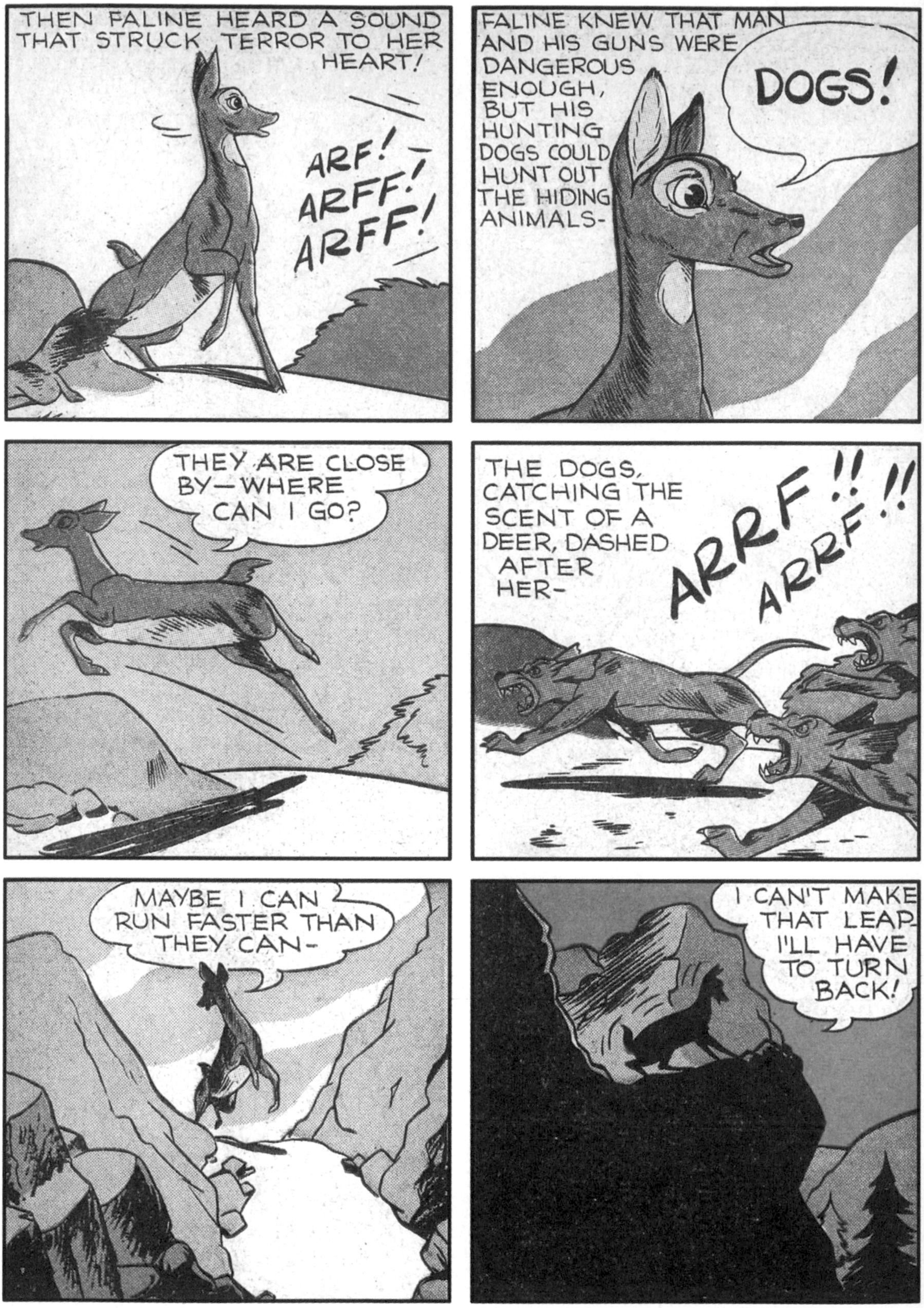
THEN FALINE HEARD A SOUND THAT STRUCK TERROR TO HER HEART!
ARF! ARFF! ARFF!
FALINE KNEW THAT MAN AND HIS GUNS WERE DANGEROUS ENOUGH, BUT HIS HUNTING DOGS COULD HUNT OUT THE HIDING ANIMALS-
DOGS!
THEY ARE CLOSE BY—WHERE CAN I GO?
THE DOGS, CATCHING THE SCENT OF A DEER, DASHED AFTER HER-
ARRF!! ARRF!!
MAYBE I CAN RUN FASTER THAN THEY CAN-
I CAN'T MAKE THAT LEAP. I'LL HAVE TO TURN BACK!

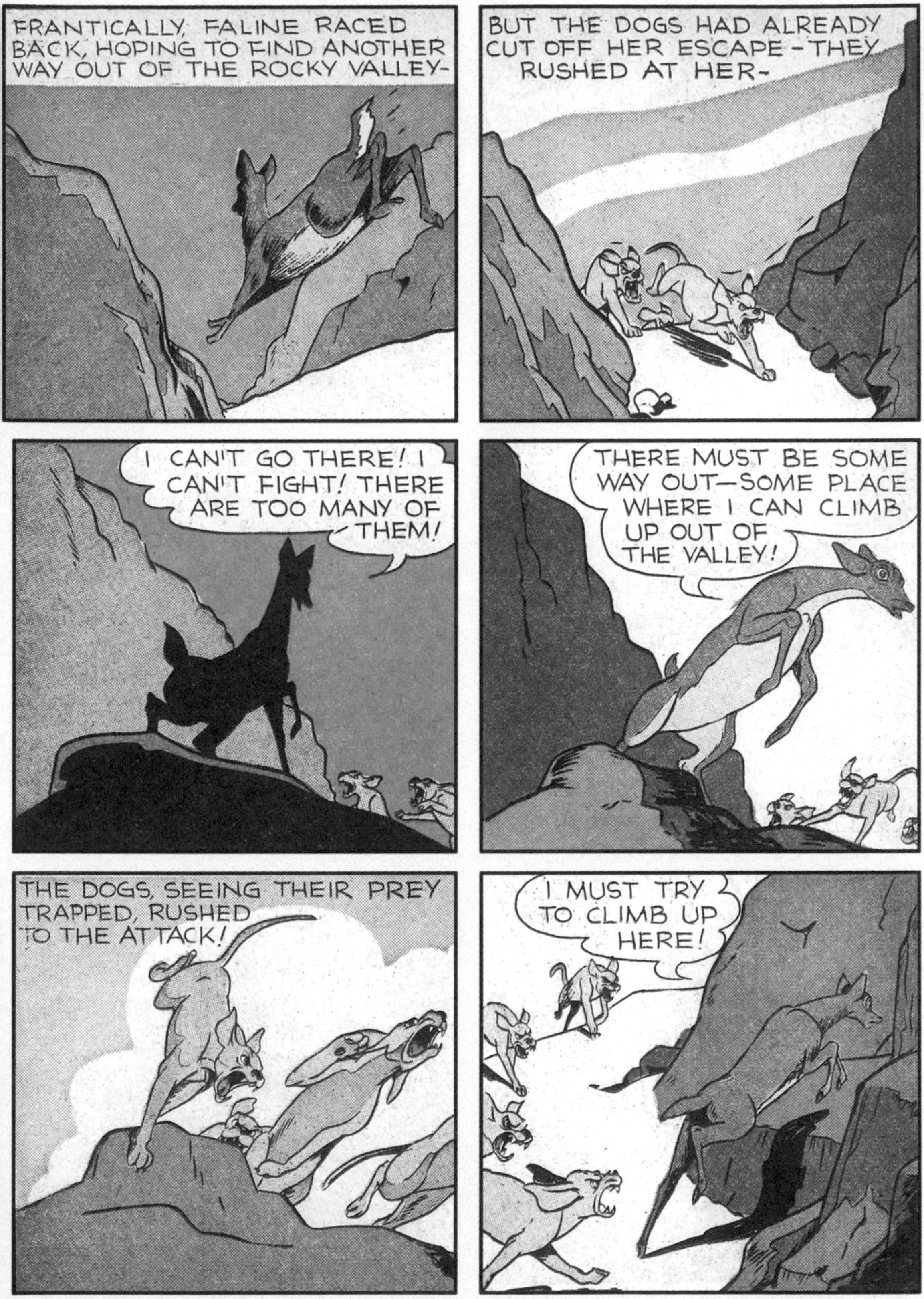
FRANTICALLY, FALINE RACED BACK, HOPING TO FIND ANOTHER WAY OUT OF THE ROCKY VALLEY-
BUT THE DOGS HAD ALREADY CUT OFF HER ESCAPE - THEY RUSHED AT HER-
I CAN'T GO THERE! I CAN'T FIGHT! THERE ARE TOO MANY OF THEM!
THERE MUST BE SOME WAY OUT—SOME PLACE WHERE I CAN CLIMB UP OUT OF THE VALLEY!
THE DOGS, SEEING THEIR PREY TRAPPED, RUSHED TO THE ATTACK!
I MUST TRY TO CLIMB UP HERE!

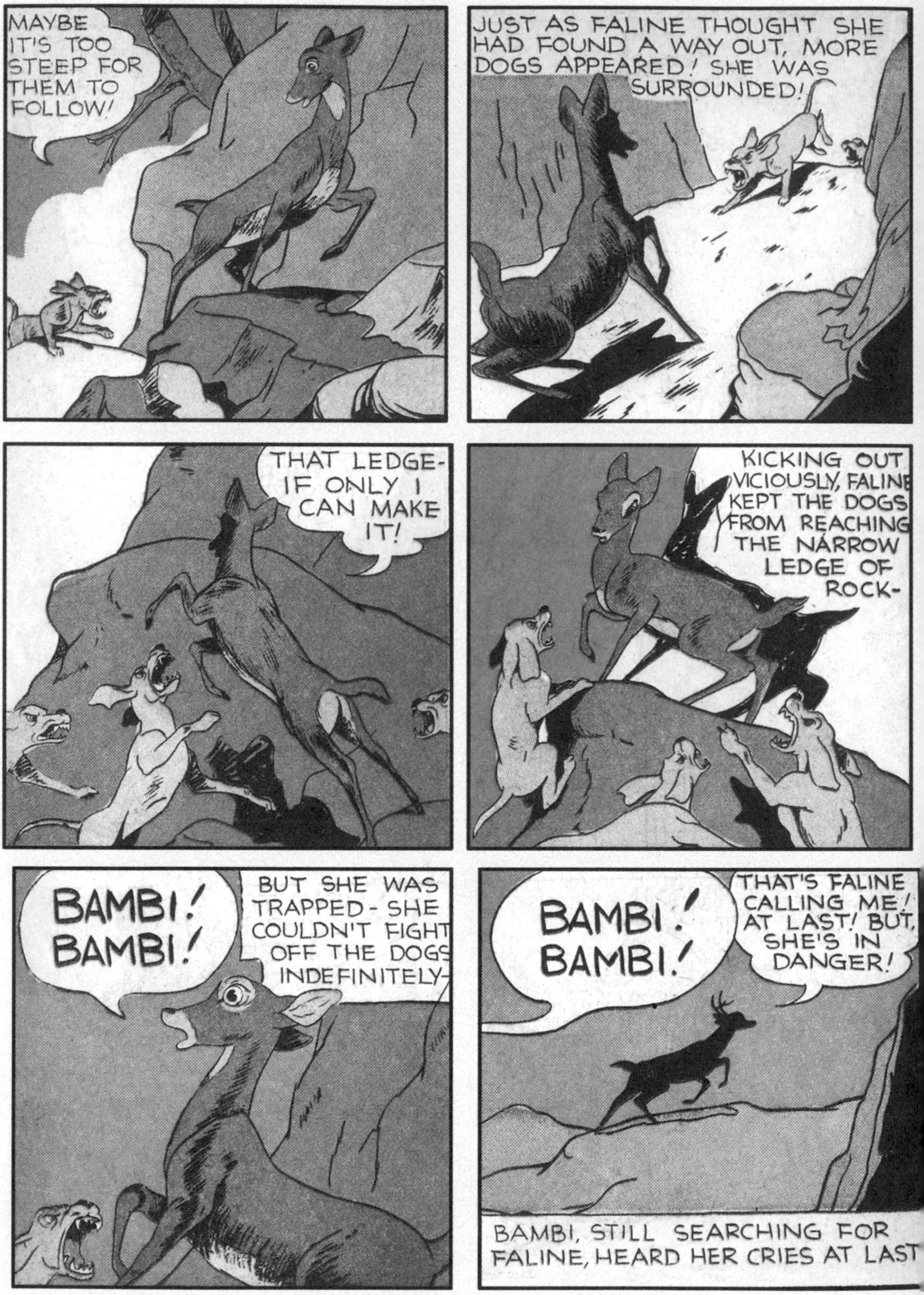
MAYBE IT'S TOO STEEP FOR THEM TO FOLLOW!
JUST AS FALINE THOUGHT SHE HAD FOUND A WAY OUT, MORE DOGS APPEARED! SHE WAS SURROUNDED!
THAT LEDGE- IF ONLY I CAN MAKE IT!
KICKING OUT VICIOUSLY, FALINE KEPT THE DOGS FROM REACHING THE NARROW LEDGE OF ROCK-
BAMBI! BAMBI!
BUT SHE WAS TRAPPED - SHE COULDN'T FIGHT OFF THE DOGS INDEFINITELY-
BAMBI! BAMBI!
THAT'S FALINE CALLING ME! AT LAST! BUT, SHE'S IN DANGER!
BAMBI, STILL SEARCHING FOR FALINE, HEARD HER CRIES AT LAST

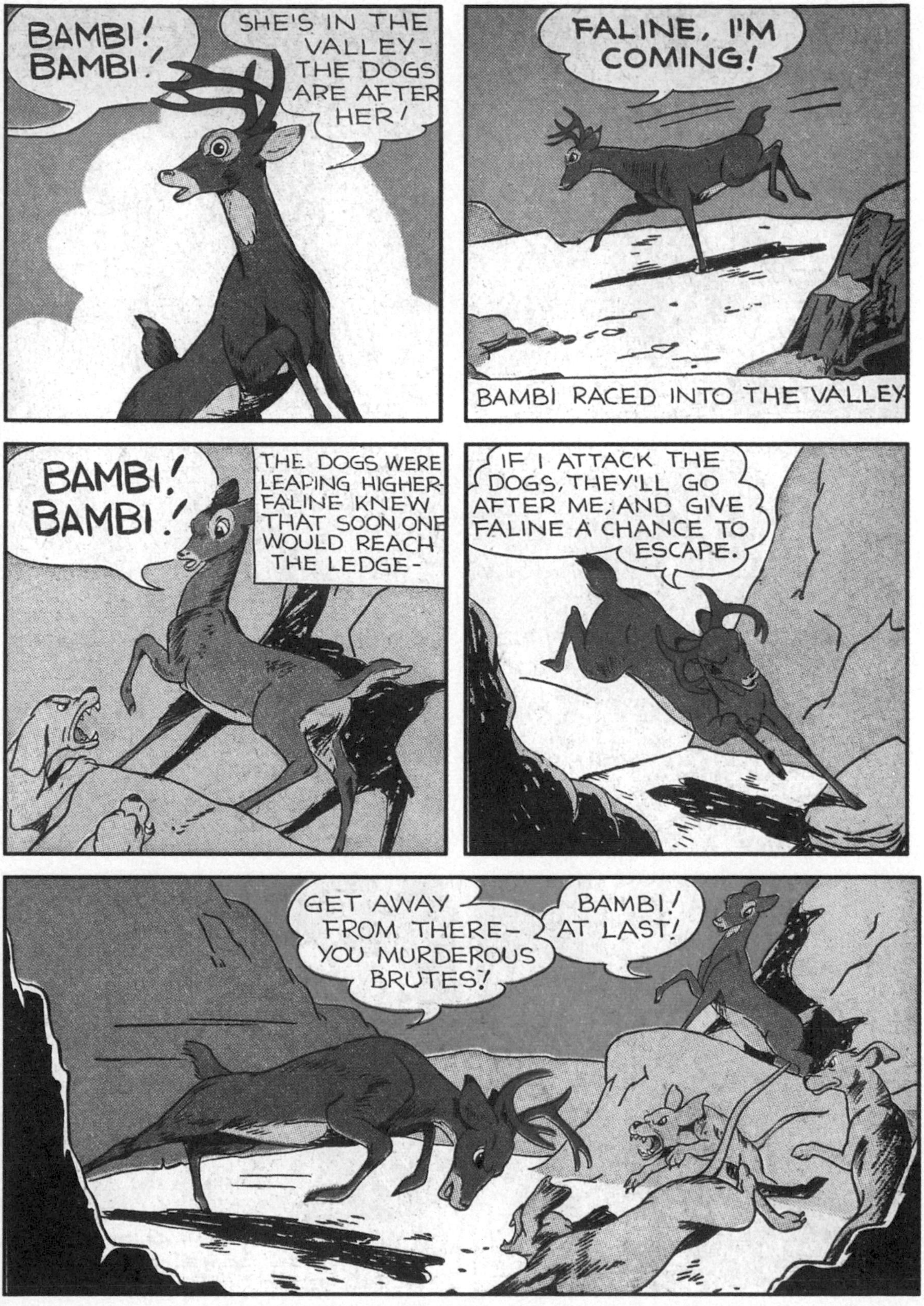
BAMBI! BAMBI!
SHE'S IN THE VALLEY- THE DOGS ARE AFTER HER!
FALINE, I'M COMING!
BAMBI RACED INTO THE VALLEY
BAMBI! BAMBI!
THE DOGS WERE LEAPING HIGHER-FALINE KNEW THAT SOON ONE WOULD REACH THE LEDGE-
IF I ATTACK THE DOGS, THEY'LL GO AFTER ME; AND GIVE FALINE A CHANCE TO ESCAPE.
GET AWAY FROM THERE- YOU MURDEROUS BRUTES!
BAMBI! AT LAST!

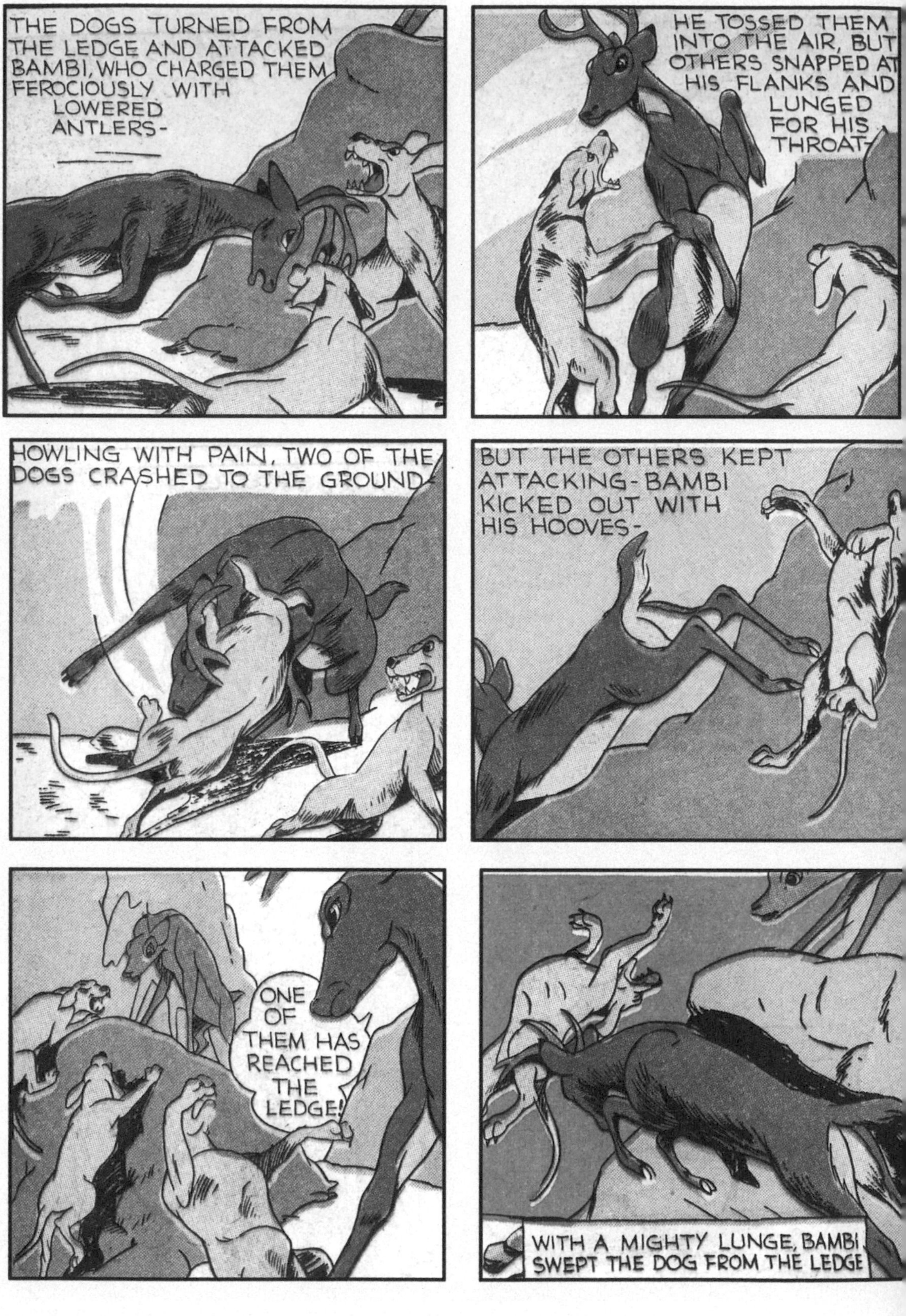
THE DOGS TURNED FROM THE LEDGE AND ATTACKED BAMBI, WHO CHARGED THEM FEROCIOUSLY WITH LOWERED ANTLERS-
HE TOSSED THEM INTO THE AIR, BUT OTHERS SNAPPED AT HIS FLANKS AND LUNGED FOR HIS THROAT-
HOWLING WITH PAIN, TWO OF THE DOGS CRASHED TO THE GROUND-
BUT THE OTHERS KEPT ATTACKING- BAMBI KICKED OUT WITH HIS HOOVES-
ONE OF THEM HAS REACHED THE LEDGE!
WITH A MIGHTY LUNGE, BAMBI SWEPT THE DOG FROM THE LEDGE

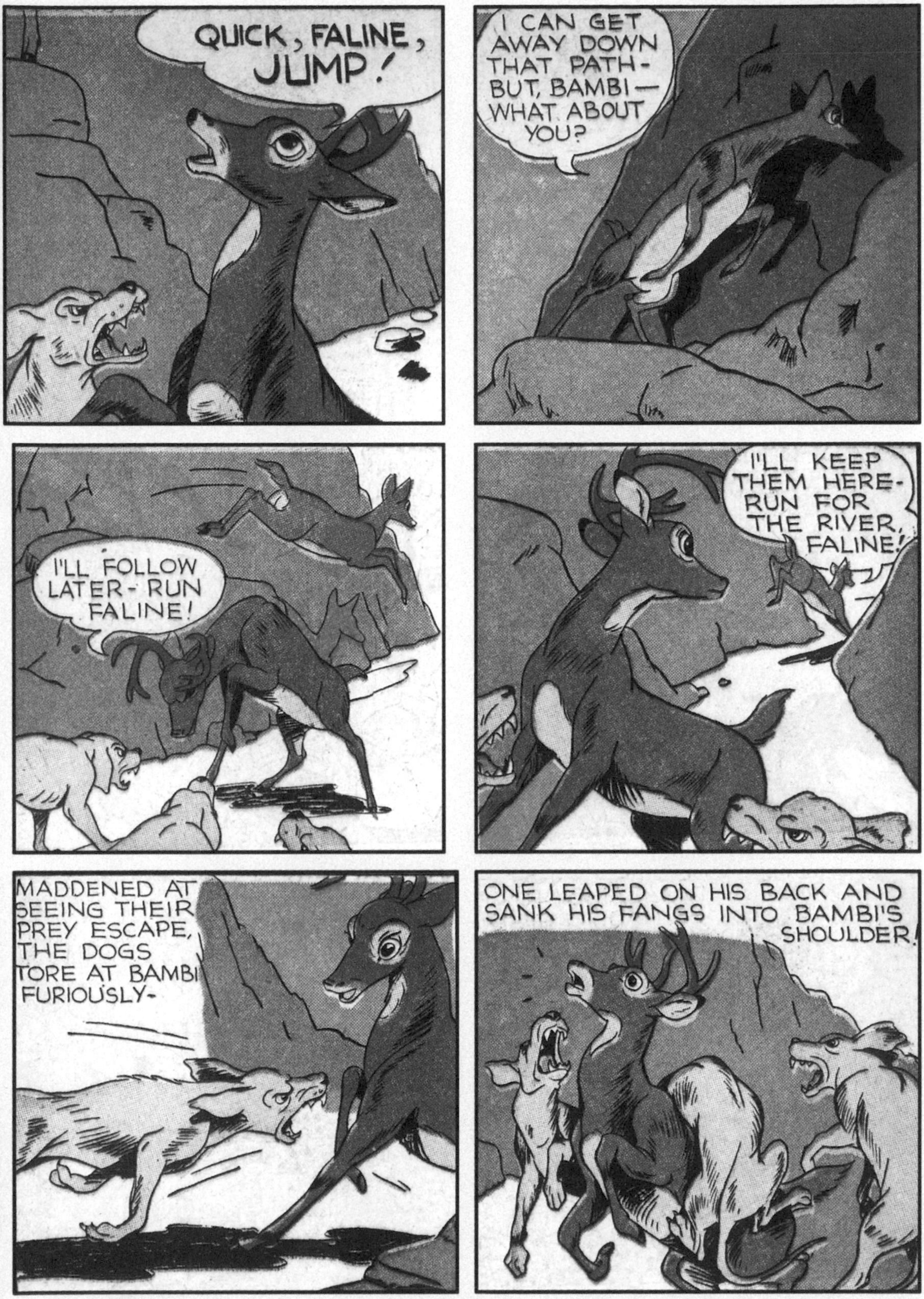
QUICK, FALINE, JUMP!
I CAN GET AWAY DOWN THAT PATH- BUT, BAMBI— WHAT ABOUT YOU?
I'LL FOLLOW LATER- RUN FALINE!
I'LL KEEP THEM HERE- RUN FOR THE RIVER, FALINE!
MADDENED AT SEEING THEIR PREY ESCAPE, THE DOGS TORE AT BAMBI FURIOUSLY-
ONE LEAPED ON HIS BACK AND SANK HIS FANGS INTO BAMBI'S SHOULDER!

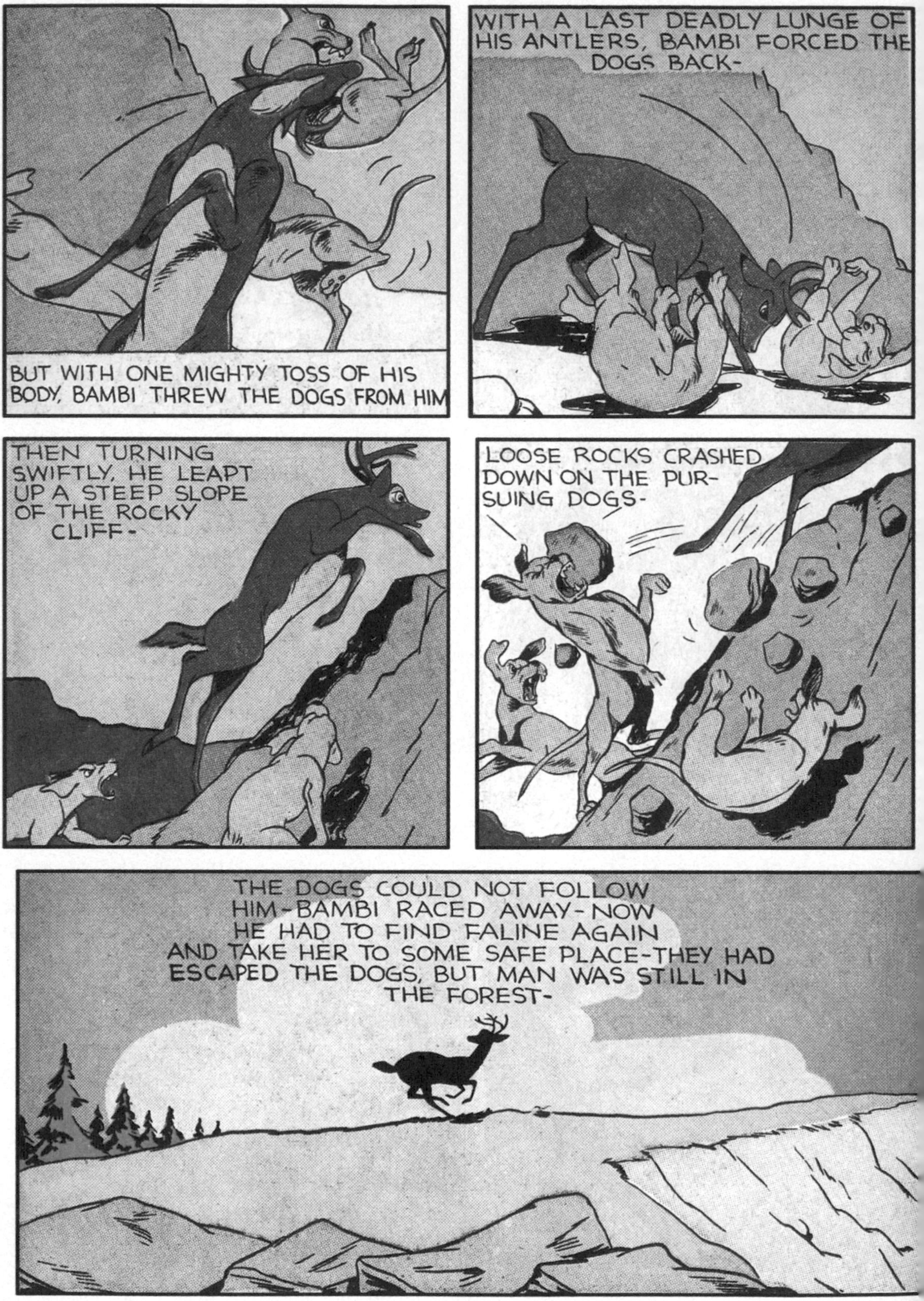
BUT WITH ONE MIGHTY TOSS OF HIS BODY, BAMBI THREW THE DOGS FROM HIM
WITH A LAST DEADLY LUNGE OF HIS ANTLERS, BAMBI FORCED THE DOGS BACK-
THEN TURNING SWIFTLY, HE LEAPT UP A STEEP SLOPE OF THE ROCKY CLIFF-
LOOSE ROCKS CRASHED DOWN ON THE PURSUING DOGS-
THE DOGS COULD NOT FOLLOW HIM-BAMBI RACED AWAY-NOW HE HAD TO FIND FALINE AGAIN AND TAKE HER TO SOME SAFE PLACE-THEY HAD ESCAPED THE DOGS, BUT MAN WAS STILL IN THE FOREST-

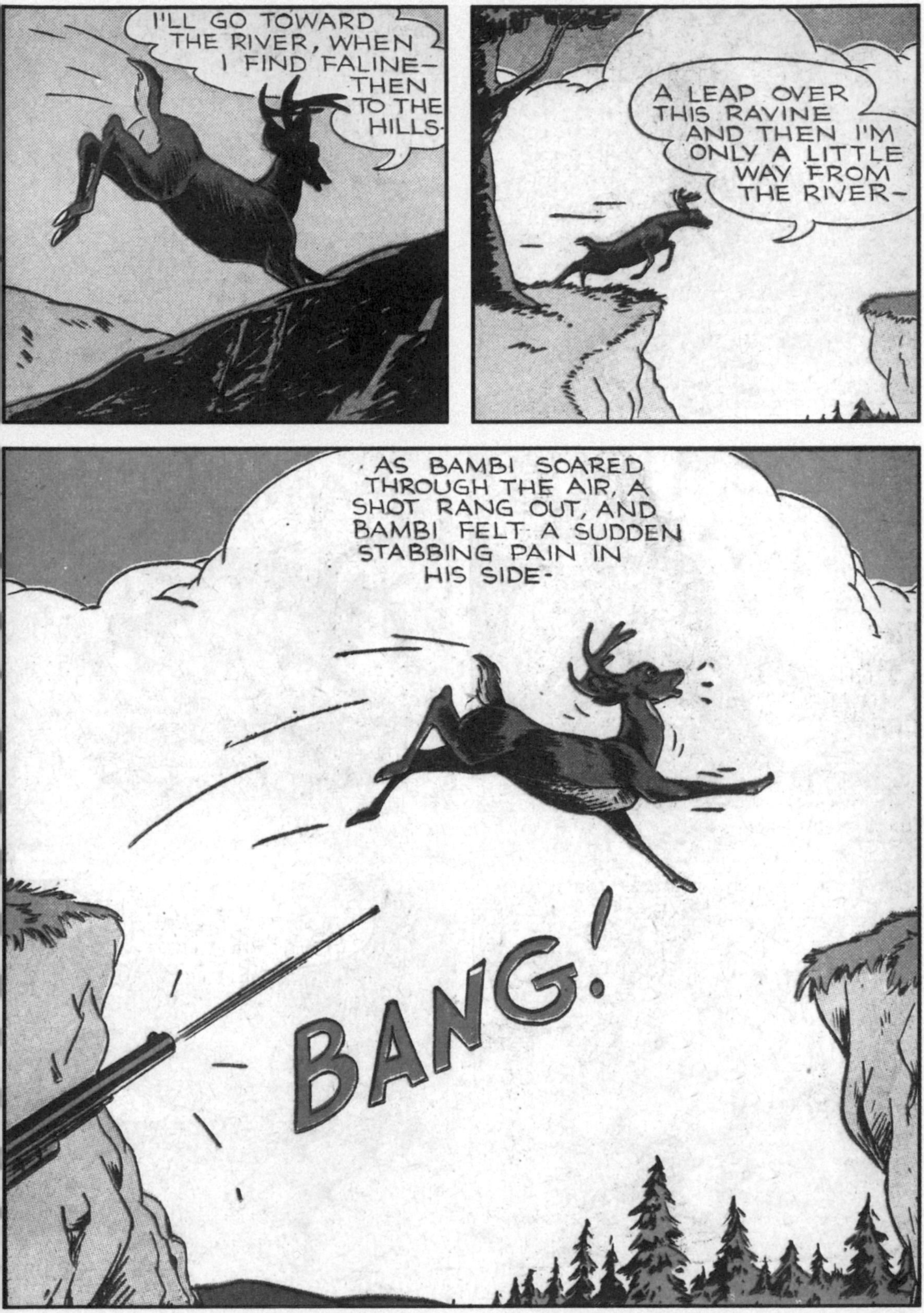
I'LL GO TOWARD THE RIVER, WHEN I FIND FALINE—THEN TO THE HILLS-
A LEAP OVER THIS RAVINE AND THEN I'M ONLY A LITTLE WAY FROM THE RIVER—
AS BAMBI SOARED THROUGH THE AIR, A SHOT RANG OUT, AND BAMBI FELT A SUDDEN STABBING PAIN IN HIS SIDE-
BANG!

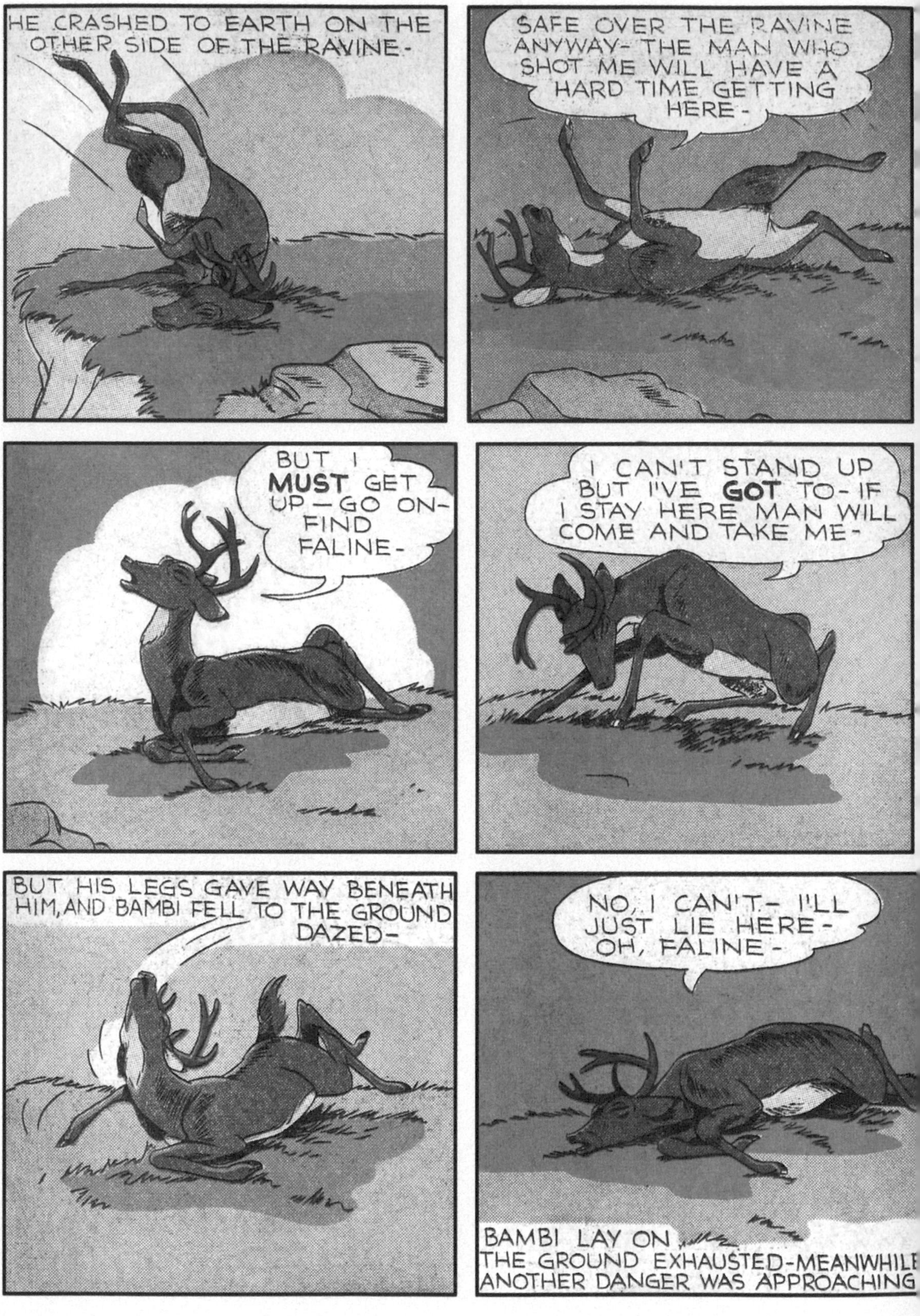
HE CRASHED TO EARTH ON THE OTHER SIDE OF THE RAVINE-
SAFE OVER THE RAVINE ANYWAY- THE MAN WHO SHOT ME WILL HAVE A HARD TIME GETTING HERE-
BUT I **MUST** GET UP—GO ON-FIND FALINE-
I CAN'T STAND UP BUT I'VE **GOT** TO- IF I STAY HERE MAN WILL COME AND TAKE ME-
BUT HIS LEGS GAVE WAY BENEATH HIM, AND BAMBI FELL TO THE GROUND DAZED-
NO, I CAN'T- I'LL JUST LIE HERE- OH, FALINE-
BAMBI LAY ON THE GROUND EXHAUSTED-MEANWHILE ANOTHER DANGER WAS APPROACHING

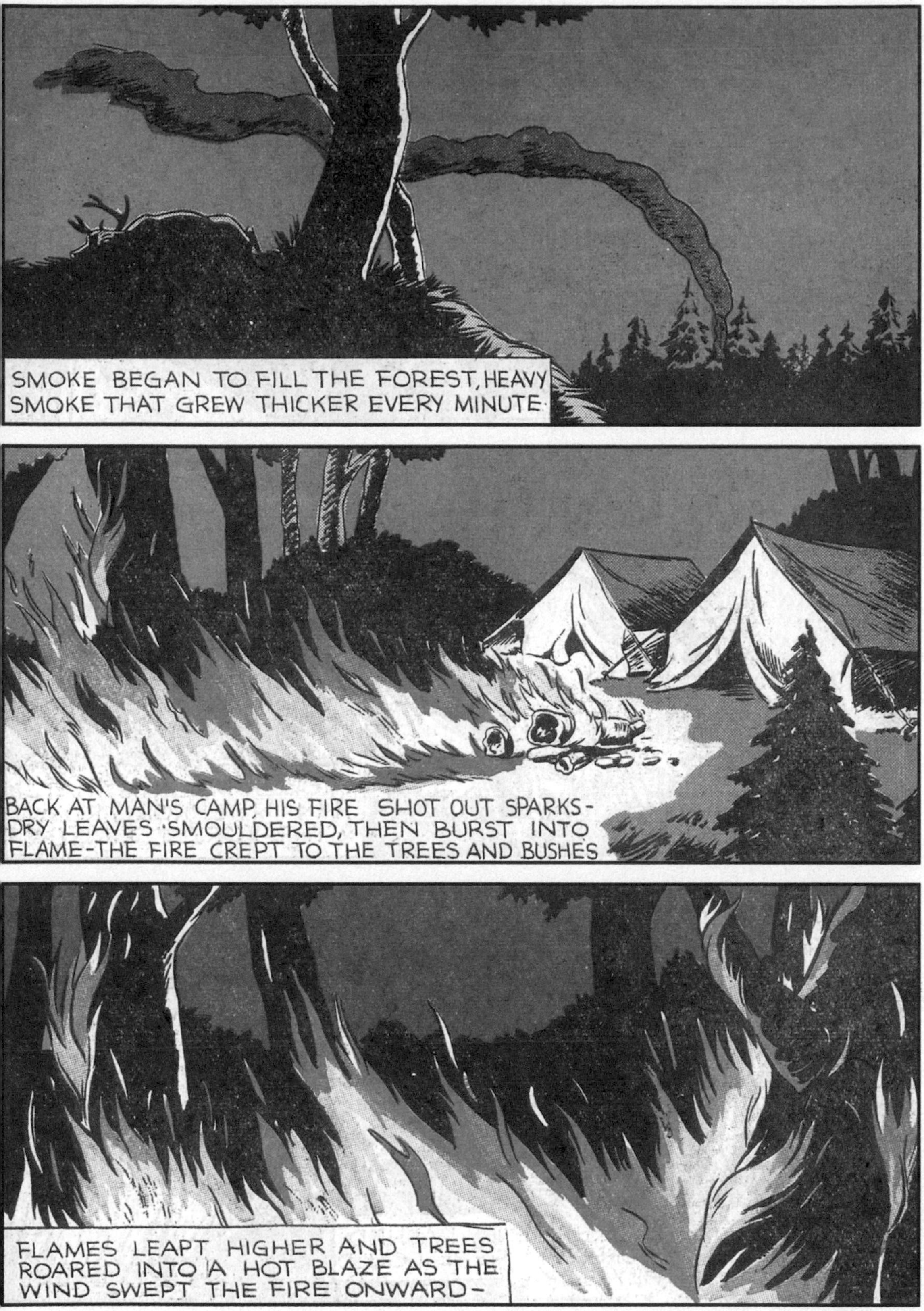
SMOKE BEGAN TO FILL THE FOREST, HEAVY SMOKE THAT GREW THICKER EVERY MINUTE.
BACK AT MAN'S CAMP, HIS FIRE SHOT OUT SPARKS- DRY LEAVES SMOULDERED, THEN BURST INTO FLAME-THE FIRE CREPT TO THE TREES AND BUSHES
FLAMES LEAPT HIGHER AND TREES ROARED INTO A HOT BLAZE AS THE WIND SWEPT THE FIRE ONWARD-

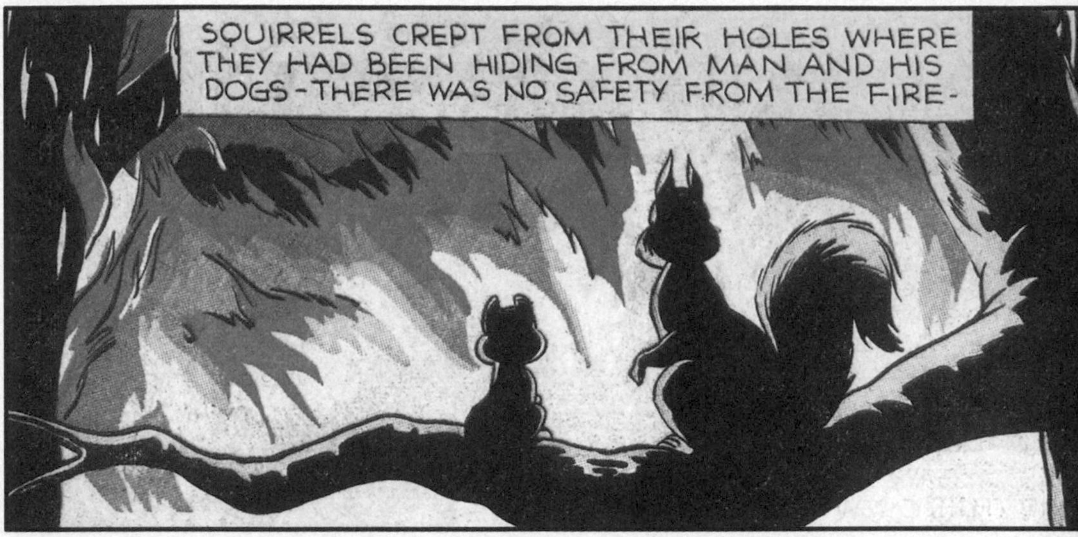
SQUIRRELS CREPT FROM THEIR HOLES WHERE THEY HAD BEEN HIDING FROM MAN AND HIS DOGS - THERE WAS NO SAFETY FROM THE FIRE-

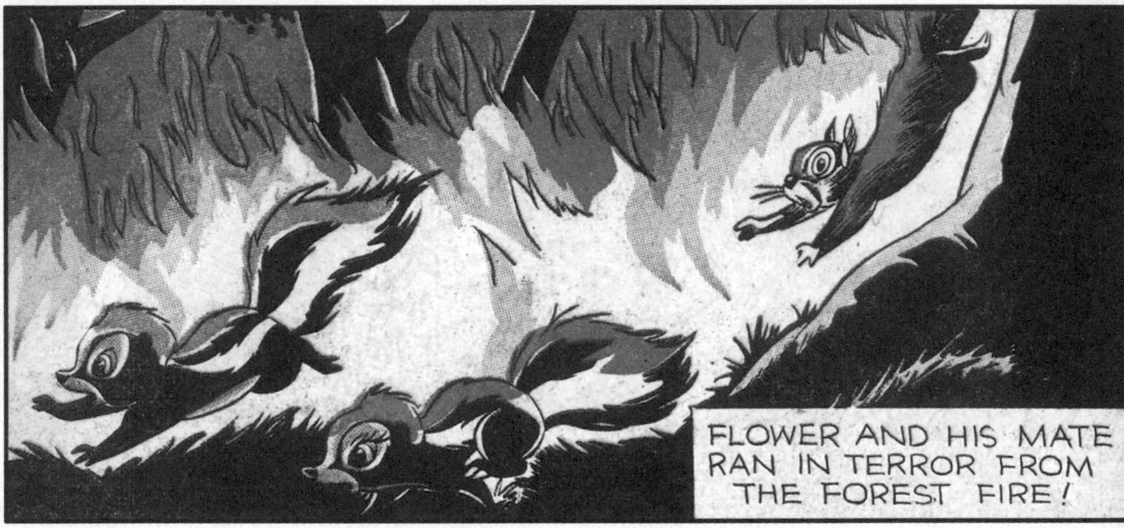
FLOWER AND HIS MATE RAN IN TERROR FROM THE FOREST FIRE!

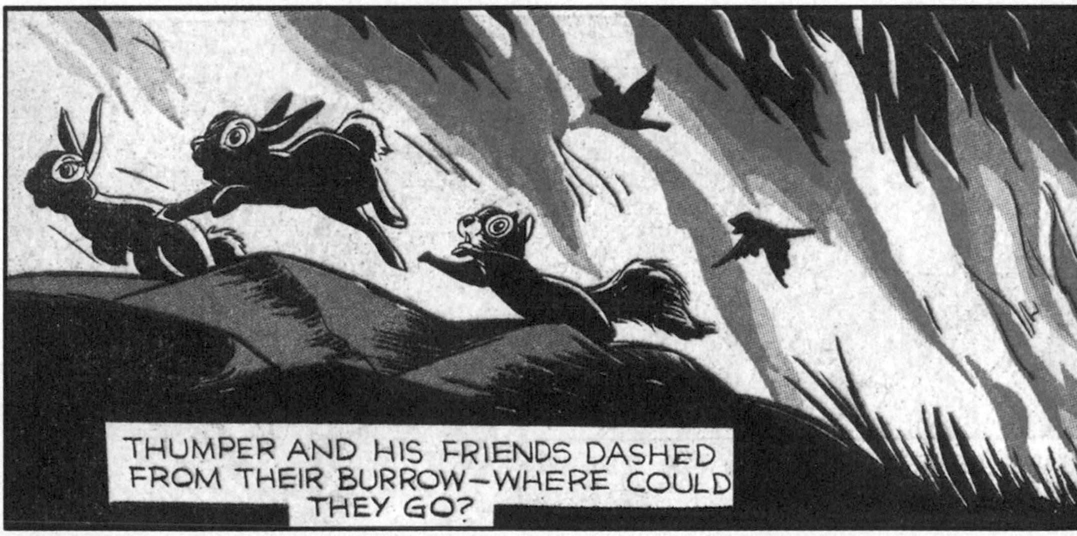
THUMPER AND HIS FRIENDS DASHED FROM THEIR BURROW—WHERE COULD THEY GO?

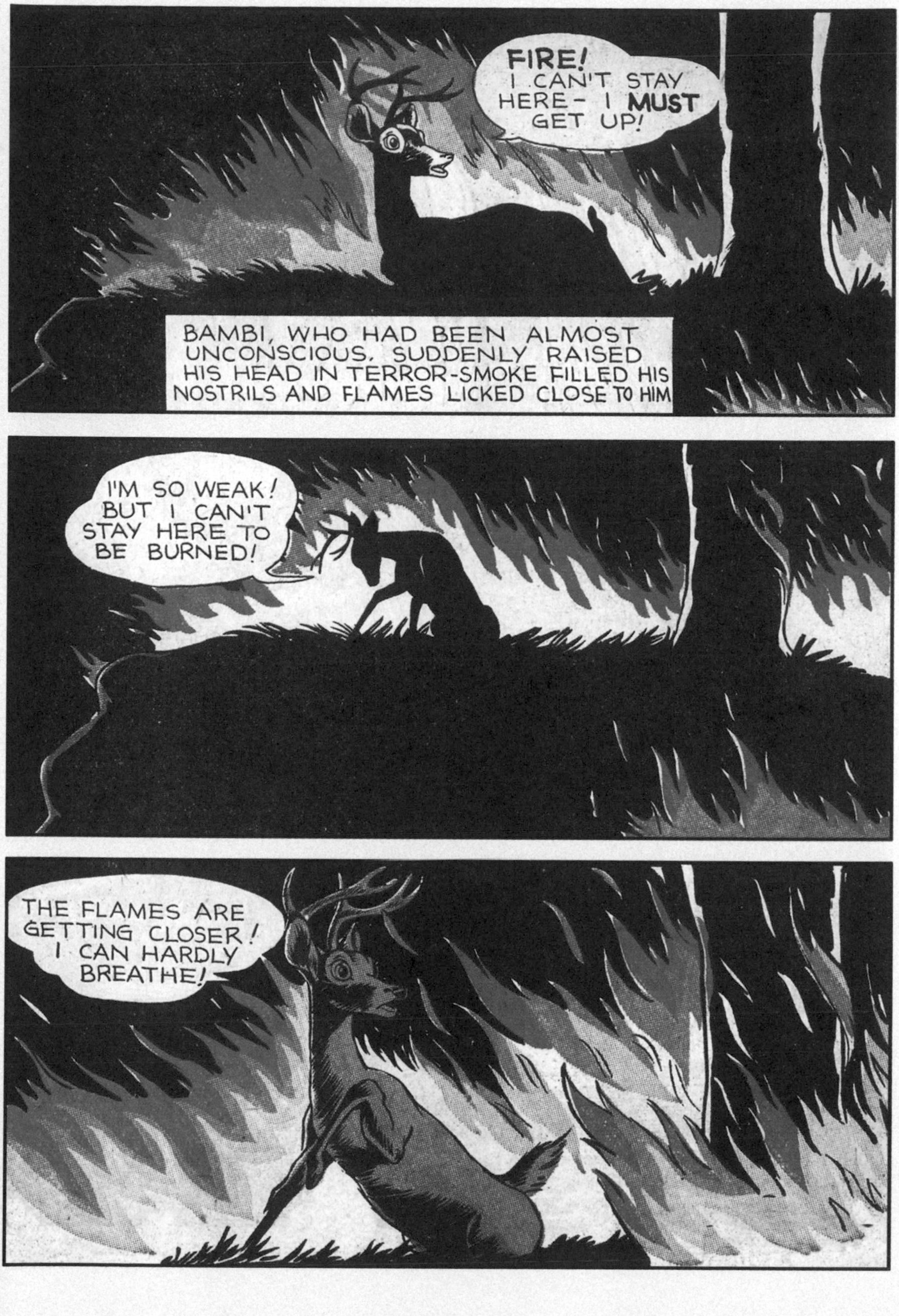
FIRE! I CAN'T STAY HERE- I MUST GET UP!
BAMBI, WHO HAD BEEN ALMOST UNCONSCIOUS, SUDDENLY RAISED HIS HEAD IN TERROR-SMOKE FILLED HIS NOSTRILS AND FLAMES LICKED CLOSE TO HIM
I'M SO WEAK! BUT I CAN'T STAY HERE TO BE BURNED!
THE FLAMES ARE GETTING CLOSER! I CAN HARDLY BREATHE!

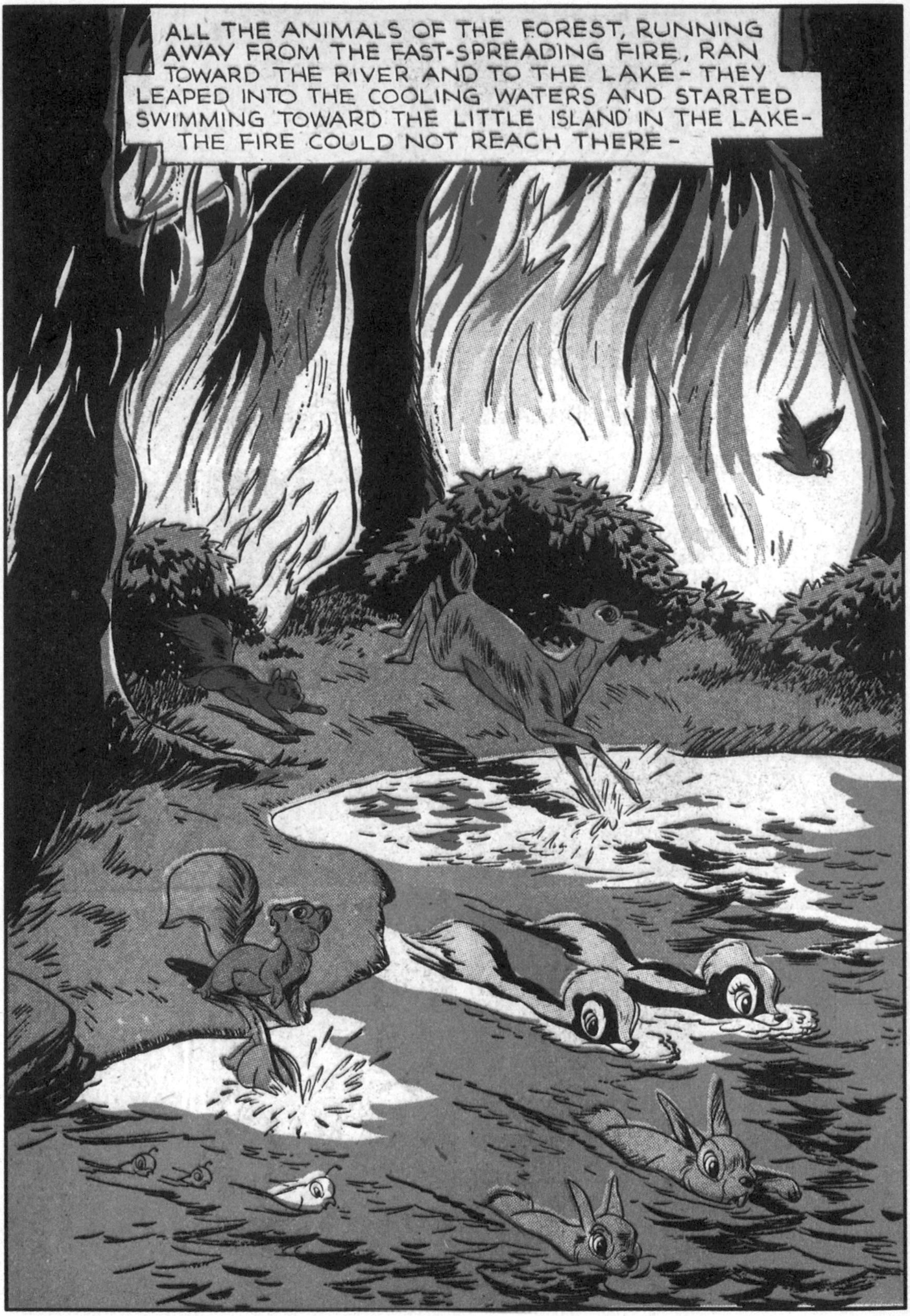
ALL THE ANIMALS OF THE FOREST, RUNNING AWAY FROM THE FAST-SPREADING FIRE, RAN TOWARD THE RIVER AND TO THE LAKE - THEY LEAPED INTO THE COOLING WATERS AND STARTED SWIMMING TOWARD THE LITTLE ISLAND IN THE LAKE - THE FIRE COULD NOT REACH THERE -

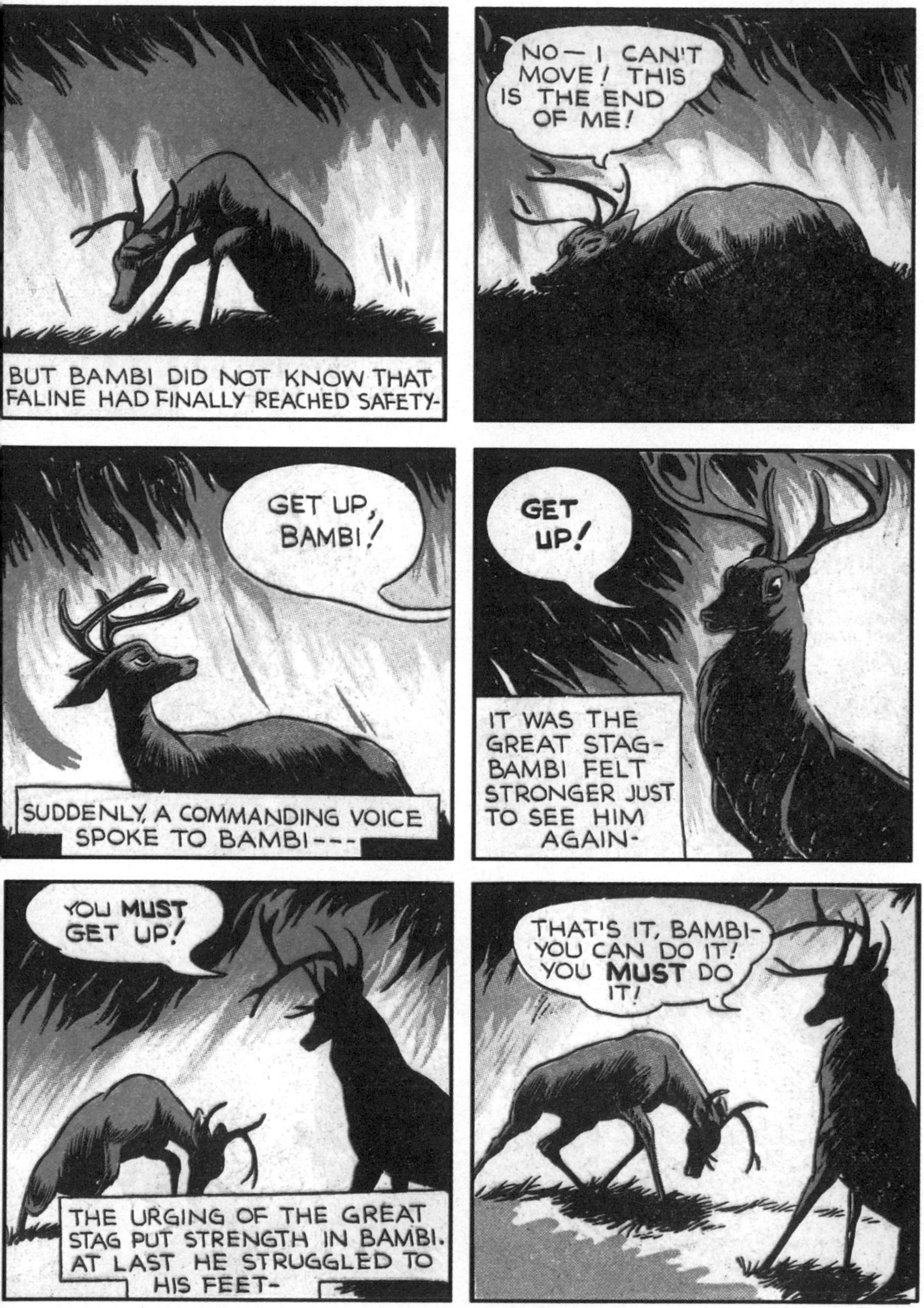
BUT BAMBI DID NOT KNOW THAT FALINE HAD FINALLY REACHED SAFETY-
NO—I CAN'T MOVE! THIS IS THE END OF ME!
GET UP, BAMBI!
SUDDENLY, A COMMANDING VOICE SPOKE TO BAMBI---
GET UP!
IT WAS THE GREAT STAG- BAMBI FELT STRONGER JUST TO SEE HIM AGAIN-
YOU MUST GET UP!
THE URGING OF THE GREAT STAG PUT STRENGTH IN BAMBI. AT LAST HE STRUGGLED TO HIS FEET-
THAT'S IT, BAMBI- YOU CAN DO IT! YOU MUST DO IT!

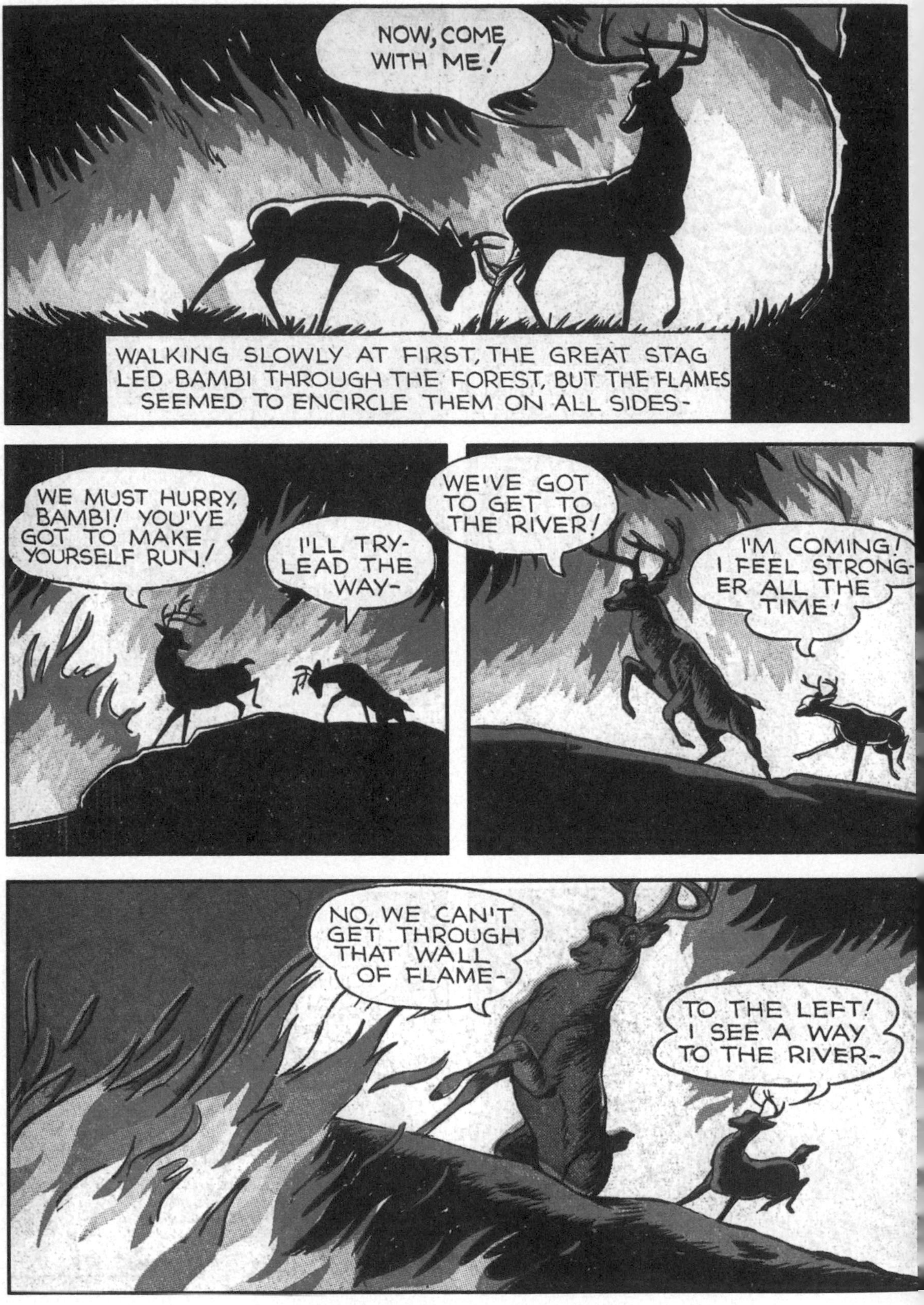
NOW, COME WITH ME!
WALKING SLOWLY AT FIRST, THE GREAT STAG LED BAMBI THROUGH THE FOREST, BUT THE FLAMES SEEMED TO ENCIRCLE THEM ON ALL SIDES-
WE MUST HURRY, BAMBI! YOU'VE GOT TO MAKE YOURSELF RUN!
I'LL TRY- LEAD THE WAY-
WE'VE GOT TO GET TO THE RIVER!
I'M COMING! I FEEL STRONGER ALL THE TIME!
NO, WE CAN'T GET THROUGH THAT WALL OF FLAME-
TO THE LEFT! I SEE A WAY TO THE RIVER-

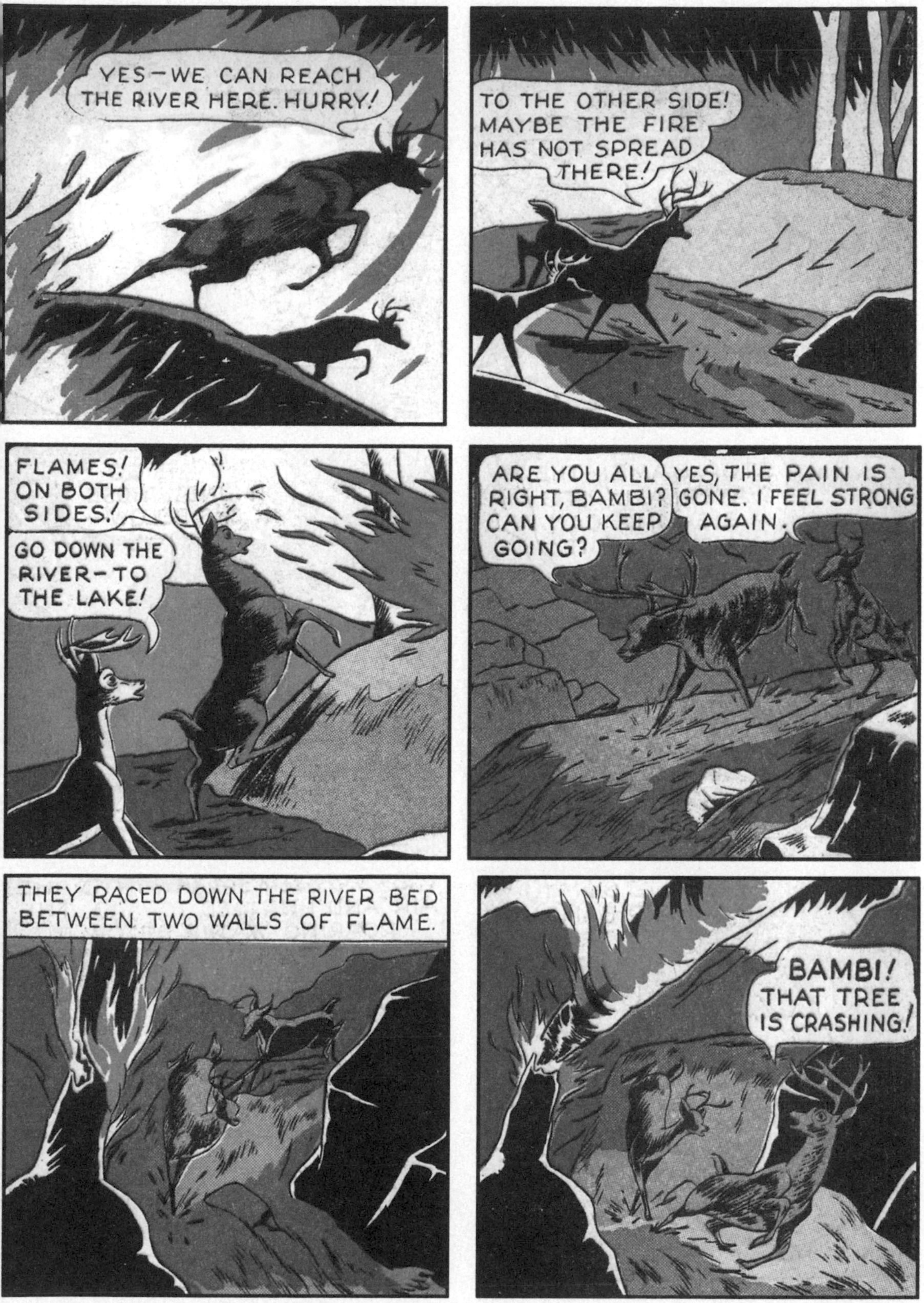
YES—WE CAN REACH THE RIVER HERE. HURRY!
TO THE OTHER SIDE! MAYBE THE FIRE HAS NOT SPREAD THERE!
FLAMES! ON BOTH SIDES!
GO DOWN THE RIVER—TO THE LAKE!
ARE YOU ALL RIGHT, BAMBI? CAN YOU KEEP GOING?
YES, THE PAIN IS GONE. I FEEL STRONG AGAIN.
THEY RACED DOWN THE RIVER BED BETWEEN TWO WALLS OF FLAME.
BAMBI! THAT TREE IS CRASHING!

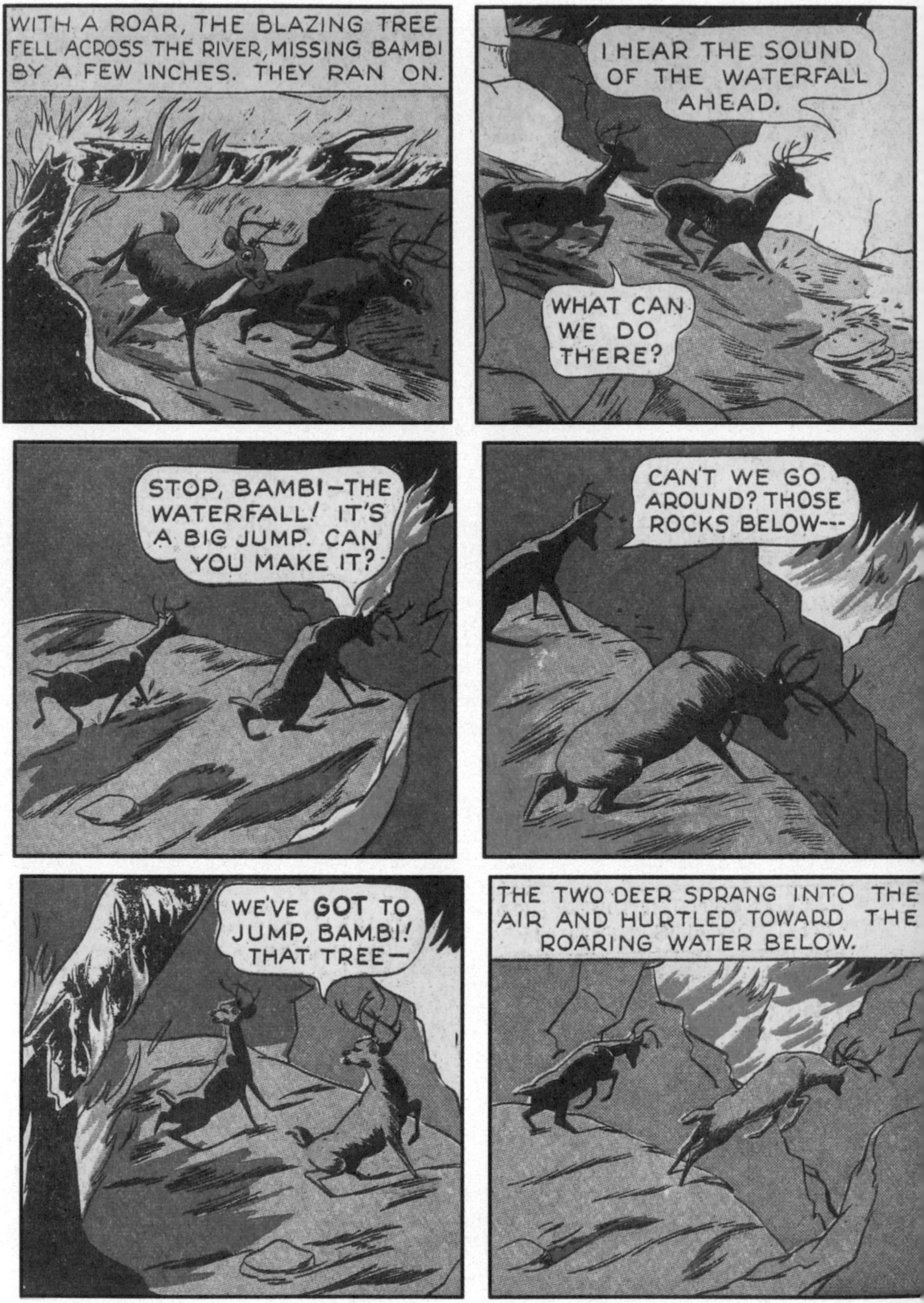
WITH A ROAR, THE BLAZING TREE FELL ACROSS THE RIVER, MISSING BAMBI BY A FEW INCHES. THEY RAN ON.
I HEAR THE SOUND OF THE WATERFALL AHEAD.
WHAT CAN WE DO THERE?
STOP, BAMBI—THE WATERFALL! IT'S A BIG JUMP. CAN YOU MAKE IT?
CAN'T WE GO AROUND? THOSE ROCKS BELOW---
WE'VE GOT TO JUMP, BAMBI! THAT TREE—
THE TWO DEER SPRANG INTO THE AIR AND HURTLED TOWARD THE ROARING WATER BELOW.

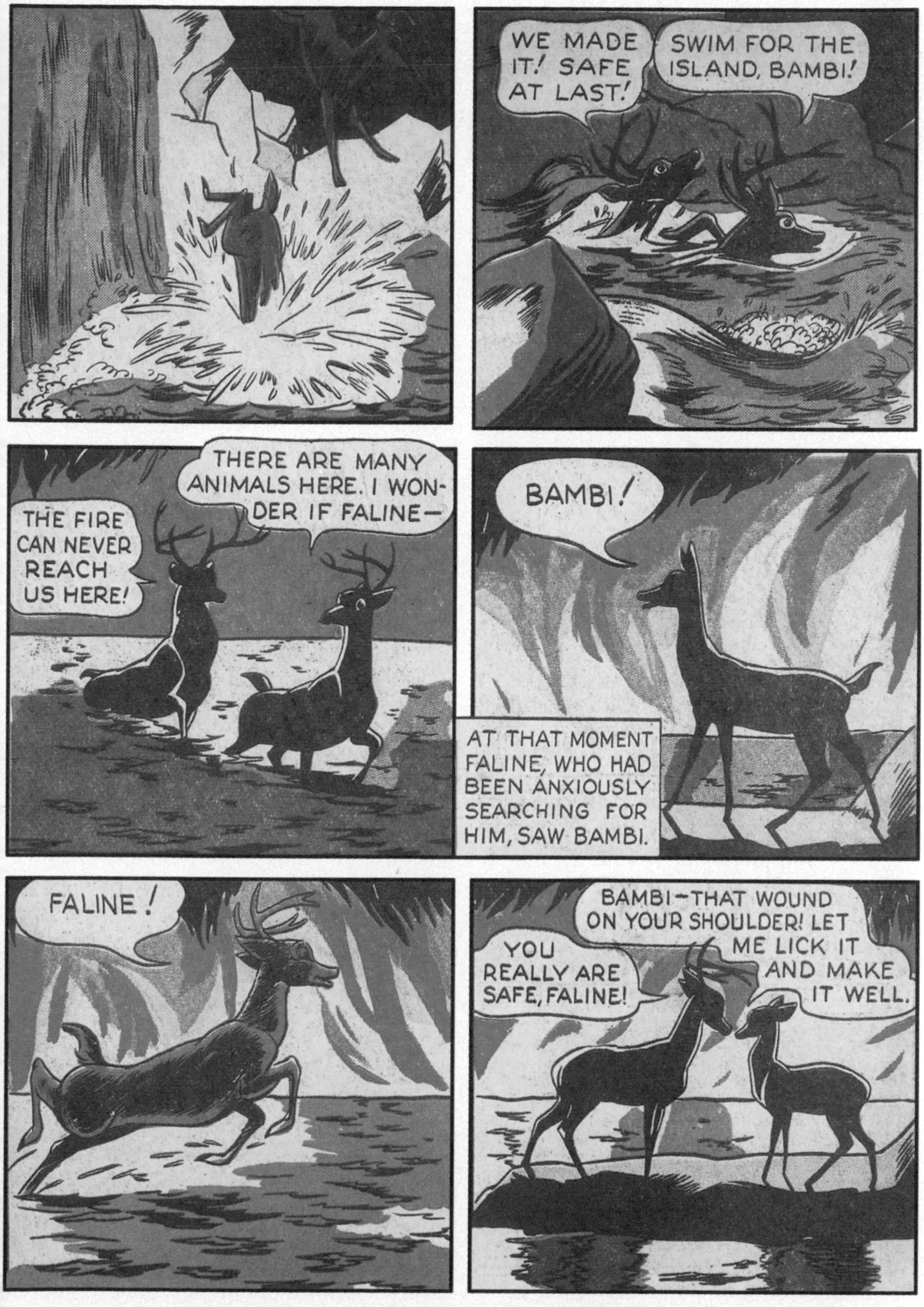
WE MADE IT! SAFE AT LAST!
SWIM FOR THE ISLAND, BAMBI!
THE FIRE CAN NEVER REACH US HERE!
THERE ARE MANY ANIMALS HERE. I WONDER IF FALINE—
BAMBI!
AT THAT MOMENT FALINE, WHO HAD BEEN ANXIOUSLY SEARCHING FOR HIM, SAW BAMBI.
FALINE!
YOU REALLY ARE SAFE, FALINE!
BAMBI—THAT WOUND ON YOUR SHOULDER! LET ME LICK IT AND MAKE IT WELL.

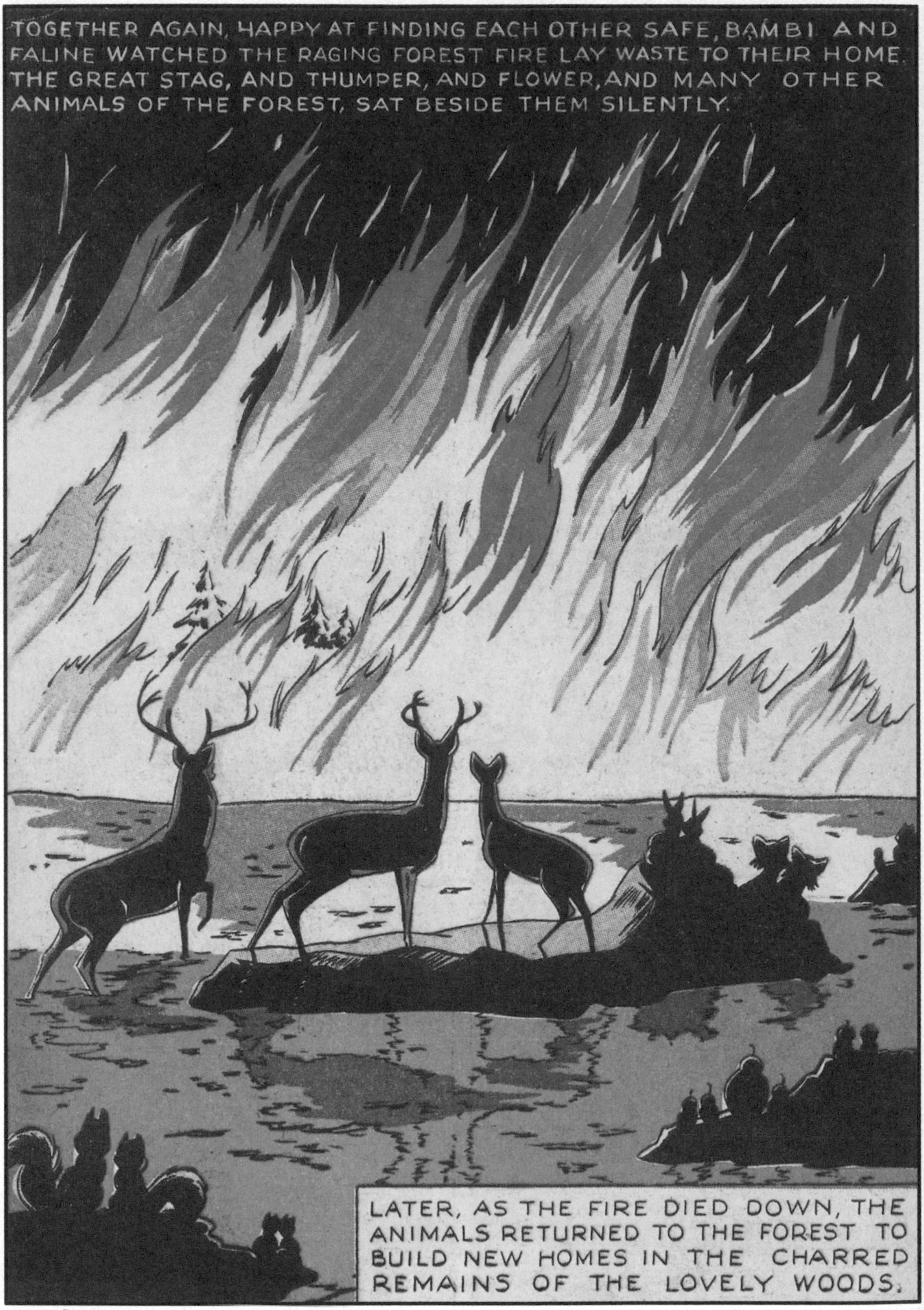
TOGETHER AGAIN, HAPPY AT FINDING EACH OTHER SAFE, BAMBI AND FALINE WATCHED THE RAGING FOREST FIRE LAY WASTE TO THEIR HOME. THE GREAT STAG, AND THUMPER, AND FLOWER, AND MANY OTHER ANIMALS OF THE FOREST, SAT BESIDE THEM SILENTLY.
LATER, AS THE FIRE DIED DOWN, THE ANIMALS RETURNED TO THE FOREST TO BUILD NEW HOMES IN THE CHARRED REMAINS OF THE LOVELY WOODS.

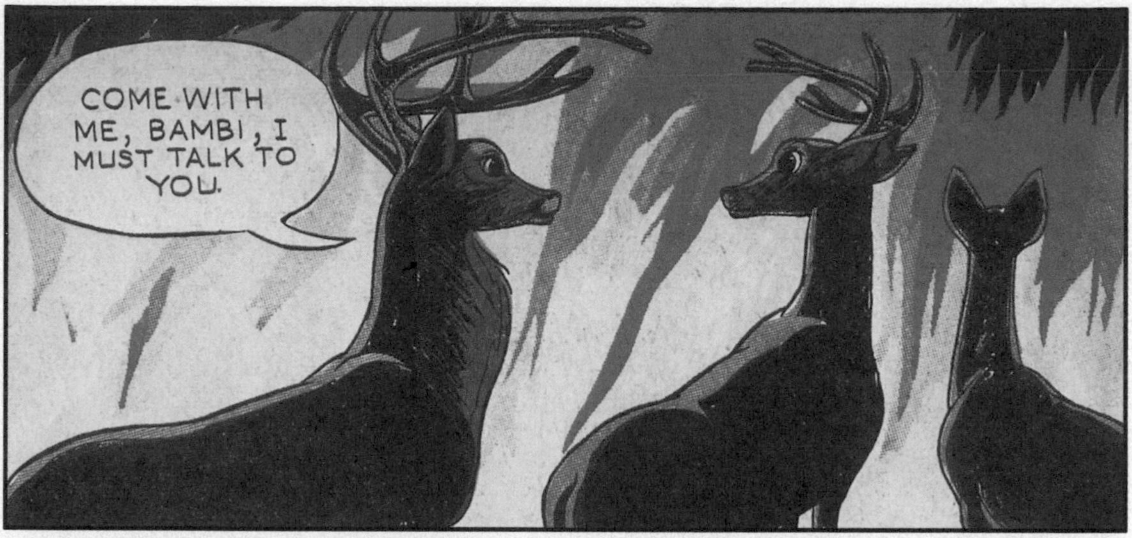
COME WITH ME, BAMBI, I MUST TALK TO YOU.

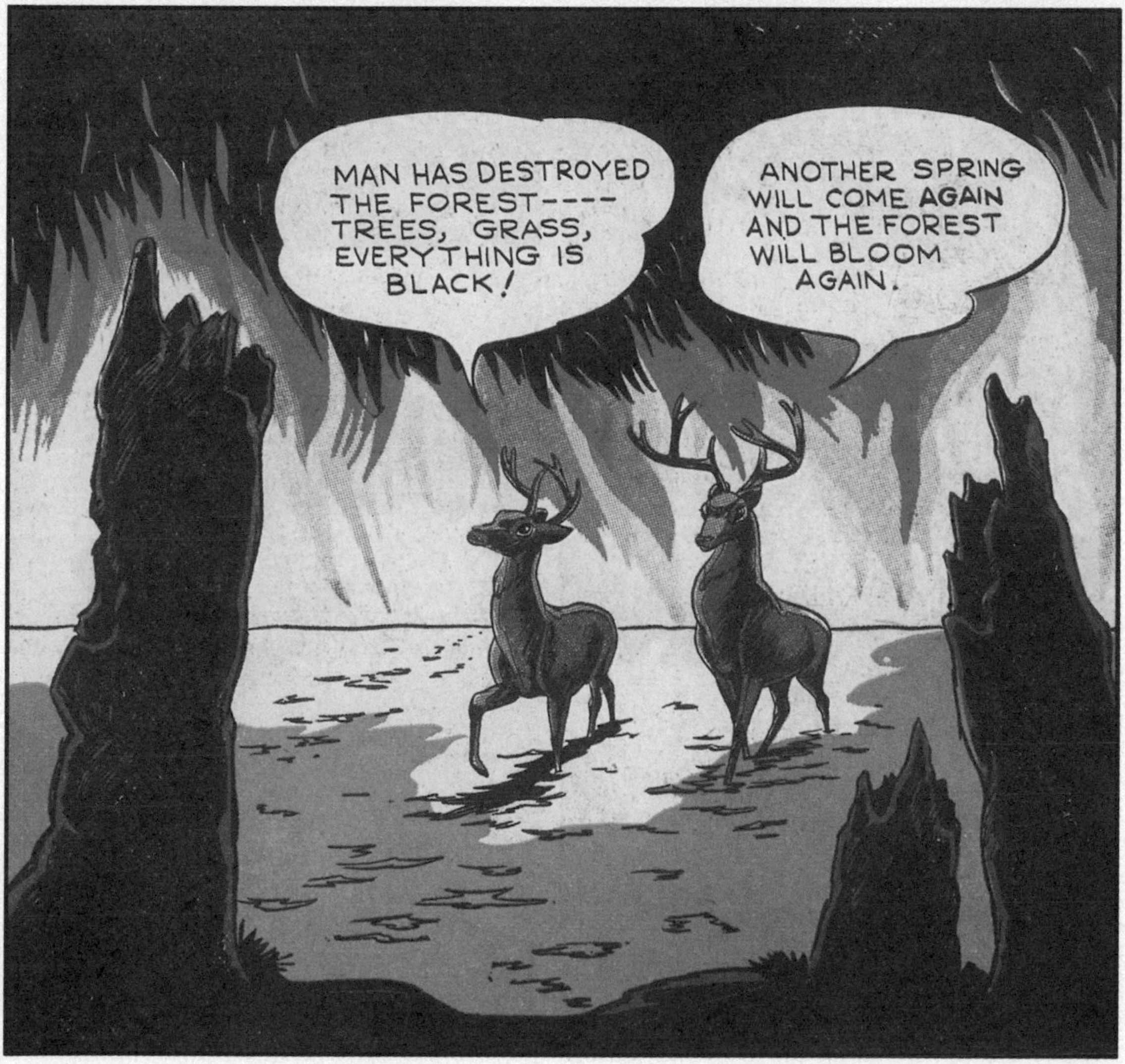
MAN HAS DESTROYED THE FOREST---- TREES, GRASS, EVERYTHING IS BLACK!
ANOTHER SPRING WILL COME AGAIN AND THE FOREST WILL BLOOM AGAIN.

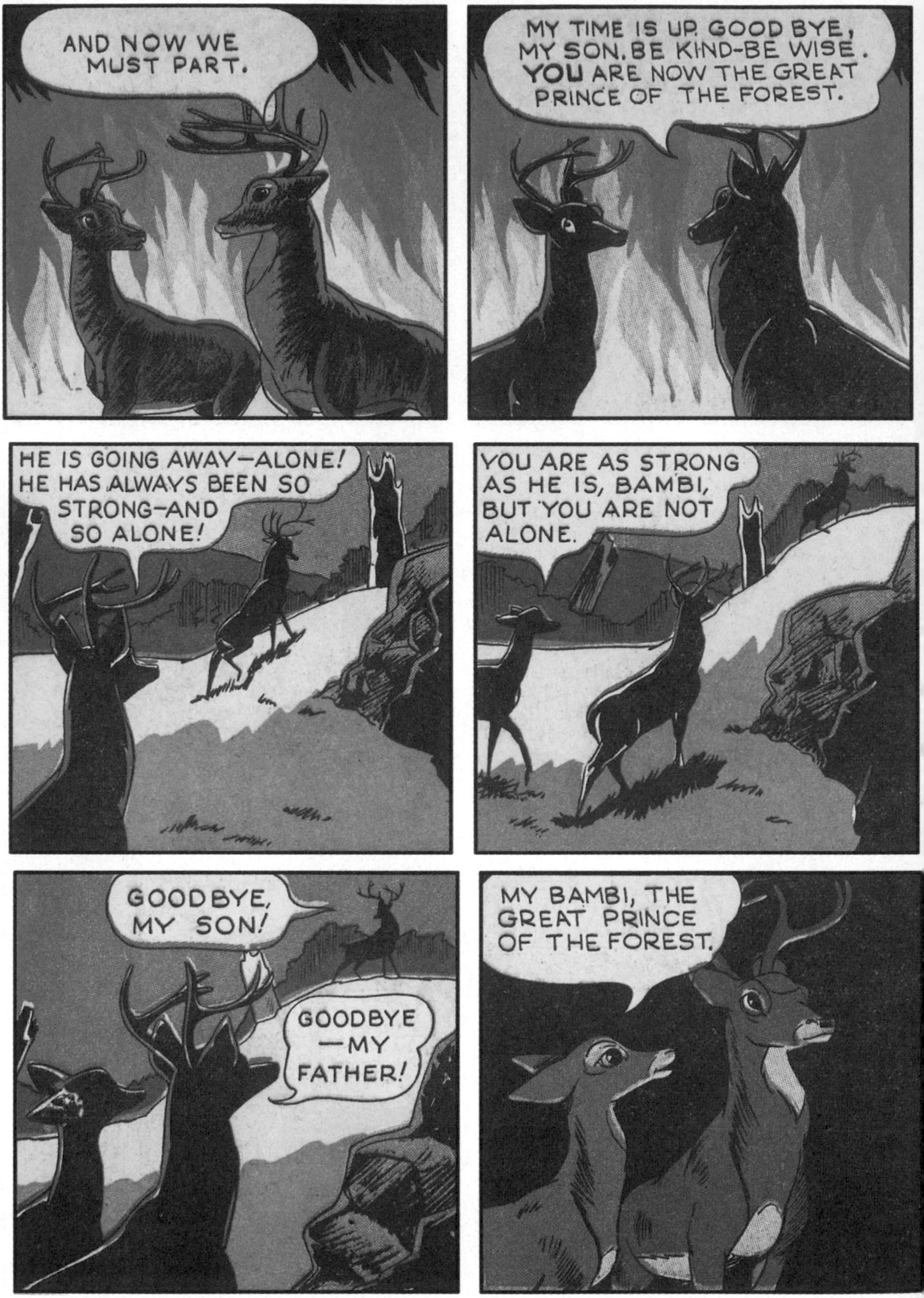

AND NOW WE MUST PART.
MY TIME IS UP. GOOD BYE, MY SON. BE KIND-BE WISE. YOU ARE NOW THE GREAT PRINCE OF THE FOREST.
HE IS GOING AWAY—ALONE! HE HAS ALWAYS BEEN SO STRONG—AND SO ALONE!
YOU ARE AS STRONG AS HE IS, BAMBI, BUT YOU ARE NOT ALONE.
GOODBYE, MY SON!
GOODBYE —MY FATHER!
MY BAMBI, THE GREAT PRINCE OF THE FOREST.

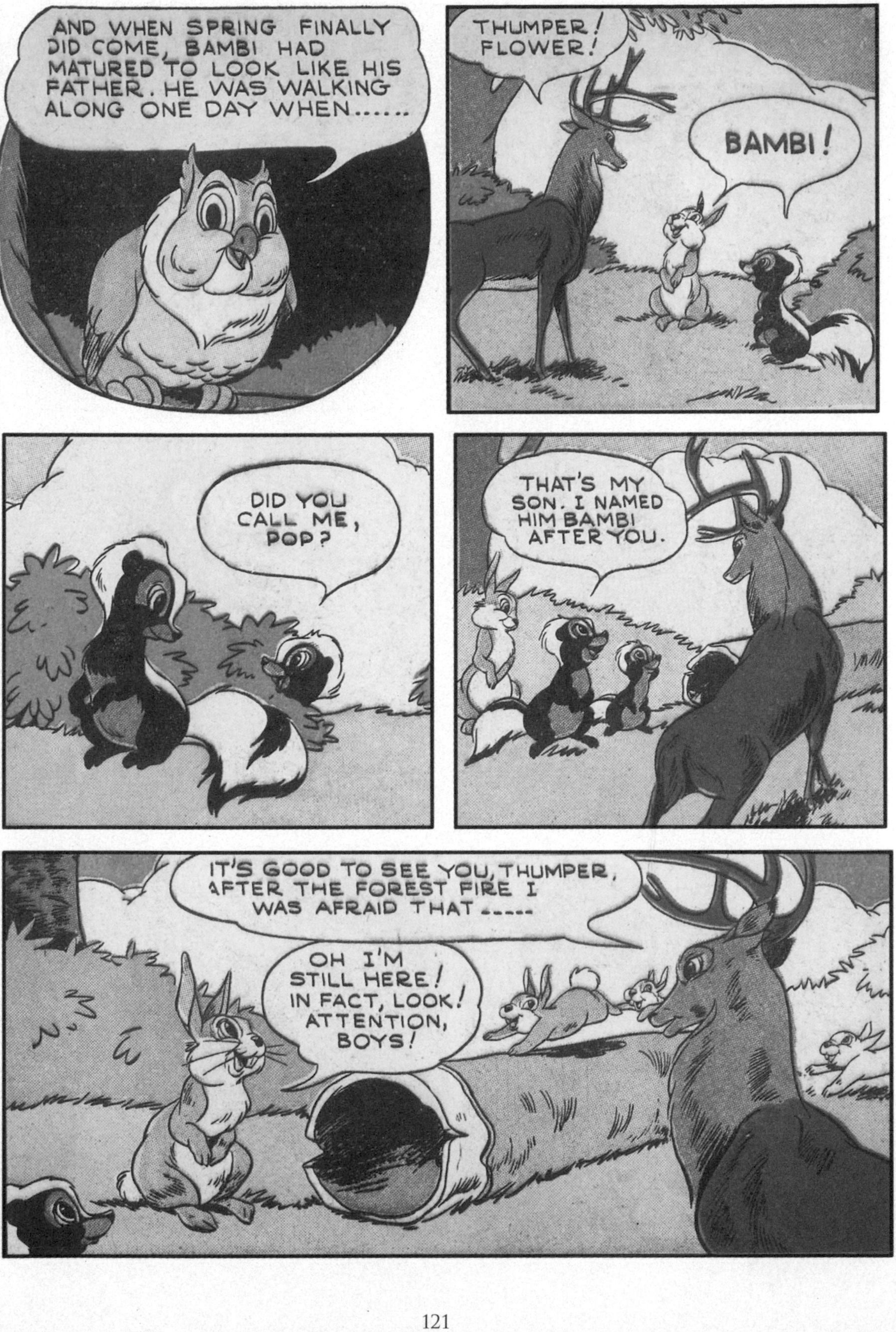
AND WHEN SPRING FINALLY DID COME, BAMBI HAD MATURED TO LOOK LIKE HIS FATHER. HE WAS WALKING ALONG ONE DAY WHEN......
THUMPER! FLOWER!
BAMBI!
DID YOU CALL ME, POP?
THAT'S MY SON. I NAMED HIM BAMBI AFTER YOU.
IT'S GOOD TO SEE YOU, THUMPER, AFTER THE FOREST FIRE I WAS AFRAID THAT.....
OH I'M STILL HERE! IN FACT, LOOK! ATTENTION, BOYS!

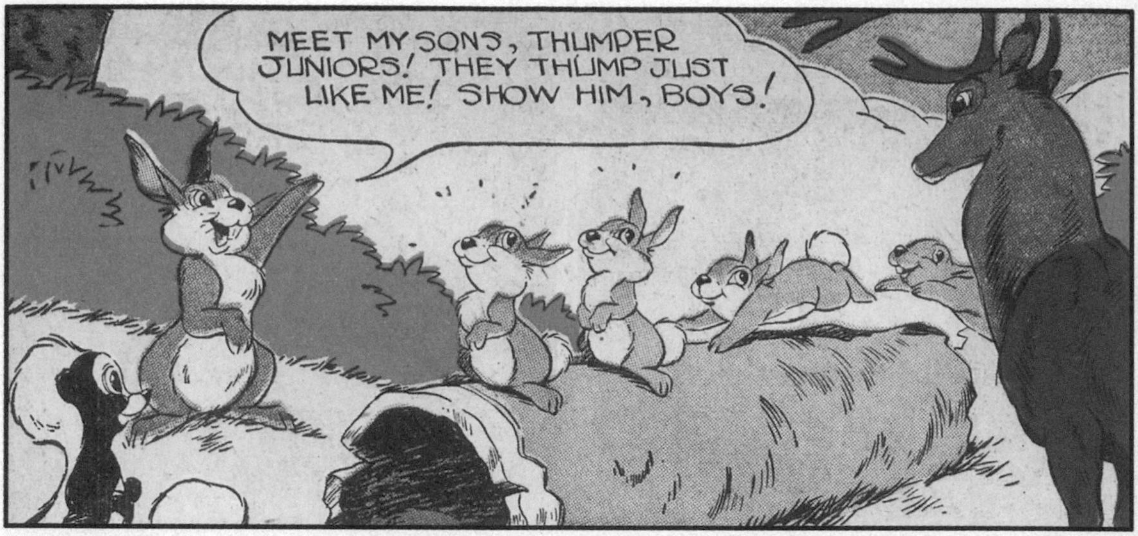
MEET MY SONS, THUMPER JUNIORS! THEY THUMP JUST LIKE ME! SHOW HIM, BOYS!

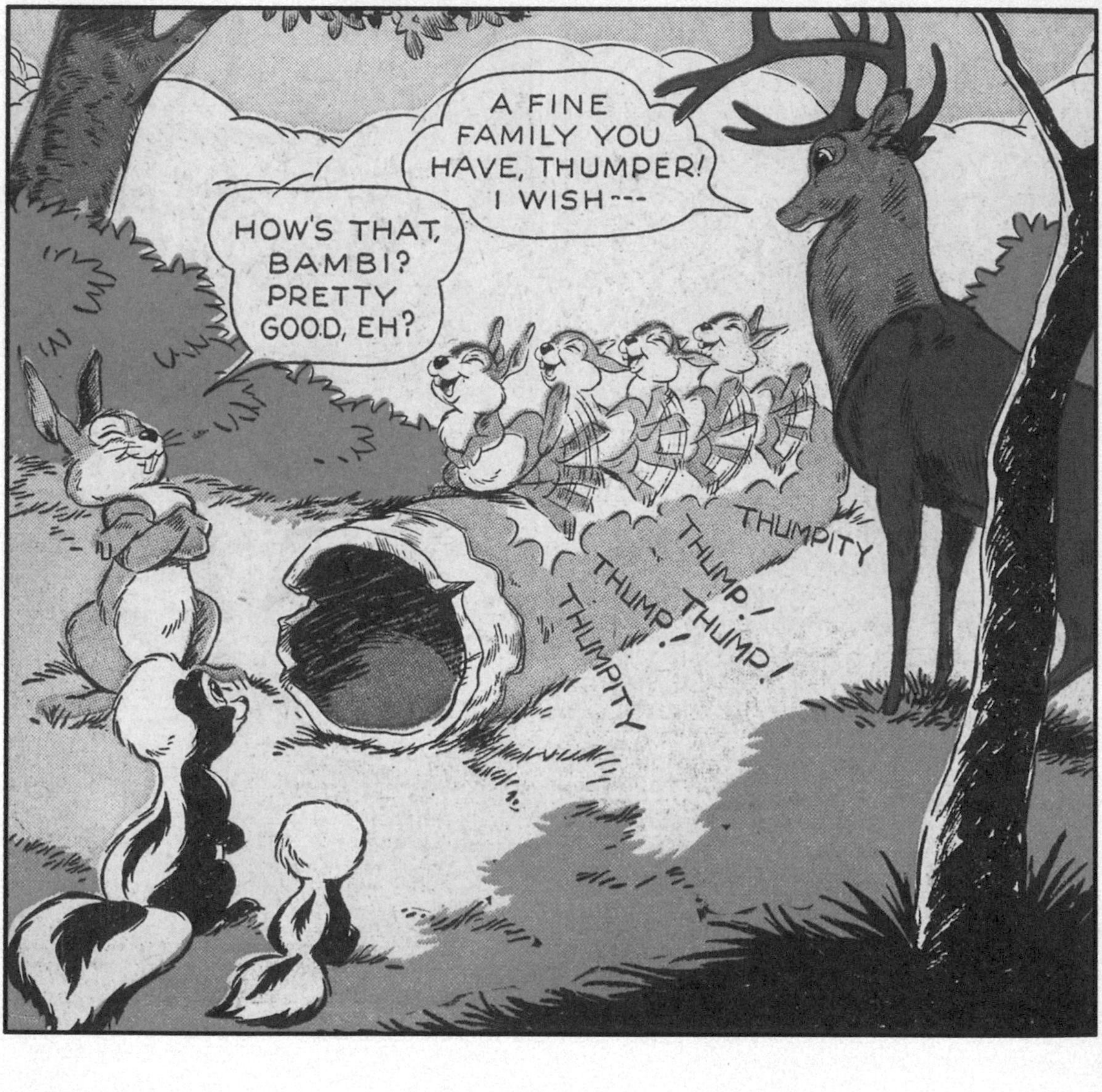
A FINE FAMILY YOU HAVE, THUMPER! I WISH---
HOW'S THAT, BAMBI? PRETTY GOOD, EH?
THUMPITY THUMP! THUMP! THUMPITY THUMP! THUMP!

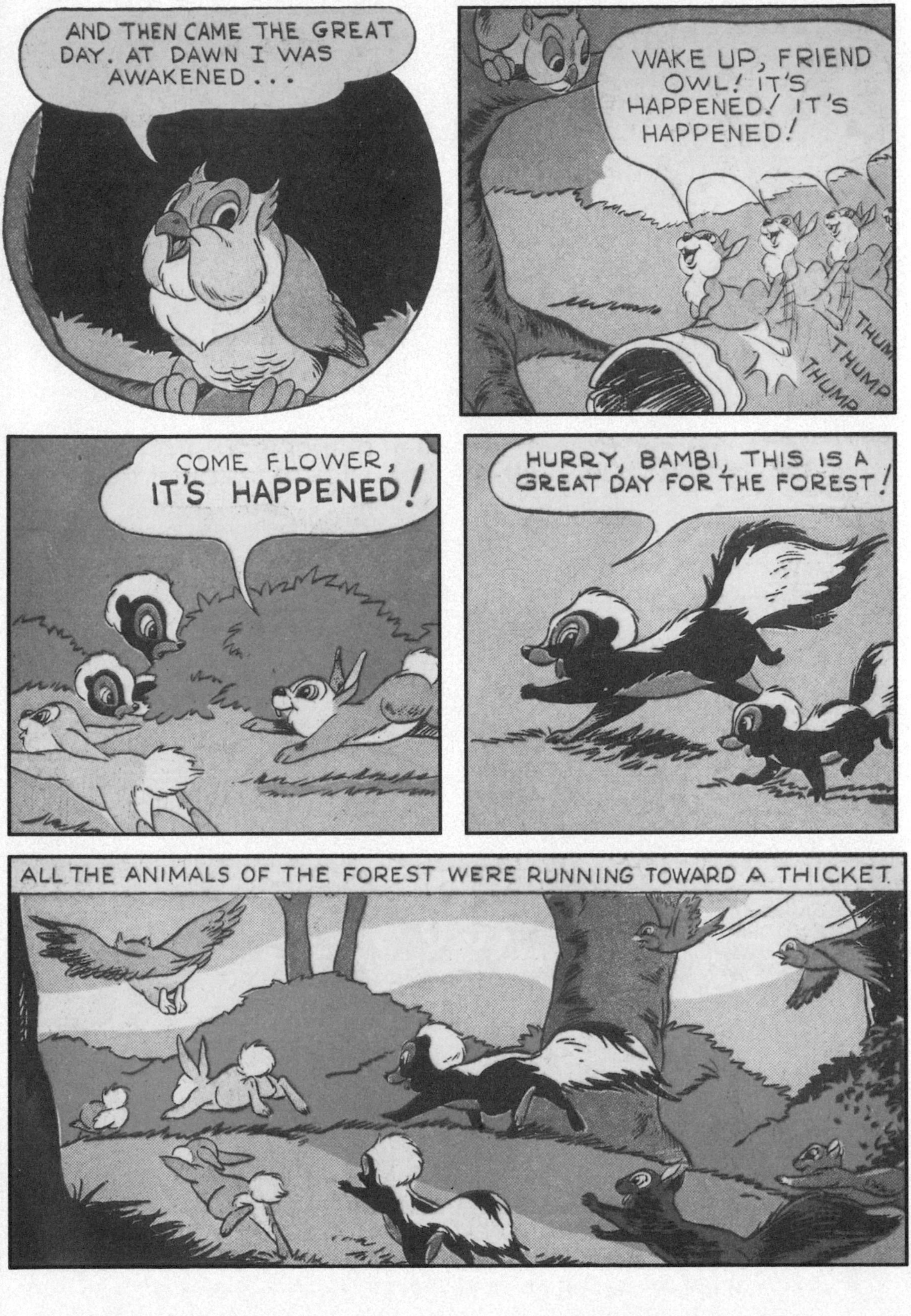
AND THEN CAME THE GREAT DAY. AT DAWN I WAS AWAKENED . . .
WAKE UP, FRIEND OWL! IT'S HAPPENED! IT'S HAPPENED!
THUMP
THUMP
THUMP
COME FLOWER, IT'S HAPPENED!
HURRY, BAMBI, THIS IS A GREAT DAY FOR THE FOREST!
ALL THE ANIMALS OF THE FOREST WERE RUNNING TOWARD A THICKET.

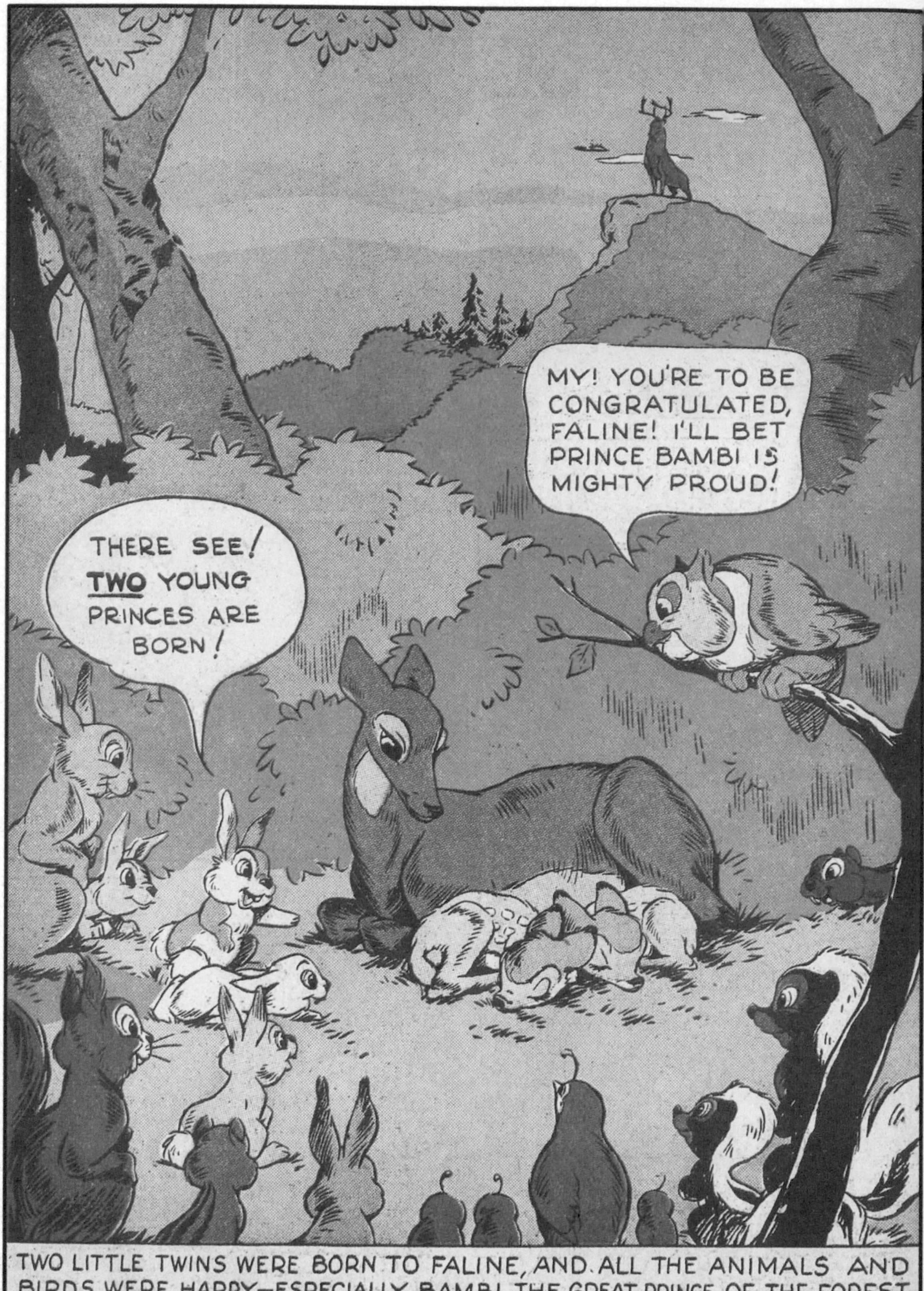
MY! YOU'RE TO BE CONGRATULATED, FALINE! I'LL BET PRINCE BAMBI IS MIGHTY PROUD!
THERE SEE! TWO YOUNG PRINCES ARE BORN!
TWO LITTLE TWINS WERE BORN TO FALINE, AND ALL THE ANIMALS AND BIRDS WERE HAPPY—ESPECIALLY BAMBI, THE GREAT PRINCE OF THE FOREST.

HELP KEEP AMERICA STRONG

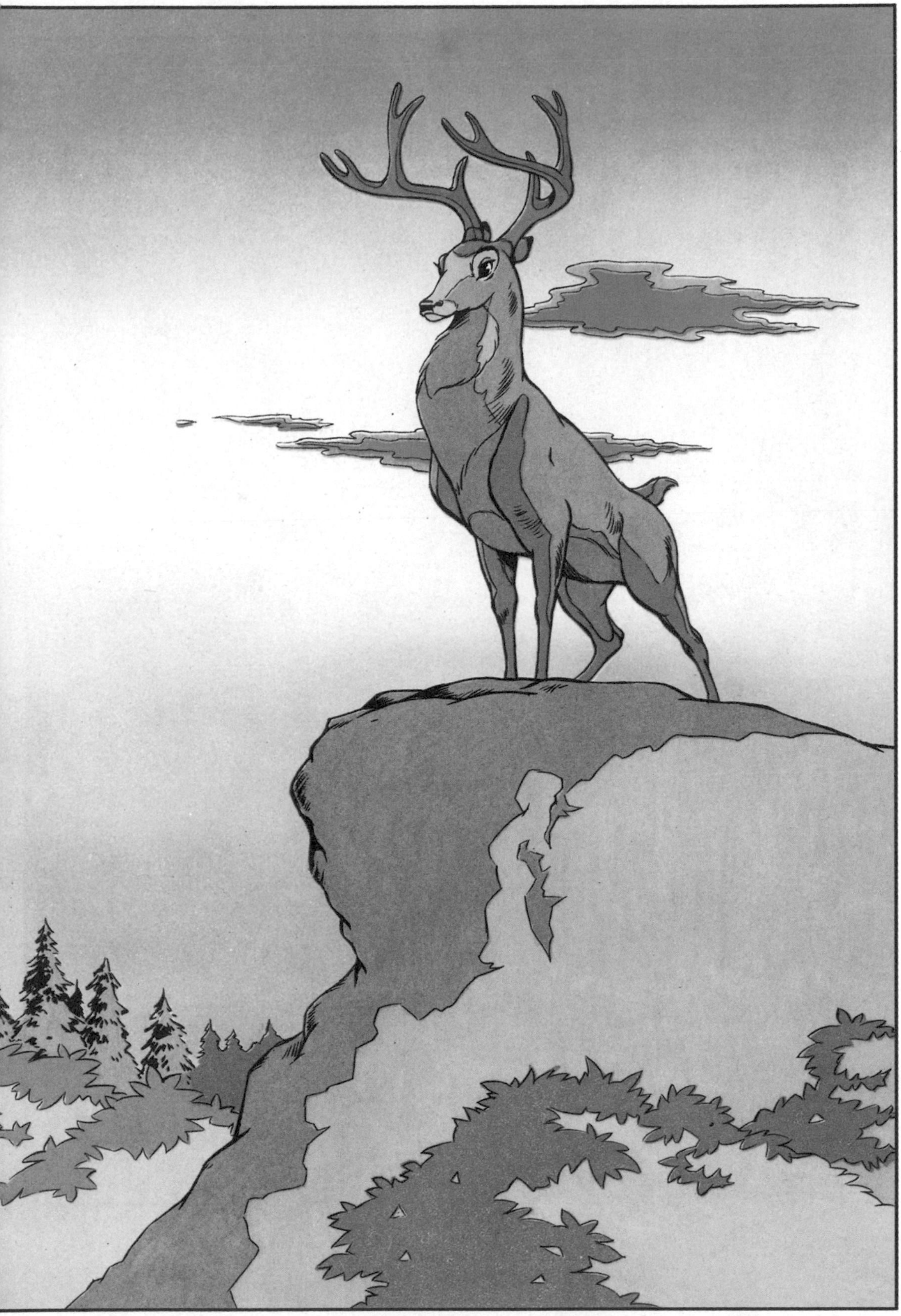

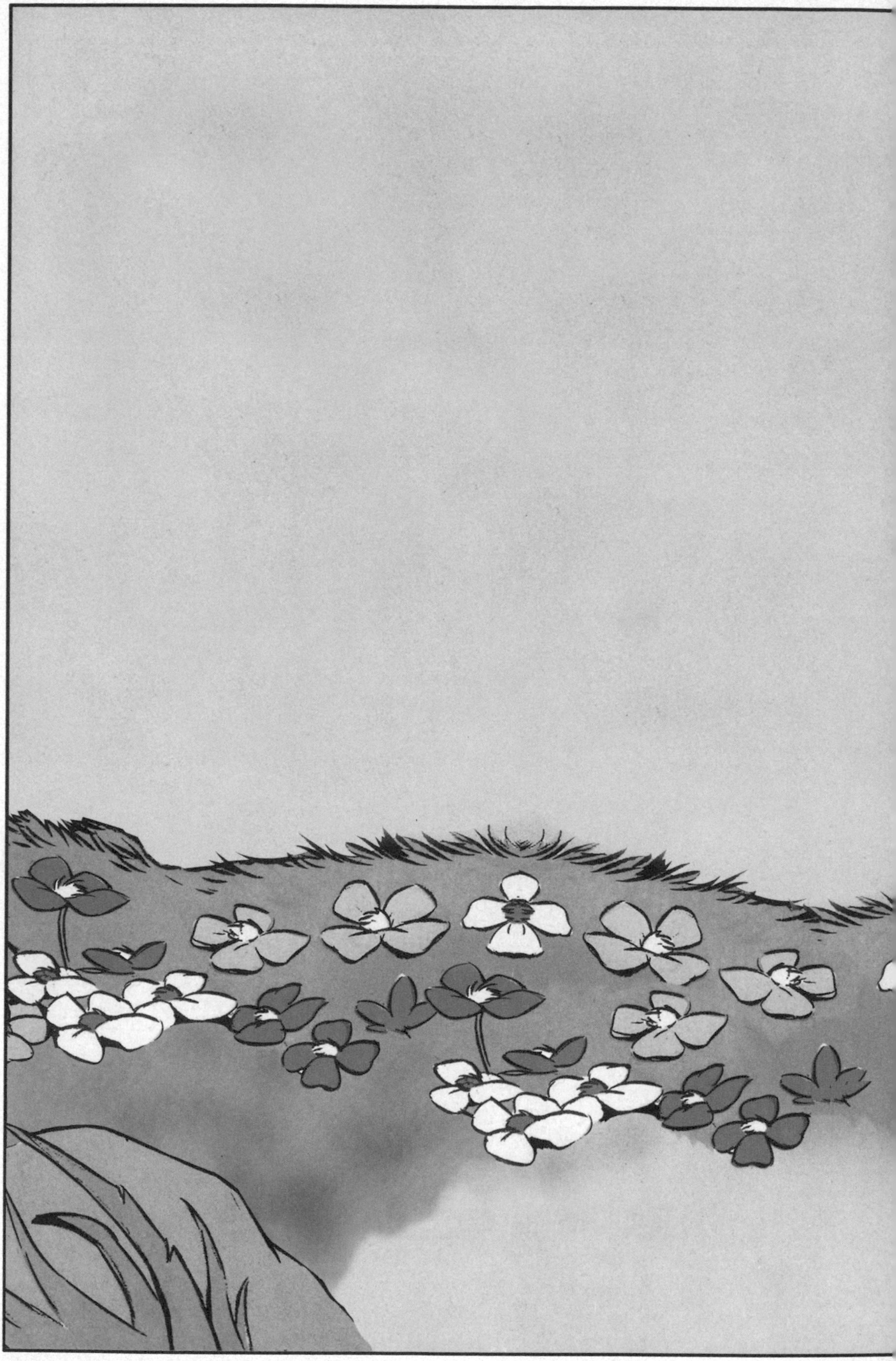

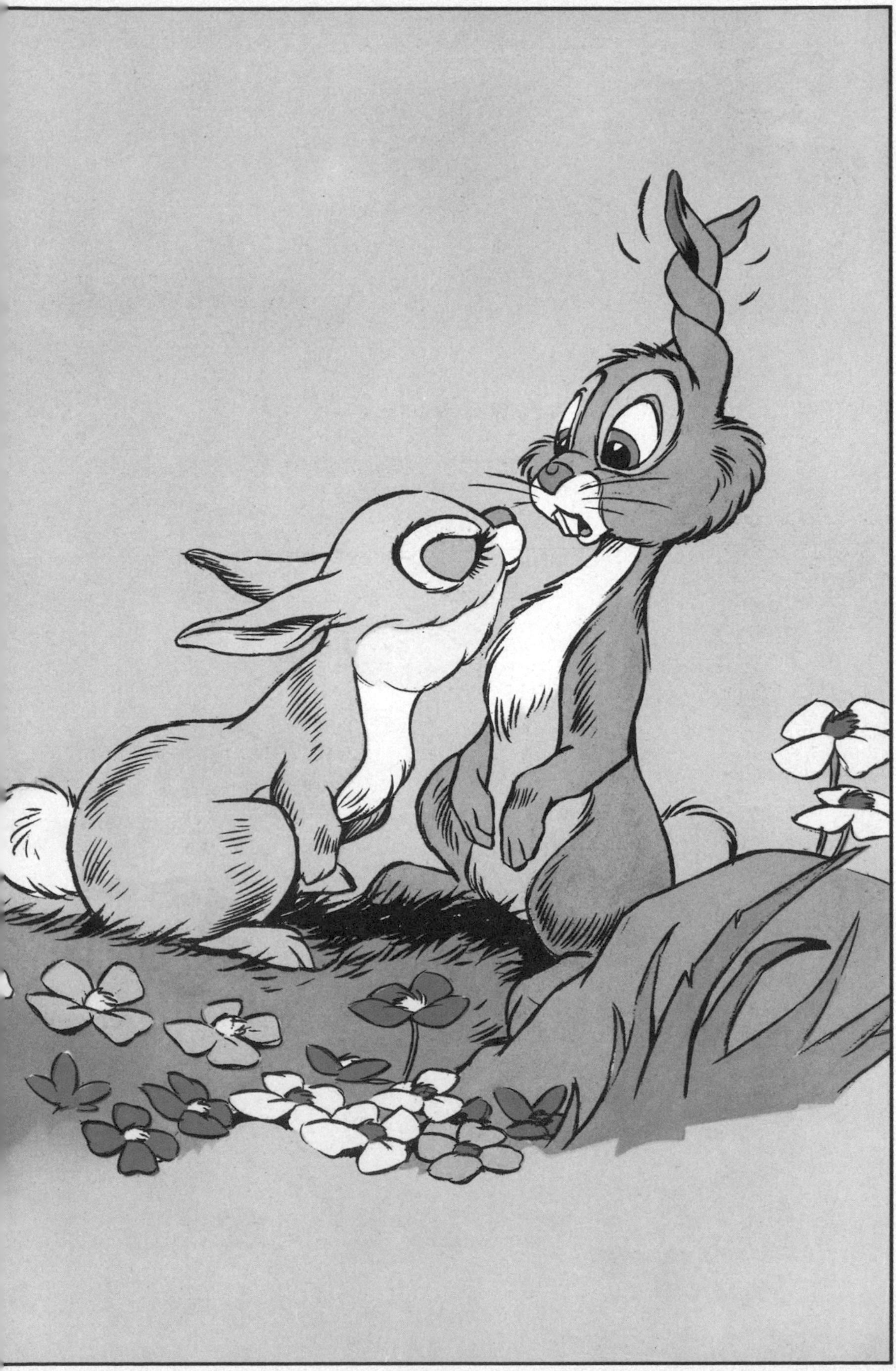

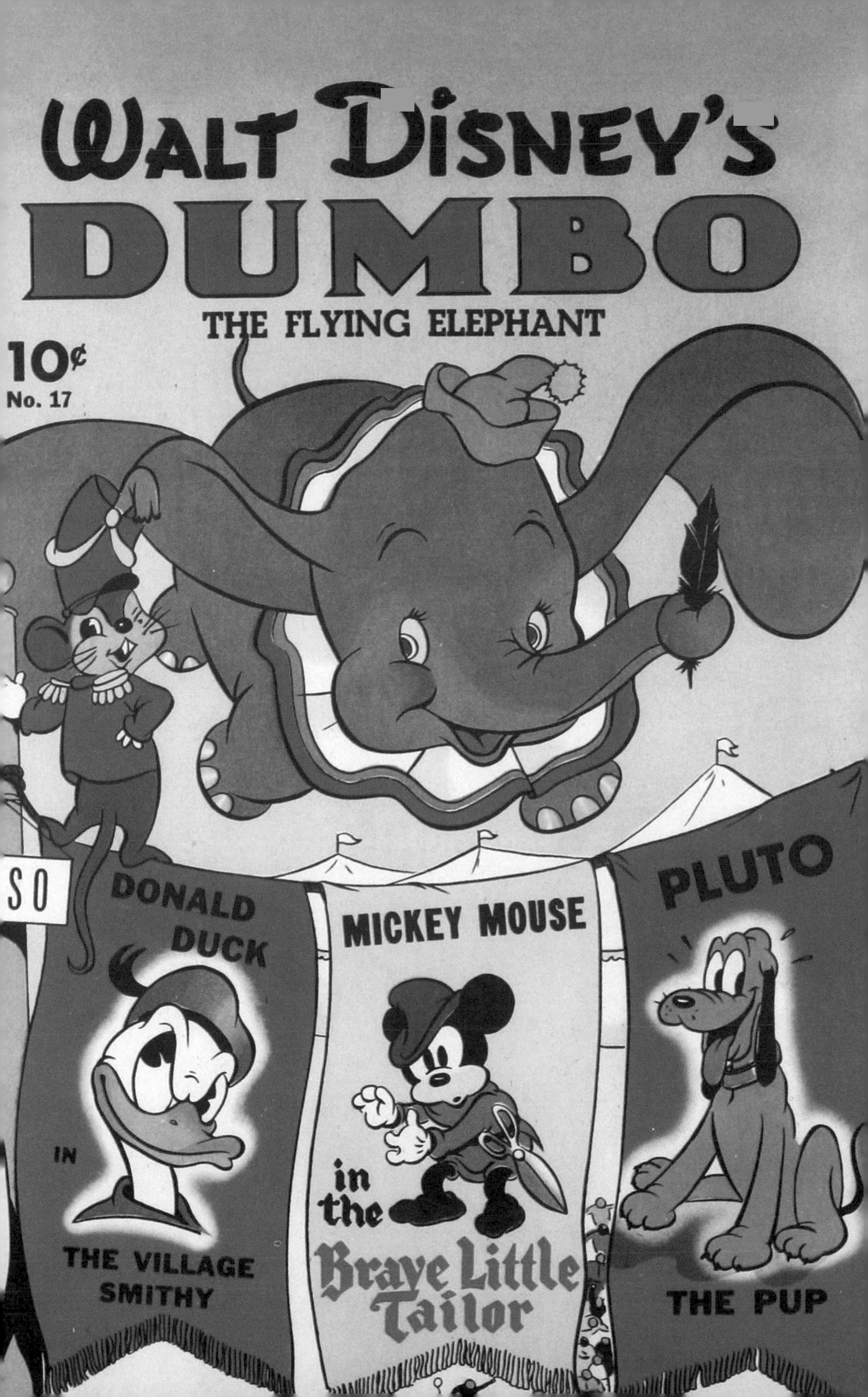

WALT DISNEY'S
DUMBO
THE FLYING ELEPHANT
10¢
No. 17
SO
DONALD DUCK
IN
THE VILLAGE SMITHY
MICKEY MOUSE
in the
Brave Little Tailor
PLUTO
THE PUP

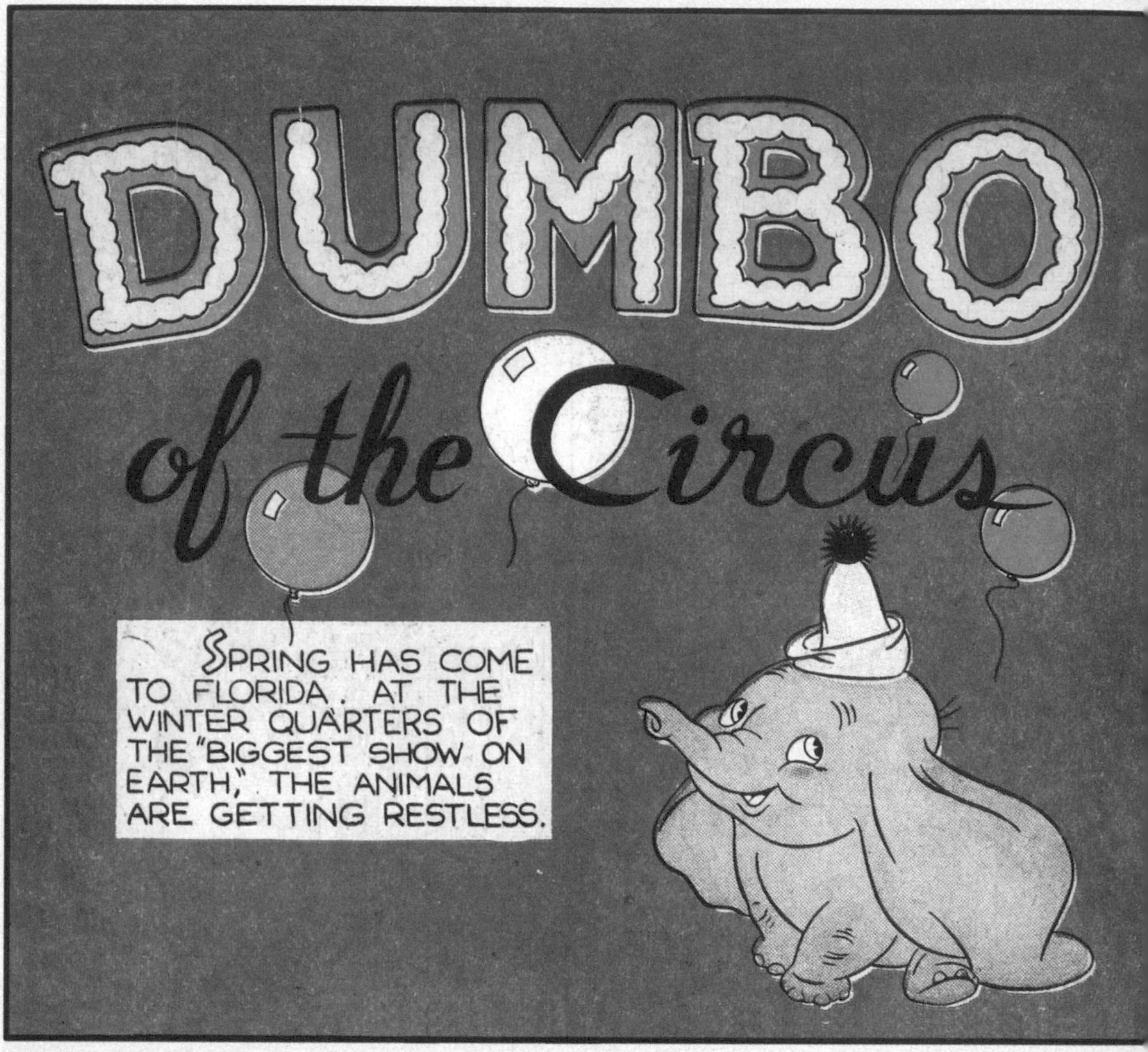
DUMBO
of the Circus
SPRING HAS COME TO FLORIDA. AT THE WINTER QUARTERS OF THE "BIGGEST SHOW ON EARTH," THE ANIMALS ARE GETTING RESTLESS.

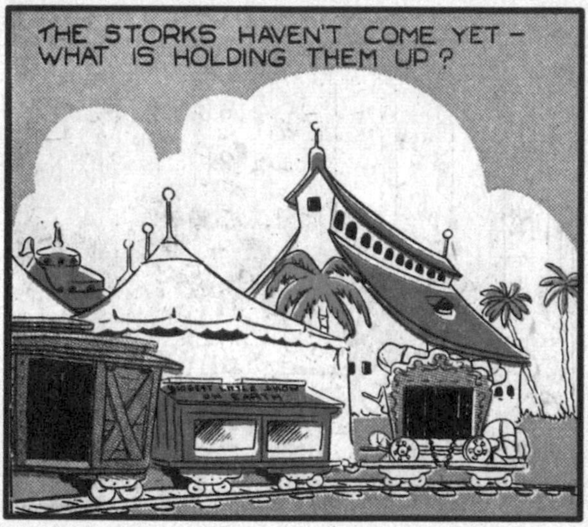
THE STORKS HAVEN'T COME YET – WHAT IS HOLDING THEM UP?

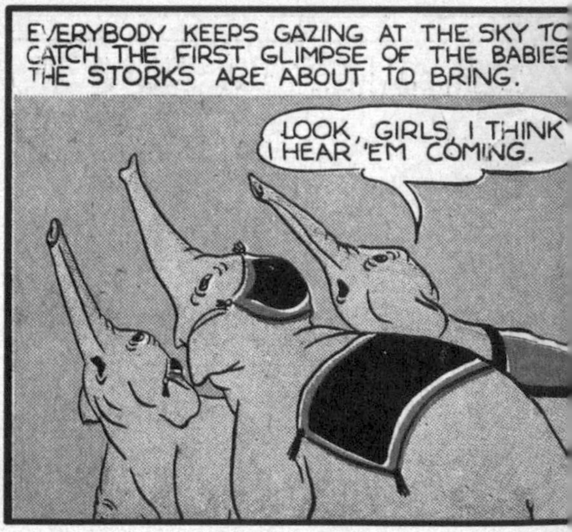
EVERYBODY KEEPS GAZING AT THE SKY TO CATCH THE FIRST GLIMPSE OF THE BABIES THE STORKS ARE ABOUT TO BRING.
LOOK, GIRLS, I THINK I HEAR 'EM COMING.

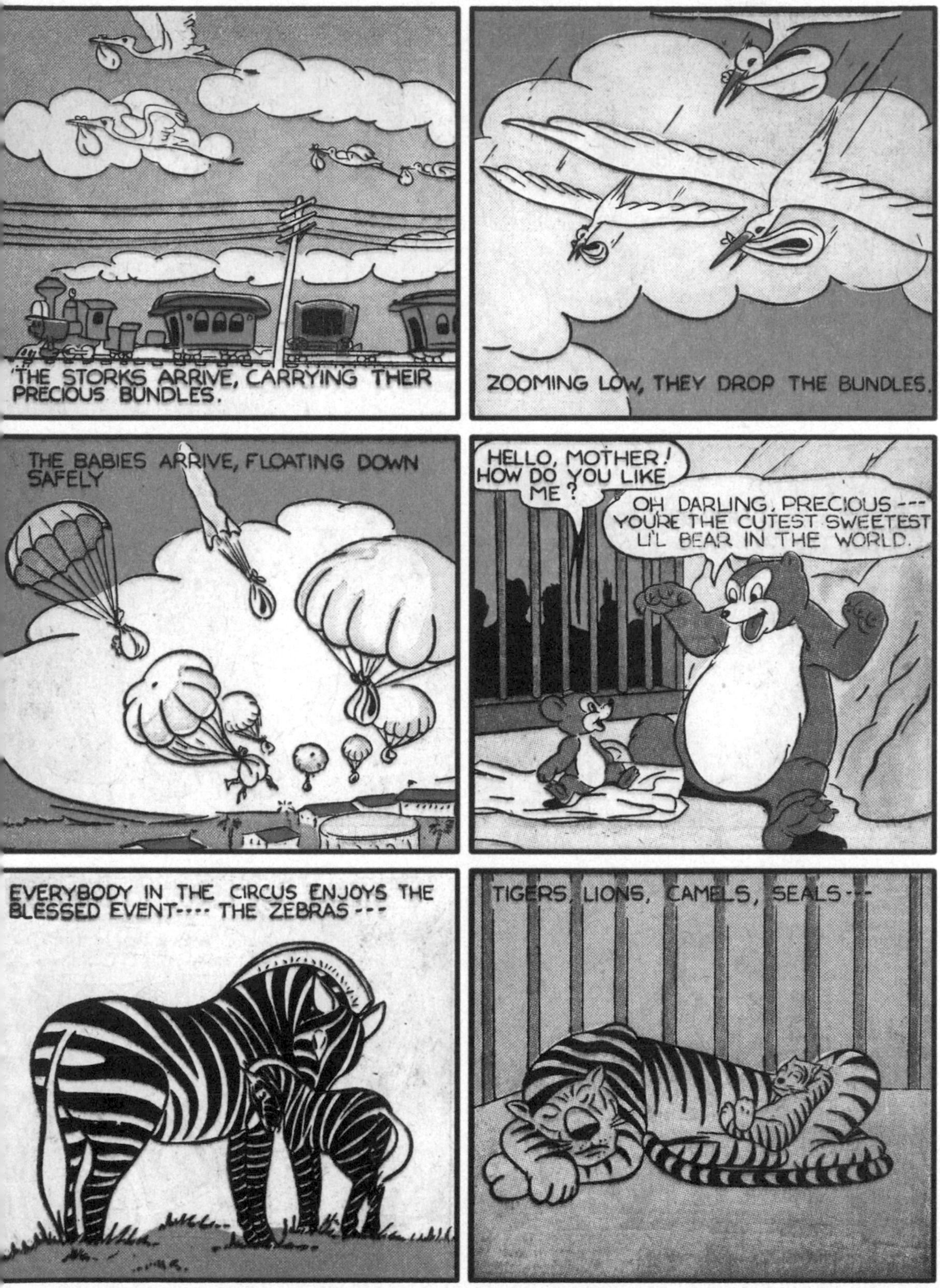
THE STORKS ARRIVE, CARRYING THEIR PRECIOUS BUNDLES.
ZOOMING LOW, THEY DROP THE BUNDLES.
THE BABIES ARRIVE, FLOATING DOWN SAFELY
HELLO, MOTHER! HOW DO YOU LIKE ME?
OH DARLING, PRECIOUS --- YOU'RE THE CUTEST SWEETEST LI'L BEAR IN THE WORLD.
EVERYBODY IN THE CIRCUS ENJOYS THE BLESSED EVENT---- THE ZEBRAS ---
TIGERS, LIONS, CAMELS, SEALS---

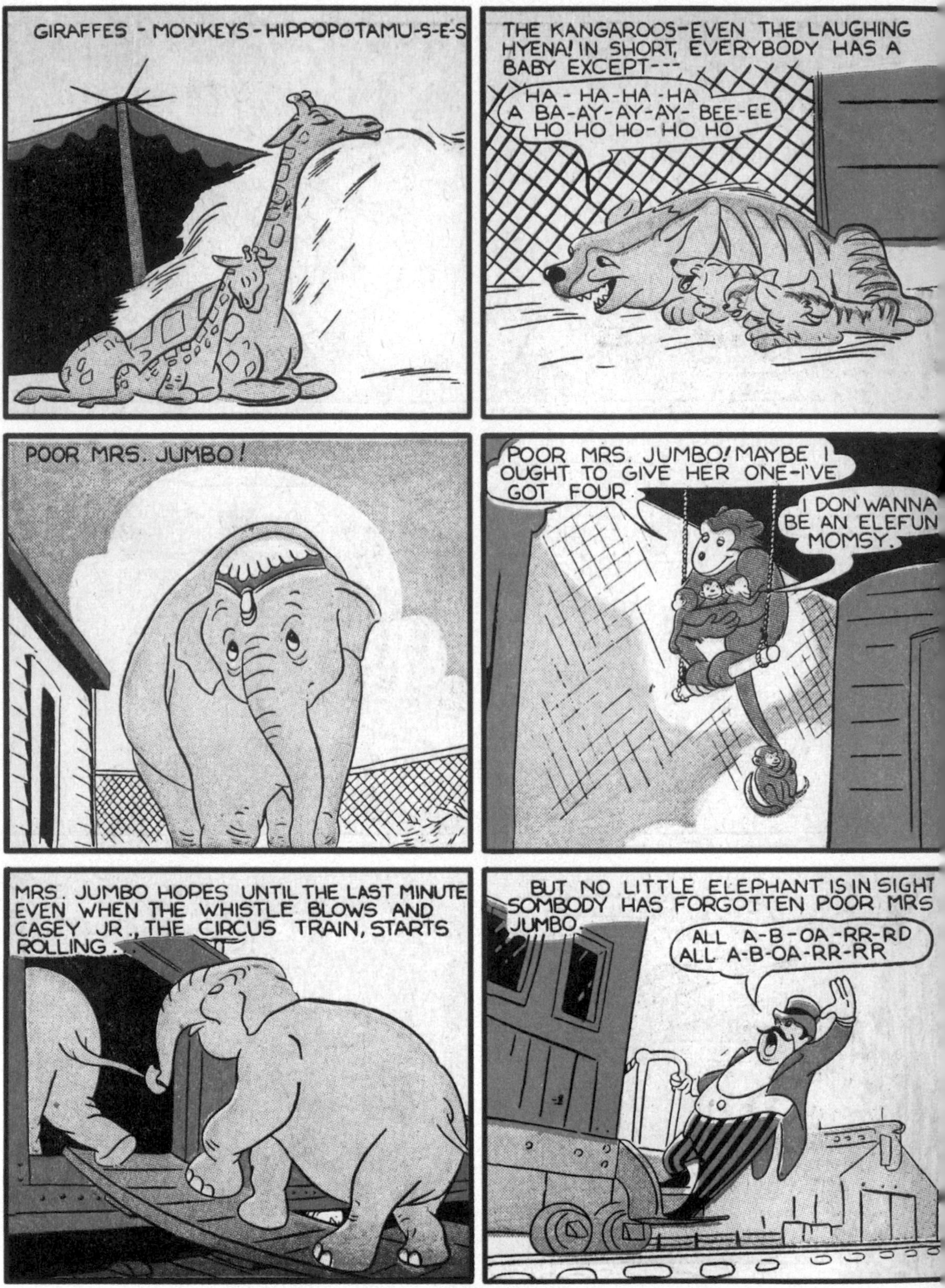
GIRAFFES - MONKEYS - HIPPOPOTAMU-S-E-S
THE KANGAROOS—EVEN THE LAUGHING HYENA! IN SHORT, EVERYBODY HAS A BABY EXCEPT---
HA - HA-HA -HA A BA-AY-AY-AY- BEE-EE HO HO HO- HO HO
POOR MRS. JUMBO!
POOR MRS. JUMBO! MAYBE I OUGHT TO GIVE HER ONE-I'VE GOT FOUR.
I DON'WANNA BE AN ELEFUN MOMSY.
MRS. JUMBO HOPES UNTIL THE LAST MINUTE EVEN WHEN THE WHISTLE BLOWS AND CASEY JR., THE CIRCUS TRAIN, STARTS ROLLING.
BUT NO LITTLE ELEPHANT IS IN SIGHT SOMBODY HAS FORGOTTEN POOR MRS JUMBO.
ALL A-B-OA-RR-RD ALL A-B-OA-RR-RR

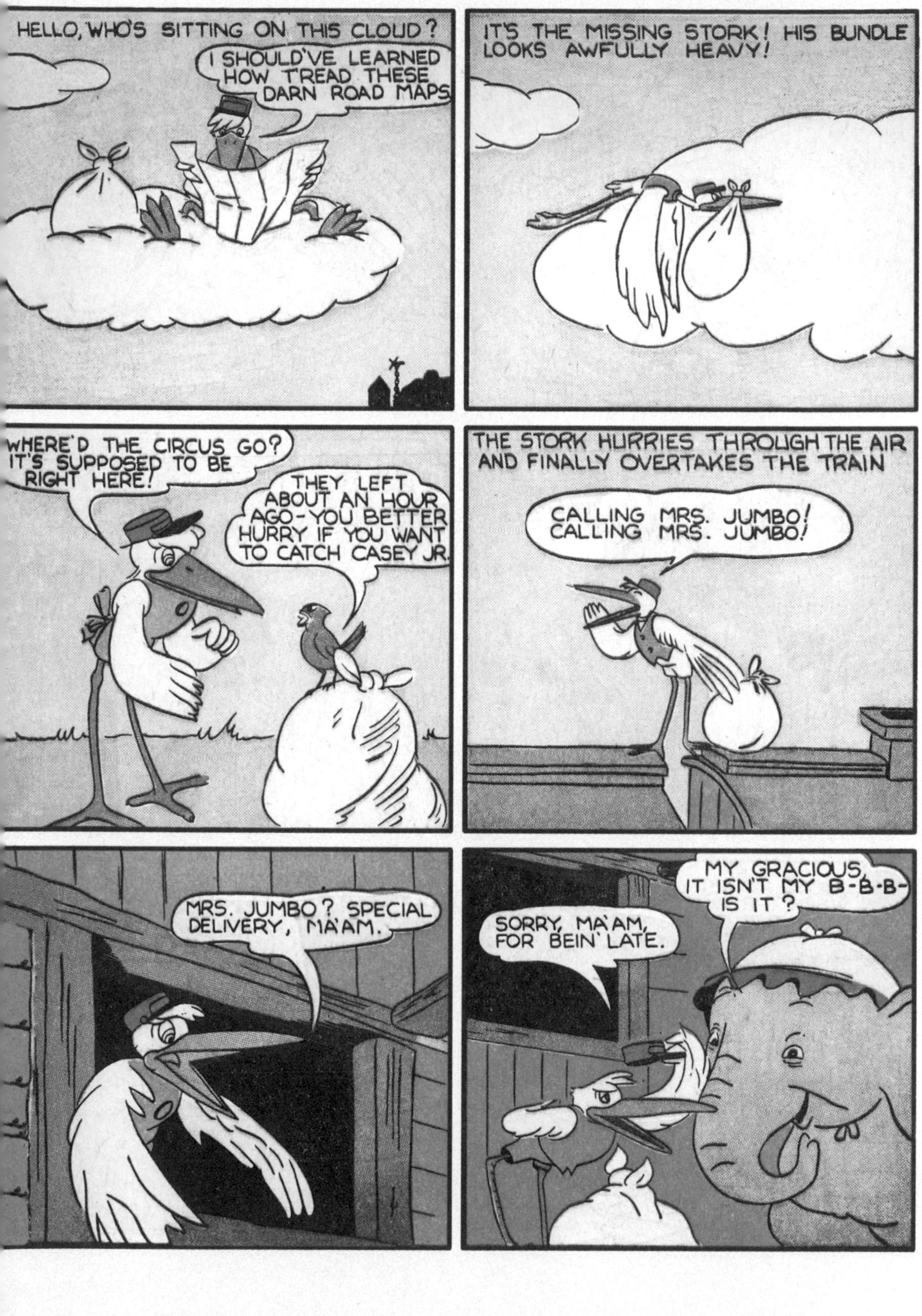
HELLO, WHO'S SITTING ON THIS CLOUD?
I SHOULD'VE LEARNED HOW T'READ THESE DARN ROAD MAPS
IT'S THE MISSING STORK! HIS BUNDLE LOOKS AWFULLY HEAVY!
WHERE'D THE CIRCUS GO? IT'S SUPPOSED TO BE RIGHT HERE!
THEY LEFT ABOUT AN HOUR AGO-YOU BETTER HURRY IF YOU WANT TO CATCH CASEY JR.
THE STORK HURRIES THROUGH THE AIR AND FINALLY OVERTAKES THE TRAIN
CALLING MRS. JUMBO! CALLING MRS. JUMBO!
MRS. JUMBO? SPECIAL DELIVERY, MA'AM.
SORRY, MA'AM, FOR BEIN' LATE.
MY GRACIOUS, IT ISN'T MY B-B-B- IS IT?

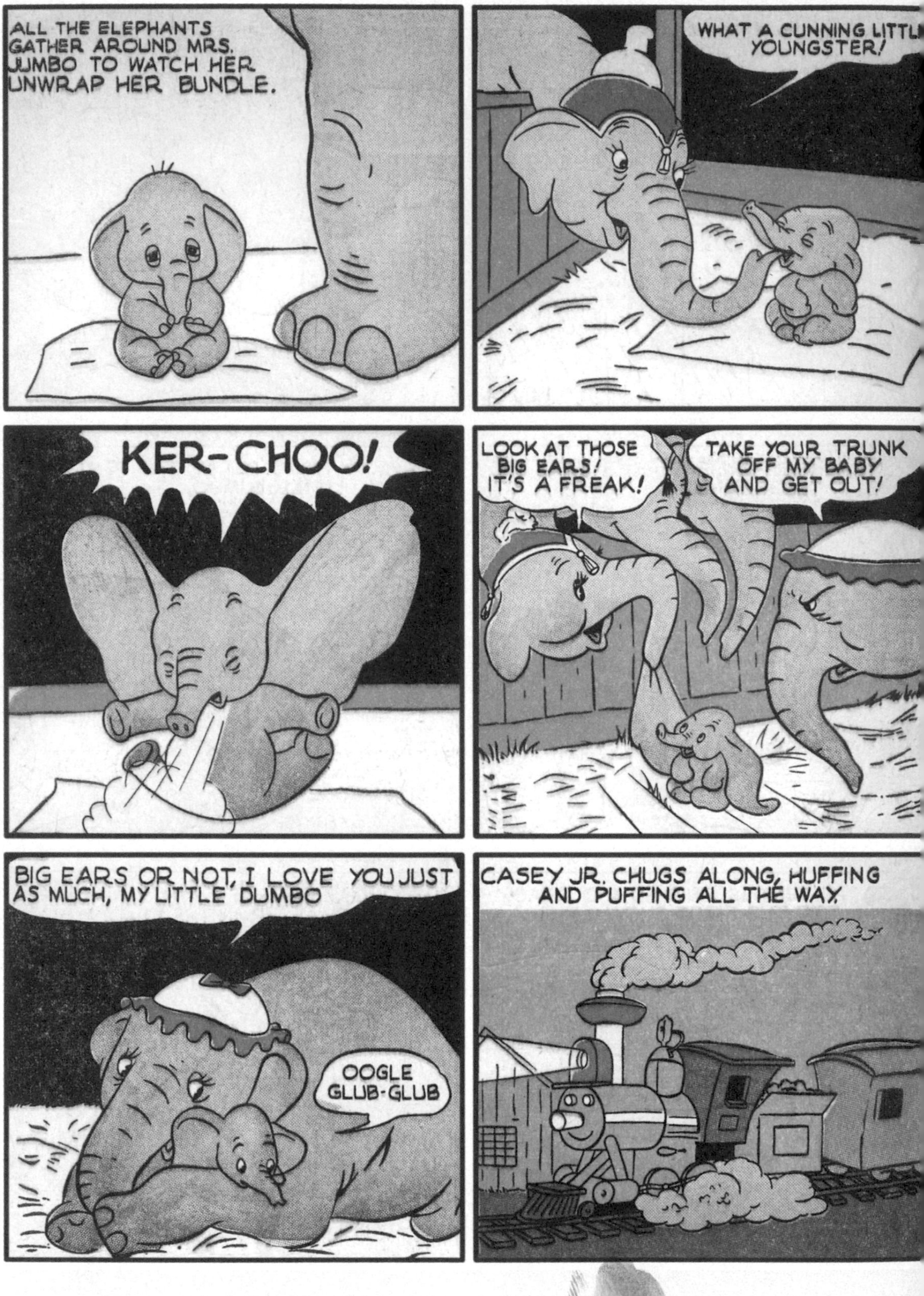
ALL THE ELEPHANTS GATHER AROUND MRS. JUMBO TO WATCH HER UNWRAP HER BUNDLE.
WHAT A CUNNING LITTL YOUNGSTER!
KER-CHOO!
LOOK AT THOSE BIG EARS! IT'S A FREAK!
TAKE YOUR TRUNK OFF MY BABY AND GET OUT!
BIG EARS OR NOT, I LOVE YOU JUST AS MUCH, MY LITTLE DUMBO
OOGLE GLUB-GLUB
CASEY JR. CHUGS ALONG, HUFFING AND PUFFING ALL THE WAY.

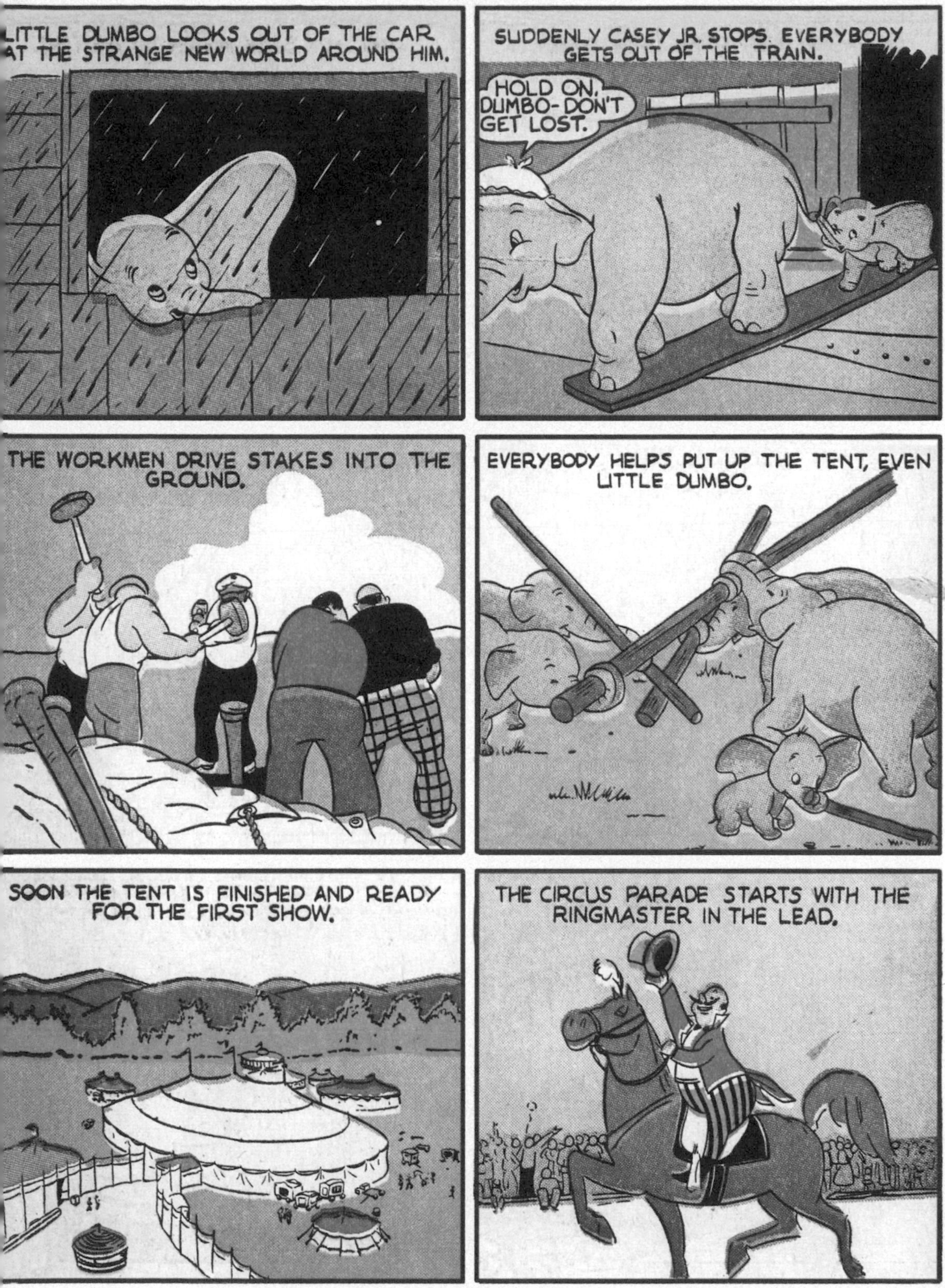
LITTLE DUMBO LOOKS OUT OF THE CAR AT THE STRANGE NEW WORLD AROUND HIM.
SUDDENLY CASEY JR. STOPS. EVERYBODY GETS OUT OF THE TRAIN.
HOLD ON, DUMBO- DON'T GET LOST.
THE WORKMEN DRIVE STAKES INTO THE GROUND.
EVERYBODY HELPS PUT UP THE TENT, EVEN LITTLE DUMBO.
SOON THE TENT IS FINISHED AND READY FOR THE FIRST SHOW.
THE CIRCUS PARADE STARTS WITH THE RINGMASTER IN THE LEAD.

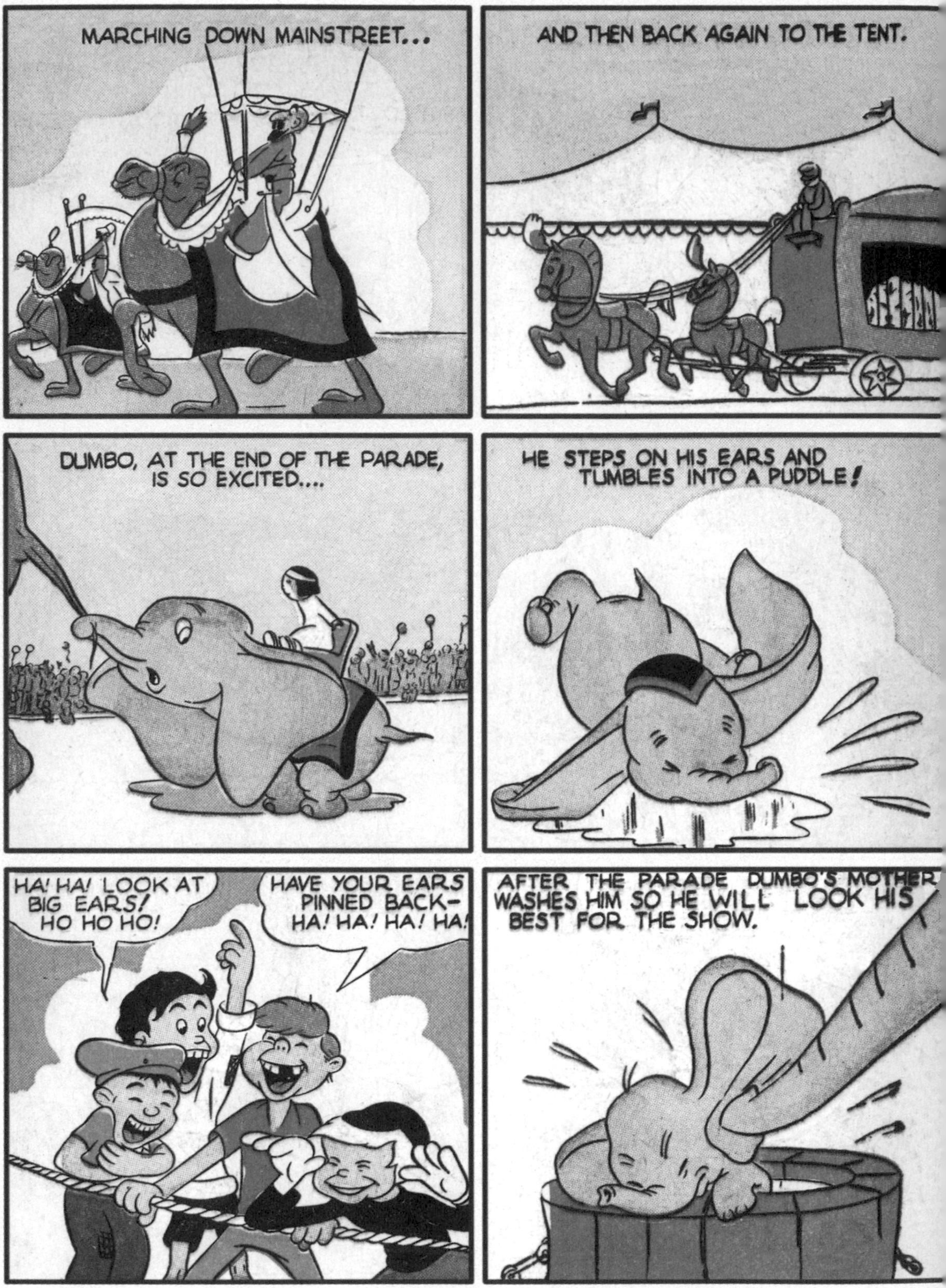

MARCHING DOWN MAINSTREET...
AND THEN BACK AGAIN TO THE TENT.
DUMBO, AT THE END OF THE PARADE, IS SO EXCITED....
HE STEPS ON HIS EARS AND TUMBLES INTO A PUDDLE!
HA! HA! LOOK AT BIG EARS! HO HO HO!
HAVE YOUR EARS PINNED BACK– HA! HA! HA! HA!
AFTER THE PARADE DUMBO'S MOTHER WASHES HIM SO HE WILL LOOK HIS BEST FOR THE SHOW.

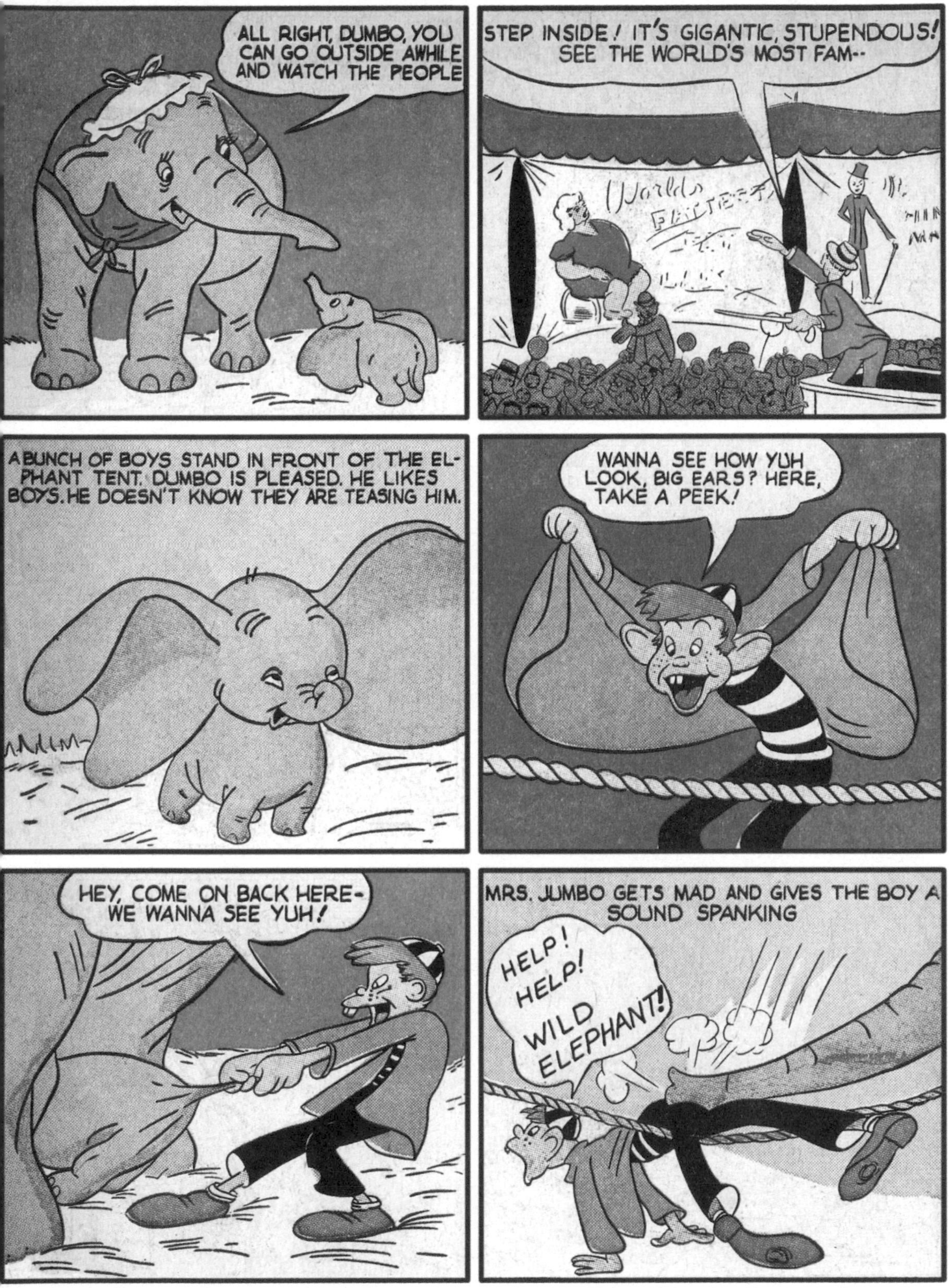
ALL RIGHT, DUMBO, YOU CAN GO OUTSIDE AWHILE AND WATCH THE PEOPLE
STEP INSIDE! IT'S GIGANTIC, STUPENDOUS! SEE THE WORLD'S MOST FAM--
A BUNCH OF BOYS STAND IN FRONT OF THE ELPHANT TENT. DUMBO IS PLEASED. HE LIKES BOYS. HE DOESN'T KNOW THEY ARE TEASING HIM.
WANNA SEE HOW YUH LOOK, BIG EARS? HERE, TAKE A PEEK!
HEY, COME ON BACK HERE- WE WANNA SEE YUH!
MRS. JUMBO GETS MAD AND GIVES THE BOY A SOUND SPANKING
HELP! HELP! WILD ELEPHANT!

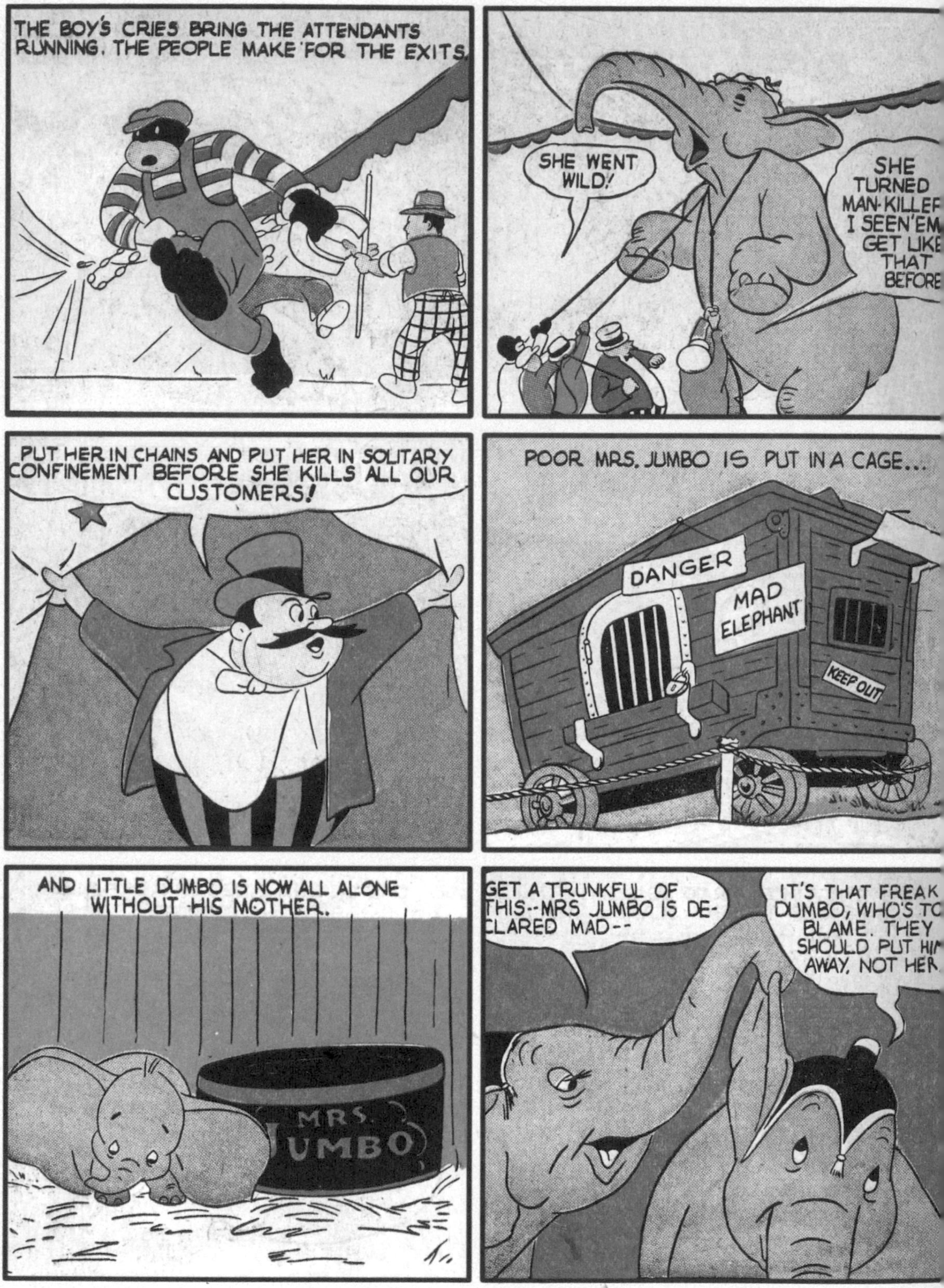
THE BOY'S CRIES BRING THE ATTENDANTS RUNNING. THE PEOPLE MAKE FOR THE EXITS.
SHE WENT WILD!
SHE TURNED MAN-KILLER I SEEN'EM GET LIKE THAT BEFORE
PUT HER IN CHAINS AND PUT HER IN SOLITARY CONFINEMENT BEFORE SHE KILLS ALL OUR CUSTOMERS!
POOR MRS. JUMBO IS PUT IN A CAGE...
DANGER
MAD ELEPHANT
KEEP OUT
AND LITTLE DUMBO IS NOW ALL ALONE WITHOUT HIS MOTHER.
MRS. JUMBO
GET A TRUNKFUL OF THIS--MRS JUMBO IS DECLARED MAD--
IT'S THAT FREAK DUMBO, WHO'S TO BLAME. THEY SHOULD PUT HIM AWAY, NOT HER.

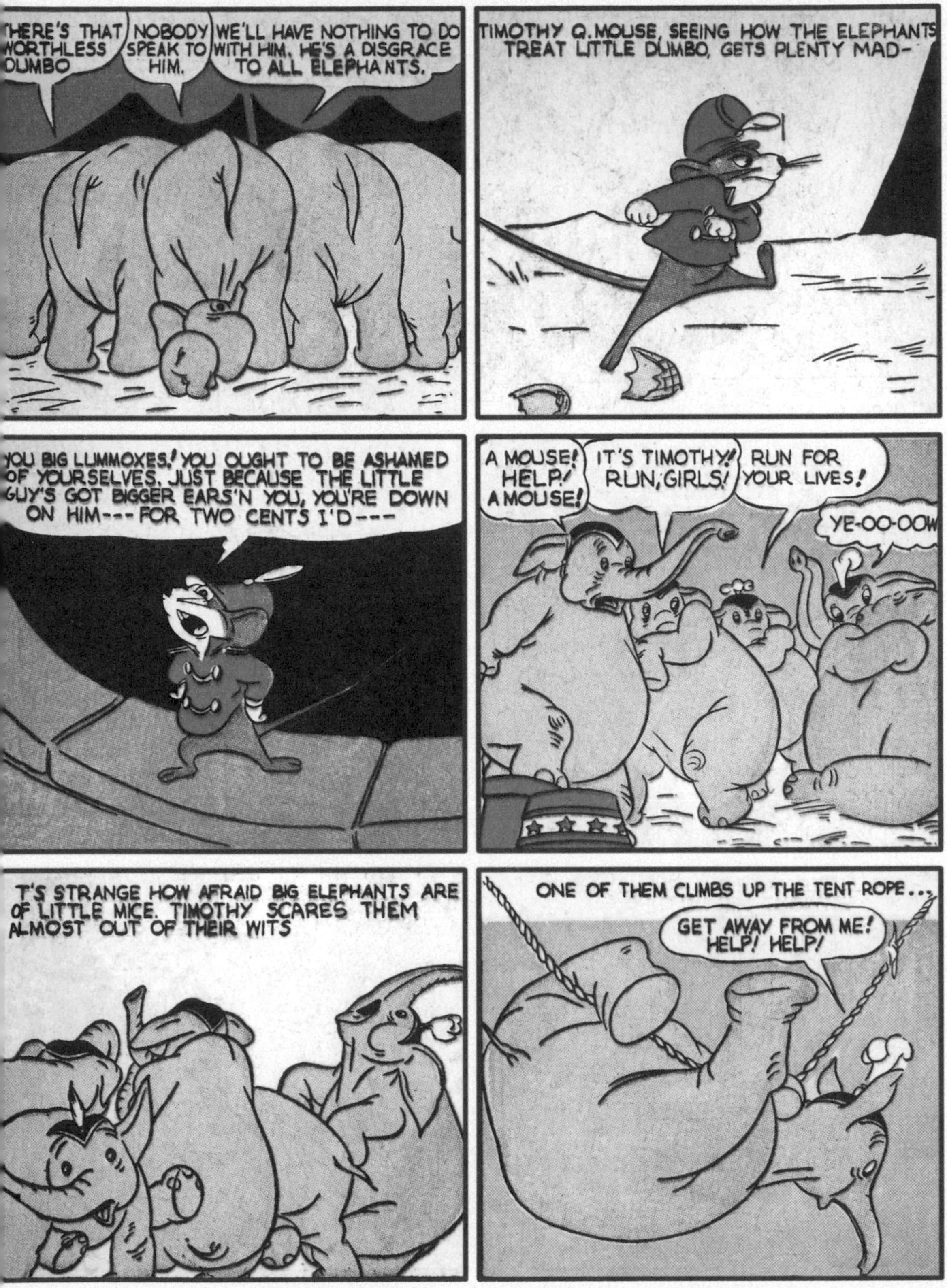
THERE'S THAT WORTHLESS DUMBO
NOBODY SPEAK TO HIM.
WE'LL HAVE NOTHING TO DO WITH HIM. HE'S A DISGRACE TO ALL ELEPHANTS.
TIMOTHY Q. MOUSE, SEEING HOW THE ELEPHANTS TREAT LITTLE DUMBO, GETS PLENTY MAD-
YOU BIG LUMMOXES! YOU OUGHT TO BE ASHAMED OF YOURSELVES. JUST BECAUSE THE LITTLE GUY'S GOT BIGGER EARS'N YOU, YOU'RE DOWN ON HIM---FOR TWO CENTS I'D---
A MOUSE! HELP! A MOUSE!
IT'S TIMOTHY! RUN, GIRLS!
RUN FOR YOUR LIVES!
YE-OO-OOW
IT'S STRANGE HOW AFRAID BIG ELEPHANTS ARE OF LITTLE MICE. TIMOTHY SCARES THEM ALMOST OUT OF THEIR WITS
ONE OF THEM CLIMBS UP THE TENT ROPE...
GET AWAY FROM ME! HELP! HELP!

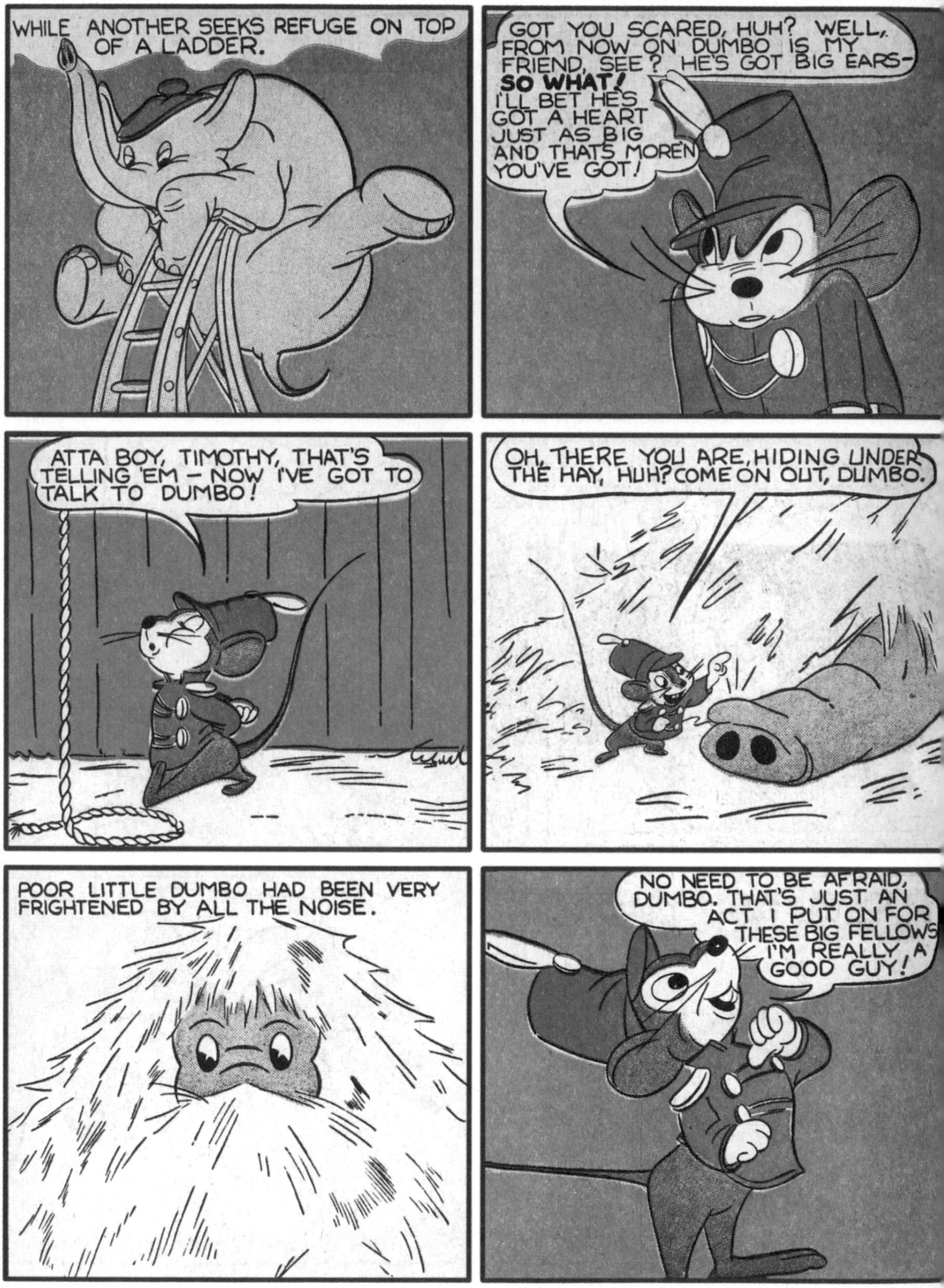
WHILE ANOTHER SEEKS REFUGE ON TOP OF A LADDER.
GOT YOU SCARED, HUH? WELL, FROM NOW ON DUMBO IS MY FRIEND, SEE? HE'S GOT BIG EARS- SO WHAT! I'LL BET HE'S GOT A HEART JUST AS BIG AND THAT'S MOREN YOU'VE GOT!
ATTA BOY, TIMOTHY, THAT'S TELLING 'EM – NOW I'VE GOT TO TALK TO DUMBO!
OH, THERE YOU ARE, HIDING UNDER THE HAY, HUH? COME ON OUT, DUMBO.
POOR LITTLE DUMBO HAD BEEN VERY FRIGHTENED BY ALL THE NOISE.
NO NEED TO BE AFRAID, DUMBO. THAT'S JUST AN ACT I PUT ON FOR THESE BIG FELLOWS I'M REALLY A GOOD GUY!

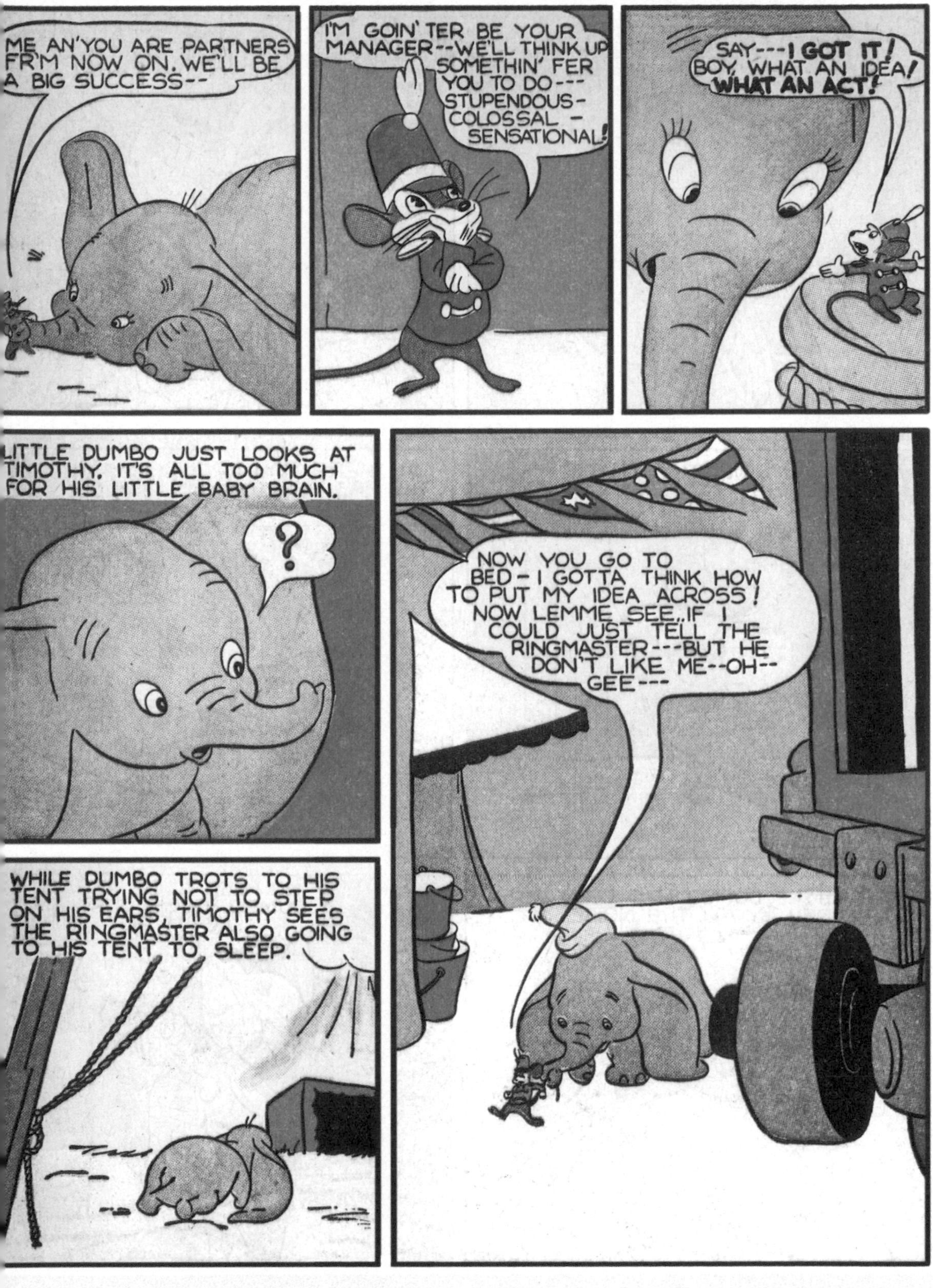
ME AN'YOU ARE PARTNERS FR'M NOW ON. WE'LL BE A BIG SUCCESS--
I'M GOIN' TER BE YOUR MANAGER--WE'LL THINK UP SOMETHIN' FER YOU TO DO--- STUPENDOUS- COLOSSAL - SENSATIONAL!
SAY---I GOT IT! BOY, WHAT AN IDEA! WHAT AN ACT!
LITTLE DUMBO JUST LOOKS AT TIMOTHY. IT'S ALL TOO MUCH FOR HIS LITTLE BABY BRAIN.
?
WHILE DUMBO TROTS TO HIS TENT TRYING NOT TO STEP ON HIS EARS, TIMOTHY SEES THE RINGMASTER ALSO GOING TO HIS TENT TO SLEEP.
NOW YOU GO TO BED - I GOTTA THINK HOW TO PUT MY IDEA ACROSS! NOW LEMME SEE..IF I COULD JUST TELL THE RINGMASTER---BUT HE DON'T LIKE ME--OH-- GEE---

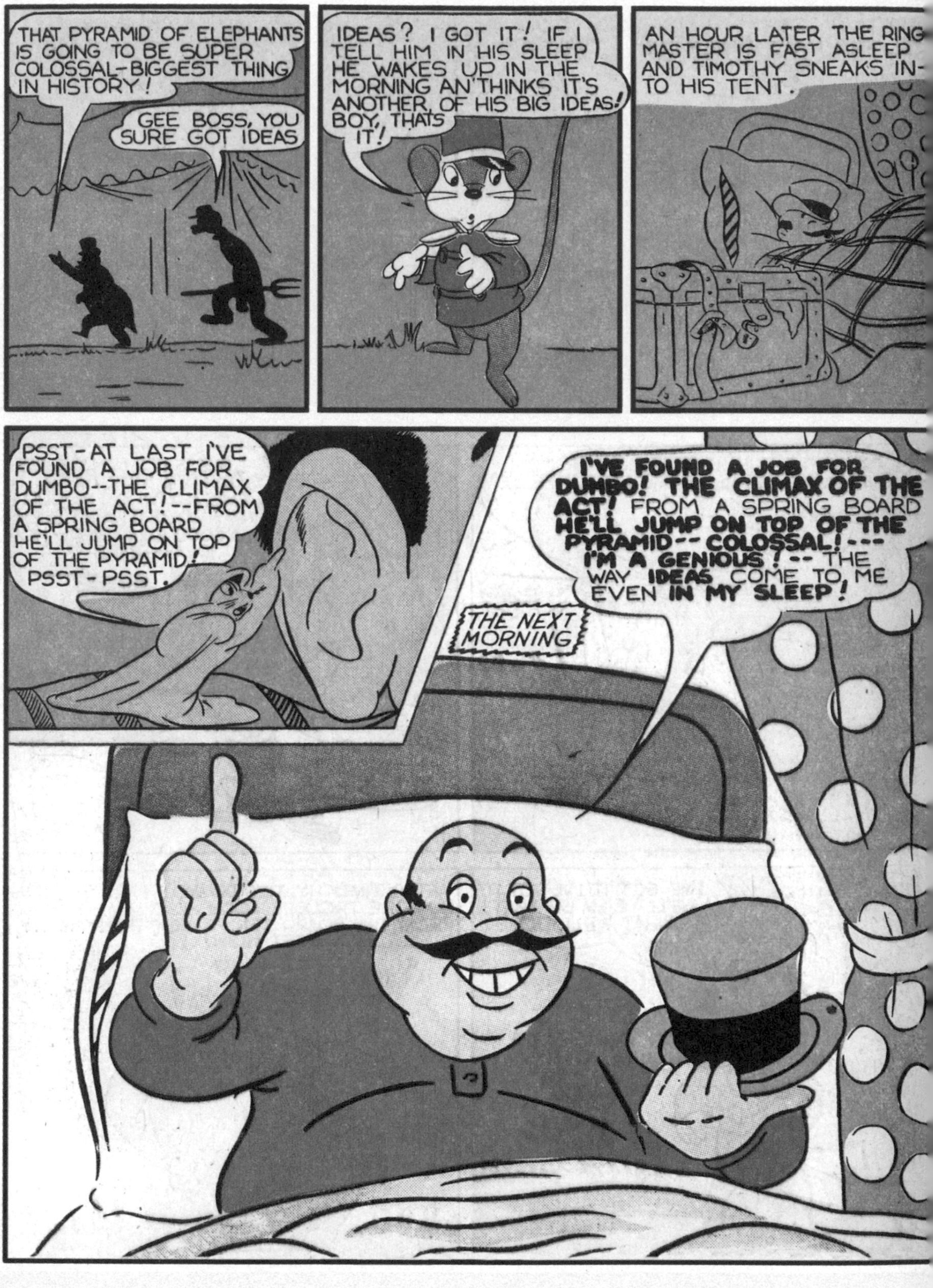
THAT PYRAMID OF ELEPHANTS IS GOING TO BE SUPER COLOSSAL-BIGGEST THING IN HISTORY!
GEE BOSS, YOU SURE GOT IDEAS
IDEAS? I GOT IT! IF I TELL HIM IN HIS SLEEP HE WAKES UP IN THE MORNING AN'THINKS IT'S ANOTHER OF HIS BIG IDEAS! BOY, THATS IT!
AN HOUR LATER THE RING MASTER IS FAST ASLEEP AND TIMOTHY SNEAKS INTO HIS TENT.
PSST-AT LAST I'VE FOUND A JOB FOR DUMBO--THE CLIMAX OF THE ACT!--FROM A SPRING BOARD HE'LL JUMP ON TOP OF THE PYRAMID! PSST-PSST.
THE NEXT MORNING
I'VE FOUND A JOB FOR DUMBO! THE CLIMAX OF THE ACT! FROM A SPRING BOARD HE'LL JUMP ON TOP OF THE PYRAMID--COLOSSAL!--- I'M A GENIOUS!-- THE WAY IDEAS COME TO ME EVEN IN MY SLEEP!

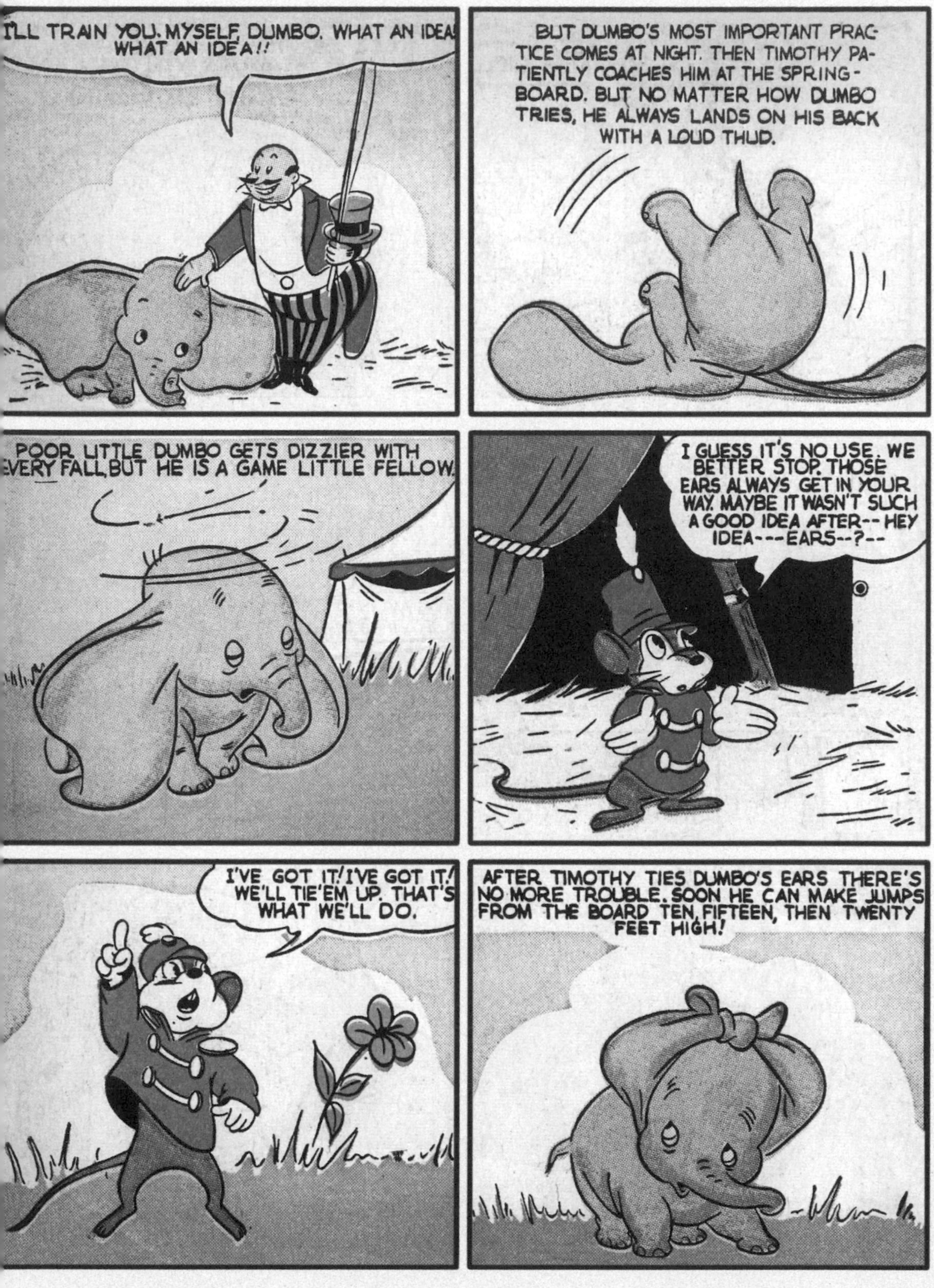
I'LL TRAIN YOU. MYSELF, DUMBO. WHAT AN IDEA! WHAT AN IDEA!!
BUT DUMBO'S MOST IMPORTANT PRACTICE COMES AT NIGHT. THEN TIMOTHY PATIENTLY COACHES HIM AT THE SPRING-BOARD. BUT NO MATTER HOW DUMBO TRIES, HE ALWAYS LANDS ON HIS BACK WITH A LOUD THUD.
POOR LITTLE DUMBO GETS DIZZIER WITH EVERY FALL, BUT HE IS A GAME LITTLE FELLOW.
I GUESS IT'S NO USE. WE BETTER STOP. THOSE EARS ALWAYS GET IN YOUR WAY. MAYBE IT WASN'T SUCH A GOOD IDEA AFTER-- HEY IDEA---EARS--?--
I'VE GOT IT! I'VE GOT IT! WE'LL TIE 'EM UP. THAT'S WHAT WE'LL DO.
AFTER TIMOTHY TIES DUMBO'S EARS THERE'S NO MORE TROUBLE. SOON HE CAN MAKE JUMPS FROM THE BOARD TEN, FIFTEEN, THEN TWENTY FEET HIGH!

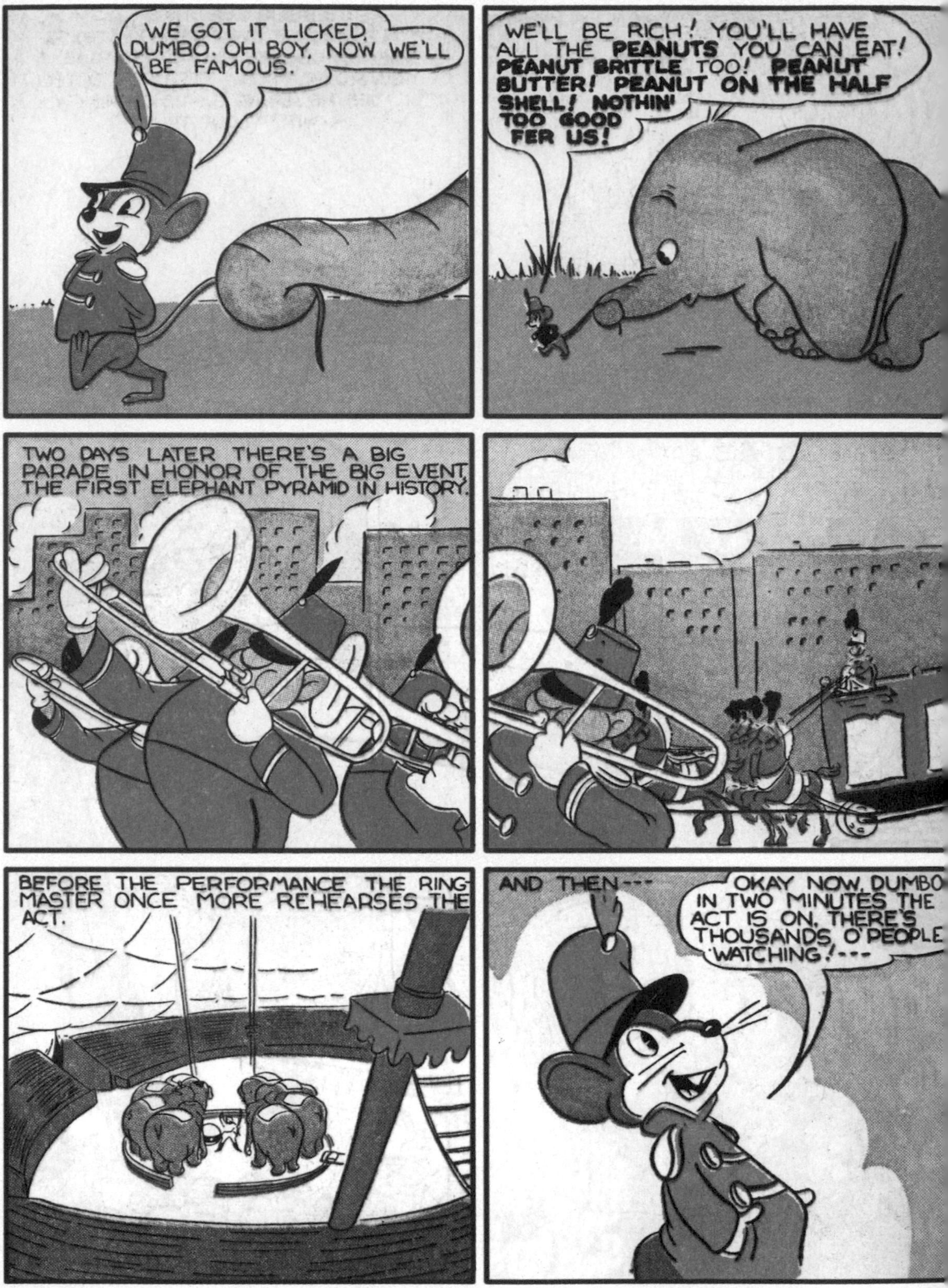
WE GOT IT LICKED, DUMBO. OH BOY, NOW WE'LL BE FAMOUS.
WE'LL BE RICH! YOU'LL HAVE ALL THE PEANUTS YOU CAN EAT! PEANUT BRITTLE TOO! PEANUT BUTTER! PEANUT ON THE HALF SHELL! NOTHIN' TOO GOOD FER US!
TWO DAYS LATER THERE'S A BIG PARADE IN HONOR OF THE BIG EVENT, THE FIRST ELEPHANT PYRAMID IN HISTORY.
BEFORE THE PERFORMANCE THE RING-MASTER ONCE MORE REHEARSES THE ACT.
AND THEN---
OKAY NOW, DUMBO IN TWO MINUTES THE ACT IS ON. THERE'S THOUSANDS O'PEOPLE WATCHING!---

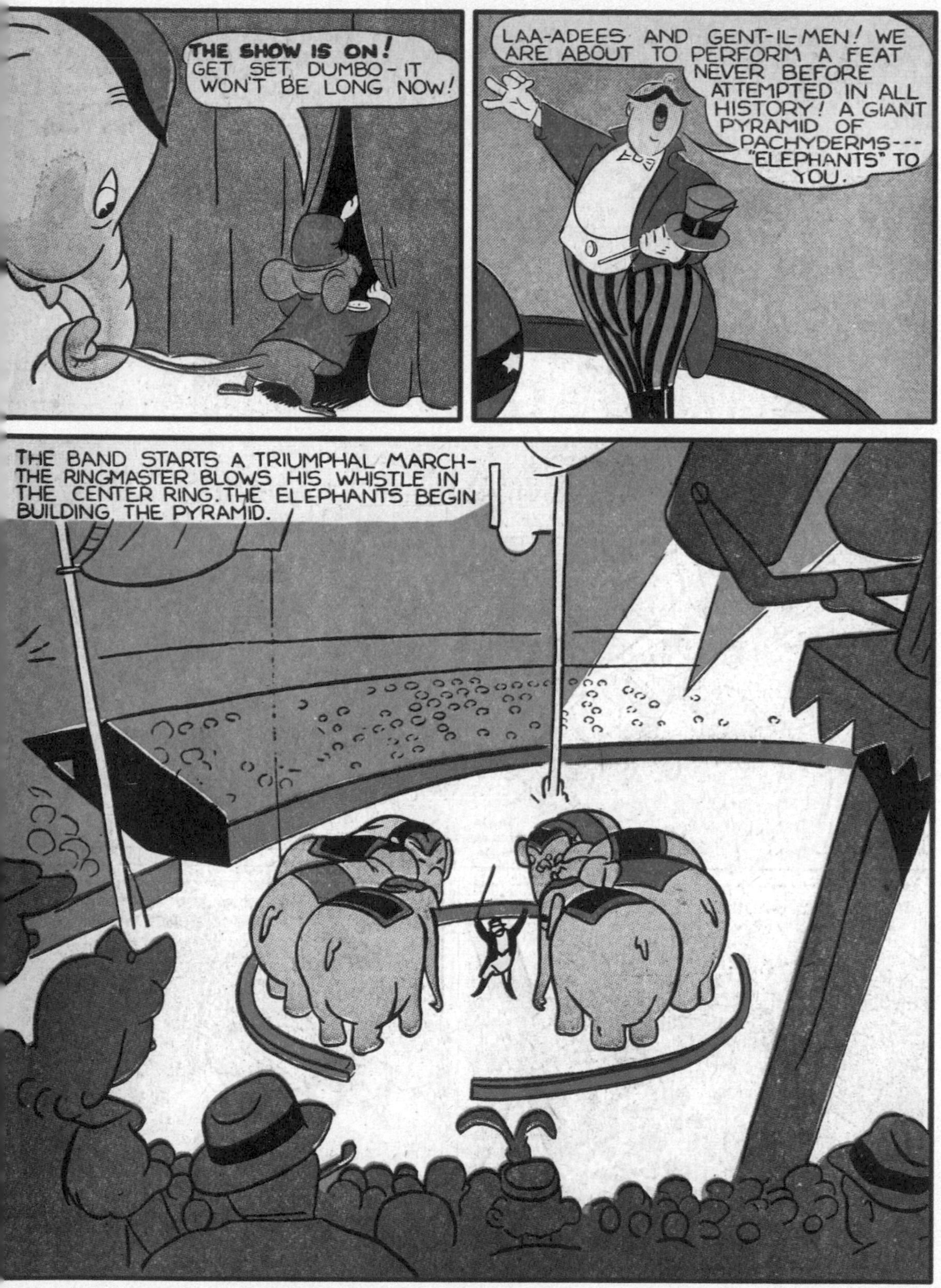
THE SHOW IS ON! GET SET, DUMBO- IT WON'T BE LONG NOW!
LAA-ADEES AND GENT-IL-MEN! WE ARE ABOUT TO PERFORM A FEAT NEVER BEFORE ATTEMPTED IN ALL HISTORY! A GIANT PYRAMID OF PACHYDERMS--- "ELEPHANTS" TO YOU.
THE BAND STARTS A TRIUMPHAL MARCH- THE RINGMASTER BLOWS HIS WHISTLE IN THE CENTER RING. THE ELEPHANTS BEGIN BUILDING THE PYRAMID.

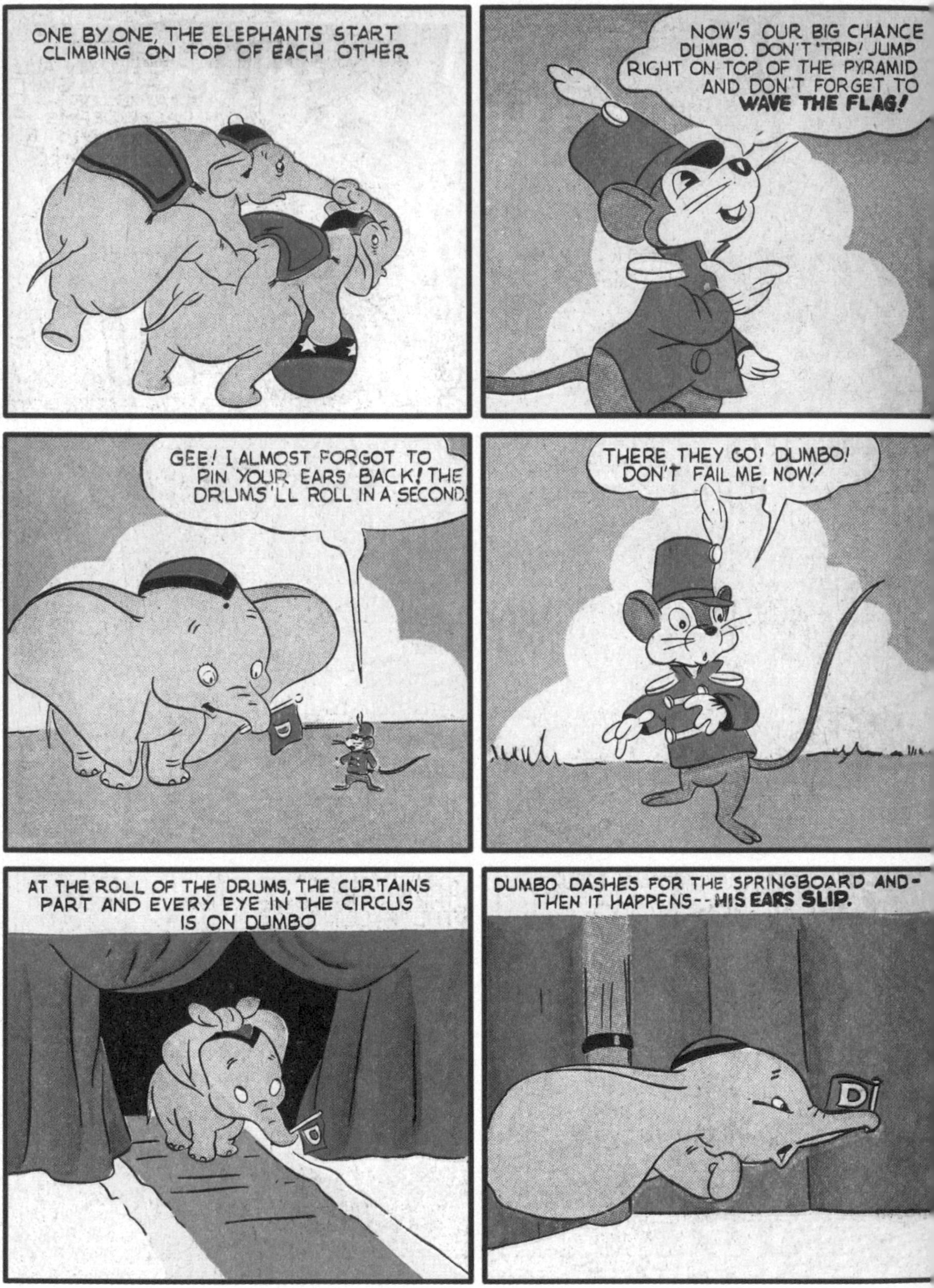
ONE BY ONE, THE ELEPHANTS START CLIMBING ON TOP OF EACH OTHER
NOW'S OUR BIG CHANCE DUMBO. DON'T TRIP! JUMP RIGHT ON TOP OF THE PYRAMID AND DON'T FORGET TO **WAVE THE FLAG!**
GEE! I ALMOST FORGOT TO PIN YOUR EARS BACK! THE DRUMS'LL ROLL IN A SECOND!
D
THERE THEY GO! DUMBO! DON'T FAIL ME, NOW!
AT THE ROLL OF THE DRUMS, THE CURTAINS PART AND EVERY EYE IN THE CIRCUS IS ON DUMBO
D
DUMBO DASHES FOR THE SPRINGBOARD AND-THEN IT HAPPENS--**HIS EARS SLIP.**
D

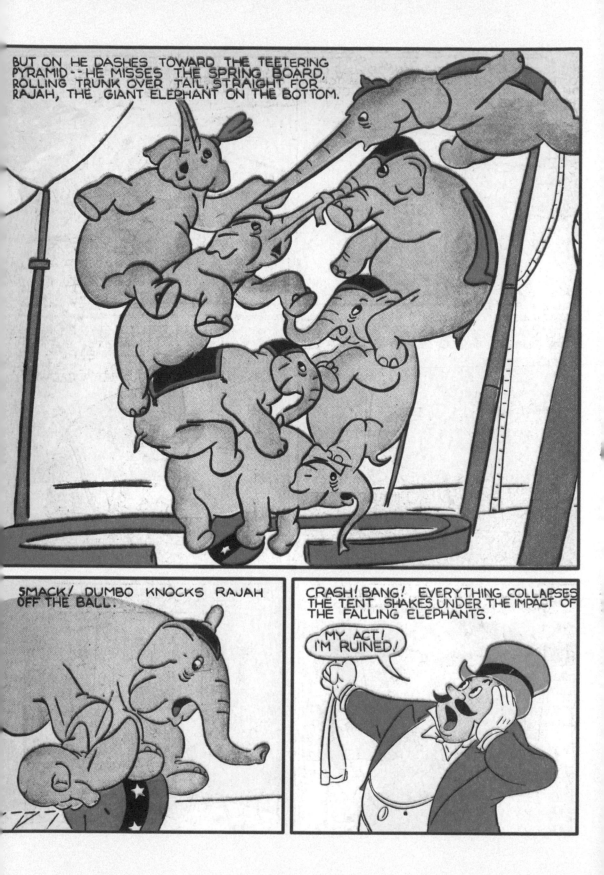

BUT ON HE DASHES TOWARD THE TEETERING PYRAMID--HE MISSES THE SPRING BOARD, ROLLING TRUNK OVER TAIL, STRAIGHT FOR RAJAH, THE GIANT ELEPHANT ON THE BOTTOM.

SMACK! DUMBO KNOCKS RAJAH OFF THE BALL.

CRASH! BANG! EVERYTHING COLLAPSES THE TENT SHAKES UNDER THE IMPACT OF THE FALLING ELEPHANTS.

MY ACT! I'M RUINED!

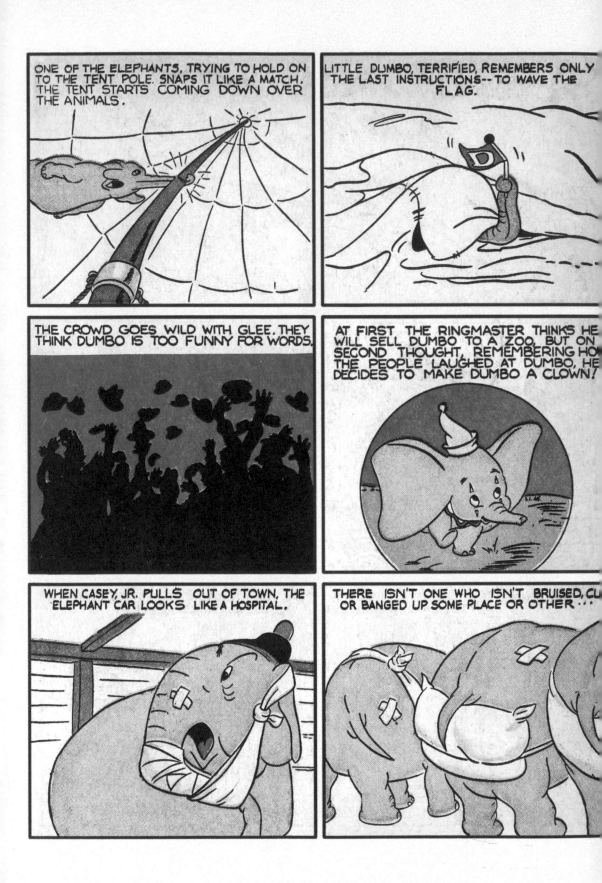

ONE OF THE ELEPHANTS, TRYING TO HOLD ON TO THE TENT POLE, SNAPS IT LIKE A MATCH. THE TENT STARTS COMING DOWN OVER THE ANIMALS.

LITTLE DUMBO, TERRIFIED, REMEMBERS ONLY THE LAST INSTRUCTIONS-- TO WAVE THE FLAG.

THE CROWD GOES WILD WITH GLEE. THEY THINK DUMBO IS TOO FUNNY FOR WORDS.

AT FIRST THE RINGMASTER THINKS HE WILL SELL DUMBO TO A ZOO, BUT ON SECOND THOUGHT, REMEMBERING HO THE PEOPLE LAUGHED AT DUMBO, HE DECIDES TO MAKE DUMBO A CLOWN!

WHEN CASEY, JR. PULLS OUT OF TOWN, THE ELEPHANT CAR LOOKS LIKE A HOSPITAL.

THERE ISN'T ONE WHO ISN'T BRUISED, CU OR BANGED UP SOME PLACE OR OTHER···

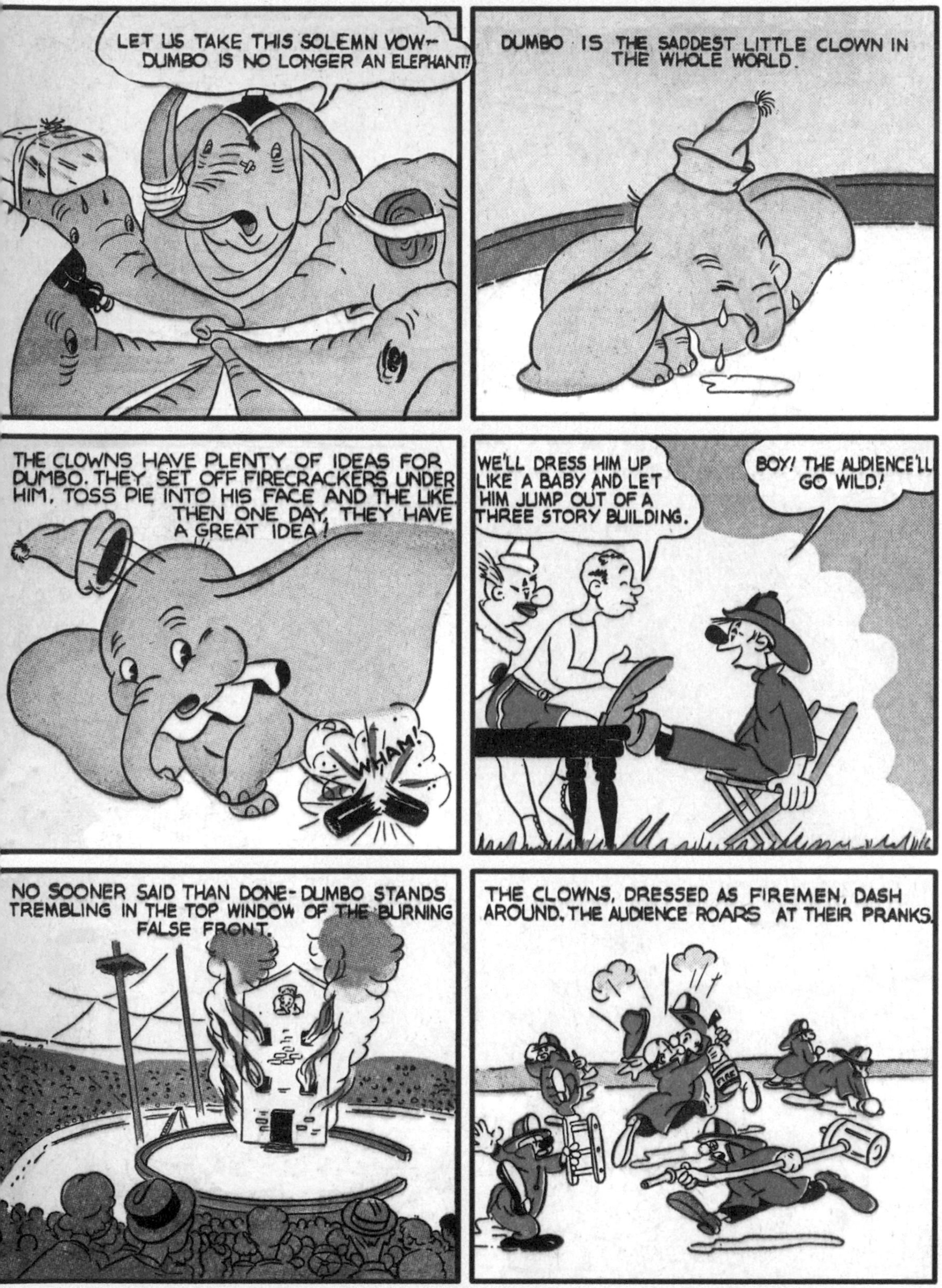
LET US TAKE THIS SOLEMN VOW— DUMBO IS NO LONGER AN ELEPHANT!
DUMBO IS THE SADDEST LITTLE CLOWN IN THE WHOLE WORLD.
THE CLOWNS HAVE PLENTY OF IDEAS FOR DUMBO. THEY SET OFF FIRECRACKERS UNDER HIM, TOSS PIE INTO HIS FACE AND THE LIKE. THEN ONE DAY, THEY HAVE A GREAT IDEA!
WHAM!
WE'LL DRESS HIM UP LIKE A BABY AND LET HIM JUMP OUT OF A THREE STORY BUILDING.
BOY! THE AUDIENCE'LL GO WILD!
NO SOONER SAID THAN DONE-DUMBO STANDS TREMBLING IN THE TOP WINDOW OF THE BURNING FALSE FRONT.
THE CLOWNS, DRESSED AS FIREMEN, DASH AROUND. THE AUDIENCE ROARS AT THEIR PRANKS.

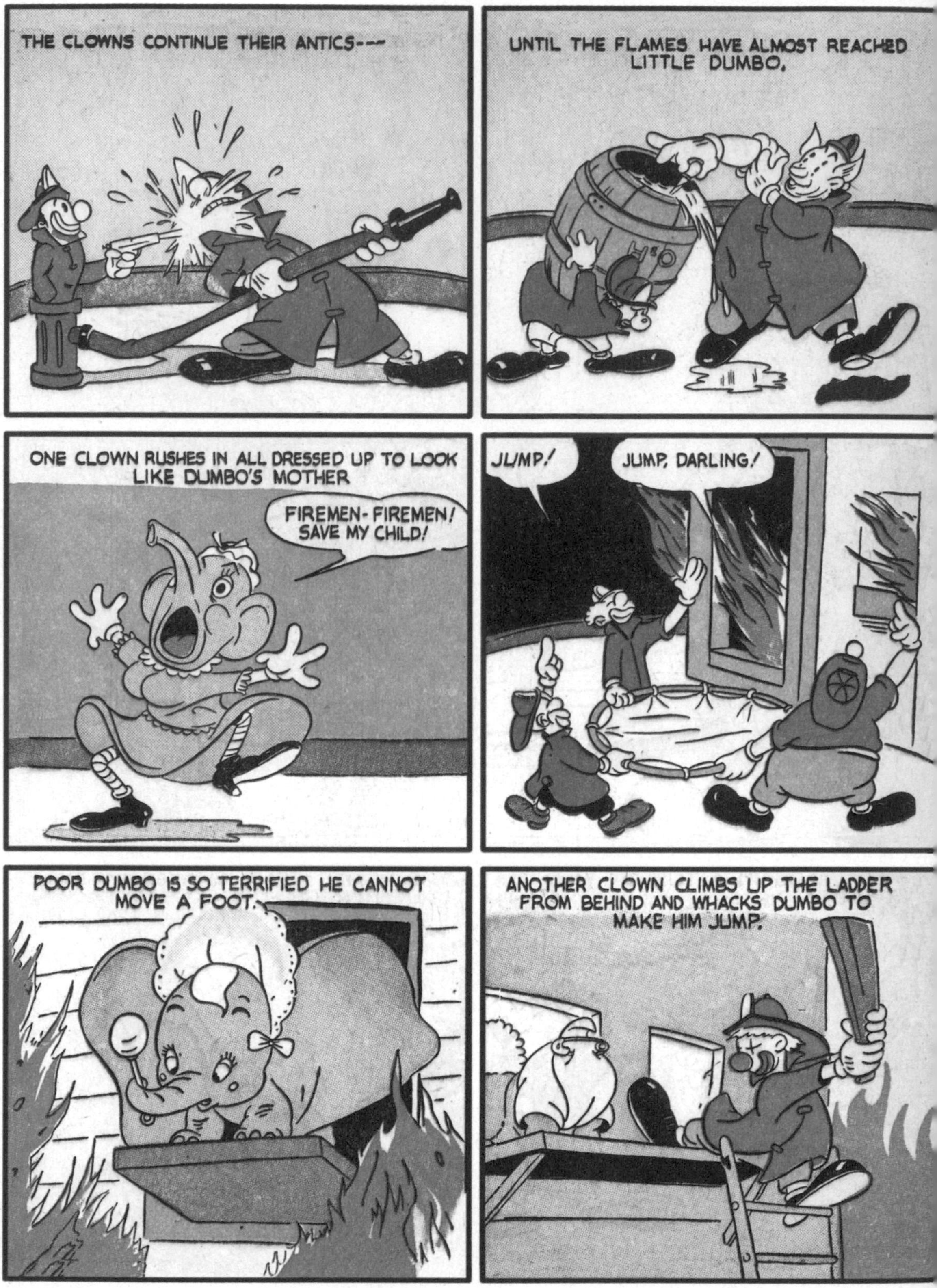
THE CLOWNS CONTINUE THEIR ANTICS---
UNTIL THE FLAMES HAVE ALMOST REACHED LITTLE DUMBO.
ONE CLOWN RUSHES IN ALL DRESSED UP TO LOOK LIKE DUMBO'S MOTHER
FIREMEN- FIREMEN! SAVE MY CHILD!
JUMP!
JUMP, DARLING!
POOR DUMBO IS SO TERRIFIED HE CANNOT MOVE A FOOT.
ANOTHER CLOWN CLIMBS UP THE LADDER FROM BEHIND AND WHACKS DUMBO TO MAKE HIM JUMP.

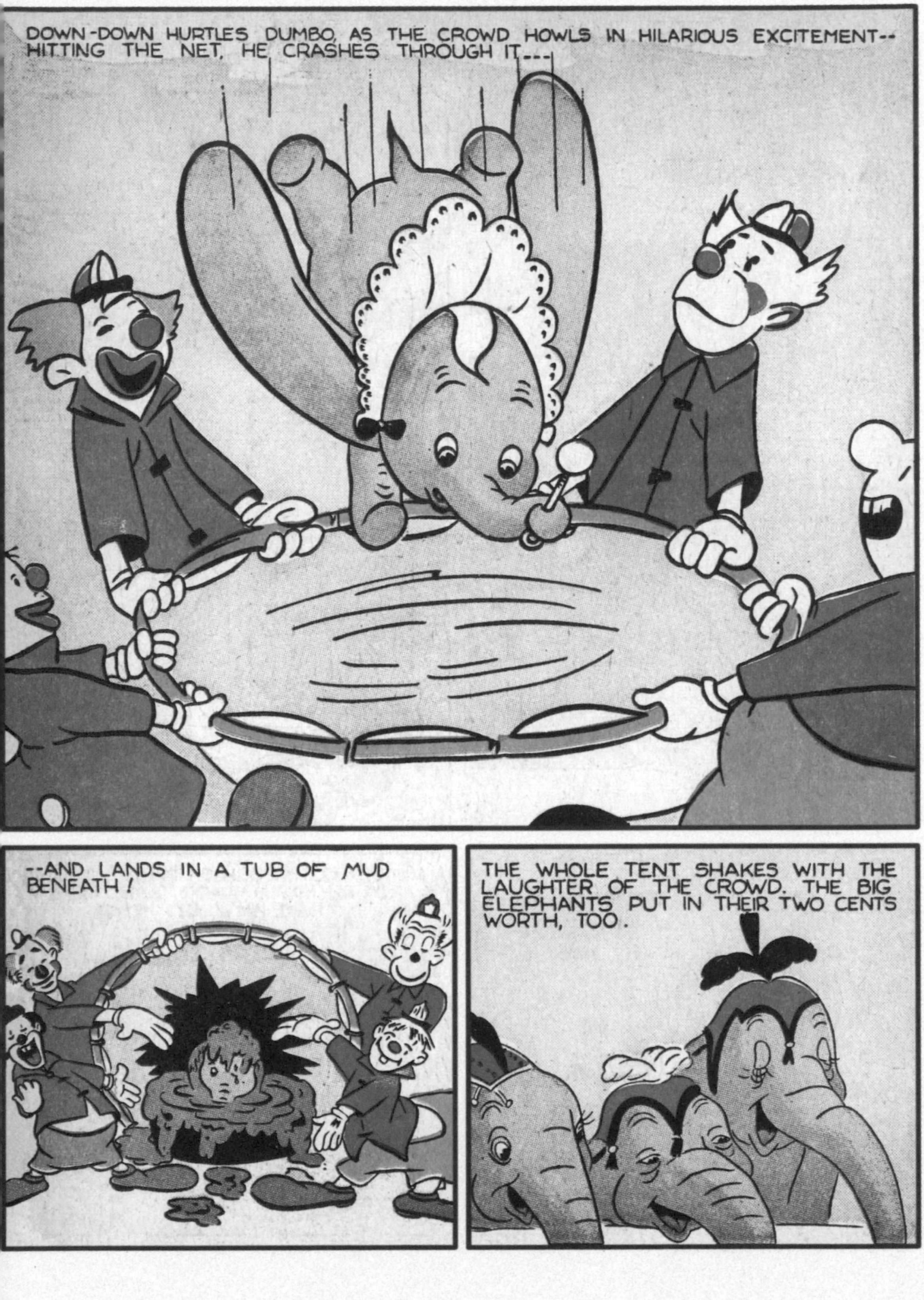
DOWN-DOWN HURTLES DUMBO, AS THE CROWD HOWLS IN HILARIOUS EXCITEMENT-- HITTING THE NET, HE CRASHES THROUGH IT---
--AND LANDS IN A TUB OF MUD BENEATH!
THE WHOLE TENT SHAKES WITH THE LAUGHTER OF THE CROWD. THE BIG ELEPHANTS PUT IN THEIR TWO CENTS WORTH, TOO.

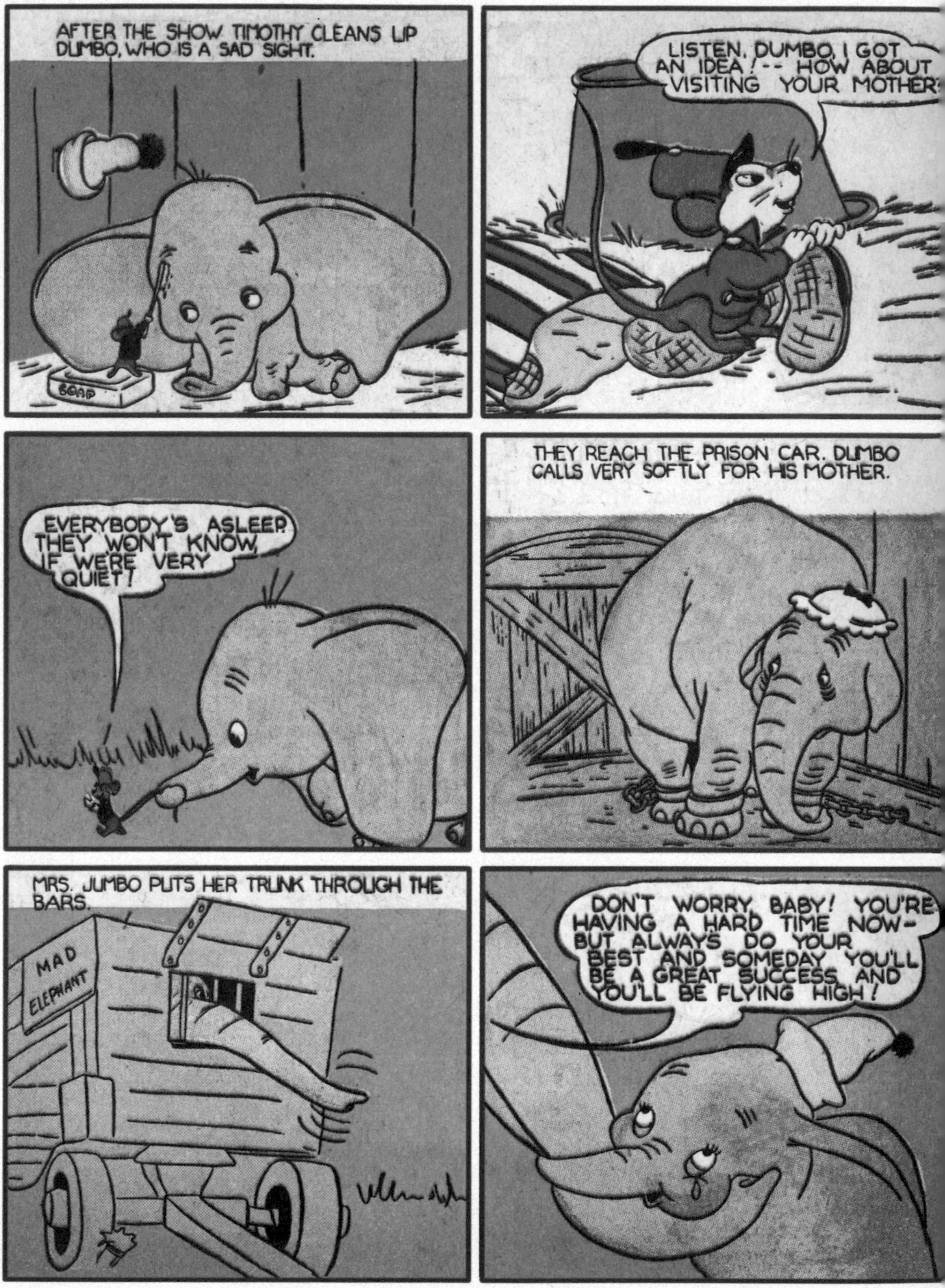
AFTER THE SHOW TIMOTHY CLEANS UP DUMBO, WHO IS A SAD SIGHT.
SOAP
LISTEN, DUMBO, I GOT AN IDEA! -- HOW ABOUT VISITING YOUR MOTHER?
EVERYBODY'S ASLEEP. THEY WON'T KNOW, IF WE'RE VERY QUIET!
THEY REACH THE PRISON CAR. DUMBO CALLS VERY SOFTLY FOR HIS MOTHER.
MRS. JUMBO PUTS HER TRUNK THROUGH THE BARS.
MAD ELEPHANT
DON'T WORRY, BABY! YOU'RE HAVING A HARD TIME NOW- BUT ALWAYS DO YOUR BEST AND SOMEDAY YOU'LL BE A GREAT SUCCESS AND YOU'LL BE FLYING HIGH!

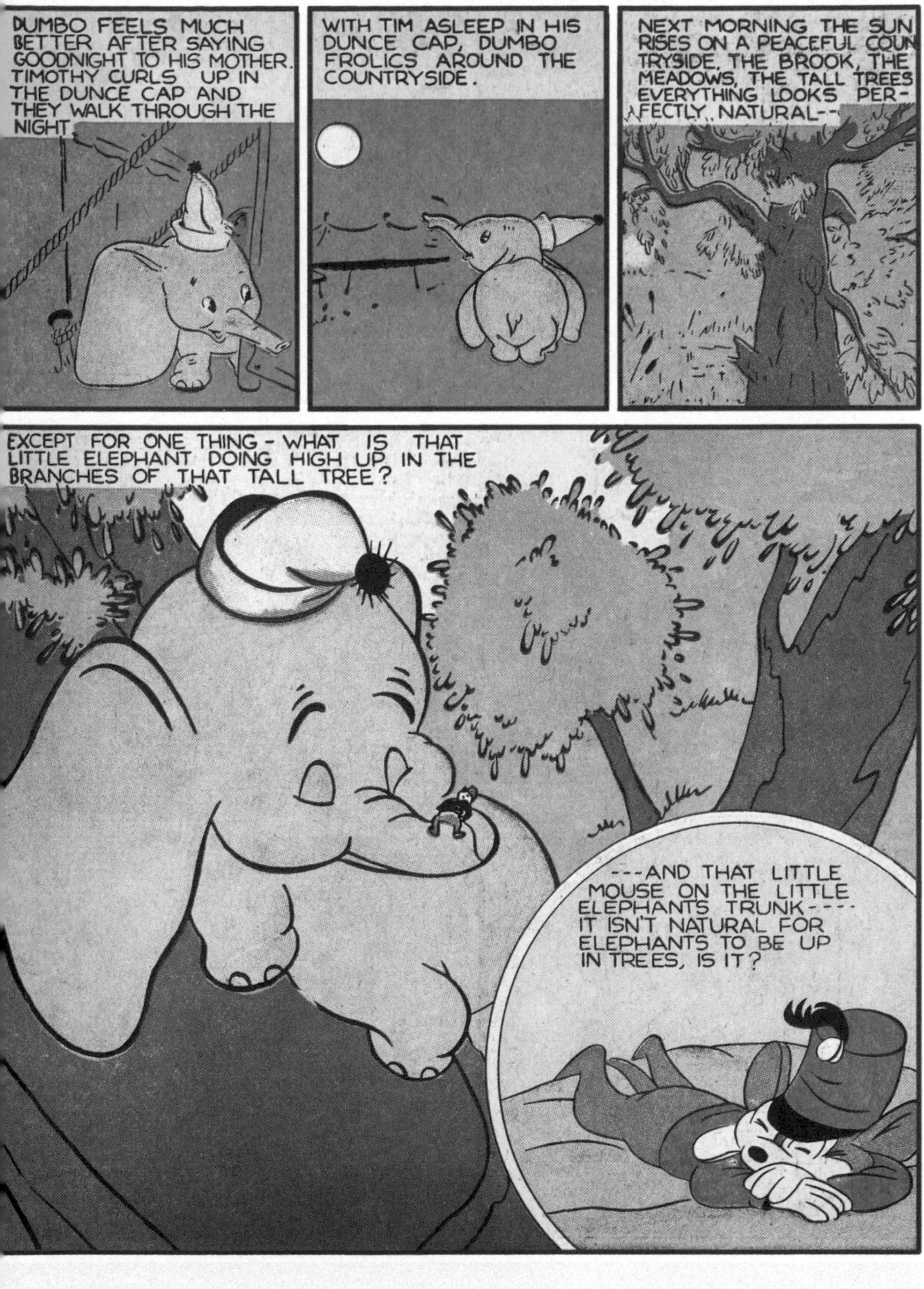
DUMBO FEELS MUCH BETTER AFTER SAYING GOODNIGHT TO HIS MOTHER. TIMOTHY CURLS UP IN THE DUNCE CAP AND THEY WALK THROUGH THE NIGHT.
WITH TIM ASLEEP IN HIS DUNCE CAP, DUMBO FROLICS AROUND THE COUNTRYSIDE.
NEXT MORNING THE SUN RISES ON A PEACEFUL COUNTRYSIDE, THE BROOK, THE MEADOWS, THE TALL TREES EVERYTHING LOOKS PERFECTLY NATURAL--
EXCEPT FOR ONE THING - WHAT IS THAT LITTLE ELEPHANT DOING HIGH UP IN THE BRANCHES OF THAT TALL TREE?
---AND THAT LITTLE MOUSE ON THE LITTLE ELEPHANTS TRUNK---- IT ISN'T NATURAL FOR ELEPHANTS TO BE UP IN TREES, IS IT?

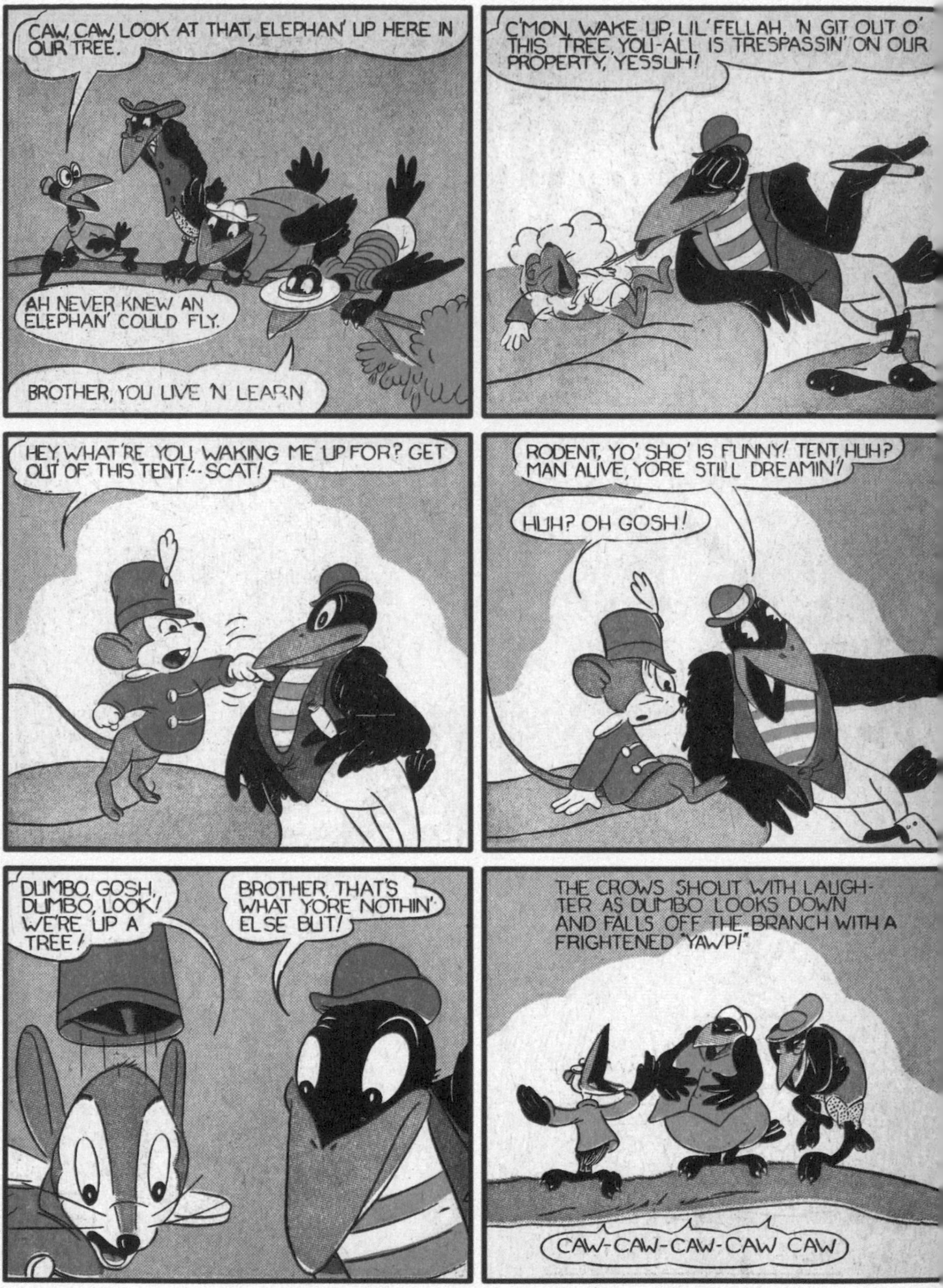
CAW, CAW, LOOK AT THAT, ELEPHAN' UP HERE IN OUR TREE.
AH NEVER KNEW AN ELEPHAN' COULD FLY.
BROTHER, YOU LIVE 'N LEARN
C'MON, WAKE UP, LIL' FELLAH, 'N GIT OUT O' THIS TREE, YOU-ALL IS TRESPASSIN' ON OUR PROPERTY, YESSUH!
HEY, WHAT'RE YOU WAKING ME UP FOR? GET OUT OF THIS TENT!--SCAT!
RODENT, YO' SHO' IS FUNNY! TENT, HUH? MAN ALIVE, YORE STILL DREAMIN'!
HUH? OH GOSH!
DUMBO, GOSH, DUMBO, LOOK! WE'RE UP A TREE!
BROTHER, THAT'S WHAT YORE NOTHIN' ELSE BUT!
THE CROWS SHOUT WITH LAUGHTER AS DUMBO LOOKS DOWN AND FALLS OFF THE BRANCH WITH A FRIGHTENED "YAWP!"
CAW-CAW-CAW-CAW CAW

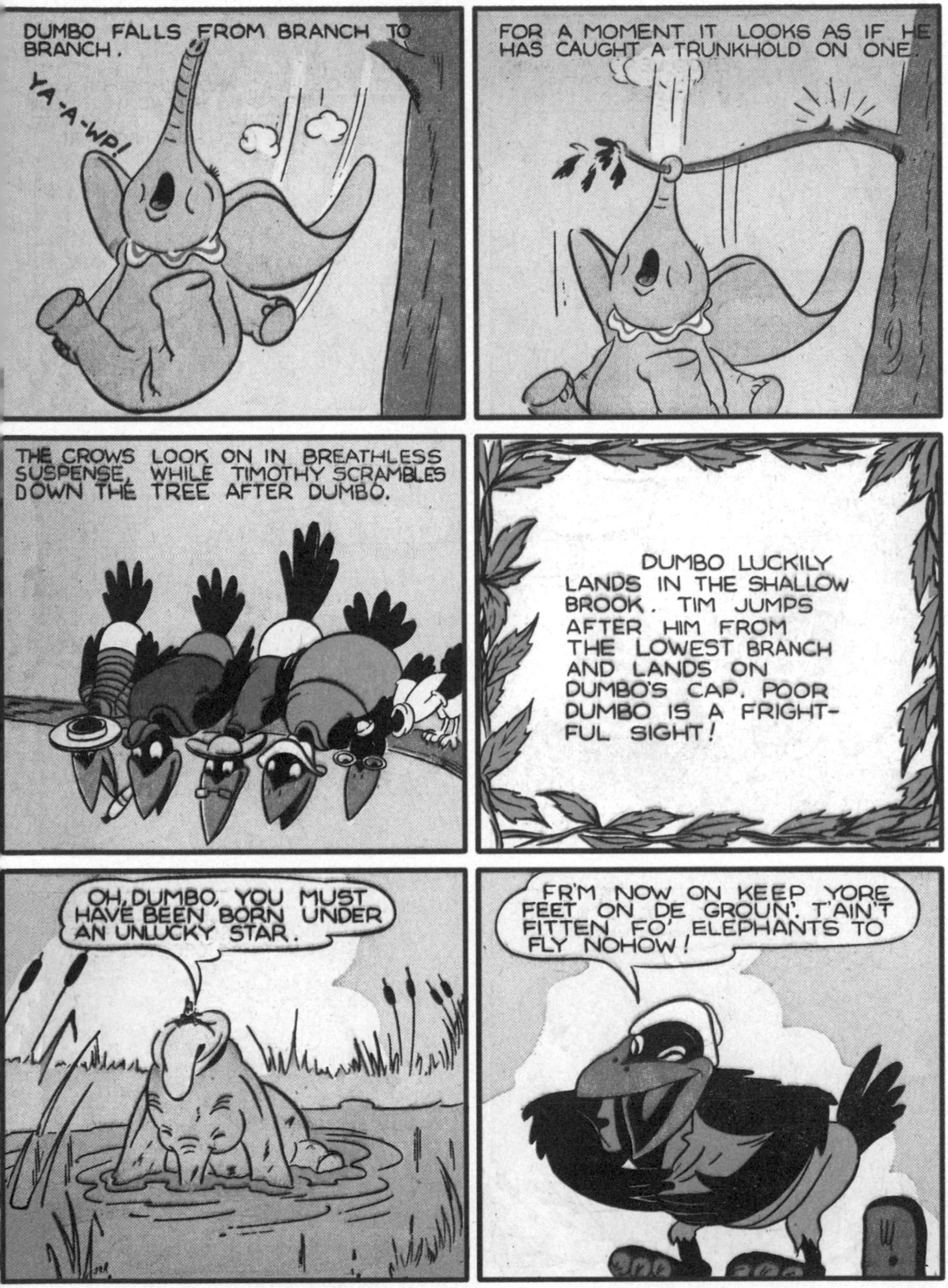
DUMBO FALLS FROM BRANCH TO BRANCH.
YA-A-WP!
FOR A MOMENT IT LOOKS AS IF HE HAS CAUGHT A TRUNKHOLD ON ONE.
THE CROWS LOOK ON IN BREATHLESS SUSPENSE, WHILE TIMOTHY SCRAMBLES DOWN THE TREE AFTER DUMBO.
DUMBO LUCKILY LANDS IN THE SHALLOW BROOK. TIM JUMPS AFTER HIM FROM THE LOWEST BRANCH AND LANDS ON DUMBO'S CAP. POOR DUMBO IS A FRIGHT-FUL SIGHT!
OH, DUMBO, YOU MUST HAVE BEEN BORN UNDER AN UNLUCKY STAR.
FR'M NOW ON KEEP YORE FEET ON DE GROUN'. T'AIN'T FITTEN FO' ELEPHANTS TO FLY NOHOW!

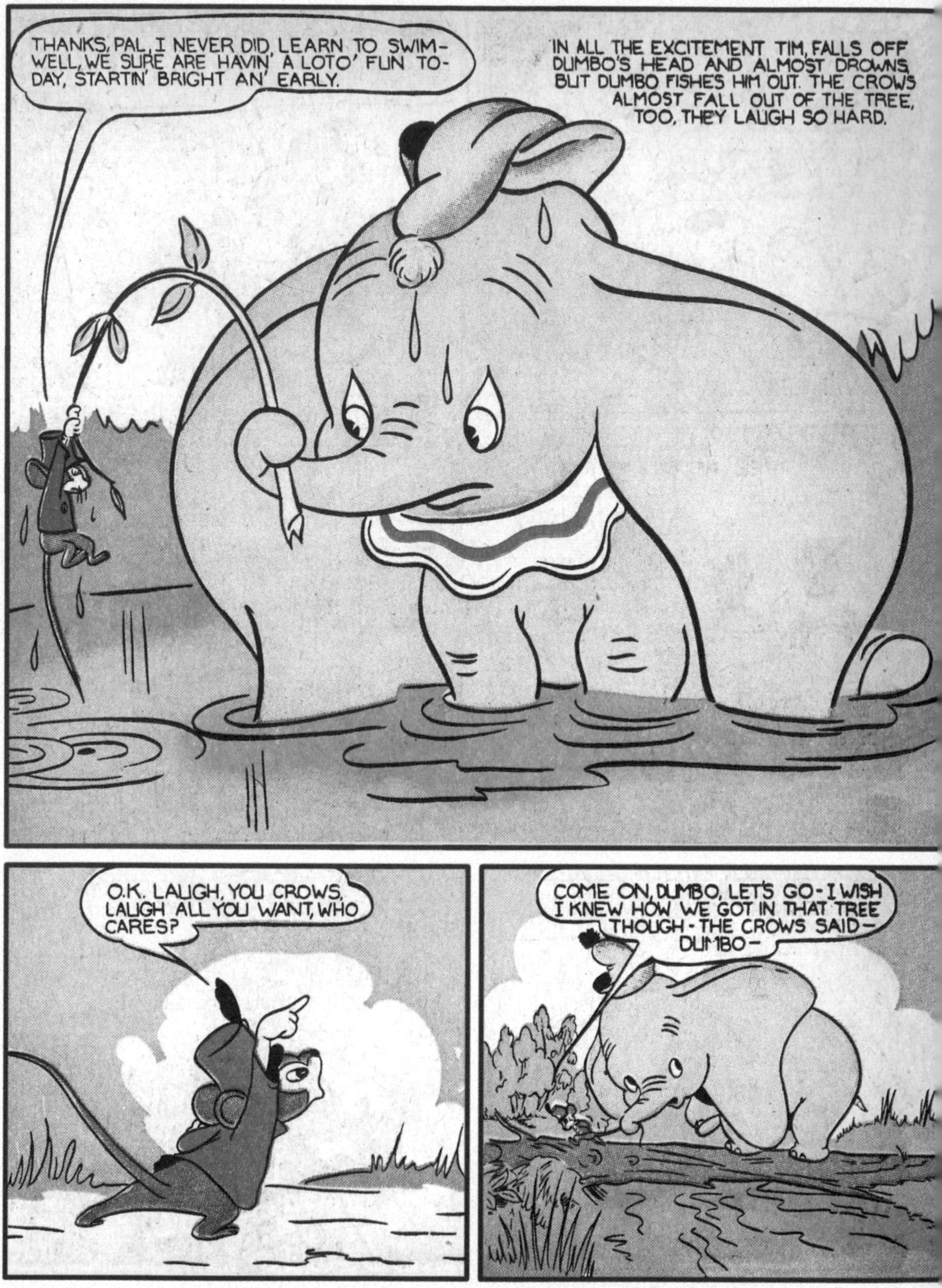
THANKS, PAL, I NEVER DID LEARN TO SWIM- WELL, WE SURE ARE HAVIN' A LOTO' FUN TO-DAY, STARTIN' BRIGHT AN' EARLY.
IN ALL THE EXCITEMENT TIM, FALLS OFF DUMBO'S HEAD AND ALMOST DROWNS, BUT DUMBO FISHES HIM OUT. THE CROWS ALMOST FALL OUT OF THE TREE, TOO, THEY LAUGH SO HARD.
O.K. LAUGH, YOU CROWS, LAUGH ALL YOU WANT, WHO CARES?
COME ON, DUMBO, LET'S GO - I WISH I KNEW HOW WE GOT IN THAT TREE THOUGH - THE CROWS SAID - DUMBO -

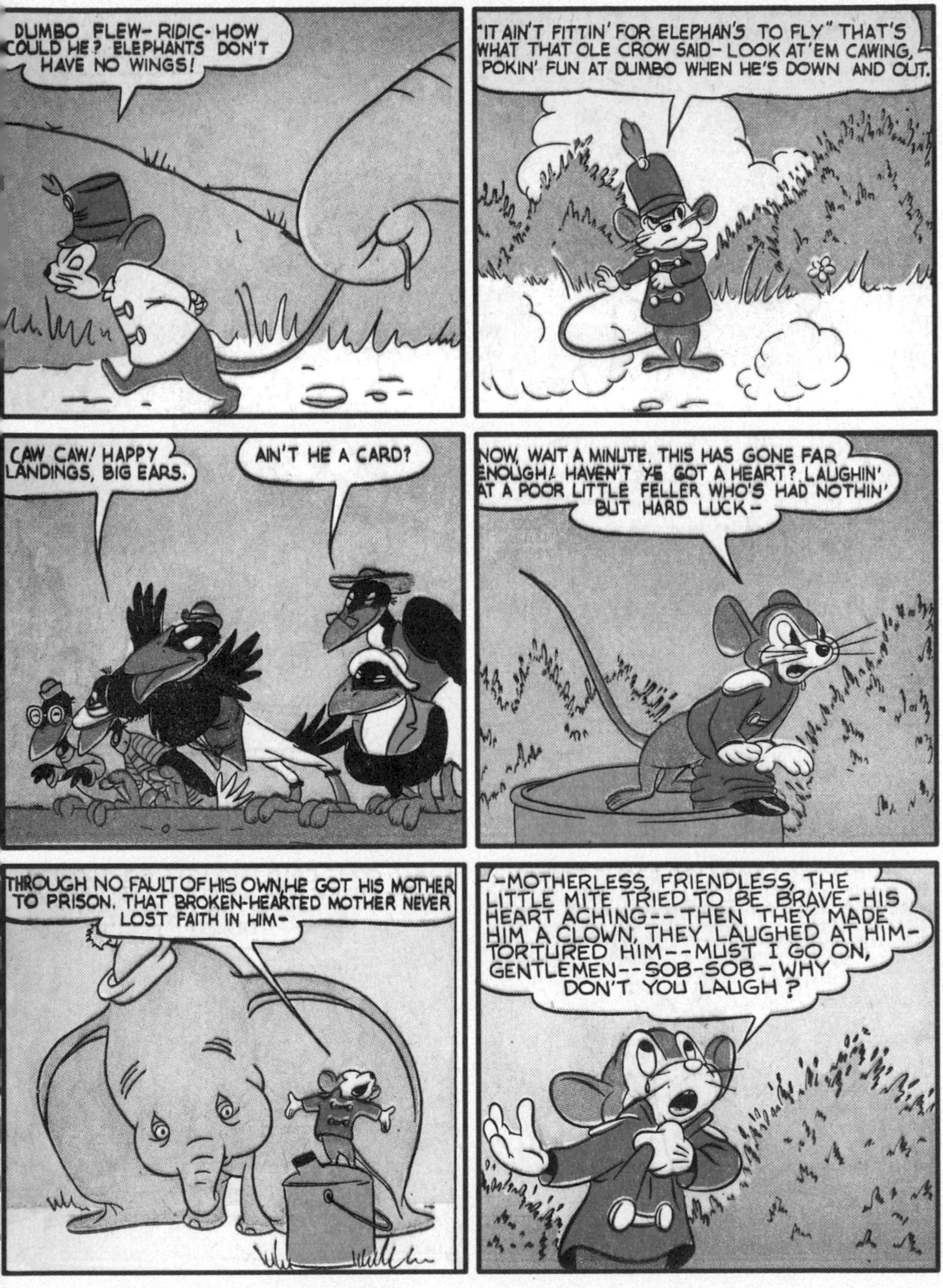
DUMBO FLEW- RIDIC- HOW COULD HE? ELEPHANTS DON'T HAVE NO WINGS!
"IT AIN'T FITTIN' FOR ELEPHAN'S TO FLY" THAT'S WHAT THAT OLE CROW SAID- LOOK AT 'EM CAWING, POKIN' FUN AT DUMBO WHEN HE'S DOWN AND OUT.
CAW CAW! HAPPY LANDINGS, BIG EARS.
AIN'T HE A CARD?
NOW, WAIT A MINUTE. THIS HAS GONE FAR ENOUGH! HAVEN'T YE GOT A HEART? LAUGHIN' AT A POOR LITTLE FELLER WHO'S HAD NOTHIN' BUT HARD LUCK-
THROUGH NO FAULT OF HIS OWN, HE GOT HIS MOTHER TO PRISON. THAT BROKEN-HEARTED MOTHER NEVER LOST FAITH IN HIM-
-MOTHERLESS, FRIENDLESS, THE LITTLE MITE TRIED TO BE BRAVE-HIS HEART ACHING-- THEN THEY MADE HIM A CLOWN, THEY LAUGHED AT HIM-TORTURED HIM--MUST I GO ON, GENTLEMEN--SOB-SOB- WHY DON'T YOU LAUGH?

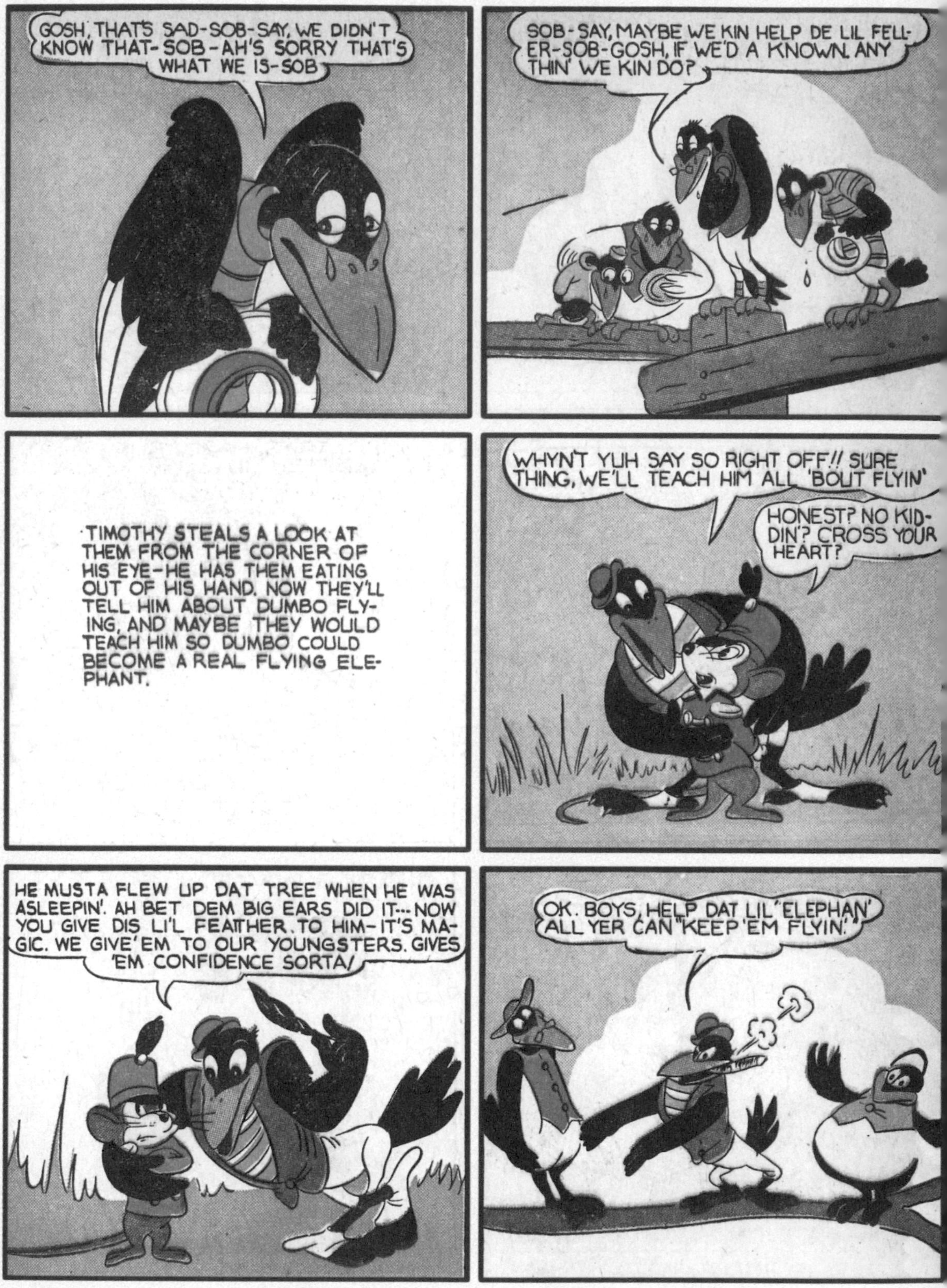
GOSH, THAT'S SAD-SOB-SAY, WE DIDN'T KNOW THAT-SOB-AH'S SORRY THAT'S WHAT WE IS-SOB
SOB-SAY, MAYBE WE KIN HELP DE LIL FELL-ER-SOB-GOSH, IF WE'D A KNOWN. ANY THIN' WE KIN DO?
TIMOTHY STEALS A LOOK AT THEM FROM THE CORNER OF HIS EYE-HE HAS THEM EATING OUT OF HIS HAND. NOW THEY'LL TELL HIM ABOUT DUMBO FLY-ING, AND MAYBE THEY WOULD TEACH HIM SO DUMBO COULD BECOME A REAL FLYING ELE-PHANT.
WHYN'T YUH SAY SO RIGHT OFF!! SURE THING, WE'LL TEACH HIM ALL 'BOUT FLYIN'
HONEST? NO KID-DIN'? CROSS YOUR HEART?
HE MUSTA FLEW UP DAT TREE WHEN HE WAS ASLEEPIN'. AH BET DEM BIG EARS DID IT--- NOW YOU GIVE DIS LI'L FEATHER. TO HIM-IT'S MA-GIC. WE GIVE'EM TO OUR YOUNGSTERS. GIVES 'EM CONFIDENCE SORTA!
OK. BOYS, HELP DAT LIL' ELEPHAN' ALL YER CAN "KEEP 'EM FLYIN'."

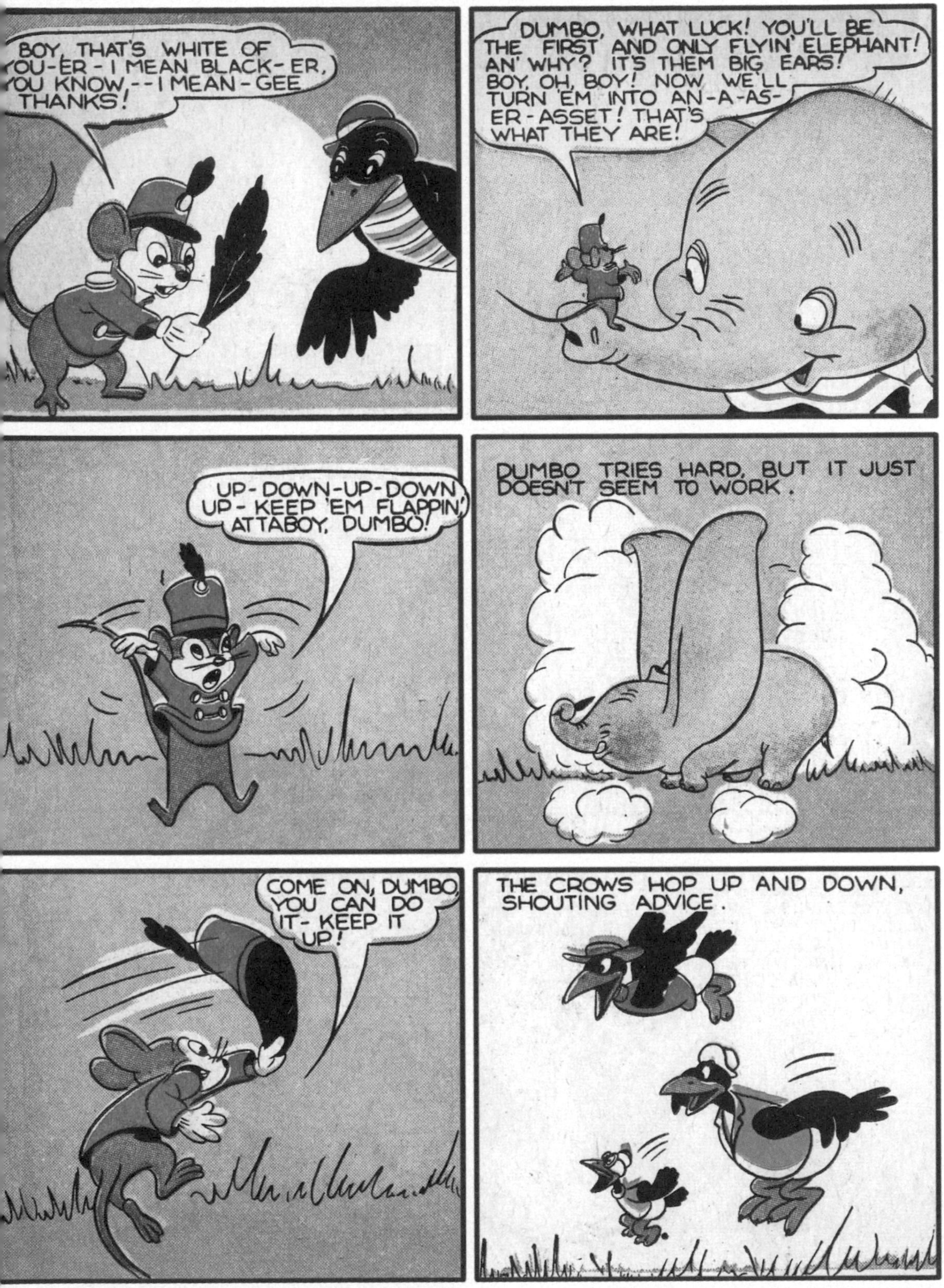
BOY, THAT'S WHITE OF YOU-ER-I MEAN BLACK-ER, YOU KNOW,--I MEAN-GEE THANKS!
DUMBO, WHAT LUCK! YOU'LL BE THE FIRST AND ONLY FLYIN' ELEPHANT! AN' WHY? IT'S THEM BIG EARS! BOY, OH, BOY! NOW WE'LL TURN 'EM INTO AN-A-AS-ER-ASSET! THAT'S WHAT THEY ARE!
UP-DOWN-UP-DOWN UP-KEEP 'EM FLAPPIN' ATTABOY, DUMBO!
DUMBO TRIES HARD, BUT IT JUST DOESN'T SEEM TO WORK.
COME ON, DUMBO, YOU CAN DO IT-KEEP IT UP!
THE CROWS HOP UP AND DOWN, SHOUTING ADVICE.

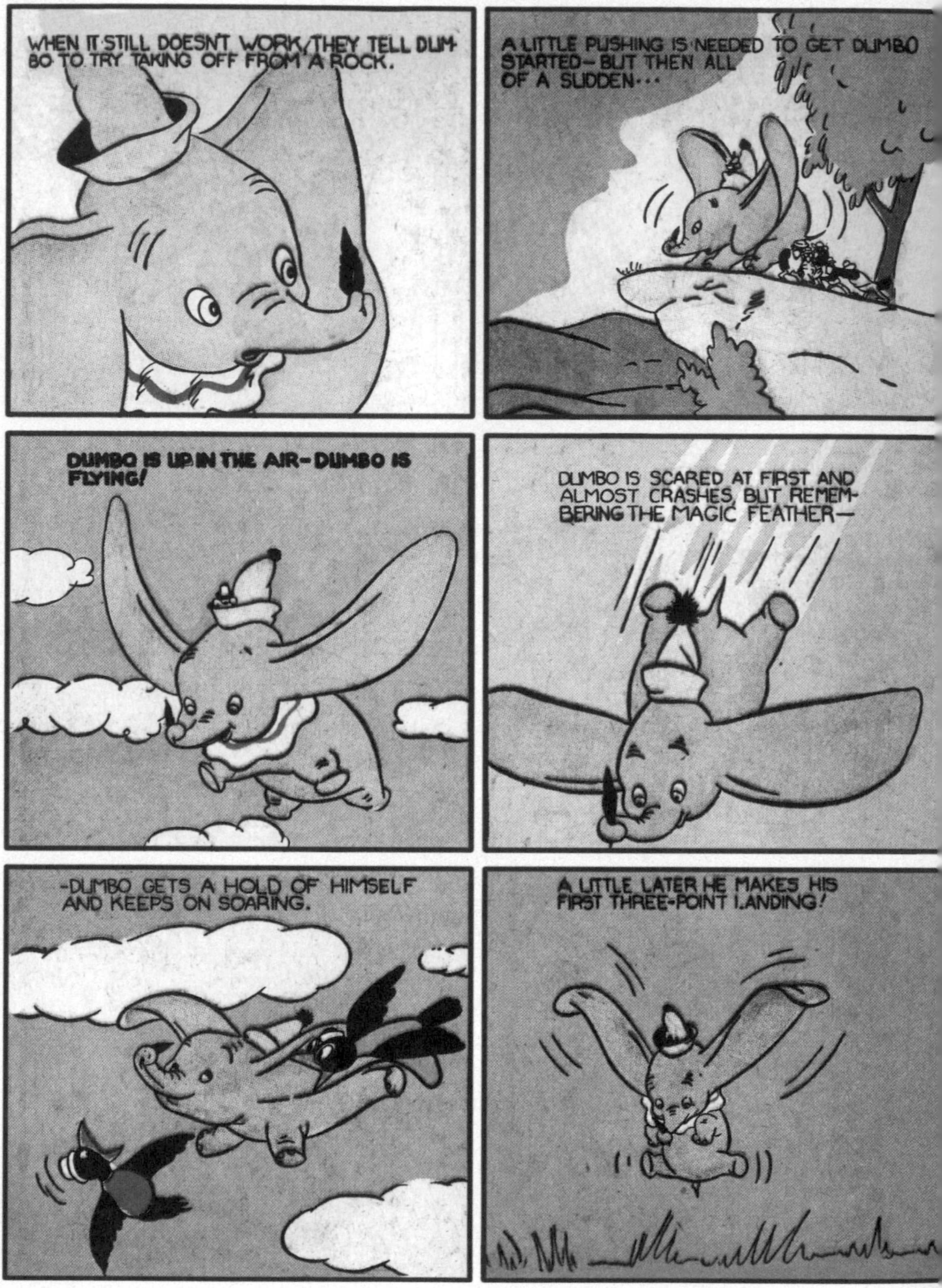
WHEN IT STILL DOESN'T WORK, THEY TELL DUMBO TO TRY TAKING OFF FROM A ROCK.
A LITTLE PUSHING IS NEEDED TO GET DUMBO STARTED—BUT THEN ALL OF A SUDDEN···
DUMBO IS UP IN THE AIR—DUMBO IS FLYING!
DUMBO IS SCARED AT FIRST AND ALMOST CRASHES, BUT REMEMBERING THE MAGIC FEATHER—
-DUMBO GETS A HOLD OF HIMSELF AND KEEPS ON SOARING.
A LITTLE LATER HE MAKES HIS FIRST THREE-POINT LANDING!

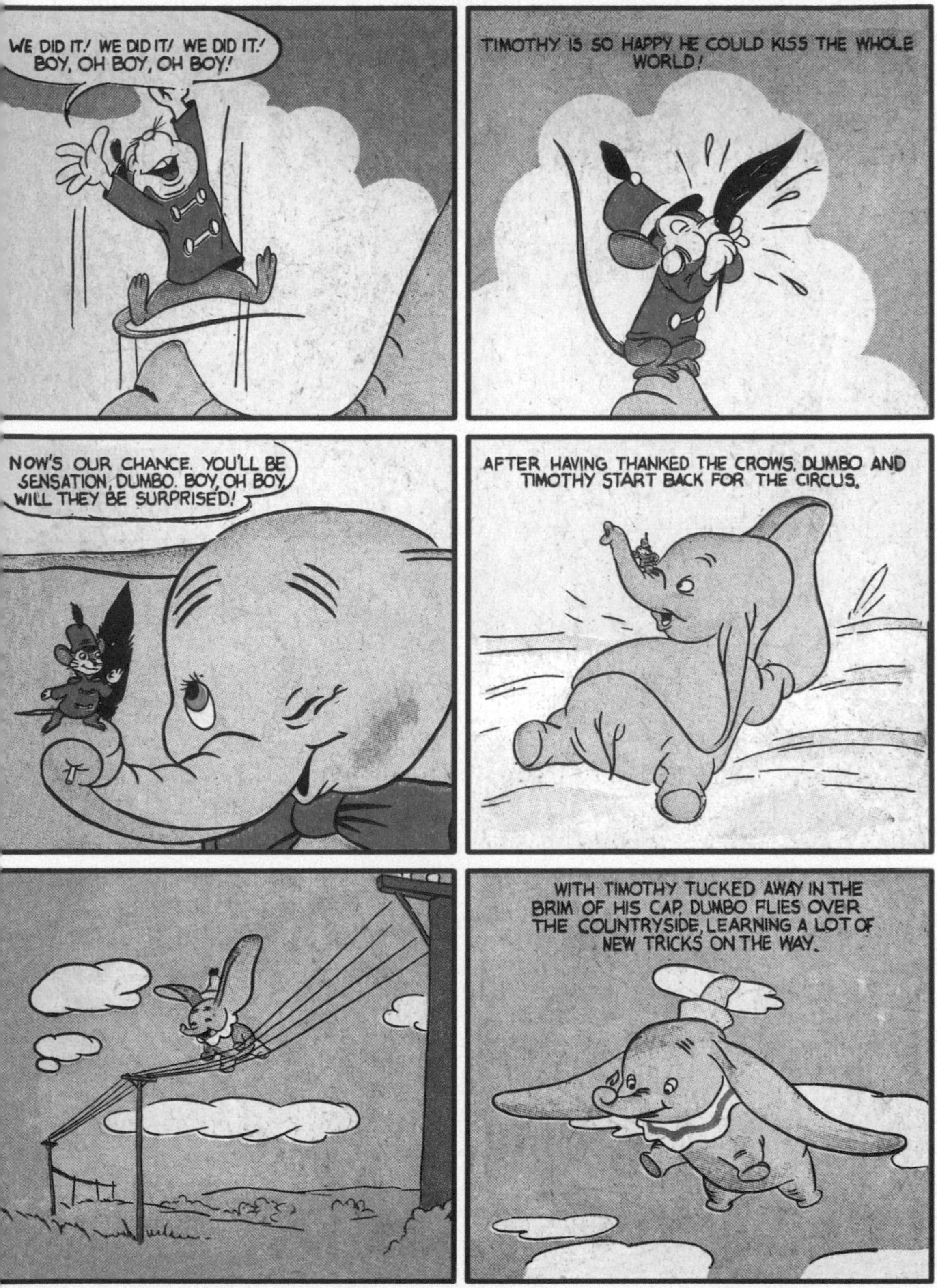
WE DID IT! WE DID IT! WE DID IT! BOY, OH BOY, OH BOY!
TIMOTHY IS SO HAPPY HE COULD KISS THE WHOLE WORLD!
NOW'S OUR CHANCE. YOU'LL BE SENSATION, DUMBO. BOY, OH BOY, WILL THEY BE SURPRISED!
AFTER HAVING THANKED THE CROWS, DUMBO AND TIMOTHY START BACK FOR THE CIRCUS.
WITH TIMOTHY TUCKED AWAY IN THE BRIM OF HIS CAP, DUMBO FLIES OVER THE COUNTRYSIDE, LEARNING A LOT OF NEW TRICKS ON THE WAY.

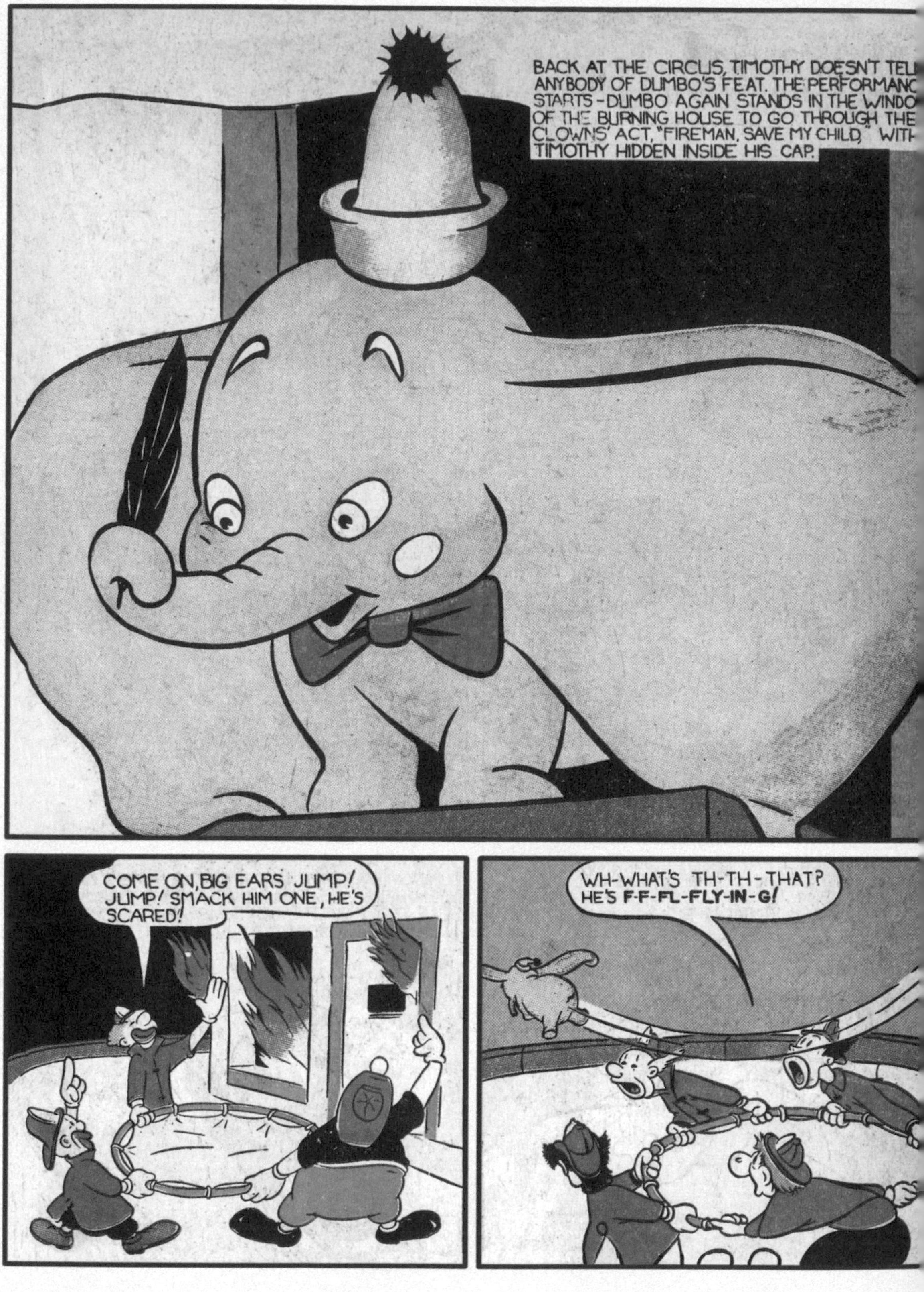
BACK AT THE CIRCUS, TIMOTHY DOESN'T TEL ANYBODY OF DUMBO'S FEAT. THE PERFORMANC STARTS - DUMBO AGAIN STANDS IN THE WINDO OF THE BURNING HOUSE TO GO THROUGH THE CLOWNS' ACT, "FIREMAN, SAVE MY CHILD," WITH TIMOTHY HIDDEN INSIDE HIS CAP.
COME ON, BIG EARS JUMP! JUMP! SMACK HIM ONE, HE'S SCARED!
WH-WHAT'S TH-TH-THAT? HE'S **F-F-FL-FLY-IN-G!**

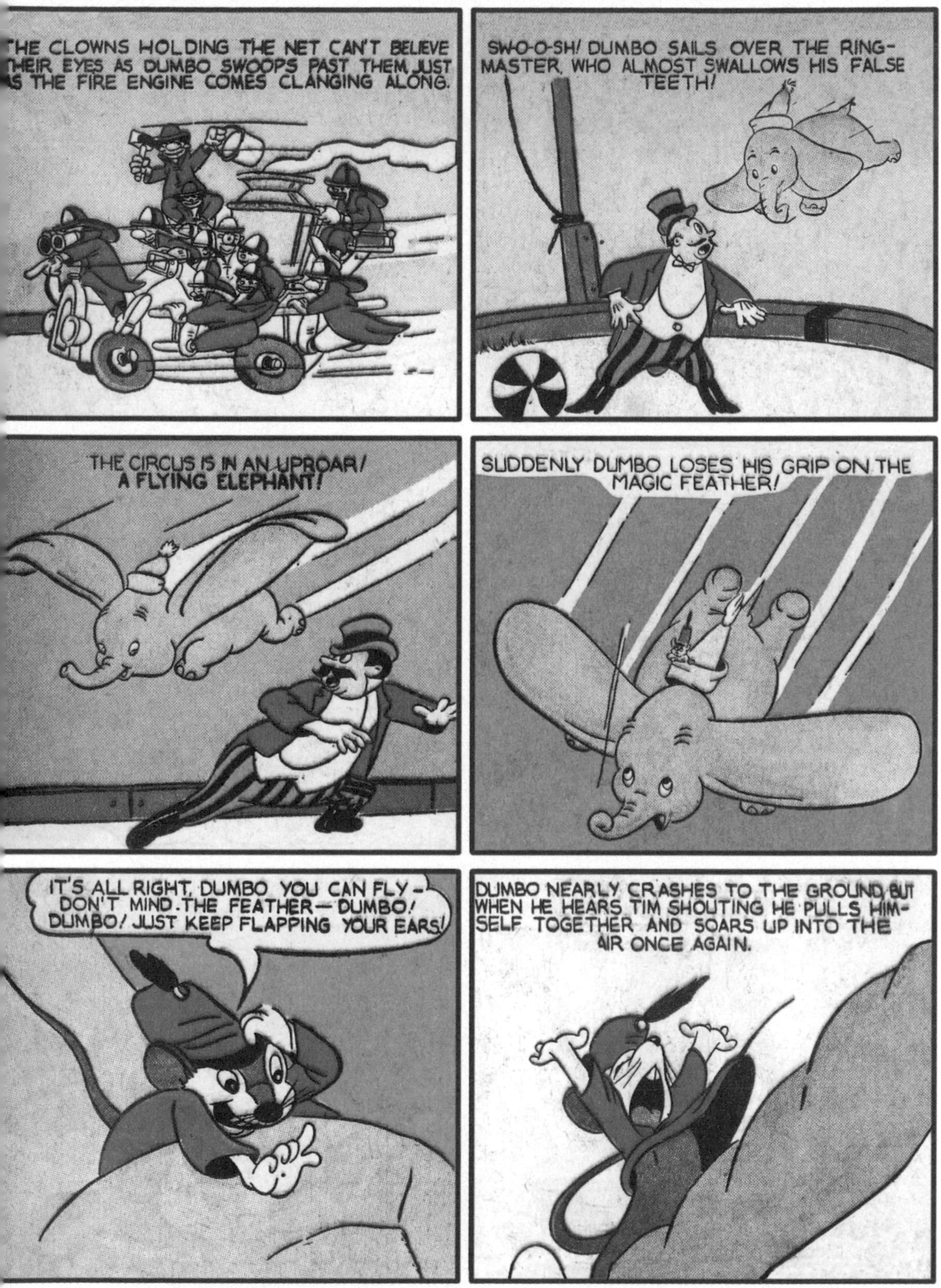
THE CLOWNS HOLDING THE NET CAN'T BELIEVE THEIR EYES AS DUMBO SWOOPS PAST THEM, JUST AS THE FIRE ENGINE COMES CLANGING ALONG.
SW-O-O-SH! DUMBO SAILS OVER THE RING-MASTER, WHO ALMOST SWALLOWS HIS FALSE TEETH!
THE CIRCUS IS IN AN UPROAR! A FLYING ELEPHANT!
SUDDENLY DUMBO LOSES HIS GRIP ON THE MAGIC FEATHER!
IT'S ALL RIGHT, DUMBO YOU CAN FLY- DON'T MIND THE FEATHER—DUMBO! DUMBO! JUST KEEP FLAPPING YOUR EARS!
DUMBO NEARLY CRASHES TO THE GROUND BUT WHEN HE HEARS TIM SHOUTING HE PULLS HIM-SELF TOGETHER AND SOARS UP INTO THE AIR ONCE AGAIN.

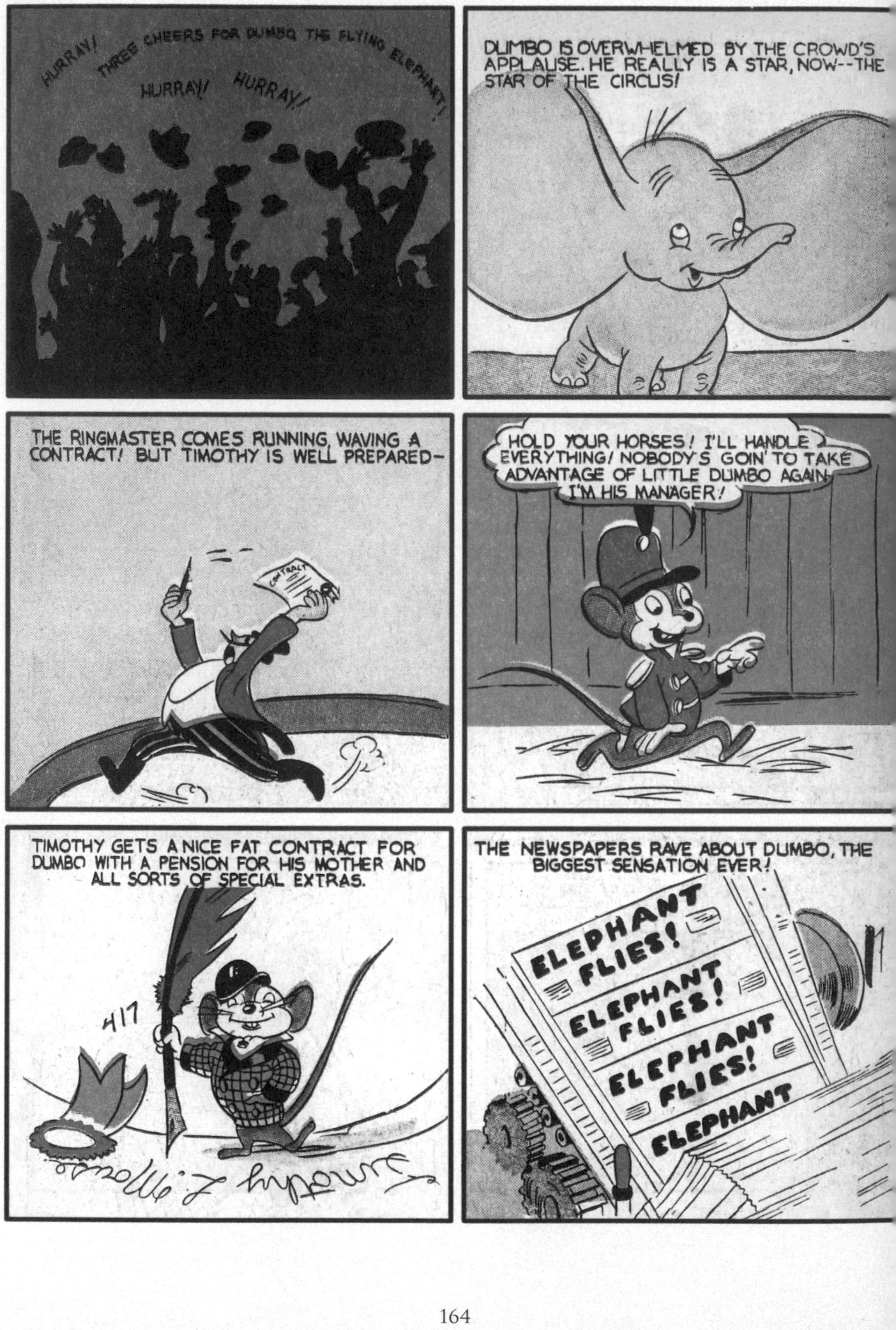
HURRAY! THREE CHEERS FOR DUMBO THE FLYING ELEPHANT!
HURRAY! HURRAY!!
DUMBO IS OVERWHELMED BY THE CROWD'S APPLAUSE. HE REALLY IS A STAR, NOW--THE STAR OF THE CIRCUS!
THE RINGMASTER COMES RUNNING, WAVING A CONTRACT! BUT TIMOTHY IS WELL PREPARED-
CONTRACT
HOLD YOUR HORSES! I'LL HANDLE EVERYTHING! NOBODY'S GOIN' TO TAKE ADVANTAGE OF LITTLE DUMBO AGAIN- I'M HIS MANAGER!
TIMOTHY GETS A NICE FAT CONTRACT FOR DUMBO WITH A PENSION FOR HIS MOTHER AND ALL SORTS OF SPECIAL EXTRAS.
THE NEWSPAPERS RAVE ABOUT DUMBO, THE BIGGEST SENSATION EVER!
ELEPHANT FLIES!
ELEPHANT FLIES!
ELEPHANT FLIES!
ELEPHANT

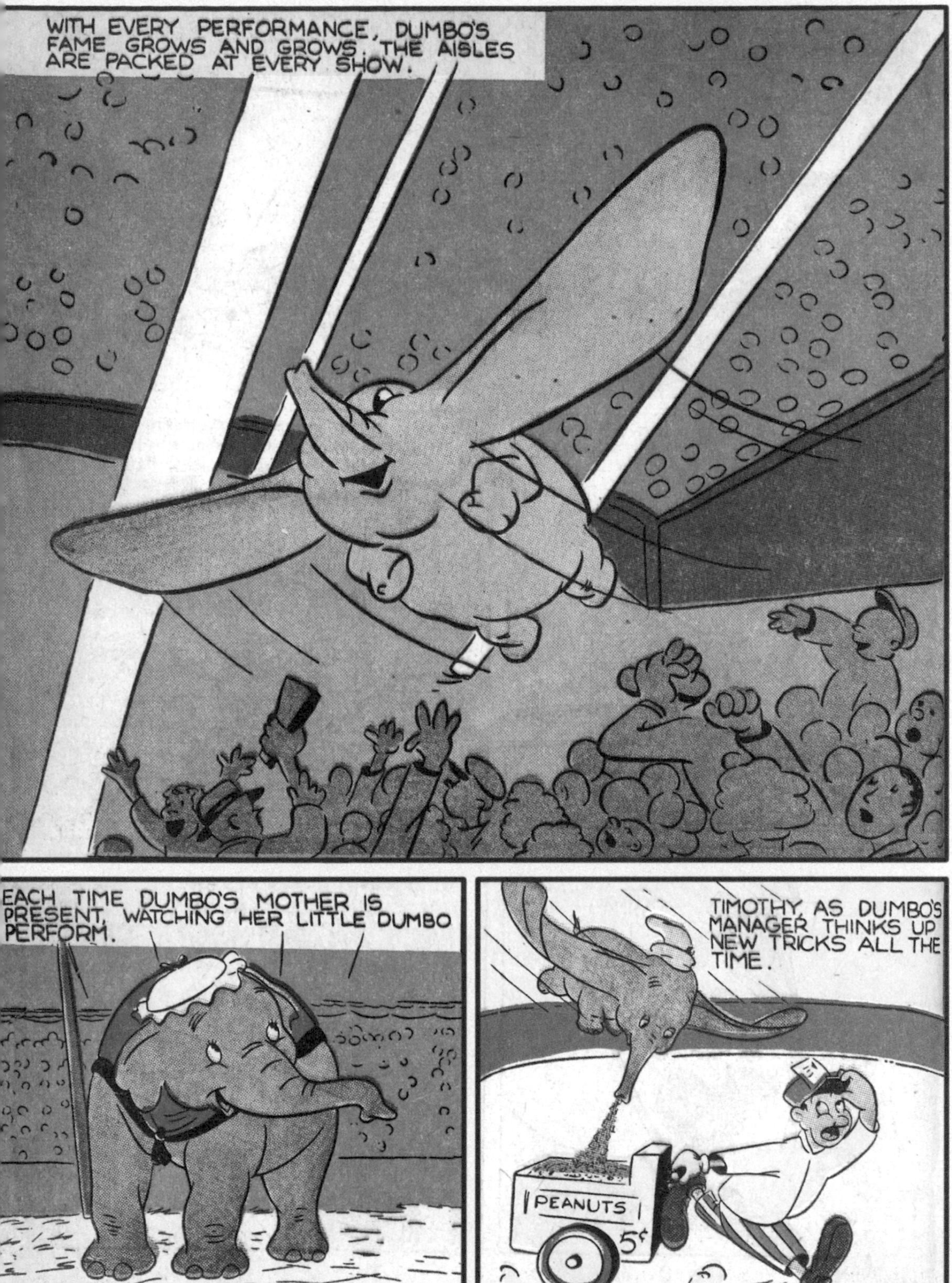
WITH EVERY PERFORMANCE, DUMBO'S FAME GROWS AND GROWS. THE AISLES ARE PACKED AT EVERY SHOW.
EACH TIME DUMBO'S MOTHER IS PRESENT, WATCHING HER LITTLE DUMBO PERFORM.
TIMOTHY, AS DUMBO'S MANAGER THINKS UP NEW TRICKS ALL THE TIME.
PEANUTS
5¢

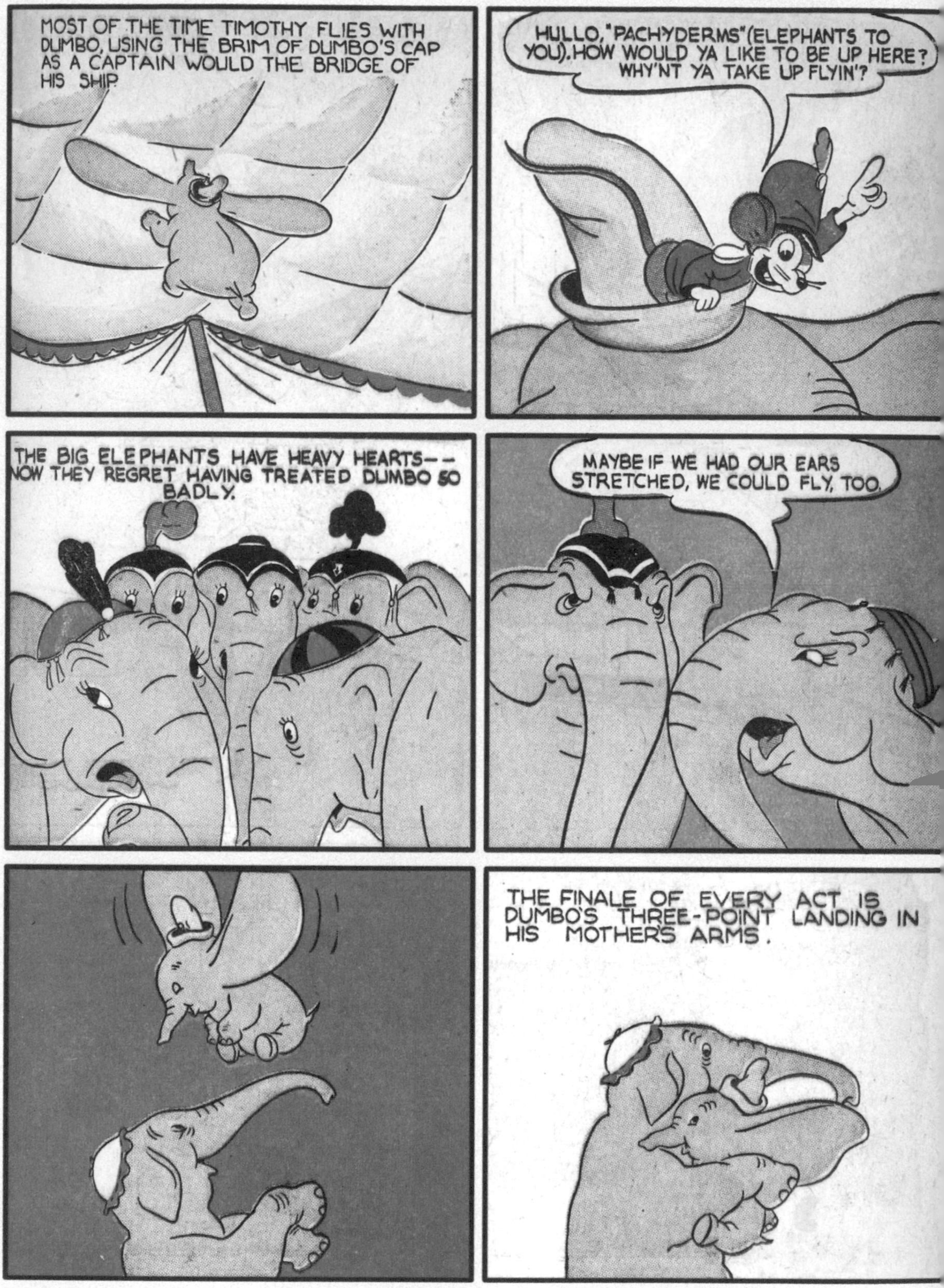
MOST OF THE TIME TIMOTHY FLIES WITH DUMBO, USING THE BRIM OF DUMBO'S CAP AS A CAPTAIN WOULD THE BRIDGE OF HIS SHIP.
HULLO, "PACHYDERMS" (ELEPHANTS TO YOU). HOW WOULD YA LIKE TO BE UP HERE? WHY'NT YA TAKE UP FLYIN'?
THE BIG ELEPHANTS HAVE HEAVY HEARTS-- NOW THEY REGRET HAVING TREATED DUMBO SO BADLY.
MAYBE IF WE HAD OUR EARS STRETCHED, WE COULD FLY, TOO.
THE FINALE OF EVERY ACT IS DUMBO'S THREE-POINT LANDING IN HIS MOTHER'S ARMS.

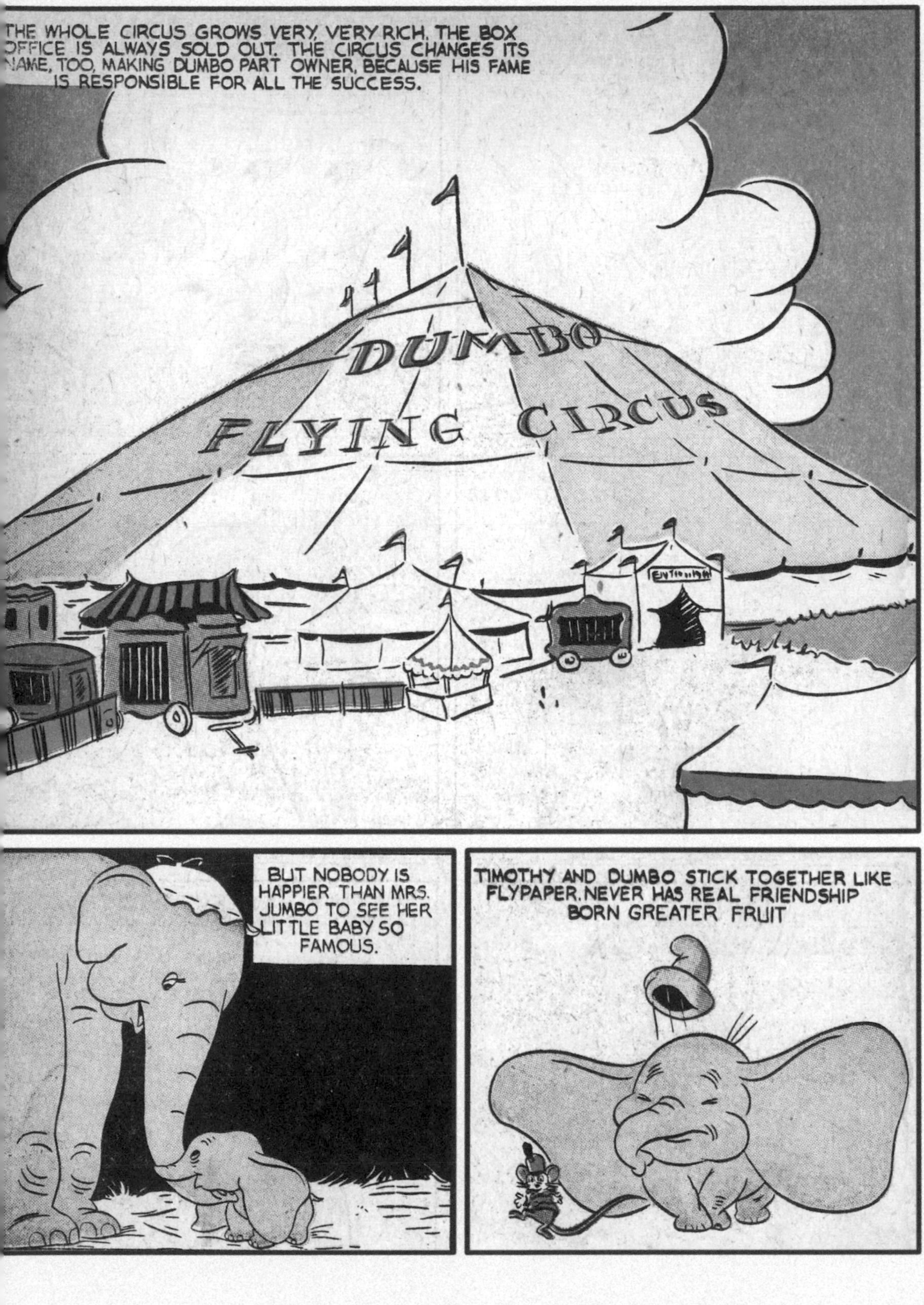
THE WHOLE CIRCUS GROWS VERY, VERY RICH. THE BOX OFFICE IS ALWAYS SOLD OUT. THE CIRCUS CHANGES ITS NAME, TOO, MAKING DUMBO PART OWNER, BECAUSE HIS FAME IS RESPONSIBLE FOR ALL THE SUCCESS.
DUMBO
FLYING CIRCUS
BUT NOBODY IS HAPPIER THAN MRS. JUMBO TO SEE HER LITTLE BABY SO FAMOUS.
TIMOTHY AND DUMBO STICK TOGETHER LIKE FLYPAPER. NEVER HAS REAL FRIENDSHIP BORN GREATER FRUIT

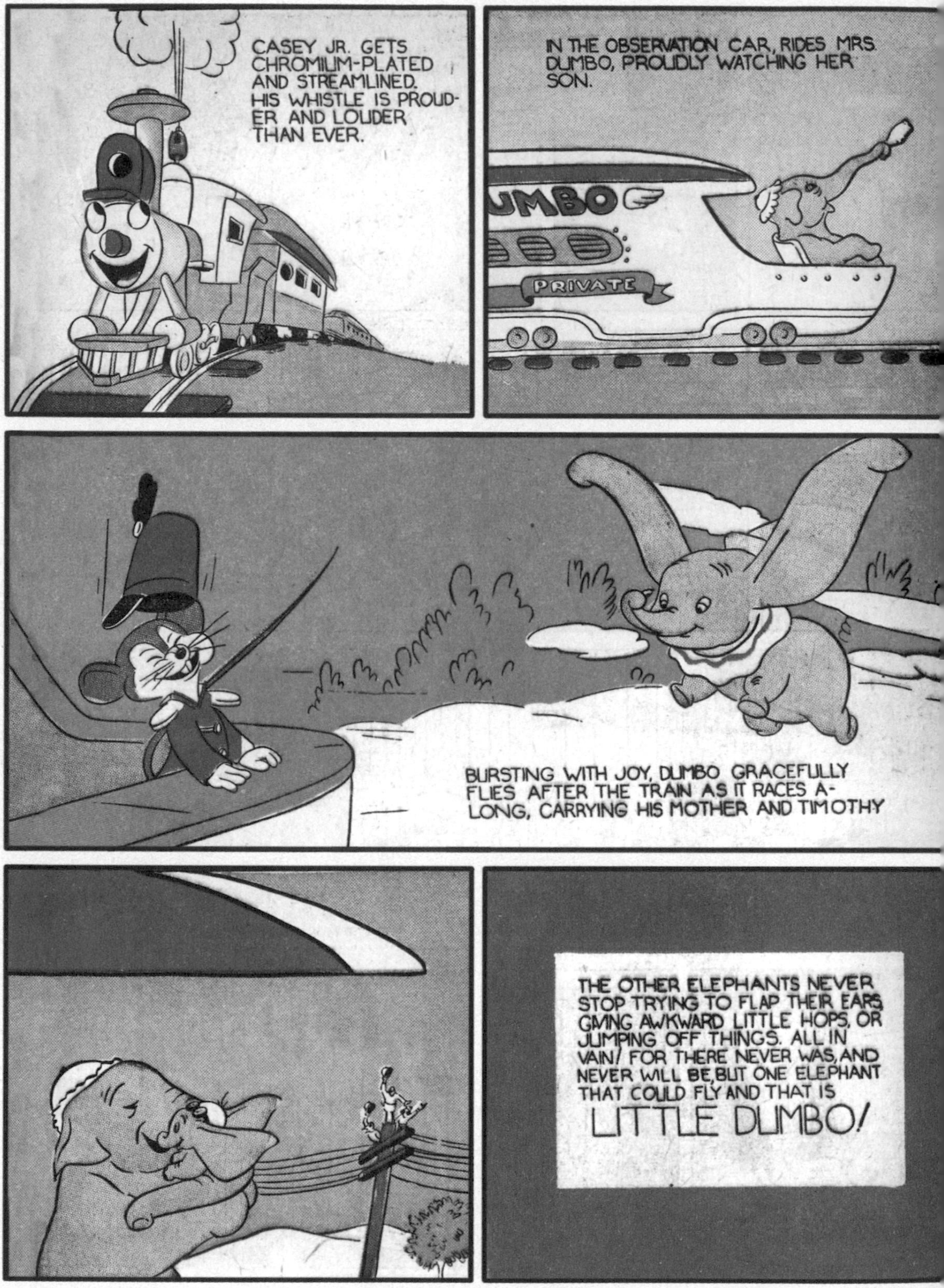
CASEY JR. GETS CHROMIUM-PLATED AND STREAMLINED. HIS WHISTLE IS PROUDER AND LOUDER THAN EVER.
IN THE OBSERVATION CAR, RIDES MRS. DUMBO, PROUDLY WATCHING HER SON.
UMBO
PRIVATE
BURSTING WITH JOY, DUMBO GRACEFULLY FLIES AFTER THE TRAIN AS IT RACES ALONG, CARRYING HIS MOTHER AND TIMOTHY
THE OTHER ELEPHANTS NEVER STOP TRYING TO FLAP THEIR EARS, GIVING AWKWARD LITTLE HOPS, OR JUMPING OFF THINGS. ALL IN VAIN! FOR THERE NEVER WAS, AND NEVER WILL BE, BUT ONE ELEPHANT THAT COULD FLY AND THAT IS
LITTLE DUMBO!

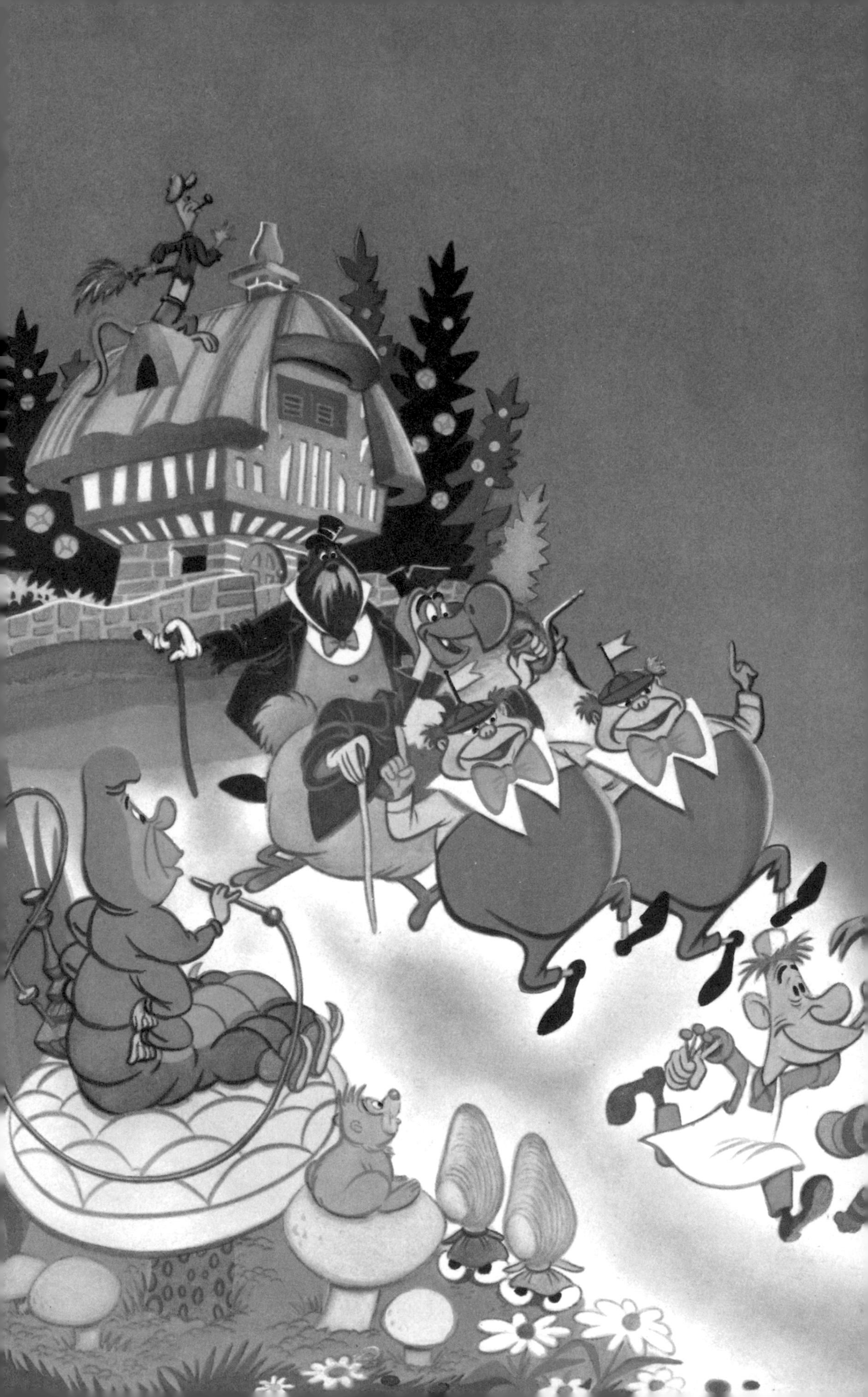

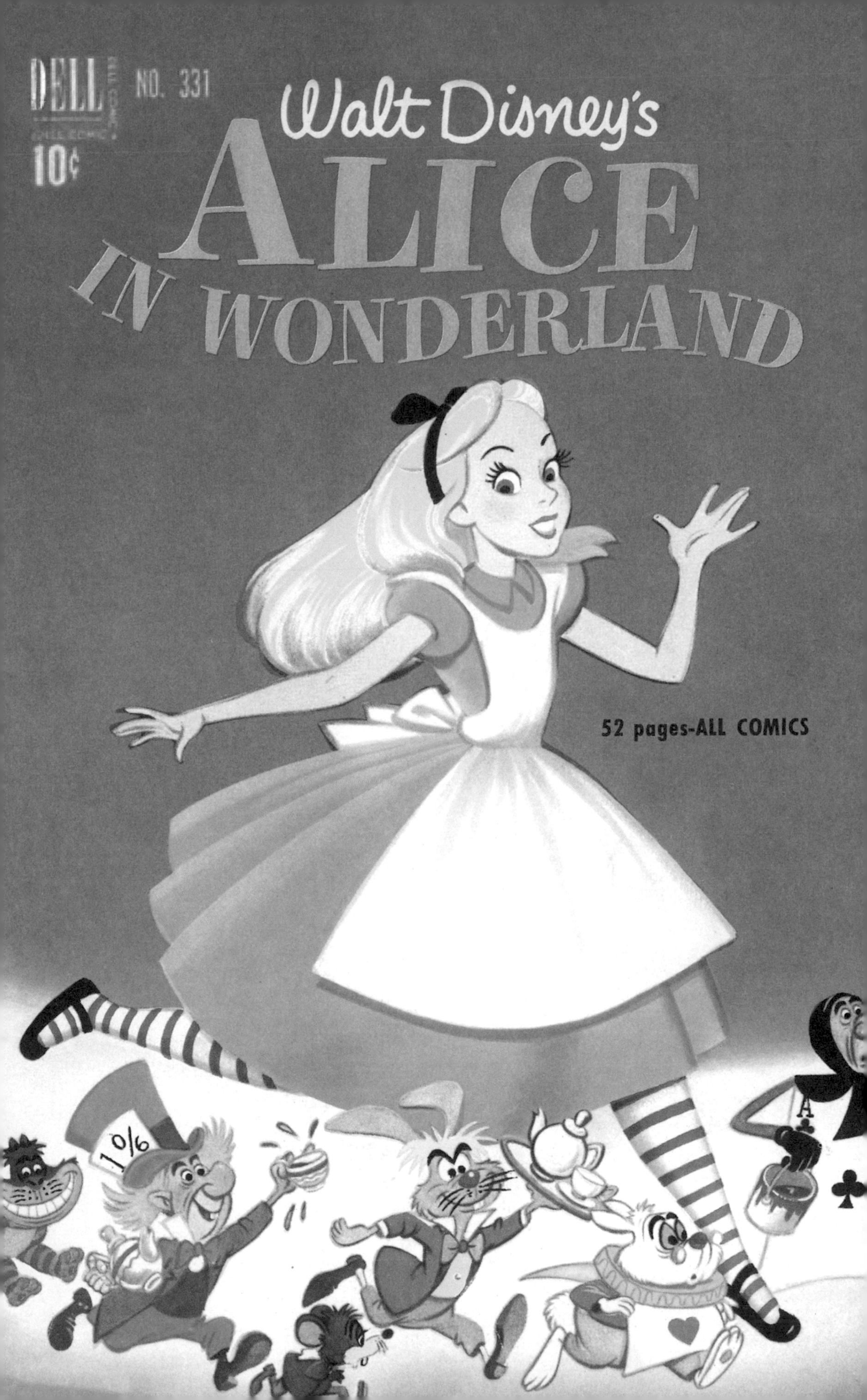

DELL
NO. 331
10¢
Walt Disney's
ALICE IN WONDERLAND
52 pages-ALL COMICS
10/6

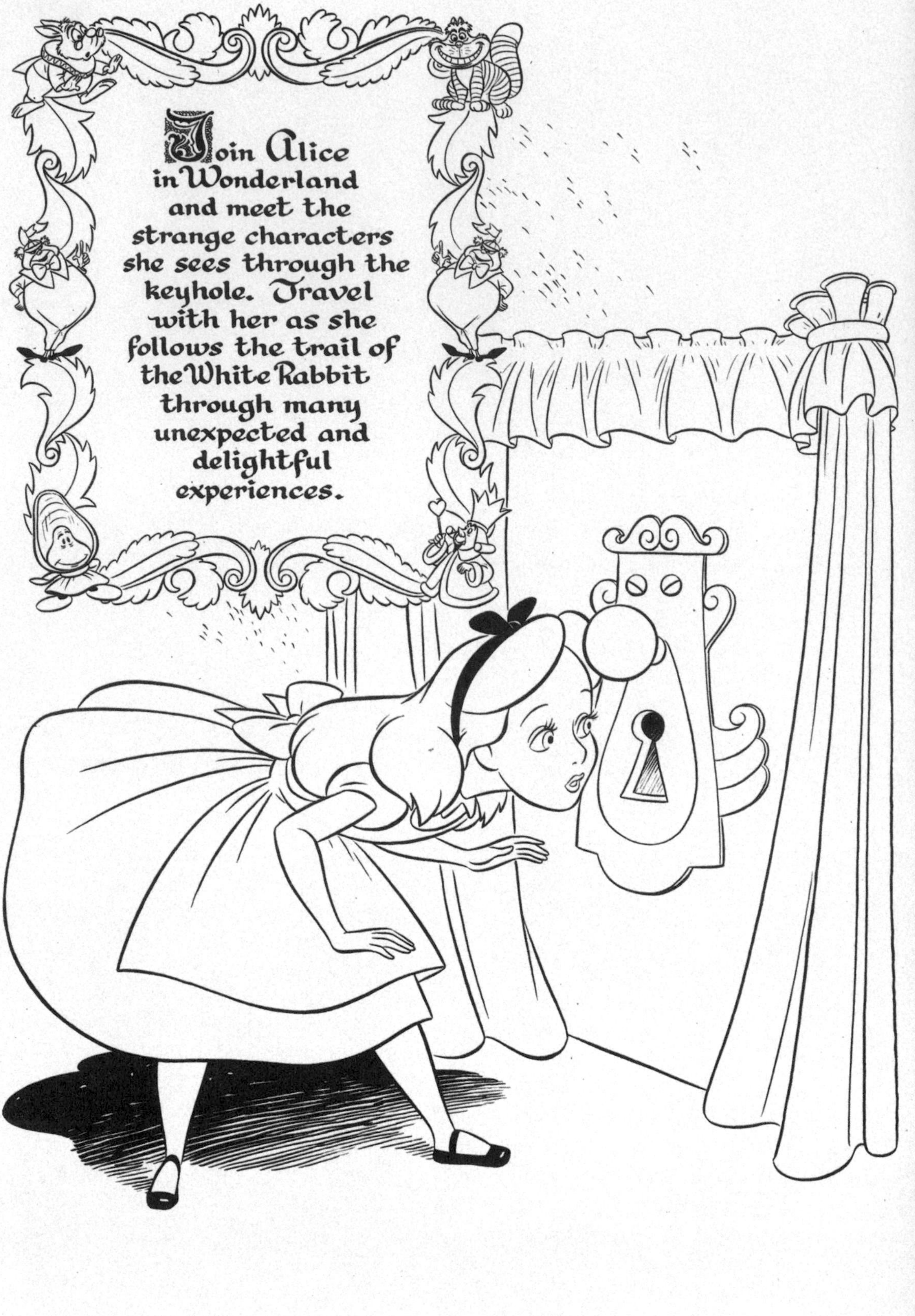
Join Alice in Wonderland and meet the strange characters she sees through the keyhole. Travel with her as she follows the trail of the White Rabbit through many unexpected and delightful experiences.

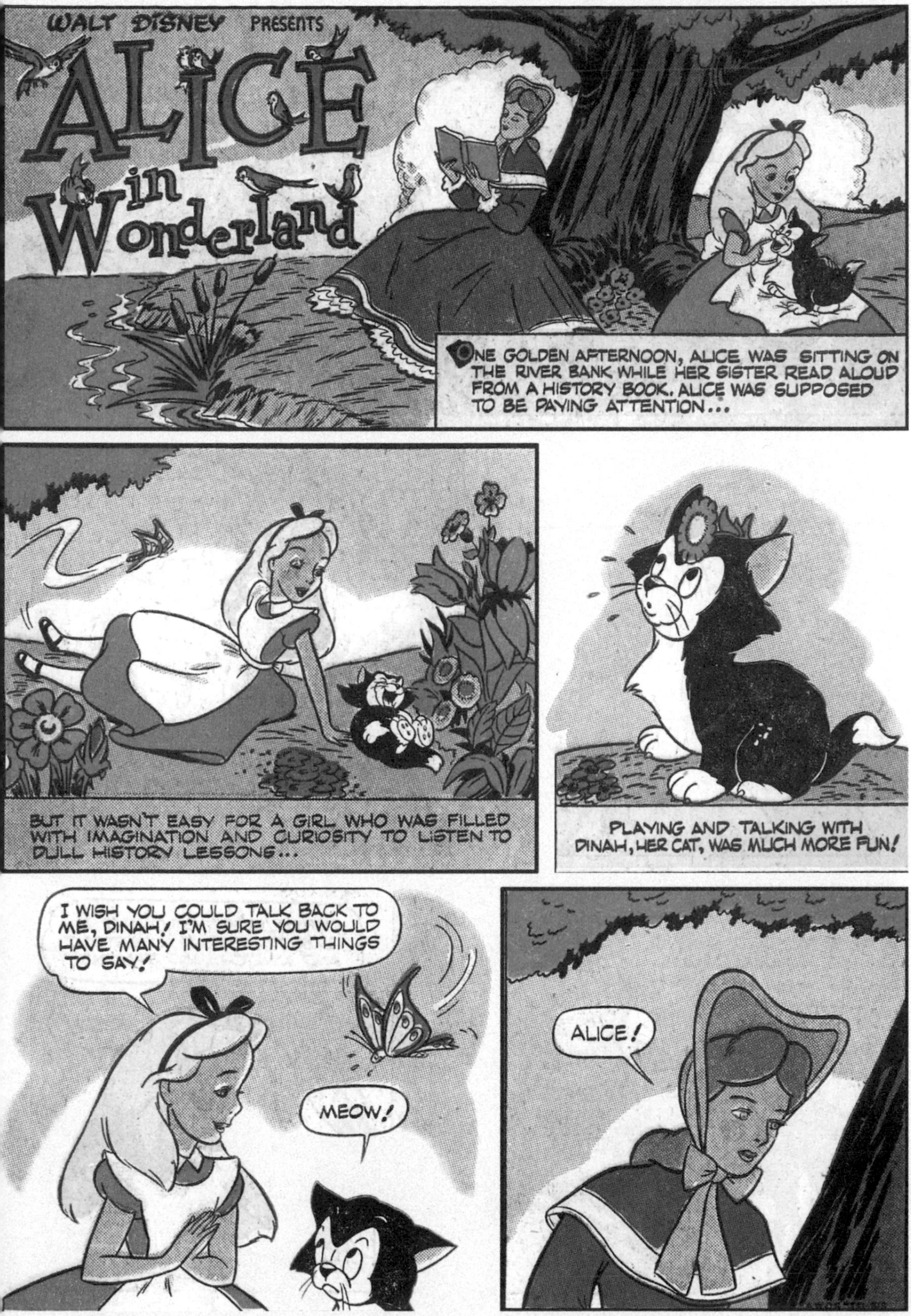
WALT DISNEY PRESENTS
ALICE in Wonderland
ONE GOLDEN AFTERNOON, ALICE WAS SITTING ON THE RIVER BANK WHILE HER SISTER READ ALOUD FROM A HISTORY BOOK. ALICE WAS SUPPOSED TO BE PAYING ATTENTION...
BUT IT WASN'T EASY FOR A GIRL WHO WAS FILLED WITH IMAGINATION AND CURIOSITY TO LISTEN TO DULL HISTORY LESSONS...
PLAYING AND TALKING WITH DINAH, HER CAT, WAS MUCH MORE FUN!
I WISH YOU COULD TALK BACK TO ME, DINAH! I'M SURE YOU WOULD HAVE MANY INTERESTING THINGS TO SAY!
MEOW!
ALICE!

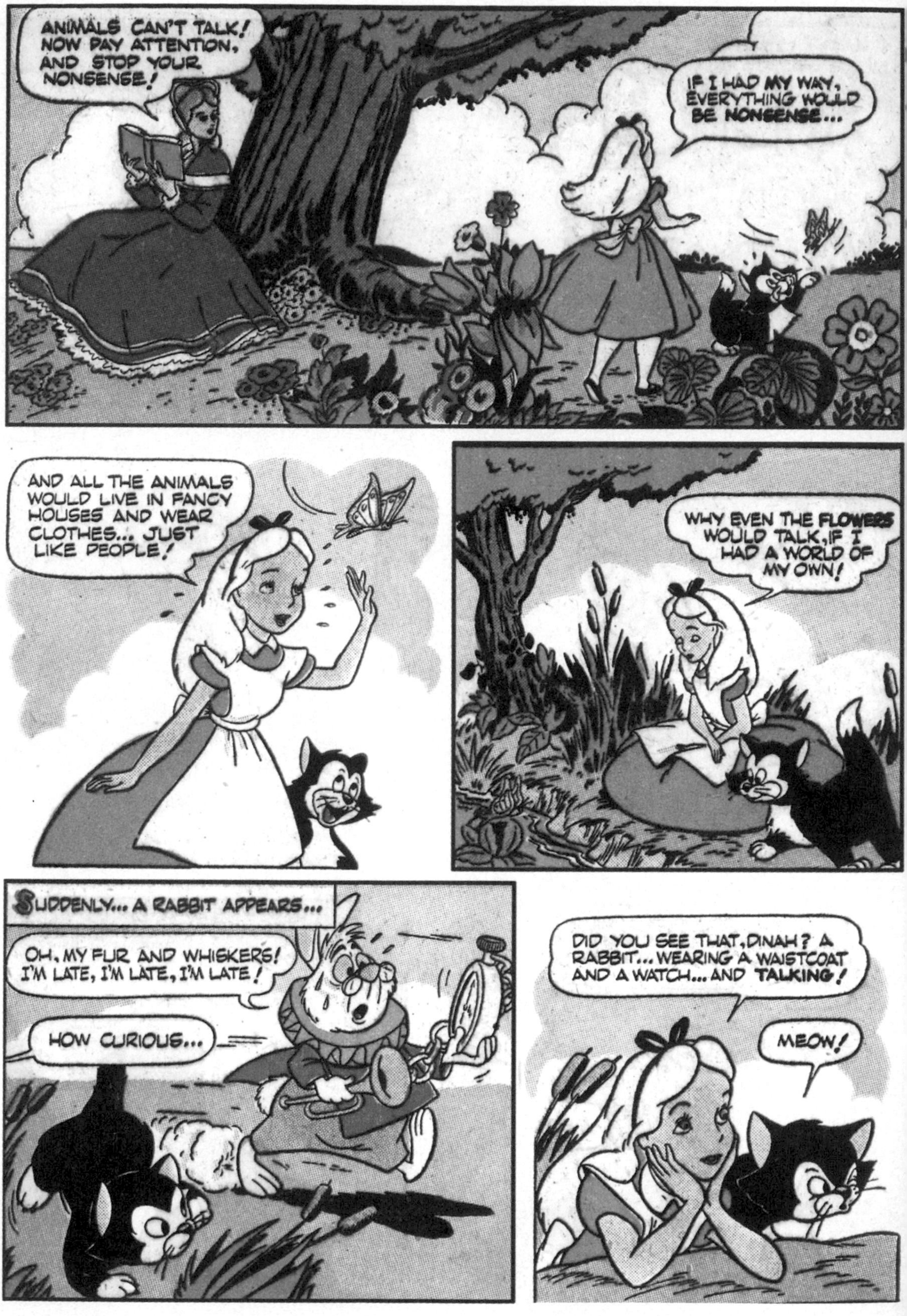
ANIMALS CAN'T TALK! NOW PAY ATTENTION, AND STOP YOUR NONSENSE!
IF I HAD MY WAY, EVERYTHING WOULD BE NONSENSE...
AND ALL THE ANIMALS WOULD LIVE IN FANCY HOUSES AND WEAR CLOTHES... JUST LIKE PEOPLE!
WHY EVEN THE FLOWERS WOULD TALK, IF I HAD A WORLD OF MY OWN!
SUDDENLY... A RABBIT APPEARS...
OH, MY FUR AND WHISKERS! I'M LATE, I'M LATE, I'M LATE!
HOW CURIOUS...
DID YOU SEE THAT, DINAH? A RABBIT... WEARING A WAISTCOAT AND A WATCH... AND TALKING!
MEOW!

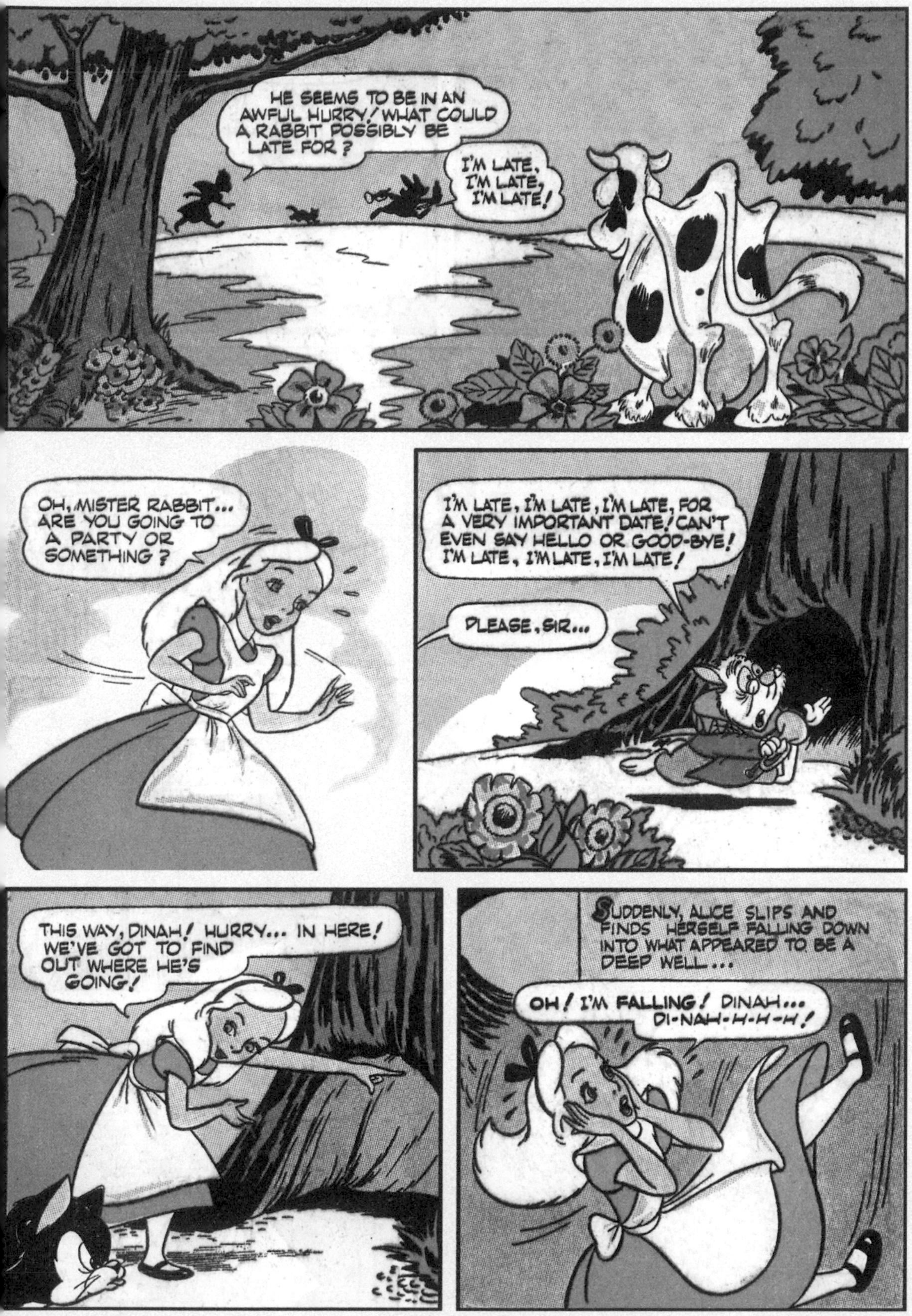
HE SEEMS TO BE IN AN AWFUL HURRY! WHAT COULD A RABBIT POSSIBLY BE LATE FOR?
I'M LATE, I'M LATE, I'M LATE!
OH, MISTER RABBIT... ARE YOU GOING TO A PARTY OR SOMETHING?
I'M LATE, I'M LATE, I'M LATE, FOR A VERY IMPORTANT DATE! CAN'T EVEN SAY HELLO OR GOOD-BYE! I'M LATE, I'M LATE, I'M LATE!
PLEASE, SIR...
THIS WAY, DINAH! HURRY... IN HERE! WE'VE GOT TO FIND OUT WHERE HE'S GOING!
SUDDENLY, ALICE SLIPS AND FINDS HERSELF FALLING DOWN INTO WHAT APPEARED TO BE A DEEP WELL...
OH! I'M FALLING! DINAH... DI-NAH-H-H-H!

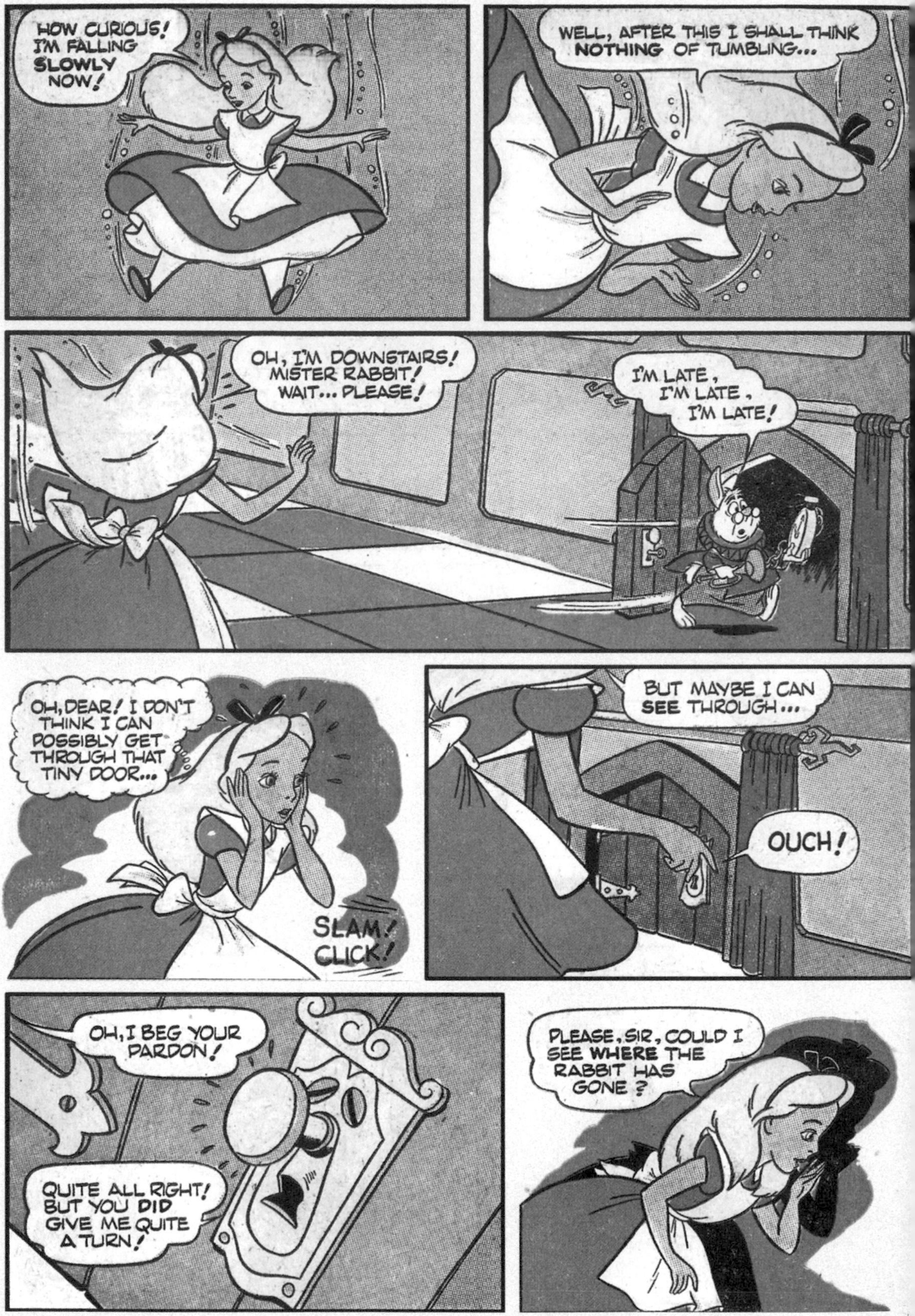
HOW CURIOUS! I'M FALLING SLOWLY NOW!
WELL, AFTER THIS I SHALL THINK NOTHING OF TUMBLING...
OH, I'M DOWNSTAIRS! MISTER RABBIT! WAIT... PLEASE!
I'M LATE, I'M LATE, I'M LATE!
OH, DEAR! I DON'T THINK I CAN POSSIBLY GET THROUGH THAT TINY DOOR...
SLAM! CLICK!
BUT MAYBE I CAN SEE THROUGH...
OUCH!
OH, I BEG YOUR PARDON!
QUITE ALL RIGHT! BUT YOU DID GIVE ME QUITE A TURN!
PLEASE, SIR, COULD I SEE WHERE THE RABBIT HAS GONE?

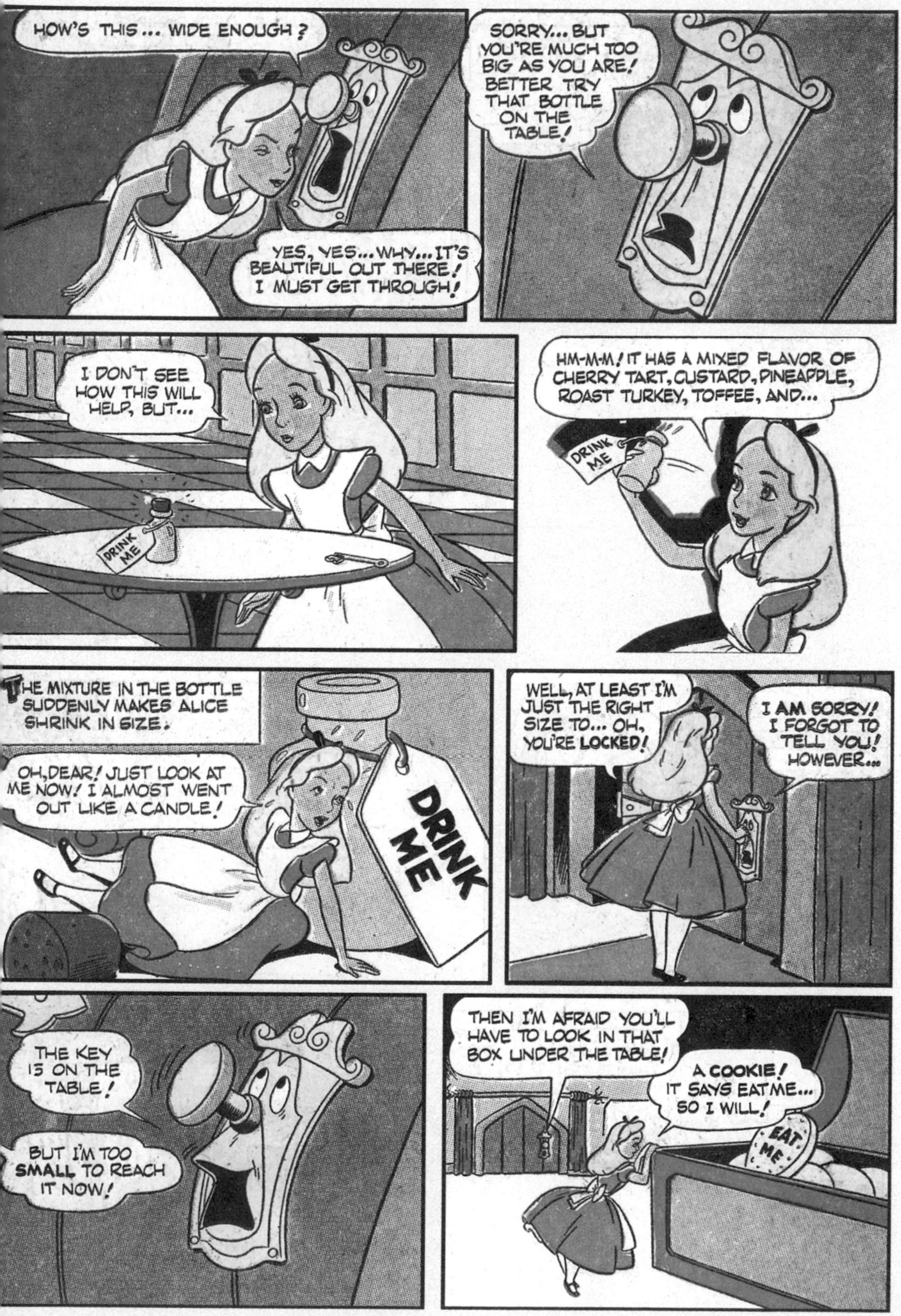
HOW'S THIS... WIDE ENOUGH?
YES, YES...WHY...IT'S BEAUTIFUL OUT THERE! I MUST GET THROUGH!
SORRY... BUT YOU'RE MUCH TOO BIG AS YOU ARE! BETTER TRY THAT BOTTLE ON THE TABLE!
I DON'T SEE HOW THIS WILL HELP, BUT...
DRINK ME
HM-M-M! IT HAS A MIXED FLAVOR OF CHERRY TART, CUSTARD, PINEAPPLE, ROAST TURKEY, TOFFEE, AND...
DRINK ME
THE MIXTURE IN THE BOTTLE SUDDENLY MAKES ALICE SHRINK IN SIZE.
OH, DEAR! JUST LOOK AT ME NOW! I ALMOST WENT OUT LIKE A CANDLE!
DRINK ME
WELL, AT LEAST I'M JUST THE RIGHT SIZE TO... OH, YOU'RE LOCKED!
I AM SORRY! I FORGOT TO TELL YOU! HOWEVER...
THE KEY IS ON THE TABLE!
BUT I'M TOO SMALL TO REACH IT NOW!
THEN I'M AFRAID YOU'LL HAVE TO LOOK IN THAT BOX UNDER THE TABLE!
A COOKIE! IT SAYS EAT ME... SO I WILL!
EAT ME

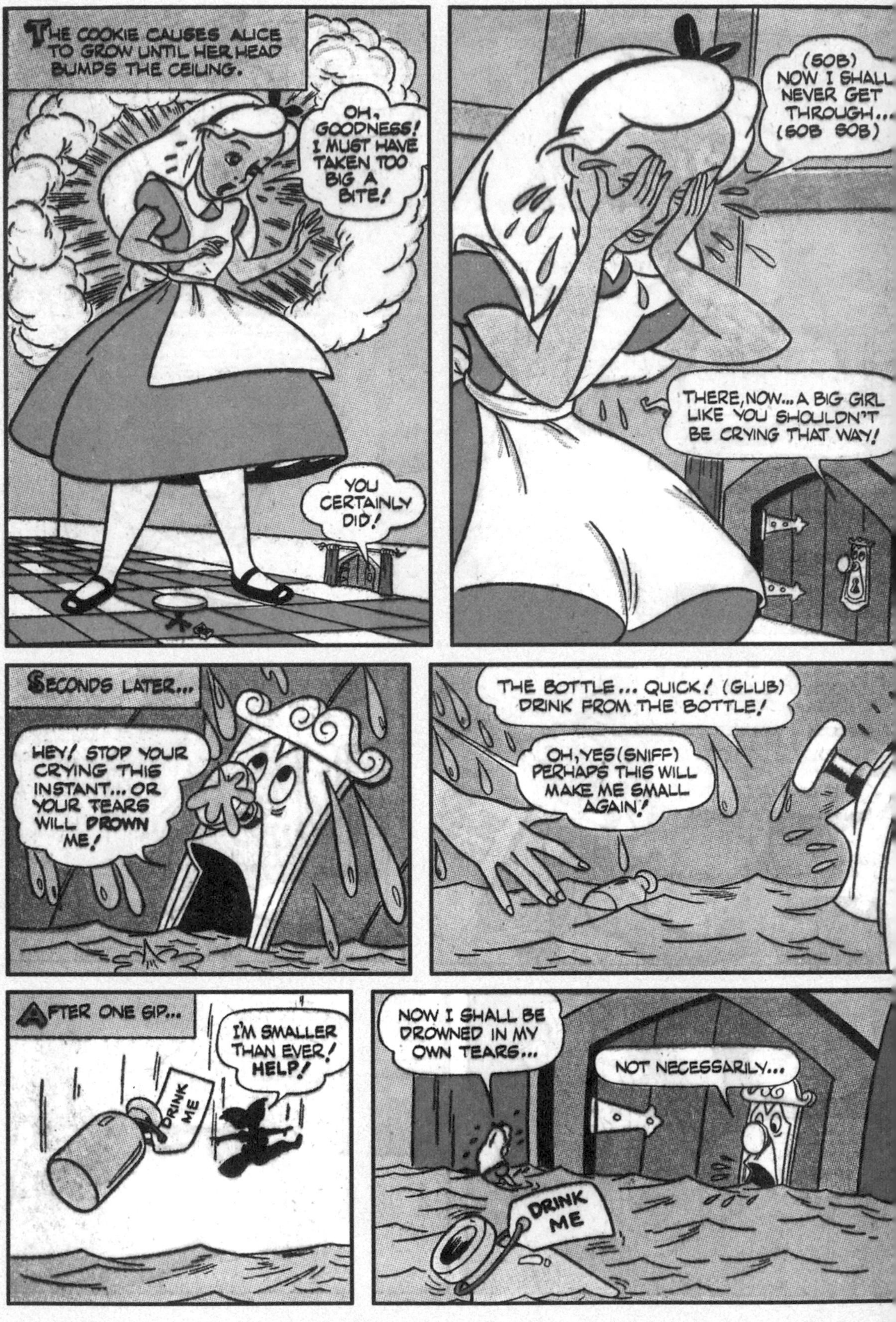
THE COOKIE CAUSES ALICE TO GROW UNTIL HER HEAD BUMPS THE CEILING.
OH, GOODNESS! I MUST HAVE TAKEN TOO BIG A BITE!
YOU CERTAINLY DID!
(SOB) NOW I SHALL NEVER GET THROUGH... (SOB SOB)
THERE, NOW... A BIG GIRL LIKE YOU SHOULDN'T BE CRYING THAT WAY!
SECONDS LATER...
HEY! STOP YOUR CRYING THIS INSTANT... OR YOUR TEARS WILL DROWN ME!
THE BOTTLE... QUICK! (GLUB) DRINK FROM THE BOTTLE!
OH, YES (SNIFF) PERHAPS THIS WILL MAKE ME SMALL AGAIN!
AFTER ONE SIP...
DRINK ME
I'M SMALLER THAN EVER! HELP!
NOW I SHALL BE DROWNED IN MY OWN TEARS...
NOT NECESSARILY...
DRINK ME

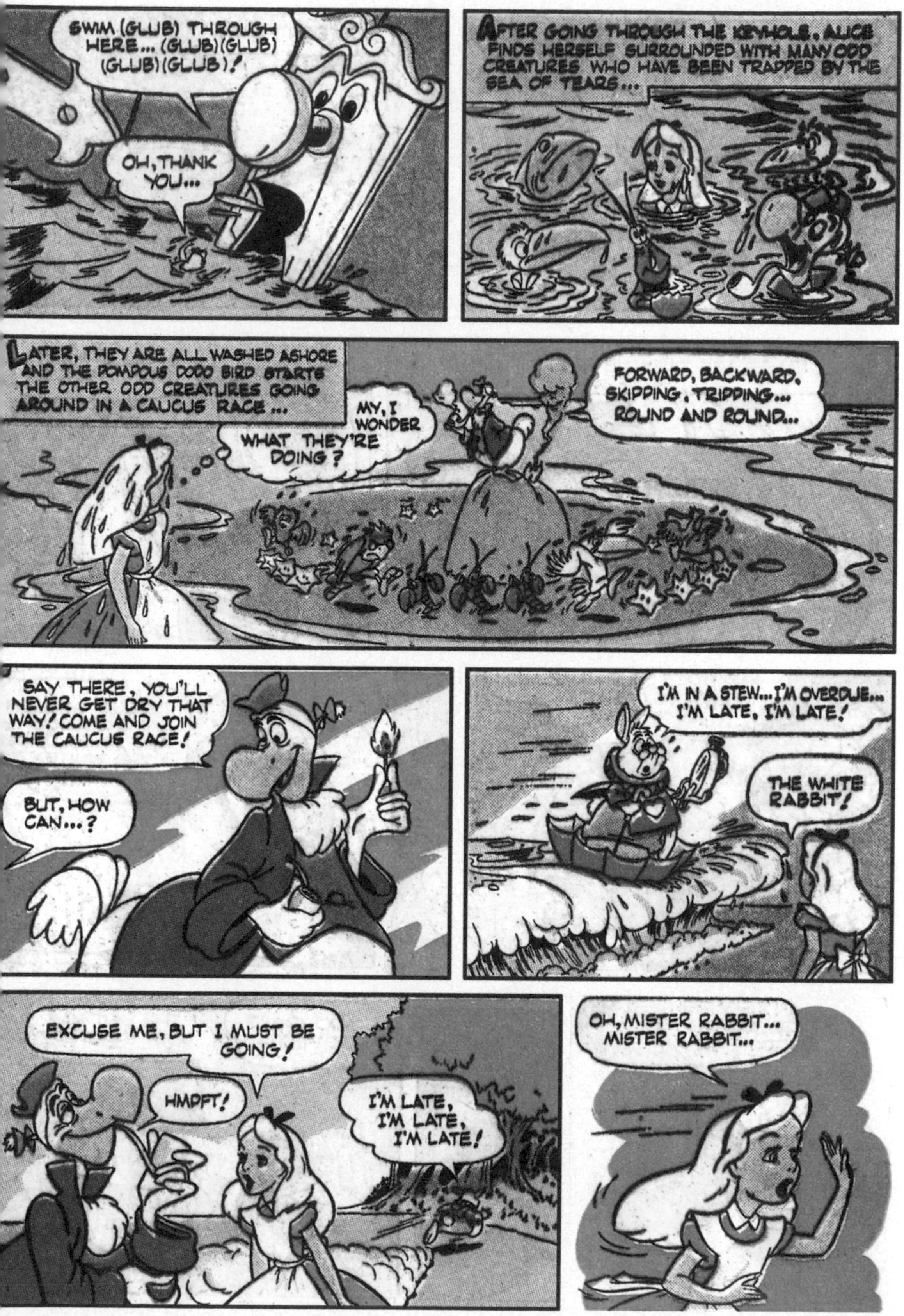
SWIM (GLUB) THROUGH HERE... (GLUB) (GLUB) (GLUB) (GLUB)!
OH, THANK YOU...
AFTER GOING THROUGH THE KEYHOLE, ALICE FINDS HERSELF SURROUNDED WITH MANY ODD CREATURES WHO HAVE BEEN TRAPPED BY THE SEA OF TEARS...
LATER, THEY ARE ALL WASHED ASHORE AND THE POMPOUS DODO BIRD STARTS THE OTHER ODD CREATURES GOING AROUND IN A CAUCUS RACE...
MY, I WONDER WHAT THEY'RE DOING?
FORWARD, BACKWARD, SKIPPING, TRIPPING... ROUND AND ROUND...
SAY THERE, YOU'LL NEVER GET DRY THAT WAY! COME AND JOIN THE CAUCUS RACE!
BUT, HOW CAN...?
I'M IN A STEW...I'M OVERDUE... I'M LATE, I'M LATE!
THE WHITE RABBIT!
EXCUSE ME, BUT I MUST BE GOING!
HMPFT!
I'M LATE, I'M LATE, I'M LATE!
OH, MISTER RABBIT... MISTER RABBIT...

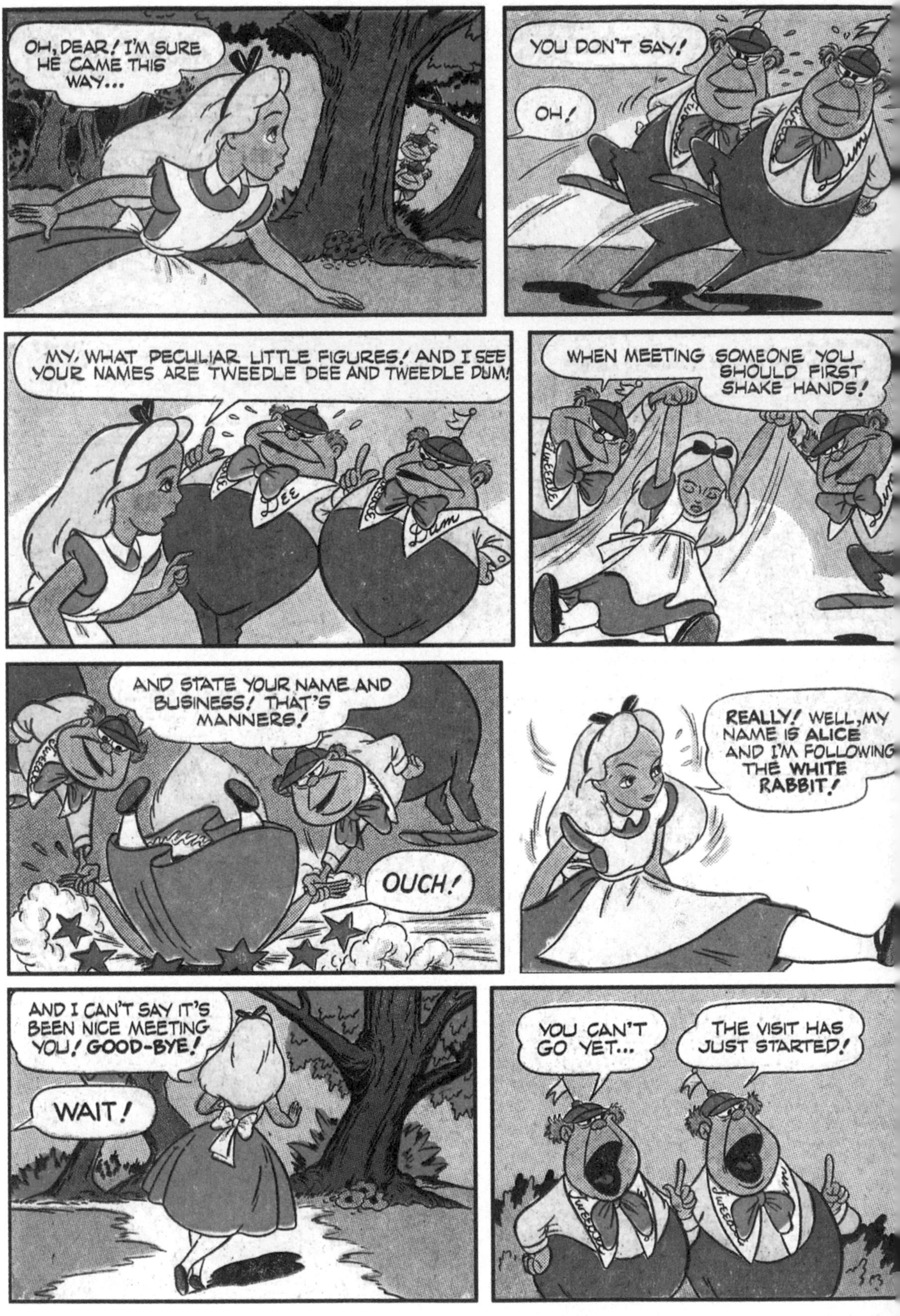
OH, DEAR! I'M SURE HE CAME THIS WAY...
YOU DON'T SAY!
OH!
MY, WHAT PECULIAR LITTLE FIGURES! AND I SEE YOUR NAMES ARE TWEEDLE DEE AND TWEEDLE DUM!
DEE
DUM
WHEN MEETING SOMEONE YOU SHOULD FIRST SHAKE HANDS!
AND STATE YOUR NAME AND BUSINESS! THAT'S MANNERS!
OUCH!
REALLY! WELL, MY NAME IS ALICE AND I'M FOLLOWING THE WHITE RABBIT!
AND I CAN'T SAY IT'S BEEN NICE MEETING YOU! GOOD-BYE!
WAIT!
YOU CAN'T GO YET...
THE VISIT HAS JUST STARTED!

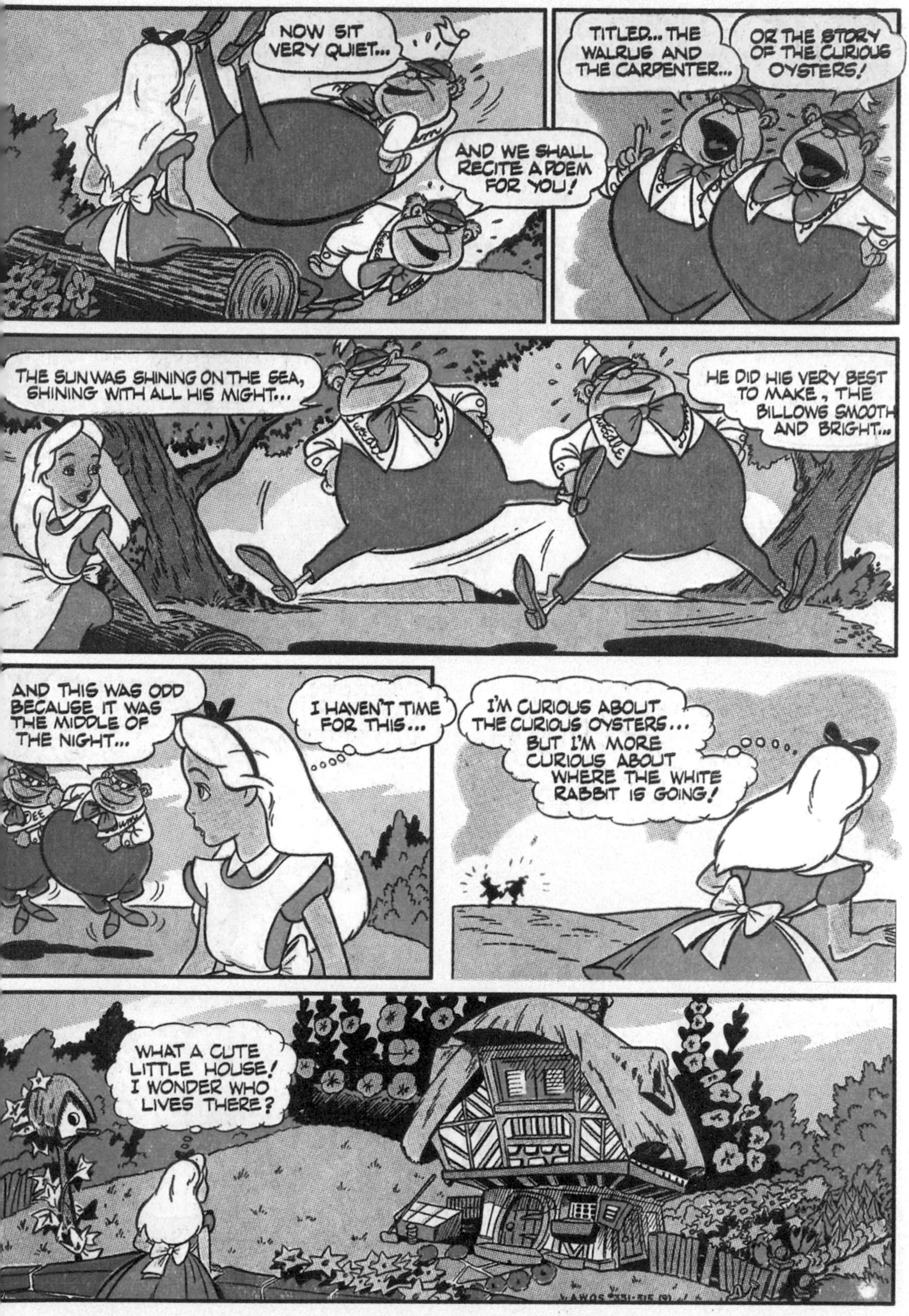
NOW SIT VERY QUIET...
AND WE SHALL RECITE A POEM FOR YOU!
TITLED... THE WALRUS AND THE CARPENTER...
OR THE STORY OF THE CURIOUS OYSTERS!
THE SUN WAS SHINING ON THE SEA, SHINING WITH ALL HIS MIGHT...
HE DID HIS VERY BEST TO MAKE, THE BILLOWS SMOOTH AND BRIGHT...
AND THIS WAS ODD BECAUSE IT WAS THE MIDDLE OF THE NIGHT...
I HAVEN'T TIME FOR THIS...
I'M CURIOUS ABOUT THE CURIOUS OYSTERS... BUT I'M MORE CURIOUS ABOUT WHERE THE WHITE RABBIT IS GOING!
WHAT A CUTE LITTLE HOUSE! I WONDER WHO LIVES THERE?

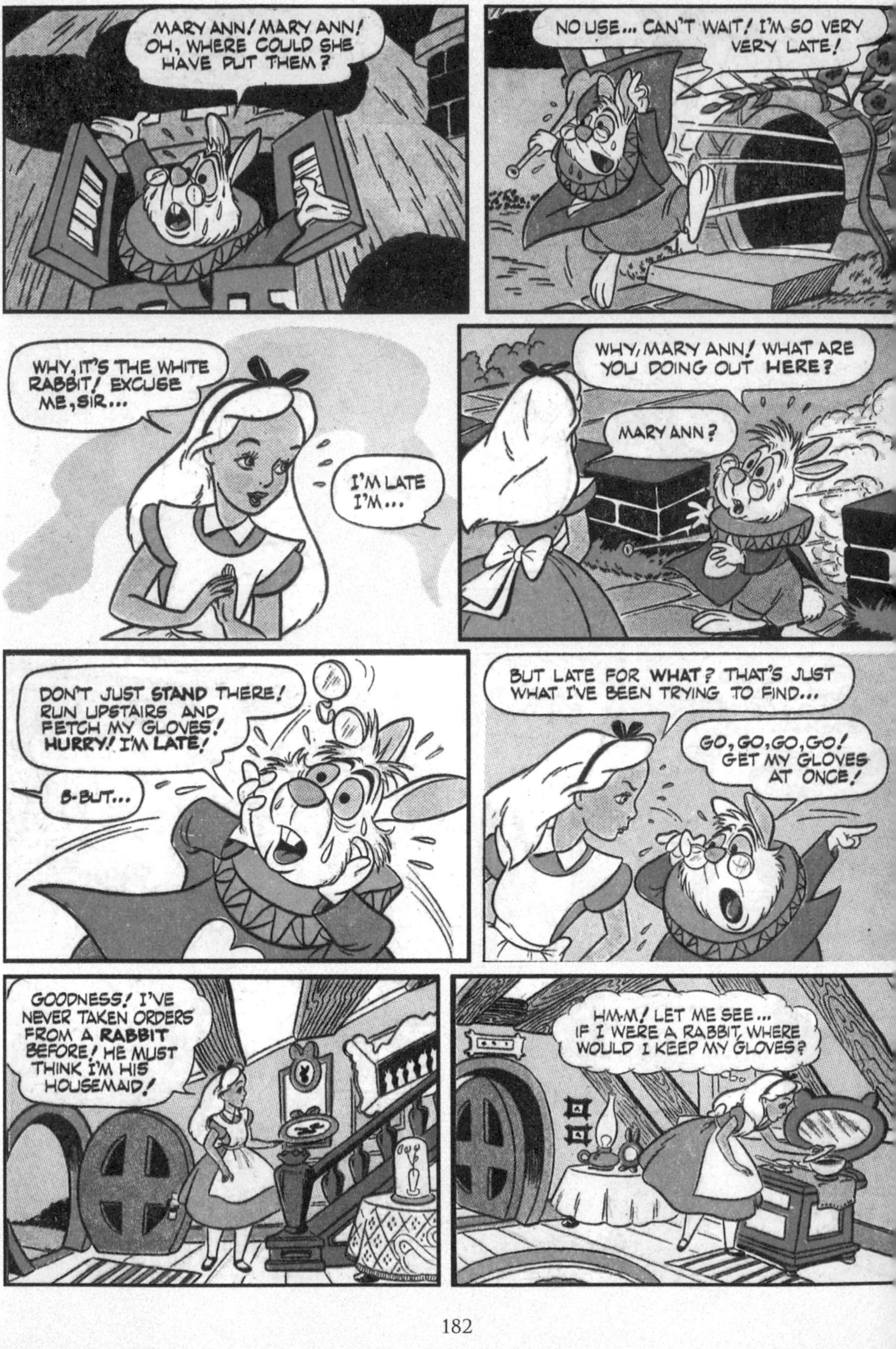
MARY ANN! MARY ANN! OH, WHERE COULD SHE HAVE PUT THEM?
NO USE... CAN'T WAIT! I'M SO VERY VERY LATE!
WHY, IT'S THE WHITE RABBIT! EXCUSE ME, SIR...
I'M LATE I'M...
WHY, MARY ANN! WHAT ARE YOU DOING OUT HERE?
MARY ANN?
DON'T JUST STAND THERE! RUN UPSTAIRS AND FETCH MY GLOVES! HURRY! I'M LATE!
B-BUT...
BUT LATE FOR WHAT? THAT'S JUST WHAT I'VE BEEN TRYING TO FIND...
GO, GO, GO, GO! GET MY GLOVES AT ONCE!
GOODNESS! I'VE NEVER TAKEN ORDERS FROM A RABBIT BEFORE! HE MUST THINK I'M HIS HOUSEMAID!
HM-M! LET ME SEE... IF I WERE A RABBIT, WHERE WOULD I KEEP MY GLOVES?

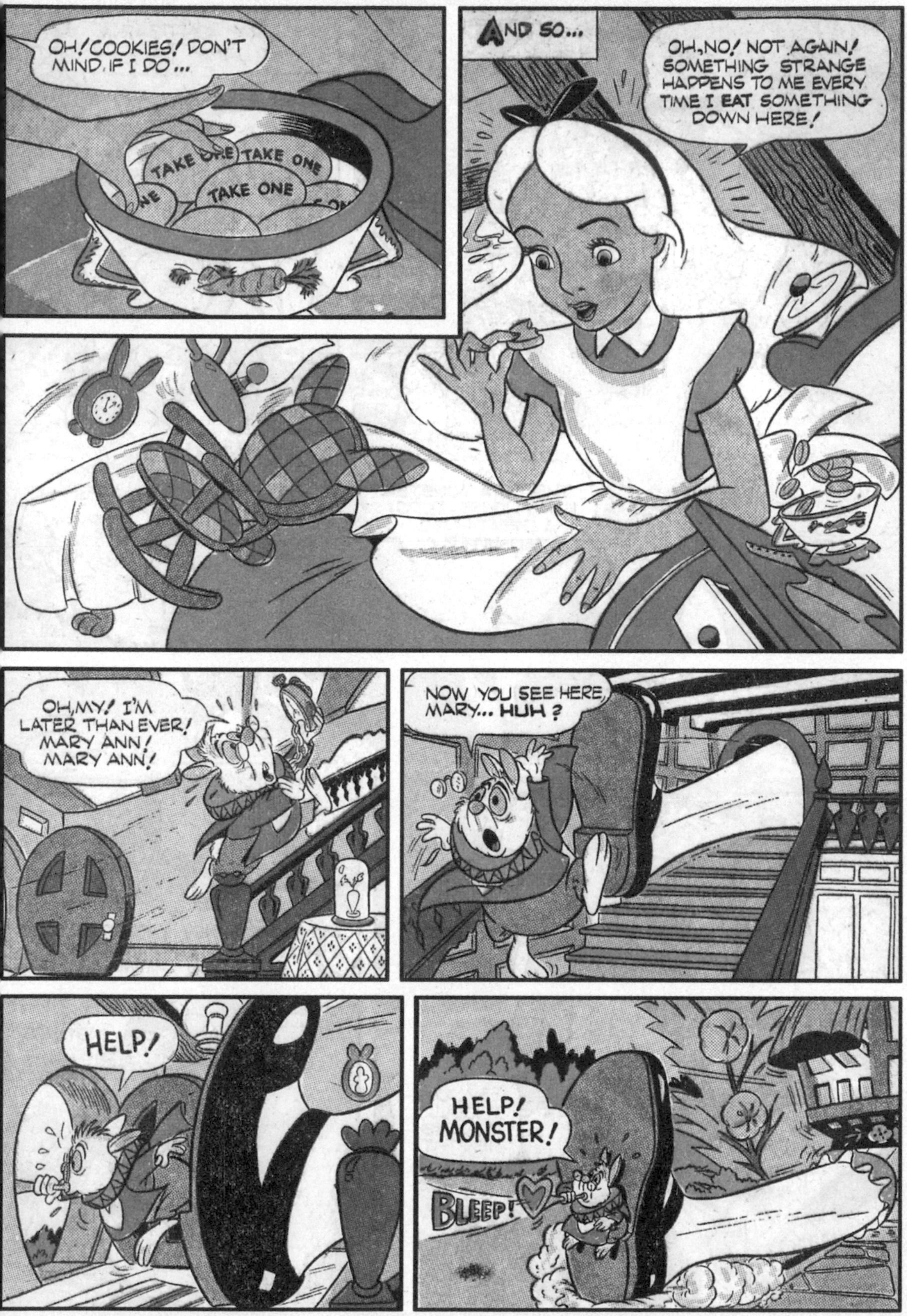
OH! COOKIES! DON'T MIND IF I DO...
TAKE ONE
TAKE ONE
TAKE ONE
AND SO...
OH, NO! NOT AGAIN! SOMETHING STRANGE HAPPENS TO ME EVERY TIME I EAT SOMETHING DOWN HERE!
OH, MY! I'M LATER THAN EVER! MARY ANN! MARY ANN!
NOW YOU SEE HERE, MARY... HUH ?
HELP!
HELP! MONSTER!
BLEEP!

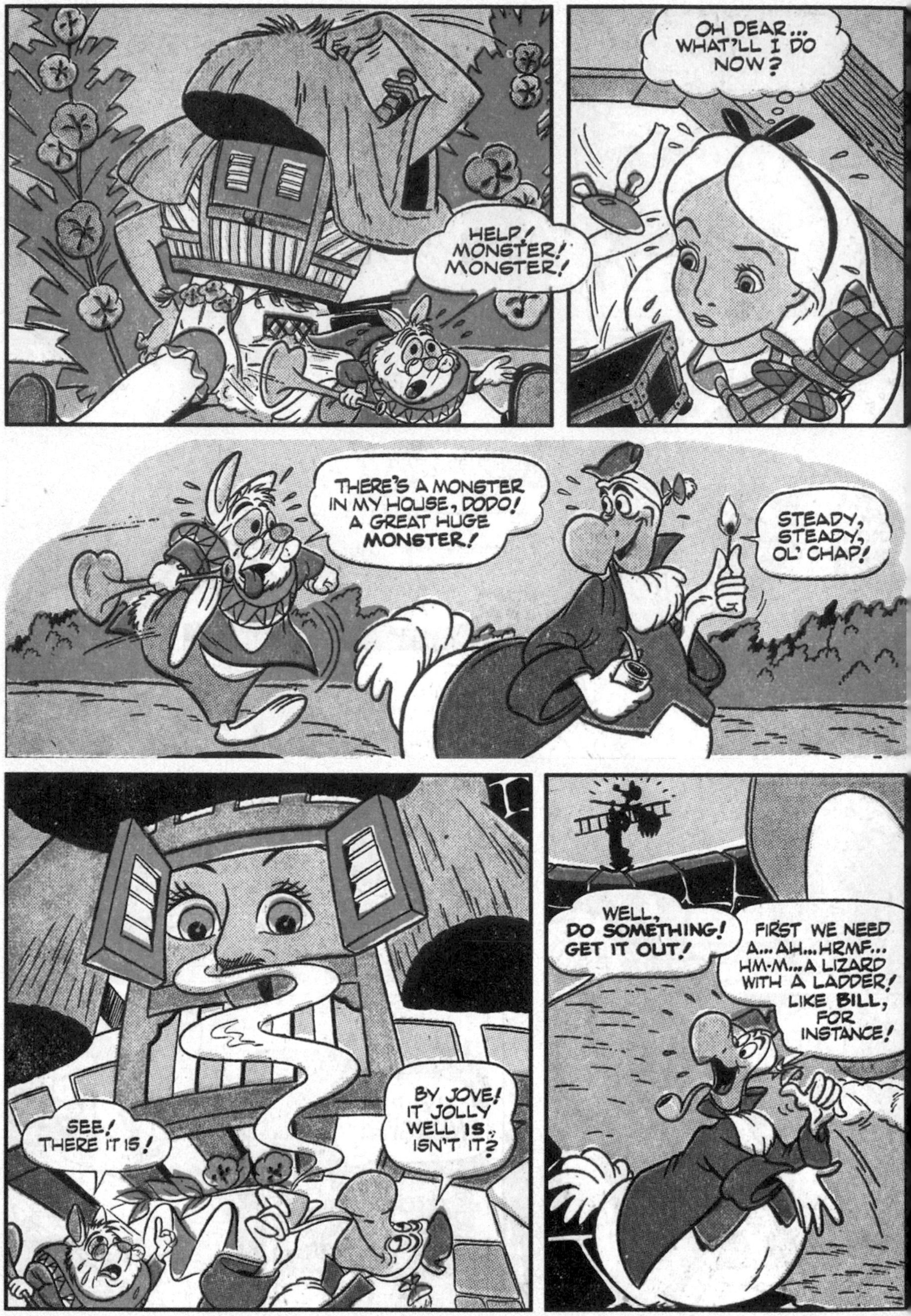
HELP! MONSTER! MONSTER!
OH DEAR... WHAT'LL I DO NOW?
THERE'S A MONSTER IN MY HOUSE, DODO! A GREAT HUGE MONSTER!
STEADY, STEADY, OL' CHAP!
SEE! THERE IT IS!
BY JOVE! IT JOLLY WELL IS, ISN'T IT?
WELL, DO SOMETHING! GET IT OUT!
FIRST WE NEED A... AH... HRMF... HM-M... A LIZARD WITH A LADDER! LIKE BILL, FOR INSTANCE!

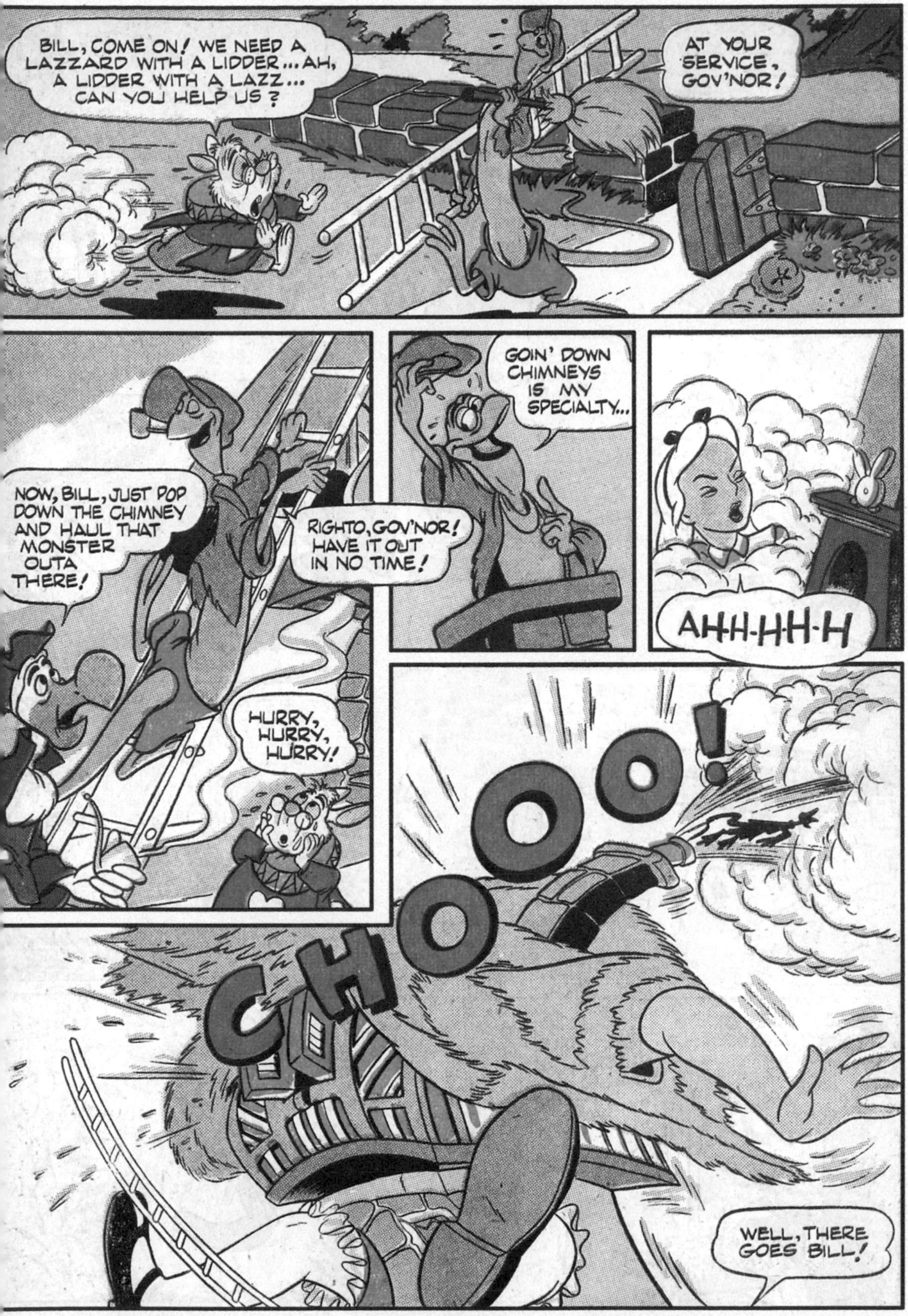
BILL, COME ON! WE NEED A LAZZARD WITH A LIDDER...AH, A LIDDER WITH A LAZZ... CAN YOU HELP US?
AT YOUR SERVICE, GOV'NOR!
NOW, BILL, JUST POP DOWN THE CHIMNEY AND HAUL THAT MONSTER OUTA THERE!
RIGHTO, GOV'NOR! HAVE IT OUT IN NO TIME!
HURRY, HURRY, HURRY!
GOIN' DOWN CHIMNEYS IS MY SPECIALTY...
AHH-HH-H
CHOOO!
WELL, THERE GOES BILL!

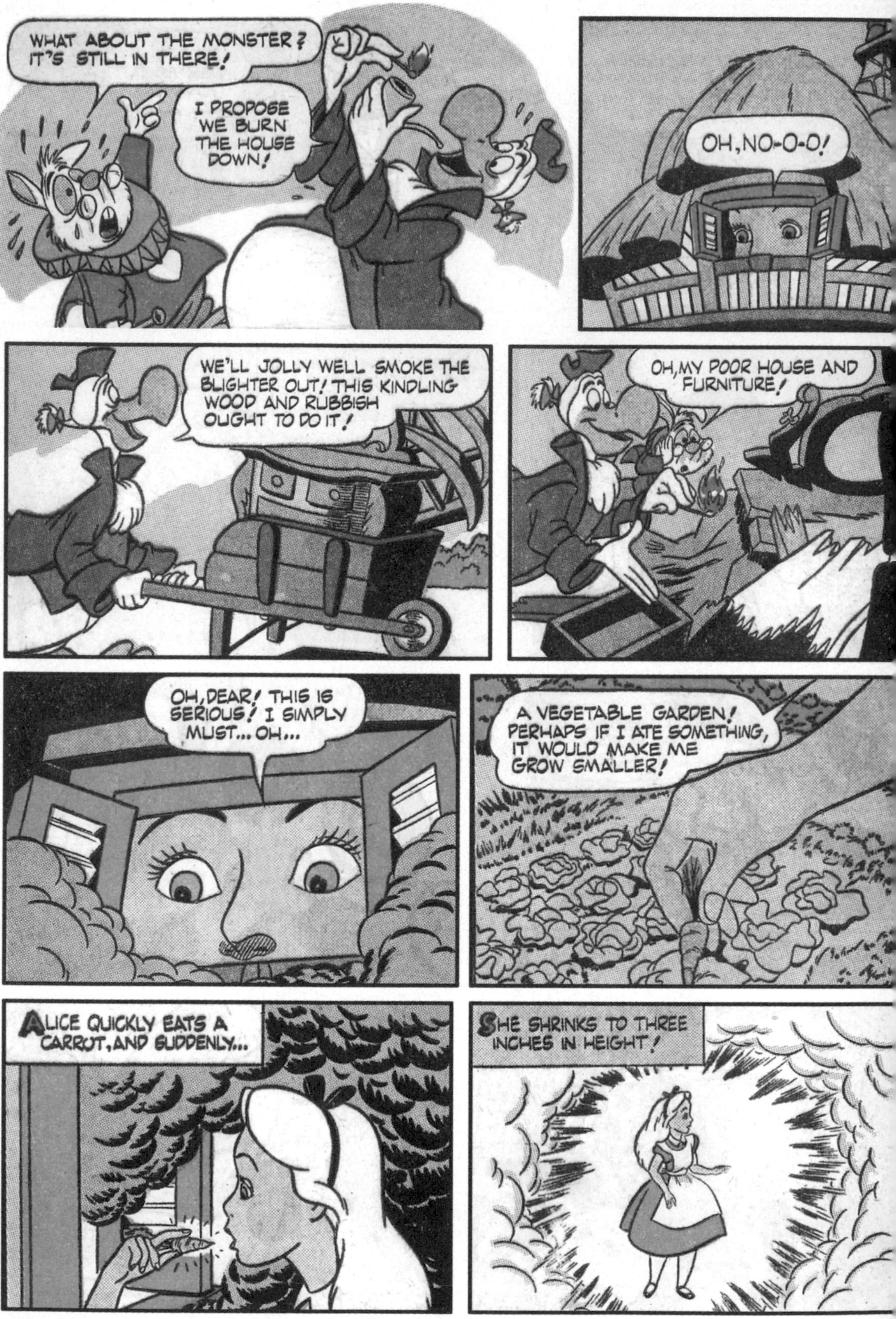
WHAT ABOUT THE MONSTER? IT'S STILL IN THERE!
I PROPOSE WE BURN THE HOUSE DOWN!
OH, NO-O-O!
WE'LL JOLLY WELL SMOKE THE BLIGHTER OUT! THIS KINDLING WOOD AND RUBBISH OUGHT TO DO IT!
OH, MY POOR HOUSE AND FURNITURE!
OH, DEAR! THIS IS SERIOUS! I SIMPLY MUST... OH...
A VEGETABLE GARDEN! PERHAPS IF I ATE SOMETHING, IT WOULD MAKE ME GROW SMALLER!
ALICE QUICKLY EATS A CARROT, AND SUDDENLY...
SHE SHRINKS TO THREE INCHES IN HEIGHT!

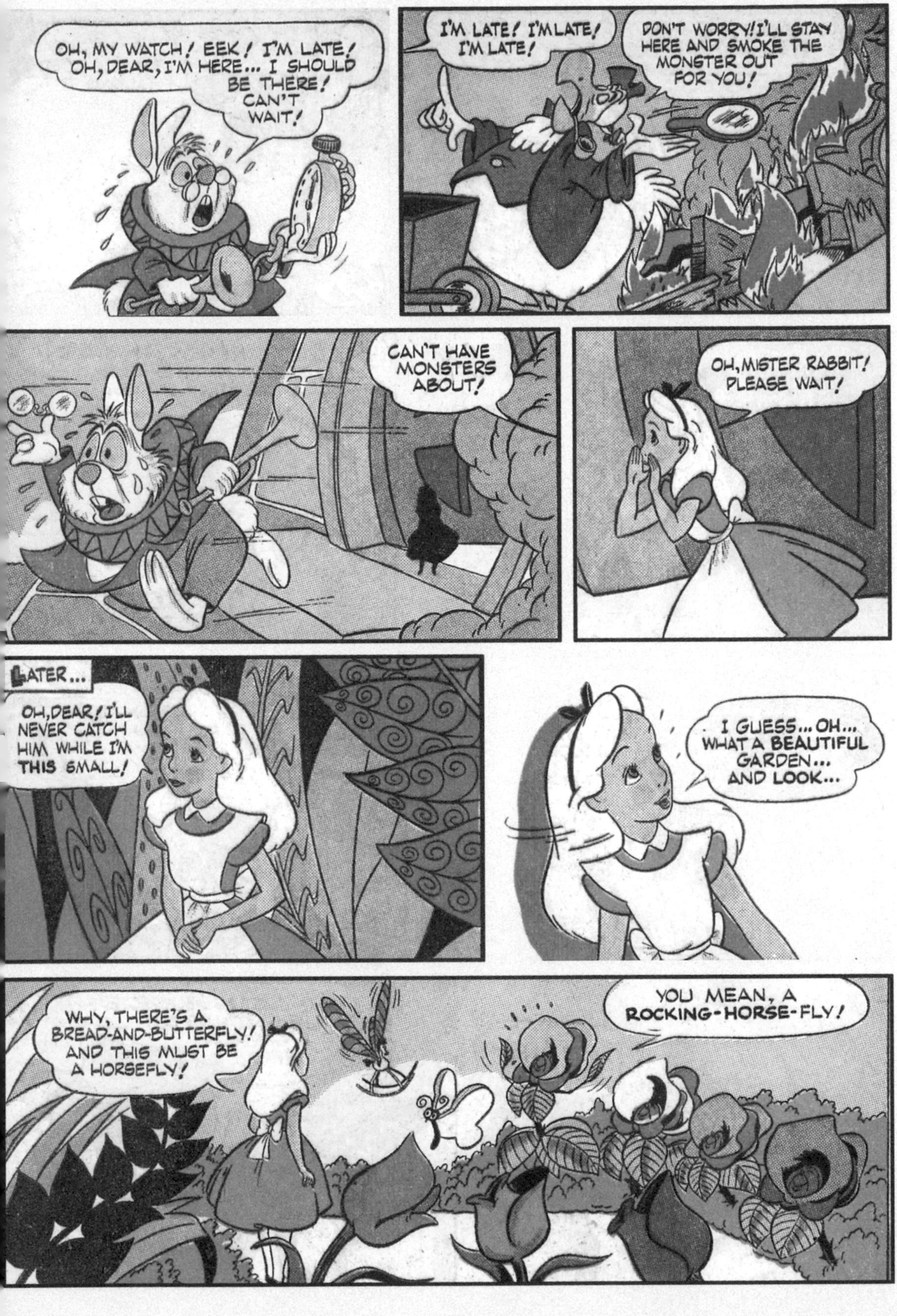
OH, MY WATCH! EEK! I'M LATE! OH, DEAR, I'M HERE... I SHOULD BE THERE! CAN'T WAIT!
I'M LATE! I'M LATE! I'M LATE!
DON'T WORRY! I'LL STAY HERE AND SMOKE THE MONSTER OUT FOR YOU!
CAN'T HAVE MONSTERS ABOUT!
OH, MISTER RABBIT! PLEASE WAIT!
LATER...
OH, DEAR! I'LL NEVER CATCH HIM WHILE I'M THIS SMALL!
I GUESS... OH... WHAT A BEAUTIFUL GARDEN... AND LOOK...
WHY, THERE'S A BREAD-AND-BUTTERFLY! AND THIS MUST BE A HORSEFLY!
YOU MEAN, A ROCKING-HORSE-FLY!

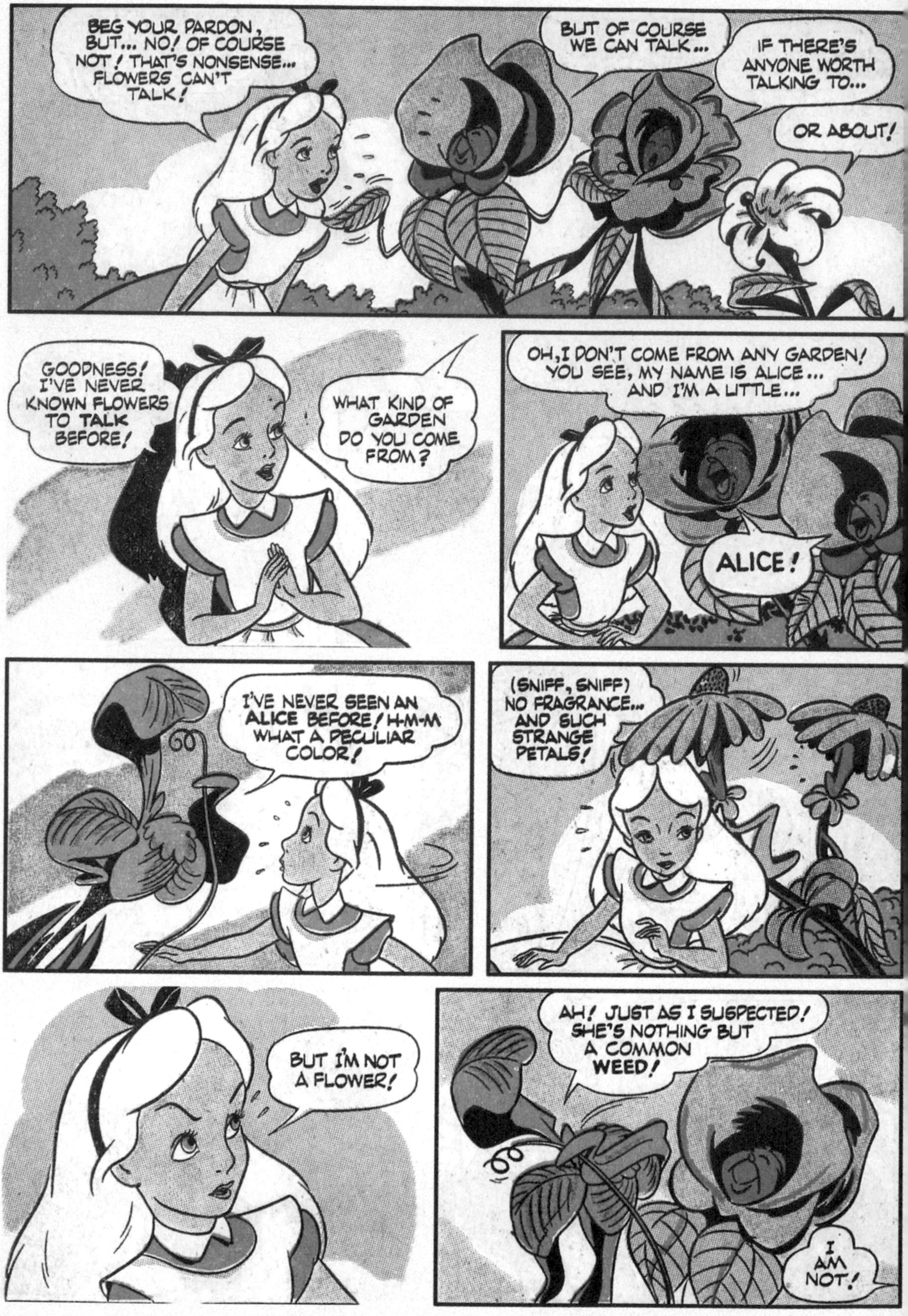
BEG YOUR PARDON, BUT... NO! OF COURSE NOT! THAT'S NONSENSE... FLOWERS CAN'T TALK!
BUT OF COURSE WE CAN TALK...
IF THERE'S ANYONE WORTH TALKING TO...
OR ABOUT!
GOODNESS! I'VE NEVER KNOWN FLOWERS TO TALK BEFORE!
WHAT KIND OF GARDEN DO YOU COME FROM?
OH, I DON'T COME FROM ANY GARDEN! YOU SEE, MY NAME IS ALICE... AND I'M A LITTLE...
ALICE!
I'VE NEVER SEEN AN ALICE BEFORE! H-M-M WHAT A PECULIAR COLOR!
(SNIFF, SNIFF) NO FRAGRANCE... AND SUCH STRANGE PETALS!
BUT I'M NOT A FLOWER!
AH! JUST AS I SUSPECTED! SHE'S NOTHING BUT A COMMON WEED!
I AM NOT!

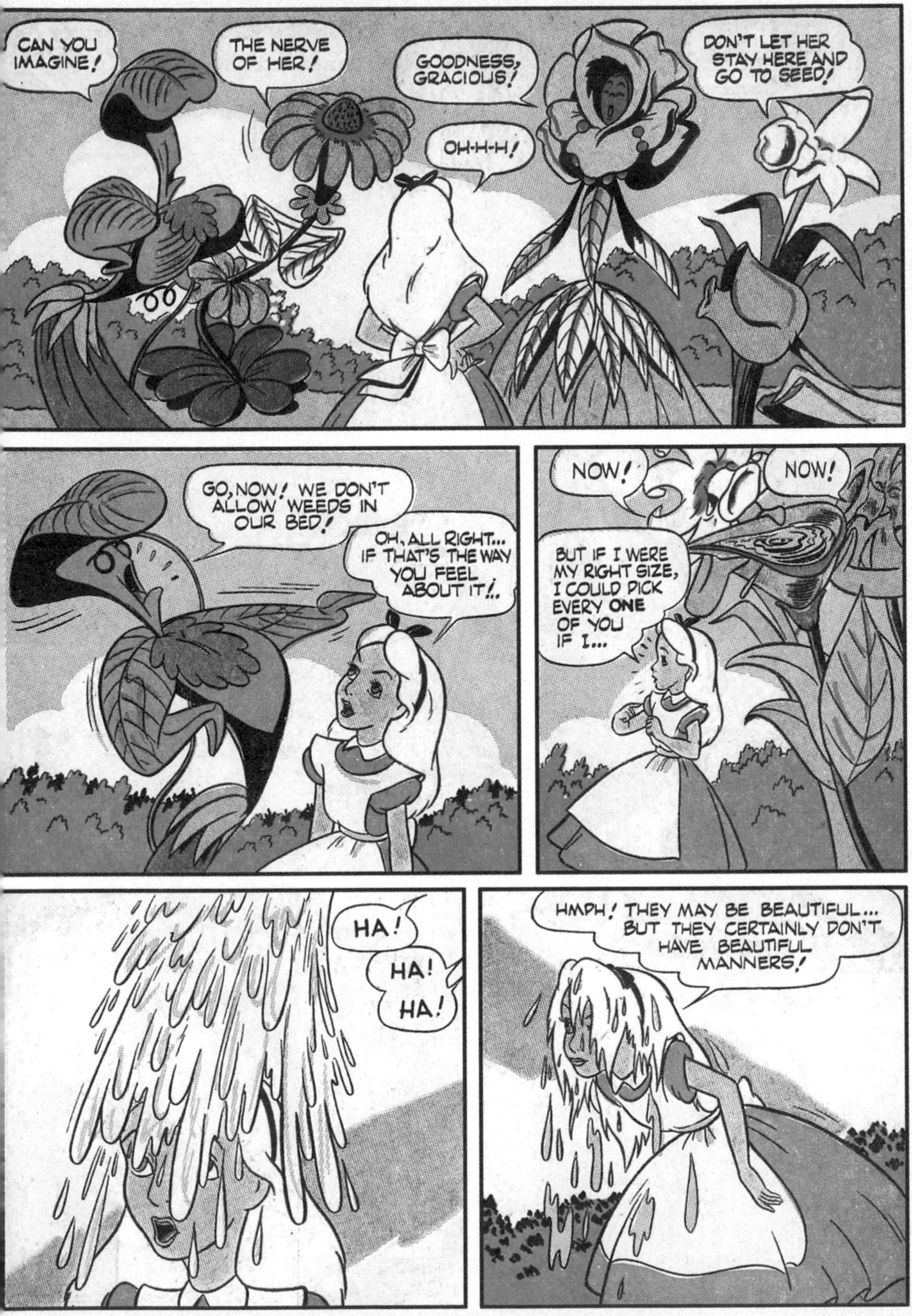
CAN YOU IMAGINE!
THE NERVE OF HER!
GOODNESS, GRACIOUS!
OH-H-H!
DON'T LET HER STAY HERE AND GO TO SEED!
GO, NOW! WE DON'T ALLOW WEEDS IN OUR BED!
OH, ALL RIGHT... IF THAT'S THE WAY YOU FEEL ABOUT IT!..
NOW!
NOW!
BUT IF I WERE MY RIGHT SIZE, I COULD PICK EVERY **ONE** OF YOU IF I...
HA!
HA!
HA!
HMPH! THEY MAY BE BEAUTIFUL... BUT THEY CERTAINLY DON'T HAVE BEAUTIFUL MANNERS!

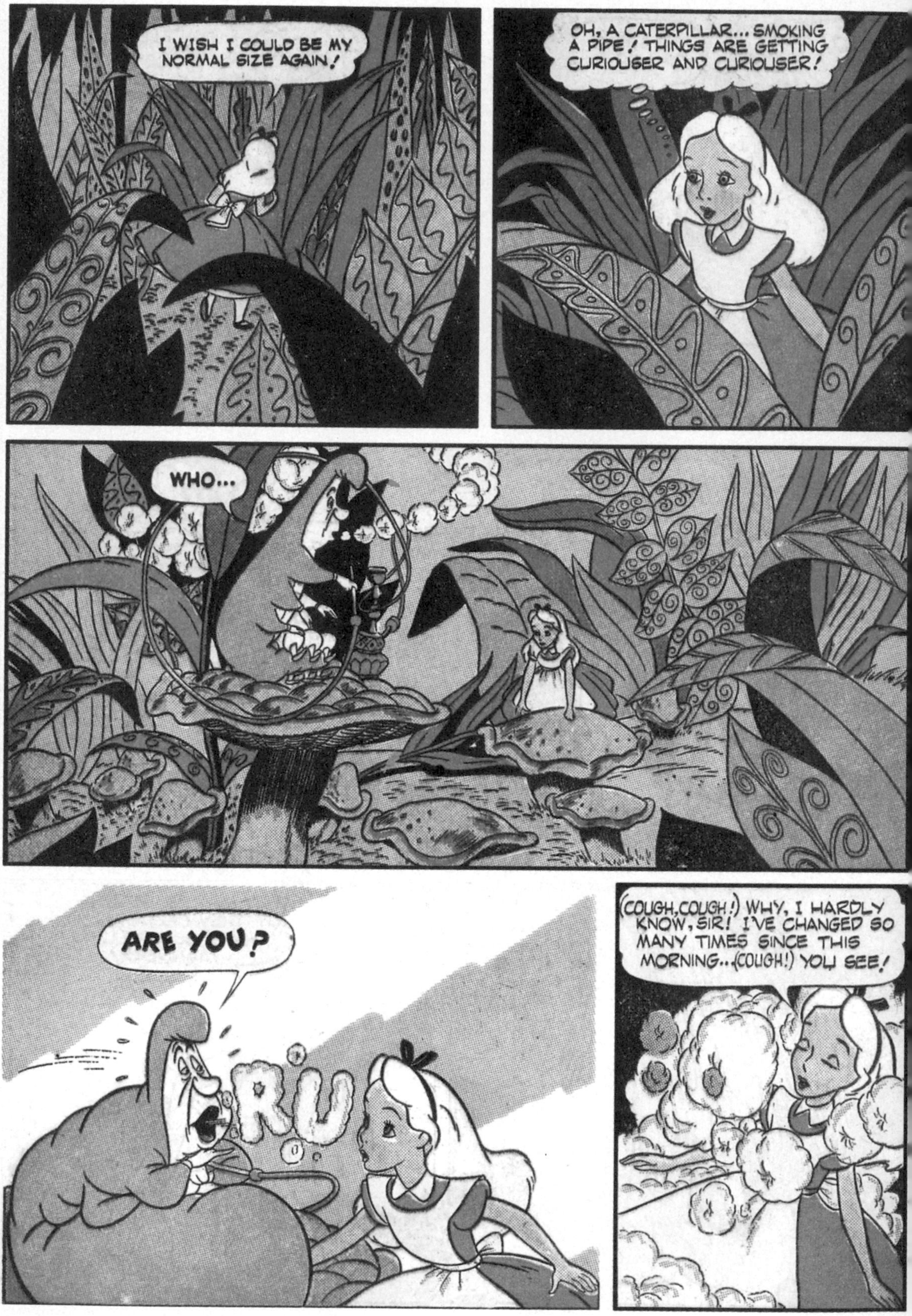
I WISH I COULD BE MY NORMAL SIZE AGAIN!
OH, A CATERPILLAR... SMOKING A PIPE! THINGS ARE GETTING CURIOUSER AND CURIOUSER!
WHO...
ARE YOU?
RU
(COUGH,COUGH!) WHY, I HARDLY KNOW, SIR! I'VE CHANGED SO MANY TIMES SINCE THIS MORNING...(COUGH!) YOU SEE!

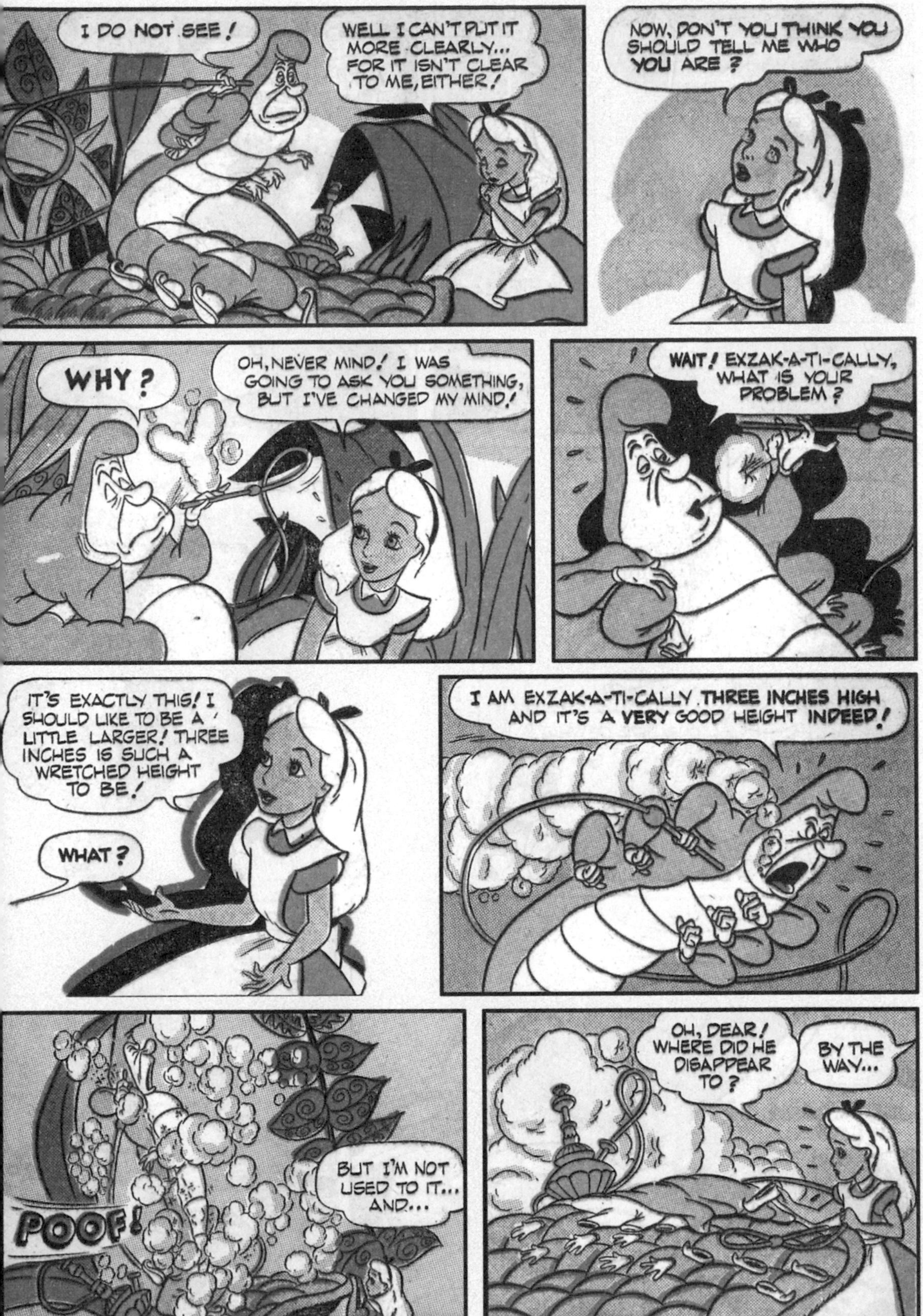
I DO NOT SEE!
WELL I CAN'T PUT IT MORE CLEARLY... FOR IT ISN'T CLEAR TO ME, EITHER!
NOW, DON'T YOU THINK YOU SHOULD TELL ME WHO YOU ARE?
WHY?
OH, NEVER MIND! I WAS GOING TO ASK YOU SOMETHING, BUT I'VE CHANGED MY MIND!
WAIT! EXZAK-A-TI-CALLY, WHAT IS YOUR PROBLEM?
IT'S EXACTLY THIS! I SHOULD LIKE TO BE A LITTLE LARGER! THREE INCHES IS SUCH A WRETCHED HEIGHT TO BE!
WHAT?
I AM EXZAK-A-TI-CALLY THREE INCHES HIGH AND IT'S A VERY GOOD HEIGHT INDEED!
POOF!
BUT I'M NOT USED TO IT... AND...
OH, DEAR! WHERE DID HE DISAPPEAR TO?
BY THE WAY...

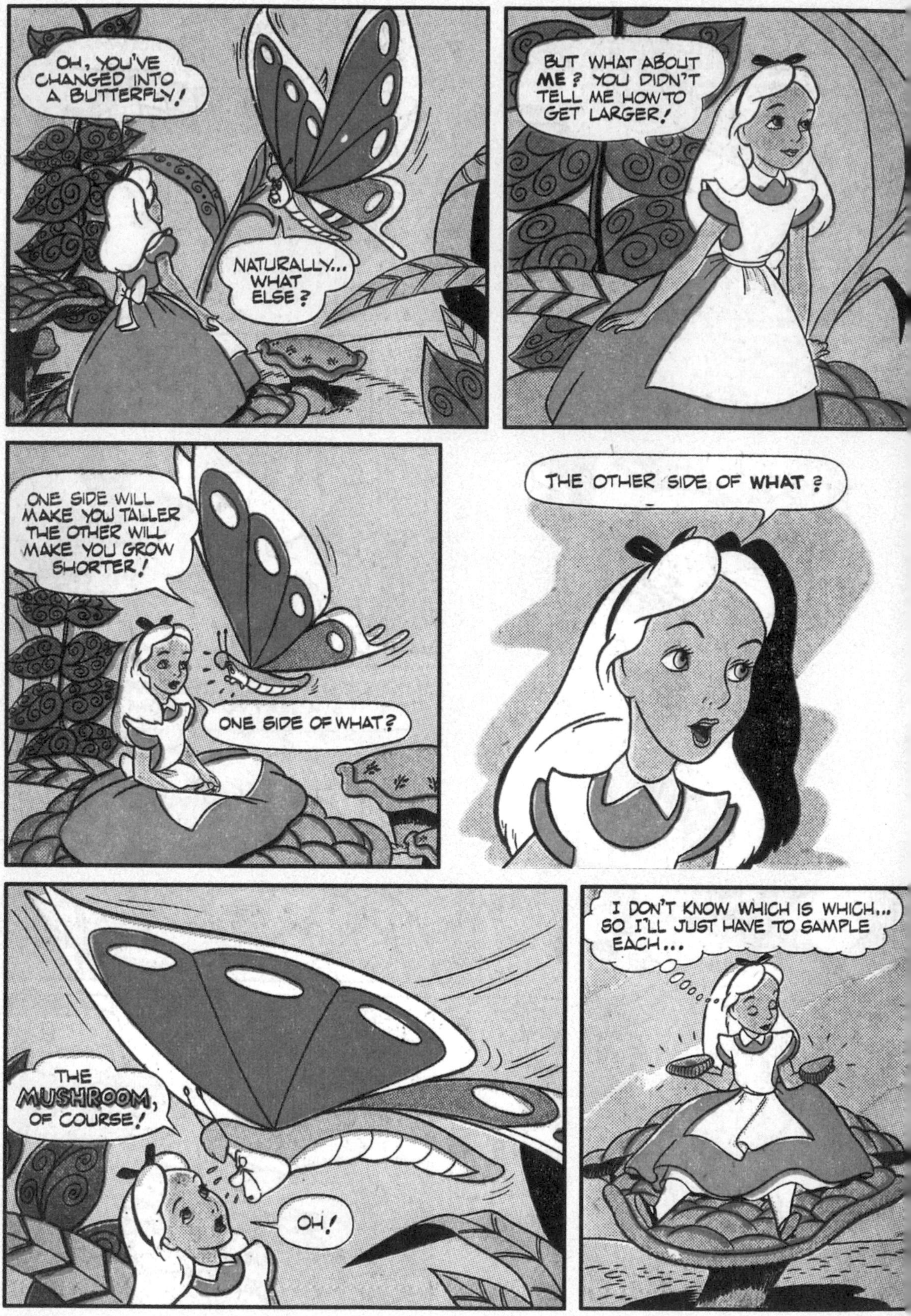
OH, YOU'VE CHANGED INTO A BUTTERFLY!
NATURALLY... WHAT ELSE?
BUT WHAT ABOUT ME? YOU DIDN'T TELL ME HOW TO GET LARGER!
ONE SIDE WILL MAKE YOU TALLER THE OTHER WILL MAKE YOU GROW SHORTER!
ONE SIDE OF WHAT?
THE OTHER SIDE OF WHAT?
THE MUSHROOM, OF COURSE!
OH!
I DON'T KNOW WHICH IS WHICH... SO I'LL JUST HAVE TO SAMPLE EACH...

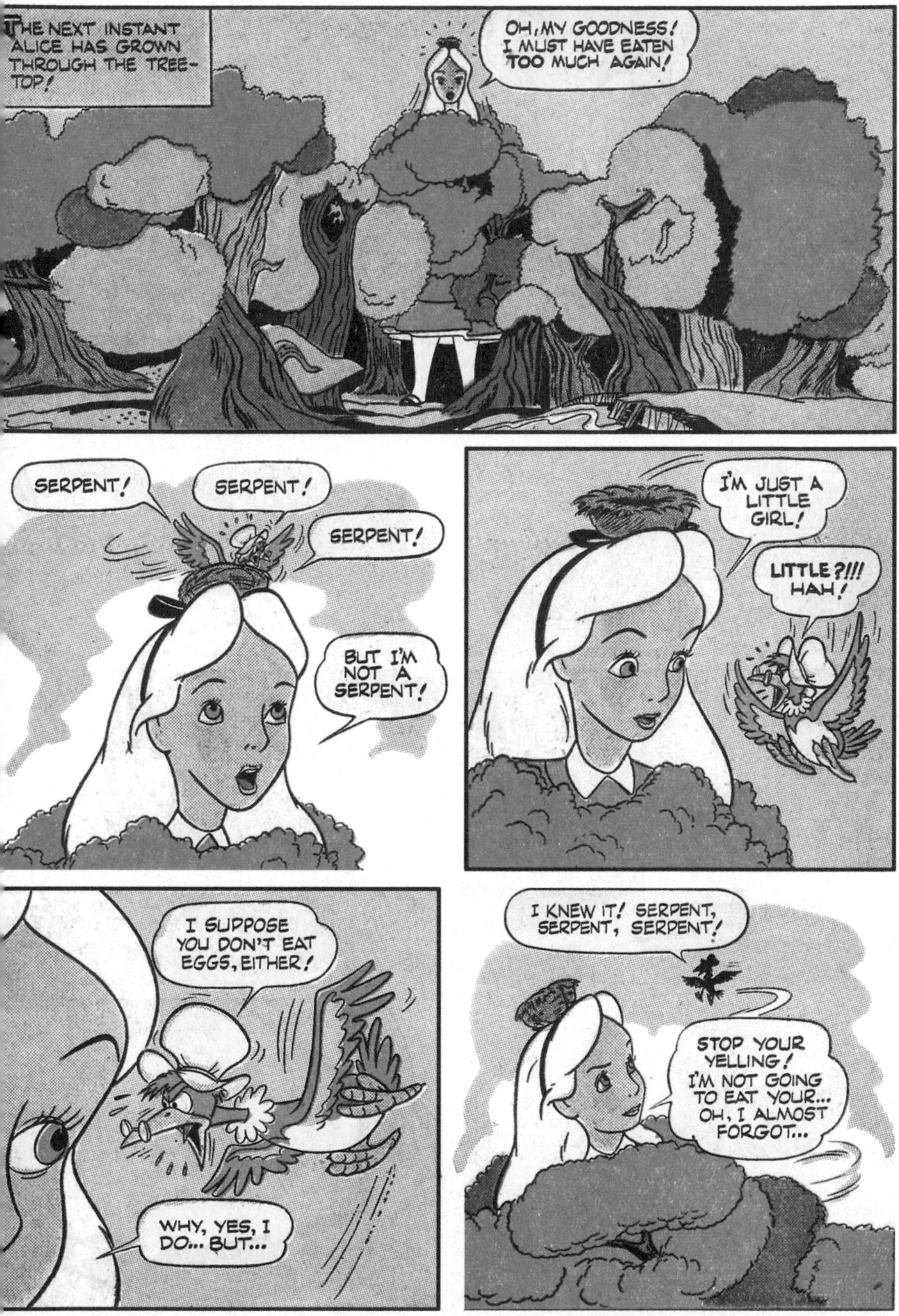
THE NEXT INSTANT ALICE HAS GROWN THROUGH THE TREE-TOP!
OH, MY GOODNESS! I MUST HAVE EATEN TOO MUCH AGAIN!
SERPENT!
SERPENT!
SERPENT!
BUT I'M NOT A SERPENT!
I'M JUST A LITTLE GIRL!
LITTLE?!!! HAH!
I SUPPOSE YOU DON'T EAT EGGS, EITHER!
WHY, YES, I DO... BUT...
I KNEW IT! SERPENT, SERPENT, SERPENT!
STOP YOUR YELLING! I'M NOT GOING TO EAT YOUR... OH, I ALMOST FORGOT...

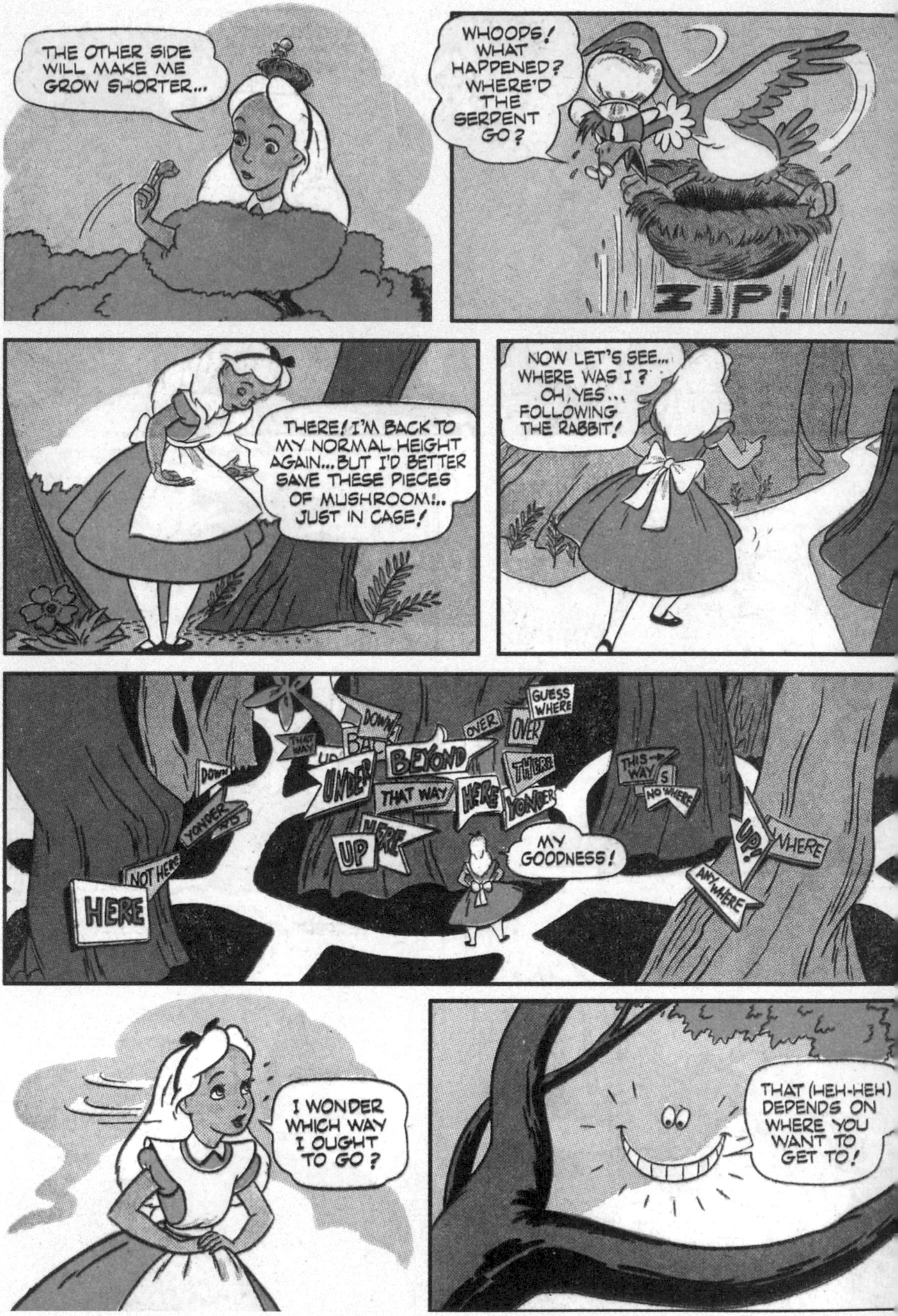
THE OTHER SIDE WILL MAKE ME GROW SHORTER...
WHOOPS! WHAT HAPPENED? WHERE'D THE SERPENT GO?
ZIP!
THERE! I'M BACK TO MY NORMAL HEIGHT AGAIN...BUT I'D BETTER SAVE THESE PIECES OF MUSHROOM!.. JUST IN CASE!
NOW LET'S SEE... WHERE WAS I? OH, YES... FOLLOWING THE RABBIT!
GUESS WHERE
DOWN
OVER
OVER
THAT WAY
BEYOND
UNDER
THAT WAY
HERE
THERE
YONDER
THIS WAY
NO WHERE
UP
UP
WHERE
ANY WHERE
NOT HERE
HERE
YONDER
MY GOODNESS!
I WONDER WHICH WAY I OUGHT TO GO?
THAT (HEH-HEH) DEPENDS ON WHERE YOU WANT TO GET TO!

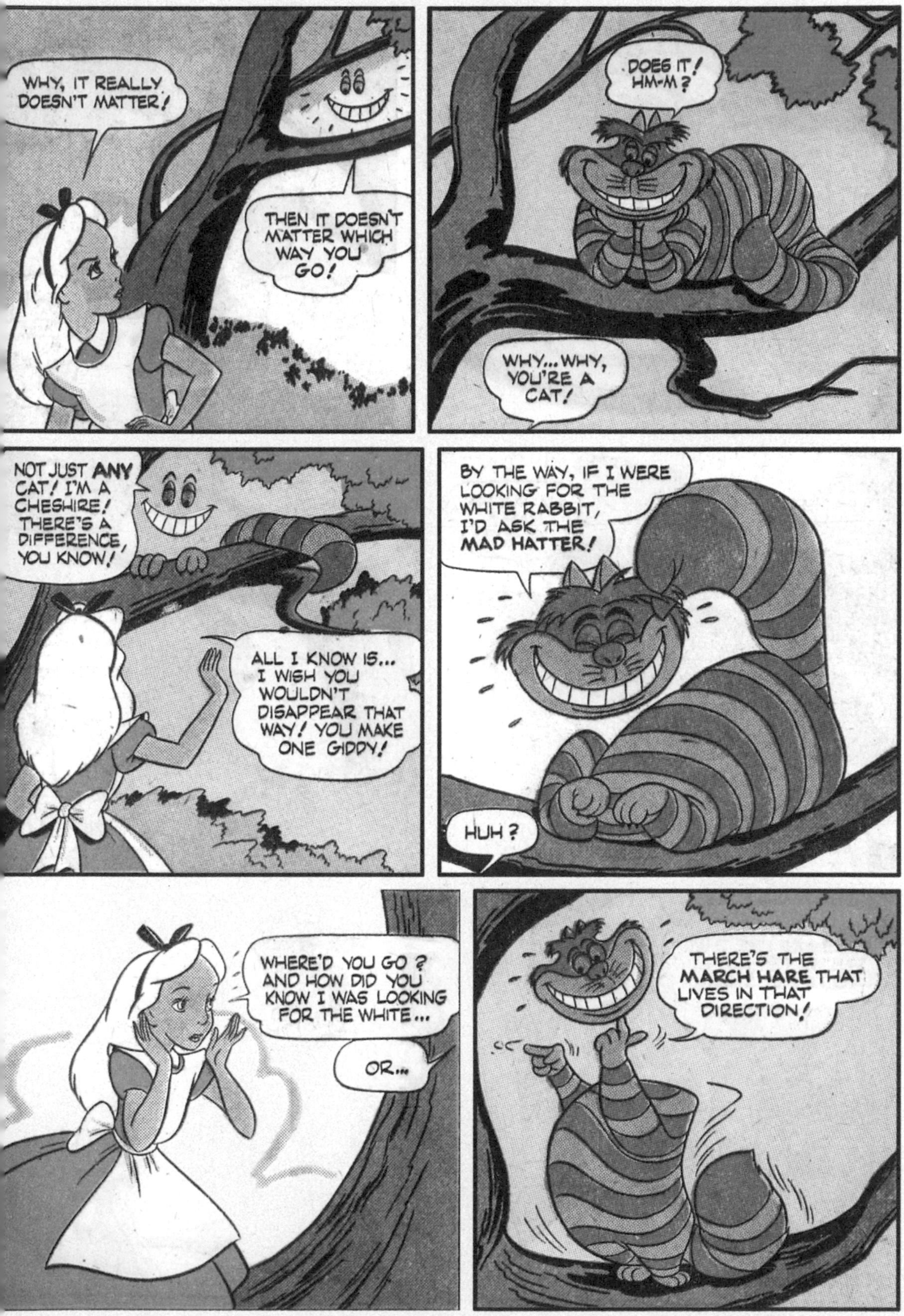
WHY, IT REALLY DOESN'T MATTER!
THEN IT DOESN'T MATTER WHICH WAY YOU GO!
DOES IT! HM-M?
WHY... WHY, YOU'RE A CAT!
NOT JUST ANY CAT! I'M A CHESHIRE! THERE'S A DIFFERENCE, YOU KNOW!
ALL I KNOW IS... I WISH YOU WOULDN'T DISAPPEAR THAT WAY! YOU MAKE ONE GIDDY!
BY THE WAY, IF I WERE LOOKING FOR THE WHITE RABBIT, I'D ASK THE MAD HATTER!
HUH?
WHERE'D YOU GO? AND HOW DID YOU KNOW I WAS LOOKING FOR THE WHITE...
OR...
THERE'S THE MARCH HARE THAT LIVES IN THAT DIRECTION!

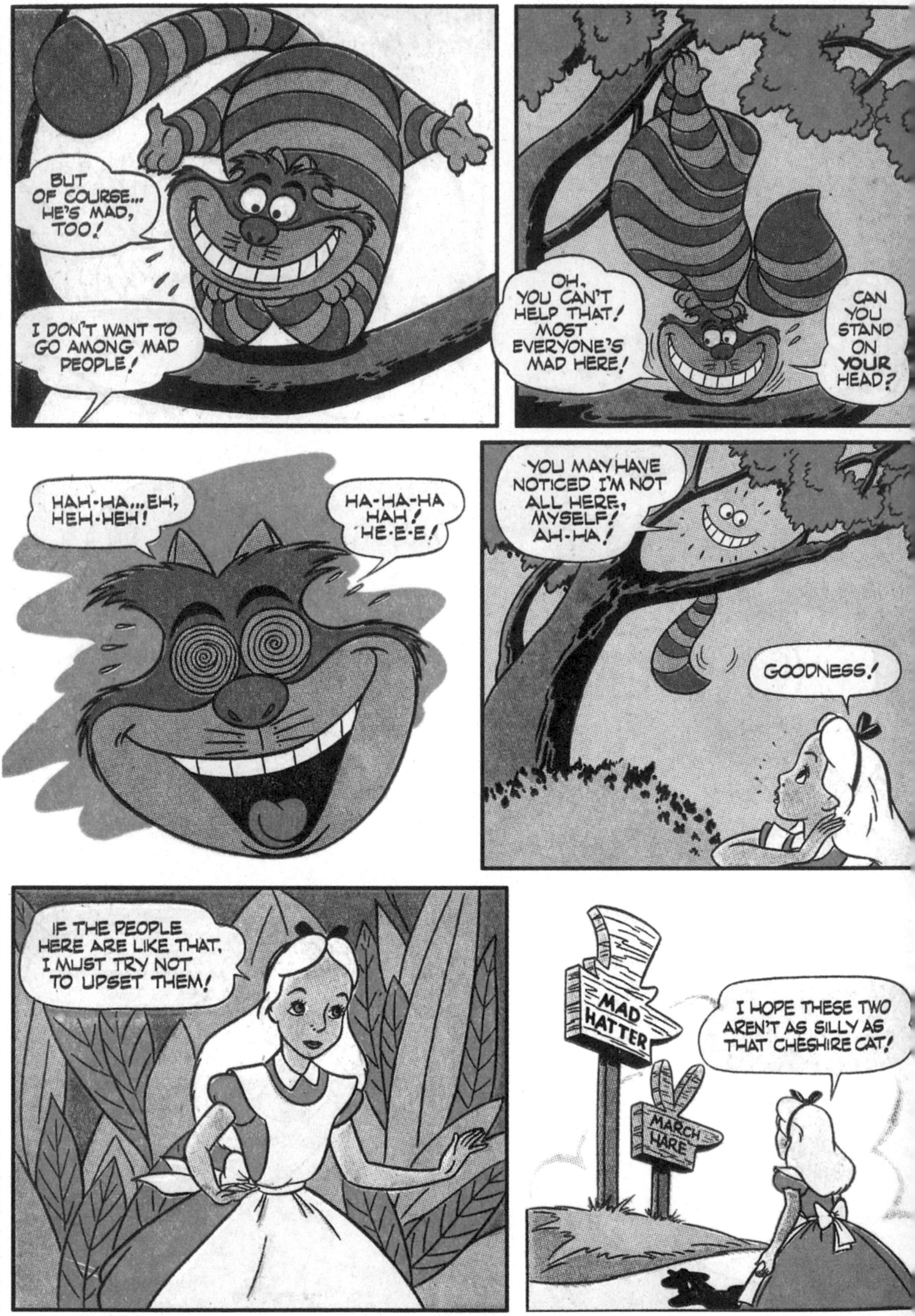
BUT OF COURSE... HE'S MAD, TOO!
I DON'T WANT TO GO AMONG MAD PEOPLE!
OH, YOU CAN'T HELP THAT! MOST EVERYONE'S MAD HERE!
CAN YOU STAND ON YOUR HEAD?
HAH-HA...EH, HEH-HEH!
HA-HA-HA HAH! HE-E-E!
YOU MAY HAVE NOTICED I'M NOT ALL HERE, MYSELF! AH-HA!
GOODNESS!
IF THE PEOPLE HERE ARE LIKE THAT, I MUST TRY NOT TO UPSET THEM!
MAD HATTER
MARCH HARE
I HOPE THESE TWO AREN'T AS SILLY AS THAT CHESHIRE CAT!

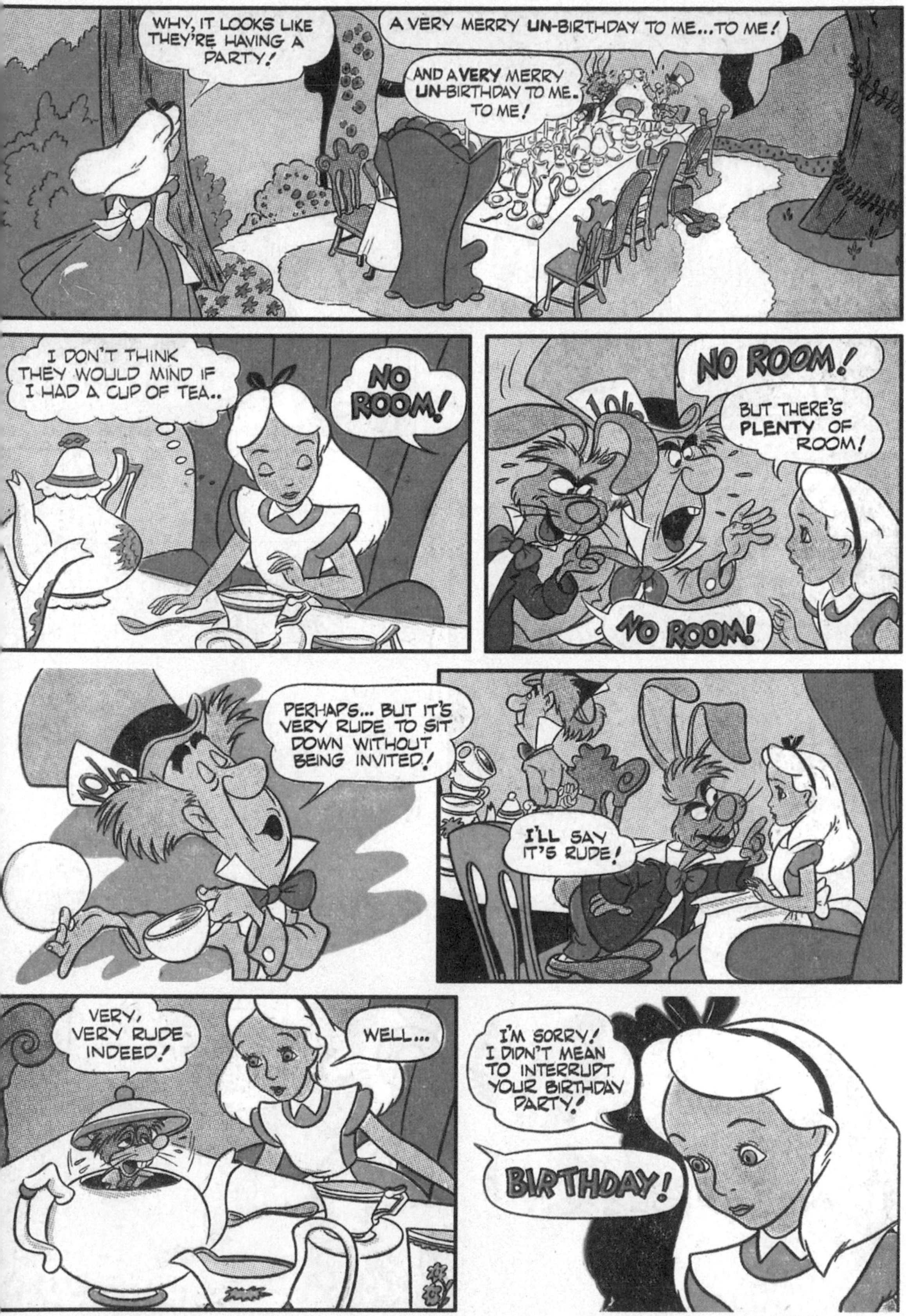
WHY, IT LOOKS LIKE THEY'RE HAVING A PARTY!
A VERY MERRY UN-BIRTHDAY TO ME... TO ME!
AND A VERY MERRY UN-BIRTHDAY TO ME.. TO ME!
I DON'T THINK THEY WOULD MIND IF I HAD A CUP OF TEA..
NO ROOM!
NO ROOM!
BUT THERE'S PLENTY OF ROOM!
NO ROOM!
PERHAPS... BUT IT'S VERY RUDE TO SIT DOWN WITHOUT BEING INVITED!
I'LL SAY IT'S RUDE!
VERY, VERY RUDE INDEED!
WELL...
I'M SORRY! I DIDN'T MEAN TO INTERRUPT YOUR BIRTHDAY PARTY!
BIRTHDAY!

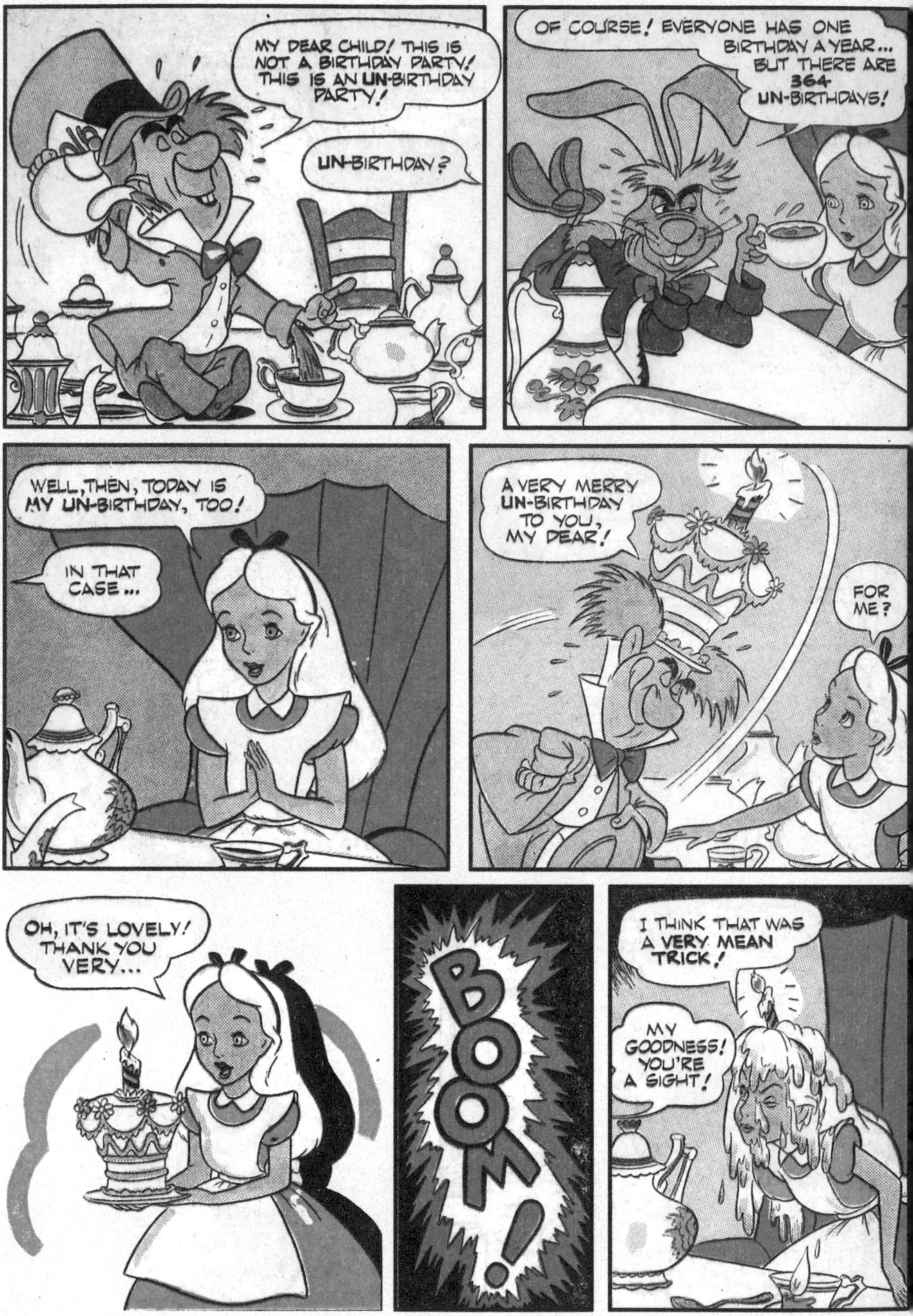
MY DEAR CHILD! THIS IS NOT A BIRTHDAY PARTY! THIS IS AN UN-BIRTHDAY PARTY!
UN-BIRTHDAY?
OF COURSE! EVERYONE HAS ONE BIRTHDAY A YEAR... BUT THERE ARE 364 UN-BIRTHDAYS!
WELL, THEN, TODAY IS MY UN-BIRTHDAY, TOO!
IN THAT CASE...
A VERY MERRY UN-BIRTHDAY TO YOU, MY DEAR!
FOR ME?
OH, IT'S LOVELY! THANK YOU VERY...
BOOM!
I THINK THAT WAS A VERY MEAN TRICK!
MY GOODNESS! YOU'RE A SIGHT!

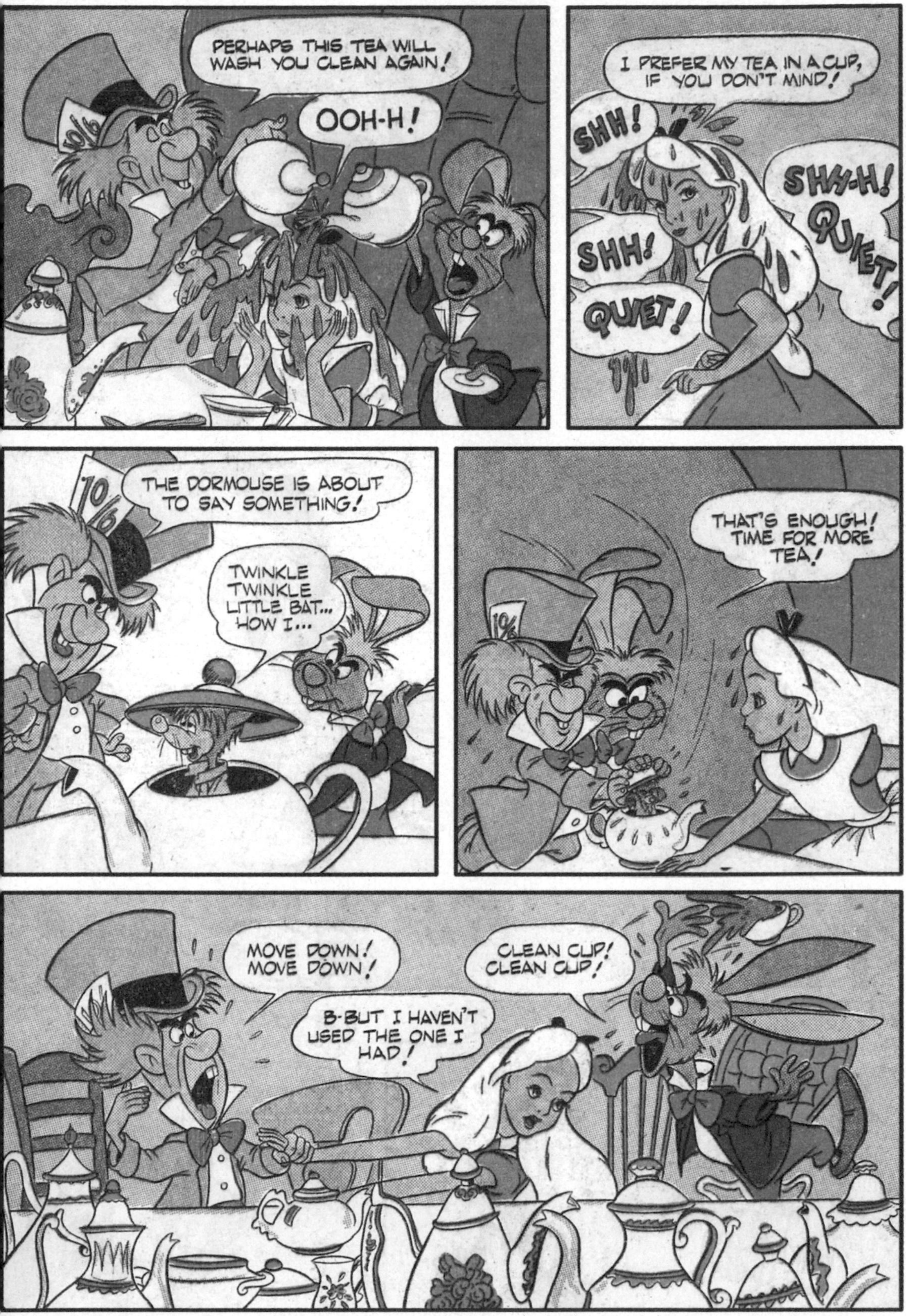
PERHAPS THIS TEA WILL WASH YOU CLEAN AGAIN!
OOH-H!
I PREFER MY TEA IN A CUP, IF YOU DON'T MIND!
SHH!
SHH-H!
QUIET!
SHH!
QUIET!
THE DORMOUSE IS ABOUT TO SAY SOMETHING!
TWINKLE TWINKLE LITTLE BAT... HOW I...
THAT'S ENOUGH! TIME FOR MORE TEA!
MOVE DOWN! MOVE DOWN!
CLEAN CUP! CLEAN CUP!
B-BUT I HAVEN'T USED THE ONE I HAD!

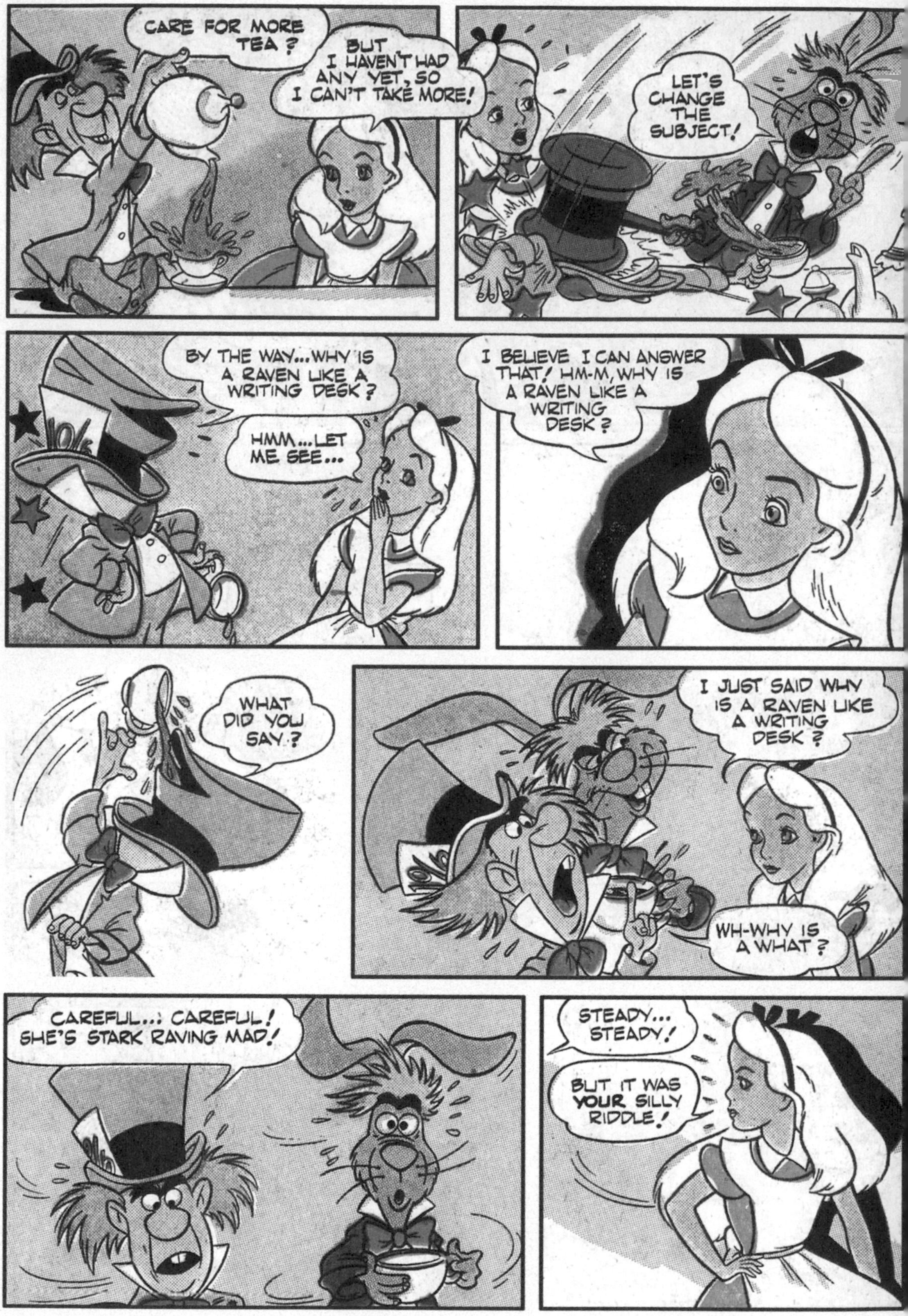
CARE FOR MORE TEA ?
BUT I HAVEN'T HAD ANY YET, SO I CAN'T TAKE MORE!
LET'S CHANGE THE SUBJECT!
BY THE WAY...WHY IS A RAVEN LIKE A WRITING DESK ?
HMM...LET ME SEE...
I BELIEVE I CAN ANSWER THAT! HM-M, WHY IS A RAVEN LIKE A WRITING DESK ?
WHAT DID YOU SAY ?
I JUST SAID WHY IS A RAVEN LIKE A WRITING DESK ?
WH-WHY IS A WHAT ?
CAREFUL...: CAREFUL! SHE'S STARK RAVING MAD!
STEADY... STEADY!
BUT IT WAS **YOUR** SILLY RIDDLE!

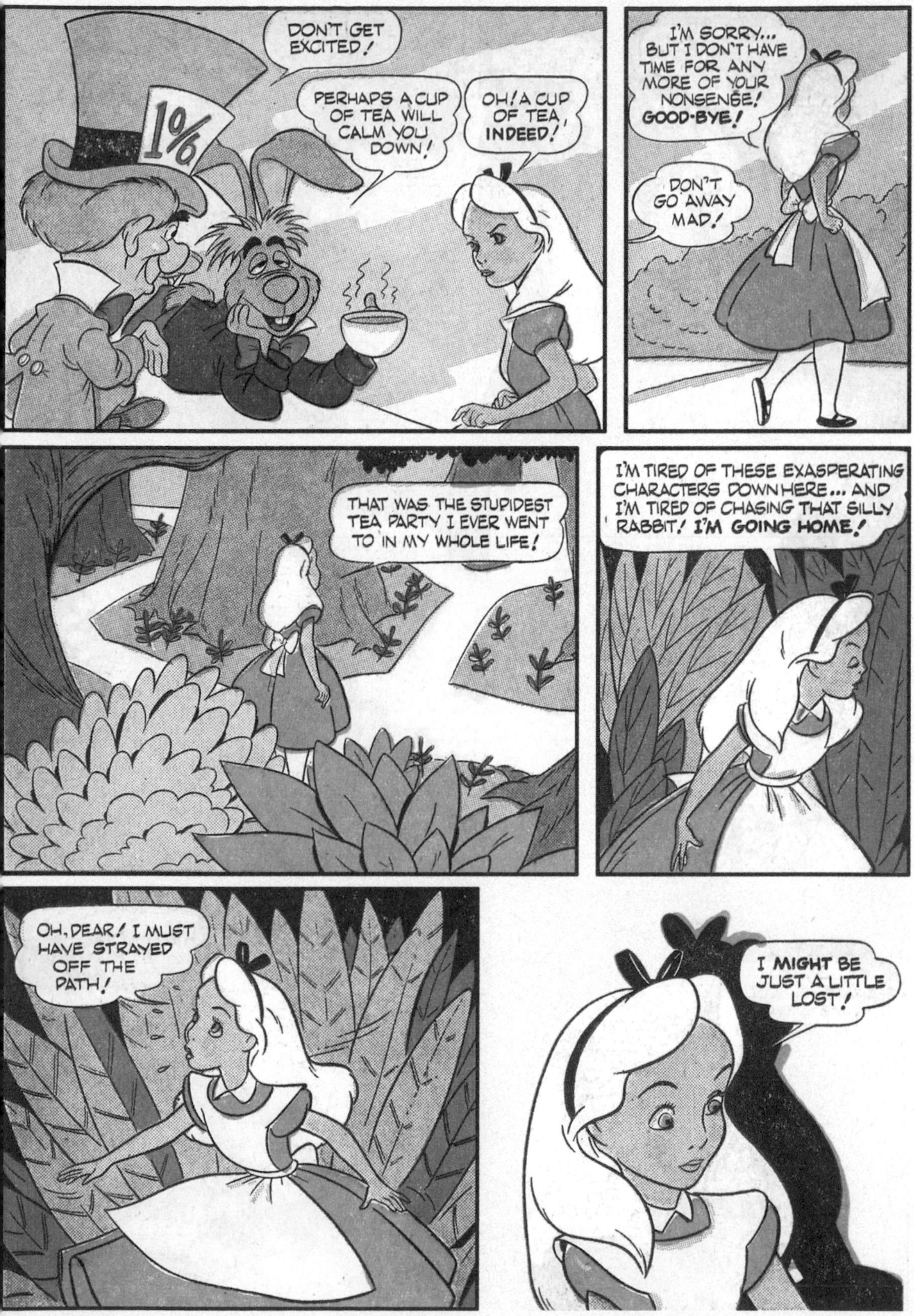
DON'T GET EXCITED!
PERHAPS A CUP OF TEA WILL CALM YOU DOWN!
OH! A CUP OF TEA, INDEED!
I'M SORRY... BUT I DON'T HAVE TIME FOR ANY MORE OF YOUR NONSENSE! GOOD-BYE!
DON'T GO AWAY MAD!
THAT WAS THE STUPIDEST TEA PARTY I EVER WENT TO IN MY WHOLE LIFE!
I'M TIRED OF THESE EXASPERATING CHARACTERS DOWN HERE... AND I'M TIRED OF CHASING THAT SILLY RABBIT! I'M GOING HOME!
OH, DEAR! I MUST HAVE STRAYED OFF THE PATH!
I MIGHT BE JUST A LITTLE LOST!

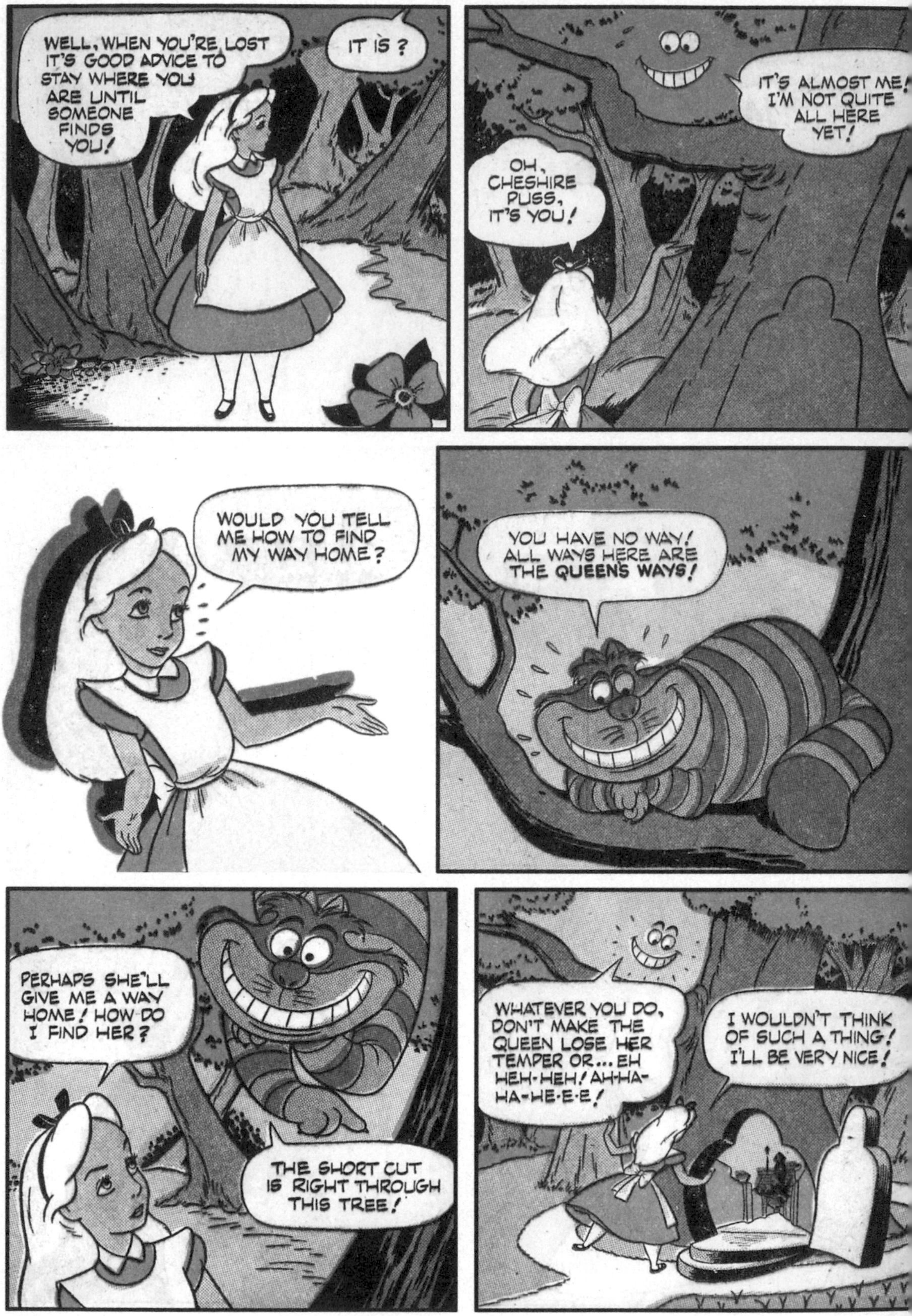
WELL, WHEN YOU'RE LOST IT'S GOOD ADVICE TO STAY WHERE YOU ARE UNTIL SOMEONE FINDS YOU!
IT IS?
IT'S ALMOST ME! I'M NOT QUITE ALL HERE YET!
OH, CHESHIRE PUSS, IT'S YOU!
WOULD YOU TELL ME HOW TO FIND MY WAY HOME?
YOU HAVE NO WAY! ALL WAYS HERE ARE THE QUEEN'S WAYS!
PERHAPS SHE'LL GIVE ME A WAY HOME! HOW DO I FIND HER?
THE SHORT CUT IS RIGHT THROUGH THIS TREE!
WHATEVER YOU DO, DON'T MAKE THE QUEEN LOSE HER TEMPER OR... EH HEH-HEH! AH-HA-HA-HE-E-E!
I WOULDN'T THINK OF SUCH A THING! I'LL BE VERY NICE!

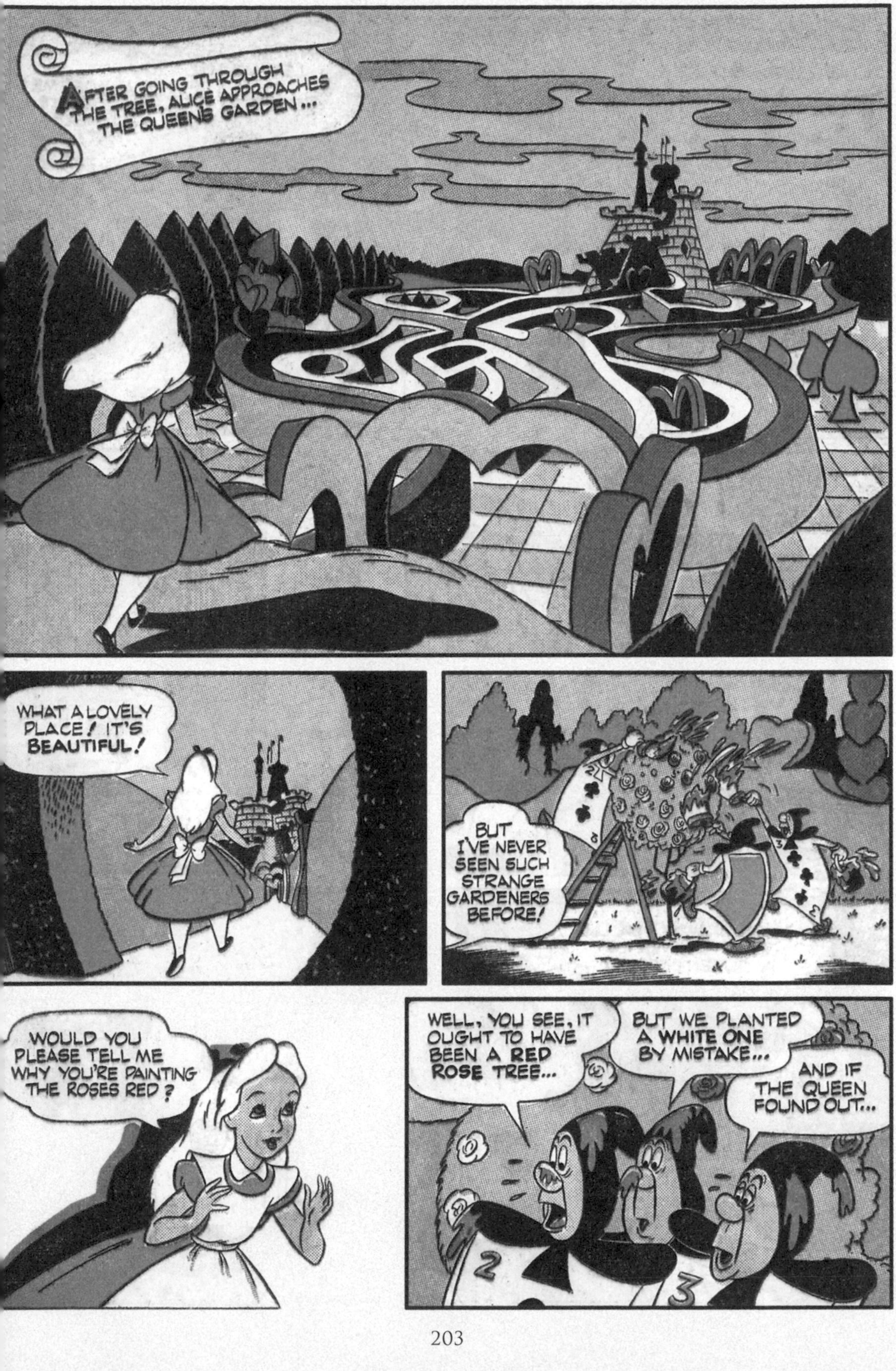
AFTER GOING THROUGH THE TREE, ALICE APPROACHES THE QUEEN'S GARDEN...
WHAT A LOVELY PLACE! IT'S BEAUTIFUL!
BUT I'VE NEVER SEEN SUCH STRANGE GARDENERS BEFORE!
WOULD YOU PLEASE TELL ME WHY YOU'RE PAINTING THE ROSES RED?
WELL, YOU SEE, IT OUGHT TO HAVE BEEN A RED ROSE TREE...
BUT WE PLANTED A WHITE ONE BY MISTAKE...
AND IF THE QUEEN FOUND OUT...

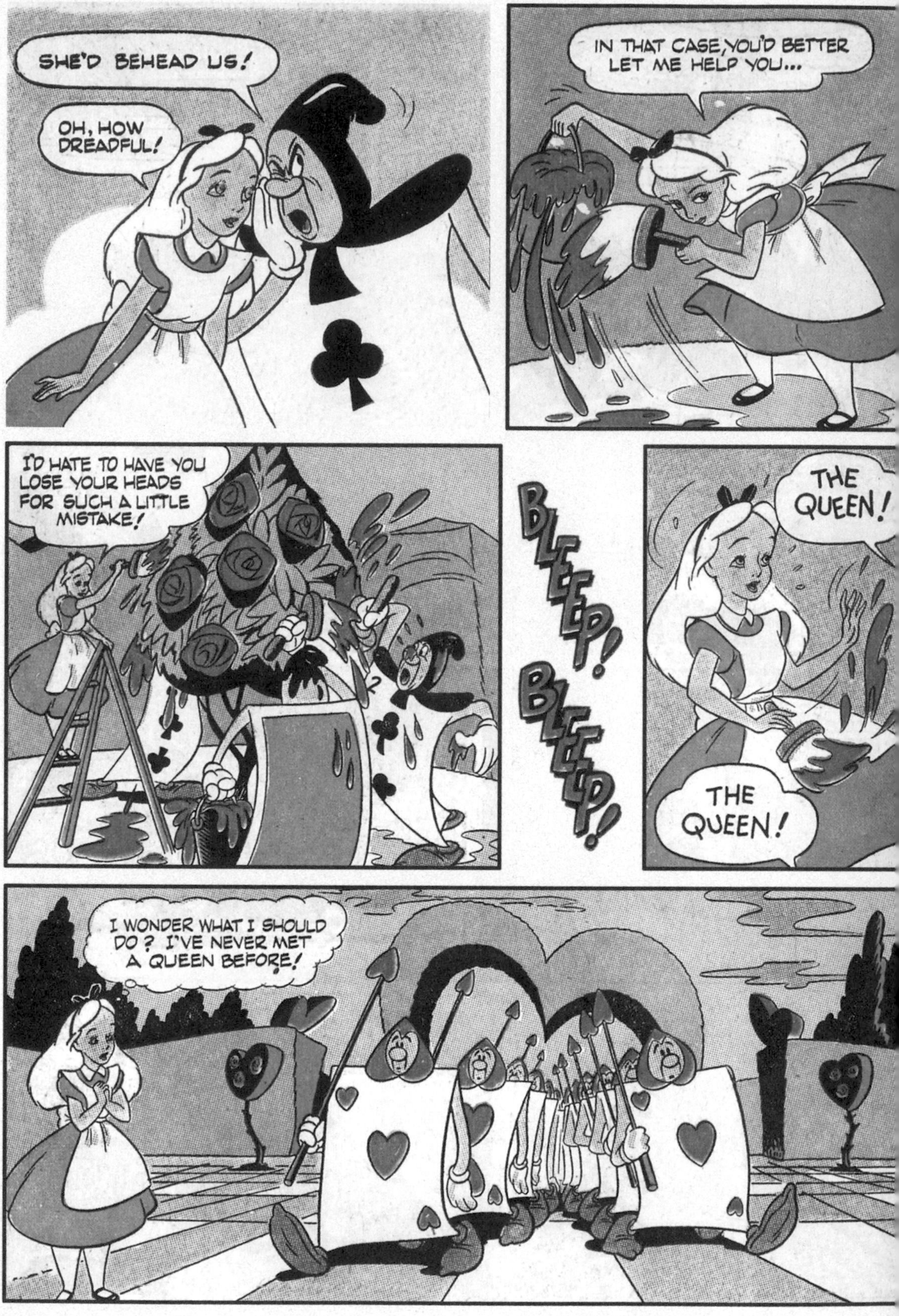
SHE'D BEHEAD US!
OH, HOW DREADFUL!
IN THAT CASE, YOU'D BETTER LET ME HELP YOU...
I'D HATE TO HAVE YOU LOSE YOUR HEADS FOR SUCH A LITTLE MISTAKE!
BLEEP! BLEEP!
THE QUEEN!
THE QUEEN!
I WONDER WHAT I SHOULD DO? I'VE NEVER MET A QUEEN BEFORE!

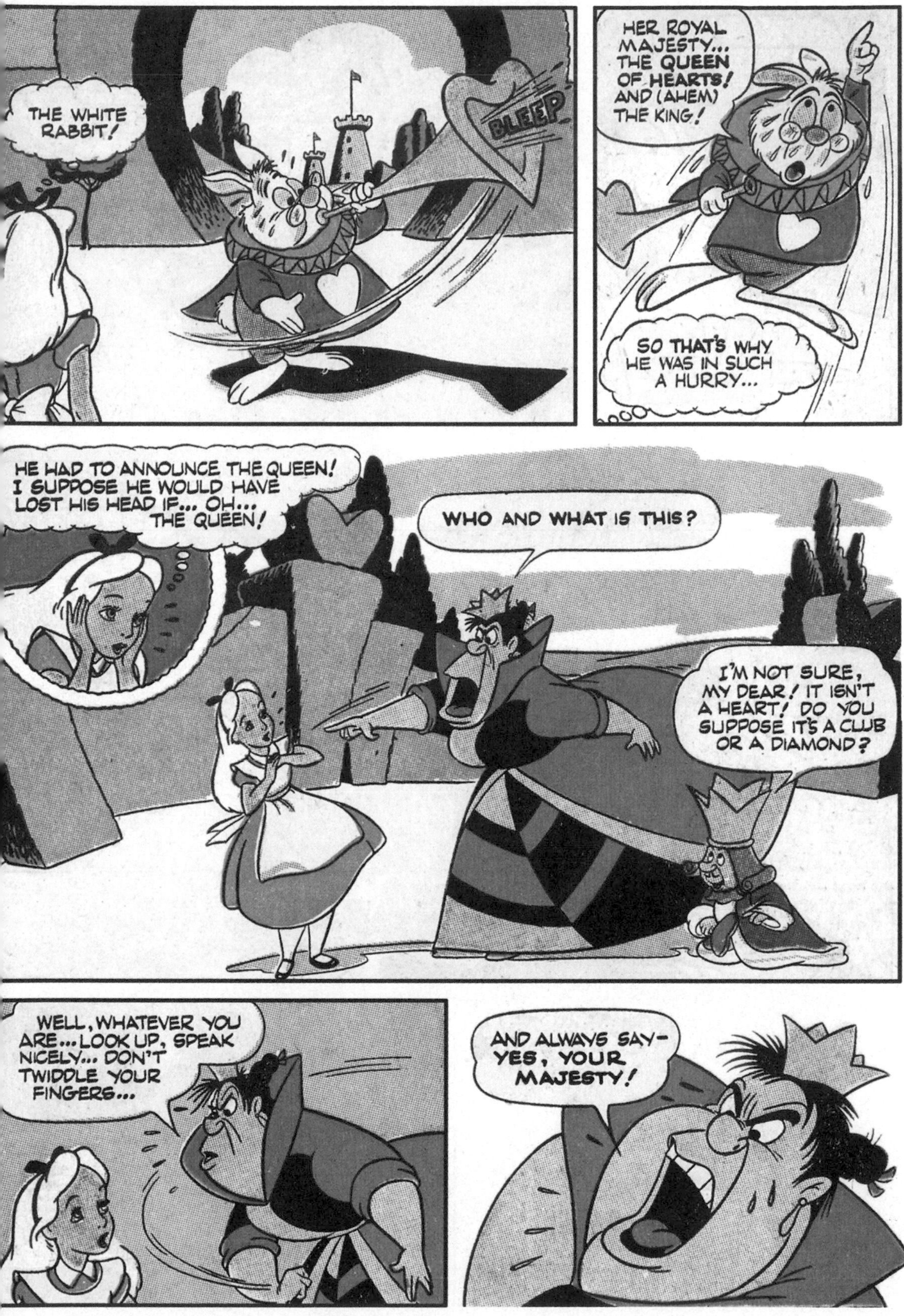
THE WHITE RABBIT!
BLEEP
HER ROYAL MAJESTY... THE QUEEN OF HEARTS! AND (AHEM) THE KING!
SO THAT'S WHY HE WAS IN SUCH A HURRY...
HE HAD TO ANNOUNCE THE QUEEN! I SUPPOSE HE WOULD HAVE LOST HIS HEAD IF... OH... THE QUEEN!
WHO AND WHAT IS THIS?
I'M NOT SURE, MY DEAR! IT ISN'T A HEART! DO YOU SUPPOSE IT'S A CLUB OR A DIAMOND?
WELL, WHATEVER YOU ARE... LOOK UP, SPEAK NICELY... DON'T TWIDDLE YOUR FINGERS...
AND ALWAYS SAY- YES, YOUR MAJESTY!

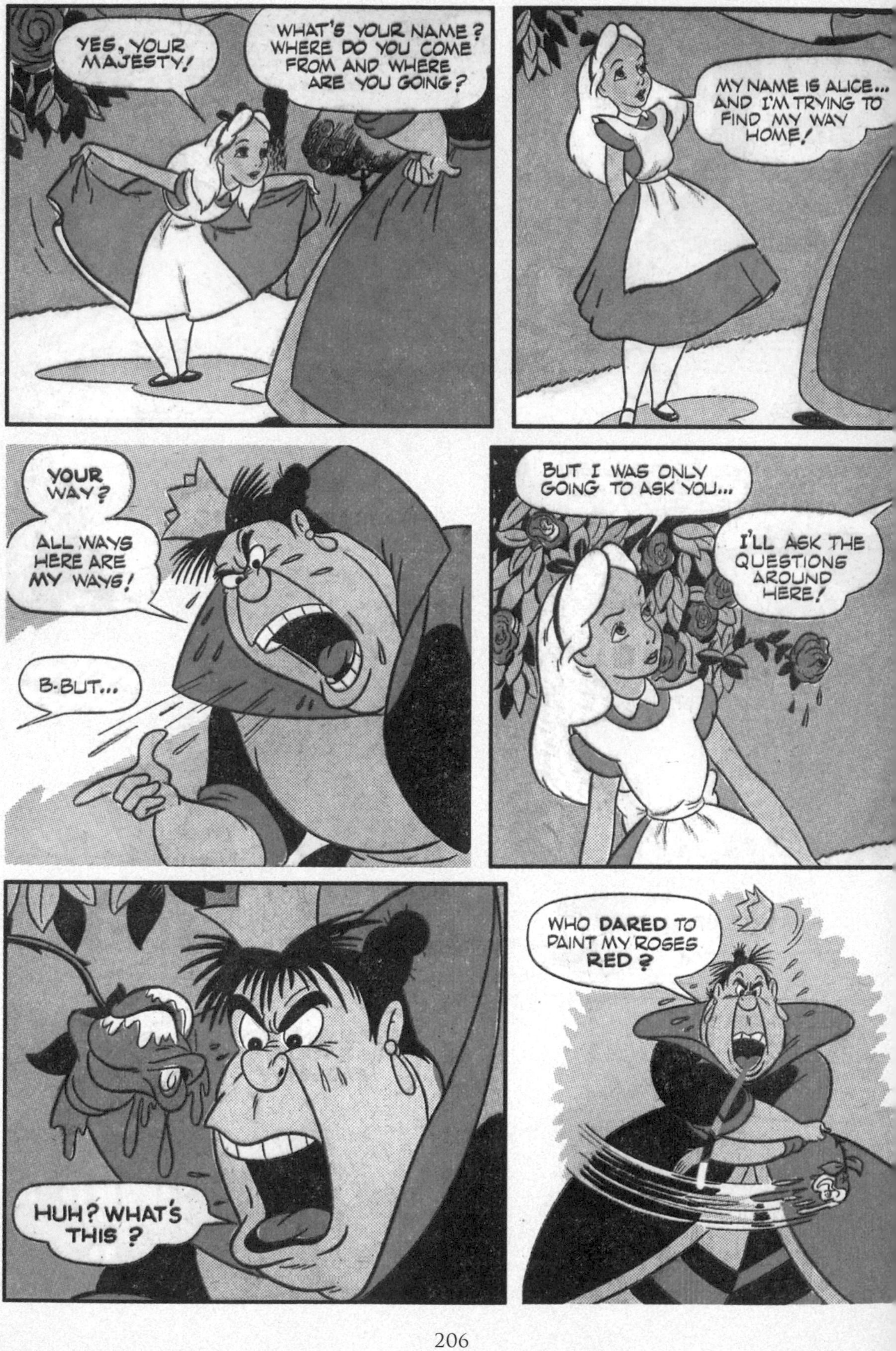
YES, YOUR MAJESTY!
WHAT'S YOUR NAME? WHERE DO YOU COME FROM AND WHERE ARE YOU GOING?
MY NAME IS ALICE... AND I'M TRYING TO FIND MY WAY HOME!
YOUR WAY?
ALL WAYS HERE ARE MY WAYS!
B-BUT...
BUT I WAS ONLY GOING TO ASK YOU...
I'LL ASK THE QUESTIONS AROUND HERE!
HUH? WHAT'S THIS?
WHO DARED TO PAINT MY ROSES RED?

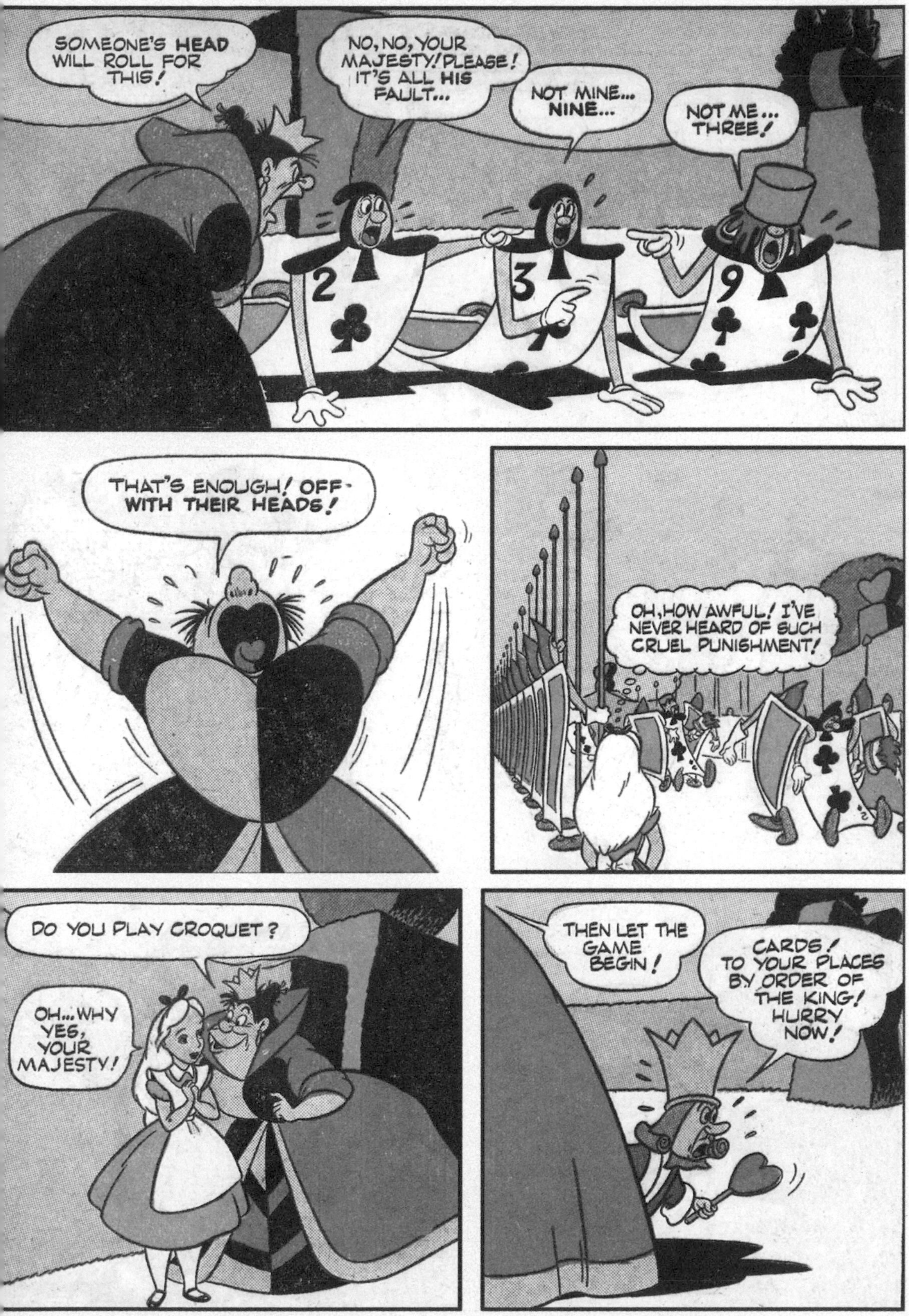
SOMEONE'S HEAD WILL ROLL FOR THIS!
NO, NO, YOUR MAJESTY! PLEASE! IT'S ALL HIS FAULT...
NOT MINE... NINE...
NOT ME... THREE!
THAT'S ENOUGH! OFF-WITH THEIR HEADS!
OH, HOW AWFUL! I'VE NEVER HEARD OF SUCH CRUEL PUNISHMENT!
DO YOU PLAY CROQUET?
OH...WHY YES, YOUR MAJESTY!
THEN LET THE GAME BEGIN!
CARDS! TO YOUR PLACES BY ORDER OF THE KING! HURRY NOW!

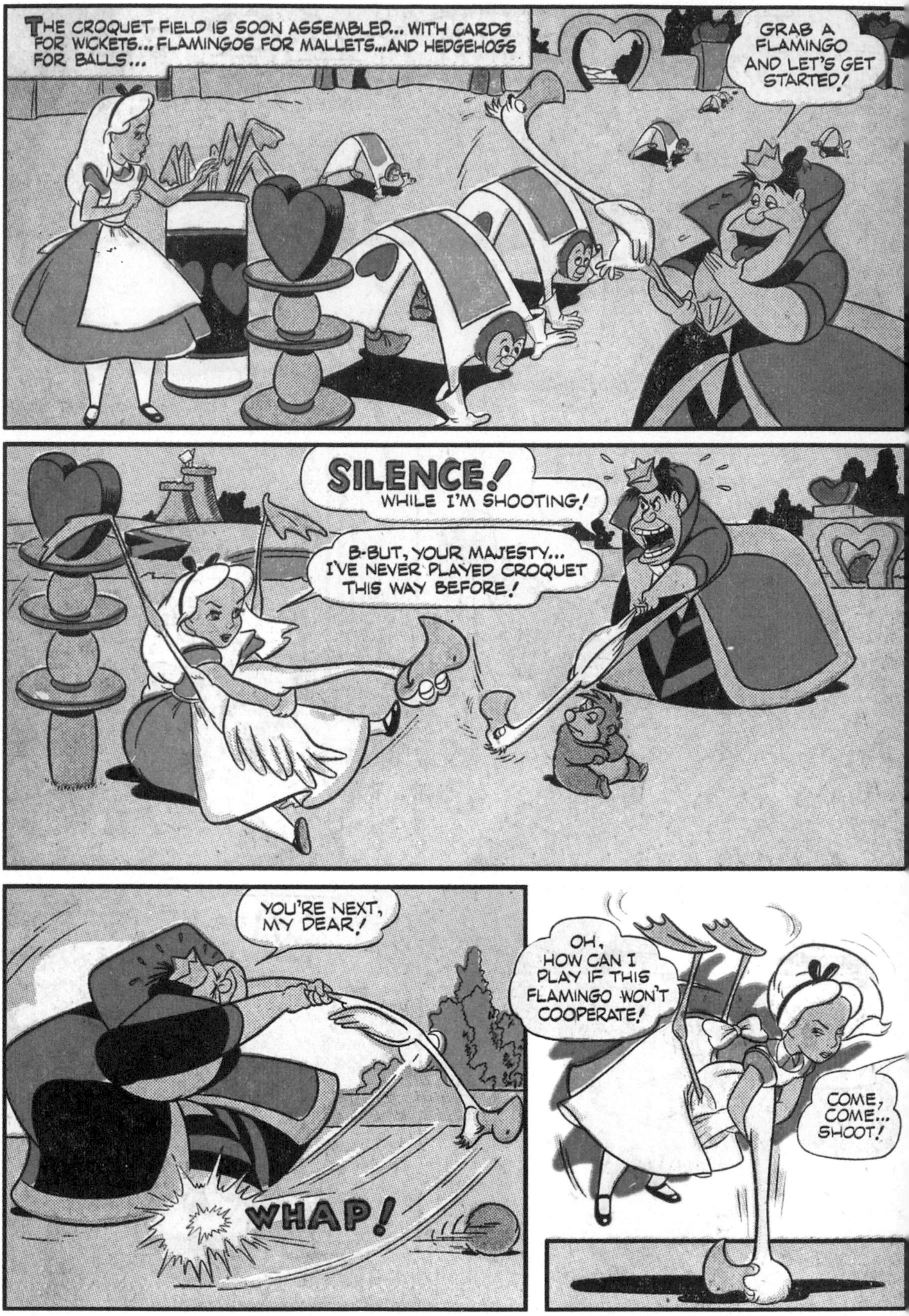
THE CROQUET FIELD IS SOON ASSEMBLED... WITH CARDS FOR WICKETS... FLAMINGOS FOR MALLETS...AND HEDGEHOGS FOR BALLS...
GRAB A FLAMINGO AND LET'S GET STARTED!
SILENCE! WHILE I'M SHOOTING!
B-BUT, YOUR MAJESTY... I'VE NEVER PLAYED CROQUET THIS WAY BEFORE!
YOU'RE NEXT, MY DEAR!
WHAP!
OH, HOW CAN I PLAY IF THIS FLAMINGO WON'T COOPERATE!
COME, COME... SHOOT!

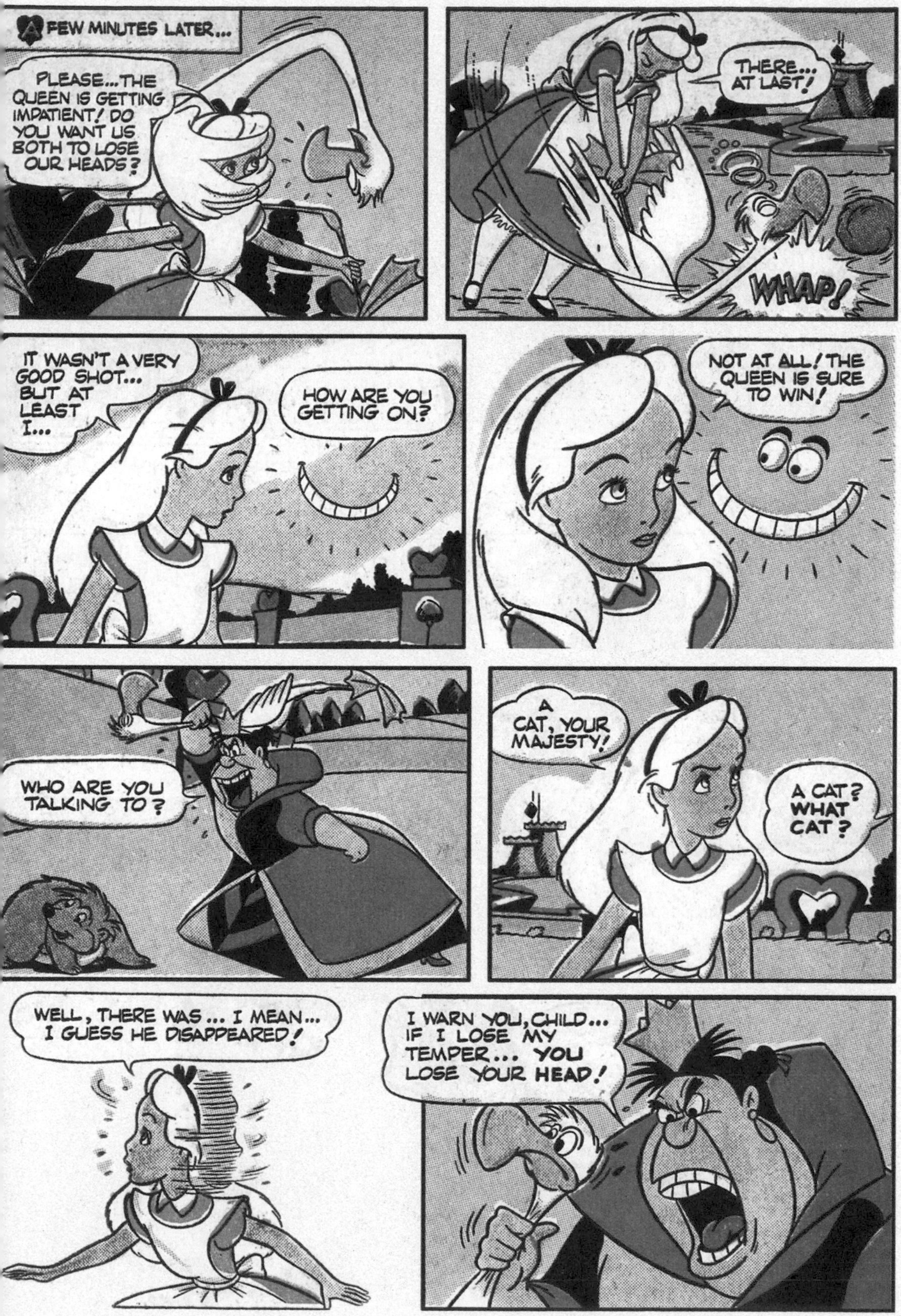
A FEW MINUTES LATER...
PLEASE...THE QUEEN IS GETTING IMPATIENT! DO YOU WANT US BOTH TO LOSE OUR HEADS?
THERE... AT LAST!
WHAP!
IT WASN'T A VERY GOOD SHOT... BUT AT LEAST I...
HOW ARE YOU GETTING ON?
NOT AT ALL! THE QUEEN IS SURE TO WIN!
WHO ARE YOU TALKING TO?
A CAT, YOUR MAJESTY!
A CAT? WHAT CAT?
WELL, THERE WAS ... I MEAN... I GUESS HE DISAPPEARED!
I WARN YOU, CHILD... IF I LOSE MY TEMPER... YOU LOSE YOUR HEAD!

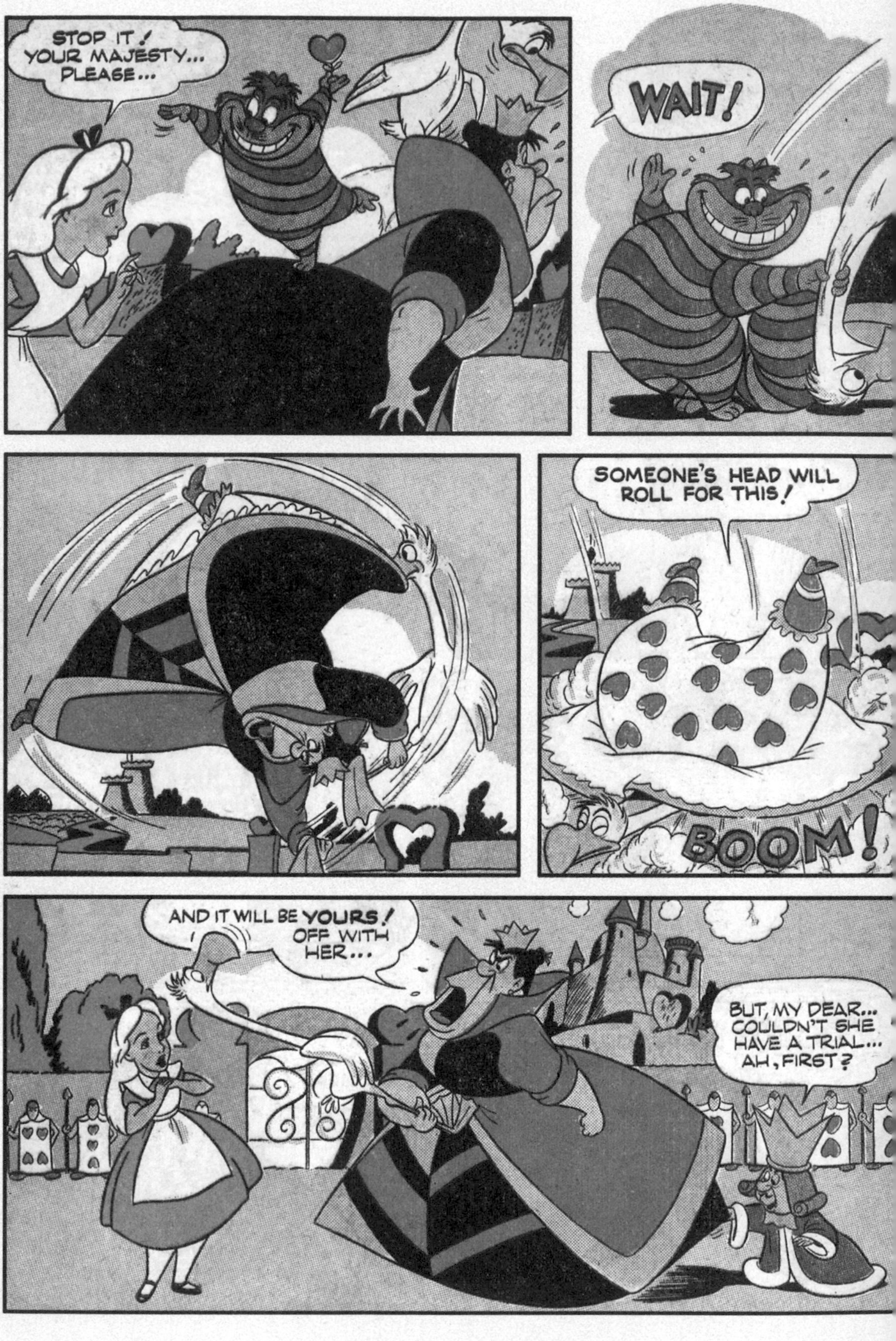
STOP IT! YOUR MAJESTY... PLEASE...
WAIT!
SOMEONE'S HEAD WILL ROLL FOR THIS!
BOOM!
AND IT WILL BE YOURS! OFF WITH HER...
BUT, MY DEAR... COULDN'T SHE HAVE A TRIAL... AH, FIRST?

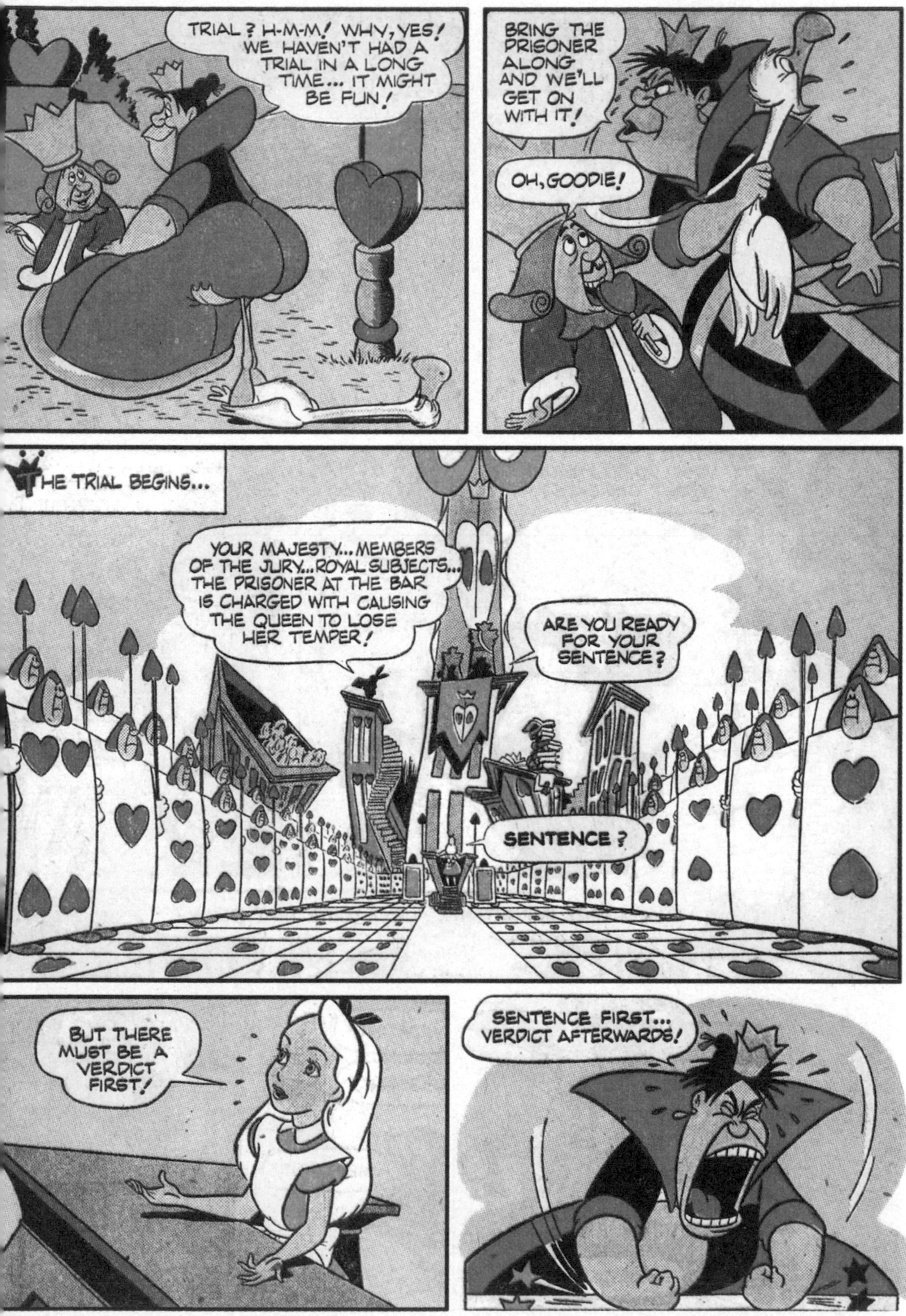
TRIAL ? H-M-M! WHY, YES! WE HAVEN'T HAD A TRIAL IN A LONG TIME... IT MIGHT BE FUN!
BRING THE PRISONER ALONG AND WE'LL GET ON WITH IT!
OH, GOODIE!
THE TRIAL BEGINS...
YOUR MAJESTY... MEMBERS OF THE JURY... ROYAL SUBJECTS... THE PRISONER AT THE BAR IS CHARGED WITH CAUSING THE QUEEN TO LOSE HER TEMPER!
ARE YOU READY FOR YOUR SENTENCE?
SENTENCE ?
BUT THERE MUST BE A VERDICT FIRST!
SENTENCE FIRST... VERDICT AFTERWARDS!

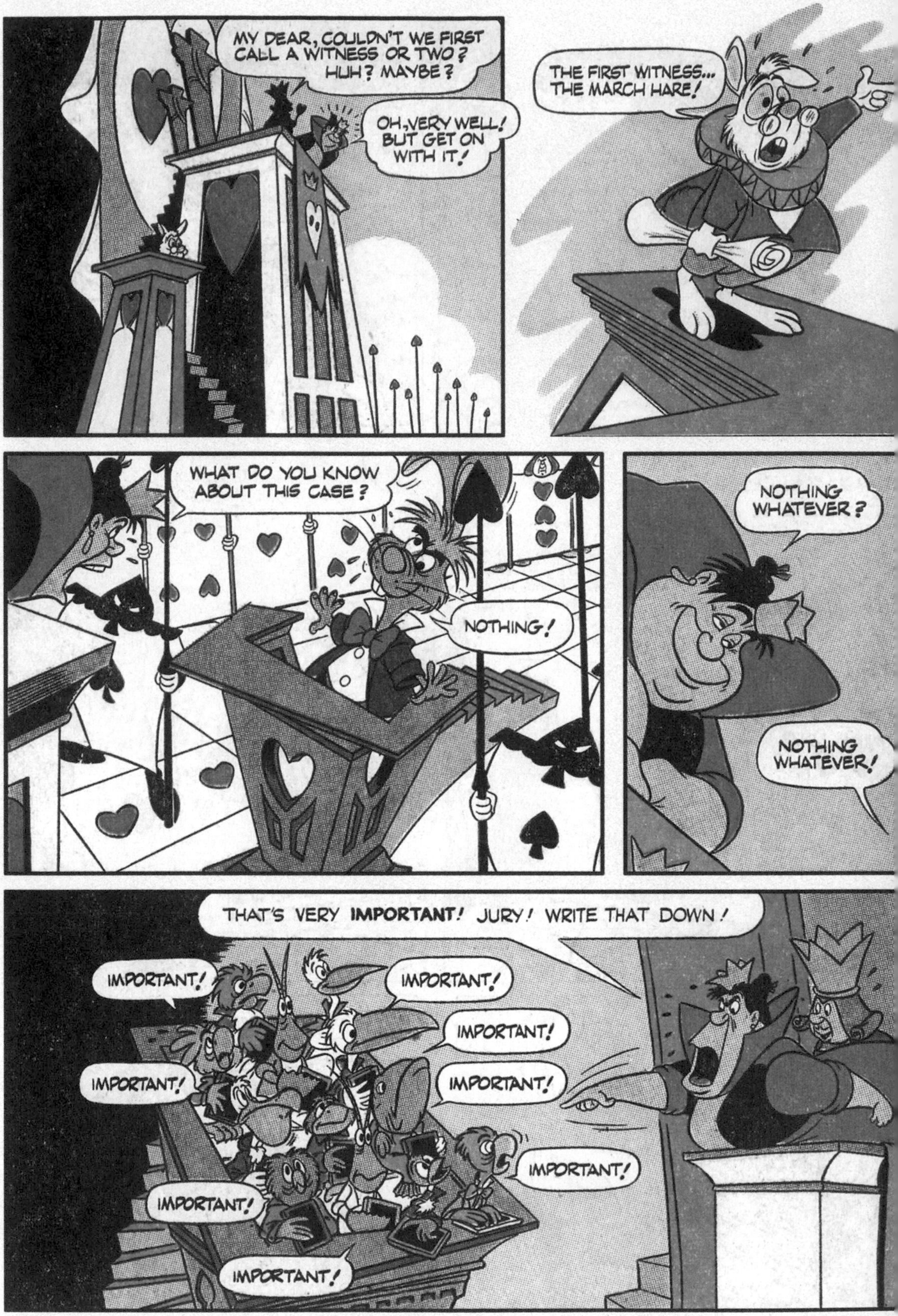
MY DEAR, COULDN'T WE FIRST CALL A WITNESS OR TWO? HUH? MAYBE?
OH, VERY WELL! BUT GET ON WITH IT!
THE FIRST WITNESS... THE MARCH HARE!
WHAT DO YOU KNOW ABOUT THIS CASE?
NOTHING!
NOTHING WHATEVER?
NOTHING WHATEVER!
THAT'S VERY IMPORTANT! JURY! WRITE THAT DOWN!
IMPORTANT!
IMPORTANT!
IMPORTANT!
IMPORTANT!
IMPORTANT!
IMPORTANT!
IMPORTANT!
IMPORTANT!

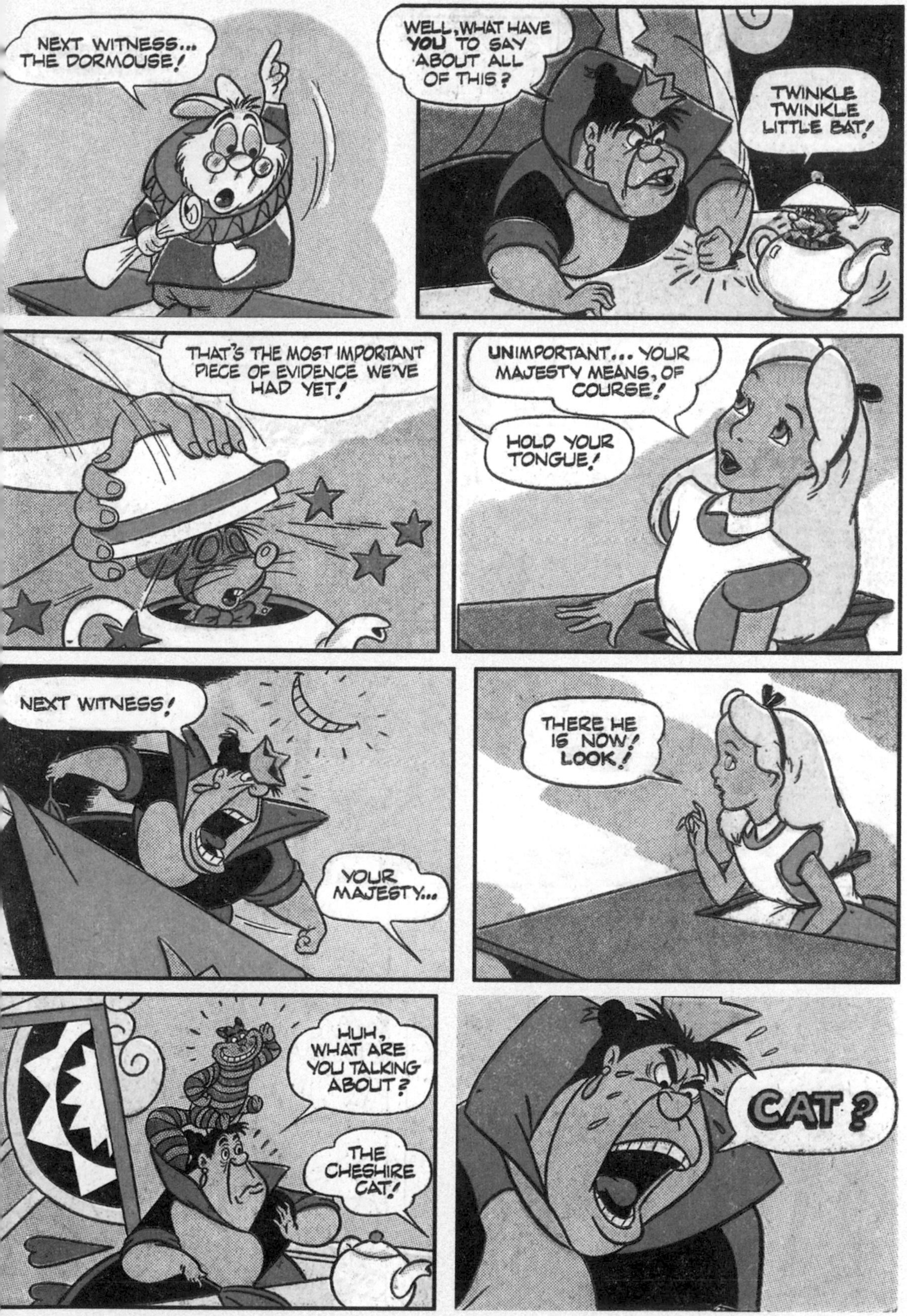
NEXT WITNESS... THE DORMOUSE!
WELL, WHAT HAVE YOU TO SAY ABOUT ALL OF THIS?
TWINKLE TWINKLE LITTLE BAT!
THAT'S THE MOST IMPORTANT PIECE OF EVIDENCE WE'VE HAD YET!
UNIMPORTANT... YOUR MAJESTY MEANS, OF COURSE!
HOLD YOUR TONGUE!
NEXT WITNESS!
YOUR MAJESTY...
THERE HE IS NOW! LOOK!
HUH, WHAT ARE YOU TALKING ABOUT?
THE CHESHIRE CAT!
CAT?

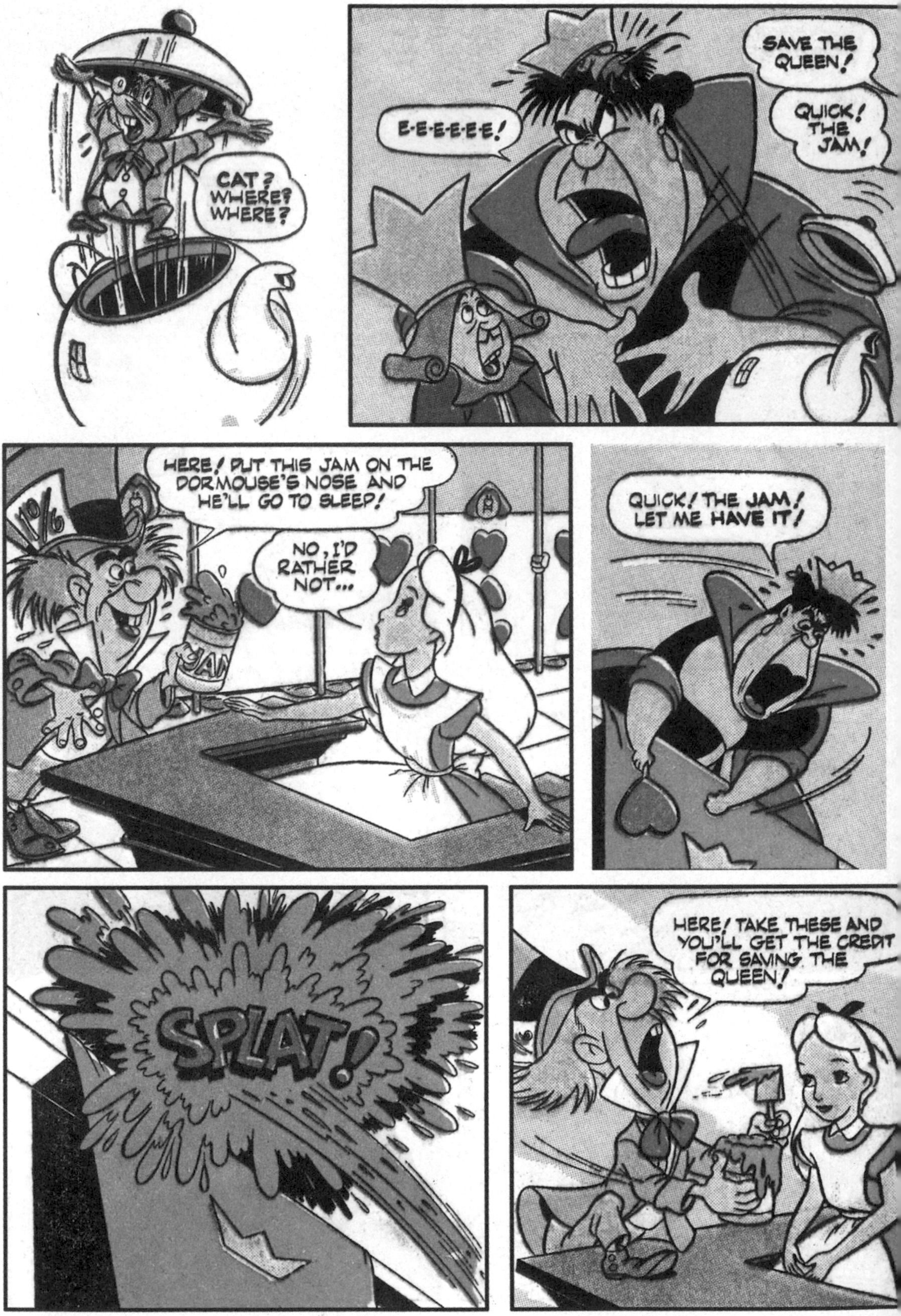
CAT? WHERE? WHERE?
E-E-E-E-E-E!
SAVE THE QUEEN!
QUICK! THE JAM!
HERE! PUT THIS JAM ON THE DORMOUSE'S NOSE AND HE'LL GO TO SLEEP!
NO, I'D RATHER NOT...
JAM
QUICK! THE JAM! LET ME HAVE IT!
SPLAT!
HERE! TAKE THESE AND YOU'LL GET THE CREDIT FOR SAVING THE QUEEN!

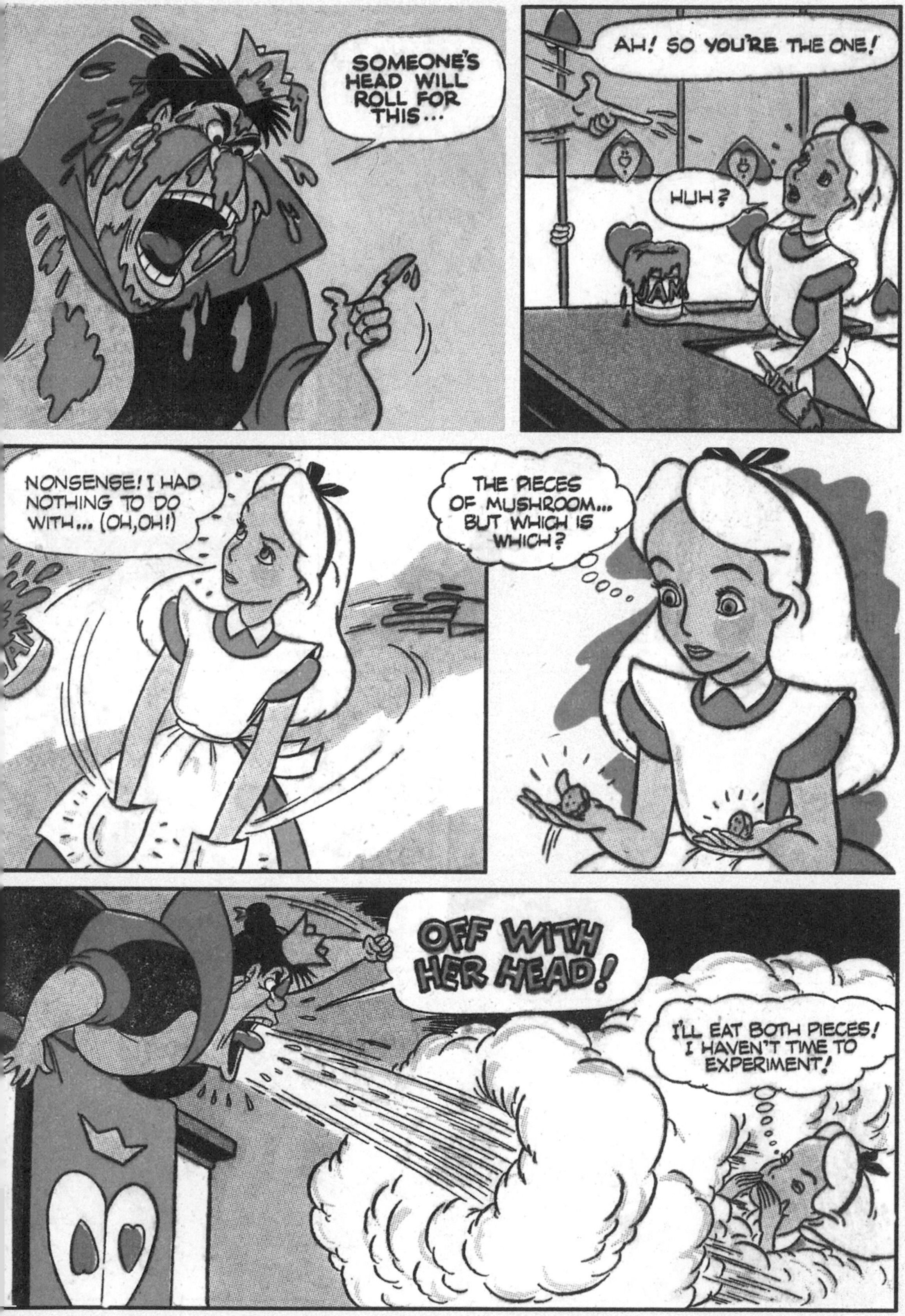
SOMEONE'S HEAD WILL ROLL FOR THIS...
AH! SO YOU'RE THE ONE!
HUH?
JAM
NONSENSE! I HAD NOTHING TO DO WITH... (OH,OH!)
THE PIECES OF MUSHROOM... BUT WHICH IS WHICH?
OFF WITH HER HEAD!
I'LL EAT BOTH PIECES! I HAVEN'T TIME TO EXPERIMENT!

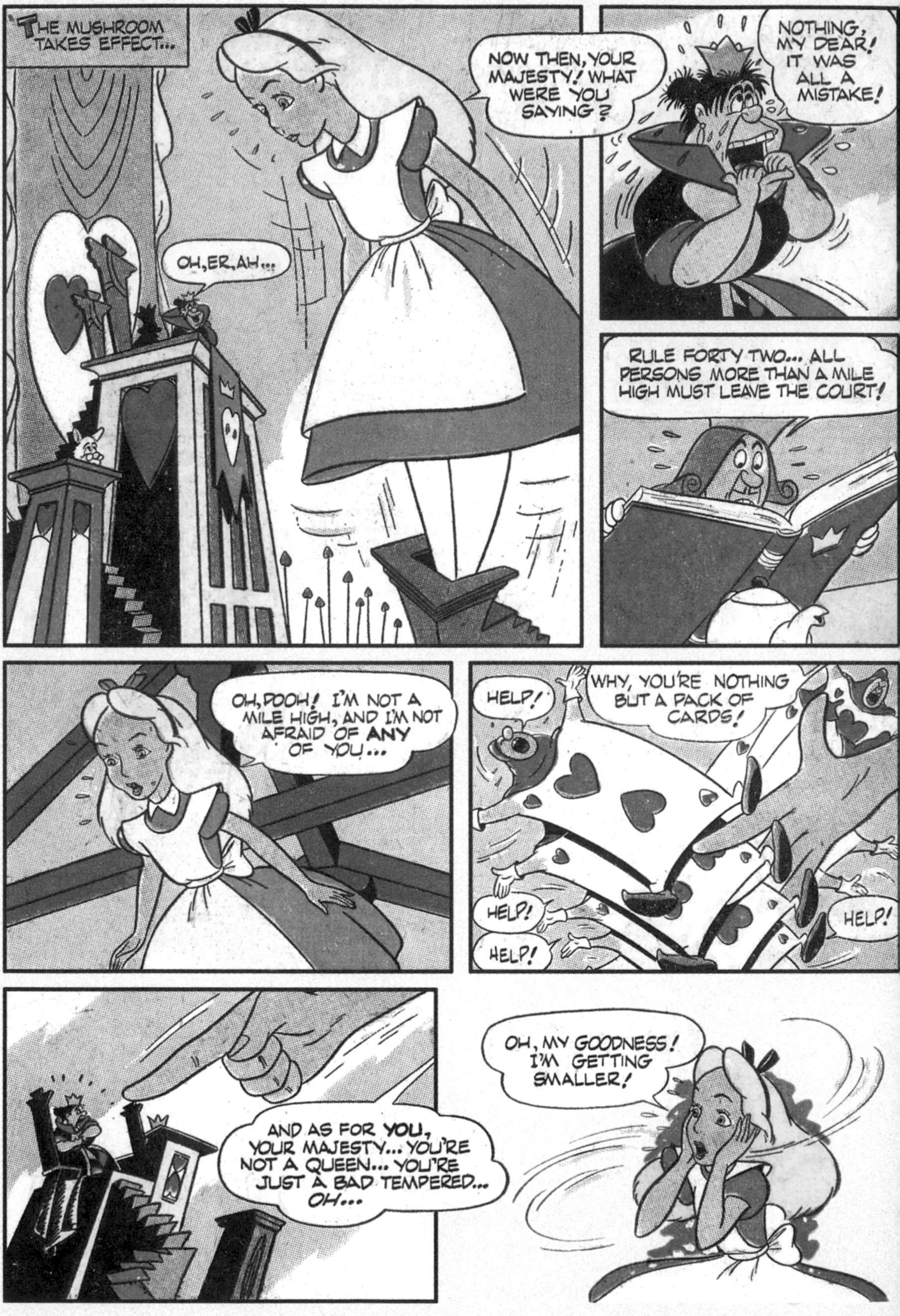
THE MUSHROOM TAKES EFFECT...
NOW THEN, YOUR MAJESTY! WHAT WERE YOU SAYING?
OH, ER, AH...
NOTHING, MY DEAR! IT WAS ALL A MISTAKE!
RULE FORTY TWO... ALL PERSONS MORE THAN A MILE HIGH MUST LEAVE THE COURT!
OH, POOH! I'M NOT A MILE HIGH, AND I'M NOT AFRAID OF ANY OF YOU...
HELP!
WHY, YOU'RE NOTHING BUT A PACK OF CARDS!
HELP!
HELP!
HELP!
AND AS FOR YOU, YOUR MAJESTY... YOU'RE NOT A QUEEN... YOU'RE JUST A BAD TEMPERED... OH...
OH, MY GOODNESS! I'M GETTING SMALLER!

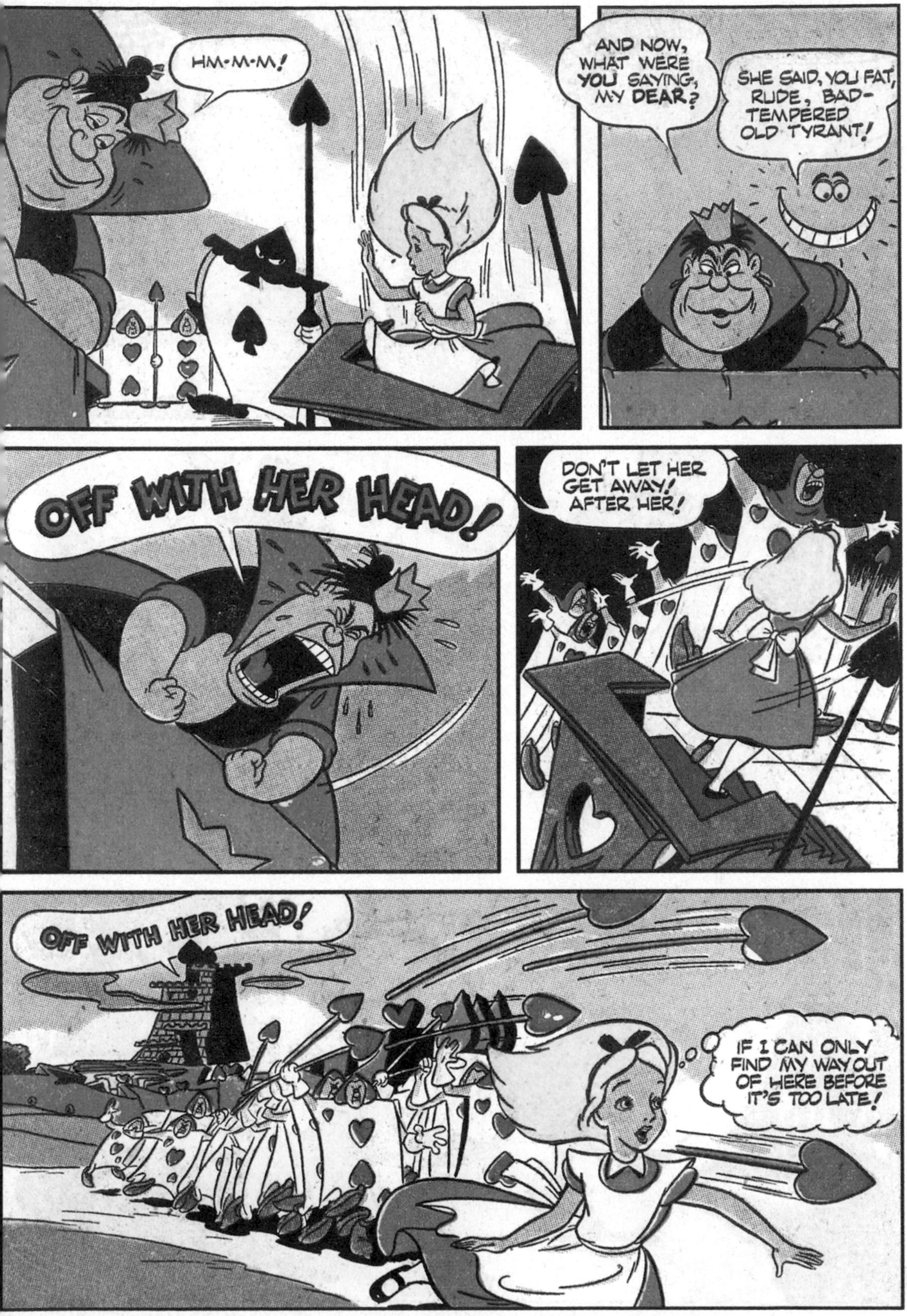
HM-M-M!
AND NOW, WHAT WERE YOU SAYING, MY DEAR?
SHE SAID, YOU FAT, RUDE, BAD-TEMPERED OLD TYRANT!
OFF WITH HER HEAD!
DON'T LET HER GET AWAY! AFTER HER!
OFF WITH HER HEAD!
IF I CAN ONLY FIND MY WAY OUT OF HERE BEFORE IT'S TOO LATE!

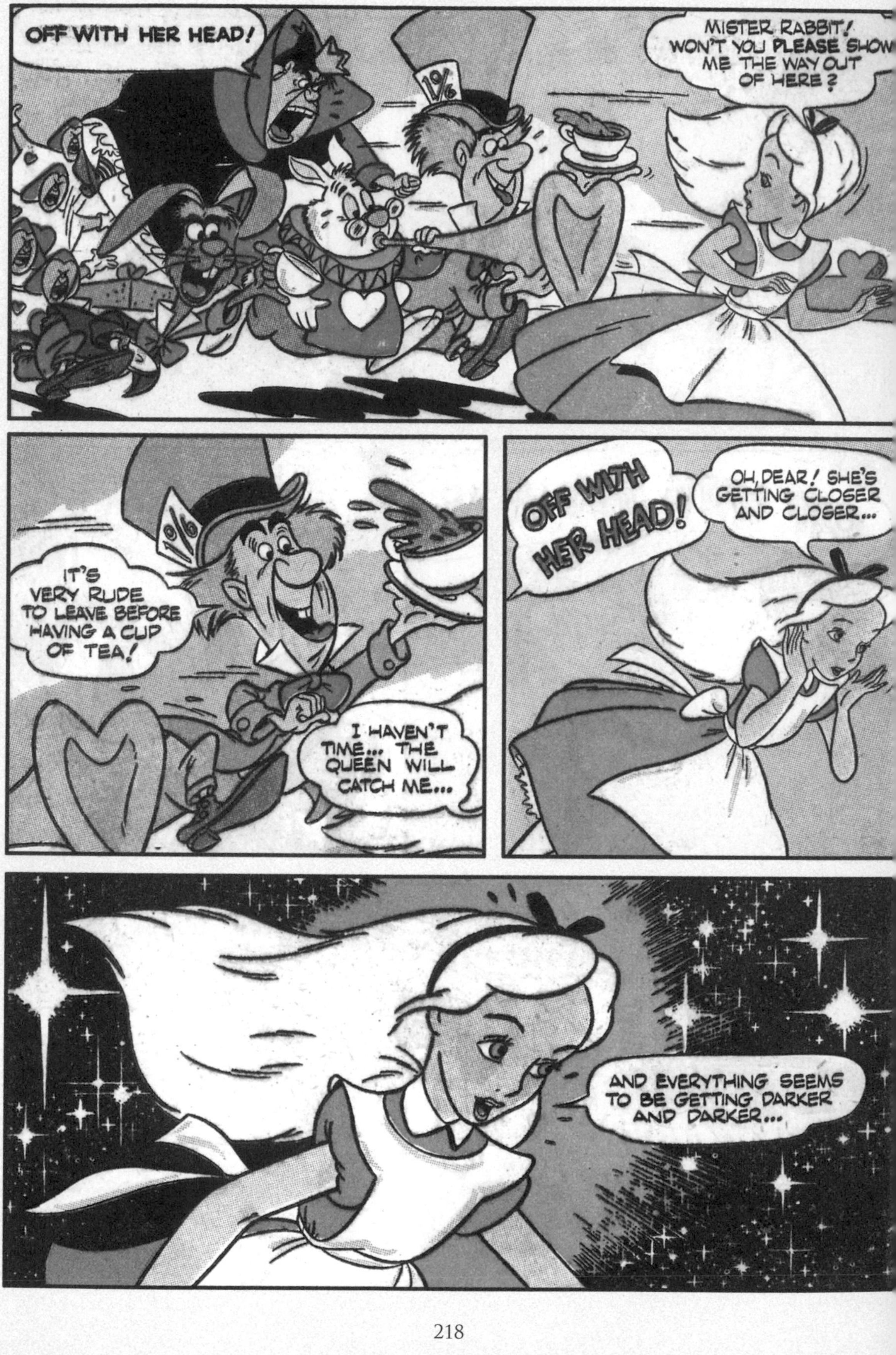
OFF WITH HER HEAD!
MISTER RABBIT! WON'T YOU PLEASE SHOW ME THE WAY OUT OF HERE?
IT'S VERY RUDE TO LEAVE BEFORE HAVING A CUP OF TEA!
I HAVEN'T TIME... THE QUEEN WILL CATCH ME...
OFF WITH HER HEAD!
OH, DEAR! SHE'S GETTING CLOSER AND CLOSER...
AND EVERYTHING SEEMS TO BE GETTING DARKER AND DARKER...

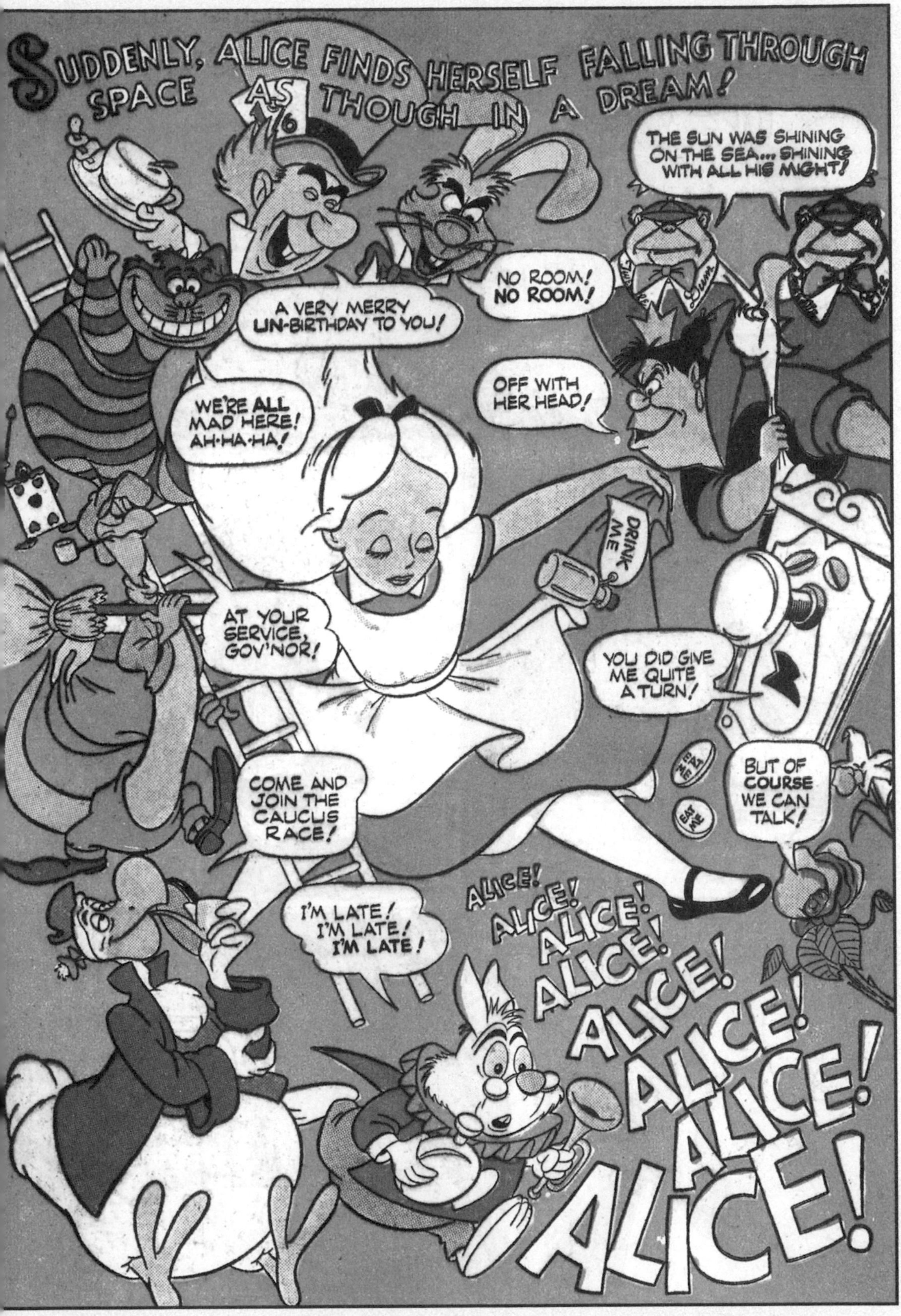
SUDDENLY, ALICE FINDS HERSELF FALLING THROUGH SPACE AS THOUGH IN A DREAM!
THE SUN WAS SHINING ON THE SEA... SHINING WITH ALL HIS MIGHT!
A VERY MERRY UN-BIRTHDAY TO YOU!
NO ROOM! NO ROOM!
WE'RE ALL MAD HERE! AH-HA-HA!
OFF WITH HER HEAD!
DRINK ME
AT YOUR SERVICE, GOV'NOR!
YOU DID GIVE ME QUITE A TURN!
COME AND JOIN THE CAUCUS RACE!
EAT ME
EAT ME
BUT OF COURSE WE CAN TALK!
I'M LATE! I'M LATE! I'M LATE!
ALICE! ALICE! ALICE! ALICE! ALICE! ALICE! ALICE! ALICE!

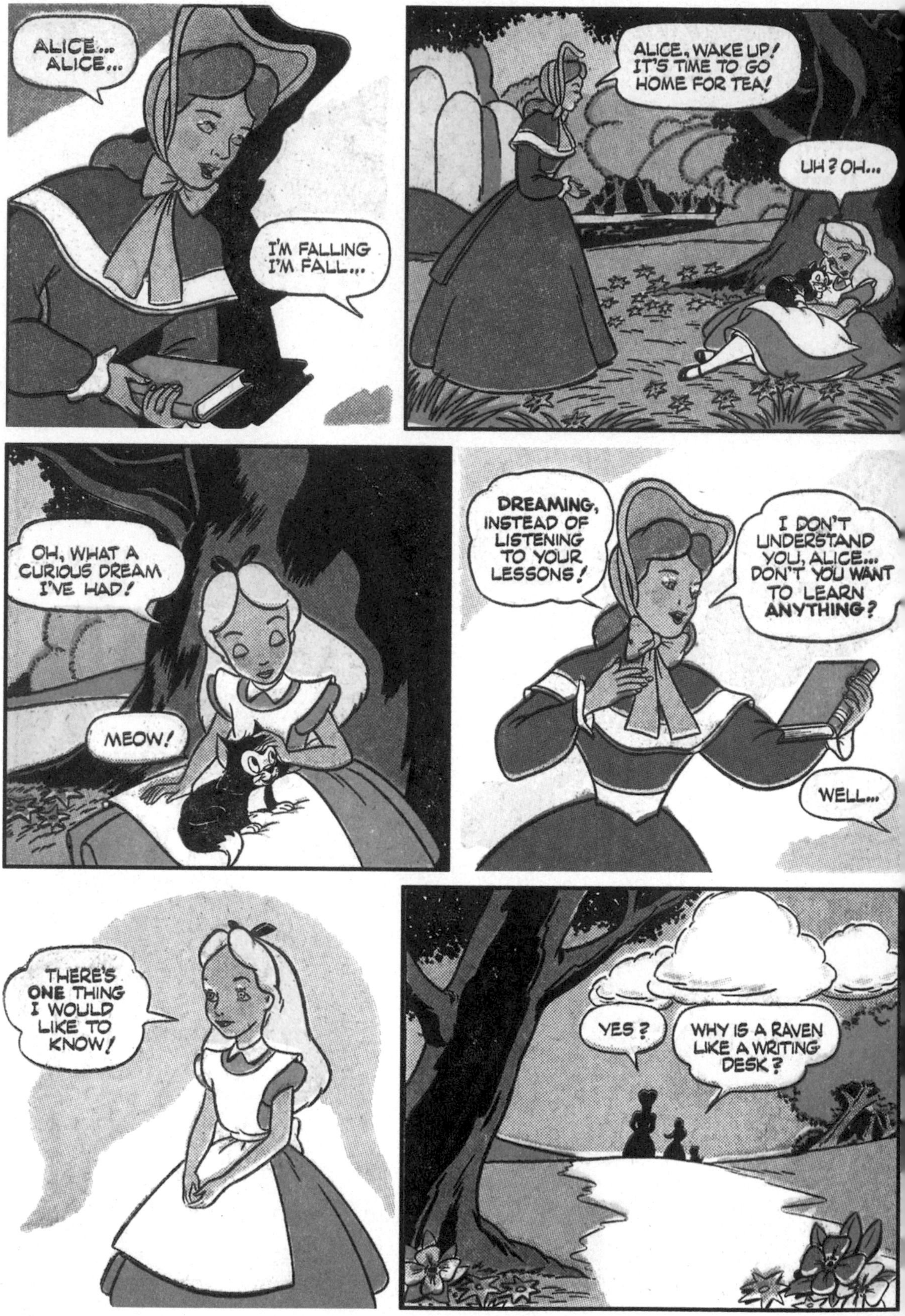
ALICE... ALICE...
I'M FALLING I'M FALL...
ALICE, WAKE UP! IT'S TIME TO GO HOME FOR TEA!
UH? OH...
OH, WHAT A CURIOUS DREAM I'VE HAD!
MEOW!
DREAMING, INSTEAD OF LISTENING TO YOUR LESSONS!
I DON'T UNDERSTAND YOU, ALICE... DON'T YOU WANT TO LEARN ANYTHING?
WELL...
THERE'S ONE THING I WOULD LIKE TO KNOW!
YES?
WHY IS A RAVEN LIKE A WRITING DESK?

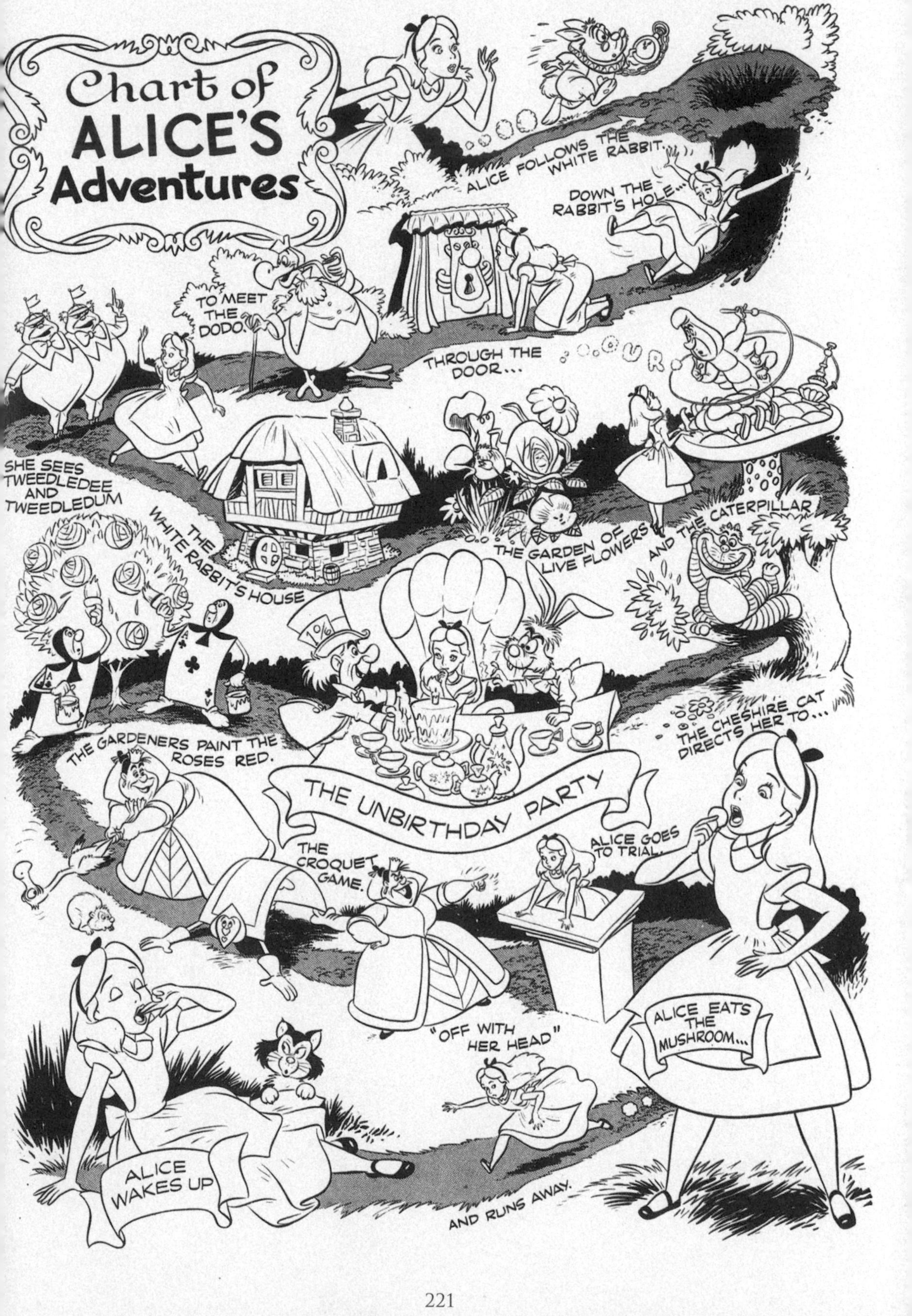
Chart of ALICE'S Adventures
ALICE FOLLOWS THE WHITE RABBIT.
DOWN THE RABBIT'S HOLE...
THROUGH THE DOOR...
TO MEET THE DODO.
SHE SEES TWEEDLEDEE AND TWEEDLEDUM
THE WHITE RABBIT'S HOUSE
THE GARDEN OF LIVE FLOWERS
AND THE CATERPILLAR
THE CHESHIRE CAT DIRECTS HER TO...
THE UNBIRTHDAY PARTY
THE GARDENERS PAINT THE ROSES RED.
THE CROQUET GAME.
ALICE GOES TO TRIAL.
"OFF WITH HER HEAD"
ALICE EATS THE MUSHROOM...
AND RUNS AWAY.
ALICE WAKES UP

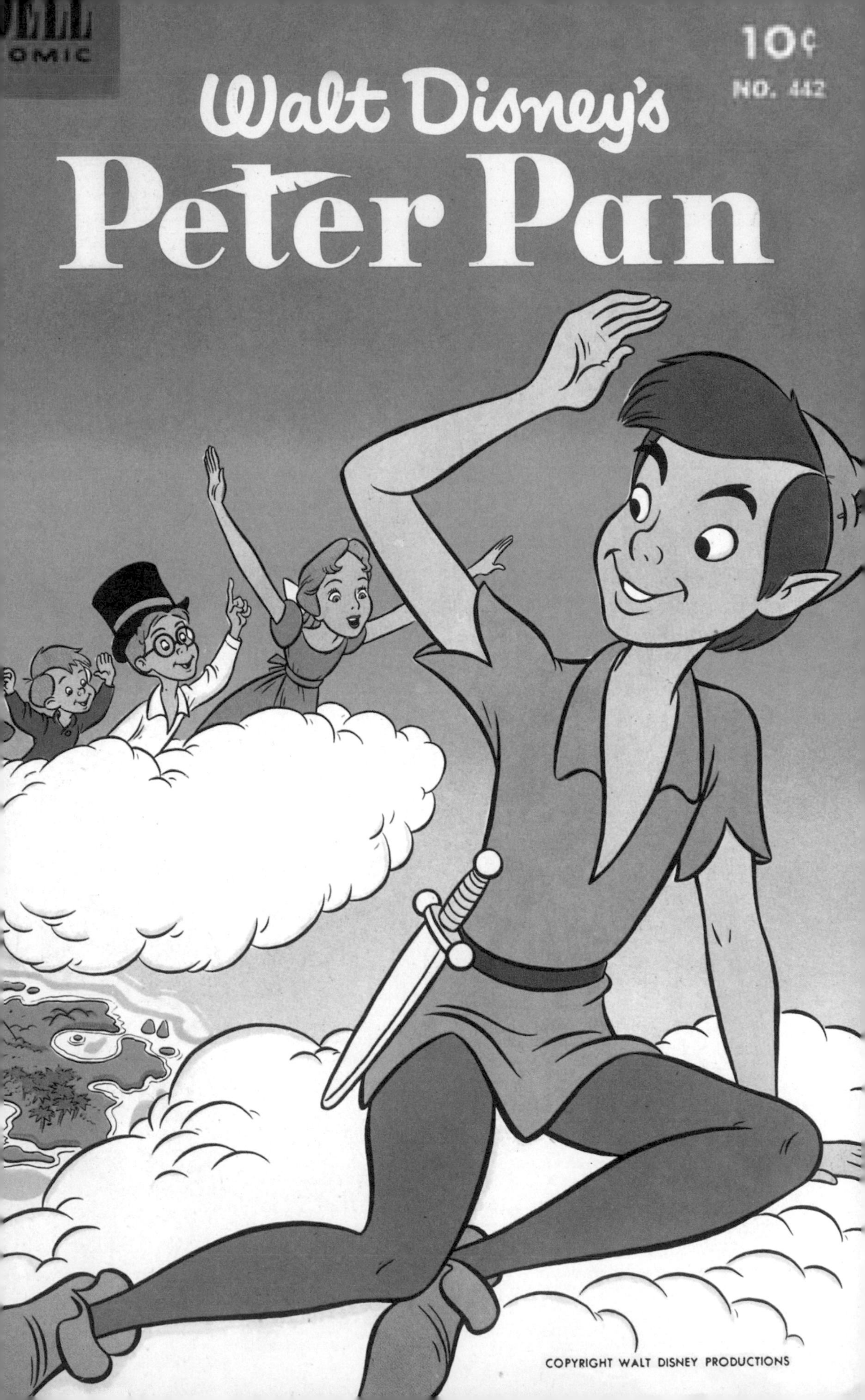
10¢
NO. 442
Walt Disney's
Peter Pan
COPYRIGHT WALT DISNEY PRODUCTIONS

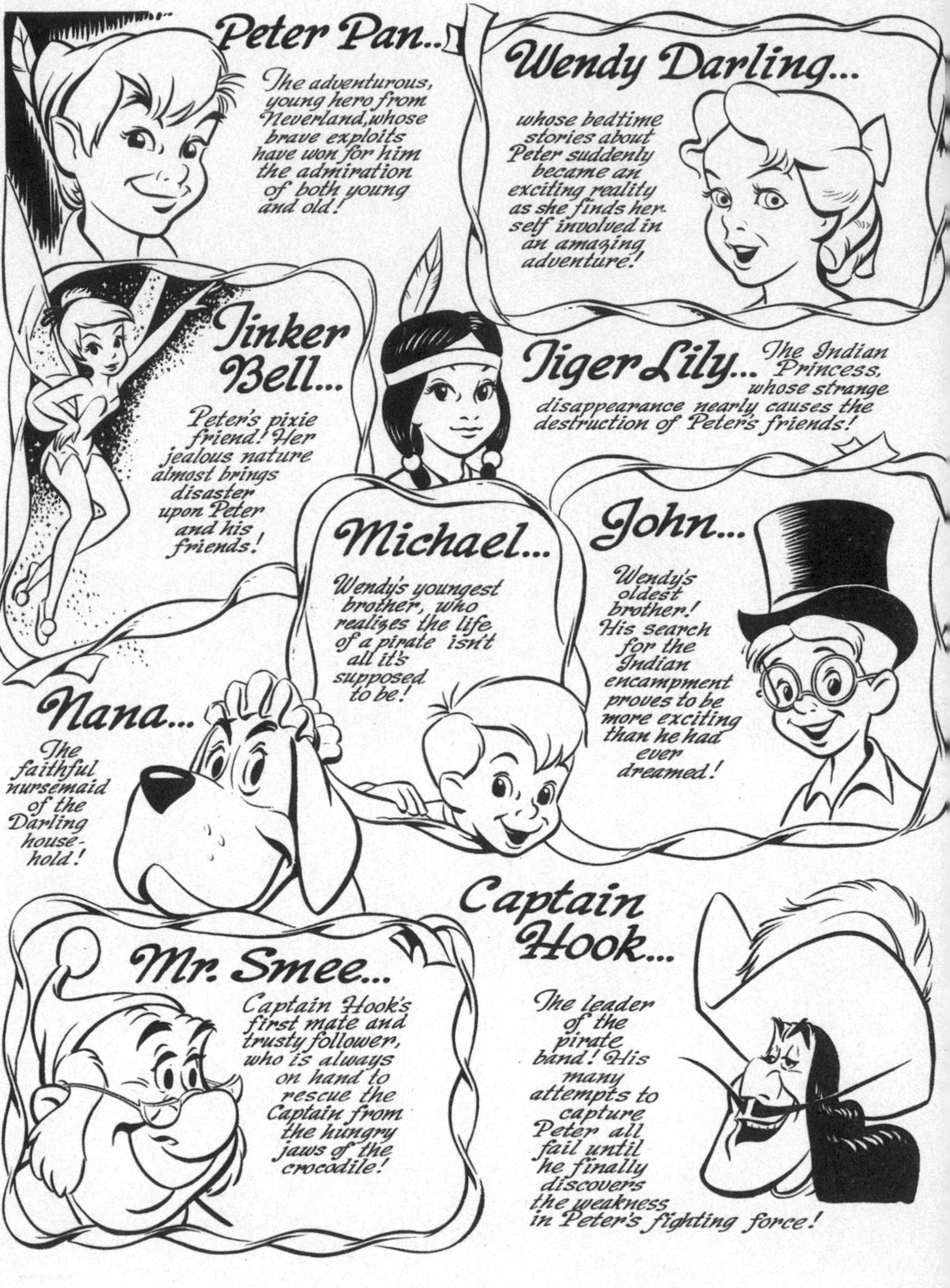
Peter Pan...
The adventurous, young hero from Neverland, whose brave exploits have won for him the admiration of both young and old!
Wendy Darling...
whose bedtime stories about Peter suddenly became an exciting reality as she finds herself involved in an amazing adventure!
Tinker Bell...
Peter's pixie friend! Her jealous nature almost brings disaster upon Peter and his friends!
Tiger Lily...
The Indian Princess, whose strange disappearance nearly causes the destruction of Peter's friends!
Michael...
Wendy's youngest brother, who realizes the life of a pirate isn't all it's supposed to be!
John...
Wendy's oldest brother! His search for the Indian encampment proves to be more exciting than he had ever dreamed!
Nana...
The faithful nursemaid of the Darling household!
Mr. Smee...
Captain Hook's first mate and trusty follower, who is always on hand to rescue the Captain from the hungry jaws of the crocodile!
Captain Hook...
The leader of the pirate band! His many attempts to capture Peter all fail until he finally discovers the weakness in Peter's fighting force!

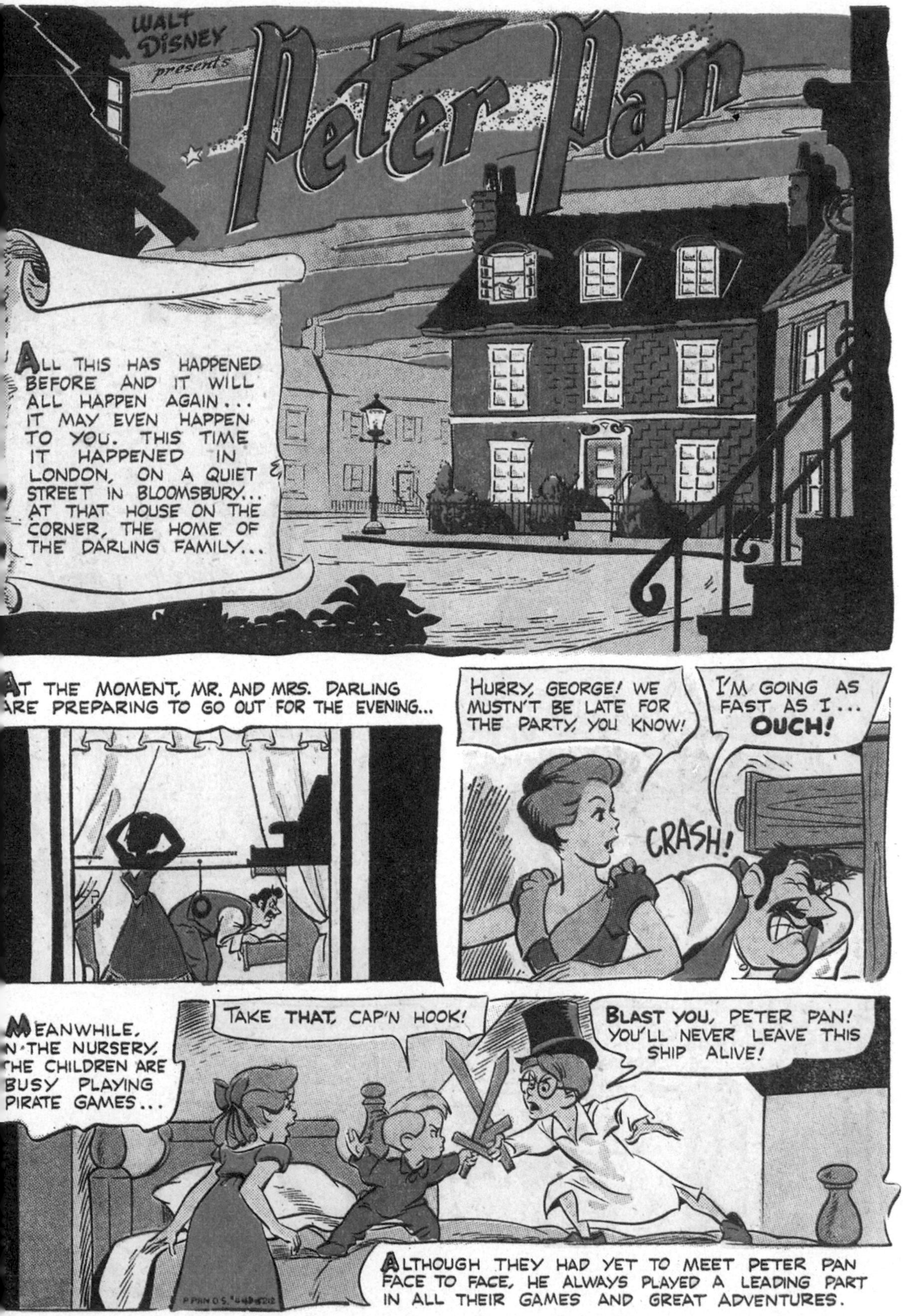
WALT DISNEY presents
Peter Pan
ALL THIS HAS HAPPENED BEFORE AND IT WILL ALL HAPPEN AGAIN... IT MAY EVEN HAPPEN TO YOU. THIS TIME IT HAPPENED IN LONDON, ON A QUIET STREET IN BLOOMSBURY... AT THAT HOUSE ON THE CORNER, THE HOME OF THE DARLING FAMILY...
AT THE MOMENT, MR. AND MRS. DARLING ARE PREPARING TO GO OUT FOR THE EVENING...
HURRY, GEORGE! WE MUSTN'T BE LATE FOR THE PARTY, YOU KNOW!
I'M GOING AS FAST AS I... OUCH!
CRASH!
MEANWHILE, IN THE NURSERY, THE CHILDREN ARE BUSY PLAYING PIRATE GAMES...
TAKE THAT, CAP'N HOOK!
BLAST YOU, PETER PAN! YOU'LL NEVER LEAVE THIS SHIP ALIVE!
ALTHOUGH THEY HAD YET TO MEET PETER PAN FACE TO FACE, HE ALWAYS PLAYED A LEADING PART IN ALL THEIR GAMES AND GREAT ADVENTURES.

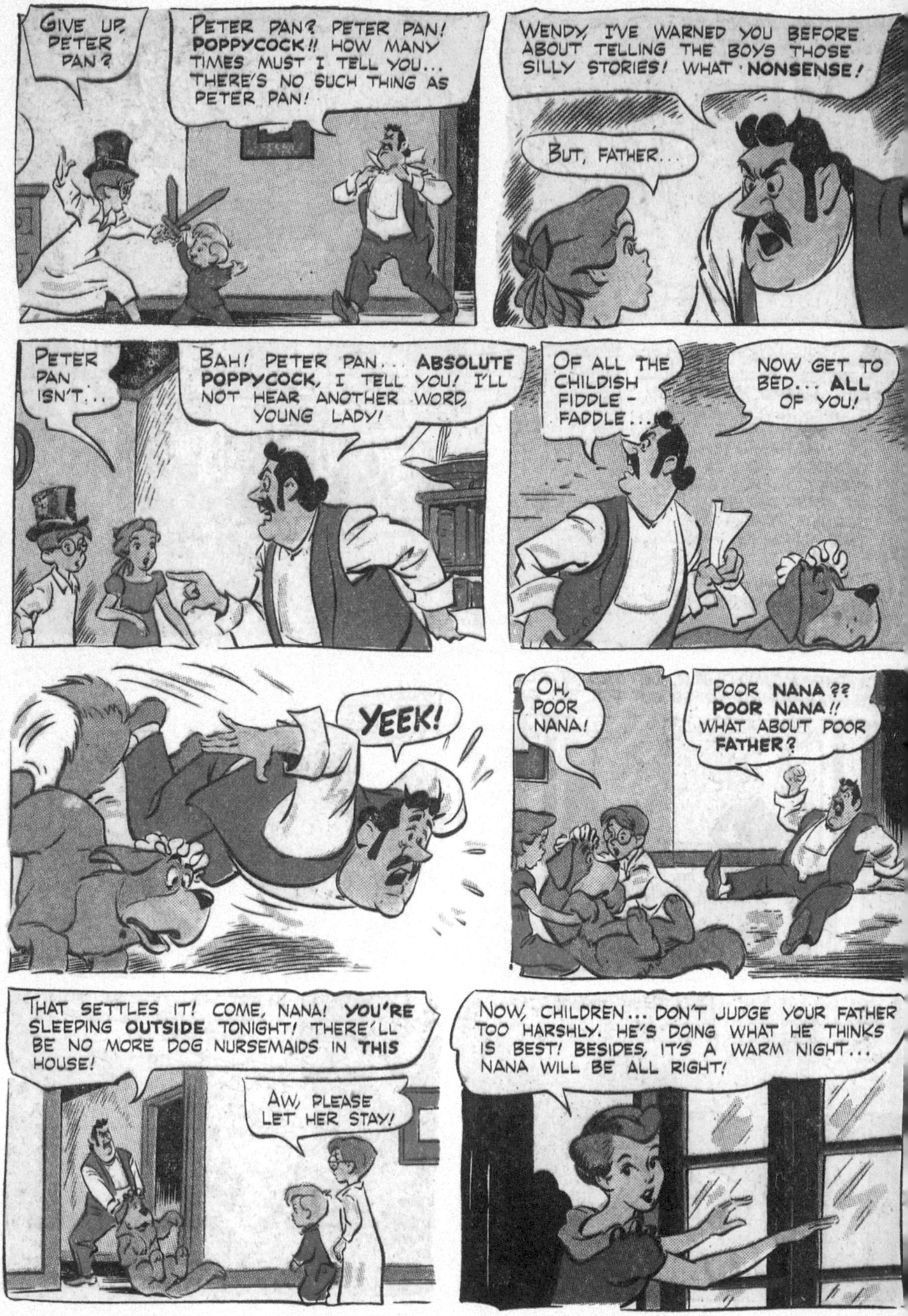
GIVE UP, PETER PAN?
PETER PAN? PETER PAN! **POPPYCOCK!!** HOW MANY TIMES MUST I TELL YOU... THERE'S NO SUCH THING AS PETER PAN!
WENDY, I'VE WARNED YOU BEFORE ABOUT TELLING THE BOYS THOSE SILLY STORIES! WHAT **NONSENSE!**
BUT, FATHER...
PETER PAN ISN'T...
BAH! PETER PAN... **ABSOLUTE POPPYCOCK,** I TELL YOU! I'LL NOT HEAR ANOTHER WORD, YOUNG LADY!
OF ALL THE CHILDISH FIDDLE-FADDLE...
NOW GET TO BED... **ALL** OF YOU!
YEEK!
OH, POOR NANA!
POOR **NANA??** **POOR NANA!!** WHAT ABOUT POOR **FATHER?**
THAT SETTLES IT! COME, NANA! **YOU'RE** SLEEPING **OUTSIDE** TONIGHT! THERE'LL BE NO MORE DOG NURSEMAIDS IN **THIS** HOUSE!
AW, PLEASE LET HER STAY!
NOW, CHILDREN... DON'T JUDGE YOUR FATHER TOO HARSHLY. HE'S DOING WHAT HE THINKS IS BEST! BESIDES, IT'S A WARM NIGHT... NANA WILL BE ALL RIGHT!

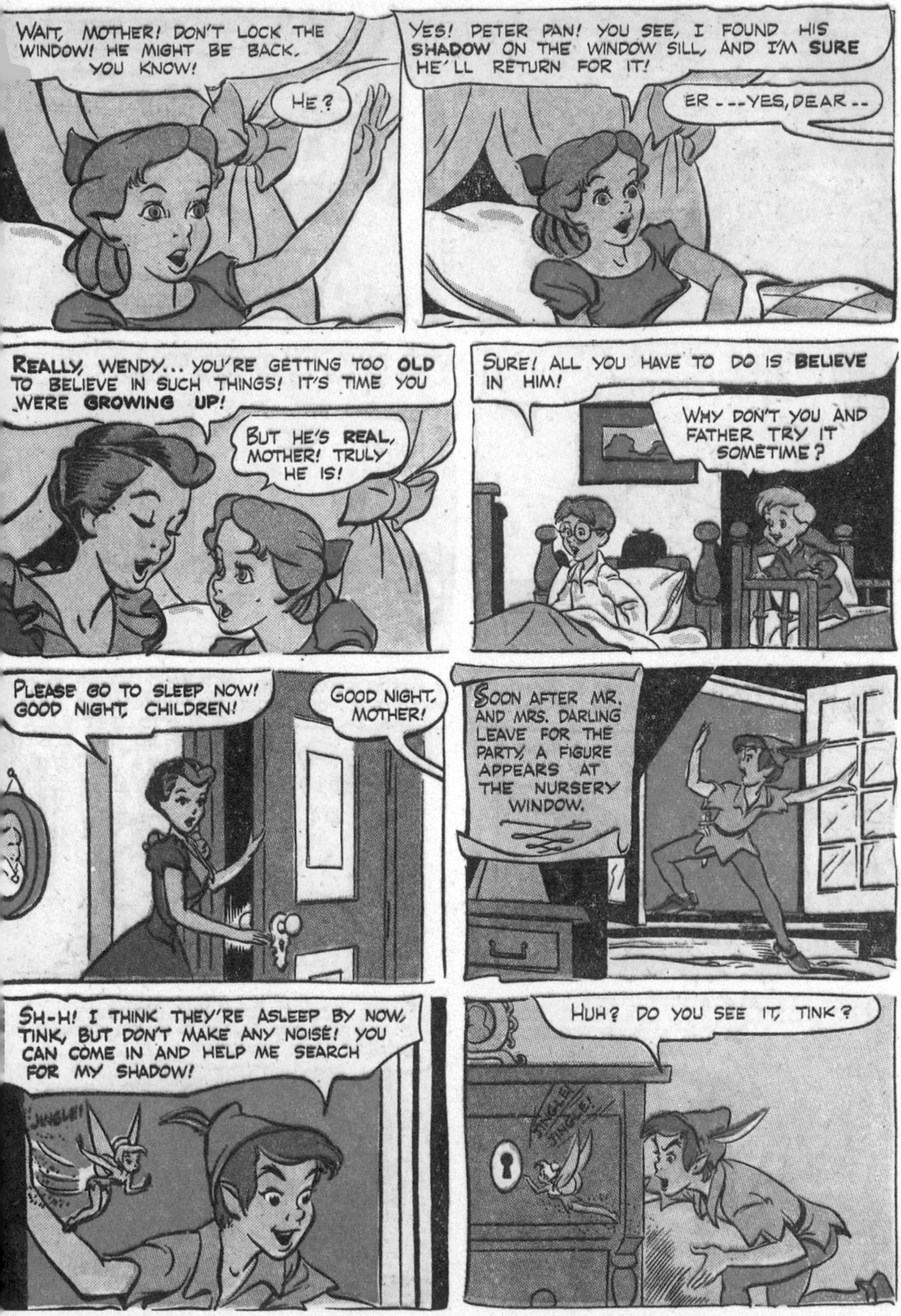
WAIT, MOTHER! DON'T LOCK THE WINDOW! HE MIGHT BE BACK, YOU KNOW!
HE?
YES! PETER PAN! YOU SEE, I FOUND HIS SHADOW ON THE WINDOW SILL, AND I'M SURE HE'LL RETURN FOR IT!
ER ---YES, DEAR--
REALLY, WENDY... YOU'RE GETTING TOO OLD TO BELIEVE IN SUCH THINGS! IT'S TIME YOU WERE GROWING UP!
BUT HE'S REAL, MOTHER! TRULY HE IS!
SURE! ALL YOU HAVE TO DO IS BELIEVE IN HIM!
WHY DON'T YOU AND FATHER TRY IT SOMETIME?
PLEASE GO TO SLEEP NOW! GOOD NIGHT, CHILDREN!
GOOD NIGHT, MOTHER!
SOON AFTER MR. AND MRS. DARLING LEAVE FOR THE PARTY, A FIGURE APPEARS AT THE NURSERY WINDOW.
SH-H! I THINK THEY'RE ASLEEP BY NOW, TINK, BUT DON'T MAKE ANY NOISE! YOU CAN COME IN AND HELP ME SEARCH FOR MY SHADOW!
JINGLE!
HUH? DO YOU SEE IT, TINK?
JINGLE! JINGLE!

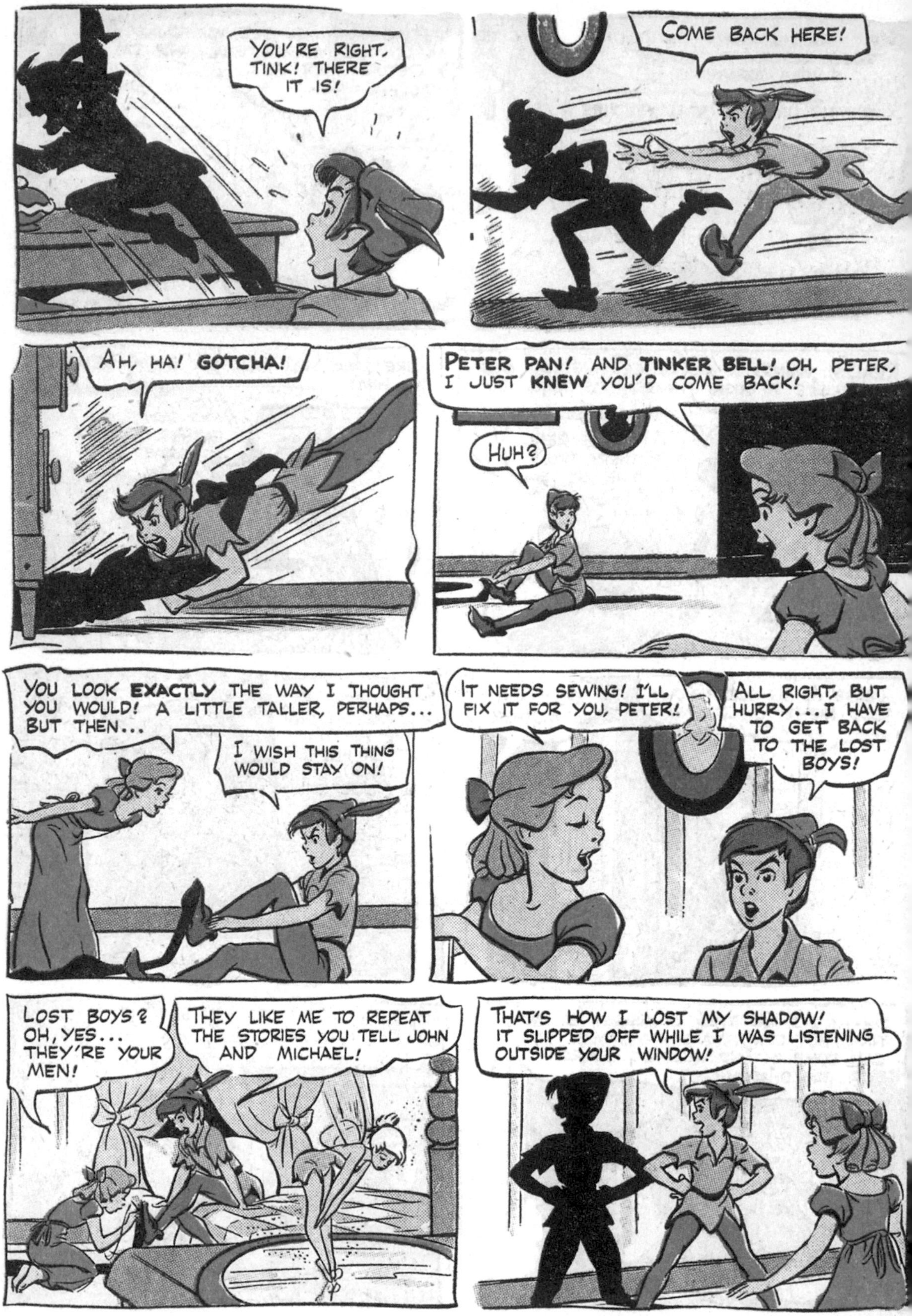
YOU'RE RIGHT, TINK! THERE IT IS!
COME BACK HERE!
AH, HA! GOTCHA!
PETER PAN! AND TINKER BELL! OH, PETER, I JUST KNEW YOU'D COME BACK!
HUH?
YOU LOOK EXACTLY THE WAY I THOUGHT YOU WOULD! A LITTLE TALLER, PERHAPS... BUT THEN...
I WISH THIS THING WOULD STAY ON!
IT NEEDS SEWING! I'LL FIX IT FOR YOU, PETER!
ALL RIGHT, BUT HURRY...I HAVE TO GET BACK TO THE LOST BOYS!
LOST BOYS? OH, YES... THEY'RE YOUR MEN!
THEY LIKE ME TO REPEAT THE STORIES YOU TELL JOHN AND MICHAEL!
THAT'S HOW I LOST MY SHADOW! IT SLIPPED OFF WHILE I WAS LISTENING OUTSIDE YOUR WINDOW!

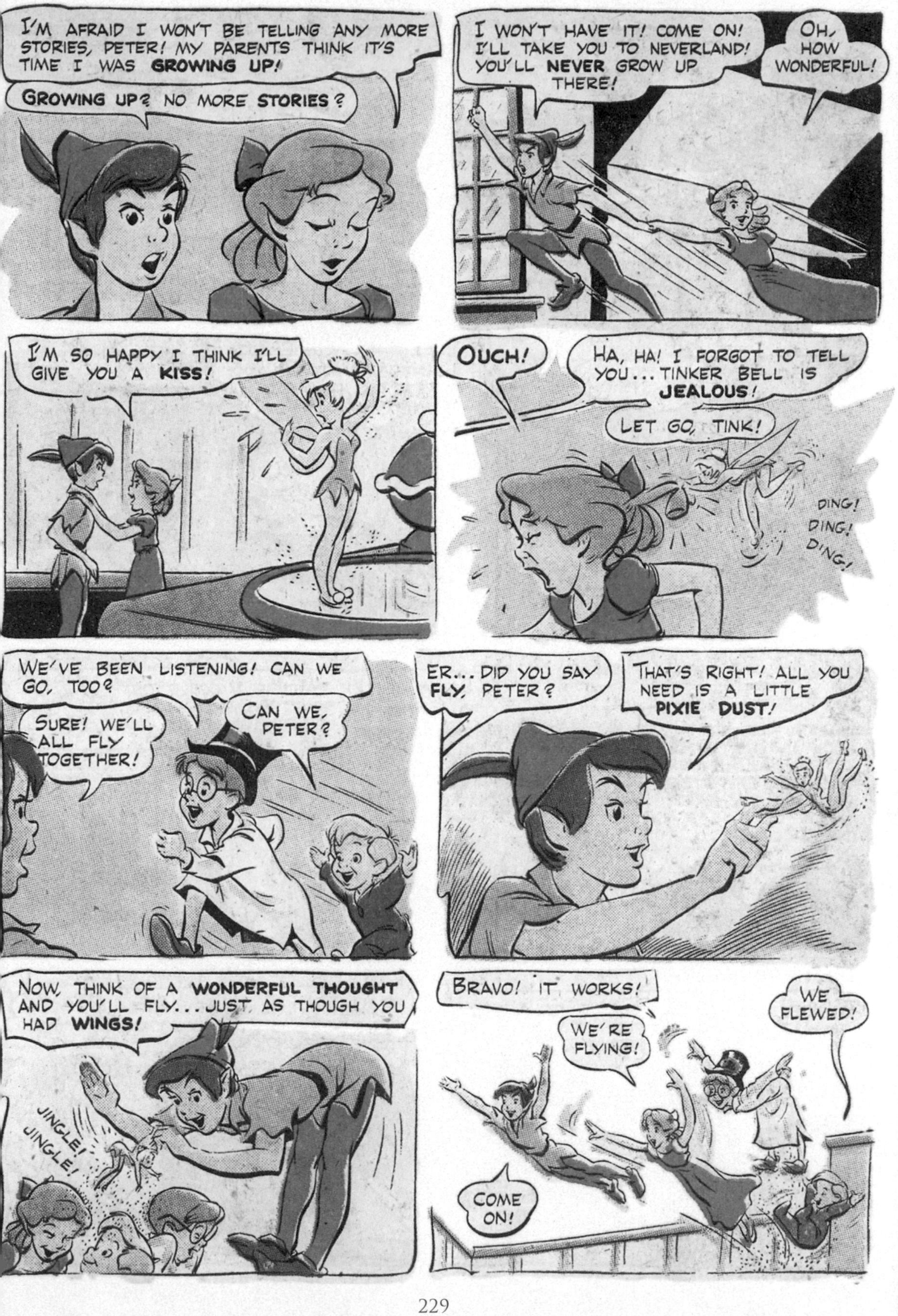
I'M AFRAID I WON'T BE TELLING ANY MORE STORIES, PETER! MY PARENTS THINK IT'S TIME I WAS GROWING UP!
GROWING UP? NO MORE STORIES?
I WON'T HAVE IT! COME ON! I'LL TAKE YOU TO NEVERLAND! YOU'LL NEVER GROW UP THERE!
OH, HOW WONDERFUL!
I'M SO HAPPY I THINK I'LL GIVE YOU A KISS!
OUCH!
HA, HA! I FORGOT TO TELL YOU... TINKER BELL IS JEALOUS!
LET GO, TINK!
DING! DING! DING!
WE'VE BEEN LISTENING! CAN WE GO, TOO?
CAN WE, PETER?
SURE! WE'LL ALL FLY TOGETHER!
ER... DID YOU SAY FLY, PETER?
THAT'S RIGHT! ALL YOU NEED IS A LITTLE PIXIE DUST!
NOW, THINK OF A WONDERFUL THOUGHT AND YOU'LL FLY... JUST AS THOUGH YOU HAD WINGS!
JINGLE! JINGLE!
BRAVO! IT WORKS!
WE'RE FLYING!
WE FLEWED!
COME ON!

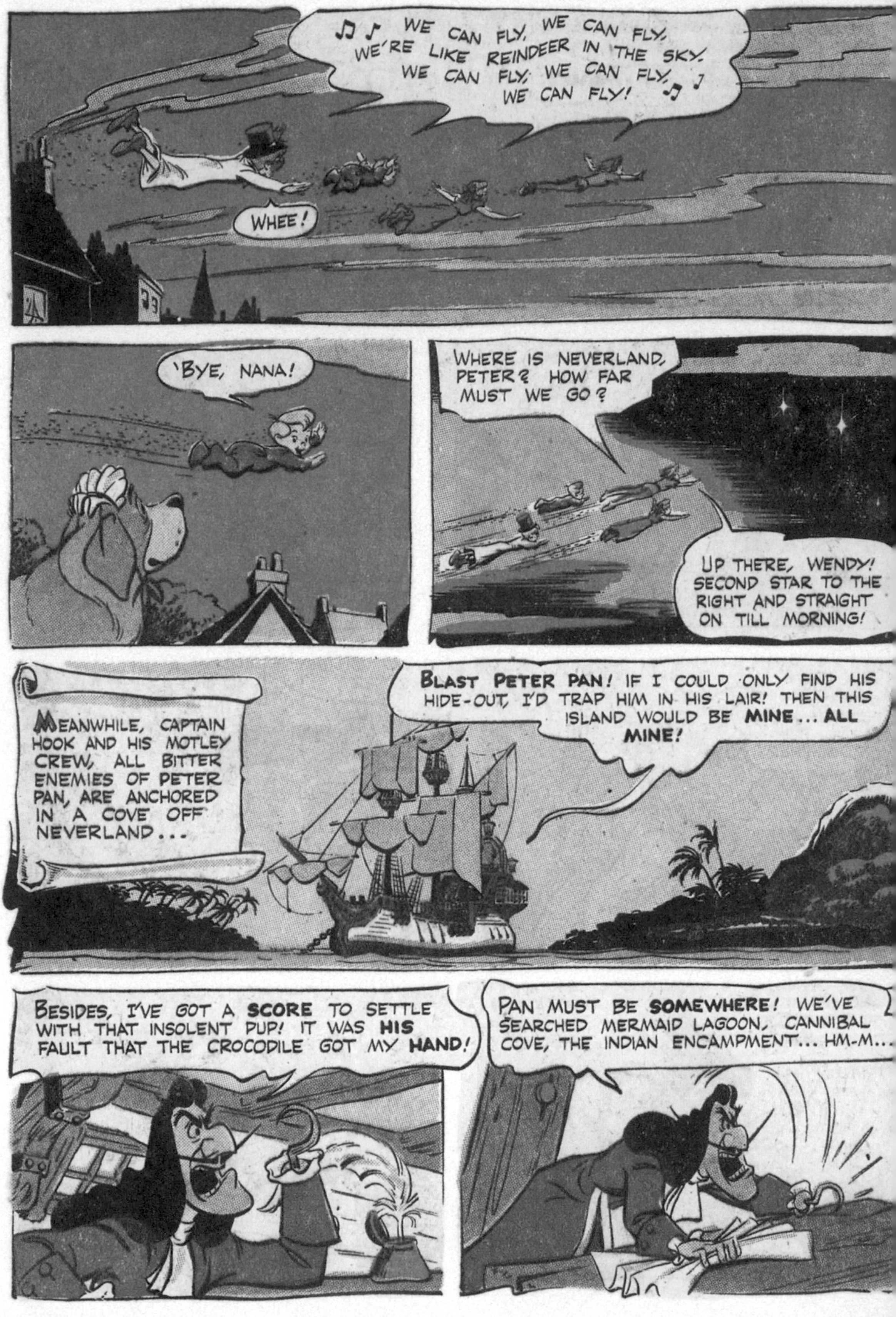
WE CAN FLY, WE CAN FLY, WE'RE LIKE REINDEER IN THE SKY. WE CAN FLY, WE CAN FLY, WE CAN FLY!
WHEE!
'BYE, NANA!
WHERE IS NEVERLAND, PETER? HOW FAR MUST WE GO?
UP THERE, WENDY! SECOND STAR TO THE RIGHT AND STRAIGHT ON TILL MORNING!
MEANWHILE, CAPTAIN HOOK AND HIS MOTLEY CREW, ALL BITTER ENEMIES OF PETER PAN, ARE ANCHORED IN A COVE OFF NEVERLAND...
BLAST PETER PAN! IF I COULD ONLY FIND HIS HIDE-OUT, I'D TRAP HIM IN HIS LAIR! THEN THIS ISLAND WOULD BE MINE... ALL MINE!
BESIDES, I'VE GOT A SCORE TO SETTLE WITH THAT INSOLENT PUP! IT WAS HIS FAULT THAT THE CROCODILE GOT MY HAND!
PAN MUST BE SOMEWHERE! WE'VE SEARCHED MERMAID LAGOON, CANNIBAL COVE, THE INDIAN ENCAMPMENT... HM-M...

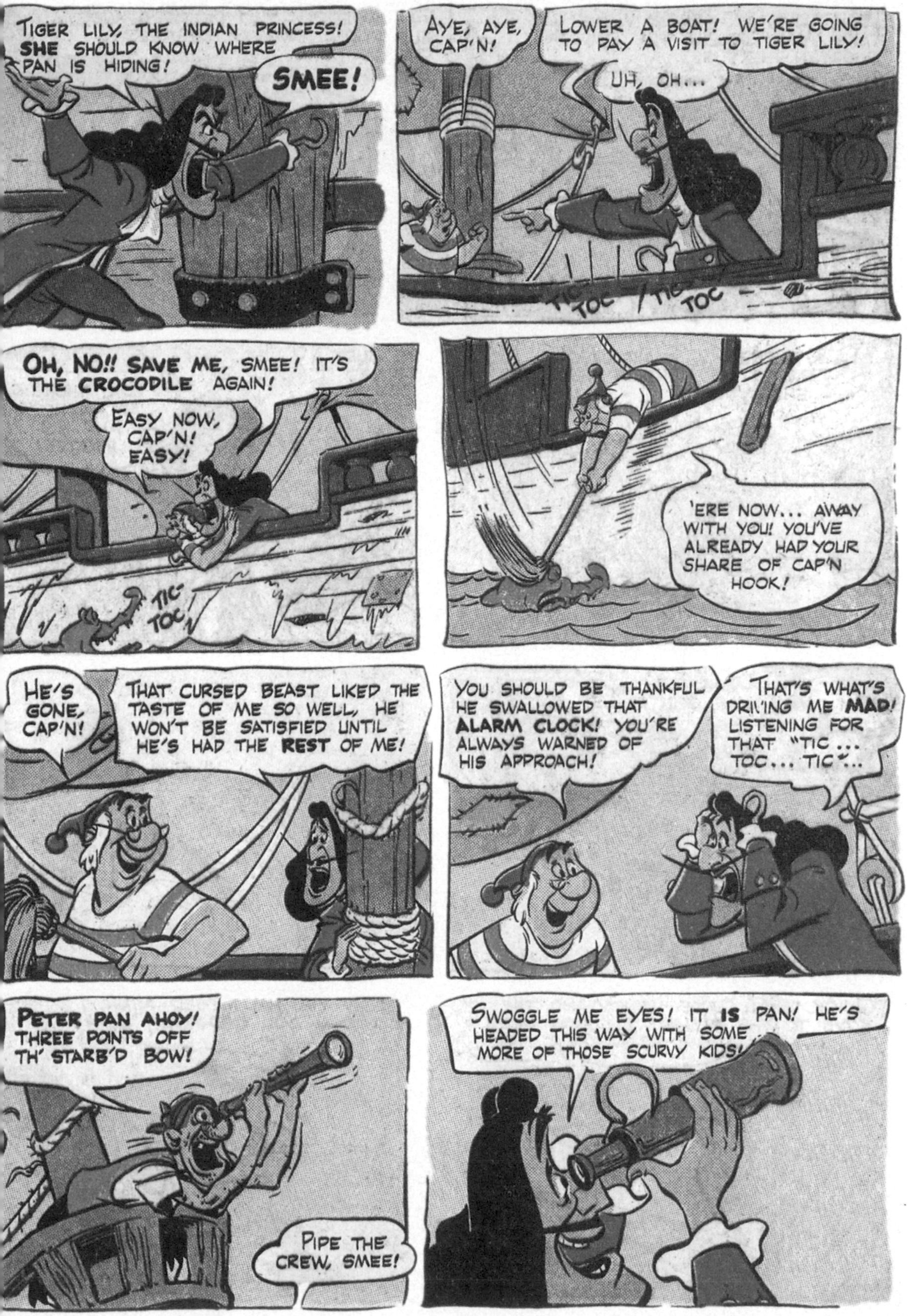

TIGER LILY, THE INDIAN PRINCESS! SHE SHOULD KNOW WHERE PAN IS HIDING!
SMEE!
AYE, AYE, CAP'N!
LOWER A BOAT! WE'RE GOING TO PAY A VISIT TO TIGER LILY!
UH, OH...
TIC TOC / TIC TOC
OH, NO!! SAVE ME, SMEE! IT'S THE CROCODILE AGAIN!
EASY NOW, CAP'N! EASY!
TIC TOC
'ERE NOW... AWAY WITH YOU! YOU'VE ALREADY HAD YOUR SHARE OF CAP'N HOOK!
HE'S GONE, CAP'N!
THAT CURSED BEAST LIKED THE TASTE OF ME SO WELL, HE WON'T BE SATISFIED UNTIL HE'S HAD THE REST OF ME!
YOU SHOULD BE THANKFUL HE SWALLOWED THAT ALARM CLOCK! YOU'RE ALWAYS WARNED OF HIS APPROACH!
THAT'S WHAT'S DRIVING ME MAD! LISTENING FOR THAT "TIC... TOC... TIC"...
PETER PAN AHOY! THREE POINTS OFF TH' STARB'D BOW!
PIPE THE CREW, SMEE!
SWOGGLE ME EYES! IT IS PAN! HE'S HEADED THIS WAY WITH SOME MORE OF THOSE SCURVY KIDS!

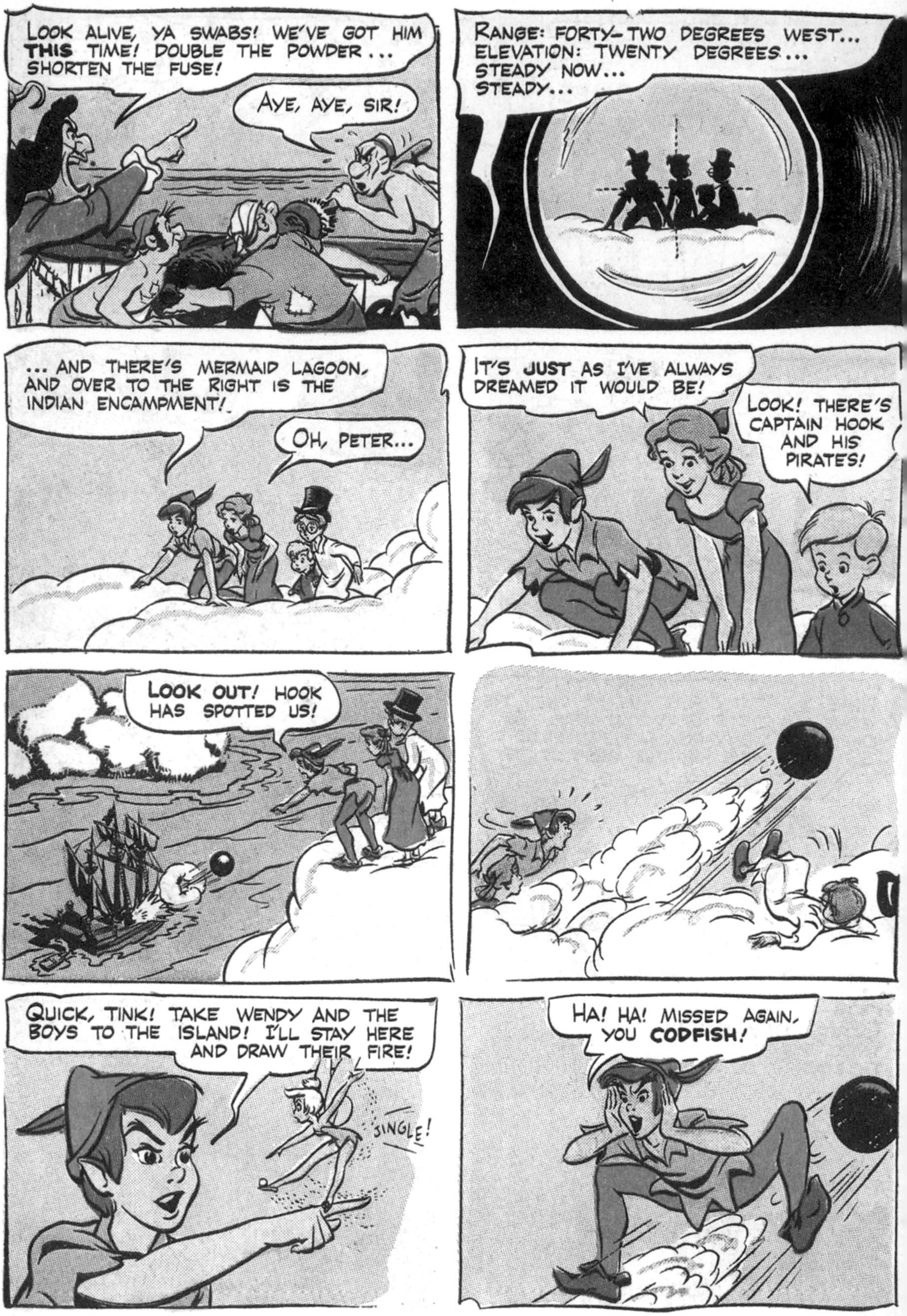
LOOK ALIVE, YA SWABS! WE'VE GOT HIM **THIS** TIME! DOUBLE THE POWDER ... SHORTEN THE FUSE!
AYE, AYE, SIR!
RANGE: FORTY-TWO DEGREES WEST... ELEVATION: TWENTY DEGREES... STEADY NOW... STEADY...
... AND THERE'S MERMAID LAGOON, AND OVER TO THE RIGHT IS THE INDIAN ENCAMPMENT!
OH, PETER...
IT'S **JUST** AS I'VE ALWAYS DREAMED IT WOULD BE!
LOOK! THERE'S CAPTAIN HOOK AND HIS PIRATES!
LOOK OUT! HOOK HAS SPOTTED US!
QUICK, TINK! TAKE WENDY AND THE BOYS TO THE ISLAND! I'LL STAY HERE AND DRAW THEIR FIRE!
JINGLE!
HA! HA! MISSED AGAIN, YOU **CODFISH**!

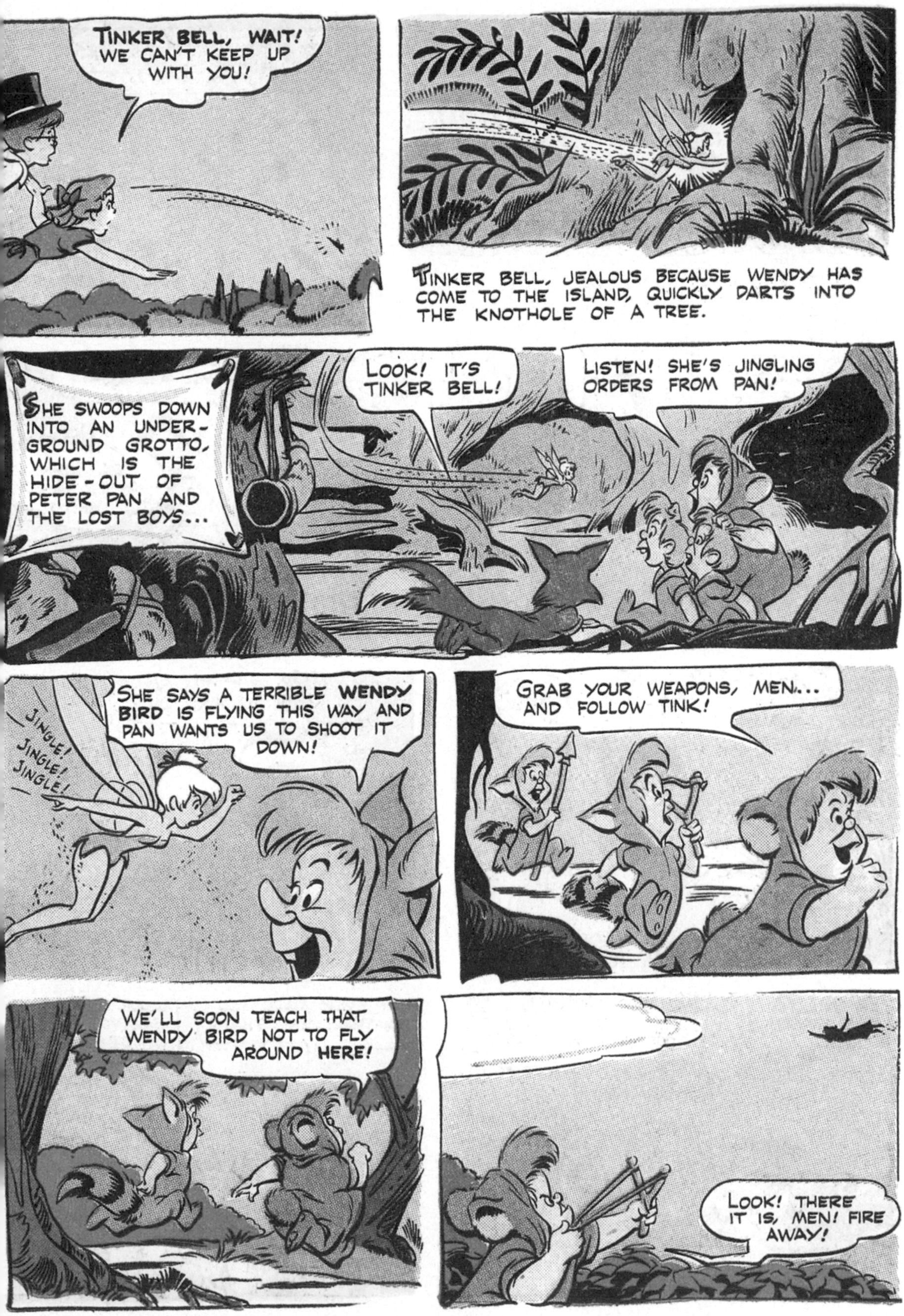
TINKER BELL, WAIT! WE CAN'T KEEP UP WITH YOU!
TINKER BELL, JEALOUS BECAUSE WENDY HAS COME TO THE ISLAND, QUICKLY DARTS INTO THE KNOTHOLE OF A TREE.
SHE SWOOPS DOWN INTO AN UNDER-GROUND GROTTO, WHICH IS THE HIDE-OUT OF PETER PAN AND THE LOST BOYS...
LOOK! IT'S TINKER BELL!
LISTEN! SHE'S JINGLING ORDERS FROM PAN!
JINGLE! JINGLE! JINGLE!
SHE SAYS A TERRIBLE WENDY BIRD IS FLYING THIS WAY AND PAN WANTS US TO SHOOT IT DOWN!
GRAB YOUR WEAPONS, MEN... AND FOLLOW TINK!
WE'LL SOON TEACH THAT WENDY BIRD NOT TO FLY AROUND HERE!
LOOK! THERE IT IS, MEN! FIRE AWAY!

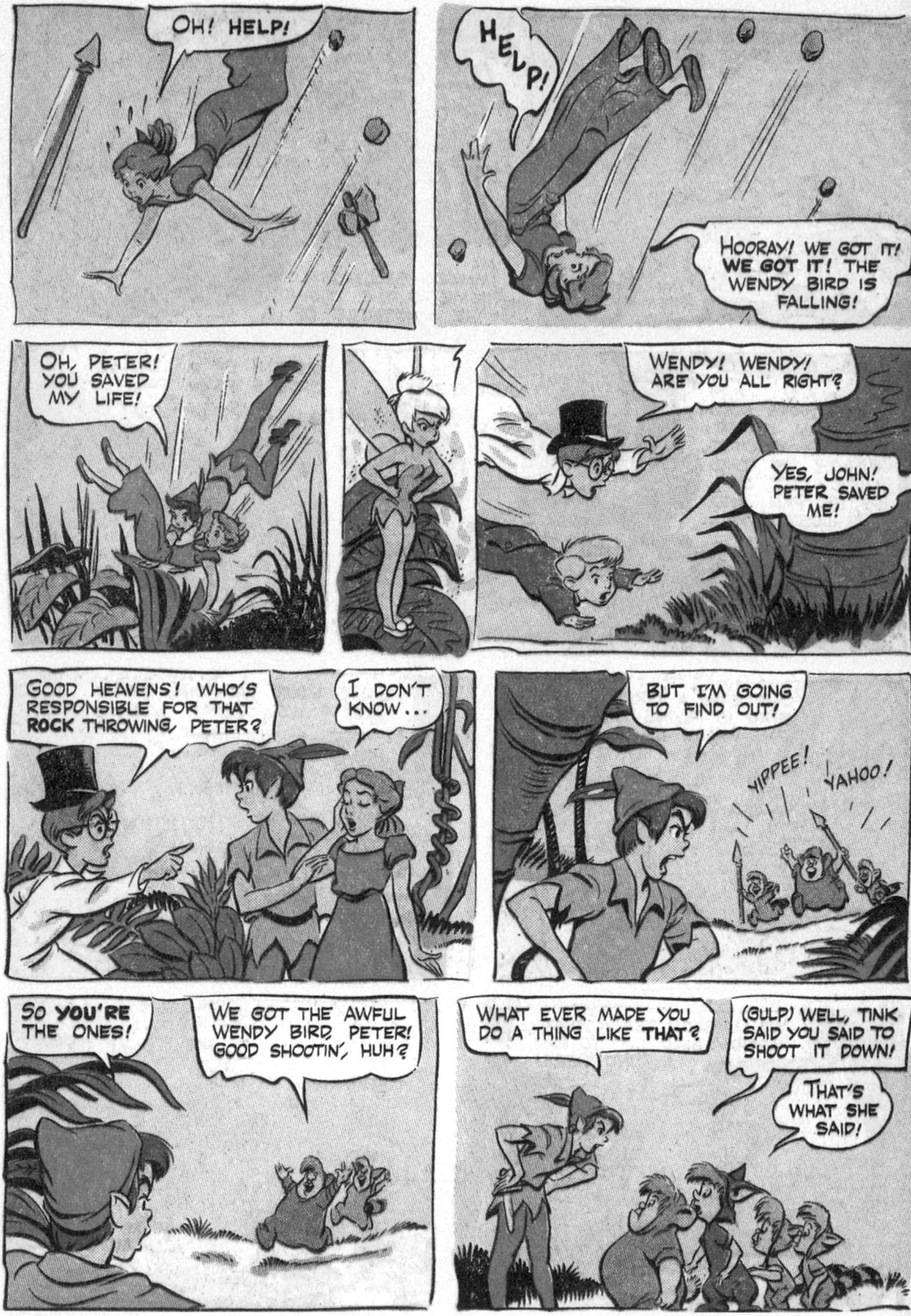
OH! HELP!
HELP!
HOORAY! WE GOT IT! WE GOT IT! THE WENDY BIRD IS FALLING!
OH, PETER! YOU SAVED MY LIFE!
WENDY! WENDY! ARE YOU ALL RIGHT?
YES, JOHN! PETER SAVED ME!
GOOD HEAVENS! WHO'S RESPONSIBLE FOR THAT ROCK THROWING, PETER?
I DON'T KNOW...
BUT I'M GOING TO FIND OUT!
YIPPEE!
YAHOO!
SO YOU'RE THE ONES!
WE GOT THE AWFUL WENDY BIRD, PETER! GOOD SHOOTIN', HUH?
WHAT EVER MADE YOU DO A THING LIKE THAT?
(GULP) WELL, TINK SAID YOU SAID TO SHOOT IT DOWN!
THAT'S WHAT SHE SAID!

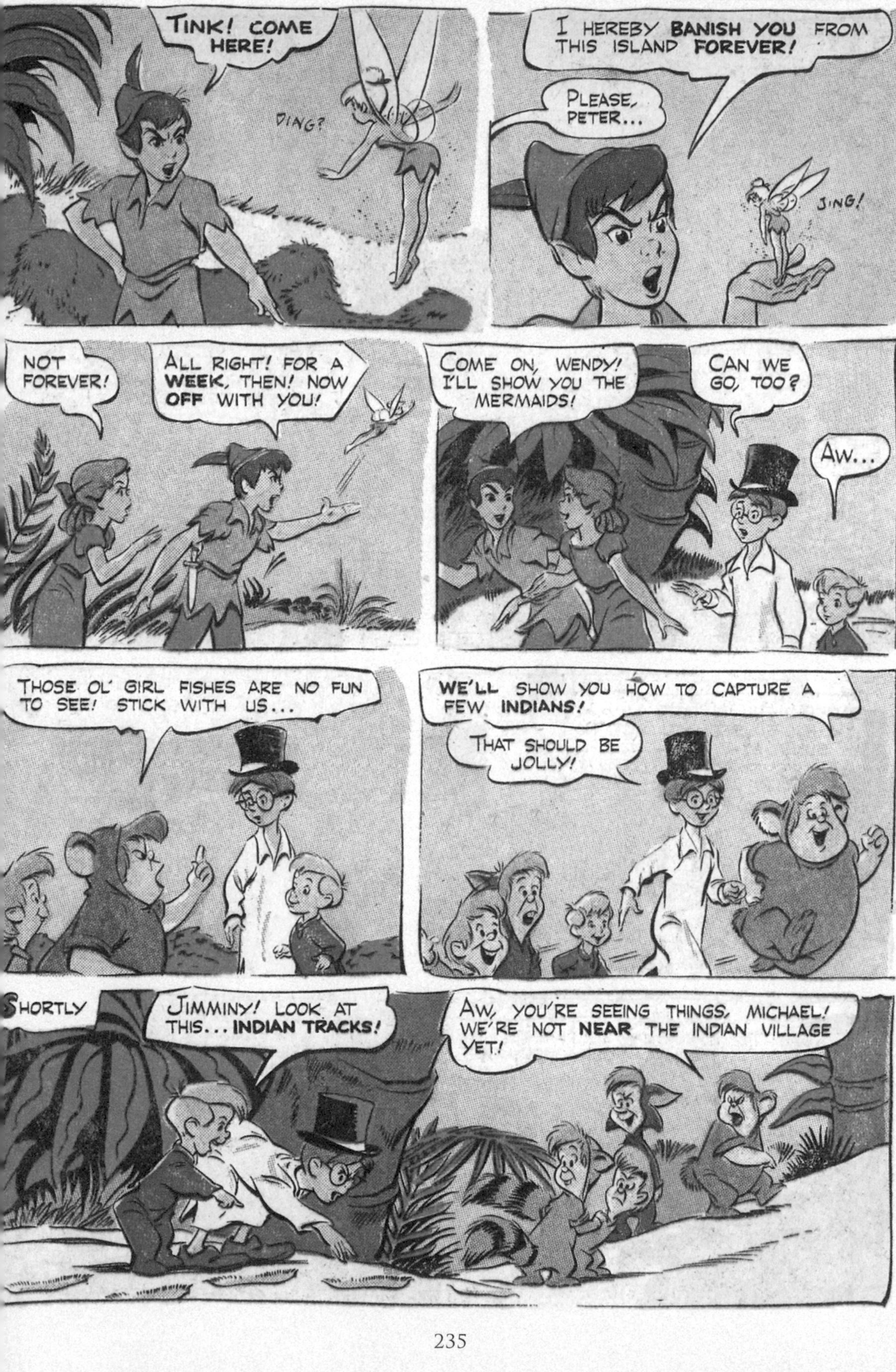
TINK! COME HERE!
DING?
I HEREBY BANISH YOU FROM THIS ISLAND FOREVER!
PLEASE, PETER...
JING!
NOT FOREVER!
ALL RIGHT! FOR A WEEK, THEN! NOW OFF WITH YOU!
COME ON, WENDY! I'LL SHOW YOU THE MERMAIDS!
CAN WE GO, TOO?
AW...
THOSE OL' GIRL FISHES ARE NO FUN TO SEE! STICK WITH US...
WE'LL SHOW YOU HOW TO CAPTURE A FEW INDIANS!
THAT SHOULD BE JOLLY!
SHORTLY
JIMMINY! LOOK AT THIS... INDIAN TRACKS!
AW, YOU'RE SEEING THINGS, MICHAEL! WE'RE NOT NEAR THE INDIAN VILLAGE YET!

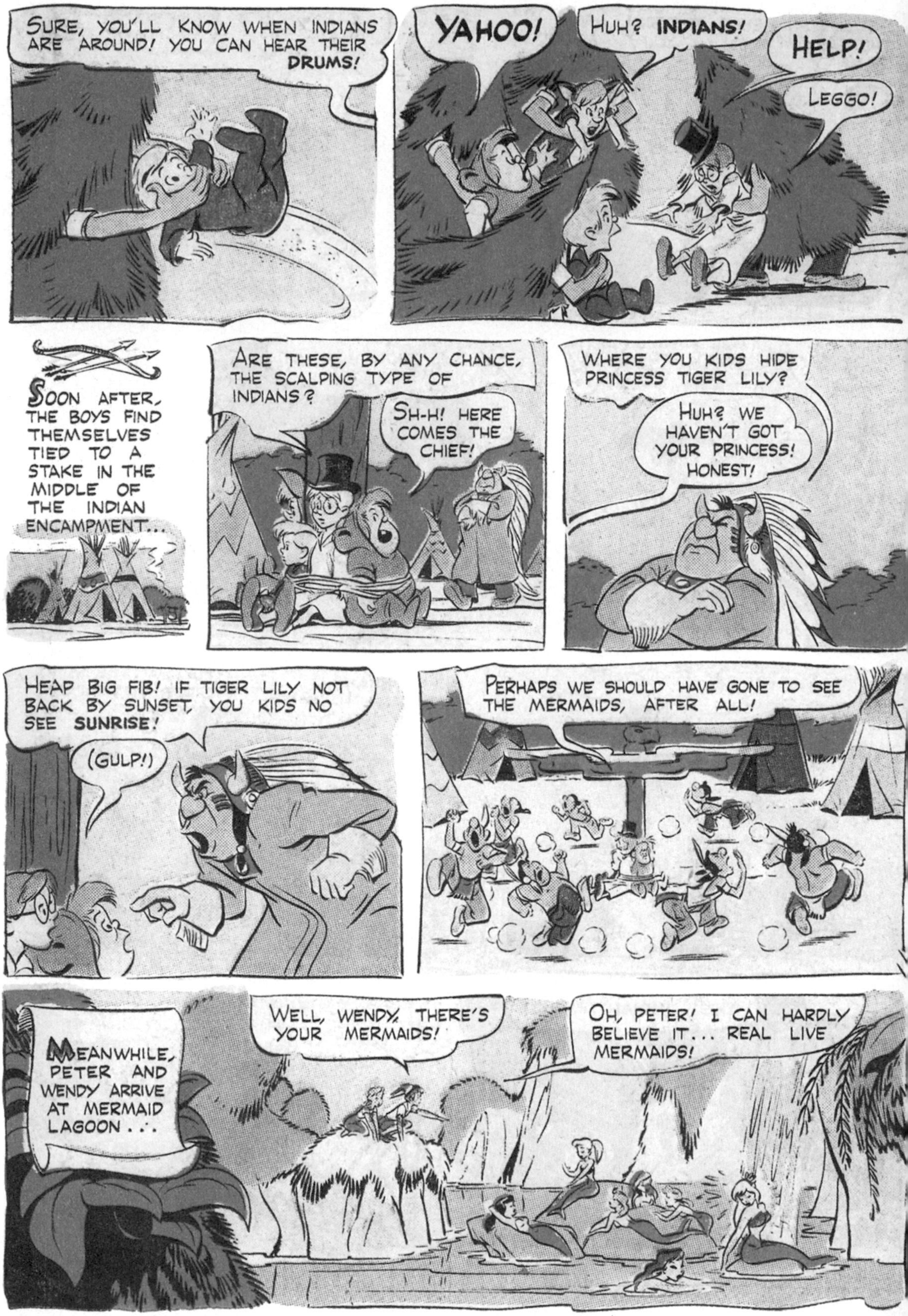
SURE, YOU'LL KNOW WHEN INDIANS ARE AROUND! YOU CAN HEAR THEIR DRUMS!
YAHOO!
HUH? INDIANS!
HELP!
LEGGO!
SOON AFTER, THE BOYS FIND THEMSELVES TIED TO A STAKE IN THE MIDDLE OF THE INDIAN ENCAMPMENT...
ARE THESE, BY ANY CHANCE, THE SCALPING TYPE OF INDIANS?
SH-H! HERE COMES THE CHIEF!
WHERE YOU KIDS HIDE PRINCESS TIGER LILY?
HUH? WE HAVEN'T GOT YOUR PRINCESS! HONEST!
HEAP BIG FIB! IF TIGER LILY NOT BACK BY SUNSET, YOU KIDS NO SEE SUNRISE!
(GULP!)
PERHAPS WE SHOULD HAVE GONE TO SEE THE MERMAIDS, AFTER ALL!
MEANWHILE, PETER AND WENDY ARRIVE AT MERMAID LAGOON...
WELL, WENDY, THERE'S YOUR MERMAIDS!
OH, PETER! I CAN HARDLY BELIEVE IT... REAL LIVE MERMAIDS!

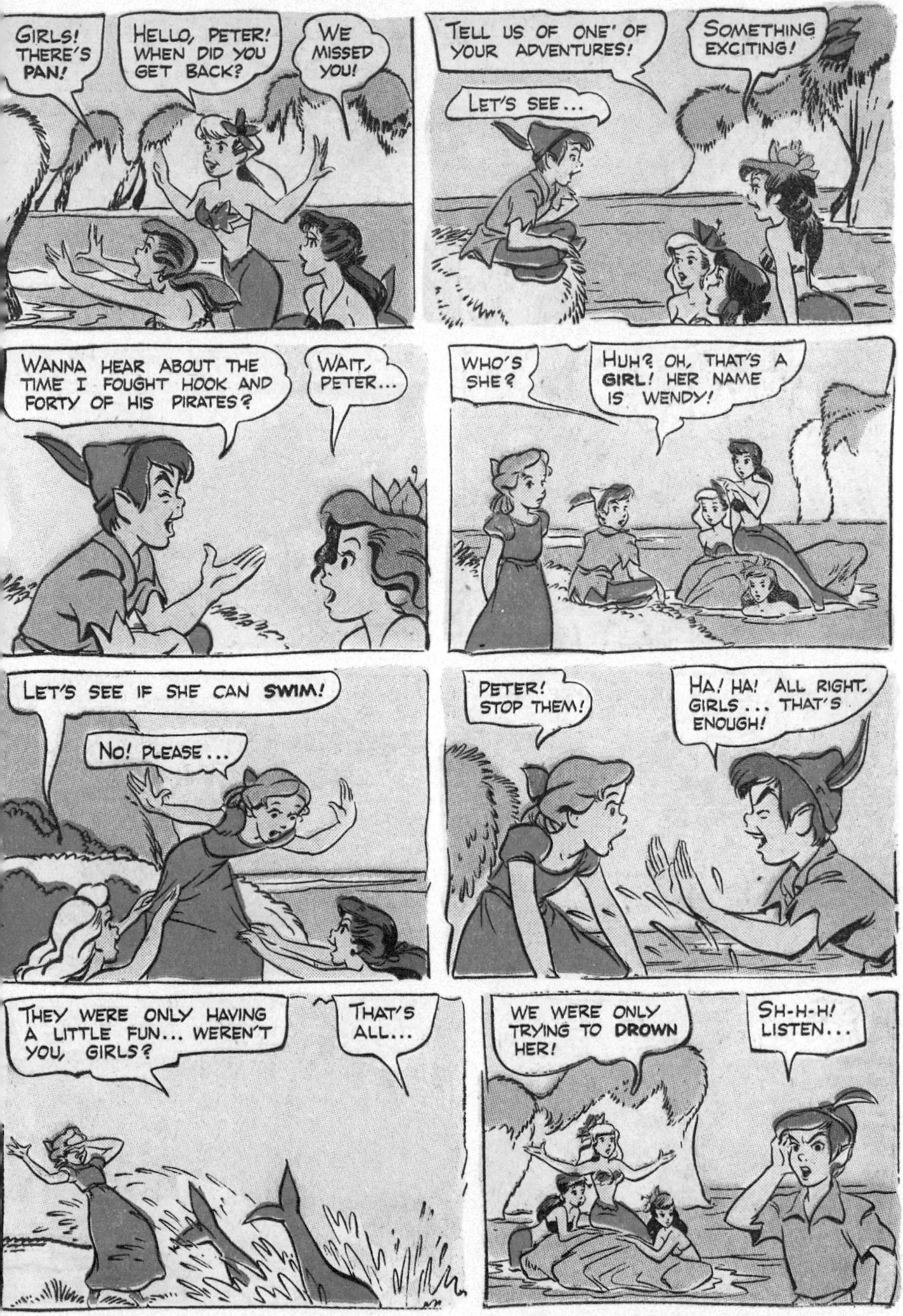
GIRLS! THERE'S PAN!
HELLO, PETER! WHEN DID YOU GET BACK?
WE MISSED YOU!
TELL US OF ONE OF YOUR ADVENTURES!
SOMETHING EXCITING!
LET'S SEE...
WANNA HEAR ABOUT THE TIME I FOUGHT HOOK AND FORTY OF HIS PIRATES?
WAIT, PETER...
WHO'S SHE?
HUH? OH, THAT'S A GIRL! HER NAME IS WENDY!
LET'S SEE IF SHE CAN SWIM!
NO! PLEASE...
PETER! STOP THEM!
HA! HA! ALL RIGHT, GIRLS... THAT'S ENOUGH!
THEY WERE ONLY HAVING A LITTLE FUN... WEREN'T YOU, GIRLS?
THAT'S ALL...
WE WERE ONLY TRYING TO DROWN HER!
SH-H-H! LISTEN...

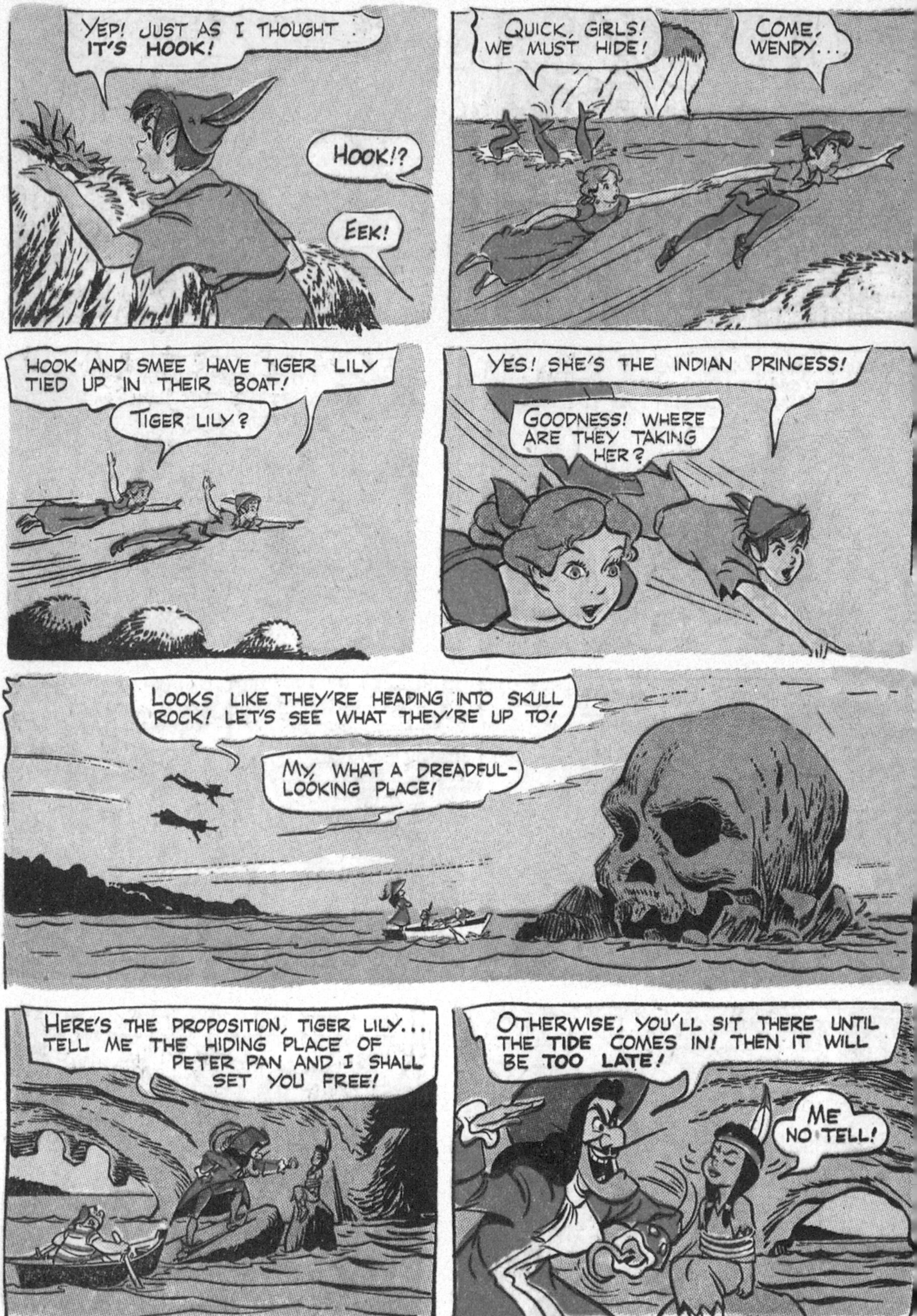
YEP! JUST AS I THOUGHT . . IT'S HOOK!
HOOK!?
EEK!
QUICK, GIRLS! WE MUST HIDE!
COME, WENDY...
HOOK AND SMEE HAVE TIGER LILY TIED UP IN THEIR BOAT!
TIGER LILY?
YES! SHE'S THE INDIAN PRINCESS!
GOODNESS! WHERE ARE THEY TAKING HER?
LOOKS LIKE THEY'RE HEADING INTO SKULL ROCK! LET'S SEE WHAT THEY'RE UP TO!
MY, WHAT A DREADFUL-LOOKING PLACE!
HERE'S THE PROPOSITION, TIGER LILY... TELL ME THE HIDING PLACE OF PETER PAN AND I SHALL SET YOU FREE!
OTHERWISE, YOU'LL SIT THERE UNTIL THE TIDE COMES IN! THEN IT WILL BE TOO LATE!
ME NO TELL!

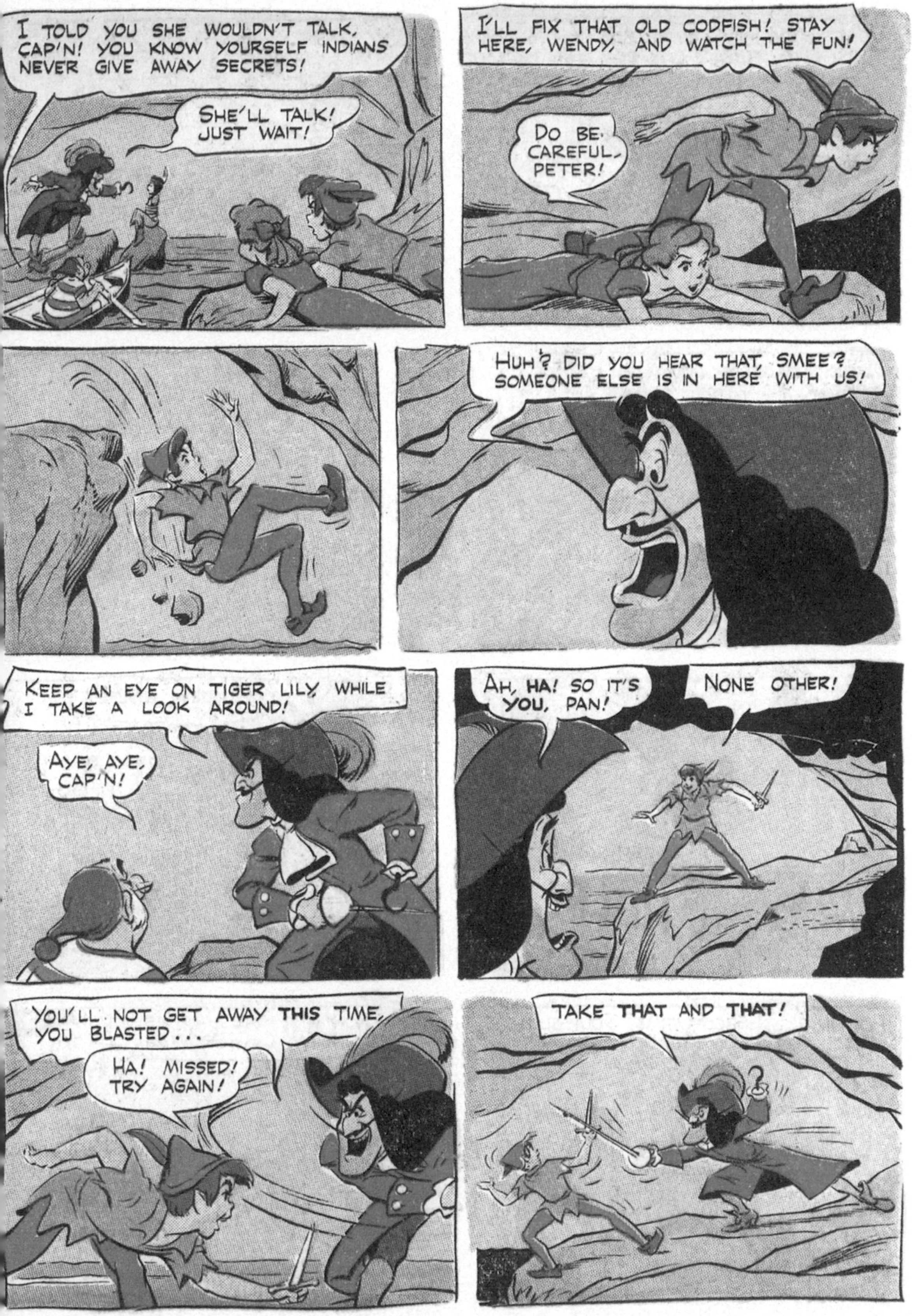
I TOLD YOU SHE WOULDN'T TALK, CAP'N! YOU KNOW YOURSELF INDIANS NEVER GIVE AWAY SECRETS!
SHE'LL TALK! JUST WAIT!
I'LL FIX THAT OLD CODFISH! STAY HERE, WENDY, AND WATCH THE FUN!
DO BE CAREFUL, PETER!
HUH? DID YOU HEAR THAT, SMEE? SOMEONE ELSE IS IN HERE WITH US!
KEEP AN EYE ON TIGER LILY WHILE I TAKE A LOOK AROUND!
AYE, AYE, CAP'N!
AH, HA! SO IT'S YOU, PAN!
NONE OTHER!
YOU'LL NOT GET AWAY THIS TIME, YOU BLASTED...
HA! MISSED! TRY AGAIN!
TAKE THAT AND THAT!

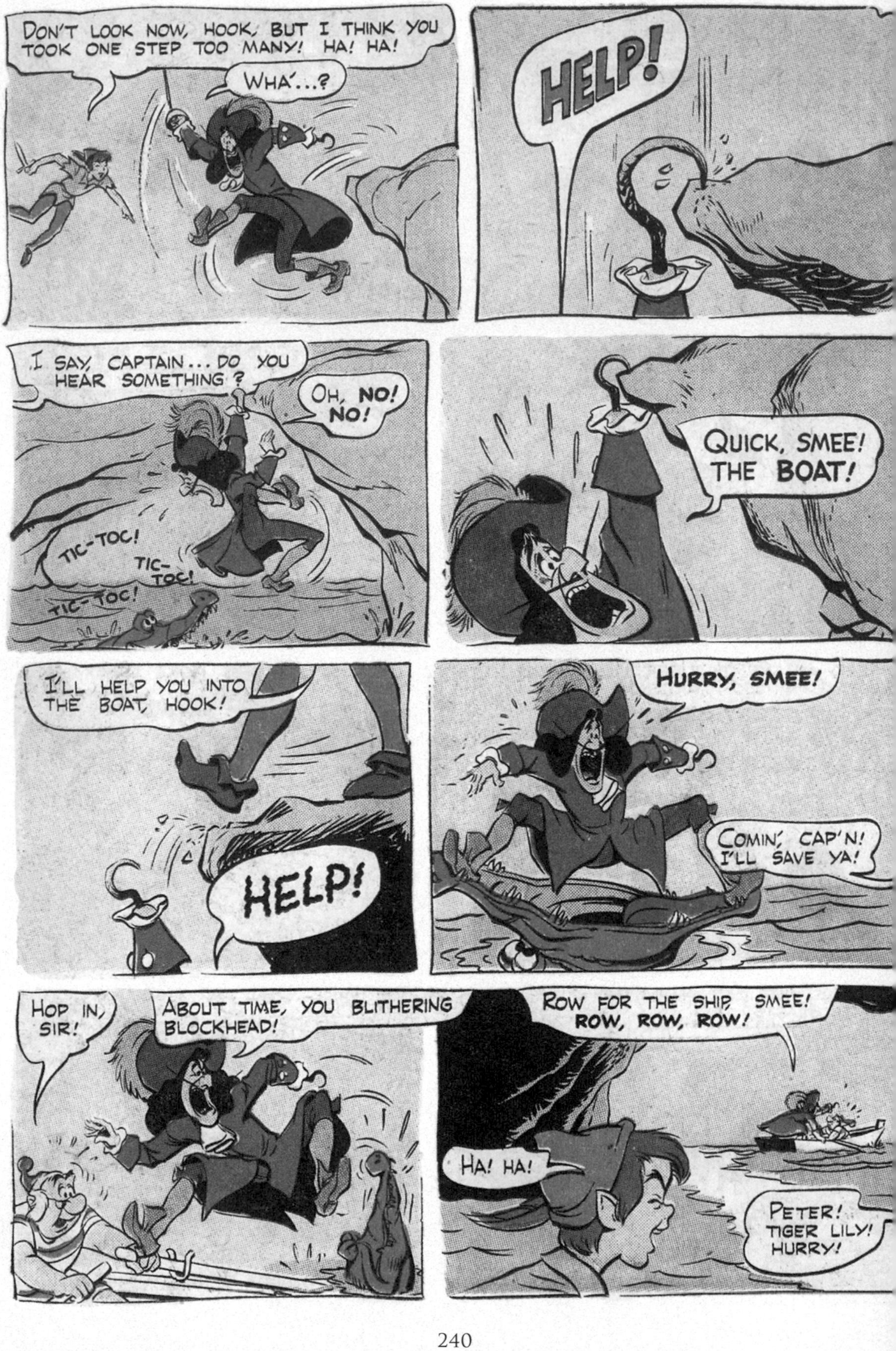
DON'T LOOK NOW, HOOK, BUT I THINK YOU TOOK ONE STEP TOO MANY! HA! HA!
WHA'...?
HELP!
I SAY, CAPTAIN... DO YOU HEAR SOMETHING ?
OH, NO! NO!
TIC-TOC!
TIC-TOC!
TIC-TOC!
QUICK, SMEE! THE BOAT!
I'LL HELP YOU INTO THE BOAT, HOOK!
HELP!
HURRY, SMEE!
COMIN', CAP'N! I'LL SAVE YA!
HOP IN, SIR!
ABOUT TIME, YOU BLITHERING BLOCKHEAD!
ROW FOR THE SHIP, SMEE! ROW, ROW, ROW!
HA! HA!
PETER! TIGER LILY! HURRY!

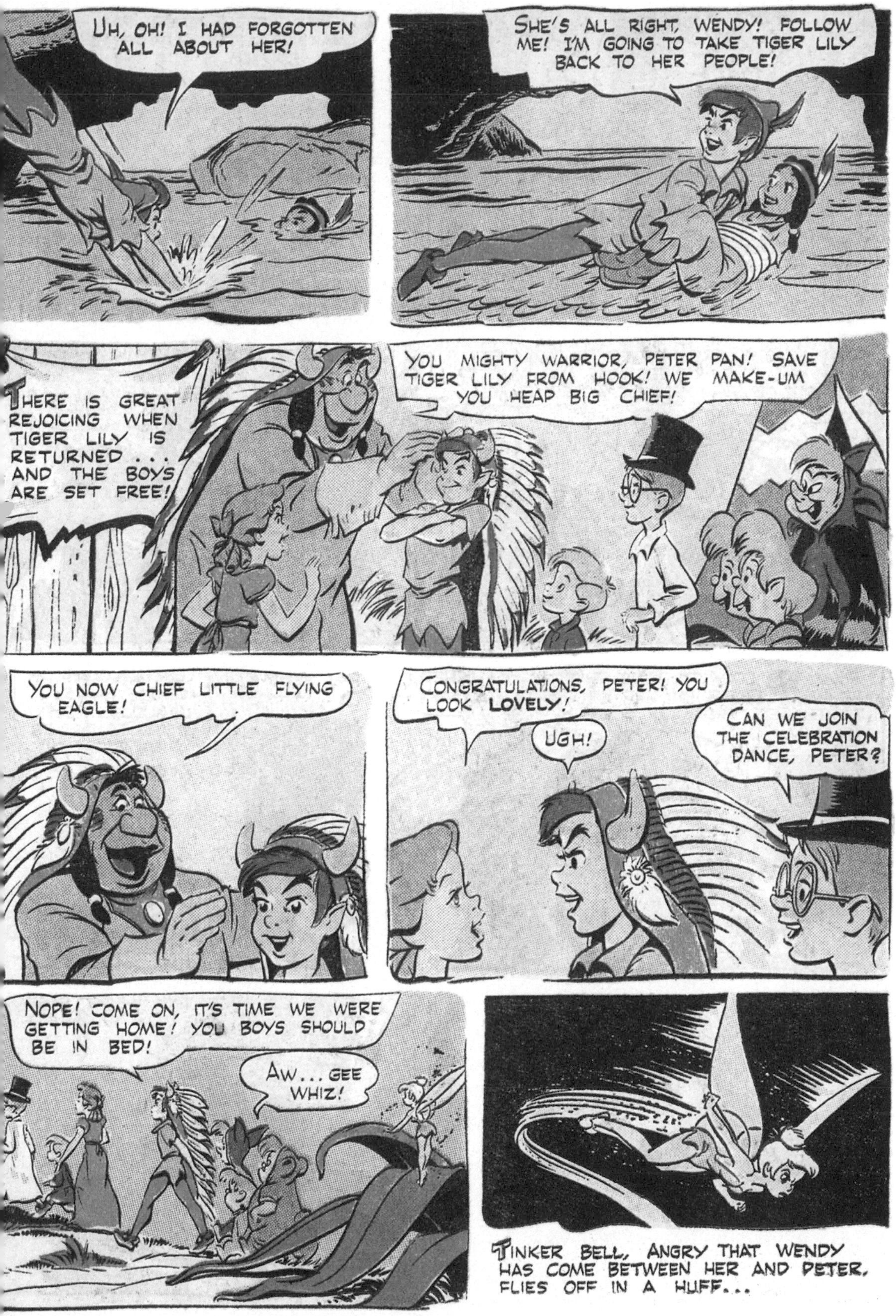
UH, OH! I HAD FORGOTTEN ALL ABOUT HER!
SHE'S ALL RIGHT, WENDY! FOLLOW ME! I'M GOING TO TAKE TIGER LILY BACK TO HER PEOPLE!
THERE IS GREAT REJOICING WHEN TIGER LILY IS RETURNED . . . AND THE BOYS ARE SET FREE!
YOU MIGHTY WARRIOR, PETER PAN! SAVE TIGER LILY FROM HOOK! WE MAKE-UM YOU HEAP BIG CHIEF!
YOU NOW CHIEF LITTLE FLYING EAGLE!
CONGRATULATIONS, PETER! YOU LOOK LOVELY!
UGH!
CAN WE JOIN THE CELEBRATION DANCE, PETER?
NOPE! COME ON, IT'S TIME WE WERE GETTING HOME! YOU BOYS SHOULD BE IN BED!
AW... GEE WHIZ!
TINKER BELL, ANGRY THAT WENDY HAS COME BETWEEN HER AND PETER, FLIES OFF IN A HUFF...

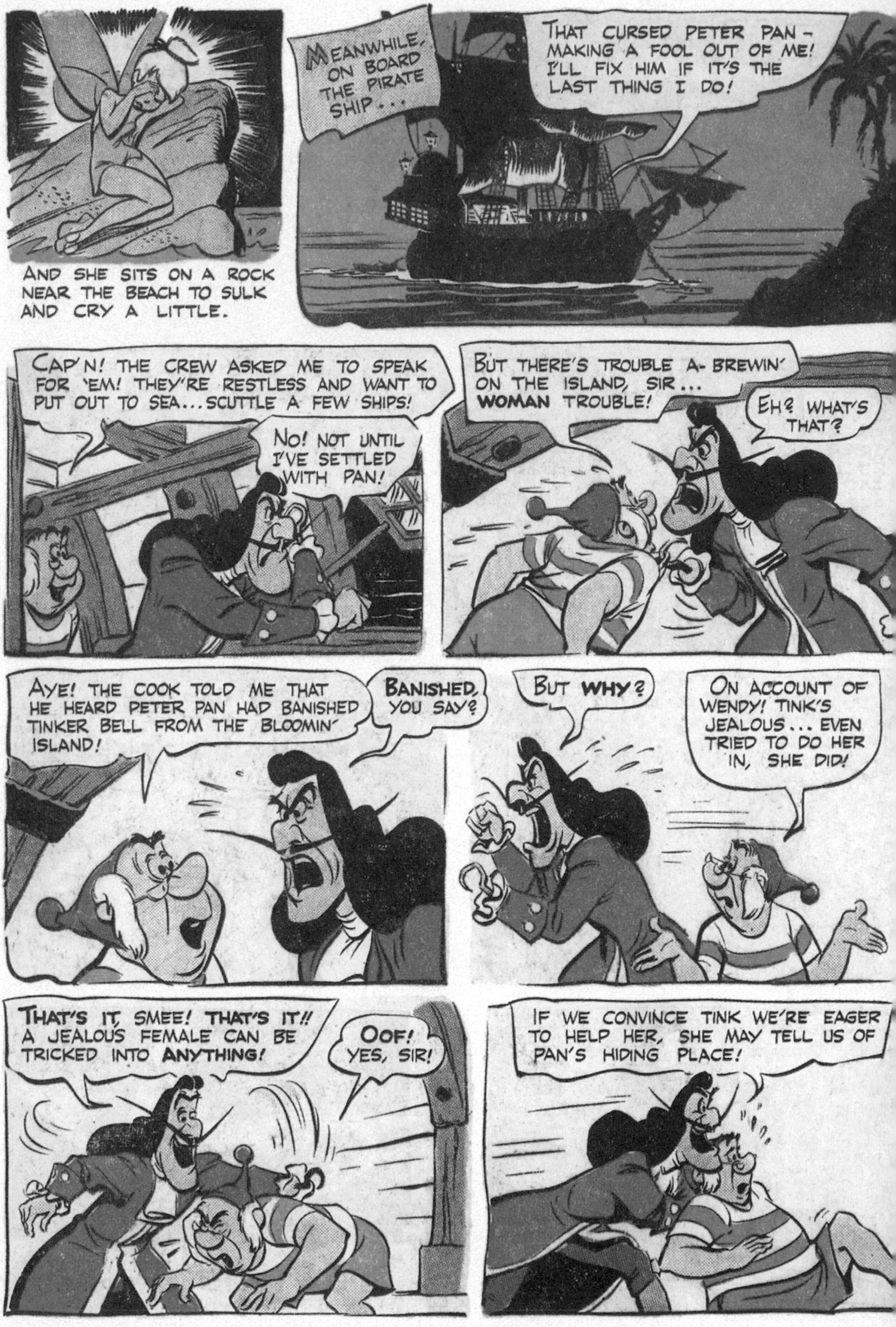
AND SHE SITS ON A ROCK NEAR THE BEACH TO SULK AND CRY A LITTLE.
MEANWHILE, ON BOARD THE PIRATE SHIP...
THAT CURSED PETER PAN – MAKING A FOOL OUT OF ME! I'LL FIX HIM IF IT'S THE LAST THING I DO!
CAP'N! THE CREW ASKED ME TO SPEAK FOR 'EM! THEY'RE RESTLESS AND WANT TO PUT OUT TO SEA... SCUTTLE A FEW SHIPS!
NO! NOT UNTIL I'VE SETTLED WITH PAN!
BUT THERE'S TROUBLE A-BREWIN' ON THE ISLAND, SIR... WOMAN TROUBLE!
EH? WHAT'S THAT?
AYE! THE COOK TOLD ME THAT HE HEARD PETER PAN HAD BANISHED TINKER BELL FROM THE BLOOMIN' ISLAND!
BANISHED, YOU SAY?
BUT WHY?
ON ACCOUNT OF WENDY! TINK'S JEALOUS... EVEN TRIED TO DO HER IN, SHE DID!
THAT'S IT, SMEE! THAT'S IT!! A JEALOUS FEMALE CAN BE TRICKED INTO ANYTHING!
OOF! YES, SIR!
IF WE CONVINCE TINK WE'RE EAGER TO HELP HER, SHE MAY TELL US OF PAN'S HIDING PLACE!

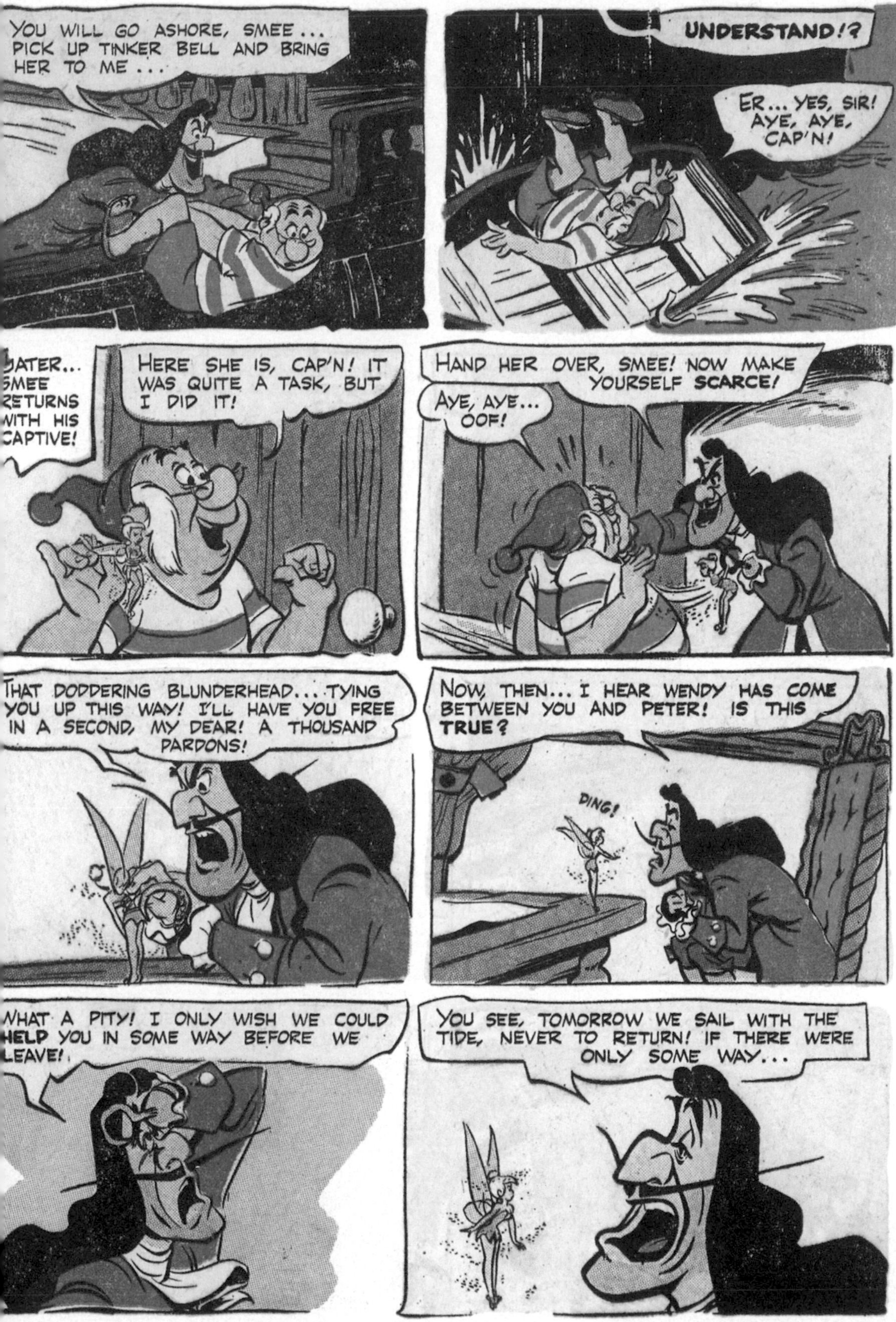
YOU WILL GO ASHORE, SMEE ... PICK UP TINKER BELL AND BRING HER TO ME ...
UNDERSTAND!?
ER... YES, SIR! AYE, AYE, CAP'N!
LATER... SMEE RETURNS WITH HIS CAPTIVE!
HERE SHE IS, CAP'N! IT WAS QUITE A TASK, BUT I DID IT!
HAND HER OVER, SMEE! NOW MAKE YOURSELF SCARCE!
AYE, AYE... OOF!
THAT DODDERING BLUNDERHEAD... TYING YOU UP THIS WAY! I'LL HAVE YOU FREE IN A SECOND, MY DEAR! A THOUSAND PARDONS!
NOW, THEN... I HEAR WENDY HAS COME BETWEEN YOU AND PETER! IS THIS TRUE?
DING!
WHAT A PITY! I ONLY WISH WE COULD HELP YOU IN SOME WAY BEFORE WE LEAVE!
YOU SEE, TOMORROW WE SAIL WITH THE TIDE, NEVER TO RETURN! IF THERE WERE ONLY SOME WAY...

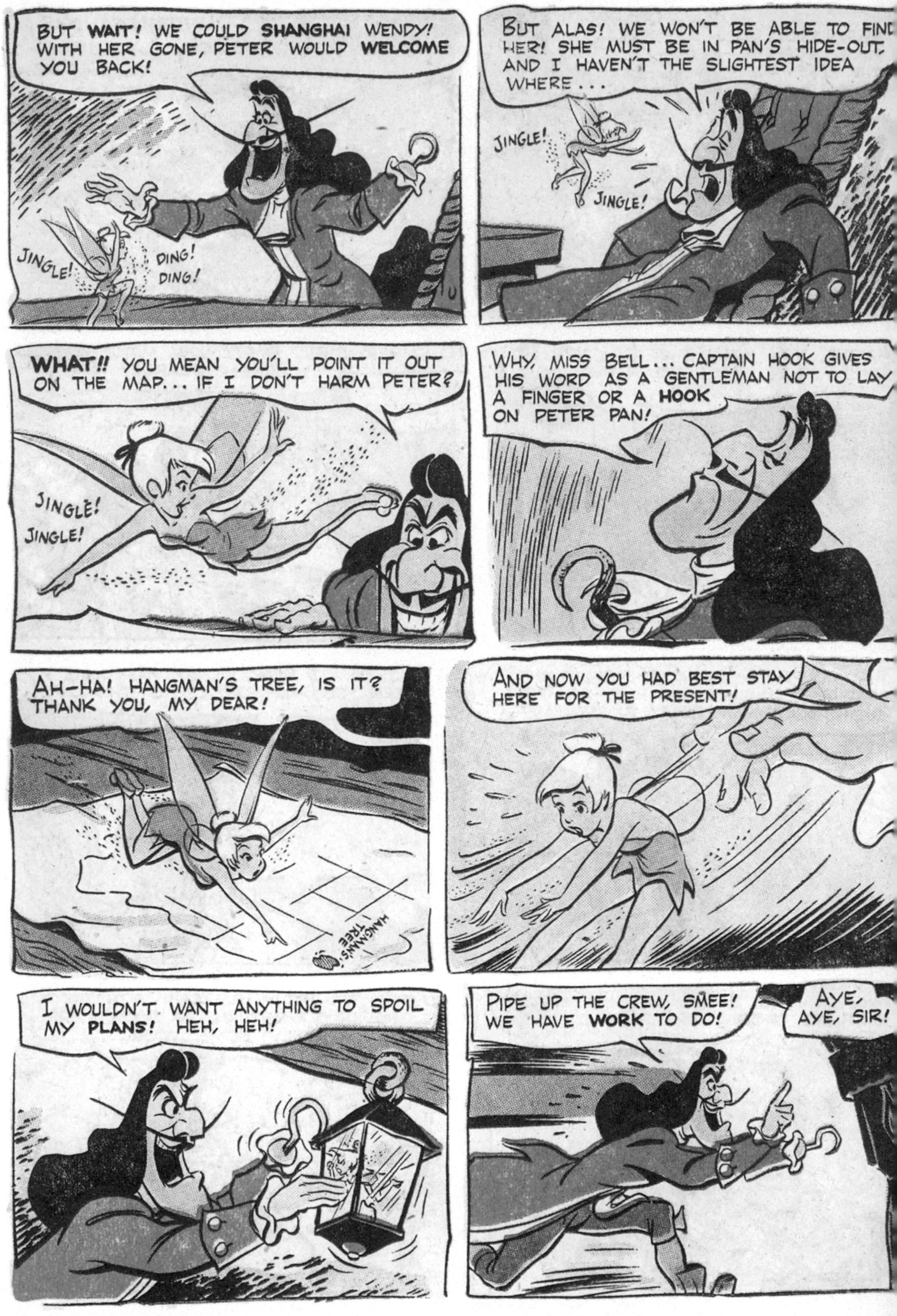
BUT WAIT! WE COULD SHANGHAI WENDY! WITH HER GONE, PETER WOULD WELCOME YOU BACK!
JINGLE!
DING! DING!
BUT ALAS! WE WON'T BE ABLE TO FIND HER! SHE MUST BE IN PAN'S HIDE-OUT, AND I HAVEN'T THE SLIGHTEST IDEA WHERE . . .
JINGLE!
JINGLE!
WHAT!! YOU MEAN YOU'LL POINT IT OUT ON THE MAP... IF I DON'T HARM PETER?
JINGLE!
JINGLE!
WHY, MISS BELL... CAPTAIN HOOK GIVES HIS WORD AS A GENTLEMAN NOT TO LAY A FINGER OR A HOOK ON PETER PAN!
AH-HA! HANGMAN'S TREE, IS IT? THANK YOU, MY DEAR!
HANGMAN'S TREE
AND NOW YOU HAD BEST STAY HERE FOR THE PRESENT!
I WOULDN'T WANT ANYTHING TO SPOIL MY PLANS! HEH, HEH!
PIPE UP THE CREW, SMEE! WE HAVE WORK TO DO!
AYE, AYE, SIR!

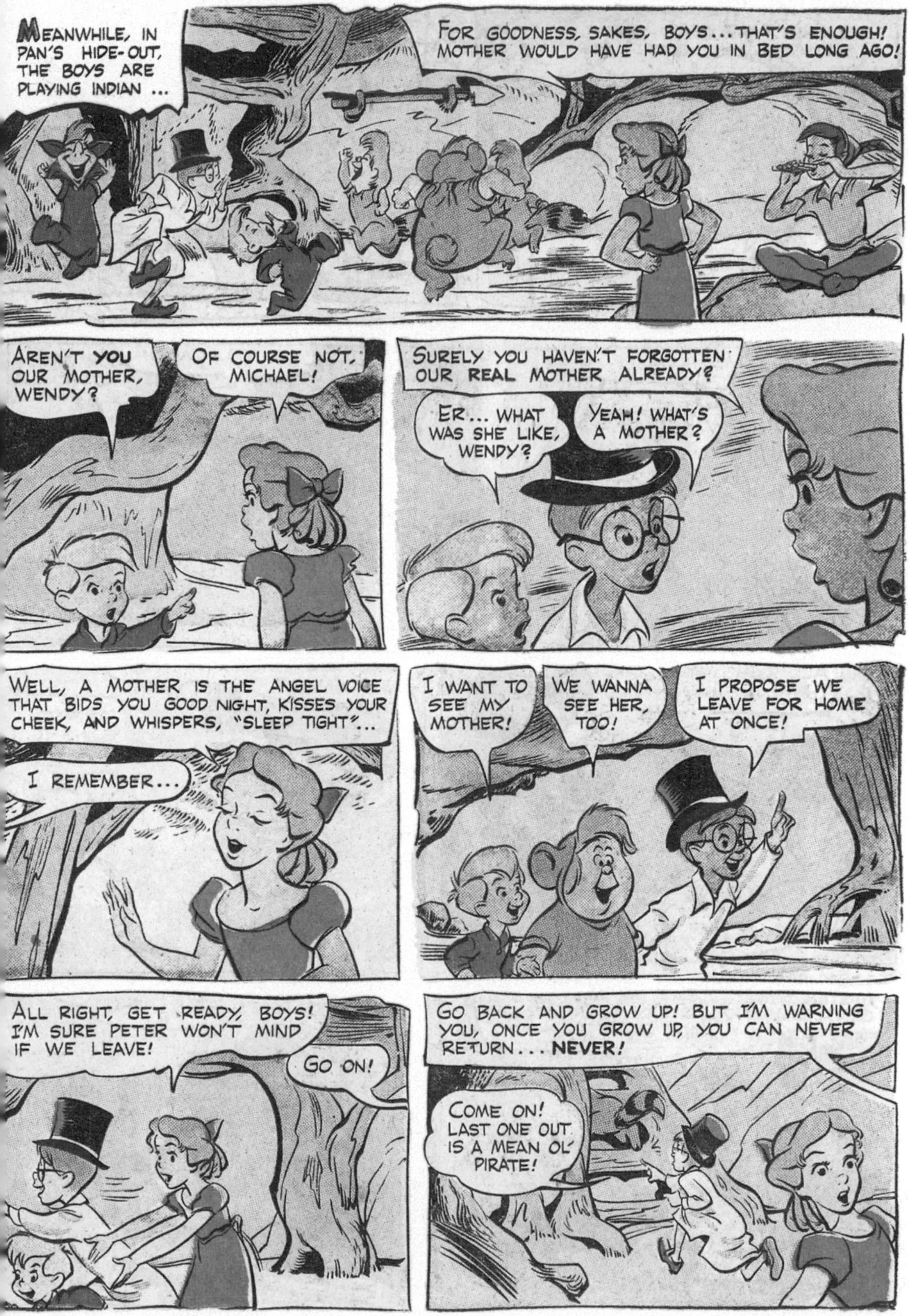
MEANWHILE, IN PAN'S HIDE-OUT, THE BOYS ARE PLAYING INDIAN ...
FOR GOODNESS, SAKES, BOYS... THAT'S ENOUGH! MOTHER WOULD HAVE HAD YOU IN BED LONG AGO!
AREN'T YOU OUR MOTHER, WENDY?
OF COURSE NOT, MICHAEL!
SURELY YOU HAVEN'T FORGOTTEN OUR REAL MOTHER ALREADY?
ER... WHAT WAS SHE LIKE, WENDY?
YEAH! WHAT'S A MOTHER?
WELL, A MOTHER IS THE ANGEL VOICE THAT BIDS YOU GOOD NIGHT, KISSES YOUR CHEEK, AND WHISPERS, "SLEEP TIGHT"...
I REMEMBER...
I WANT TO SEE MY MOTHER!
WE WANNA SEE HER, TOO!
I PROPOSE WE LEAVE FOR HOME AT ONCE!
ALL RIGHT, GET READY, BOYS! I'M SURE PETER WON'T MIND IF WE LEAVE!
GO ON!
GO BACK AND GROW UP! BUT I'M WARNING YOU, ONCE YOU GROW UP, YOU CAN NEVER RETURN... NEVER!
COME ON! LAST ONE OUT IS A MEAN OL' PIRATE!

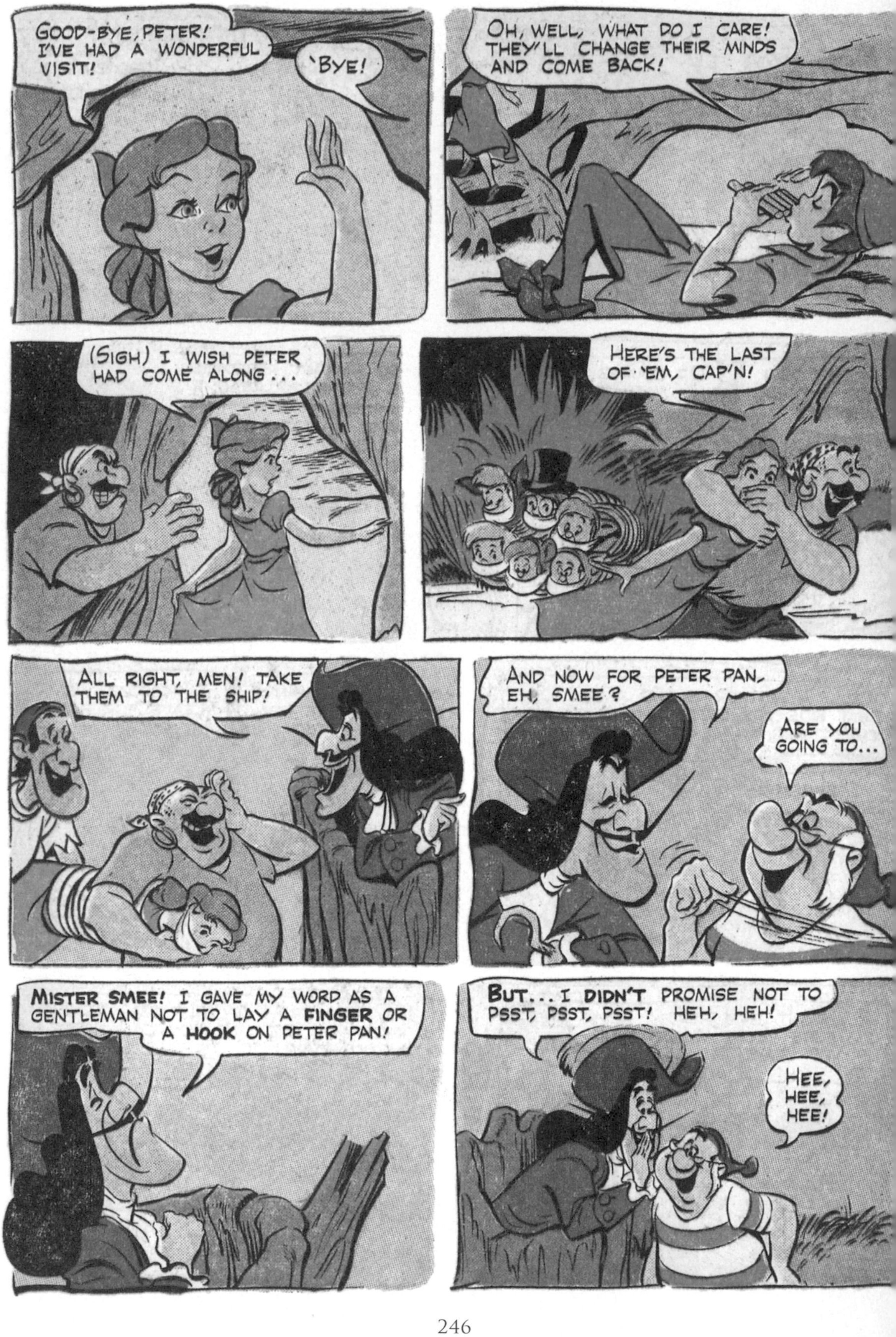
GOOD-BYE, PETER! I'VE HAD A WONDERFUL VISIT!
'BYE!
OH, WELL, WHAT DO I CARE! THEY'LL CHANGE THEIR MINDS AND COME BACK!
(SIGH) I WISH PETER HAD COME ALONG...
HERE'S THE LAST OF 'EM, CAP'N!
ALL RIGHT, MEN! TAKE THEM TO THE SHIP!
AND NOW FOR PETER PAN, EH, SMEE?
ARE YOU GOING TO...
MISTER SMEE! I GAVE MY WORD AS A GENTLEMAN NOT TO LAY A FINGER OR A HOOK ON PETER PAN!
BUT... I DIDN'T PROMISE NOT TO PSST, PSST, PSST! HEH, HEH!
HEE, HEE, HEE!

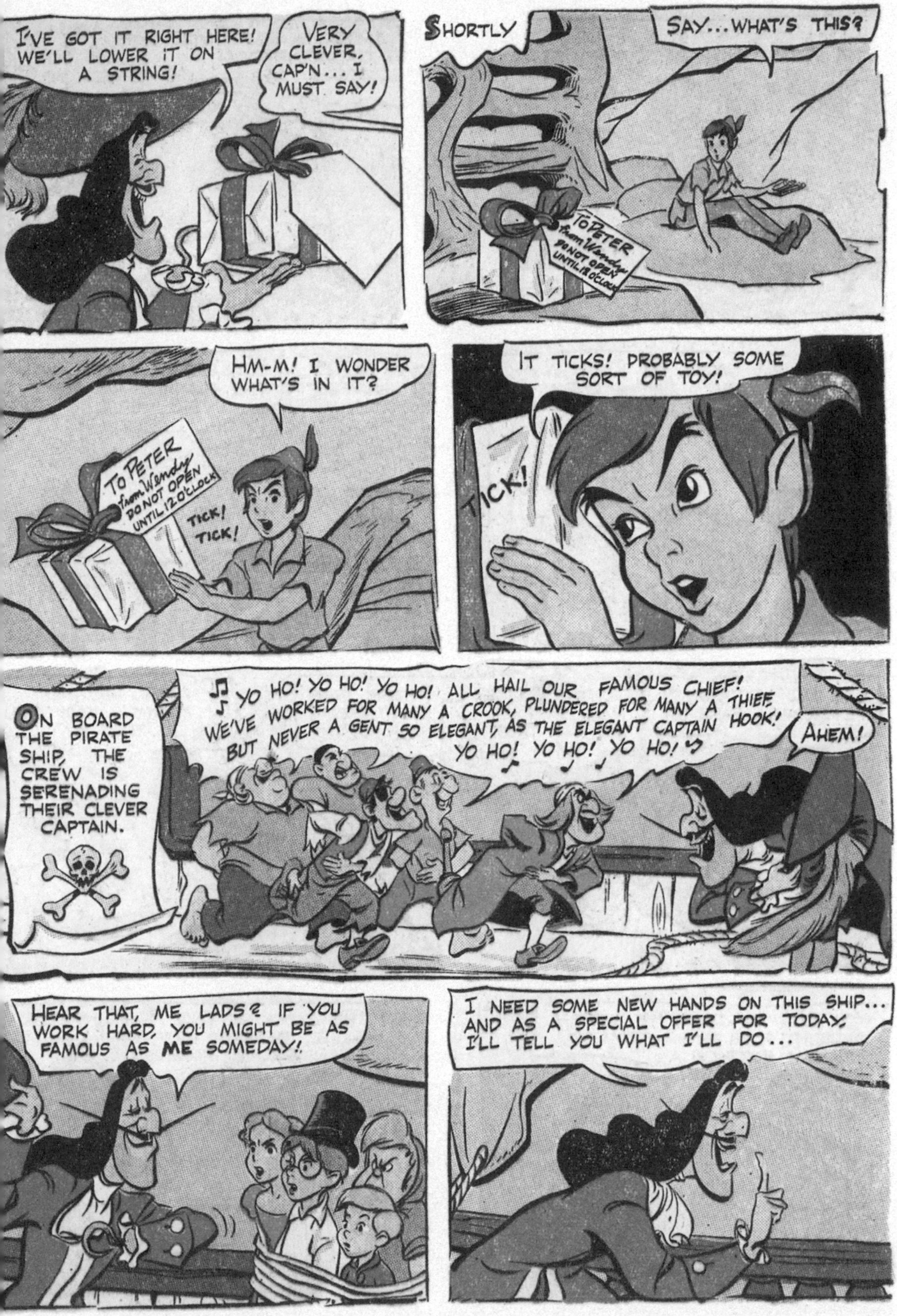
I'VE GOT IT RIGHT HERE! WE'LL LOWER IT ON A STRING!
VERY CLEVER, CAP'N... I MUST SAY!
SHORTLY
SAY...WHAT'S THIS?
TO PETER from Wendy DO NOT OPEN UNTIL 12 O'CLOCK
HM-M! I WONDER WHAT'S IN IT?
TO PETER from Wendy DO NOT OPEN UNTIL 12 O'CLOCK
TICK! TICK!
IT TICKS! PROBABLY SOME SORT OF TOY!
TICK!
ON BOARD THE PIRATE SHIP, THE CREW IS SERENADING THEIR CLEVER CAPTAIN.
YO HO! YO HO! YO HO! ALL HAIL OUR FAMOUS CHIEF! WE'VE WORKED FOR MANY A CROOK, PLUNDERED FOR MANY A THIEF, BUT NEVER A GENT SO ELEGANT, AS THE ELEGANT CAPTAIN HOOK! YO HO! YO HO! YO HO!
AHEM!
HEAR THAT, ME LADS? IF YOU WORK HARD, YOU MIGHT BE AS FAMOUS AS ME SOMEDAY!
I NEED SOME NEW HANDS ON THIS SHIP... AND AS A SPECIAL OFFER FOR TODAY, I'LL TELL YOU WHAT I'LL DO...

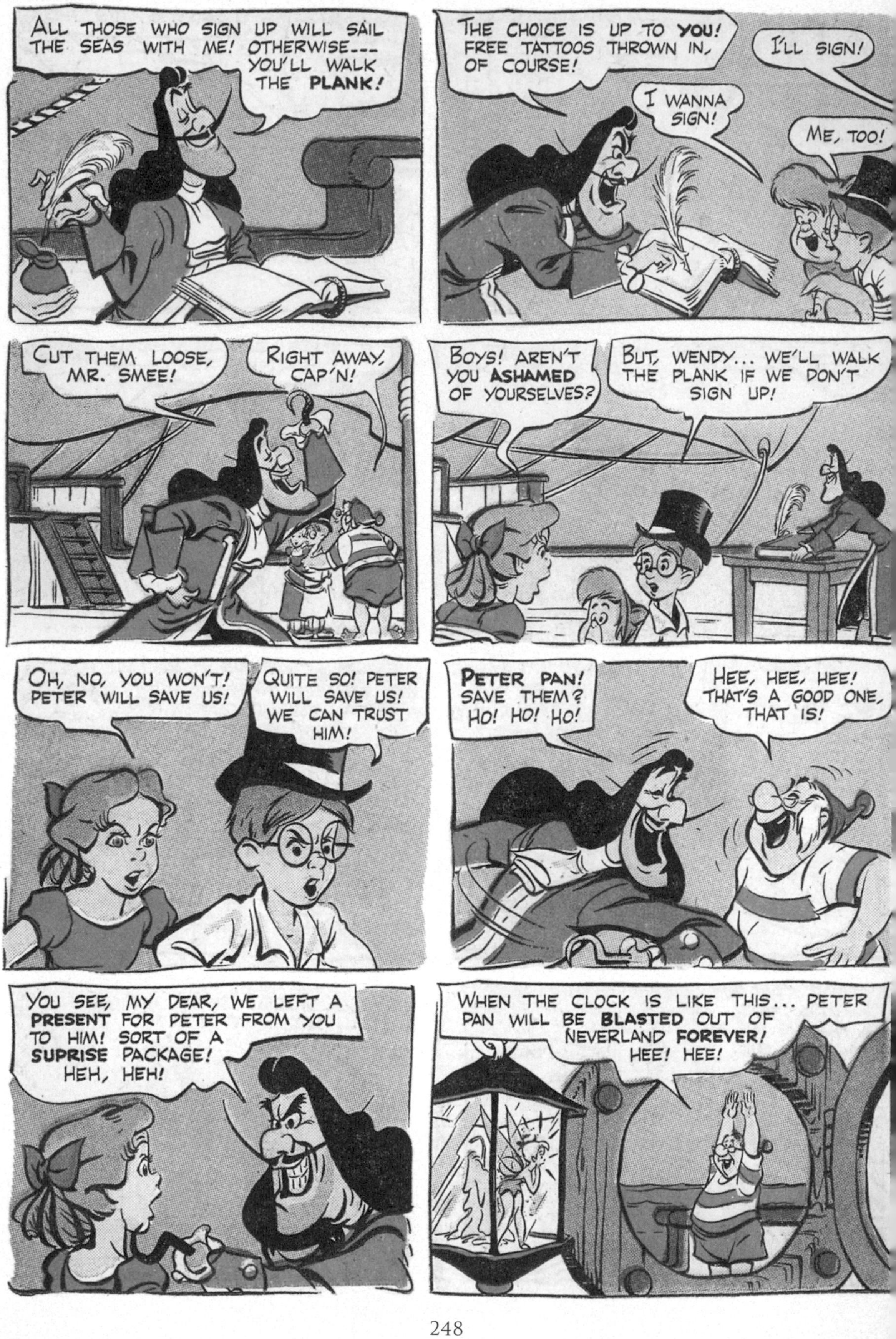
ALL THOSE WHO SIGN UP WILL SAIL THE SEAS WITH ME! OTHERWISE--- YOU'LL WALK THE PLANK!
THE CHOICE IS UP TO YOU! FREE TATTOOS THROWN IN, OF COURSE!
I'LL SIGN!
I WANNA SIGN!
ME, TOO!
CUT THEM LOOSE, MR. SMEE!
RIGHT AWAY, CAP'N!
BOYS! AREN'T YOU ASHAMED OF YOURSELVES?
BUT, WENDY... WE'LL WALK THE PLANK IF WE DON'T SIGN UP!
OH, NO, YOU WON'T! PETER WILL SAVE US!
QUITE SO! PETER WILL SAVE US! WE CAN TRUST HIM!
PETER PAN! SAVE THEM? HO! HO! HO!
HEE, HEE, HEE! THAT'S A GOOD ONE, THAT IS!
YOU SEE, MY DEAR, WE LEFT A PRESENT FOR PETER FROM YOU TO HIM! SORT OF A SUPRISE PACKAGE! HEH, HEH!
WHEN THE CLOCK IS LIKE THIS... PETER PAN WILL BE BLASTED OUT OF NEVERLAND FOREVER! HEE! HEE!

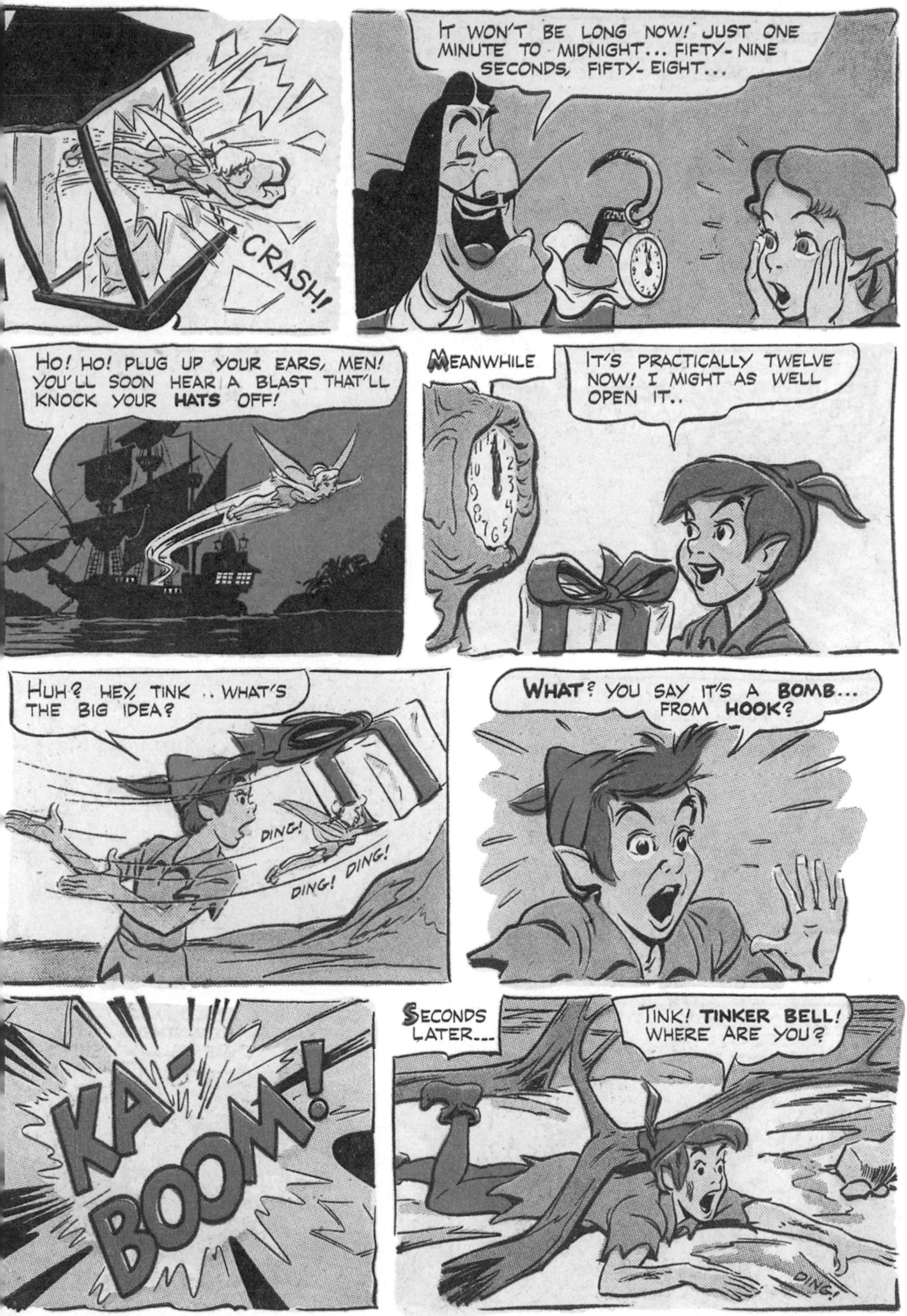

CRASH!
IT WON'T BE LONG NOW! JUST ONE MINUTE TO MIDNIGHT... FIFTY-NINE SECONDS, FIFTY-EIGHT...
HO! HO! PLUG UP YOUR EARS, MEN! YOU'LL SOON HEAR A BLAST THAT'LL KNOCK YOUR **HATS** OFF!
MEANWHILE
IT'S PRACTICALLY TWELVE NOW! I MIGHT AS WELL OPEN IT..
HUH? HEY, TINK .. WHAT'S THE BIG IDEA?
DING!
DING! DING!
WHAT? YOU SAY IT'S A **BOMB**... FROM **HOOK**?
KA-BOOM!
SECONDS LATER...
TINK! **TINKER BELL**! WHERE ARE YOU?
DING!

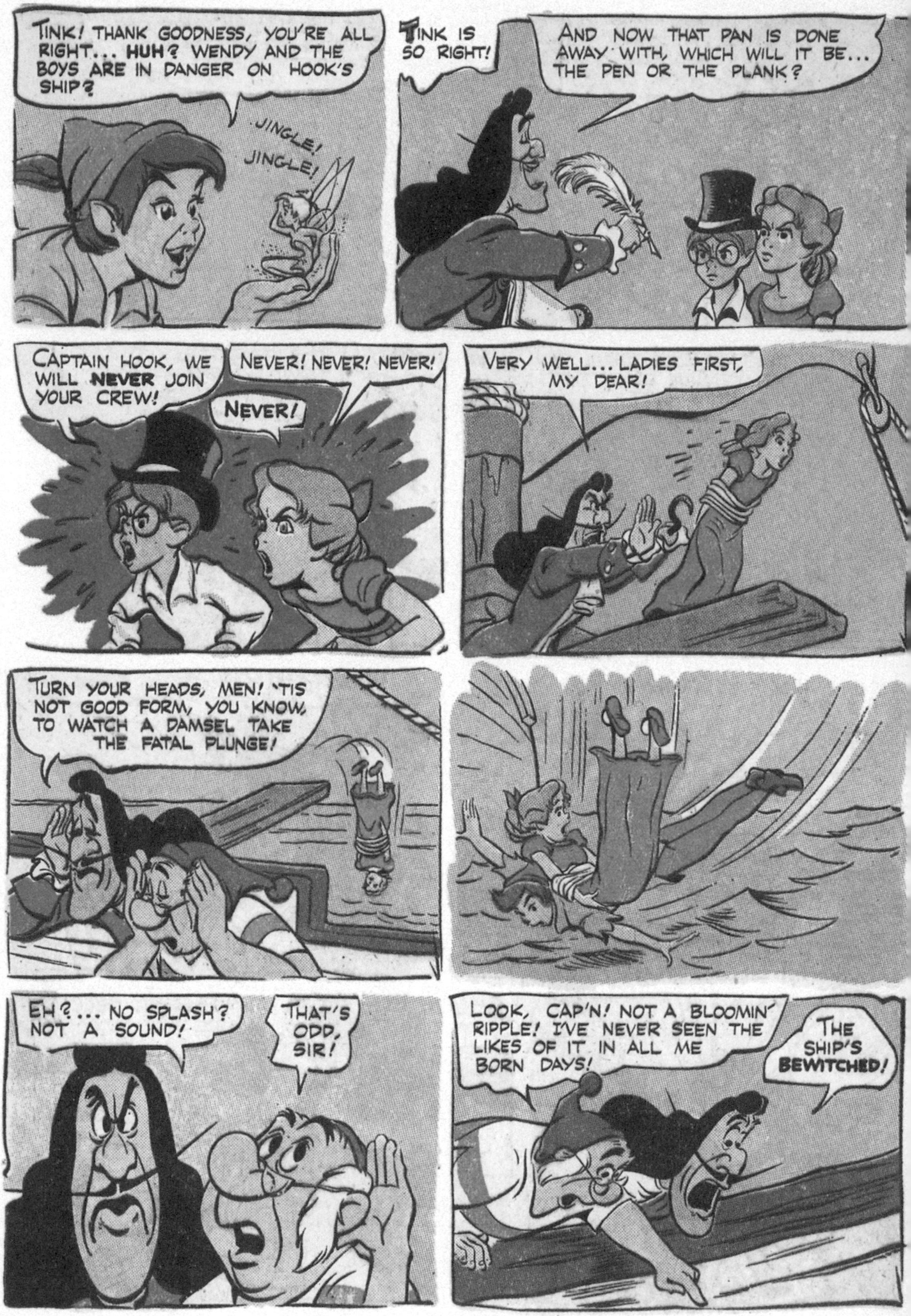
TINK! THANK GOODNESS, YOU'RE ALL RIGHT... HUH? WENDY AND THE BOYS ARE IN DANGER ON HOOK'S SHIP?
JINGLE! JINGLE!
TINK IS SO RIGHT!
AND NOW THAT PAN IS DONE AWAY WITH, WHICH WILL IT BE... THE PEN OR THE PLANK?
CAPTAIN HOOK, WE WILL NEVER JOIN YOUR CREW!
NEVER! NEVER! NEVER!
NEVER!
VERY WELL... LADIES FIRST, MY DEAR!
TURN YOUR HEADS, MEN! 'TIS NOT GOOD FORM, YOU KNOW, TO WATCH A DAMSEL TAKE THE FATAL PLUNGE!
EH?... NO SPLASH? NOT A SOUND!
THAT'S ODD, SIR!
LOOK, CAP'N! NOT A BLOOMIN' RIPPLE! I'VE NEVER SEEN THE LIKES OF IT IN ALL ME BORN DAYS!
THE SHIP'S BEWITCHED!

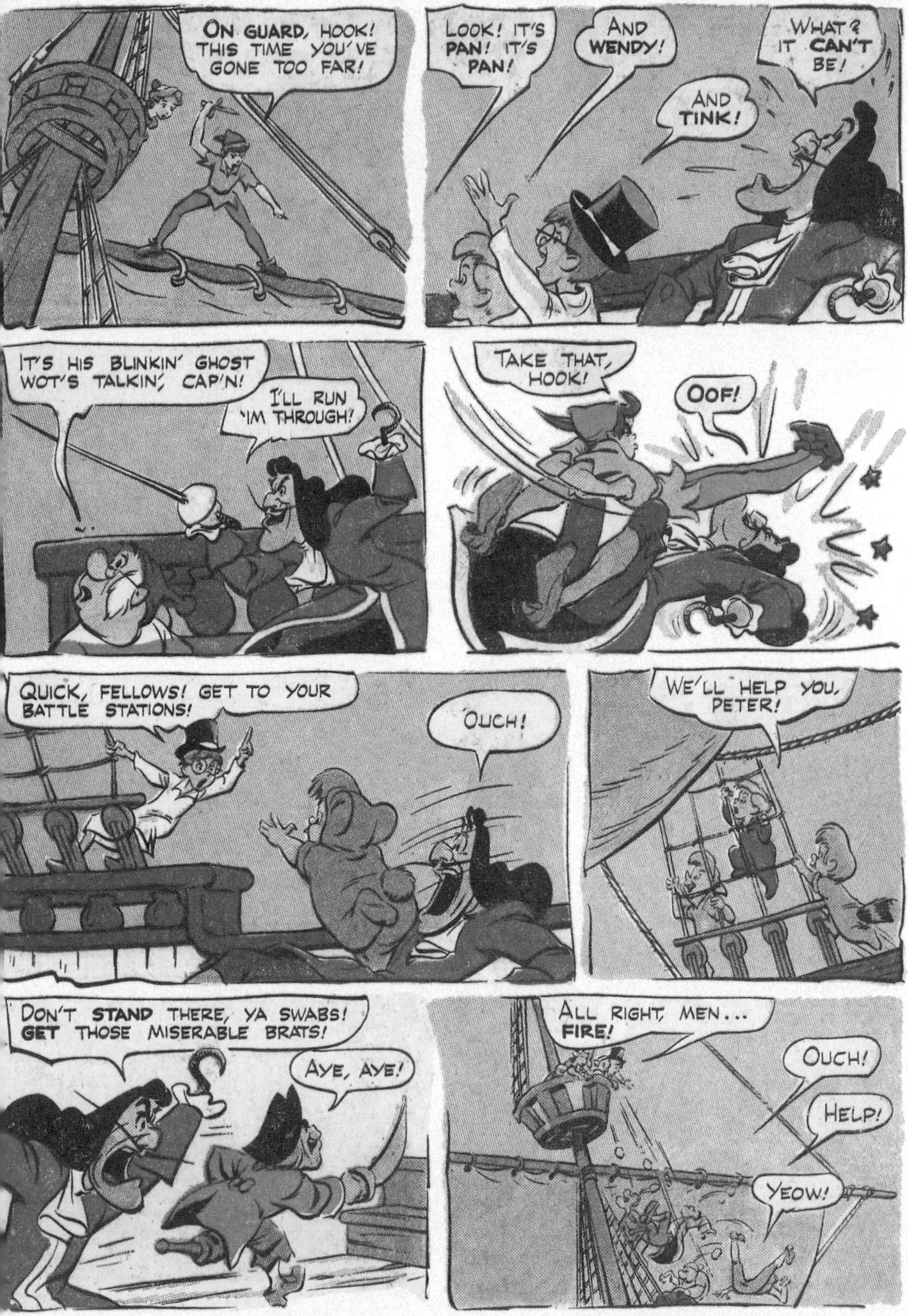
ON GUARD, HOOK! THIS TIME YOU'VE GONE TOO FAR!
LOOK! IT'S PAN! IT'S PAN!
AND WENDY!
WHAT? IT CAN'T BE!
AND TINK!
IT'S HIS BLINKIN' GHOST WOT'S TALKIN', CAP'N!
I'LL RUN 'IM THROUGH!
TAKE THAT, HOOK!
OOF!
QUICK, FELLOWS! GET TO YOUR BATTLE STATIONS!
OUCH!
WE'LL HELP YOU, PETER!
DON'T STAND THERE, YA SWABS! GET THOSE MISERABLE BRATS!
AYE, AYE!
ALL RIGHT, MEN... FIRE!
OUCH!
HELP!
YEOW!

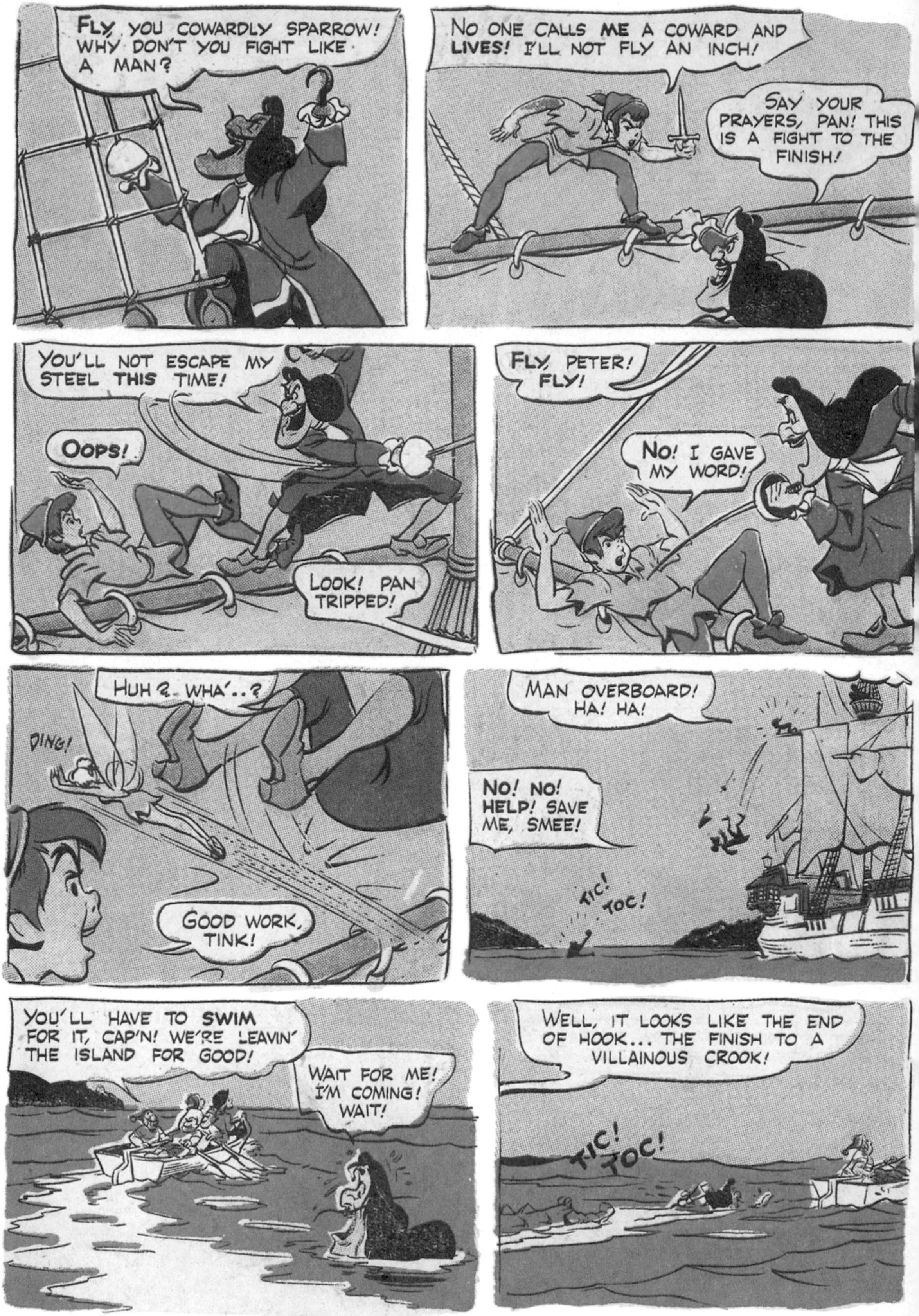
FLY, YOU COWARDLY SPARROW! WHY DON'T YOU FIGHT LIKE A MAN?
NO ONE CALLS ME A COWARD AND LIVES! I'LL NOT FLY AN INCH!
SAY YOUR PRAYERS, PAN! THIS IS A FIGHT TO THE FINISH!
YOU'LL NOT ESCAPE MY STEEL THIS TIME!
OOPS!
LOOK! PAN TRIPPED!
FLY, PETER! FLY!
NO! I GAVE MY WORD!
HUH? WHA'..?
DING!
GOOD WORK, TINK!
MAN OVERBOARD! HA! HA!
NO! NO! HELP! SAVE ME, SMEE!
TIC! TOC!
YOU'LL HAVE TO SWIM FOR IT, CAP'N! WE'RE LEAVIN' THE ISLAND FOR GOOD!
WAIT FOR ME! I'M COMING! WAIT!
WELL, IT LOOKS LIKE THE END OF HOOK... THE FINISH TO A VILLAINOUS CROOK!
TIC! TOC!

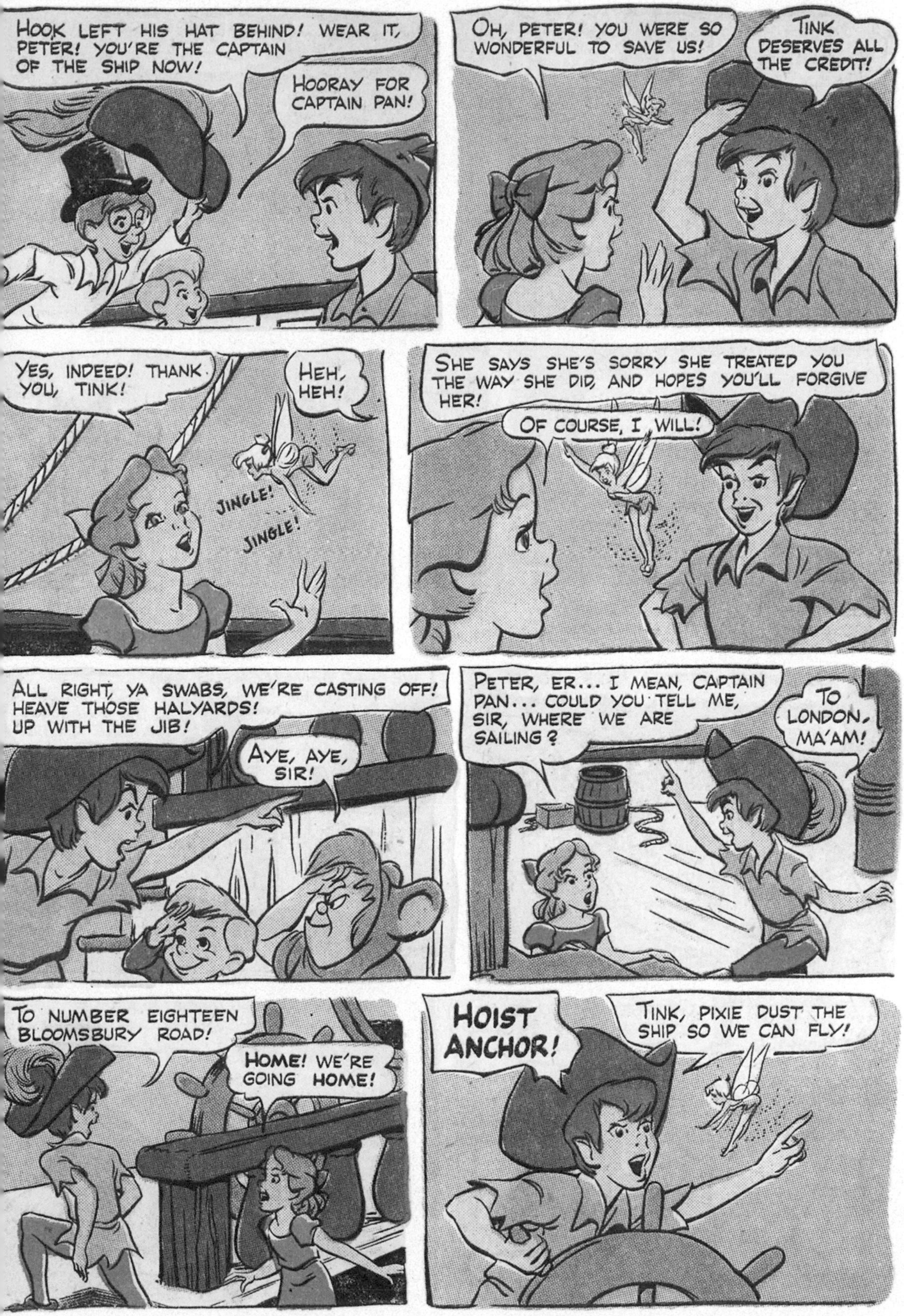
HOOK LEFT HIS HAT BEHIND! WEAR IT, PETER! YOU'RE THE CAPTAIN OF THE SHIP NOW!
HOORAY FOR CAPTAIN PAN!
OH, PETER! YOU WERE SO WONDERFUL TO SAVE US!
TINK DESERVES ALL THE CREDIT!
YES, INDEED! THANK YOU, TINK!
HEH, HEH!
JINGLE! JINGLE!
SHE SAYS SHE'S SORRY SHE TREATED YOU THE WAY SHE DID, AND HOPES YOU'LL FORGIVE HER!
OF COURSE, I WILL!
ALL RIGHT, YA SWABS, WE'RE CASTING OFF! HEAVE THOSE HALYARDS! UP WITH THE JIB!
AYE, AYE, SIR!
PETER, ER... I MEAN, CAPTAIN PAN... COULD YOU TELL ME, SIR, WHERE WE ARE SAILING?
TO LONDON, MA'AM!
TO NUMBER EIGHTEEN BLOOMSBURY ROAD!
HOME! WE'RE GOING HOME!
HOIST ANCHOR!
TINK, PIXIE DUST THE SHIP SO WE CAN FLY!

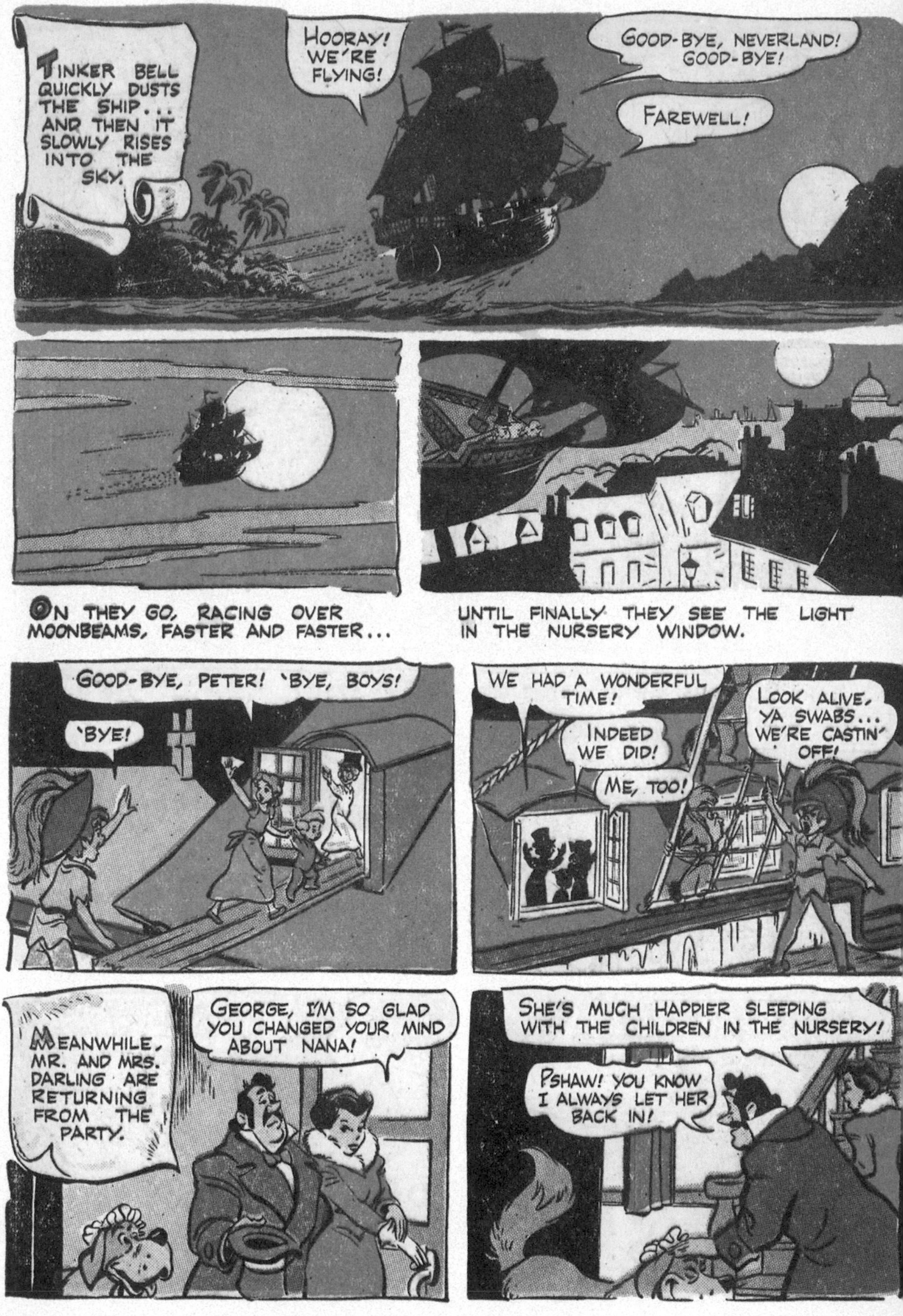
TINKER BELL QUICKLY DUSTS THE SHIP... AND THEN IT SLOWLY RISES INTO THE SKY.
HOORAY! WE'RE FLYING!
GOOD-BYE, NEVERLAND! GOOD-BYE!
FAREWELL!
ON THEY GO, RACING OVER MOONBEAMS, FASTER AND FASTER...
UNTIL FINALLY THEY SEE THE LIGHT IN THE NURSERY WINDOW.
GOOD-BYE, PETER! 'BYE, BOYS!
'BYE!
WE HAD A WONDERFUL TIME!
INDEED WE DID!
ME, TOO!
LOOK ALIVE, YA SWABS... WE'RE CASTIN' OFF!
MEANWHILE, MR. AND MRS. DARLING ARE RETURNING FROM THE PARTY.
GEORGE, I'M SO GLAD YOU CHANGED YOUR MIND ABOUT NANA!
SHE'S MUCH HAPPIER SLEEPING WITH THE CHILDREN IN THE NURSERY!
PSHAW! YOU KNOW I ALWAYS LET HER BACK IN!

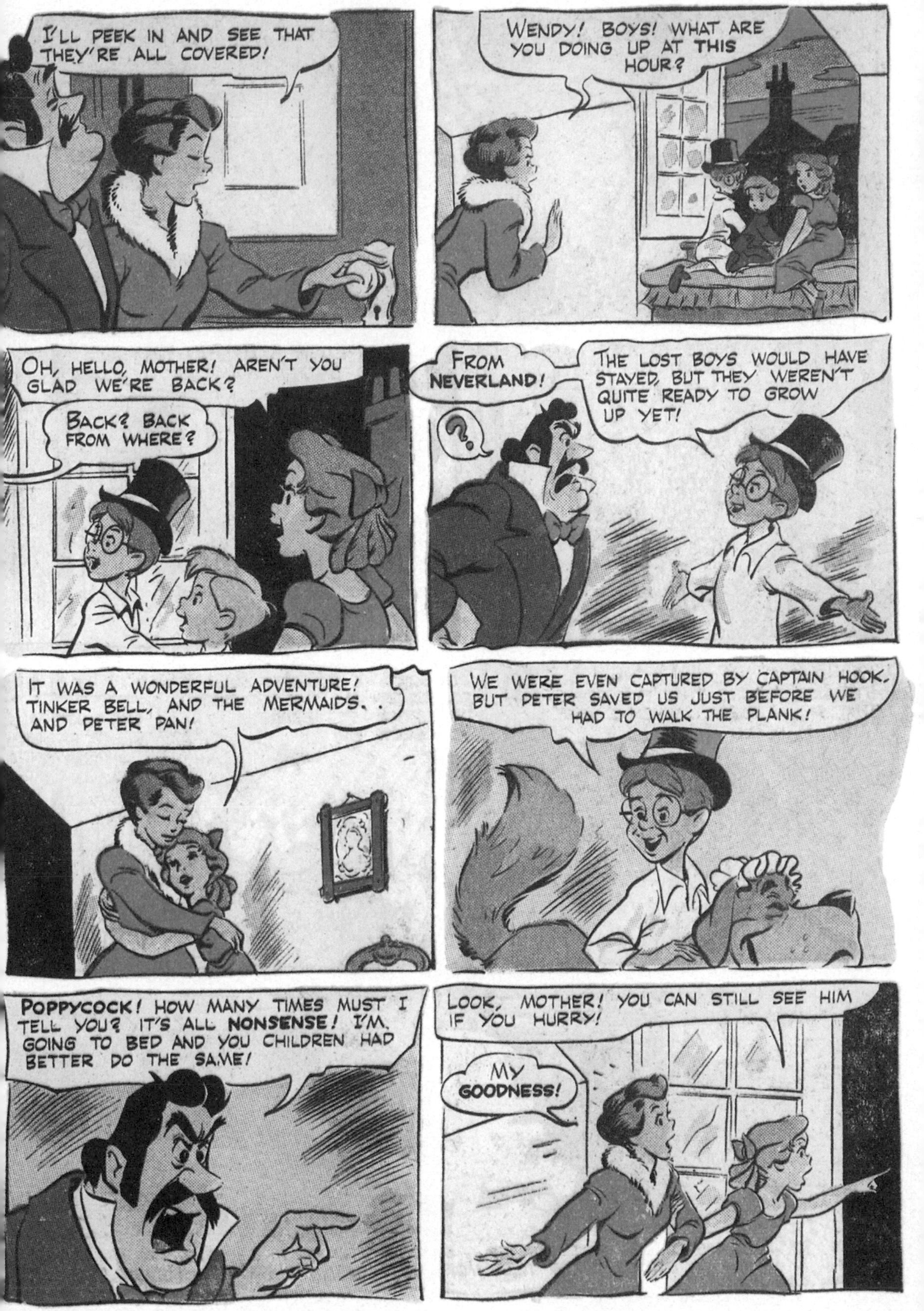
I'LL PEEK IN AND SEE THAT THEY'RE ALL COVERED!
WENDY! BOYS! WHAT ARE YOU DOING UP AT THIS HOUR?
OH, HELLO, MOTHER! AREN'T YOU GLAD WE'RE BACK?
BACK? BACK FROM WHERE?
FROM NEVERLAND!
?
THE LOST BOYS WOULD HAVE STAYED, BUT THEY WEREN'T QUITE READY TO GROW UP YET!
IT WAS A WONDERFUL ADVENTURE! TINKER BELL, AND THE MERMAIDS. . AND PETER PAN!
WE WERE EVEN CAPTURED BY CAPTAIN HOOK, BUT PETER SAVED US JUST BEFORE WE HAD TO WALK THE PLANK!
POPPYCOCK! HOW MANY TIMES MUST I TELL YOU? IT'S ALL NONSENSE! I'M GOING TO BED AND YOU CHILDREN HAD BETTER DO THE SAME!
LOOK, MOTHER! YOU CAN STILL SEE HIM IF YOU HURRY!
MY GOODNESS!

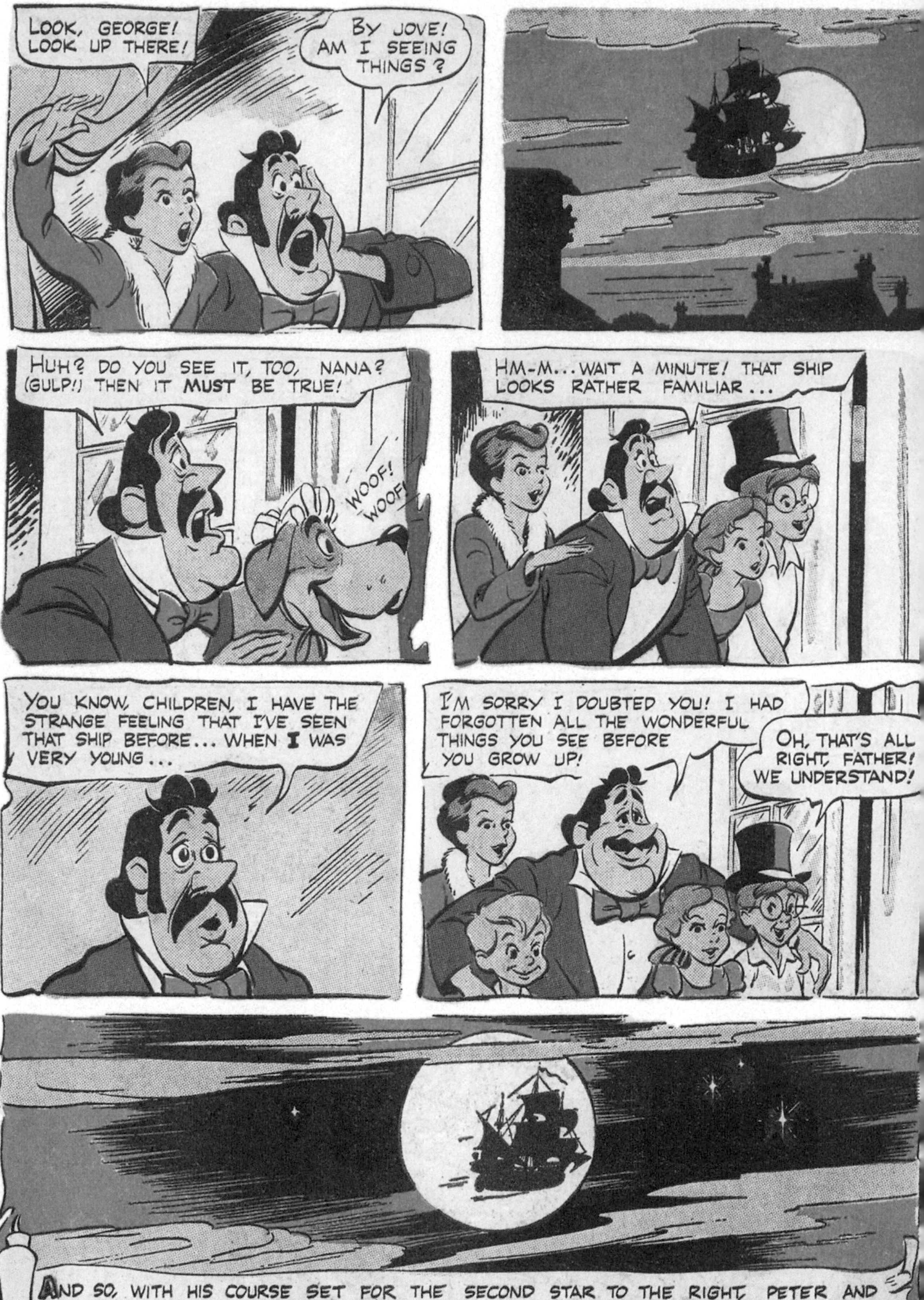
LOOK, GEORGE! LOOK UP THERE!
BY JOVE! AM I SEEING THINGS?
HUH? DO YOU SEE IT, TOO, NANA? (GULP!) THEN IT **MUST** BE TRUE!
WOOF! WOOF!
HM-M...WAIT A MINUTE! THAT SHIP LOOKS RATHER FAMILIAR...
YOU KNOW, CHILDREN, I HAVE THE STRANGE FEELING THAT I'VE SEEN THAT SHIP BEFORE... WHEN **I** WAS VERY YOUNG...
I'M SORRY I DOUBTED YOU! I HAD FORGOTTEN ALL THE WONDERFUL THINGS YOU SEE BEFORE YOU GROW UP!
OH, THAT'S ALL RIGHT, FATHER! WE UNDERSTAND!
AND SO, WITH HIS COURSE SET FOR THE SECOND STAR TO THE RIGHT, PETER AND HIS CREW SAILED STRAIGHT ON TILL MORNING... STRAIGHT BACK TO NEVERLAND.